DARKSIDE

MICHELLE ROSIGLIANI

Editing by Elizabeth Wright
Book Cover Design by Damonza.com

To *M*

For inspiring me to create and persevere.

Contents

Acknowledgments

Writing this book has been quite a journey, and there is no doubt that the help and understanding of some very amazing people made this story what it is today. I am profoundly grateful to all of you, and I hope you all know that.

To my parents, Monica and Dan, thank you for your patience, understanding, and support. I know I am not the easiest person to deal with when I am immersed in a story, so thank you for sticking with me and believing that I can do it.

To Liz, who has known and cherished the story since the very first moment, when the characters had other names and the plot was slightly different (or completely). Your continual support, friendship, and encouragements are dearly valued. I don't think I could have done this without you.

To Diana and Lori, thank you for your countless questions and timely feedback. Your input helped me develop this book from a few ideas to a full-blown novel.

To Elizabeth, thank you for taking my words and chiseling them into a better story. Your keen eye for detail and unbelievable suggestions were tremendously helpful and appreciated.

To Damonza, thank you for the awesome cover design. It is everything I wanted, and yet, so much more than I ever hoped for. I simply love it.

Last but not least, I would like to thank all the people who at some point taught me or influenced me to pursue the fascinating world of creating.

And thank you, dear reader, for giving *Darkside Love Affair* a chance. I hope you will enjoy reading it as much as I enjoyed writing it.

Preface

I did not believe in Fate.
I believed in choices and that in making them, we triggered a series of events that chiseled the path that led to the final curtain. I had devised my outcome, so why was I surprised that it had come to this?

The lights went out, and my long-forgotten nightmares came to life. In the dark, among the falling ceiling and through the chaos that had been unleashed, I fumbled for his touch.

But there were no warm, soothing hands waiting for mine, no tender lips to brush across my forehead and urge me to be brave, nor strong arms to protect me. There were only piles of concrete, broken glass, and splintered wood.

And the flames. They grew thick and merciless and scorched everything in their wake.

The firestorm had taken an ugly, painful form. And from its untamed flames stepped the perverted killer I had been hunting for.

It was he who hunted me now, and he was ruthless.

With eyes full of hatred, he pointed his gun at my head.

Then my world exploded in tiny, scattering pieces.

Chapter 1

Charlotte

he black sedan stopped at the curb, and the back door opened to reveal the Armani clothed figure of a man I knew all too well. James Burton did not waste time on loving gestures or false pretenses. With a single detached wave, he ordered me to join him inside the somber luxury of his car.

"Father," I greeted him rather stiffly as I shut the door and the car rolled into motion. "What was so pressing that it couldn't wait until Monday?"

Impenetrable brown eyes surveyed me before he pulled a leather dossier out of his briefcase. His motions were curt but elegant, as was the man himself. James Burton had naturally creamy skin, so perfectly smooth that he could have been the envy of the most pampered woman. His features were severe yet unreachably beautiful, with a hint of nobility that only heightened his innate power. His body, even in his mid-fifties, was agile, fit, and imposing.

Reaching for his cigarettes, he placed the dossier in my lap. The small flame of the lighter trembled for an instant before the tip of the cigarette caught fire, and the smell of tobacco penetrated my nostrils. I frowned and massaged my temples, watching the circles of smoke coiling and drifting in the enclosed space of the car.

"I trust you don't mind," he replied, remorselessly bringing the cigarette to his lips, then pointing somewhat impatiently to the dossier. "Open it."

Inside the folder, there was a single sheet of paper that looked like it had been meticulously creased. It was a contract signed with a flourish by Mitch Stewart, the mayor of Washington, D.C. When I finished reading the paper twice, I looked up at my father in confusion.

"Mayor Mitch Stewart hired Burton & Associates to be co-counsel on his son's case?"

My father nodded with a sly twist of his lips that had me straightening my spine almost defensively.

"Why are you giving me this, Father?"

An unwelcome chill ran up and down my spine when he finally extinguished his cigarette, inched closer, and spoke. I knew by the look in his eyes that I wouldn't like whatever he had to say.

"It's been three months since you were promoted to Junior Partner, and you haven't had any notable cases yet. Jack Stewart's case will put your name on the map. That is why I'm giving you this opportunity."

"But, Father…"

"Before you say anything reckless," he went on resolutely, speaking in that tone that allowed little objection, "please appreciate the fact that I am offering you the spotlight, Charlotte. Now it's time to prove that you deserve this promotion. Imagine the opportunities this success will bring you."

I had little faith that Jack Stewart's story would be a successful one because I had little faith in him. It was my duty as a lawyer to listen to my client and reserve all judgment for myself, but defending a man accused of murdering his own fiancée went against each and every one of my convictions.

"I believe Isaac would be a better fit for this case, and you know it."

"Isaac doesn't want the case."

"You mean you talked him into passing on this case so you

could give it to me."

"Let's make something clear, Charlotte. In my firm, I say what happens, and the rest of you act in accordance."

"Jack Stewart is accused of murdering his fiancée," I cut him off, which I rarely did and almost always regretted afterward.

James's eyes darkened, and his lips pressed into a thin line. I was testing his patience, but that seemed less important when faced with the possibility of losing my peace of mind over an unwanted case.

Being a lawyer had never been my choice, but in time, I had learned to appreciate the benefits such a profession granted and recognize the good it allowed me to do. I had drawn gratification from the many people I had been able to defend, but I had never used my abilities in favor of criminals. I had never dived into that dark aspect of my profession, and I hated that my father forced me to begin now.

"He is innocent until proven guilty, Charlotte. It's your job not to let that happen. I hope you will make me proud."

"I don't feel comfortable accepting this case."

"There's really no room for argument here," he said, emphasizing each word while glancing out the window as if he had already forgotten that I was sitting beside him. "You should be called to D.C. soon."

It was clear there was no room for argument, but there was no room for any other conversation either.

"Please, stop the car."

"Don't be absurd, Charlotte."

"I'd like to walk, please. Stop the car."

I climbed out of the car, slamming the door on my father's commanding plea to come back. He had that annoying way of turning even the most heartrending request into an order, and for tonight, I just wanted to shut him out. He had ordered me enough.

It seemed fitting that such a disastrous day ended with a thorough downpour. Rain-laden clouds rolled languorously on the ashen sky, and thunder echoed somewhere in the distance.

It was unnaturally cold for an early summer evening. The wind was brutal as it slapped me mercilessly across the face. Its chill was feral as it turned my lips into a trembling mess of purple flesh.

I felt the rage of the storm approaching in my very bones, and for a short second, I regretted having traded the warm interior of my father's car for those cold, dark streets. Hastening my pace and wrapping the flimsy coat tighter around myself, I hoped I would reach the safety of my apartment before the heavens split open.

"Damn it," I cursed silently when my feet didn't carry me fast enough.

I was not particularly sensitive, but I was definitely weather-sensitive. When it was cold and rainy, I got headaches, seasoned with joint and bone pains that extended from such an inoffensive, little ache in my left knee, all the way to my faulty spine. Even my muscles felt loaded with a burning kind of tension. The nagging pain plagued me as I hurried down the darkened alley that was the only shortcut to my apartment building.

No more than two minutes passed before I lamented the decision to forsake the main street, adequately illuminated and sufficiently populated, in favor of an isolated, empty alley that was dimly lit and saturated with a bothering reek of sewers.

"Hey, sugar, where are you going?" I heard a male voice coming from somewhere threateningly close.

I tensed but neither turned to see who was calling nor slowed my pace. If anything, I started walking even faster, which earned me their obnoxious jokes. The sound irritated me as much as it awakened self-preservation instincts that I had not been aware I possessed.

Fear pumped a strange current through my blood. I was the prey, so I sensed the danger. They were the predators, so they smelled my fear. And thus, they were incited.

While their laughter reached horrible peaks and the distance between us was eradicated, my heart beat faster, my hands became sweaty and trembling, and my mind throbbed with one single thought. Run.

"Come on, hon, don't run away," another one sneered.

"You'll make us think you're a frigid little one and nobody likes that." Another voice, another threat.

When the first drop of water finally hit my forehead, I shivered.

There must have been at least three men after me, but I didn't dare to check. I wasn't nearly close enough to safety, and I could almost feel them breathing down my neck. I shivered again, but it had nothing to do with the chill. I shivered with fear.

"We just want to have a chat with you," one of them continued as they caught up with me.

I could see them. There were indeed three, and if their voices almost bordered on boyhood, their appearance had nothing to do with that of a boy.

All three of them were tall and intimidating. One was taller than the rest, with dark, shaggy hair covering his forehead and a slenderer figure, while the other two were blonde-haired, had a slightly robust construction, and looked so much alike that I suspected they were brothers, or at least related. Underneath their loose clothes, their muscular bodies were threateningly shaped. I gulped down my anxiety and struggled to make my feet move faster, but the fear started having a paralyzing effect.

"Come on, sugar, don't be so pretentious," one of the blondes said, catching me by the elbow and dragging me to him.

He was well-built and reasonably beautiful, but his eyes lacked kindness, and his lips were curled over his teeth, revealing a brutal desire to cause harm. And he was categorically keen on inflicting it. On inflicting it on me.

I shook off his hand, but he only made a low, annoyed sound in his throat and grabbed my hips, pushing me without mercy against the wall of the building behind us. The sudden impact made me gasp, and my spine protested with a painful crunching noise. It was going to bruise.

"You smell good," he mumbled while the others sneered loudly from close by.

I struggled against his groping hands because that was the only thing I could do, yet my effort and perseverance were sorely outshined by panic.

Time and time again, I had heard stories of harassed women, or worse, abused and humiliated girls who had their innocence mocked by strangers. I actually used to defend abused women and fight until they received justice. Yet, I had never imagined I would ever be one of them.

I guarded myself. I didn't talk to strangers or stick my nose in somebody else's business. I opted for the illuminated street and not the dark alley. But tonight, I had made a mistake that I was apparently going to pay for. And only now did I come to clearly understand that no amount of justice would erase the horror, the pain, the shame, or the following nightmares.

My limbs turned cold as my captor's hold tightened around my wrists, and he leaned in to trace his tongue up and down my neck. I whimpered and writhed, but the more resistance I offered, the more driven he became. By the time the rest joined us against the dampened wall of the building, my captor was utterly plastered against me, so I could feel that my struggles and pleas provided no real excitement for him.

"Dude, I think you should let her go," one of them muttered, but I was already too panicked to recognize who had spoken.

I felt nauseous and feared that rape might not have been the worst of his intentions. The other blonde bent closer until his nose was nestled in my hair and his hand fisted at my nape. They reeked of alcohol, and while their inebriated minds could be more easily tricked, they could also get stronger and meaner if they were riled.

The dark-haired one finally inched close enough so that his arm brushed against mine. A pair of hands slipped beneath my coat and my shirt, fondling my flesh with blatant sexual purpose, but I wasn't sure who they belonged to. I knew my chances to escape were getting slimmer by the minute, so I had to do something immediately. Instinct took over, and a piercing scream exploded from my chest.

My loud outburst bothered them at first, but any shred of worry they might have experienced vanished quickly. They outnumbered me, and from that they drew confidence. The blonde one who scared me the most covered my mouth with his hand, and his eyes shot daggers at me. When minutes elapsed and I realized that nobody had heard my plea for help, I became desperate.

My ineffective struggles only amused my attackers.

"See, you're being difficult," the other blonde snickered. "We just wanted to talk, have some fun…"

"I don't want to talk," I managed to push past my trembling lips.

"Oh, no? Now you're being naughty. You want more than that, don't you?"

"No. Just let me go," I pleaded.

I hated that my voice sounded so weak, but my very blood was infected with panic, and nausea was slowly replaced by dizziness.

"Let's make a deal. Let us have some fun, then we'll let you leave...for now."

They all started laughing, and despite the cold claws almost strangling me, I took advantage of their momentary lack of attention. The slender one, with the brown hair, was closest to me, so I kicked him hard in the gut. He doubled over and hissed, but I didn't stay back to assess the damage I had done, if I had done any significant damage at all.

I launched forward, prepared to run, when a sinewy, ruthless arm caught me by the waist and angrily dragged me back, pushing me once more against the wall. Air left my lungs in a rush when my eyes locked on clouded, angry ones. It was the mean guy, looking meaner than ever.

"Now, you're downright rude. Why did you have to hurt our poor friend, hm?"

"Please, I—just let me go. I have nothing to give you."

"Oh, but I think you do," he snarled. "You have to pay for what you have done, don't you think?"

I had nothing to threaten him with. I had nothing to defend myself with. And this time, I was probably not going to get another way out. If they wanted to make me pay, if they were going to be merciless, if they wanted to hurt me, they could.

"Okay, that's enough," somebody said in a calm, casual voice that sounded almost bored.

My head automatically snapped to my right, where the voice had come from, to see another man detach himself from the wall. He might have stood there throughout my whole assault.

He was even taller than the other three, with intimidatingly broad shoulders, strapping arms that he kept folded over a well-built chest, and legs that seemed endless. The way he was dressed—

black leather jacket, black jeans, black sports shoes—he looked like a biker, threatening and mean and much scarier than his friends.

"I said, that's enough," he growled to the man still pressing me against the wall.

Slowly and with lethal grace, he approached us and coolly removed my captor's hands from my body, giving him a shove until he was forced to step aside. Then a pair of fire blue eyes fixed me for an interminable moment. It wasn't just the strength of his body that intimidated me but also that of his demeanor. Power and control exuded from him, so fiery and potent that when he walked closer, I felt scalded.

"Are you okay?" he asked, ducking his head to better see my face.

No, I was not okay. Despite my efforts, I was trembling, and more infuriatingly, my eyelids were stinging and my nose was prickling, a taunting warning before I started crying.

All I wanted to do was crawl beneath a blanket in the safety of my room and forget all about what had happened in that dark alley. But the man currently standing before me had other intentions.

"I know you have a tongue because you have just spoken to these idiots…" he continued, coming even closer to me as I shrank back.

He assessed me, then he straightened to his full height and stepped back. He knew I was scared, but he wasn't set on acting on my fear. That surprised me.

"Look, I am not trying to scare you. I just want to know if you are okay. Are you?" he pressed when I still said nothing.

It was odd that moments ago I had been able to beg his less likable friends to release me, and now, I was entirely incapable of forming an answer to a simple question. Instead, I nodded. He continued watching me as if not absolutely sure I was telling the truth, but eventually, he nodded too. If he had witnessed the whole ordeal, he knew that his friends hadn't done anything more than thoroughly scare me and teach me to never choose a shortcut in my life.

"They weren't going to hurt you," the blue-eyed man explained, motioning absently to the retreating figures of my three assailants.

"They just have a strange way of spending their time. And you got scared much too quickly, which only… entertained them."

"I'm glad they enjoyed themselves," I muttered in a low voice, hardly hearing myself.

His eyes snapped to my lips before they locked on my own. His stare was torrid and harshly intent. Then a broad smile pulled up the corner of his lips and lit his eyes so brightly that they seemed spotlights in the growing darkness.

I looked away, and seeing that he didn't corner me like a predator, I dared to move. He didn't stop me when I began walking away, but he did follow.

"Let me walk you home," he asked, the side of his body almost touching mine. "I need to be sure that nothing else happens to you tonight."

"That is not necessary."

"Please."

His fingers locked around my wrist, briefly stopping me in place, absently caressing the skin there. The contact didn't last more than a second, but it electrified me. I snatched my hand back and cradled it to my chest as if he had burned me. My reaction brought a frown to his face, knitting together his well-defined brows.

I set off once more, not sticking around to inspect his facial changes. "That is not necessary," I repeated, even more curtly than before.

"Maybe that's better," he concluded, finally letting me leave.

I hugged myself and struggled to walk as fast as possible, which in my anxious state was not fast at all. And suddenly, the weird urge to turn and catch a last glimpse of that man pulsed furiously in my blood. I was so tense, so edgy, that when he called out, I all but shrieked.

"Aren't you going to get your bag?"

Instinctively, I reached for my bag, which was not hanging on my right shoulder anymore. Hesitation stopped me in place. When I turned, I found him standing in the exact same spot where I had left him, holding my purse and urging me with his wayward stare to go and get it.

I finally mustered the courage to return for my bag, feeling his searing blue eyes on me with each step that I took. Reaching for the handbag, I made the mistake of touching his fingers, and the contact sent a flaring jolt of awareness through my system.

I pulled on the strap with more rudeness and more force than necessary, but his grip matched my brusqueness with an unflinching strength. I looked up into bright, singularly beautiful eyes that narrowed just a bit as he tried to figure me out, like I was a mystery that he needed to solve.

When I prepared to yank at the bag again, the stranger let go, a quietly amused smile flapping defiantly across his features. He didn't say anything more. He didn't expect me to say anything more either. He just disappeared, and so did the scare his friends had given me.

Or so I thought.

Chapter 2

Marcus

I glared up at the clouds and stepped outside *L'Affaire* onto the already wet sidewalk. I favored the idea of a storm before or during a race as much as I liked that Kai, Bryson, and Brayden were going to ride in their inebriated states.

Brayden tripped over his own feet then ran into a strawberry blonde girl, who was clutching her coat around her frame and her bag to her chest as if she were holding her entire life in that small sack. As she tottered on her feet and almost fell, she looked up, her eyes finally leaving the ground where they had been riveted. She seemed young and much too innocent for what was coming.

"Hey gorgeous," Brayden said, settling his big hands on her narrow waist.

The girl blinked in confusion, then, despite the growing chill outside, her cheeks warmed up and her eyes returned to the rain-dampened ground. So she wasn't just innocent, she was also timid—a heady concoction for Brayden's obnoxiousness.

"I'm sorry," she murmured then tried to push Brayden's hands to the side so she could leave.

"No need to apologize, sugar," Bryson cut in with a big grin that matched his brother's. "I assure you he enjoyed tremendously how you bumped against his—ahem—chest."

Brayden threw his head back and howled with deafening laughter, clapping Bryson's shoulder, who joined in his brother's antics. While Brayden and my cousin, Kai, were three years younger, Bryson was my age, but sometimes, he seemed the most stupid and reckless of us all. Watching him enabling his little brother and turning a blind eye to his dangerous and morbid habits was no surprise anymore. In fact, what stunned me was Kai, who sneered at the girl and joined Brayden's never-ending vicious cycle.

Kai was reckless in his own way but never disrespectful and never cruel to those weaker than him. He tolerated Brayden's habits, but he never contributed to his idiocy. Alcohol might have been clouding his mind but not so badly as to turn him into a different man unless other things were weighing on his mind.

"I didn't mean to—I was just not paying attention—"

Their amusement grew while the girl was almost brought to tears. She clutched her bag tighter to her body as if it could protect her. Her chin was burrowed to her chest, and her shoulders shook with repressed tears and mounting fear. The image of a vulnerable girl, who I doubted was even of age, held no amusement to me.

"You should be paying attention," I told her coldly then pushed each man behind, offering her a clear way out.

She blinked then fastened her gaze on me. Her pupils dilated, and her lower lip quivered slightly but enough to show me that she was more scared by my voice than she had been by Brayden and Bryson's approach. Typical.

"Now try to get home without any other incidents, darling."

"But…" Brayden interrupted, vexed by my interference. They knew that when I usually interfered, it was to break their little party and not join it.

"But…" I muttered, mimicking his expression. "Put one leg in front of the other and walk."

"Dude," Bryson said, clamping my shoulder, "you didn't have nearly enough alcohol yet."

I shoved his hand and glowered until the grin slipped off his face. "I don't drink before a race."

I hadn't had the best of days. In fact, all I wanted was to forget all about the past day, or better, the past month, and the only way I could achieve that was by racing.

When I was on my motorcycle, with the wind in my face and the speed making my heart pump faster and my blood run hotter, the adrenaline gave me strength.

When I raced, I felt so powerful that nothing could break me or bring me to my knees. Nobody could take the control from my hands. And walking the thin line between life and death added a shade of danger that only made everything better.

When I raced, I could forget, even if for a short while, that my own father was the man aiming to put me behind bars.

"Dude, are you listening?" Kai demanded, elbowing me in the ribs.

I ran a hand over my face, a habit to both hide my emotions and scatter the upsetting thoughts that crammed my mind. I looked at Kai without a clue, and with an arch of my brow, I prompted him to speak although I didn't have the slightest interest in whatever he had been discussing. My interest was solely focused on getting to the race where I could shut off my brain.

"What?"

"Liv just called. She said she needs your help. Stat."

"What? Why?" I hissed. "What's wrong?"

"Dude, chill," Bryson sighed, rolling his eyes in exasperation. "There's just a power outage in the neighborhood. I don't know why she doesn't just call somebody else."

I allowed myself to breathe a sigh of relief. Every time Liv called, I expected that something dreadful had happened, and though a power outage for her must have been horrible enough, at least I knew she was safe.

It was in that short moment of relief that I picked up on Kai's irony. What he had meant was that she didn't need me immediately but was only being capricious. I didn't agree. She truly needed me. And I was always going to be there for her. No matter what.

I veered right on a narrow dark alley before they could say anything to stop me. I knew they were following just by the sound of their cadenced footsteps on the pavement. I wished they hadn't because sooner or later they were going to do or say something that tested my patience.

"Dude, the race?" Kai called.

"I have time," I threw over my shoulder and hurried to Liv.

"You are a complete idiot," Bryson sighed again but kept his distance. He knew better than all of them that when Liv called, they should mind their own business.

"Oh, but what do we have here?" Brayden growled dramatically. He looked like a predator on the hunt.

My eyes followed his gaze to stumble upon the hurried silhouette of a woman. At first, I feared it was the same unfortunate girl from earlier, but this one was unmistakable even if she only graced us with her back.

She was slightly taller than the girl we had encountered earlier and definitely womanly-shaped. Her hair, draped over one shoulder, stood out against the cream of her coat and was a wild halo of long chocolate waves.

Brayden licked his lips and walked her way. He had a softness for long-haired women and an obsessive desire for revenge directed toward all the wrong targets. It didn't surprise me that he planned to harass her too. Unfortunately for his new prey, I wasn't going to stick around to get him off her when he would cross the line. Because he would.

"For God's sake, don't go,' Bryson tried one more time as Brayden followed the woman. "Let's have fun. Let's meet that girl. Let's go to the race."

"Have fun," I muttered and walked off. By now, Liv must have been hysterical.

I didn't stop when I walked past the woman and saw her scared expression as Brayden, Kai, and Bryson cornered her. They might have been half-drunk and too obnoxious for her taste, but they weren't going to actually harm her.

Raindrops started falling faster, but despite the thrumming of the rain, I could hear the woman's pleas to be left alone.

I was not a decent man. I was not particularly kindhearted either. I rarely empathized with somebody else's fear or pain. But while Brayden had a tendency to scare innocent-looking women and enjoy doing so, I had the tendency to protect them.

Liv was my first, sometimes my only priority. Protecting her was both duty and instinct, but though she was waiting for me, the big brown eyes of the woman I had just passed in the alley flashed before mine and made my step falter. I had seen her for only a fraction of a second. I had hardly noticed anything about her other than the fear and despair soaking her sight, but I was going back for her.

Brayden's laughter echoed gruesomely loud. If he had scared the strawberry-blonde girl from earlier, he frightened his current plaything to the point that she was shaking and struggling to breathe.

"Please—I—just let me go. I have nothing to give you," she pleaded. Her eyes shone with unshed tears, and I couldn't comprehend how a man, tipsy, drunk, or sober, could enjoy such fear.

"Oh, but I think you do," Brayden told her sharply, towering over her while she grew smaller. "You have to pay for what you have done, don't you think?"

Finally close enough to watch every emotion dancing chaotically on her face, the woman was fascinating despite her anxiety. I leaned against the wall where they had her pinned, adopting a leisurely attitude when, in fact, I only wanted to slap the idiocy out of the three of them.

I heard a groan and looked past Brayden and Bryson, who were cornering the young woman, to see Kai holding his guts. I almost laughed. So she was a fighter. I liked that. And respected it.

Then I observed her. She had a pale complexion, which I wasn't sure whether it was her natural skin color or a temporary pallor caused by the panic that she emanated in almost tangible waves. Those big brown eyes looked even larger now that I was closer, and the long eyelashes adorning them fanned her cheeks softly.

She had a beauty spot that contrasted with her pale skin just above her upper lip, near the left corner of her mouth, and her mouth... Well, her mouth was delightfully shaped with voluptuous lips that were red and tempting.

She was not the most beautiful woman I had ever seen, but there was something about her that felt intoxicating, addictive. Once my attention was distracted by her feminine appeal, I knew it was time to cease the scrutiny.

"Okay, that's enough."

Kai and Bryson stepped back with a roll of their eyes, wobbling away as if nothing had ever happened. Brayden, however, didn't even acknowledge me. But the woman did.

Her eyes found me and glided erratically over my body. When her features deepened with fear, it didn't surprise me that I scared her more than her assailants. I was used to it by now. If only I had looked like Hulk or Frankenstein, I would have understood where this fear was always coming from.

"I said that's enough," I ordered and straightened, taking a step closer so I was standing right behind Brayden.

His determination to scare the woman wavered, but that didn't mean he complied with my command, so I physically removed him from sight. The glare I gave him as I did so efficiently shut him up.

"Are you okay?" I asked the stranger, but no words came out of her mouth. She only shivered. "I know you have a tongue because you have just spoken to these idiots…"

I had returned only to make sure that Brayden and the rest gave up on their attempt to disturb her, but all I had managed was to scare her further. And our proximity didn't do anything to help matters.

Once more, I ran a hand over my face and stepped back. She needed her space as much as I needed her to assure me that those morons hadn't harmed her.

"Look, I am not trying to scare you. I just want to know if you are okay. Are you?"

Still no answer. Although the woman's fearful attitude could have been amusing, at the moment it was becoming annoying. Couldn't she understand that I didn't mean her any harm?

"They weren't going to hurt you," I spoke, seeing as she didn't plan on saying anything. "They just have a strange way of spending their time. And you got scared much too quickly which only… entertained them."

"I'm glad they enjoyed themselves."

So, besides being a fighter, she was also a smart-mouth. I liked that more than I wanted to admit, and because of that, I needed to part ways with her as quickly as possible.

"Let me walk you home," I told her instead, frowning as I realized what I had just said. Liv was waiting for me, for God's sake, but despite that, I kept walking by the woman's side. I didn't even know her name. "I need to be sure that nothing else happens to you tonight."

"That is not necessary."

"Please," I pressed, my hand reaching for hers.

As my fingers brushed her skin, her appeal turned even more powerful. It invaded me. The brief contact, however, seemed to only appall her as she recoiled and stared at me like I had just taken advantage of her innocence.

"That is not necessary." She strode off, wrapping her arms around herself.

"Maybe that's better," I muttered more to myself than to her. She was nobody to me, so I was not responsible for her safety. But I was responsible for getting her belongings back.

"Aren't you going to get your bag?" I shouted after her. She turned cautiously, her eyes immediately lowering to the bag she hadn't noticed I had picked up off the ground and carried for the several steps we had walked together.

It might have been more comfortable for her if I had walked up and handed her the bag, but I was done facilitating matters for her. If she wanted her purse, she'd better come and get it.

After a long moment of hesitation, I was confident she wouldn't, but that rebellious flash of determination returned to her eyes, and just like that, she was before me, reaching for her purse. Only I found I wasn't prepared to let go. Or maybe now that our ways were meant to split, I discovered that teasing her was a bottomless source of enjoyment.

When she recovered her bag from my grasping hand and stormed off, all drenched and furious, with her makeup running and those haunting eyes frowning, I couldn't help but chuckle. And follow…

She might not have agreed to let me accompany her, but that

didn't mean I had to listen to her. Before long, I realized that we were headed in the same direction. How ironic was it that this unknown, mysterious woman lived in the same apartment building as Liv? How strange was it that we had to meet under these circumstances rather than bump into each other while one exited the elevator and the other one climbed in? And how likely was it for us to meet again?

Wiping a smile off my face, I allowed her to enter the building, waited for five minutes, and then followed. The doorkeeper greeted me with a nod when I stepped inside. He already knew where I was going, so he didn't stop me to ask questions. During the short meeting with the brown-eyed woman, my mood had shifted, and I was suddenly not prepared to face Liv. But she had called, and I owed her.

By the time I knocked on Liv's door, the power was back on, and no sound came from her apartment. Usually, when I stopped by, I only needed to knock once, and she would open the door wide with a cautious expression plastered upon her face like she had been waiting a minute too long for my arrival. Now, an austere, annoying silence greeted me. I knocked again and again and was getting ready to knock the damn door down when a click resonated in the silence.

She unlocked the door but didn't open it which struck me as strange—much too strange for Liv. A claw of fear seized my throat and prevented air from getting to my lungs as I gripped the door handle and pushed the door open. She wouldn't have dared to do something foolish. She couldn't have.

Liv was standing in the middle of the living room, facing the window and hugging herself. In the course of time, I had learned all her gestures and habits. She was both anxious and irritated. And if memory served me well, each time she was irritated, she somehow managed to unleash all that anger on me. But tonight, I was too drained of energy to be the buffer that absorbed her mood swings.

"Liv…are you okay? The power is on…"

"If I'm okay," she mumbled under her breath and made an agitated gesture with her hands, then spun around like a tornado.

"You ask me if I am okay? I've been here all alone, scared. It was dark and you—you—I called you, but you didn't come. You weren't here."

"Liv, I'm sorry. I wasn't close enough to get here in time—" I trailed off, the lie leaving a foul taste on my tongue.

"Lately, you're never close enough," she accused, struggling to walk back and forth as tears bathed her face. My eyes immediately settled on her left leg, which she absentmindedly rubbed as she limped on.

"You know that is not true, Liv."

"Is it not?" she snapped, her glare confronting my weary stare.

"No, it is not," I retorted firmly and closed the gap between us.

When I pulled her into my arms, her whole body quaked with sobs. Sometimes it was difficult to discern whether my absence or my embrace made her more vulnerable.

"I was scared," she repeated, fisting her small hands in my jacket.

"I know, baby. I am here now," I assured her, kissing the top of her head while my hands stroked her hair.

Chapter 3

Charlotte

I despised lack of punctuality, so being the cause for delaying a meeting was not on my list of favored accomplishments. When said meeting was with James Burton himself, the whole problem turned into a nightmare.

Drumming my fingers on the counter, I struggled to keep up a formal expression as the barista fumbled with the coffee machine. I had been waiting for more than ten minutes to get a miserable cup of coffee, and the girl behind the counter had yet to take my order. Somewhere in the depths of my mind, I realized she was as stressed and as busy as every citizen around her, but understanding her problems didn't lessen my own.

"Yes, Miss?" the girl behind the bar said eventually, straining to make her voice sound pleasant. She couldn't be older than twenty.

"A medium espresso, no sugar, please."

Luckily, the firm was a five-minute walk, but the girl's working speed, or lack of, lessened any chances I might have had of getting there before my father. As soon as she put the cup on the counter, I grabbed it and shoved the money into her hands, not waiting for any change.

It was a small pleasure to wrap my fingers around the hot paper cup and bring it closer to my nose so I could savor the poignant aroma of the coffee, but it was a real annoyance to take the first sip and be invaded by a sickly sweet taste that almost made me nauseous.

I was already by the door, and the interminable line of people waiting for their hopefully well-prepared coffee discouraged me from returning and asking for another cup, precisely as I had ordered it. My mood hadn't been a spectacular one to start with, but now it was worsening by the second.

I pushed the glass door open with my shoulder, determined to dump my coffee in the first trash bin I encountered when a solid black mass slammed into me, knocking the breath out of my lungs. Almost instantly, I felt the hot contents of my cup soaking through my formerly white suit jacket, burning my skin until I shrieked and let the cup fall from my fingers in a desperate attempt to peel the scalding clothes from my body. But no matter how much it burned, I couldn't undress in the middle of the jam-packed New York streets.

I had been somewhat ill-humored ever since Friday night, so I wasn't surprised to have reached the limits of my patience so soon and so fast. I ceased my agitated movements and snapped my head up to the idiotic person who hadn't been watching where he was going, ready to unleash the most acidic retort I could muster. When my eyes focused on the man's face, I gasped and swallowed my words.

"Dude, she's the—"

"I know who she is," the solid black mass snapped, his eyes not leaving mine.

I knew the young man behind him because now in the full light of day I could see him for what he actually was—a boy who had yet to grow up. He was one of the three hoodlums who had attacked me Friday night, one of the three who had made me fear for my safety. But now, as he peered at me as if I were a freak of nature, he almost amused me. Almost....

And I also recognized the man standing between us, because he was one hundred percent purely, terrifyingly male. He was the one who had made the other three stop, the one who had scared me the most.

"Unbelievable," I muttered and threw my hands in the air.

The likes of them were exactly what I needed for a Monday morning. I sidestepped them, praying that I could get to work without any more incidents, but of course, they had to follow. Although people surrounded me from all sides, one presence stood out—that of the man walking to my right, smoothly matching my hurried strides.

"I'm sorry, I just didn't see you," he tried to explain. "Are you okay?"

The man had a tendency and a liking for stupid questions. I was drenched in hot coffee, I was late for work, and I reeked. I had him and his friend following me and reminding me of Friday night. I was due to listen to my father's lecture on responsibility and endure an impossible day in an impossible outfit. How was I supposed to be okay?

"Kai, can you ask her if she is okay or if she needs help? She tends to speak to you more than she does to me," he said casually.

Although I kept my eyes stubbornly trained forward, I could feel his eyes even more stubbornly trained on me.

"Miss, are you…"

"Oh, shut up," I snapped, not slowing down my pace. "I heard him perfectly. And the only thing you can help me with is to stop following me."

"It's not my fault that you are so small that I didn't even see you," the taller one said defensively, shoving a hand through his hair.

"Unbelievable," I scoffed, unable to keep myself from looking up at him.

He couldn't have known, but he had struck where it hurt. I wasn't so short as to be considered petite, but my height had always frustrated me. In a world so big, I had always felt much too small. The fact that he was mocking me was infuriating.

"You are not only assaulting me but also offending me."

"I wasn't trying to offend—For God's sake, can you stop for a moment?"

"Just stay away from me," I ordered harshly and walked away.

When I finally managed to get to work and stepped out of the elevator, my assistant's eyes were like saucers and her mouth slightly agape. She cleared her throat and jumped to her feet but couldn't quite disguise her shock at seeing me all disheveled and late, to top it off.

"I will bring your spare suit immediately," Sofia offered and set into motion. But there was something odd about her, and it had nothing to do with seeing me in such disastrous shape.

"The meeting has already started, hasn't it?"

It was a customary meeting that my father held each Monday for all the partners. He was updated about the ongoing cases and also addressed any possible issues regarding the firm. It was so customary that it had become a downright bore, but James Burton wouldn't even think of canceling such meetings, let alone accept the absence of one of his partners.

"Yes," she replied without really meeting my eyes. "Mr. Burton was furious."

Sofia was professionally detached but tremendously loyal, and sometimes, she took my father's fits as if they were directed at her instead of me. It was evident from the tense lines around her eyes that she had already undergone such an outburst. She made no complaints, however, and five minutes later she knocked on my office door with my spare suit in her hands.

When I made it to the conference room, the partners were already filing out, and my father was standing at the end of the table, pinning me through the glass wall with hardly concealed irritation. I groaned and tried to gather the courage to face his wrath.

"Father, I'm so—"

"I don't want to hear it," he cut me off and motioned me to sit. "At least you are not late for the most important part."

My brows shot up in confusion, but he didn't consider it appropriate to enlighten me. Moments later, however, when Mayor Mitch Stewart entered the room, the situation was clear enough. My absence at the meeting hadn't really been missed since it was mandatory now.

"James, thank you for accommodating me on such short notice," the mayor greeted my father and shook hands vigorously. "Nonsense, it is our pleasure."

"The pleasure is all mine," the mayor continued and turned to me. "Char–Can I call you Charlotte? You are riveting. I wanted to personally thank you for agreeing to join my son's legal team. He is extremely fortunate to have you."

Only he didn't have me. My eyes traveled to my father, who continued to fix me with his censorious stare. He knew I hadn't accepted the case, and this was his way of ensuring I had no option but to say yes.

My cheeks colored, and my eyes burned with rage, but although I hated my father's smugness, I wasn't about to undermine his authority in front of the mayor of Washington, D.C. I swallowed the bitter taste in my mouth and plastered a cold smile on my face.

"I'll do my best so justice will prevail."

The mayor gave me a wink that contorted his whole face. He was too old to be attractive but possessed that particular appeal that politicians do, which rendered him charismatic and mysterious. His eyes were big and colorless behind his clear glasses, and his hair was gray and thinning. He stood stiffly, with his chin slightly lifted and his chest inflated beneath the expensive jacket of his suit.

I extended my hand to shake his, but Mitch Stewart caught my fingers and brought them to his lips, all the time surveying me with a shadow of mischief, the kind that was not playful but downright evil. I suppressed a shiver and removed my hand from his grasp.

"Now, let's talk business," the mayor said and took a seat across from me.

I wasn't prejudiced, but I did have killer instincts and an uncanny ability to read people. The mayor looked and behaved like a proper gentleman, but it was only a very classy façade. He was quietly aggressive and wore the armor of a man who possessed enough power to make him untouchable. He was influential and fearless, but he was not indomitable, and he certainly was not above the law.

"For the duration of my son's trial, we'd like to have you move to D.C. It would be more convenient if you worked at Cameron Drake's firm than here."

"Mr. Stewart, I understand the importance of your son's case, but I do have other cases that require equal attention on my part."

"I'm sure we will be able to properly reconcile Jack's case with Charlotte's other commitments," my father intervened. My jaw clenched, and I was convinced they had heard the sound of my teeth clinking together.

"I see. But you will have to be present for all the meetings, and I'm afraid that is non-negotiable."

"Of course."

"We can't wait for you to join us. Anything you might need for your stay, please let me know. I will personally ensure your requirements are met."

I nodded but did not fall for his chivalrous act. The more he talked, the more strained his courtesy seemed. He was the man that others pleased, not the one who met people's requirements. And then it dawned on me why he accepted me on his team. While Cameron Drake was lead-counsel, I was the publicity stunt.

One of my father's many attempts to convince me that being a lawyer was the best thing I could do with my life had been striking a deal. For any high-level case I successfully settled, I could work on any pro bono case of my choosing. And I chose those who couldn't or didn't know how to defend themselves. I chose battered women and exploited children, and for once, I drew satisfaction from my job.

Before long, I had built a reputation for being fair and dangerously determined to put abusers behind bars. So, being the one to defend someone accused of the ultimate form of abuse had to raise some questions like maybe he wasn't guilty after all? I was the figure who was going to make his son look good.

"And there's something else I came here for."

The mayor pushed a folder across the table, and I opened it with reluctant fingers. They wanted me to gather evidence and testimonies that Jack Stewart was an upstanding citizen. While such proof wasn't going to acquit him of the crime he was accused of, it was undoubtedly going to sway the jury in his favor.

"I'll get to work. It was nice meeting you, Mr. Mayor."

My back was rigid as I walked out of the conference room. Nothing about today was nice, and I got the horrible feeling that things weren't going to be nice for a long while. When my father followed me into my office, his face tight and bleak, it was evident that the worst part of my day hadn't passed yet.

He sat in one of the two leather chairs in front of my desk and regarded me with a narrowed look that was the only indication of his disappointment.

"Charlotte..." he began somberly, lacing his fingers together and resting his hands on his chest. He was able to make even my own name sound like a reprimand.

When he looked at me with that intent, reproachful stare, I didn't feel like a full-grown woman but a little girl who tried time and time again to please a father who could not be pleased. Irritation and discomfort mingled together, and eventually, the annoyance won.

"I don't appreciate you strong-arming me into accepting a case."

James Burton was not accustomed to being confronted, especially not by his daughter, but he was experienced enough to quickly school his expression into a neutral mask as he stood and glared my way. His stare was somber and implacable as he pointed his finger in my direction.

"I don't appreciate you being ungrateful, so get your act together and start preparing Jack Stewart's defense."

"I already told you that I am not comfortable accepting this case, not when I work daily with abused women and do my best to defend them from the likes of Jack Stewart. You can't ask me to work for somebody I don't believe in."

He didn't even listen. He gestured irritably then pinned me with a conclusive stare.

"There is a big difference between tolerating your little hobbies and turning a blind eye to you sabotaging your career. This is a high-profile case that will serve as a launching ramp for you."

I couldn't entirely control my disbelieving gasp, nor bring myself to care about the disapproving daggers in his eyes. The pro bono work I did was one of the few satisfactions I had from being a lawyer. That my father considered it a hobby both hurt and angered me.

"How will I be of any service to Jack Stewart if I don't have his best interest at heart?"

"By holding judgment," he snapped. At that moment, James Burton looked more like a stranger than my own father. "I wasn't making a request, Charlotte. You will take the case, and you might hate me if that pleases you, but mark my word, darling, the day will come when you will thank me."

"I doubt that," I whispered to myself and lowered my eyes in defeat.

It took that small gesture of acquiescence for my father to recover his harmonious disposition. He rounded my desk, cupped my cheeks, and pressed a fatherly kiss on my forehead, allowing me to dream that he was a warm understanding father. Then he straightened his silver suit jacket and walked past me without another glance.

"And Charlotte," he added in that same authoritative, cool voice before he reached the door. "In this firm, I am not your father. I am your boss. Do not be late again."

"Yes, sir!" The words came out drily, with just a shade of hurt.

I closed my eyes, rubbing my eyelids with the heels of my hands, probably smearing my makeup in the process. Tears gathered in the corners of my eyes, but I refused to let them spill. I didn't deserve to be crying. After all my sacrifices, the least my father could grant me was a pleasant environment to work in.

What he thought he was granting me, though, was the honor of working with some of the best lawyers in the country. While I had never dreamed of nor desired such an honor, my destiny had been written before I was even born.

I walked to the glass wall behind my desk and looked outside. My office, unlike my father's, was not on the top floor of the building, but it still offered a spectacular view over Central Park. From this far up, I could only see the treetops, but the tranquility that small part of nature exuded managed to calm me when nothing else in the office could.

I breathed once more, longing for a cleansing run by the lake, but in the end, I let out a sigh and returned to my duties. It was going to be a stressful day.

BY LUNCHTIME, MY HEAD WAS throbbing with a dull ache, and my stomach churned painfully, but I didn't dare leave my office for a quick meal. My father's earlier admonishment had been more than enough, so when my step-sister waltzed in, unannounced and with her baby daughter in her arms, I was afraid to even hope I could enjoy half an hour of their company.

Christina was four years older than me, and the only parent we had in common was specifically the father she nearly despised, and I dreaded. James had married Christina's mother, Julie, for a brief period, his reasons uncertain as were the reasons he'd had for filing for divorce six months later.

Three months after the divorce, Christina was born, but my father had stubbornly and repeatedly refused to recognize her.

While Julie had always refused to allow a DNA test, Christina had accepted it as soon as she became of age, but by that time, my father had burned bridges and inflicted wounds that couldn't be mended. By the time he accepted that Christina was his first daughter, she had already grown to love another man as her dad and had built a life which James Burton was not a part of.

Thankfully, she was not as rancorous as to not allow me to be a part of her life. Although my father hadn't allowed me to spend much time with Christina when I was young, he hadn't cut her out from my life altogether, so we developed an excellent relationship long before a test result told us that we were indeed sisters.

"Hello, pumpkin," Christina chuckled as she sat little Marie on the black leather sofa in the far corner of my office.

I couldn't help but laugh. She had been calling me that ever since we spent our first Thanksgiving together, and I ate a whole pumpkin on my own. I really liked pumpkin, I thought, and my empty stomach instantly reacted.

"Hi," I sang, a sincere smile lighting my expression as I gave her a warm hug then swiftly bent to press a kiss on top of my adorable niece's head. "Nobody announced you two. Hello, Marie. Did you miss me, precious?"

"Did we need an announcement?" Christina asked, falsely upset.

"No, of course not, but…"

"Bah-bu-oon…" Marie muttered, coming into my arms eagerly as soon as I sat near her on the sofa. The girl had an innate talent for making you instantly fall in love with her.

"What's she trying to say?" I asked Christina.

"Balloon," Christina laughed and rolled her eyes. "Logan spoils her too much. Now the entire house is full of balloons."

Marie was an exact replica of Christina when she had been a baby. I could even see a small resemblance to me, which meant that our father's genes weighed more than Christina wanted to admit. She was a peewee with dark curls and big almond eyes that conquered you with their brown depths. But it was the broad, childish smile she displayed all the time that stole your heart. It was unbelievable how such a small creature could control all the adults around her. And we let her do so freely because she was tremendously loved.

"So any reason in particular why you are visiting me?"

We saw each other almost daily, but she had a determination to not cross our father's path, which I never questioned. To see her come willingly into his territory where she could bump into him at any moment was more than surprising. It was strange.

"To take you out to lunch, of course."

"Chris, I don't know—I don't think I should today. Father is already upset with me."

"When is he not?" she scoffed, struggling to hide her distaste. "But anyway, you are entitled to a lunch break, so that's where we're going. I know this place close by. They make a salmon salad to die for."

"Chris, I am serious. I don't want to fight with him anymore."

"You won't fight with him, I promise."

A sudden sadness crossed her chocolate eyes, the same color as my own, as our father's, but then the sadness was gone. What she had meant was that James would not fight with me if she were close by so he could fight with her.

I hated that he had never let her in, never tried to love her, never offered her the place she deserved in his heart, in his life, and in his family.

Marie clenched her little fists in my hair and bumped her small feet against my knees, happiness dancing in her astonishing eyes. I wished I were so carefree, so happy.

I was so accustomed to always pleasing my father that I was ready to put work before family.

"Let's go."

Chapter 4

Marcus

*A*lthough I knew I was making a fool of myself, the stupid grin I had been wearing all day simply didn't want to wane. How likely was it to meet the same woman by accident twice in less than a week when I had never met her before? And why was I still thinking of her?

Or maybe I wasn't thinking of her but of those fascinating brown eyes that glimmered with emotion. Bravery and fear fused together in their depths. She blinked and hinted at the mysteries she was sheltering. Mysteries, especially when they wore the disguise of a beautiful woman, rendered a man's fantasy wild.

"Earth to King Marcus," Bryson shouted smacking me right up on the head.

"Touch me again, and I don't guarantee you'll keep your hand."

"Oooh, don't taunt the tiger," Brayden laughed, throwing his head back and slapping his knees repeatedly, something he always did when he was amused.

L'Affaire was once again packed with strident people. Sitting quietly in such a place was more likely to attract attention than Brayden's howling laughter. Despite the intoxicating smoke and the tart smell of alcohol filling the air, I liked being there.

The clamor of the place, the agitation, and the different personalities created a unique vibe that pulsated with the music. It was a pleasant mixture that drowned out my dark thoughts. I couldn't think of my problems when I was here, but apparently, I could think of Brayden's Friday night prey. Having them know that I was thinking of her was the last thing I wanted.

"Who won the race Friday night?" I asked to distract myself from pursuing my line of thought and them from asking unsolicited questions.

They all exchanged a look while Kai sighed dreamily. Suddenly, there was no need for an answer as I suspected who must have won the damn race.

"It was The Fox. She won by a minute."

"She won because you are complete drunken idiots. That's why," I cut in bitterly.

I was not misogynistic. A woman could win a motorcycle race just as efficiently as a man if she was properly trained and had the skill to tame her bike. But The Fox was not just a woman. She was the monument of everything I despised in a female, and for that, I simply could not conceive of the fact that she had earned the satisfaction of winning a race or anything else for that matter.

"The woman is just...unbelievable," Kai sighed again, a far-off look in his eyes.

My cousin was not an idiot, but he wasn't far from being one either. I was perhaps the only one who had noticed his fondness for The Fox, whose real name few actually knew, and I was also the only one to warn him against developing or pursuing that attachment. After all, how could I counsel my own blood to court a woman who had been openly trying to seduce me? The only reason I hadn't welcomed her advances was that I refused to be the toy of any woman. I was not a plaything, and what she wanted was exactly that.

"The woman is just...treacherous," I corrected him with a frown.

"Exactly," Brayden joined in with bitter enthusiasm. "Women are treacherous, and they treacherously stab you in the back."

"I didn't mean all of them."

I knew Brayden was still hurting because of what Harper had done to him. I knew he could taste her betrayal every day because, despite everything he said or did, he still loved her stupidly and that was why it hurt that bad.

I could see his wounds, raw and bleeding, but that didn't mean he was right in treating all the women passing through his life like they were garbage. Some women cheated and messed up a man's life, but just as well, some men broke hearts and destroyed destinies. I was one of them.

"What do you know?" he spat, standing and kicking off his chair. With a look of sheer disgust, he walked to the bar for another night of drowning his sorrows in alcohol.

"I know that you are so enraged that the right person might walk into your life and you might just miss her," I shouted after him, knowing that whoever else heard me would not give a damn.

"Then you know nothing. There's no such thing as the right person, you idiot."

"Great," Kai exhaled, falling back in his chair and locking his hands behind his head.

Kai was the one who hated conflict the most. Maybe out of all of us, Kai was the one with the highest potential and the kindest heart. Too bad for him that he kept us as company.

"He'll get over it eventually," Bryson mumbled, his eyes trailing to his brother.

They might have been acting more often than not as complete idiots, the idea of responsibility might have been foreign to them, but when it mattered the most, they were there for each other, and they were there for Kai and me too. We might have brawled and disagreed, but in the end, the bond that united us was stronger than any argument.

"What's up with you, though?" Bryson asked, his whole attention suddenly focused on me.

At first, I thought he was referring to my earlier reflective mood, but when I caught sight of his openly concerned expression and slightly knit brows, I knew he was referring, in fact, to my father.

"You mean what's up with Isaac?" I simply couldn't call him father. He was not a father to me. A father wouldn't do to his son what he was doing to me. "He's still trying to put me in jail. He's still frustrated that he's failing."

"The bastard," Bryson growled under his breath, clenching his jaw after another shot of alcohol. "How long is he going to persecute you like this?"

"Until I subject myself to his damn wishes," I sighed and gulped the remainder of my glass of whiskey.

Although I didn't usually drink before races, I allowed myself those few sips. The liquid burned my throat and rushed down to my stomach like a serpent of fire.

"Who's racing tonight?" I asked, eager to change the course of the discussion.

"The Fox," Kai mumbled almost inaudibly yet loud enough for me to hear. When my fist connected with his shoulder, he didn't even flinch.

"Cut him some slack, dude," Bryson laughed. "The idiot is falling in love."

"That's what I'm afraid of."

"Hey, I'm still here," Kai protested. I could have sworn the slightest tinge of red had already colored his cheeks.

I left *L'Affaire* roughly an hour later. I needed to clear my mind before the race and make sure that nobody was tailing me. My father knew about my questionable habit and had made quite a lot of attempts to expose me to the authorities, but I was not going to facilitate his work and let him discover that easily where or when the races took place.

I was passing Paris Theater when a flash of royal blue caught my eye, and a familiar feminine voice reached my ears. Actually, the voice was not familiar at all. It hadn't even been a whole week since the first time I heard it, so the fact that it already sounded familiar should have worried me. But for now, I was too intrigued by my brown-eyed mystery to care.

I turned around and fully watched her. She had been remarkable when frightened. She had been appealing when furious. But now, as she laughed and her long brown locks bounced around her head, she was mesmerizing.

A man wrapped an arm around her shoulder and kissed her

temple as she continued laughing at whatever he was telling her. I tried ignoring the rash displeasure caused by their proximity and instead focused on her.

She didn't wear anything out of the ordinary, just a blue chiffon blouse and a pair of white pants, paired with high stilettos that could have stirred any man's imagination, but the simple attire complimented her in all the right places.

The man let go of her and put his arm protectively, dominantly even, around the waist of another woman, who had just joined them, holding tickets. I breathed with a relief I didn't expect to feel, and suddenly, I made a decision I had never expected to make. When they turned to enter the movie theater, I followed and bought my own ticket. After all, how could I have allowed a beautiful woman to feel like the third wheel next to a couple of lovebirds?

Judging by the price I had to pay for that little piece of paper and by the crowd filling the hall, there must have been the preview of some movie. I didn't even bother to check the name. My attention was solely focused on the woman with the blue blouse.

By the time I made it inside, she had already sat with her friends in the eighth row. Although my seat was three rows behind, I hurried to catch the empty chair to her left. I had a little plan I needed to carry out—I needed to find out the name of my mystery.

A girl headed for my seat, innocently believing she could claim it, but froze when she bumped into me. With a furious blush, she scurried away as soon as she took notice of my glare. She slid in the closest seat to the wall and risked another look at me, only to find me glaring some more for good measure.

Although my first instinct had been to plump down noisily, anticipating my mystery's predictable startle, I sat as quietly and discreetly as possible. I reined myself in for two reasons: one, I had already startled her on our previous two meetings and the outcome hadn't been pleasant, and two, I knew I would enjoy more a look of incredulous surprise than a jerk of apprehension.

"One of these days your sister is going to give me diabetes," the man sitting next to her was saying, causing the other woman to instantly protest. So my mystery had a sister. Had I not been so intrigued and enraptured by her, maybe I would have adequately appreciated the beauty of her sibling.

"That is not true. And the only reason you might get diabetes is that you can't get enough of my cakes."

"True," my mystery spoke. "And I'll get fat before getting diabetes."

I bit my tongue to stop from interfering and telling her that she was anything but fat and that I was willing to keep her fit myself. A stupid grin covered my face just when the opening credits started playing and the lights dimmed.

I set my arm on the armrest between us and waited for her reaction. It wasn't long until she accidentally touched me, or rather, scratched the skin off my hand, then whirled in her seat to apologize.

At first, she wore a magnificently apologetic expression, which was quickly tinted by that incredulous surprise I had expected. Then, the funniest shade of revulsion settled from the depths of her brown eyes to the tilt of her rosy lips. I bit the inside of my cheek to keep from laughing. She was truly delightful.

"Unbelievable," she muttered, but in the silence that had fallen, her voice sounded too loud.

"Oh, what a surprise," I answered, falsely shocked. My smile simply didn't want to leave my face.

"What are you trying to accomplish?" she hissed. Once more, her voice was too loud for the silence surrounding us.

"What's that?" the man next to her asked, leaning into my mystery, which only caught the attention of the other woman. All of a sudden, the three of them were facing me—my mystery with a vexed look on her face and her two companions with skeptical surprise sparkling in their eyes.

"Hi. I apologize for being late," I told them as if we were old acquaintances and held out my hand. "I'm Marcus King."

"Mm—Hi," the man answered, still skeptical but shaking my hand briskly. "Logan Barrett."

"Christina," the sister said and shook my hand in a very feminine way, displaying a blooming smile she couldn't quite suppress. "I didn't know you invited someone, sis."

"I didn't…" she objected, this time so quietly that I hardly heard her. The disgust on her face, however, was beyond visible and beyond amusing.

"Now," I whispered, inching closer to her as Logan and Christina returned their attention to the big screen. "Aren't you going to tell me your name, sugar?"

"I am not sugar, and I am not—" she trailed off, struggling to keep her voice down.

"If you don't tell me your name, I have to call you something."

She kept her eyes fixed on the screen although I doubted she was paying any attention to the movie. She sat rigidly by my side, but thankfully, there wasn't any trace of panic. Maybe her body knew better than her mind that I didn't mean her any harm.

"Ignoring me isn't going to work," I whispered in her ear.

I had a height advantage over her even if we were sitting, so I was able to catch every twist of her features without moving my head. I got the distinct impression that she wasn't as revolted as she let on. And I liked that. It meant that I had a chance to creep past her defenses.

"I am here to watch a movie, Mr. King. I would appreciate it if you let me."

"See? That is not fair. You already know my name, but I don't know yours. I like equality."

"Charlotte," she snapped in a whisper. "Satisfied? Are you going to let me watch the movie now?"

I hadn't expected that my smile could grow any wider. I liked her name. And truth be told, I liked the woman too. Perhaps that was why I felt so intrigued by her.

Yet pursuing her was dangerous.

Memories that felt dreadfully real flashed in my mind, and for a fraction of a second, they overwhelmed me. Charlotte seemed a lovely, decent woman—a woman who should not have me in her life. So I promised myself tonight was all I allowed myself to have—just a few hours of innocent fun.

"I will try," I replied, letting the hand I had kept on the armrest between us invade her space. She didn't flinch but merely watched my hand, anticipating my next move. "But are you going to watch it?" I teased her.

Instead of answering my question, she crossed her legs and folded her arms on her chest, stubbornly looking ahead, although we both knew that she wasn't watching the movie.

Knowing that I distracted her pleased me. Trying to decipher why it pleased me was a matter I did not want to consider at the moment. So I mimicked her posture and watched her while she obstinately ignored me. I was going to miss another race because of this woman, and I just couldn't bring myself to care.

Chapter 5

Charlotte

"**I**s this supposed to be a horror movie?" Marcus murmured, appalled, shifting in his seat until his arm was pressed against mine.

I should have been the one appalled for thinking of him as Marcus as if he were an old acquaintance. I should have been even more troubled that I had told neither my sister nor her husband that he was practically a stranger. Yet the proximity between us didn't bother me as much as it should. And because of that, I was frustrated with myself and even more so with him.

"Look, I don't trust you or your intentions," I said, leaning against the armrest.

Despite the darkness, despite the fact that each time I dared to look up at him, his eyes were directed forward, I was confident he had been watching me. I could feel those blue eyes stuck to my skin as if they had been flames burning through me. His insistence should have scared me, or at least offended me. And because I just felt stupidly flattered, I got defensive, which might have been a flaw of mine, but after all, I couldn't be blamed. I hardly knew the man and stalking me didn't help his cause.

"Why?" he rumbled, sounding genuinely scandalized when I

knew he wasn't. "Is it my jacket?" he continued, touching the black leather jacket he was wearing like he was seeing it for the first time in his life and wondered if it was offensive or not.

With theatrics that weren't required, he removed his jacket, flexing all too unnecessarily his muscles and scattering around his scent of spice and musk, then let it drop on the empty seat to his left. He turned his head back to me with a cocky grin that should have annoyed and insulted me. Instead, it made me blush, and the darkness shrouding us did little to hide my discomfort.

"Problem solved," he chimed proudly.

He was wearing a raisin black V-neck shirt that pulled tautly around his torso and complimented his muscular arms. I had noticed his strength since the first time we met, but having him so close, his arm brushing mine and his smug confidence stunning me, the virility he radiated intimidated as well as enticed me.

What was wrong with me? He was a stranger in a crowd, and that was how he should remain. I didn't befriend just anybody or pay attention to whoever tried to pick me up on the street. In fact, that type of person caused enormous red flags to pop in my head.

I didn't trust the likes of him, so why was he different? Why was he silently tempting me to play his game?

"And you aren't funny either," I retorted. Maybe if I were mean enough, he would give up, and I would not be forced to battle with the temptation he embodied.

"No? Not even a little?"

He bent so low that his lips nearly brushed my temple. Once again, I tried to focus on the movie, but it was easier to let myself inhale his scent. He smelled of conifers, musk, and lavender, all wrapped around his natural manly fragrance. His warmth enclosed me, and not only did it enhance his dizzying perfume, but it also increased my own body temperature.

I had been truly thankful that it was dark enough to not be properly seen until my eyes flicked to my right to see Christina gazing at us with a conspiratorial gleam and a silly grin that made her look like someone who belonged in a circus.

"What?" I mouthed, glaring.

"You look gorgeous," she mouthed back.

Winking, she let her head rest on Logan's shoulder. She had been trying for so long to push me into some Prince Charming's arms that I wouldn't have been surprised if she decided she liked Marcus enough to start with her usual romantic plots.

"Of course, we do," Marcus whispered, making me shudder.

"I bet you have a great time at my expense."

"No, not at your expense. I'd like to have a great time with you."

A sinewy and equally warm arm enfolded my shoulders and slightly pulled me to him. He was acting with such an arrogant ease while I tensed and felt my whole body catching fire. I'd like to have been that type of woman who flirted easily, who trusted quickly, who had one-night stands without regrets, but I wasn't.

I was cautious, and I trusted people with difficulty because when I did care about someone, I did so completely. I jumped headfirst, without restraints, without holding back. When I loved, I loved with every cell of my body, with every drop of my blood. I loved with a passion that consumed me, and for that, I needed to be careful. I needed to guard my heart.

"You're crossing the line," I hissed.

"Am I? Because you can always shake my arm off, which you haven't done yet."

I convinced myself that I wasn't shaking off his arm because I wanted to be civilized and not cause a scene. And I also convinced myself that I couldn't feel his warmth soaking through my blouse. But in spite of how hard I coaxed myself to ignore him, and certainly, to his immense pleasure, I was completely aware of him.

"I'm trying very hard to be polite, but you're making it difficult."

"Hissing at me is not exactly polite," he chuckled. His fingers started a slow dance on my right shoulder. If I was growing stiffer and stiffer in my seat, he was becoming absolutely, annoyingly comfortable. "But let's continue being civilized. Tell me something about yourself."

"I don't share my personal life with strangers."

"Then, I'll start," he went on cheerfully, tirelessly. "I'm twenty-nine and a Scorpio, allegedly the most sexual sign. I wouldn't dare object."

I was about to faint. I couldn't believe my ears. Nobody could be that obstinate or conceited, surely? I glared up at him before I could stop myself. After all, we both knew I had never quite ignored him. My aversion, however, didn't bother him in the slightest but merely entertained him.

"I've had a wonderful relationship for six years now with Kinga…my dog. I have an unexplainable but troubling fear of insects. My favorite color is… well, right now there's a battle between the tempting chocolate shade of your eyes and the blue of your blouse."

Marcus traced his index finger from my right shoulder all the way to my elbow. "It complements your skin so wonderfully."

I shuddered and struggled to escape his touch. If I evaded his caress, I would press closer into him, to his chest. If I kept enduring his stroking fingers, then he would realize that his touch affected me more than I wanted to admit. He was creating a blaze that smoldered within me.

No, it was the embarrassment that caused the blaze, I assured myself.

"While your chitchat is very entertaining, I'd like to pay attention to the movie."

"I like a woman who makes me work for her affection," he continued, unaffected by my continual crossness.

"I don't like a man who takes pleasure in getting on my nerves."

"I'll make sure to keep such a man away from you if I see one."

"I was talking about you," I muttered, looking up at him. He stared back with a concentration that momentarily stole my breath.

"What would life be if the man beside you agreed with you on everything? Don't you think you'd miss the spice that makes life interesting?"

"I think that would be a very peaceful, harmonious life."

"And a very boring one," he concluded.

He finally fell silent, and the abruptness with which he did so, or the absence of his husky voice ringing in my ear, startled me. I should have felt relieved that he had finally deigned to shut up. I should have been able to regain a modicum of composure and cool my burning skin. But I was still sitting stiffly in my seat with my arms folded on my chest, which made Christina chuckle against Logan's shoulder. Moreover, the fact that Marcus seemed to have suddenly become low-spirited didn't make me feel any better.

"So you enjoy being in conflict with people? That's how you spice up your life?"

I was stunned with myself that this time, I was the one seeking to break the silence. Thankfully, Christina had chosen seats close to the wall where it wasn't too crowded. Still, although our entire conversation had been very quiet, it was a small miracle that nobody had come to escort us outside.

"Not necessarily in conflict," he replied in that deep, slightly raucous voice of his that made one's blood pump and rush in strange ways. "But I do believe that divergent minds can create spectacular situations and achieve unexpected outcomes. I do believe that opposed characters are inevitably drawn to each other. Because what you lack, I can offer you, and where I'm faulted, you can mend me."

"Hypothetically speaking," I hurried to interject. He couldn't talk about him and me. There was no him and me.

"Hypothetically speaking," he agreed softly, his breath fanning across my face. I could feel the smile in his voice and the heat in my cheeks. "We aren't strangers anymore now, are we? You know all about me."

"Don't be modest, Mr. King. You certainly can't be summed up in so few words."

Courageous was the last epithet I would have used to describe myself, but just for tonight, he made me want to be so courageous as to take part in his little game. For one short night, I just wanted to leave caution aside and put fears to sleep.

"I have a Mechanical Engineering degree to my father's absolute dismay," he told me, this time on a more serious note than before.

"Oh," I breathed, truthfully taken aback.

I wasn't prejudiced, but I hadn't expected him to have a degree, let alone such a complex one. Indeed, he could have lied just to impress me, but I didn't believe he had. Perhaps it was his alluring voice or his confident attitude, driven to a maddening point, but when he spoke, he made me believe him entirely.

"Let's say your surprise flatters me," he trailed off, a smile still playing across his face. His voice, though, didn't sound entirely pleased.

"I didn't mean to offend you," I hurried to explain. "But I really didn't expect you to—"

"What did you expect then? How did you see me?"

"A motorcyclist," I replied without a second thought.

"I am," Marcus admitted nonchalantly as if being on a motorcycle was the most common thing when to me, it was something so outlandish that I didn't even dare to think of it. My father had made sure from early on that I was always busy studying or engaged in some intellectual activity. I had never even learned how to ride a bicycle. "What are *you*, Charlotte?"

"Me?" I almost stuttered, once again startled by his blunt approach. My eyes were hardly focused on the screen now but searching again and again for his face. "I'm not so daring."

"I think you are not allowing yourself to be," he whispered against my temple, making my skin tingle.

When he fell silent again, I knew it was because this time he expected me to take the first step—to be daring. He was patient, letting me digest his words. He was also cunning, testing me, challenging me to be as daring as I had said I couldn't be.

"And how would you describe a daring woman?"

"A woman who is determined and not afraid of taking what she wants, yet not a woman who is a ruthless manipulator. A woman who is strong enough to admit she might be weak at times. A woman who is not afraid to show her vulnerability. A woman who ventures to dream strange, impossible things. A woman who will go against the world to defend her ideals. A woman who is willing to be put out of her comfort zone. A woman willing to explore her limits even though she is not sure of the outcome."

That woman he was talking about was not me. That woman was the type of person I could only wish to become because plain, wary me could not measure up to such heights.

"You like daring women." It was rather a statement than a question, but after he scanned my profile minutely, he answered nonetheless.

"I do. As much as you like annoyingly tenacious men."

"Have you found someone matching your description?" I

inquired, choosing to ignore his comment.

"Not yet."

The people around us seemed honestly awestruck by the movie and relatively scared, but my mind was entirely someplace else. Marcus's words kept ringing in my head. His voice was still filling dark and hidden corners of my mind. And his eyes were positively haunting me. Instinctively, I turned to look up at him, but he was watching the movie, or pretending to.

The psychopath in the movie meandered his way down a dark corridor, a demented look in his eyes. The music in the background thudded in the speakers, creating a gripping atmosphere. Suddenly the psychopath appeared behind his prey, pushing her brutally against the wall behind them and pressing a blade against her throat. Somewhere behind us, someone yelped and made me give a start. To my left, Marcus chuckled.

"You should act scared, Charlotte," he told me, inching closer for the umpteenth time. The way he had said my name was as if he had savored it before letting it out. "The movie is about to end."

I realized a few minutes later as the ending credits rolled on the screen and the lights came on that I had no idea what the movie had been about. I exceedingly hoped that Christina or Logan would not ask me if I liked the movie or something in particular about the action. In fact, now that the movie didn't prevent them from questioning me about Marcus, I suddenly became as tense as I had been the second I found him next to me. What was I supposed to say about him? That we met the night his friends had assaulted me?

We left the theater in near silence. I saw my sister and her husband kissing lightly on the lips every few steps they took, with such a warm ease, such loving familiarity that it made me wonder how it would feel to have somebody to wake up to—somebody to wake up for?

Yet, it was Marcus my eyes strayed to every so often. Now that we had left the theater, he was going to vanish any moment.

"Frowning doesn't suit you," I heard him saying. He had put his leather jacket back on, and his right arm rubbed against mine. "It makes you look older."

"You're awful at complimenting a woman." My voice came out

in a rash, severe breath, just like I knew it would.

"I wasn't trying to compliment you. It does make you look older when you frown because when you don't, your eyes have the power of making a man melt on his feet."

I hoped he hadn't heard me groan. He was tireless. And although I had ignored his earlier comment, although I forbade myself to agree with it, I was flattered.

When Logan's phone rang, I felt saved by the bell. I turned my back on Marcus, skimming Logan and Christina's faces as Logan spoke swiftly into the phone and my sister leaned to hear what the person at the other end of the line was saying. Sighing, I wished that Marcus's body heat hadn't traversed the space between us and seeped right through me.

The conversation was short and efficient, my father would have said. As soon as Logan put the phone back into his pocket, he whispered something to Christina and her face fell. Something was wrong with Marie. Nothing else could have made her turn pasty white out of the blue. Nothing could have affected her in such a manner.

"Is everything alright?" I managed to ask, closing the space between us.

"It's Marie," Logan confirmed my suspicions. "She's got a fever. Apparently, she's been crying all night and feeling bad. We should go home, Chris."

"Yes—I—" she stammered, and her eyes almost filled with tears.

It was odd to see my warrior sister crumbling so fast, just thinking about her daughter being in pain. Then, with agitation twisting her features, she turned to me apologetically. I already knew what she was about to tell me.

"Are you okay if we cut the night short?"

I nodded and kissed her cheek. Although they were going to leave me alone with a man I hardly knew, I could take care of myself. Marcus might not have been my friend as he had pretended to be all evening, but I wasn't in danger with him either. I knew criminals, and he wasn't one. He might have been too persistent, too intense, and too obstinate, but he was not a man intent on harming me.

"Yes," I answered when Christina stared at me warily and unconvinced. "You can go. I'll manage."

They exchanged pleasantries and hastened to their car. My previous bravado that I would manage wavered as soon as I remained alone with Marcus, who hadn't fled yet. He was frowning when I turned to him.

"Frowning doesn't suit you either, Mr. King."

"Will they be okay?" he asked, genuinely concerned.

It would have been easier if he had made some rude joke that would have gotten on my nerves. It wouldn't have made me feel guilty for pushing him away unkindly.

"Yes," I responded, starting the short walk to my own car.

He nodded then walked confidently by my side. "You have been unpredictably bashful for our first date."

In a very deep corner of my mind, I knew this was his way of lightening the mood. But he was relentless. And the things he was saying… Certainly, he was that persistent and that audacious because my embarrassment amused him. I wondered if I was just another woman on a long list of conquests.

"This hasn't been a date," I growled, a horrid sound even to my own ears. "God—"

Back there in the movie theater, I had fallen under his spell. I had played his game. But now, back outside in the blaring city night, back in the vortex of people passing by, back to real life, the real *me* returned, and guardedness prevailed. I could see it in his eyes that he had spotted the precise moment when walls rocketed up around me like armor.

"It was to me," he said. The smile he had on his face suddenly didn't seem as genuine or cheeky as before.

"You were very funny in there, but we should stop pretending."

"I wasn't pretending, Charlotte. I wanted to know you," he cut in, almost sternly. His laidback demeanor was gone. Instead, the brilliant, intimidating man I had seen Friday night walked unbendingly beside me.

I was both grateful and sorry that we were about to permanently part ways. I pretended that I was focused on fishing the car keys out of my purse, but I was completely aware of him standing next to me. I also knew that as soon as I looked up, he would say something else in that deep, sensual voice of his, forcing me to reply rudely just to make sure I would get rid of him.

But did I want to get rid of him? Couldn't I persist under his spell for a little while longer? Couldn't I try to be that daring woman he had told me about?

"Charlotte, I'd like—" he started the instant I pulled the door open, blocking my escape with a firm hand pressing the door shut.

When his voice died down, and he removed his hand from the door without me having to tell him anything, I looked up to find him once more frowning. His eyes were directed to the passenger seat where I had forgotten a folder with the logo of my father's firm and my name at the top.

"Charlotte Burton—Burton & Associates? Are you a secretary or something?"

"No. I am a lawyer. And I could have you arrested for assault and stalking."

I hadn't meant a word of what I said, but the words dripped maliciously off my tongue anyway. If Marcus had known me, he would have recognized my defense mechanism. He would have known that I was rude only to push the temptation away and make sure I wouldn't be hurt. He would have known this was the coward *me* operating. But he did not know me, and I was too scared to let a stranger in.

His face fell, and the frown I had found between his brows when I looked up disappeared too. Instead, his expression settled into a placid mask that seemed out of place on his face. His blue eyes were meant to sparkle with mischief and amusement. His lips were supposed to be tilted up into a smile. And I had made the amusement disappear and the smile wither. I couldn't keep him at arm's length and pleased all at the same time.

"Actually, no, Miss, you can't. To accuse me of assault, I should have caused bodily harm to you, and I—I haven't caused you a scratch."

His voice had sounded purposefully harsh, lacking in the calm tone I was accustomed to him using with me. He even took a step backward, looking at me as one looked at a mistake he regretted having made. I shouldn't have felt so deeply ashamed of my attitude, but I did. And I honestly wanted to apologize, but my tongue spoke completely different words.

"It suffices that you intentionally or knowingly caused me to fear imminent bodily injury."

My voice was smug as the lawyer took over, but my cheeks burned with remorse when I saw him flinch and roll his jaw. I should have simply told him to leave me alone. Maybe we would have parted ways politely.

"Careful, sugar. Defamation is also punishable by law."

Chapter 6

Marcus

I had a foul taste in my mouth as if I had eaten something rotten, but food was not the cause of my sickness. It was the taste Charlotte Burton had left me. It was the very same taste my father left me each time we met.

I kept walking as fast and as far away as possible from the woman who now had a name, a profession, and a life that had nothing to do with me. I had asked her if she was a secretary because the alternative was too abhorrent to consider. But of course, she was not a secretary. She was a Burton—James Burton's daughter.

Marching through the night, I laughed bitterly. My father had constantly praised the bright and hard-working daughter of his partner. He had always resented me that I wasn't more like her, more compliant, more sharp-sighted. I had known about her ever since I was a boy, and yet, I had to meet her by accident while my stupid friends were attacking her.

Life had an ironic way of defying me, of haunting me. Who would have imagined that the first woman who held my interest in such a long while, who intrigued me to such extent that I had been unable not to pursue her, was nothing else but a lawyer and the daughter of my father's business associate?

As I walked, I clenched my fists so hard that the skin covering my knuckles grew thin. Automatically, I checked my phone. It was almost midnight, and I had twelve missed calls and four messages. The calls were from Bryson and Kai, and the messages were from different women who attended the races, telling me how much they missed me. By now, the race must have been over, and I had no other way to uproot the anger that was tightening around me like a vice.

"I could have you arrested…" she had sneered. In my mind, her voice merged with my father's—the same coolness, the same superiority, the same detachment.

The brutal way in which we had parted should have sufficed to get her out of my mind. In fact, it should have awakened in me at least a feeble desire to avenge my trampled pride. But it didn't. It was her calm expression from the movie theater and the blush adorning her cheeks that popped in my head.

She hadn't known that she was striking precisely where it hurt the most. She hadn't known she was touching insecurities I strived to keep hidden, insecurities that my own father had created. And she definitely couldn't have known that her words had rubbed salt in old festering wounds.

I had allowed myself one night with her, escaping my dark world to step into a world where I was a simple stranger talking to a beautiful mystery. The night was over, and so was our acquaintance. Tomorrow she was going to forget me, and I was going to do the same.

Despite her coldness, her spitefulness even, I couldn't bring myself to regret my spontaneous decision to follow her inside that movie theater. Because this was how I was—I lived on the edge, I sought danger, and I took chances. Sometimes I failed, sometimes I got broken by those exact decisions that I had made, and sometimes I defeated all odds and succeeded. Charlotte Burton was that kind of memory that I locked in a corner of my mind to stop it from haunting me. She was in the past now.

I knew as soon as I unlocked the door to my flat that something was wrong. Kinga's usual bark didn't greet me. In fact, the silence that reigned over my apartment was disconcerting. If I had paid attention to the movie, and if I had been a white-livered man, I might have been scared. I turned the lights on, about to call out Kinga's name, when my eyes landed on the loveseat in my living room. And there was Isaac King with his linked hands resting in his lap.

"Have you finished your little race, Son?"

As if my night wasn't already bad enough, my father effortlessly made it worse. I clenched my fists again, and my father's hawk eyes caught the tension-loaded gesture with a smirk. Arching an eyebrow, he glanced at my balled hands and challenged me to act on my frustrations.

Despite everything he was keen on doing to me, I had never considered raising a hand against my own father. I wasn't so stupid as to give him the perfect excuse to press charges against me. The thought made me groan, made me remember a delightful pair of brown eyes that had held for me nothing but contempt.

"I have no idea what you are talking about, Isaac," I replied icily. "To what do I owe the displeasure of having you in my apartment?"

"Visiting my son was not a crime last time I checked."

To my utmost irritation, his response was calm and aloof. As he always was. The blue eyes I had unfortunately inherited from him checked steadily every twist of my emotions. Where he was poker-faced, I must have been a volcano on the brink of erupting.

"You should know everything about crimes," I muttered under my breath, so low that I doubted he had heard me. "Let's drop the pretenses, Isaac. Because you have donated your semen, doesn't make me your son, or you my father."

"You lost the race, I assume?" he queried as if he hadn't even heard me. "I would show my regret, but that would not be genuine. I am glad you did. The more you lose, the more you'll realize that is not your place."

"Get to the point and get out of here."

It didn't matter how sternly, how coldly, or how disdainfully I talked to him. He was always going to treat me as if I were a little child throwing a tantrum.

Isaac rose to his feet and fastened his suit jacket. His height dominated the room, and I felt like a child before I remembered that I was a man on my own two feet now, that I should never cower before him again. The fact that he refused to accept it was his problem.

"You are not in the position to throw me out of my own house, are you?" he demanded, a victorious smirk taking over his features.

"I am here because it's time for you to know the truth."

"What truth are we talking about?"

Suddenly, my palms grew clammy, and an unwelcome lump rose in my throat. The last time Isaac King had told me that I should know the truth, said truth had devastated me. The short-lived glimpse of sympathy I caught in his eyes told me he was thinking the same thing I was.

My frown deepened, and my jaw clenched as my father hesitated for the briefest of seconds. His chin twitched, then pride sharpened his features.

"I am not just a lawyer, with common ambitions," he started.

"What are you then?"

"I am an agent. An undercover FBI agent."

At first, the shocking news hardly touched me, then numbness morphed into lethal fury. I strained to remain calm but knew I would fail.

The man I had known my whole life, the man my mother had married, was suddenly a complete stranger. I spun around and fisted my fingers in the hair at the nape of my neck, concentrating on my breathing, struggling to reduce the chaos inside me to a quiet unrest. When I sneered and slammed my fist against a wall, both Isaac and I were startled.

"I knew you were a despicable man, but I never imagined you'd turn out to be a fraud."

Isaac King didn't welcome insults, not even when he deserved them. His blue eyes chilled, and his full lips thinned into a line that whitened at the ends. Then his firmly controlled expression turned into raw emotion. Was it frustration I saw in his stare?

"I'm undercover for a reason. I couldn't parade with that

information for everyone to know. It would have been dangerous for me as well as for you."

"Is King even my last name?" I burst, ignoring his attempts to reason with me. He only rolled his eyes.

"Of course, it is."

I couldn't even look at him. I feared if I did, the night would turn out much more terrible than it had already been. I feared the man's mere stare would push me over the brink.

"My intention has never been to put you behind bars or make of you an ordinary lawyer at the mercy of petulant clients," Isaac went on, almost conciliatory. "But you were always too rebellious and too stubborn to abide by any rules. You still are. So I will use any leverage I have, any threat I can hold against you."

"I will never be your puppet."

"I want you to become a man who controls the world around him, not a failure who is wasting his time," he growled and stepped closer, a menacing stance that failed to intimidate me.

I scoffed and struggled not to let his words affect me. But how could they not, when for once, I agreed with him. I was a failure, not because I refused to comply with his wishes but because everything I had ever touched eventually turned to dust.

"I only want what's best for you. And I can give you the best, Marcus, as long as you give me what I need in exchange. Put your influence with these questionable circles you frequent to good use. Find the information and evidence I need. Become more than just a criminal. Become an…"

"You want me to become an agent?" I shouted.

My skin crawled and my blood boiled in my veins. Isaac wanted me to become a man with a ruined life, just like his. He saw me as a failure, but he was not far from being one himself. If anger was still profoundly locked inside me, contempt oozed freely.

"That's priceless. You have worked so hard to keep me from racing, and now, you're asking me to do that exact same thing?"

Isaac nodded, his eyes shining for the shortest of moments with something akin to human emotion, then his cool, commanding mask slipped masterfully into place.

"You know what I want and that I will get it by any means

necessary. I am tired of fighting, so ultimately, the decision is yours. You have a week to decide, but make no mistake, this time I will not tolerate rebellion."

"No need to give me a week," I snapped. "My decision is already made. I am not becoming a damn agent, and I have no intention of cajoling your ego."

My mouth pursed, the skin whitened around my knuckles, and my heart beat violently in my chest. I needed an outlet for my growing anger before it consumed me from the inside out.

"It is beyond my imagination how you can be so stubborn," Isaac all but growled. The only thing betraying his own rage was the fire burning quietly in his eyes. "But let me remind you. This house belongs to me and so does your inheritance unless you get married, which we both know is unlikely. How would you live, if you were to be denied all of these?"

"You forget I have a very well-paid job, Father."

"Do you?"

He smirked, wordlessly reminding me of his power, of how little he had to do to make my life a living hell. It was definitely the worst possible time to taunt me, but he drew pleasure from poking and prodding at my sanity. The smirk turned into a full sneer, and I finally exploded.

"Get out!"

I didn't care if he took away the money or the apartment, and he knew it. He also knew that the only thing that would truly affect me was losing everything I had invested in my career. I hadn't become an engineer to defy him. It was one of the few things I did naturally and better than most.

"One week, Marcus."

He dismissed me and strode to the door. His hand was already on the doorknob when he looked over his shoulder and spoke in a measured voice.

"Losing your money and your miserable job is only the beginning. I can take everything, including your freedom, until you come begging for a deal. I truly hope you will not force me to take such actions."

With that, he finally left.

To say that I was angry wouldn't have been just an understatement but a lie. What I felt was too much and too hard to put into words. If it was anger, it was so intense that it bordered on madness.

I felt my skull about to explode from an invisible pressure. I was a ticking time bomb. I was about to do something really, really stupid. I wanted to—I wanted to do something, anything, just to dismantle the burden pressing on me.

My phone rang, and I answered before thinking twice. Maybe if I picked an argument with whoever was calling, I would feel better in the end. Perhaps it was Kai calling to tell me that Brayden had picked another fight and that they needed me to stop him. I was ready to throw some punches myself, both at Brayden and at whoever he might have been fighting with. But the voice that greeted me was not Kai's.

"Marcus? Marcus, are you alright?"

"Liv…" I mumbled instead of hello. My voice sounded beaten even to my own ears.

"Are you alright?" she repeated, almost shouting. There was an edge to her voice that made her sound panicky. From the noise playing in the background, I could tell she was outside and moving. Why was she out at this hour?

"Yes, I am. Is something wrong? Liv, where are you?"

Now she was starting to worry me. And tonight, I really didn't want to be worried on top of everything else. I needed something to help me forget, even if for a little while. I didn't usually get drunk, but all of a sudden, the idea carried a unique appeal.

"Of course, something is wrong. You haven't been answering your phone, and I got worried and—Open the damn door already."

I turned toward the door at the same time Kinga came out of nowhere and started barking. Then, a fraction of a second later, the door handle was forced, and a sharp banging echoed. Liv was here.

She almost never came to me but always called me to her whenever she needed me. I opened the door, and she flung herself into my arms, her hands going around my neck like they used to do so long ago.

"You are alright," she murmured, caressing my shoulders, my

head, whatever she reached. "You had me so worried. I thought—
I knew tonight was a race night—and I thought—"

"Liv, sweetheart, I am alright," I told her, taking her face in my
hands. She looked as if she wanted to cry but couldn't. "I haven't
been at the race."

"No?" she demanded incredulously and frowned with
suspicion. "Why not? And argh, keep that dog away from me."

Liv had never liked Kinga much. In fact, she couldn't stand
being too close to live animals. They scared her, she always told
me, and since I had developed the habit of keeping away from her
anything that might have upset her, I did as she demanded.

"Kinga, sit," I snapped a little harsher than necessary. Kinga
whined, looked at me pleadingly, but in the end, she sat by the
closed door with her head on her paws.

"You're upset," Liv stated, her searching eyes not allowing me
to hide anything.

"You could say that."

"Baby, what's the matter?" she asked quietly, sounding like the
old Liv, like the Liv I used to love.

She cupped my cheek and settled the other hand on my hip to
balance her bum leg. Her lately empty eyes were suddenly filled
with emotion. There were these rare moments when she showed
her vulnerability and her care, when she revealed that she was still
human and capable of feeling, that drew me back to her.

"Isaac gave me an ultimatum."

I didn't need to tell her anything more. She was intimately
acquainted with the tension between my father and me. She knew
that I would not relent, and she also knew what would happen if I
didn't. What was sickening was the fact that she tended to agree
with him.

"Good Lord, Marcus, why do you keep fighting him?" she
asked, a flicker of impatience crossing her eyes. She was always
impatient lately. "Wouldn't it be better if you just pleased the man
and went on with your life?"

What she couldn't comprehend was that, if I obeyed my father,
I would not go on with my life but with his. I wanted to have a say
in my own life. I wanted the decisions I made to be made because

that was what I wanted not because I had been forced. I wanted to have a life in which my father had no say and no right to dictate.

"I don't want to fight with you too, Liv," I warned her, and just like that, she softened against me, a timid reassuring smile pulling her lips upward. It looked just the tiniest bit made-up.

"I don't want to fight either. I want to take care of you."

Liv pushed me back until I fell like a boneless heap of muscles onto the sofa, then she cautioned me with a finger to wait for her. She limped her way to the kitchen and returned minutes later with a hot mug of cinnamon tea. She walked back to me slowly, careful not to trip and spill the drink. The thought that she was so vulnerable made me clench my jaw until it hurt.

"Cinnamon tea, to help you relax and improve your mood," she said lightly, handing me the mug and gingerly snaking her way onto my lap.

I froze. Once, Liv used to be the sweetest and most affectionate woman I had ever known. Nowadays, she rarely displayed any form of affection and seldom allowed any sort of closeness. To have her take the first step staggered me.

"Thank you."

I took a sniff and a careful sip of the hot liquid. It was unlikely to improve my mood although cinnamon was an aphrodisiac as potent as any other. I wondered if that had been Liv's explicit intention or if she had made me cinnamon tea just because she preferred it. With her, I never knew.

We remained in silence. The rage within me hadn't subsided, but having her in my lap, with her fingers playing in my hair, on my face, on my lips like she was discovering me for the first time, helped, or rather forced me to restrain whatever violent emotions I might have held on to.

She knew me well. She might have been unable to calm me completely, but she was able to distract me. Her small hands traveled to my neck where she kneaded the tight knots in my muscles. She made me feel so good that I let my head fall back against the headrest and my eyes close. When I groaned in grateful pleasure, she giggled like a high school girl. Despite my unbalanced mood, the sound made me genuinely smile. Then there was silence again, a loaded silence that foresaw the storm.

I still had my eyes shut when her mouth molded around mine and her hands firmly secured my head as if she couldn't bear the idea of me facing away from her. It was a slow, exploratory kiss but not a shy one. With her soft lips, she was preparing me, coaxing me for the avalanche that we knew was about to come.

I felt a small hand fisting the hair at the back of my head and the other traveling from my face, down my throat, past my collarbone, and to the first button of my shirt. It fell open easily. Her tongue languidly traced the seam of my lower lip, tasting me, allowing me to sample her sweet, flowery taste.

Then all languor was over. My hands found her narrow waist, and I pulled her even closer. My head came off the headrest, and my mouth collided with hers almost harshly. My heat mingled with hers as I recognized the signs—we were going to consume each other.

"Liv—" I began, but she didn't seem willing to talk anymore.

"Let me take care of you," she mumbled between kisses.

An instant of tension made me remember our last amorous encounters. They had been few and far between, and as if following a pattern, they had always happened when I found myself in a disastrous mood and had always been initiated by her.

This was her way of showing me that she still cared, that she wanted to appease the demons within me, but this was also a pattern that had to be broken before it completely tore us apart.

"This has to stop, Liv," I told her with a sternness that sounded weak even to me.

"Not tonight," she both pleaded and commanded.

"Not tonight," I agreed.

I stood with her in my arms. My mouth devoured hers while I decided that this was our last time together. It had to be. We had to break a circle that was leading us nowhere but to more heartache and disillusions. Tonight, though, we were going to fool ourselves that we were still whole.

I laid her on my bed carefully, knowing that any brusque movement would hurt her leg. That was the only gentleness I granted her, and she didn't want me to coddle her either. Liv might have changed a lot over the last couple of years, but some things never truly changed. She had never been shy in bed. She had never liked slow lovemaking. And she had never tried to muffle the fire that burned between us—that *burned us.*

I grabbed her shirt by the collar and wrenched it open so hard that the buttons fell all around the room. Liv hadn't put on a bra like she had known she would not need it. What invited me to go on were not her full breasts or their stiff peaks but the transfixed look in her green eyes.

I stroked her waist and found her hips to better position her underneath me, then I bent to nibble on her throat while my hands massaged her breasts just like she had rubbed my neck earlier.

She moaned, but when my fingers lingered over the scar on her left hip, she went still. The scar on her body didn't hurt anymore, but the one in her mind and soul hadn't even started to heal yet.

Her eyes were fixed on mine, silently telling me that she didn't need to be romanced. She needed to be taken. But whereas she refused to feel, I was curious to find once more how it felt when pleasure and love fused together.

Chapter 7

Charlotte

I *was much too upset to think straight. My hands trembled around the steering wheel, but my foot pressed firmly on the gas, and so, the black sedan I was driving became a blur in the night. I was crying, but I didn't know exactly why. There were too many emotions overwhelming me, and the lump in my throat made it difficult to breathe.*

When a Range Rover passed by my car, almost wrenching my side mirror in the process, I let out a shriek. I was not only upset but also painfully tense. I feared the slightest disturbance could make me shatter. Of course, when I had thought about disturbances, I hadn't imagined bullets flying toward my car and almost shooting me in the head.

A thunderous noise split the night, and it took me a while to understand that it was the echo of my own scream. Driving was a challenge. Another car was following me closely with a man leaning out of the passenger's window, holding a gun and pointing it at me. The shooting started soon after.

It was too dark for me to distinguish more than the ruffled dirty blonde hair covering the man's head, and it would have been entirely useless even if I had been able to catch any other particulars. I had the grim feeling that I wouldn't make it out…alive.

Although panic was slowly settling in, I swallowed past a dry throat and willed myself to stay calm. New York was famous for brutal gangster crimes, but I had never imagined I would be one of their victims. I didn't entertain peculiar relationships, so nobody should have had a reason to want me dead. Unless I represented a reminder of someone who had in truth wronged my attacker.

I knew I was crying because I could feel the wetness on my cheeks. My heart sped and slowed at the same time as it became terrifyingly clear that I was running out of time.

I had to leave this darkened, empty road and drive someplace where crowds still swarmed the streets even at that hour. There, somebody had to save me. But it felt like the darkness was swallowing me.

And then everything stopped. I only heard a great blast like a bomb had just exploded before the car halted. My body was violently plunged forward. The airbag opened and cushioned my torso and face. I was dazed for a long moment, then I felt a sharp pain from my hip all the way to my knee. When I looked down, I saw blood stain my pants.

My first instinct was to scream for help, but then, I saw flashlights behind my car, and the sound froze on my tongue. I debated whether I should play dead or not when I caught a glimpse of the silhouette of a man approaching my car. In the darkness that surrounded me, all I could see was that same blonde hair that sent chills down my spine.

Then the man without a name hurled my door open and ducked his head so he could see me. An evil, pleased smile spread on his face as he pinned me with his cruel eyes.

"Hey, sugar," he said as he dug his fingers in my throat.

His grip loosened slightly as somebody grabbed him from behind and shoved him away. Crying and shivering, I looked up into ocean blue eyes.

"You…" I managed to mumble before I choked.

I WOKE UP SCREAMING AT the top of my lungs. Sweat coated my nape and wetted my pillow. My hands were trembling just as they had been doing in my dream. My chest felt constricted like a heavy weight was pressing down on it. I struggled to take one breath at a time and gain some semblance of composure, but the whole dream still felt terribly vivid. Especially since it reminded me of that Friday night.

My first nightmare with the nameless blonde had been on that Friday night. I had assured myself then that it was a typical stress release and that through that first nightmare I had gotten rid of the last remnants of fear I had felt in that empty, dark alley.

But apparently, I had been wrong.

Fear clawed at me until a pair of electric blue eyes mysteriously settled me down. Then, remorse filled the hole that fear had dug into my chest. In my memory, Marcus's gaze shifted from purposely charming and leisurely amused to unexplainably wounded.

I had been rude to him, and at some point, I had suspected he had read right through my façade, but in the end, my severity hit him in a way that erased all humor from his eyes.

I was a stranger to him. My words and my actions shouldn't have had the power to hurt him like they had. And surely, the wound I had caused shouldn't have affected me the way it did.

I writhed in my bed, impatiently trying to fall asleep, but now that the vividness of the nightmare had dispersed, it was Marcus, or rather the guilt I felt toward him, that kept me awake.

I had been rude only because I had felt threateningly close to believing in his charming act. That was my survival mechanism. That was how I managed to remain detached. But what was survival if it lacked in emotions of any kind? And why had I even bothered to push him away so harshly if now I had this nagging feeling that I had been wrong?

I rolled on my side, and my eyes landed on the clock resting on the nightstand. It wasn't even 6 o'clock yet, but I was completely awake. And furious with myself. Why couldn't I act normally? Why couldn't I just dare to take a risk and befriend a mysterious and annoying stranger? Why wasn't I that daring woman he had told me about?

I sighed, defeated, trying to erase from my mind the image of Marcus King, but remorse refused to be appeased. I knew one way to burn the negative energy that coursed through my veins like wildfire. Running. I always ran, and frequently, I ran away from...feeling.

Central Park was quiet enough, but it could have howled with life for how much attention I paid it. With the hood of my sweatshirt over my head and my earphones in my ears, I listened to orchestral music, and I ran—I ran until the muscles in my calves started protesting, until my heart seemed to expand so it occupied my whole ribcage, until the air burned my lungs and my breaths came out jaggedly.

And despite the exertion, despite my stubbornness of concentrating only on my footing as I ran, it was Mr. King returning to the forefront of my thoughts. He was haunting me. And perhaps the persistent recollection of him was my punishment for having been so mean that, in the end, I had almost felt cruel.

"Actually, no, Miss, you can't," I recalled his voice with such clarity that I had to stop myself from turning around to check for him. *"To accuse me of assault, I should have caused bodily harm to you and I—"*

The way he had phrased his sentences had sounded quite intriguing for an ordinary man. It wasn't the way a scoundrel or a lowlife would have talked. His words couldn't have been anything else but the argument of a man who knew what he was talking about, of a man who knew the law.

I sighed with renewed regret and frustration. I should have realized my mistake last night. I should have understood that he wasn't a rogue, or at least not a complete one, and tried to part ways politely. But sometimes the best and easiest defense was a great offense.

I jogged back to my apartment building, preparing myself mentally for a new work day, but today of all days, dealing with my father or the murder case he had so kindly dropped on my plate sounded utterly dreadful.

I felt a throbbing pain in my chest and in my left shoulder before I realized I had bumped into someone. My hood fell off my head, and the earphones dropped from my ears. A pair of long-fingered masculine hands grabbed my hips to steady me.

I gasped, recognizing the hands, and as I did so, I tried to convince myself that it was only my imagination playing tricks on me. But when I looked up, there he was, half frowning, half looking startled himself. *Marcus.*

"I'm sorry, *Miss,*" he apologized, emphasizing his last word coolly.

He removed his hands from my hips immediately, as if I had burned him, and retreated with clenched teeth. His jaw rolled, and a vein, long and thick like a rope, crossed his forehead. He hadn't expected to see me again.

The hood of my sweatshirt had covered my identity until it had been too late. With another pang of regret, I realized he would have avoided me if he'd had the chance.

"Marcus," I called, my hand reaching of its own accord and grabbing his arm.

He started walking away but stopped in midstride and fixed that peering stare of his on my face. My impulsive reaction surprised us both, but this might have been truly the last time I saw him. I wanted—no, I needed to apologize. For some unknown reason, I just needed him to know that I wasn't a mean city girl like he certainly imagined—like I had made him imagine.

"About last night," I started, releasing his arm when he fully faced me.

I was a lawyer for a reason. I was able to talk to crowds. I was able to make a judge see my point and convince a jury of someone's innocence. Sometimes, I could speak so much that I bored myself. Marcus, though, rendered me speechless.

He watched me quietly, folding his arms over his chest and keeping his expression still, detached.

"The way I behaved toward you last night was completely bad-mannered," I tried again, proud that my voice hadn't wavered this time. But the apology had sounded empty, and it certainly hadn't gained me his forgiveness.

"There is no need for you to apologize, Miss Burton. I have been rude in the first place. I have stalked you."

His distantly polite words had been the perfect reply to my ineffective apology. His once sensual voice now sounded like frost. I gritted my teeth and shut my eyes. I was not used to apologizing, let alone to explaining myself or the reasons I acted in a particular way. Although still a stranger to me, I wanted him to understand— I wanted him to accept my apology. But most of all, I didn't want to be just a bad memory in his life.

"No, you weren't rude. You took me by surprise, and then, you got truly persistent. I am by nature a suspicious person, and I don't trust people who approach me the way you did. So I acted the way I know best. I made sure I pushed you away. I didn't realize that in my attempt to create a barrier, I offended you. Please accept my apology."

He arched an eyebrow and studied me at length. He had the expression of a man who analyzed each word I said. He had the power to make me feel as nervous as I did before I received a verdict. My eyes darted to his mouth when he stuck his tongue out to wet his lips, then I all but gasped when he shook his head and began walking away.

"No," he answered calmly but continued to walk away.

"Why not?" I demanded. I couldn't believe that I was following him. Next thing I knew, he would accuse *me* of stalking.

"I don't like barriers."

"But—That is ridiculous."

I knew as soon as the words left my tongue that my voice had sounded everything but apologetic. The man frustrated me. Couldn't he just accept the apology? It all got worse when his lips quirked up. Once again, I amused him.

"Careful, sugar," he cautioned. "You sound dangerously close to being outraged, which is not at all a justly remorseful attitude."

"Stop calling me sugar," I hissed before correcting myself. "Look, you don't know me, so you don't know how difficult it is for me to express regret, but I am truly sorry for the way I behaved last night. I wish we had parted on better terms, and I know it is my fault that we didn't. Can you forgive me for that?"

"I'll accept your apologies," he said abruptly, stopping in the middle of the street, almost making me bump into him again.

"Thank you," I breathed with just a tint of exasperation.

His eyes, framed by long, dark lashes, remained fixed on me, so long that I all but started squirming. He had an intensity about him that stole your breath away, that hint of mystery that offered him a dark side, and yet, in spite of the way we met, he wasn't as dangerous as my mind had wanted to make him.

"Not so fast, sugar. I'll accept your apologies if you have lunch with me tomorrow."

I was sure that my mouth was hanging open. I didn't know exactly whether he had sincerely accepted my apology or was simply trying to get his revenge by ridiculing me. Another infuriating quality about Marcus King: he excelled at keeping me off balance.

"No." It wasn't only a negative response but a protest. And yet, why did I want to say yes?

"Then your apologies have no meaning to me."

His flat words hit me like a kick in the gut. Then, once again, he turned around and walked away, and I, to my rising frustration, kept on following him. Somewhere in a corner of my mind, I wondered what it was about him that compelled me to earn his forgiveness. In any other case, with any other person, I would have already given up and probably wouldn't have even cared.

"But I honestly—"

"Lunch. Tomorrow," Marcus repeated with an edge of finality. "You can choose the location. Somewhere with lots of people, preferably, and maybe a few policemen, just to be sure."

I didn't like his sarcasm, but I deserved it, so I kept my tongue in check. He took my left hand in his, and with his right, he pulled from his pocket a small pen that was tacked to his keychain and started scribbling on my skin.

"Text me the address," he instructed as if I had already accepted to go out with him. His confidence was irritating. It was suspicious. It was completely alluring. "And, Charlotte, stop thinking so much. You'll implode."

Then he left.

In a matter of seconds, his silhouette got lost in the growing crowd. His bottomless, blue eyes, though, remained stuck in my brain even as he disappeared from sight. I could still see the fierce determination that had flickered in them just before he departed. Marcus King was not good for me, not good to keep around.

"But I can't," I breathed in his wake, staring at the phone number he had written on my palm.

I couldn't stop thinking, and I dreaded that if he wanted, he could make me stop thinking altogether.

The prospect of simply feeling horrified me.
It impelled me.

Chapter 8

Marcus

threw a quick glance at myself while instinctively clutching the handles of the motorcycle. The black waistcoat I was wearing suddenly squeezed me so tightly that breathing became difficult. The matching trousers seemed too long, too loose, and too elegant to suit me. Even my lacquered shoes shined disgustingly clean.

I scoffed at my own appearance and instantly missed the comfort of my black jeans and black leather jacket. This man dressed to the nines was not me, and yet, I had dressed purposefully so to impress her.

I was pitiable.

What was going on with me, and what was so special about Charlotte Burton that lured me back for more? The demon on my shoulder, who fed off my darkest side, reminded me of the anger she had awakened only two nights ago, the demeaning way her eyes had looked at me, and the throbbing blisters that she had so carelessly poked.

The reasonable side of me, which at times was so small and so wavering that I feared it had ceased to exist, wisely prompted that Charlotte didn't even know who I truly was, so how could she have known the damage she had done? Moreover, she had been adorable while apologizing.

But why did I still pursue her?

She liked harmony, while I was chaos itself. She was a damn lawyer, while I partook in questionable events as a form of relieving stress. She sought calm waters, while I craved the adrenaline of a storm. She was north, and I was south. She was all I never wanted to become, and I was everything she disapproved of in a man. There was no common ground to bind us, but hadn't I been the one to say that opposed characters were inevitably drawn to each other?

I chided myself for not having severed our relationship once and for all, then I recalled the tremble of her lower lip when I refused to accept her apology. She had been delectable, so much so that I just couldn't deprive myself of seeing her one more time.

The front door of the building opened. I could feel the cold texture of the grille as if it were my own hand pushing it open. The last time I held that door, it had been for Liv. Groaning and willing the memory out of my head, I straightened on my motorcycle and folded my arms on my chest, adopting a casual attitude that had nothing to do with me presently.

My former mystery and current temptation walked toward me somehow hesitantly, her eyes shifting from me to the motorcycle I was straddling to the clothes I wore. She was surprised, and I was baffled. What did she have that all other women I had met in the past couple of years hadn't? What pulled me to her when I should have stayed away?

"Hello, sugar."

I drank her in, wondering how Charlotte Burton would have acted if we had met under different circumstances. If we had known each other from childhood, for instance?

Her jaw tightened, and her eyes turned suddenly defiant. With her, it was difficult to decide whether I wanted to please or taunt her. But I got the feeling that, whereas she turned into wildfire when angered, she would open like a delicate night flower when properly cared for. She could satisfy both the need of the mindless beast and that of the protective warrior that hid and battled for supremacy within a man.

"How should I explain to you that I do not like to be called like that?"

"Nicely?"

"You're funny already," she scoffed and bowed her head to hide her expression. Nevertheless, I still caught a glimpse of a smile playing on her lips.

"How should I call you then?"

I decided, perhaps instinctively, that I did not want to annoy her, so I was going to play by her rules.

"Charlotte."

Her name as well as her quiet yet determined voice invaded me. *Charlotte*—I feared it was not a name that could be easily forgotten.

"Well, Charlotte, I need to tell you something first. I do know you. Not personally, obviously, but I do know of you. My father is Isaac King. He told me many things about you."

At first, her eyebrows flew so high that I feared they wouldn't go back down, then she pressed her lips into a thin, red line. Lastly, as she bit her lower lip and settled her stare on me, understanding seemed to sink in.

"I wondered about the coincidence of your name," she admitted. "But I never imagined you were truly Isaac's son."

"I'm not his best feat," I replied with a shade of bitterness that I was unable to hide. I got that all too often—people who knew my father couldn't comprehend how one like me was his son. Sometimes I couldn't either.

"Nor should you be. You are his son, not some achievement."

I was so used to my bitterness that I didn't miss her own. In the depths of her chocolate eyes had clearly shone a form of support that could only be mustered by somebody who had undergone similar emotions, by somebody who had lived a life of not feeling enough, of always fighting and failing to live up to somebody's too high or misplaced expectations.

She empathized with this part of me. Yet, I couldn't understand why the precious and sublime Charlotte Burton felt any trace of resentment.

"Now that we settled this, we should get going."

"I texted you the address of the restaurant. Shouldn't you—"
But she trailed off, her attention focused on the black Yamaha
underneath me.

Confusion, trepidation, and excitement mingled together,
rendering her all the more beautiful. I imagined how she would feel
riding behind me, her arms locked around my waist. Would she
tremble, scream, or stiffen with the fear of the first ride? Or would
she embrace her curiosity and enjoy the wind blowing in her face
as the motorcycle moved at full speed?

"That wouldn't have been very gentlemanly of me," I laughed
but eyed her carefully. I was pretty sure her vision of me was
anything but that of a gentleman.

"Then I should get my car," she mumbled hesitantly.

"Oh, no. Letting you ride your own vehicle wouldn't be very
gentlemanly either."

"I am not getting on this—thing," she hurried to say, her voice
shrill with the slight hint of panic.

I forgave her for having called my baby a *thing* because she was
too gorgeous. I leaned against the steering handlebar and locked
my eyes with hers. Had her pupils just dilated?

"You should know one thing about me, Charlotte. I will never
allow you to hold back. You are curious about being on *this thing*,
so you will get on it."

She swallowed with some difficulty, eying the motorcycle
tentatively but not fully convinced. I climbed off and took the only
step that separated us. From this close, she was small but soft and
curvy in all the right places. She was neither too slender nor had
any more weight than a woman should. She moved, and the sudden
impulse to touch a lock of her hair and inhale her scent
overwhelmed me. She smelled of tuberoses and enticement.

"I will keep you safe," I said.

As soon as the words left my mouth, my jaw clenched. I felt a
tingling down my spine and a stiffness that contracted my whole
body. Was I really the best man to keep a woman safe?

When I showed her the helmet, Charlotte eyed it dubiously but
with the same excitement she could not conceal. There was a battle
inside her between reason and recklessness, between curiosity and

restraint, between the known and the unknown.

"Okay," she muttered, seeming to will herself to be brave. "But drive within the speed limit."

"I will," I promised.

Driving within the speed limit for her must have been customary. For me, it was a rarity. With a woman like her, however, tightly pressed against my back, so tight that her warmth became my own, forsaking the speed that freed me wouldn't be as torturous as it would have if I were on my own.

I got on the motorcycle first to steady the lissome beast then held out a hand for Charlotte. She straddled the bike, endearingly hesitant. I waited for her to wrap her arms around my body, but when she just remained frozen behind me, I guided her arms slowly around my torso.

Letting my hands linger on her soft skin, I chuckled when she didn't manage to intertwine her fingers but instead tightened her hold on my hips. She didn't reject my caress, maybe because she was too edgy to manage a protest or maybe curiosity just gave her courage. There was still a part of me that hoped that she enjoyed the connection as much as I did.

"Hold tight, Charlotte," I instructed her although I doubted she would let go once the bike was in motion. She nodded against my back, then we were off.

Within the speed limit.

When we arrived at the restaurant that Charlotte had chosen, I hurried to place our orders so my attention could be entirely focused on her. The short ride had brought a flush to her cheeks, and the helmet had marvelously mussed her formerly perfectly styled hair. This way she looked more human, more reachable—and definitely less lawyerly.

"Now it is your turn to talk," I told her as soon as the waitress left our table.

During our movie encounter, which, in truth, had been anything but a proper date, I had been the one who talked, the one who avoided pressing her for answers of her own, the one who had unconsciously sought her trust. Now I wanted to listen, to watch her while she opened up to me, even for a little bit.

Charlotte's eyes widened as though my statement had somehow surprised her, then the color in her cheeks deepened slightly but enough to reveal that she didn't enjoy being in the spotlight. That stunned me. A woman like her should always be in the spotlight.

"That was—something else," she said and glanced across the road where I had parked my motorcycle.

"You can breathe now. You are on solid ground," I teased, and Charlotte surprised me with a sheepish smile.

When she became aware of my scrutiny, the small smile vanished from her face, and she slightly stiffened. She didn't like to be scrutinized, but that was a side of me I simply couldn't change.

When something interested me, my full attention and endeavors were dedicated to that particular target. I wanted to capture even the smallest facial change or the quietest of sighs.

"Tell me about yourself, Charlotte."

"I don't even know how to ride a bike," she confessed with a laugh and pulled a lock of hair behind her ear—a nervous gesture that made her even more gorgeous.

I couldn't help but enjoy the change in her attitude, yet at the same time, my own suspicions stirred, creating a nagging feeling inside me. Was her sudden eagerness and confidence based on the knowledge that I was Isaac King's son, or had she decided to take a chance on me, regardless of whose son I was?

"Afraid of them?"

"I don't think so," she answered, shaking her head. "But when I was little, there never seemed to be the proper time for learning that. And now I think it is too late."

"It's never too late although I hope you understand my dislike for little, skinny bikes." She rolled her eyes, and I grinned, faking a shudder. "So what did you have time for when you were little? And don't tell me studying."

"All my time has always been for studying," she said, the same bitterness I had detected earlier staining the delicate tone of her voice. "But I did do something else. I liked to dance. I never did it professionally, though."

"That was your form of freedom."

I still had trouble connecting the Charlotte Burton my father had always told me about with the woman sitting across from me. The Charlotte Burton my father praised was an untouchable woman, an accomplished professional with a career he approved of. The Charlotte Burton sitting across from me seemed to be a woman with emotions and vulnerabilities, with regrets and wishes she didn't dare to seize. I wondered who was the real Charlotte, the one my father had always been on familiar terms with or the one I was beginning to know?

"And riding is your form of freedom?"

"Yes."

The waitress returned with a salad for Charlotte and steak for me, but eating was the last thing I was interested in doing. Before she picked up her fork, she subtly rolled her left shoulder then brought her fingers to gently massage the flesh covering the bones. Ever so fleetingly, a trace of discomfort flashed in her eyes. Then it was gone.

"So what else is there to know about the mysterious Charlotte Burton?"

"I'm twenty-six and a Cancer, allegedly the most emotional sign. I would like to protest, but unfortunately, it is the truth."

I grinned idiotically while she hid behind a forkful of salad. So she had listened to me that night, and she remembered. That shouldn't have pleased me so much, but it did. She might have been reluctant, but what if she was as intrigued by me as I was by her?

"I'm weather sensitive, and I cannot stand the winters. I love the ocean, but I am utterly unable to swim. And yes, I know. As a water sign, I should have learned long ago."

"Not necessarily. I am a water sign too and half my life I have been terrified of deep waters. I learned how to swim on a dare...and to avoid drowning."

"W-what?" she gasped and nearly choked. Her surprise brought a bright smile to my face. I had walked the thin line between life and death on more occasions than I could count.

"I was fifteen, I think, at my cousin's lake house. We were a large group of stupid boys playing around. We were on the pier, and they dared me to jump in the lake because the water was freezing cold. When I said I wouldn't do it, somebody shoved me off the pier, and I was forced to kick and slap at the water to keep afloat. After that, I was determined to learn to swim only to avoid similar situations."

The truth was that I had learned to swim to avoid the embarrassment. I had fallen in love for the first time that fall. It had been the first time I wanted to impress and be in the good graces of a girl, and Kai had ruined everything for me that night as he jostled me into the dark waters. He had been remorseful ever since, but of course, not because he had embarrassed me before the girl I liked, but because he had almost killed me.

"Similar experiences of your own?"

"No," she replied. I wasn't certain if her voice sounded outraged or just panicky. "I told you I am not so daring."

"I do not believe you. You are daring. I can see it in your eyes. You only have to understand that yourself."

"What else can you see?" she asked, slightly breathless.

Her fingers returned to her left shoulder, massaging the pain away. It was then that I remembered how her small body had slammed into mine the previous day. For me, it hadn't even been a slight discomfort, but for her fragile feminine frame, the impact must have been harrowing.

"You have locked the true Charlotte within yourself, so deeply that perhaps even you have forgotten who she truly is. I would really like to come to know that woman."

That resentment that I had recognized earlier and often felt myself fluttered over her delicate features. I was right. There was another Charlotte deep within her. She had sealed away a woman full of dreams and hopes, and the idea of setting that person loose terrified her.

I was more than politely empathic. I was curious to bring that woman to life, and when I was curious, matters turned very tricky. When I got curious, I got determined. When I got determined, I got relentless. When I got relentless, I started feeling. And feeling something for Charlotte Burton could be very dangerous for a man that was already broken.

"Why did you go to law school?" I asked her all of a sudden.

"Why are you asking me this?"

"I'm curious."

"I didn't have any other option. I come from a family of lawyers. My profession had been chosen for me before I was even born."

She talked like the answer was clear as daylight and I was an idiot for even asking in the first place. Revolted, I flexed my fists on the table. I wanted to tell her that there was a choice—that there should always be a choice. I wanted to tell her that her life shouldn't be dictated by her family—that her life should be lived according to her own judgment. But I knew the story. It was my own.

If she had stuck by her own choice and lived life according to her own judgment, she would have been in constant war with her family. If James Burton resembled my father even a tiny bit, I did not see his daughter facing his wrath daily. I didn't want her to. Yet, I hated that she had complied with a choice that had been forced on her.

"Is your aversion directed only toward law school or lawyers altogether?" she asked, taking me aback.

"Toward my father," I explained honestly but hurried to change the subject. Any discussion involving my father wasn't going to finish well. "But tell me, what would you have liked to do, if you weren't a lawyer?"

"It doesn't matter now," Charlotte trailed off, meditating. She brought her hand to her shoulder, slightly grimacing as she dug her fingers too harshly into the flesh. Her eyes caught the light and turned into the warmest shade of brown. "I had always known I would never really do anything else."

Her eyes lowered to her wristwatch, and immediately, her brows puckered. I didn't need a degree to understand that she had to leave. Although I hated her profession, I didn't want to keep her from her duties. Charlotte hesitated, but eventually, she looked up. I could swear she blushed.

"It's okay if you have to go," I told her. "I will just resume stalking you."

"Very funny."

She rolled her eyes but couldn't muffle the chuckle or the light that shone in her eyes. Then she stunned me. It was only fair if I enjoyed disconcerting her, that she liked doing the same thing to me.

"I did want to ask you one question. Why are you pursuing me?"

"I don't know, Charlotte," I sighed. I wished I knew the answer myself. "I really don't know."

The way she searched me for any trace of a lie was comical, but it also showed that she was used to always finding the truth. And that particularity about her should have bugged me since it reminded me so much of my father.

Then I realized that my father was not in a continual search for the truth but a quest to achieve his goals, no matter the costs. Charlotte was nothing like my father. She was nothing like the lawyers I knew.

"I could ask you the reverse. Why are you letting me pursue you?"

"I don't know, Marcus," she answered, almost mimicking me. The way my name had sounded on her lips brought all my innermost instincts to life. I just wanted her to say it one more time.

Charlotte stood then, offering me the satisfaction of seeing a shade of regret imprinted on her features. In the beginning, she had tried pushing me away, but did she still want that?

I couldn't stick to the promise I had made myself in that movie theater. I didn't want to remove her from my life. On the contrary.

"Charlotte," I called, just after she smiled apologetically and turned to leave. "If you want to get another taste of *that something else*, I'd like to show you something this Saturday. If you are available, of course."

"Maybe I am available, but I am not willing."

"Then Saturday it is."

Chapter 9

Charlotte

"How is your shoulder doing?" Marcus asked matter-of-factly.

He stood behind me and leaned close enough that his lips almost brushed my ear. His warm breath made the nape of my neck tingle, and his scent invaded my senses. He was huge, powerful, and utterly male. The combination made me groan, aware of how small and defenseless I was.

My fingers automatically curled around my shoulder. I hadn't realized he had noticed my discomfort, but most importantly, I hadn't imagined he would care enough to ask.

Some women might have been flattered when they received flowers or expensive gifts, while others when they were the cause of constant compliments or reckless deeds. I, on the other hand, was flattered by these small gestures that showed when a person cared. My cheeks heated, and I had to clench my hands by my sides to keep from covering my face.

"How did you know?"

"You almost knocked me over, remember?"

"No, I didn't," I protested, spinning around. Yes, I had bumped into him—roughly—but he had hardly been affected by the collision, whereas I had fully felt the merciless impact of his stone chest. It had been exactly like hitting a wall. "And the shoulder is much better, thank you."

"Good,' he said firmly, with a nod of his head.

He took the helmet and placed it on my head. He was too close, and those sky-blue eyes of his were inspecting me relentlessly. I looked away, but judging from the low, almost inaudible growl rumbling in his chest, I suspected he didn't approve of my inability to confront his inquisitive stare. If he disliked my self-consciousness, he said nothing.

"Why do I have to wear a helmet and you don't?"

"Because I promised to keep you safe."

His eyes, his voice, his whole demeanor didn't brook any argument.

"Now, we already played by your rules," he continued, his voice exquisitely husky, rendering me aware in ways that panicked me— that made me throb with new life. "Are you ready to play by my rules?"

"Not exactly."

His wicked smile held no form of comfort. I had no idea what Marcus wanted to show me. I had no idea why I had accepted his invitation. And I definitely had no idea why I was so eager to set off, but when he straddled the motorcycle and held his hand for me, I swung my leg over the bike without any objections.

We were in motion before I even sat properly behind him. My hands settled on his chest, a little higher than where he had placed them the last time we drove together. The recollection of his warm, calloused fingers around mine was as real as his heartbeats currently reverberating under the palms of my hands. His heart beat strong and steady—a man's untamed heart.

A lump rose in my throat, and my blood went cold, so how could I, at the same time, feel lighter and burn hotter? It must have been the adrenaline rush, the same thing Marcus certainly sought each time he climbed on that speeding bullet.

I rested my head against his shoulder because it shielded me from the wind blowing past us with an almost suffocating speed, but mostly because the closeness calmed me.

When he finally exited the city, he increased speed little by little. I suspected he did that only because he wanted to spare me a panic attack. Then, we were floating over the roadway, and pure energy invaded my bloodstream like a virus.

What I had considered earlier an adrenaline rush had hardly been tiny, little nerves compared to what I was feeling now.

Marcus straightened slightly to absorb the wind embracing us, and my arms flexed involuntarily around him. He was so large that it was nearly difficult to encircle his muscle-packed torso with my arms.

The motorcycle bowed under Marcus's steadfast control. He rode with confidence, with unleashed enthusiasm, and an unperturbed smile on his lips merged with a concentrated look in his eyes. He infused me with his addiction.

"How does it feel back there?" he chuckled.

As he spoke, he settled his left hand on my own, the touch electrifying, then he promptly placed it back on the handlebar.

All the tension I had accumulated in my system throughout the week seemed to simply disappear. I had never imagined that speed would grant me freedom and strength in equal measure. The faster the motorcycle moved, the more invincible I felt, like no force was stronger than me, like nothing could make me crumble.

Then there was also a shadow of dread nagging at the back of my head that only heightened the experience. I could almost taste the air blowing in my face. In spite of the frightening speed, I was still able to see with stunning clarity everything we left behind. And, when my fingers touched Marcus's chest, I could feel everything from the softness of his shirt to the hard planes of his muscles, to the cadenced beating of his heart. So instead of answering, I thought I should show him how I felt.

I loosened my hold on him slowly. The gesture was sluggish, teasing, and probably not something I would have done with anybody else, perhaps not even with him if I hadn't been infected by this burst of energy.

My legs tightened against his thighs, then I gingerly stretched my arms open like I wanted to clinch the wind and become as weightless as it was. I moved my arms slowly in the air, watching my own motions, watching my fingers as they tried to seize the unseizeable. I wanted this sensation to never end.

"What are you doing?" I heard Marcus hiss.

But the question was: what had he done to me? He had made me do things I never imagined I would do. A little more than a week ago, I hadn't believed that I would entertain a relationship with a stranger or trust him enough to ride his motorcycle.

He had snapped me out of my tight cage of rules and responsibilities. He had made me want to be reckless like I had never wanted to. So I never expected his harsh, nearly aggressive reaction.

"Put your arms back around me, Charlotte," Marcus snapped. "Now."

There was something in his commanding tone that left no room for argument. In my haste to obey, I lost my balance just a little. The noise coming from the engine couldn't muffle the growl that exploded from Marcus's chest. I wrapped my hands once more around his body, but the previous carefree Marcus was just a memory. He was hard as stone and tense as a spring.

He said nothing more, but I knew he was mad, and I felt responsible and embarrassed, just like I used to when I was little and did something wrong. I held on tight and buried my head once more in his shoulder. Soon, I noticed that the tighter I squeezed him, the more relaxed he became. I had worried him.

"You didn't tell me where we're going," I said out loud after a while. Rather than making small talk, I wanted to make sure that he wasn't upset anymore.

"We're going to deliver a pack of cocaine," Marcus answered loud enough so I could hear him.

His voice sounded business-like, but he was trying hard not to laugh at me. After all, wouldn't it have been downright ironic that a lawyer transported illegal substances? Apparently, he wasn't upset anymore but in the mood for making awful jokes.

"Don't mock me," I hissed and slapped his chest hard but not so hard as to make him lose concentration. He laughed loudly, maybe releasing the earlier tension I had caused. Luckily, he didn't hold grudges either. "You're not a criminal."

"How do you know that?"

"I can see it in your eyes."

Using his own words against him, something I did often and well, but generally with the purpose of incriminating the person in the stand, made me smile broadly against his leather jacket. To make use of such a tactic under different circumstances was refreshing.

"I see you like quoting me. Isn't there a law for copyright?"

"Yes, there is. Sue me."

"I don't think it's wise. You'll just sue me for—what was it? Assault?"

The ease which he drove the motorcycle with and still talked, the posture of his body—animal-like in appearance, but wildly sensual in essence—the deep hoarse voice that reached me despite the whistling of the wind or the roar of the engine proved distracting.

When his words finally penetrated my consciousness, I had to restrain myself from slapping his chest again. Maybe he didn't hold grudges, but he certainly knew how to tease a person with old mistakes.

"Argh. You already forgave me for that," I complained.

"I did."

I breathed a sigh of relief.

Marcus had crept beyond defenses that I hadn't been aware I had erected. More disturbingly, he seemed to have an influence over me that few people had had over the course of time. With that power, he had managed to snake into my life and slowly reveal a Charlotte I was hardly acquainted with.

Sometime before we arrived at our destination, I figured we were headed toward the Hamptons. When I came of age, my father bought an impressive estate in a small but exclusive village, where we generally went on weekends or for a few weeks during the summer if we were lucky.

Although the property was in my name, I had never felt it was my own. There must have been another half an hour ride to my holiday house, but I decided against mentioning it. Whatever

Marcus had planned on showing me, it sounded definitely more appealing.

"Crescent Moon Ranch," I read the big sign hanging over the entrance.

Marcus drove past the gate with the certainty and confidence of a man who knew his way. He parked the motorcycle next to a black Land Rover then helped me climb down. When my eyes met his, he was smiling broadly, if not a little uneasily like he was nervous about something.

I looked around curiously, knowing that all the while his blue gaze was searching me. A concoction of smells greeted us, and it was difficult to single out just one. The smell of seaweed and salt water blended with the specific scent of horses. Freshly cut grass merged with the earthy notes of dust and splintered wood. It even smelled a little like rain. I took a deep breath and smiled too. This was nature unhindered.

"The owner's son was my roommate during college," Marcus explained. He put a hand on the small of my back and directed me away from the improvised parking lot. "He has been tormenting me ever since, so the least he can do is offer me preferential treatment on his family's ranch."

"That's highly unethical."

Marcus smirked, utterly undeterred by my remark. With a simple grin, the dangerous man from a few minutes ago had turned into a cheerful boy.

"I like to visit during the summers. They provide a special indulgence of an interest of mine."

Before long, the special indulgence he referred to became clear as we stopped in front of a wooden stable. The scent of horses wafted from inside, and Marcus filled his lungs with it.

Against my better judgment, I admired the confident stance of his body and his stealthy allure that entangled a woman's senses. His eyes paused on my face, catching emotions I would rather have kept to myself. He flustered me, and he enjoyed it. I feared that to some extent I did too.

"Mr. King," someone called, and we both turned to see a workman jog to us.

"Hi, Marina. Is Weston home?"

My mouth all but hung open. The workman with dusty clothes and riding gloves was, in fact, a woman. Marcus threw me an amused glance, probably reading my mind, while Marina didn't even acknowledge my presence.

I feared my poorly hidden surprise at her gender had offended her, but then I noticed how her eyes sparkled and her body softened near Marcus. If I had offended her with anything, it was being Marcus's companion.

On closer inspection, it was truly absurd that I had mistaken her for a man. Behind the short-cropped hair, the manly clothes, and the rough edges of her attitude, she was all woman.

"No. He left this morning for London, but he said that he can't wait to catch up."

"Sure. Maybe we can spend a quiet evening together sometime if Charlotte agrees."

Two sets of eyes, one mischievous, the other bored, turned in my direction, causing my cheeks to redden and my lips to pull up into a self-conscious smile. While the woman still refused to acknowledge me, Marcus's gaze seared through my armor, demanding entrance where barriers did not separate us.

"So can I help you with anything?"

"Actually, I can manage. I will take 5 and 7."

"Just call if you need anything."

The woman turned around and disappeared just as fast as she had arrived. I hadn't understood much from her conversation with Marcus, except that they were on very familiar terms. When Marcus faced me, I felt the need to look away, like I had just witnessed something I shouldn't have.

"Marina does not have an interest in me."

Marcus's blunt and unexpected statement made me gasp and stagger back a step. His fingers instantly wrapped around my elbow to steady me and his formerly laughing eyes turned severe.

"You are not required to clarify your sentimental affairs," I replied detachedly, which only made him remove the little space between us. Ducking his head so we were almost of the same height, he whispered.

"I do not like when you assume this defensive attitude, Charlotte. Especially when you have no reason to. The one Marina is having an affair with is Weston, not me."

"Oh…" was all I managed to say.

"Oh, indeed. Are you calmer now?" he teased but stepped back, allowing me to breathe.

"I was calm before."

"Good. Let me show you something now."

He took my hand in his, and for a short instant, I froze. There was an intimacy in simple actions such as holding hands or kissing, sometimes even more significant than the actual act of lovemaking.

A man could sleep with a woman without any feelings or emotions attached to the act whatsoever beyond the fleeting pleasure. But the warmth and closeness of holding hands or the tenderness of feeling soft lips pressing against yours until they molded perfectly could only spring from caring, from craving the other's touch, from wanting, at all moments and all costs, to feel the person you cared for.

I struggled to regain my former disposition, but my cheeks were flaming. Why had I even started entertaining such ideas? They definitely did not apply in Marcus's case. We hardly knew each other, and certainly, his gesture had been merely instinctive and lacking in importance, but instead of letting my hand go, he squeezed it tighter as if willing me to wrap my fingers around his hand too.

When I looked up at him, he was watching me with that pungent intensity that made me shiver. He brought to life sides of me that had been dormant for far too long.

"Crescent Moon Ranch," I read again the inscription written on each stall gate, impatient to steer his attention away from my person. "Why did they choose this name?"

"Elizabeth, Weston's mother, is the one who practically founded the ranch, or rather her passion was. Crescent Moon was her first pony when she was seven years old. Unfortunately, she died within 3 years."

I nodded sadly. It was harder sometimes to watch an animal die than a human because they died in silence and often in agony.

There was a suffering about them when they passed away that was not expressed through complaints but through rough whimpers and pain-filled eyes.

Marcus opened a stall and carefully motioned me inside. A chestnut-colored horse with white legs and soft, compelling eyes lifted its head and instantly seemed to recognize Marcus. He sauntered to the horse and put both his hands on its head and a kiss right on the white star between its eyes.

He was a peculiar sight—all dressed in black, with the precise attitude of a rebellious, rugged man and yet with a softness in his stare and so many hidden aspects to his character that I was left astounded.

"She's Ilona," Marcus said, stroking the horse's head "I found her a few months ago, not far from here. She was malnourished and had cuts all over her body. Her hind legs were especially injured, but she is all better now."

"You took care of her." It was more of a statement than a question. The devotion pouring from his eyes and the trust that Ilona gifted him with could only originate from a help that had been given when most needed.

"I did," he admitted then held his hand back to me. "Give me your hand."

"Mm, I'm not sure—"

I did love horses. I loved animals in general, but that didn't mean I was brave enough to go near most of them.

Marcus turned around with a wicked grin that only widened when I retired a step. He stalked me without hesitation, his hands settling on my shoulders. Swallowing heavily, I followed the trail of his hands as they stroked down my arms and finally locked around my wrists.

"I am trying to familiarize you with her because we'll go for a little ride along the seashore. Besides, she'll love you."

"There's no point in protesting, I suppose?"

"You suppose right," he grinned, without the smallest trace of regret.

Then suddenly he was behind me. His knowing hands settled firmly and unapologetically on my waist, guiding me forward to

Ilona. Marcus took my hands in his and ever so slowly placed them on Ilona's head. She felt warm and slightly apprehensive but a little curious. As was I.

I found myself smiling, looking between Ilona and Marcus, who appeared delighted. When he laughed, there was no trace of the intimidating man I had met on that Friday night. When he laughed, his whole face glowed, and my heart pounded a tiny bit faster.

The fleeting impression I'd had about Marcus being a jovial innocent-looking boy vanished altogether. His arms tightened around me, nearly knocking the breath out of my lungs. Before I realized what was happening, he had already set me on top of Ilona's back. The terrorized look I gave him only earned his undiluted amusement.

"Marcus, I'm scared. She'll feel it," I said. My voice sounded high-pitched and trembling at the same time. "I told you I never rode a bike. Do you really think I have ever been on horseback? I don't know what to do."

"She has been scared too, but she is strong now. She'll teach you."

He gripped my knee and held my gaze. He challenged and encouraged me to overcome my fear. And in the end, he gave me that strange, nagging sensation that I could not, did not want to disappoint him. When I complained no more, he placed the reins in my hands and headed toward the stall numbered 7.

"If you want to get revenge because I offended you," I called, my throat feeling dry already. "I think you might succeed."

My jaw was clenched so tightly that the words hardly came out discernibly.

"The last thing I want to do to you, Charlotte, is get revenge. Besides, the score is even."

His eyes hardened with the memory of a night I imagined he had already forgotten. But I had guessed wrong. Marcus was far from being a perfect man, but it seemed he lived by a personal code that made him more respectable than most.

"I never blamed you for what your friends did. I wanted to, but I never could."

My admission seemed to have eased the sudden tension that had gripped him, and his eyes turned soft once again. He planted his foot in the stirrup and mounted a pure black stallion. The man and the beast were a perfect match, one a natural continuation of the other.

"Starling, lead the ladies outside," Marcus ordered and took the reins while sending me a playful yet encouraging wink.

By dint of great effort and sheer stubbornness, I managed to guide Ilona out of the stalls although I suspected she merely followed a well-known path. Between Marcus's instructions and the snickering of the horses, we followed a secluded trail that led to the seashore.

My edginess, however, never diminished. It was Ilona's steady trot and the sound of the crashing waves that eventually helped my nerves settle.

"You like riding things," I commented, trying to discard the last remnants of anxiety.

The most mischievous smile appeared on Marcus's face, and I nearly caught fire. I looked away frustrated with myself and with my choice of words, but fortunately, he made no improper remarks.

"Each experience is unique in its own way."

We were riding side by side now, and water occasionally bathed Ilona and Starling's legs. Marcus leaned close, so close that I felt his voice reverberating in my flesh. We both knew that he wasn't thinking about motorcycles or horses anymore. When he fixed his gaze on my face, I realized for the first time that the man facing me was only a censored, restrained version of his true self.

"I'd like to know the true Marcus King too," I said, remembering his own words from days ago.

I wondered how those flames blazing in the depths of his eyes would stir him if he embraced them. Then I stiffened at my own thoughts, at my own admission. I was more reserved than this— that was how I had always kept myself whole. It was foolish to suddenly let my guard down.

"Nobody has wanted that in such a long time that I am afraid I don't know how to show it anymore."

Chapter 10

Charlotte

There was no discomfort in the silence that followed. I focused on the tempestuous sound of the waves crashing against the shore and the footprints the horses left in the wet sand until eventually, my thoughts drifted back to Marcus and to the absurdity that we hadn't met before although our fathers were longtime friends.

His tongue poked out to lick a mouth made for sin, and my skin sizzled despite the cool breeze. The inexplicable pull between us was insane. It was paradoxical. I was all for following the rules, so how could I be attracted to a man who surrounded himself with an entourage that was capable of such horrible things?

A chill passed over me while flashes of gruesomeness returned to my mind. My inability to get rid of my nightmares was frustrating, and I wondered if what triggered them was keeping Marcus around since he was the only link I had to that Friday night.

I could tell he was not a criminal, but I couldn't be so sure about his friends. They were systematically haunting my subconscious.

In the end, I speculated what Isaac King might have told his son about me. *'He told me many things about you,'* Marcus had said, but although he had tried to make it sound pleasant, I doubted there was anything of the sort behind those words. He had sounded bitter like he always did when he mentioned his father. Like I did when I mentioned my own.

"You look beautiful when you ruminate. Certainly, you will look even more so when you don't."

Marcus's whole face shone with an inscrutable smile under the soft twilight sun. The intensity that never left him ensnared me in its sweet, tempting trap, and so, my cheeks warmed, and my heart vibrated like a wild flapping of wings, yet my mind never stopped working.

It was not the first time he was telling me to think less, but it was simply not in my power to achieve that goal. Thinking was what I did best. Without it, I felt lost, vulnerable, and on foreign ground.

"What are you thinking about?"

"Your father," I said and almost regretted my honesty. His eyes hardened, but he quickly schooled his expression in a neutral one.

"Problems at work?"

"I was thinking about you and him. You said he told you things about me. You didn't sound pleased."

"My displeasure doesn't involve you, Charlotte."

Marcus looked away, a frown marring his handsome face. It was frightening how attuned I was to his changing disposition. A brutal violence lay beneath the thin layer of his skin and spread into his very bloodstream.

In an attempt to regain his composure, he bent over and stroked Starling's skin. Clenching his teeth, he tightened his hand around the reins. A muscle in his jaw ticked, and his entire body tensed until he finally looked back at me. The practiced look of composure might have fooled me if I hadn't shared his inner violence and frustrations so many times before.

"My father truly praises you. He never said anything about you that he shouldn't have. But Isaac and I—we never got along, so disliking what he liked has always been second nature to me. You seem to be the exception, though. I cannot *not* like you. I've tried. And I've failed."

"Isaac has always seemed so—good-natured. I'll admit he might be ruthless in a courtroom, but—"

"But that is not the man I know. I know an ambitious man, prepared to do whatever it takes to accomplish his goals. I have never shared his ambitions. Hence I am no more than a failure to him."

"Marcus, you are not a failure."

The stern and chiding tone of my voice startled us both. Failure was not something I could attribute to Marcus King.

"I think you might be stubborn and very persistent, and perhaps you are used to going against your father, but he certainly doesn't see you as a failure—"

"Do not defend him to me," he snapped. A violent storm altered the blue of his eyes, almost turning them to black.

"I wasn't," I appeased him. I reached for his hand and was pleased when he didn't pull away. His skin was cold now. "But to me, you are not a failure. I do not know you well, Marcus, but failures don't grow into men like you."

"Are you flattering me, Charlotte?"

"I guess I am," I laughed, and this time I was the one to look away.

Starling and Ilona moved slowly through the crashing waves as if they knew a faster pace would disturb the moment. Marcus's fingers found my chin, and he gently turned my head back to face him. He assessed me in that quiet manner of his that made you squirm, that made it difficult to breathe, and that turned my thoughts into a confused mess.

"Let's not talk about my father. He brings out the worst in me, and I don't want to show you that."

"You should talk," I pressed, against my better judgment. "You should let everything out until it doesn't affect you anymore."

"It doesn't," he said between clenched teeth. But it did. "The man is my father only because I inherited his genes and his name. Otherwise, he is a stranger."

"Your quarrel with your father has to have a deeper foundation than just irreconcilable differences."

I recognized my bold lawyerly tone, but sometimes I didn't

know how to disguise it. And Marcus recognized it too. He just smiled.

"The foundation of our quarrel runs deep, and the differences between us are innumerable, but this is not the proper time to spring it all on you."

"There's never a proper time. Tell me." Instead, I wanted to say, *'Trust me.'*

I refused to believe that his father was the only reason I had decided to take a chance and trust Marcus. The decision to trust him had been made perhaps unconsciously, but the only one who had garnered it had been Marcus himself. So in return, I wanted to earn his trust too. I wished to calm the storm in his eyes and watch the sun come out.

"There were times I tried to find excuses, explanations for his behavior toward me. But there are not. He simply wanted a son that I am not. He wanted a replica of himself, and he tried so hard to imprint all his beliefs in my brain that I started despising them. I always wanted things of my own, and each time I did, he corrected me, forced me to follow the path he had designed for me. So I rebelled. I defied him. That maddened him. I live with the consequences every day."

"What consequences?"

A lump had risen in my throat and was preventing me from breathing properly. The only consequences coming from the Isaac I knew could have been a cold shoulder to his son. The Isaac painted by Marcus, however, seemed to be capable of things much worse than that.

"Nothing special, actually. He will disown me, have my job, and eventually manage a way to put me behind bars so he can teach me a lesson."

"He will never do something like that."

"My father doesn't make threats in vain. He will get his way, and I suspect that will happen fairly soon."

I couldn't tell for sure what outraged me more between his joking tone or his father's threats. How deep could Isaac's wrath run? How far was he willing to go before he went too far and ruined Marcus's life?

I resented my own father for many things, but I didn't imagine resenting him the way Marcus did. And I couldn't blame him. At the moment, I disliked Isaac too.

I convinced myself the only reason for the growing anger throbbing in my blood was the unfairness Marcus had lived with for so long. As a lawyer, unfairness enraged me. That had to be the reason my spine was ramrod stiff and my hands fisted against Ilona's neck.

"I guess I should have also warned you that I am the errant son."

There was doubt in his eyes and fear of being rejected for what he truly was, for how he truly felt. Words sometimes were bare of power and unable to collect the intensity and depth of one's feelings, so I didn't bother to explain to him that I could never judge him for having made his own choices. That was the thing I most appreciated about him.

Instead, I reached for his hand and stroked it gently, hoping he would understand that his doubts and fears were misplaced. Marcus held himself tautly as he observed me with suspicion, expecting anything but what he received.

The day had quickly run into night, and the air had turned chilly enough to create goosebumps on my unclothed arms. Yet, when Marcus's fingers interlaced with mine and his expression lightened up into a guarded smile, warmth exploded in every cell of my body.

"Why would he do that, though?" I started fiercely. It was easier to focus on his problem than on the unexpected, alarming sensations that he was awakening in me. "What reason does he have? Unless you did give him reasons and—"

His eyes had never left my face. If anything, they only developed a quiet concentration that gave me the disquieting sensation that I was laid bare before his scrutiny. I had metamorphosed so easily into my lawyer self that I was afraid I had gone too far, that I had crossed a line he wasn't ready to cross yet. I knew *I* wasn't prepared to cross many lines just yet.

"I'm sorry. Sometimes I get inquisitive, but I meant well."

"I know."

He accepted my apology with a wink, his hand tightening

around mine in reassurance. The low quality of his voice made it sound illegally sensual—forbidden. My attention strayed to his barely parted lips before returning to his eyes.

How could my heart do that crazy somersault just because I was the object of his unaltered concentration? It was a small relief to discover that confusion haunted him too.

"How do you know?" He didn't strike me as the most gullible of men, so his quick concession surprised me.

"Because I can feel you," he replied quietly like it was the most obvious answer. The idea of Marcus feeling anything regarding me made me shudder, and it wasn't exactly a bad kind of shudder.

On the horizon, streaks of fire unfurled on the rusty sky and drowned into the ocean. The sunset made me think of Marcus. There was fire in his eyes, a force hidden in their depths that calmed you like the liquid touch of the ocean and yet burned you with the fierceness of leaping flames.

By the time we brought Ilona and Starling back to the stables, the two horses seemed bored and hungry. And they were not the only ones who were hungry. Marcus's stomach rumbled so loudly that I couldn't help but laugh at the top of my lungs.

"Poor boy, are you hungry?" I teased.

His eyes glinted dangerously, their usual lightness turning darker as if they had caught the shade of the night. Marcus stalked toward me, his expression intent, his stance threatening yet infuriatingly appealing. Those compelling eyes of his never left mine as he grabbed my chin between thumb and forefinger.

"I am no boy, Charlotte."

Marcus towered over me, his maleness on sweltering display. My throat felt dry, and suddenly, swallowing was impossible. My palms dampened, and my pulse accelerated under his merciless survey. I had never felt so tiny in my life.

"But I am hungry. And so are you."

When his thumb lingered for the shortest moment on my bottom lip, I was sure his words had nothing to do with our empty stomachs.

Only when I was once more on the motorcycle behind him, my arms wrapped around his torso, did I realize that I was not only hungry but also cold. I shuddered.

"Let's get you warmed up," he said minutes later, parking before a grandiose, expensive-looking mansion that swarmed with people, light, and clamor.

The instant we climbed off the motorcycle, he wrapped his leather jacket around my shoulders, and his hands were kneading the tension out of my muscles. The mansion or the uproar of music and voices coming from inside ceased to hold my attention. Only Marcus's breath fanning across my cheeks and his hands resting on my shoulders existed.

"Where are we?"

"I have no idea. But we're starving, and there seems to be a party inside, so let's go have dinner."

"Marcus, stop," I dragged on his left arm, but he just intertwined his fingers with mine, stirring me forward despite my shocked expression and feeble attempt to hinder his progress. "We cannot go to a party where we haven't been invited. We don't know anybody."

"We can't? Why not?"

The genuinely shocked voice he mustered made me laugh. A satisfied grin spread on his face, which confirmed that I had just encouraged him in his reckless intentions.

"Marcus, for God's sake, let's just find a restaurant."

"That wouldn't be nearly as fun as this, would it?"

He walked inside the mansion unhindered, bringing me with him. His ease to blend in would have made you believe that he was at least best friends with the owner of the house. I, on the other hand, when I was not staring at my own shoes, cheeks aflame and lips pressed in a taut line, was looking around apologetically, prepared to hear someone calling the police.

"Try to look less outraged. You'll ruin our cover."

Marcus just pushed through the crowd with a cocky twist of his mouth. He even nodded to some people who were staring at us curiously then turned to wink at me smugly. People made small talk and danced but remained completely unaffected by the intruders among them.

I realized he had been looking for the kitchen only when we

found it. Dim lights illuminated the ample space, and the loud music that reverberated around the house was merely a discordant noise in the distance. The area was empty, and a glass door that led to the back porch was left ajar.

My last hopes of convincing Marcus to leave vanished when I turned to see him opening the fridge and helping himself shamelessly.

"We really can't do this. It's—"

"Charlotte."

Marcus walked to me, placing on the countertop three casseroles he had picked from the fridge. His posture, as well as his eyes, exuded authority, the kind of authority that was flattering in a man and appealed to a woman.

"Today you are not a lawyer. Today you are just Charlotte eating in a stranger's kitchen. Completely outrageous."

"Why do I have the feeling that you are incorrigible?" My voice was stern, but the smile that started shaping on my face diminished the sting of my words. He touched my cheek with the back of his index finger and smiled wistfully.

"Because you are a very perceptive woman."

We ate standing, or rather nibbled at a few Shanghai chicken strips, a Cesar salad, and zucchini rolls. When my belly was properly and illegally fed, I allowed myself to laugh. I had never kept a list of outrageous things I wanted to do because I had always known I would never get the chance to achieve such goals.

With Marcus, however, it seemed that such a list wrote itself without planning or preventing it. In spite of the recklessness, he showed me a side of freedom that I hadn't hoped for.

"Hi, gorgeous, I haven't seen you around here before."

We both turned at the same time, our mouths full and our eyes wide. Leaning drunkenly against the doorway, a leggy blonde winked at Marcus. Her appearance seemed jumbled, and her makeup was a combination of running mascara and unflattering stains of sweat, foundation, and eye shadow, but I could tell she was a fine-looking woman.

Her tall, willowy figure managed to seem graceful even as she swayed uncertainly. She approached Marcus with the confidence of someone who hadn't encountered refusal in her life. Her hand settled on his chest and played with the first button of his shirt until she finally freed it. I had to clench my jaw not to hiss.

"And you probably won't see me again."

Marcus caught her wrist and let her hand fall, then with a conspiratorial wink, he grabbed my hand and whisked me out of the kitchen and back into the crowd. Satisfaction pulled my lips into a grin that soon froze in place.

In the middle of the vast living room that had been turned into a real dance floor, among countless strangers swaying on the soft notes of a sensual song, Marcus spun me in a pirouette and caught me tightly in his arms. If earlier I had been breathing, I certainly didn't remember how to do it now.

"Surely, we are leaving."

"I want this dance, Charlotte," he breathed against my ear. "I am rarely willing to relinquish what I want. Tonight is not one of those times."

His arms like iron bands around my waist didn't allow me an inch of distance. My hands settled gingerly on his shoulders, and my eyes followed of their own accord the path to his lips. They were red and freshly dampened. They were parted and always letting out words that enthralled me.

"Dance with me," Marcus urged, bowing indecently, enticingly close to me. "And stop thinking. Aren't Cancerians based on feeling?"

"We have to think more than others exactly because when we do feel, we feel too much and we don't know how to stop."

Marcus's eyes were wilder than ever, and his body incited mine to move, to sway, to surrender to the gripping rhythm of the music. I closed my eyes and leaned my head against his shoulder only because his intense stare was robbing me of strength. It made me feel bare, vulnerable.

An arm remained firmly wrapped around my waist while a hand enfolded my nape and kept me impossibly close to his chest. I could smell him—all pure, fierce man. His warmth transcended the barrier of clothes and mingled with my own increasing body temperature. Then, regardless of the seductive music creating an orgy of the senses, what I heard the clearest was his steady, harmonious heartbeat. I loved the sound. And that terrified me.

"Are you scared of feeling, Charlotte?"

He secured my head with one hand, while his lips brushed against the shell of my ear. Suppressing a moan, I shivered.

"Sometimes."

What Marcus had intended to show me today had nothing to do with the horses, the ride by the sea, the enchanting sunset, or with the fact that we could infiltrate among the guests of a private party. He had intended to show me a part of himself that I didn't imagine existed and that probably not many had the chance to see.

He had intended to lure to the surface a side of me that I was afraid of exploring. He had let himself in, crumbling barriers that I had perfected and few managed to cross. He had enticed me, and he had done it wonderfully.

It was late and dark when we eventually returned to his motorcycle. I felt drained, but it was a good kind of tiredness that overwhelmed my body. I felt confused, but it was an arousing kind of bewilderment that turned my thoughts upside down and affected the usual order and monotony of my mind.

"Charlotte," Marcus called, once I was safely behind him. "I promised you that I would keep you safe. Don't force me to break my promise."

His displeasure was wild as he recalled our earlier ride and my complete recklessness. I nodded obediently against his back and tightened my hold around his waist, offering a comfort I instinctively knew he needed.

While we split the night at bullet speed, I got the electrifying sensation that being kept safe by a man like Marcus could be equally soothing and dangerous.

Chapter 11

Marcus

"I have a plan, and you are going to help me," I told Kai, two days after I last saw Charlotte. Kai watched me stroll self-assuredly around his studio apartment, unaffected by my intrusion.

The place was more of a mess than usual. Piles of clothes were scattered from the foot of the bed all the way to the balcony door. Empty casseroles with putrid leftovers and myriad of painting utensils were forgotten on every available surface. Even the air was sour and stifling. And Kai himself was covered in paint and filth from head to toe.

Between slanted eyes, he inspected my impatient movements before returning his attention to the canvas. He continued painting with fast but confident strokes, utterly unimpaired by the disarray his artistic fits were leaving behind. Taking a step back to evaluate his yet unfinished work, Kai finally deigned to speak, although his attention was entirely focused on whatever he was coating in color.

"Does your plan involve your moving into my apartment? Because I'll have to pass. I have guests tonight."

"I imagine," I scoffed, picking with my index finger a pink bra from a pile of clothes and holding it up for Kai to see. He only smiled thoughtfully then placed his brush on the tall work stand by the easel and opted for a small knife, which he dabbled in paint and started sketching furiously across the canvas. "But no, I am not going to move in with you, hon. Maybe next time."

"You're breaking my heart, baby," he teased back, making me laugh but not lose focus. When I had a purpose, it was very difficult to be diverted from my path.

"I want you to set up a race. Tomorrow night if possible."

"Beg your pardon?"

Kai placed his tools on the stand and stepped away from the easel, for once his attention entirely disrupted. With suspicion and concern, his eyes skimmed me, then he scowled. I had missed the last two races for reasons that eluded him, and now I was urgently summoning another race. It was preposterous and yet intoxicating that the only reason for everything was Charlotte herself.

She was the kind of woman who, unaware of her own power, got under your skin and made you do reckless things. Days had passed since I last saw her, but she was there, haunting my mind, spurring me to take actions that I had never imagined I would ever take. She was the kind of woman who not only thickened the blood in your veins but also made you lose reason altogether.

I had fooled myself that one sociable night, sprinkled with some innocent fun and teasing, would be all I wanted and got from an association with Charlotte Burton. But perhaps I had known then as well as I did now that I couldn't be deterred once she tempted me.

First, she had ignited my protective instincts, then she had fueled my curiosity until she gained my yearning. Unfortunately for her, the yearning of a Scorpio was not something that went away quickly or was dealt with lightly.

I wanted Charlotte, and the depth of my growing desire scared me more for her sake than for my own. I was a man who could easily be ignited but whose interest was difficultly kept. I was a man utterly unable to find comfort and peace hence equally so in providing it. I was a man who had rebelled from childhood and whose very proximity to a woman like her was dangerous, but at the same time, I was a man who never relented and never backed off.

I was the most improper man for her, and yet my mind raced with possibilities. Conquering her defenses would be hard, because like a true Cancerian, she had many, behind which she frequently hid to protect herself.

That only lured me more. Because the more she recoiled, the more I wanted to discover her; the faster she disappeared inside her shell, the more fiercely I wanted to discover the passionate woman inside, with all her facets and emotions.

"I want you to set up a race," I repeated although I knew he had heard me perfectly the first time.

"What does your plan have to do with a race? Why not wait until the next one?"

"I have a deadline and no time for waiting. Can you help me? Can you orchestrate a race?"

Kai scowled at me suspiciously, if not somewhat crossly. He was an artist to the bone, but deep inside his soul, he had a dark side he could only unleash when he was on the back of a motorcycle, leading his pack. He was the bandmaster of each race, and consequently, he felt responsible for all those who trusted him and always joined his races. He was also a marvelous judge of character and knew that my intentions weren't as transparent as I let on.

"I trust you have the means and influence to gather enough men for a race," I pressed when he gave me no answer.

"I might, but I don't think I want to lead my people into something I am not even aware of."

"My plan involves only me, and you have nothing to worry about. Please, Kai, I need to do this."

He shook his head, confused and still unconvinced, but I had no doubt he would help. Just like Charlotte, he was a worrier, and because of that, the less he knew, the better it was going to be for everybody involved. Truth be told, I was afraid he would shut down my plan before it was even set in motion if he knew exactly what I truly plotted.

"Before I make a decision, I need to kn—"

"Just send me the details, Kai, and stop whining," I admonished, walking to the door.

He shot me a glare right before I shut the door behind me. Something massive crashed against it then crumbled to the ground with a dull thud. I laughed then called loud enough so Kai and everyone else within earshot would hear, "And please... Clean up that mess."

ONE EVENING LATER, I dismounted on the outskirts of the city, feeling the blood pumping in my veins. While leather-clad motorcyclists welcomed me with the usual clap on the back, Kai pinned me with a cold glare and promptly turned his back on me. He was in a dangerously lousy mood.

The Fox intercepted him and slid an arm around his waist, all while sending me a defiant and annoyed look over Kai's shoulder. She didn't attempt a more intimate contact, but my grim suspicions were already confirmed, not by the confidence and familiarity with which she touched Kai but by the way he relaxed and sought more of the comfort she offered. Only I doubted such a treacherous creature could offer any comfort at all.

As if my concern hadn't already reached dangerous peaks, Kai settled his hands on her hips and bowed in quest of her mouth.

"Aww," he groaned and covered his left side, which she had so vilely struck. "What was that for?"

"Don't overstep, Reed," she warned with a pointed finger and danced her way out of his grasp.

A veil of fire floated in the air as she swung a leg over her motorcycle. She stopped the white beast right in front of Kai, admiring his cowering posture with a satisfied, conceited grin. Out of nowhere, her hand fisted in his leather jacket, and she pulled him close enough that their mouths hovered a mere whisper away. Whatever she had told Kai had the calculated intention of making his blood boil.

When she sped away to the starting line, Kai's lustful gaze followed her. His clear eyes, however, darkened as soon as they landed once more on me.

He zipped his jacket with unnecessary brutality and climbed on top of his bike with one sharp movement. He had gathered a good handful of riders and a nice, enthusiastic crowd, but he was far from happy.

He drew his motorcycle to an abrupt halt in front of me and spoke through clenched teeth while pinning me with a scowl.

"I know you are not telling me everything. There's another reason behind all this stupidity so do not take me for a fool."

There was a reason, one that had brown eyes, rosy lips, and a laugh that enthralled the senses, but just now, Kai didn't need to know that.

The sound that signaled the start of the race blasted in the night. As usual, Kai had planned everything with the artistry of a bandmaster, but if my plan was going to work, tonight his well-thought-out orchestrations had to fall apart. Casting him an apologetic look, I shot forward, riding my motorcycle at a vengeful speed.

By the time we reached the first intersection, I was leading the convoy with Kai closely behind me and Tucker and Sean flanking us. We were halfway to the finish line when Kai stormed past me and the appalling sound of sirens echoed in the distance. It grew louder and louder as it chased us.

A collective growl drowned out the boom of angry engines and the shriek of tires against pavement. Crouched over my motorcycle, clenching the handlebars in taut fists, I growled too. Everything could go very wrong, very fast.

"Split up," Kai shouted.

Warning police lights closed in on us while the sirens screamed in our heads and brought us to the dangerous edge of panic.

I started counting in my head to keep myself calm. This race provided adrenaline in abundance but not a modicum of freedom. There was no pleasure or strength to draw from the speed that drove us across the streets like demons unleashed. There was only a strategy I had to see through.

Calvin and Xavier sped up then veered left onto a narrow alley. Tucker took an abrupt turn, snaked through the complaining, scared people on the sidewalk, and finally disappeared down an improperly lit street, followed by his brother, Sean.

Kai pushed on straight ahead, now and again throwing worried glances over his shoulder. I realized I had dropped behind only when Colt and Samuel reached my flanks then went flying like missiles.

Samuel looked behind, his eyes fixed past my shoulder on the police car that hunted us, and aligned his motorcycle with Colt's. The blood in my veins boiled furiously as it became clear that escape was no longer an option for me.

I smirked, not with satisfaction but with defiance. Samuel balanced his weight over his speeding bike, and with economical grace, he flung himself behind Colt. I only had time to see them speed up along the road.

I didn't see Samuel's abandoned motorcycle coming my way but heard the blast of the collision like a grenade exploding inside my ears. Then, I felt the collision my own body produced once it hit the cold, unwelcoming ground.

Protecting my head with my arms, I landed hard on my left side, the bones in my shoulder giving a loud, crunching noise that tore through my muscles and throbbed in my blood.

My body rolled harshly, the cement tearing my leather clothes and scraping at my flesh until I felt the sting of open bleeding wounds. But nothing could rival the aching severity of cracking and dislocated bones or the hammering pain pulsating at the back of my head. Maybe I hadn't protected my head that well after all.

IT STARTED AS A TROUBLING discordance of sounds until it turned into an earsplitting clatter that had the same effect of shards cutting into my ear drum. I struggled to peel my eyelids open, but light quickly attacked me like a snake injecting its poison into my sockets. I tried to speak and demand whoever was producing that awful noise to stop, but my jaw wouldn't move.

"Wake up, Marcus."

I was not surprised that I was not in a hospital room but in a cute little prison cell. I became aware of how cold and poorly lit my surroundings actually were before my eyes drowsily landed on Isaac King. His stare hardly conveyed any concern or regret for his son's condition. Instead, his expression was a perfect portrayal of smugness.

I groaned with pain and irritation. The bed I was sprawled on felt grimy and skeleton-like. In the far corner of the room, a metal toilet and a small sink were lined side by side. There was no trace of a doctor, and I terribly needed pain meds.

Pain was a creature that had taken over my body and tormented it viciously, but my father showed no sign of caring. I knew what he was doing, and why I was in a cell instead of a hospital. He was sending a message. He was the man wielding the power. He could toy with my life. He could go to any extent, and I could not stop him.

"A dislocated shoulder, a sprained wrist, and bruised ribs," Isaac enumerated. "For what? For an illegal race that puts at risk not only your safety but the safety of innocent people around you?"

"Spare me the lecture, Father. You came to gloat. Consider the deed done."

I hated his hypocritical attitude more than ever. Racing was dangerous and illegal and monstrous, but if I had been his obedient puppy, playing undercover, then everything would have miraculously been fine.

He pushed his hands into his pockets while his empty eyes inspected me. Although his self-confidence didn't fail to annoy me, for the time being, I had no interest in wiping the triumph off his face.

"In fact, I came to reason with my son." The disdain lacing his words confirmed what I had always known. I was the son he had never desired. "I came to offer you a last chance, Marcus. I don't want to see you in this position any more than you do."

"Certainly." My sarcasm earned a cutting glare from him, but otherwise, he refrained from any comments.

"You will cease every rebellious pursuit immediately. This last disaster you've caused is a new low I am not willing to tolerate." His eyes narrowed, his lips pursed, and the line of his jaw sharpened, yet the flash of irritation died out just as quickly as it had appeared.

"Are you done? Magnificent. My answer is still no. You can take your leave now."

"You managed to lose not only my trust but that of men far above me," he went on, unmindful of my intervention. "Yet, you are my son, Marcus, so give me your word, and you walk out of this cell immediately. You refuse, and there's nothing I can help you with."

"Have you ever had any trust in me?" I snapped. "You know what I think, Father? I think you never trusted me and perhaps you never will, no matter what I do. I think you need me, and for that, you are willing to play a charade, but I am not. I have a life that has nothing to do with yours. I will not put an end to all I have been working for, all I have accomplished on my own, just to please a father who has never cared for me. I have a damn degree that has nothing to do with FBI or your absurd demands. I have a job that I love and am very proud of. So go ahead, try to take it all away. I promise I will fight like a rabid dog. If you imagine I will be the one who's sorry in the end, you are sorely mistaken."

Isaac ground his teeth, his eyes flashing dangerously, yet he retained his detached demeanor. He had me cornered, and I was supposed to submit to whatever outrageous demands he had. I was reckless enough to taunt him even in this situation, but my reason for doing so was not only to garner his irritation but to make my eventual capitulation seem as genuine as possible.

"If I leave, I will not return to make the same offer again. If I leave, the offer leaves with me. And I assure you, Marcus, you will not leave too. I will make sure this cell becomes your permanent residence."

"You cannot keep me locked up forever. You might have a strong influence over men capable of putting me behind bars, I'll grant you that, but there's little you can accuse me of, Father. There have been no victims. You missed the right race for that."

The bitterness of memories I carefully kept locked behind the bars of my own brain threatened to tamper with my indifference. I shot to my feet, ignoring the pain and dizziness, and started pacing back and forth, making Isaac retreat a few steps as if I were a plague he'd rather not touch. Frustration shimmered in his gaze. He knew his power was not as extensive as he wanted to make it seem.

"True. But when you eventually get out you will have a criminal record, no job, no money, and nowhere to live. I promised you that, and I keep my promises, Son. Now, be reasonable and do not test me."

I pushed a hand through my hair, feeling the pain dripping from my skull all the way to the tips of my fingers. I hugged my left side and focused on breathing evenly. Isaac's stony glare tried to demean me, but I glared right back with obstinacy. Surprisingly, it was he who finally sighed and broke our tacit quarrel.

"You will not become an agent overnight, and I, indeed, need you, so the least both of us deserve is a compromise." Isaac feigned nonchalance, but he studied me with the interest of a man about to achieve his goal.

"What are you suggesting?"

"I only seek to have an agreement with you, something that will satisfy none of us entirely but that will have to do." He rolled his neck and inhaled deeply before resuming. "You need to come to the realization that this is the life for you, and that cannot happen if you live in a whole different world. So I want you to come and live in my world. Give me your word, and you are a free man. Nobody will bother you or come asking questions about this— disaster that you've caused."

He flicked a hand in my direction, more annoyed by the disturbances I've caused than by the damages I suffered. My bruises, my grunts, or my limping passed completely unnoticed.

"I still don't understand," I said and gave up on standing. My knee and hip hurt too badly.

"You will take a plea deal, and I will convince the prosecutor to drop all charges against you."

"In exchange for?"

"You will plead guilty, of course, then you will do your community service at Burton & Associates. The firm offers an internship, led by James's daughter. I will make sure she welcomes your participation in her program."

My whole body stiffened, pain seeping out as desire replaced it. It was a struggle to keep my emotions hidden from Isaac's prying eyes. I feigned disinterest that bordered on disdain, a reaction I had gifted him with plenty all my life, so he was neither suspicious nor particularly offended.

"Be a part of her team, get a taste of our life, and prove that you can be as trustworthy as I hope you can be. Moreover, becoming part of her program will acquaint you with the main case she is working on. Once my supervisor and I regain our trust in you, we will provide you with further information. Until then, I sincerely hope you will reconsider your decision and choose more wisely."

I wouldn't, but he didn't have to know that.

Shock had me staring blankly into space. My plan all along had been to get caught by the police then contract Charlotte's legal services to get out of whatever hole my father made sure I landed in.

So I had never expected Isaac to cut me a deal. I hadn't hoped for the easy way out. In the end, my father, without knowing or even intending to, had offered me a better outcome than what I had envisioned. And though I was dying to laugh in his face, I was forced to enjoy my victory without the merest sketch of a smile.

"But I'm not a lawyer, remember? How will I become an intern at a law firm?"

"You could do paralegal work, and *how* does not concern you."

I had never dreamed he would voluntarily take me so close to Charlotte. But any reasons he might have had were completely irrelevant as long as I got to spend time with her.

"Don't believe for a moment that I will suddenly become pliable to your desires or that I will allow you to interfere in any aspect of my life."

His greedy eyes fixed me like a wild animal fixing its prey before attacking and seizing its reward. Then his stare attained a more contemplative quality. Eventually, he smiled self-assuredly, almost pityingly.

"You are in no position to make threats or demands, but let's say I agree for the moment. I will not intervene in any aspect of your life, but make no mistake, in the end, you will become pliable to my desires."

We both smiled, each defying the other. His jaw clenched again. One of the things Isaac hated the most was to be faced with another man's arrogance or confidence. I showed off my insolence shamelessly. While he thought he was playing with my mind, I was playing with his.

"You'll start Monday, and don't evade your responsibilities, Marcus. Don't try to deceive the trust I am placing in you. I assure you that you'll live to regret it."

Perhaps I was about to make some mistakes, but underestimating my opponent was not one of them. Isaac King was capable of anything to achieve his goal, and his first mistake was thinking that he had fathered a son who didn't share the same stubbornness.

I intended to hit two birds with one stone. I was going to let my father think that I complied with his wishes, and in the process, I was going to get something far more valuable—time with Charlotte.

He turned to leave when I decided I wasn't done tempting fate. "You forget something, Father. Men who consider themselves invincible are all the easier to break."

He smirked. "That is nonsense and time will prove it."

"It will."

The triumph in his eyes was soon going to be dismantled, but by that time, I hoped to enjoy not only Charlotte's affection but also complete freedom from my father's clutches.

Chapter 12

Charlotte

A peculiar restlessness had been defying my power of control for days. I was irritable, impatient, and most importantly, incapable of gathering my thoughts. I was exhausted from lack of sleep and frustrated for reasons I failed to pinpoint, and so, the usually polite, thorough, and efficient Charlotte was replaced by an aberrant form of herself that rather resembled a mindless, hot-tempered ghost.

Drumming my fingers on the desk, I struggled to make sense of the papers scattered in front of me, but there was no room in my mind for anything except... *Marcus*. Infuriated and exhausted, I rubbed my temples, willing myself to concentrate on my responsibilities. The fact that I failed should not have surprised me.

I was worried about a man I had known for roughly two weeks. The last and only message I received from him didn't alleviate the unexplainable state of apprehension I experienced each time my mind returned to him, which happened more frequently than I cared to admit.

'I need to take care of a problem. Don't forget about me, sugar,' he had said in a cryptic message then completely disappeared.

I stood and wandered to the enormous windows behind my

desk, considering for the umpteenth time whether I should ask Isaac about his son, but for the umpteenth time, I refrained. If Marcus had made anything clear about his father, it was that their relationship resembled a landmine that could detonate at the first misstep.

Just as I brought my fingers to my throat, rubbing furiously as if I could mollify the lump blocking my airways, a sharp sound sliced the silence. I had forgotten to turn off that damn phone and the shrilling noise it emitted only aggravated my volatile temper. I frowned at the black receiver, contemplating smashing it, but eventually gave up on my violent intentions and simply answered when it reached its fourth chime.

"What is it?" I demanded.

"Miss Burton, I am sorry to disturb you. Your two o'clock appointment is here." Sofia, my secretary, waited for an answer, but when it didn't come, she added helpfully: "For the internship. Should I let him in?"

"Of course."

I sighed, pinched the bridge of my nose, and tossed the receiver back in its cradle. The Burton & Associates internship program had been my father's first strategy of introducing me to the family business before he made me go to law school. Later, he had appointed me as manager of the program only to make sure that even my free time was dedicated to his firm.

At the time, the appointment had brought me more frustration than joy, but later on, I had learned to take pleasure in teaching others who were visibly eager to delve into the secrets of lawyerly life. Today, however, I was not in the mood to answer countless questions from a wannabe.

The knock at the door startled me. I resumed my seat, busying myself with organizing the scattered files on my desk. Absentmindedly, I noticed Sofia leading the way and placing in front of me a dark blue dossier with Isaac King's name at the bottom.

"Mr. King requested his incorporation into the program." Sofia bent and explained in a low whisper. "Everything is explained in the fo—"

"Welcome to Burton & Associates, Mr.—" I cut Sofia off impatiently and finally lifted my head to meet my intern. And as soon as I did so, I regretted it.

Marcus stood mere feet away from my desk, with his arms folded casually over his chest and his amused blue gaze sizing me up. As usual, he was wearing a black leather jacket, which looked new, and all black beneath.

His muscular body was beyond imposing, and his tall stature was actually frightening. In the enclosed space of my office, he looked even taller, even bigger, so much so that his mere presence dwarfed his surroundings.

The black he was so fond of highlighted his eyes, but it also gave him a dangerous touch that I supposed he enjoyed projecting. Men like him fascinated as much as they frightened. In fact, his mischievous smile and warm gaze were the only things that kept him from resembling a criminal.

Maybe because the circumstances of this meeting were utterly different from the previous ones, I saw him in a new light. At first, I came across his silky hair arranged in a concoction of dark locks that fell over his brow, then I saw what the hair was covering, and I frowned.

A purplish bruise contrasted unhealthily with his tanned skin and spread from the corner of his left eye, upward to his forehead. The need to go to him and touch his battered skin shocked me.

"King," he said almost smugly.

"He's Mr. King's son," Sofia explained in a hushed voice. Marcus's grin grew even wider, and he almost winked.

"Thank you, Sofia. You can go now."

Once Sofia left, I snatched the folder she had brought me and skimmed through it. The worry I had been feeling shifted into the initial tingling of anger.

"What are you doing here, Marcus?" I snapped. I could swear he looked surprised.

"I believe all the answers about my presence here are contained in that folder you're almost tearing apart."

I slapped the folder against the desk, struggling to get a hold of my escalating frustration. I was annoyed mostly because Marcus was able to create this cacophony of feelings inside me, whereas he remained calm and amused. I was annoyed because something wrong was happening right under my nose, and I couldn't pinpoint it. I was annoyed because he had simply disappeared, and I—I had foolishly missed him.

"You are involved in illegal races."

I skimmed through the pages with a frown that deepened and threatened to develop into a nagging headache. Then I stood and resumed my nervous habit of pacing. I was too edgy to be sitting, and movement helped ease my agitation.

"Is it true?"

"Yes."

"Your father requested your participation in this program in order for you to complete a stage of probation and forced labor."

"Yes."

His continual agreement irritated me more than if he had been arguing. He took several steps toward my desk without invitation or approval which only served to aggravate me further, but I didn't comment on it.

"I would say I have been waiting for you, but I was not aware you'd be interested in taking an internship in a law firm of all places."

There were many reasons why I couldn't picture Marcus in an internship program, but the one that stood out with blinding starkness was precisely his repugnance toward his father's profession, and I dared say, toward the man himself.

"I would say I have been waiting to get here, but I haven't. I have been anxious to see you, though."

All of a sudden, I glared, recalling the concern he had made me feel for the last few days. *Not anxious enough,* I thought. Then I glanced once more at the bruise his hair couldn't hide completely. I hadn't been wrong in worrying. I fisted my hands to prevent myself from reaching for him.

"Why are you really here, Marcus?"

I sighed and looked away. He had his own admirable profession, his own hopes and goals. Moreover, he despised complying with his father's commands, so I couldn't imagine Marcus simply giving in to Isaac's demands unless he pursued his own objective. Having him this close, day after day, wasn't going to be precisely innocuous for me.

"I think you know." He walked closer until his fingertips touched the edge of my desk and his eyes held mine with that hypnotizing intensity that had my lips parting on a gasp.

"I don't, actually. That is why I am asking."

As if he had done it million times before, Marcus took a seat and placed an ankle against his knee. His demeanor was casual, confident. While he developed a fondness for watching me fixedly, I developed chronic impatience.

"Isaac found a way to force my hand. It was jail or working here. Knowing you were here facilitated my decision. What's better than mixing business with pleasure?"

I stiffened. My chin lifted of its own accord, and my left brow arched challengingly.

"I do not mix business with pleasure. If you counted on that, then you made the wrong decision."

Suddenly, his blue eyes sparkled with danger and mischief. "That doesn't mean I have to follow the same rules."

He bit his bottom lip and wrapped his fingers around the armrests, wordlessly but purposefully pushing me to take notice of his plump red lips, of the way his chest rose and fell, of how the shirt beneath his jacket hugged his body intimately.

Marcus's presence not only made me aware of how unguarded I was next to a powerful man such as him, but it also brought to life all my feminine instincts until a fine tingling coursed through my whole body.

"What happened?" I demanded and made a touchy gesture toward his head.

Closing my eyes and pinching the bridge of my nose, I let out a breath, struggling to control the topsy-turvy course of my thoughts. He was teasing me, and he enjoyed it.

"Oh, this? This is the least of my pains."

He smiled and pushed his hair back, pointing to the abused skin that once wholly revealed looked worse than I had imagined. The dark purple bruise had an irregular shape, looking more like a collection of bruises than a single one. Above his eyebrow, there was a semicircular cut that still shone bright red. It was going to leave a scar, but I suspected Marcus was no stranger to those.

"I do race," he resumed. "And I do know it is not legal, but I don't do it out of a desire to resist authority. I do it because it gives me freedom. It gives me purpose. It gives me the opportunity to not think."

He looked up at me, his momentary contemplative countenance vanishing. When his jaw clenched and his chin jerked upward defiantly, I realized I had been frowning. And I also realized that he must have been thinking that I was judging him. I definitely did not agree with his notion of a pastime, but for reasons entirely unrelated to his presumption.

The mere notion of *racing* combined with the ugly bruise on his forehead brought a sense of danger that made me shudder with apprehension. Although I had enjoyed the dazzling speed and subsequent exhilaration while riding with him, I couldn't fathom the risk a race implied. Yet, I could understand the desire to purge his mind of thoughts.

"It also gives you an adrenaline rush."

"I am not an adrenaline junkie." His voice was stern, castigating. And so were his eyes. It was unnerving how he managed to make me feel ashamed of my assumptions. "I do enjoy the adrenaline rush, but I am not addicted to it."

"So you do it out of competitiveness?"

"It's an interesting theory." Surprise colored his gaze, then he nodded as if he acknowledged my idea for the first time. "Charlotte, some people consume their energy through drinking or engaging in fisticuffs. I race. It's as simple as that."

"Okay. Let's make something clear."

Apparently, Marcus didn't completely impair my defensive mechanism. The impulse to draw a barrier between us pounded at my brain like a vicious headache. And in spite of that, there was nothing I wished more than to be rid of all the formalities and professional responsibilities my position entailed. I continued, however.

"While you are within this building, I am your handler, so I am not Charlotte. I am Ms. Burton."

"Oh, so this is how it's going to be?" A cocky grin split his face in two, revealing a row of perfect, white teeth. Licking his bottom lip, he dared me to answer. He tantalized me.

"Yes."

Under his never-ending inspection, my knees grew weak. Hoping for nonchalance, I resumed my seat only to find myself eye level with him. I swallowed hard, and his smile deepened.

I could see it in his stare that he intended to prove me wrong and unsettle my determination. I knew if he wanted, he would succeed.

"You don't strike me as the man to be caught if he doesn't want to be," I commented, and refused to meet his intrusive stare.

"Sometimes I can be caught off guard too."

His voice was low and warm, almost seductive, like he had meant to transmit a message with double meaning. Still, I kept my eyes stubbornly trained on his folder and began scribbling his first tasks.

"Somebody must have tipped the police off. Everybody sought their own way out of the mess, and in the resulting chaos, I collided with an abandoned motorcycle. I crashed. My father was absolutely delighted with the whole ordeal. And, as you can see, I was in a tough spot. I chose what suited me best."

I stiffened and felt a chill running down my spine and taking over my whole body. My painfully vivid imagination put on display disturbing images of Marcus crashing, hitting the asphalt headfirst, blood spilling everywhere. I could almost hear the sound of cracking bones and smell the reek of gasoline.

I clenched my teeth until my jaw hurt, but the images refused to evaporate. I couldn't worry about him. He didn't have the right to make me worry. I rubbed my temples to force the horrid images out of my head and rein in my thoughts. It didn't work.

"Say something, Charlotte."

"There's something you are not telling me." It might have been a sixth sense or simply his cryptic tone of voice, but I was certain he was hiding something. "If you are to work with me, if I am to write an accurate report at the end of this internship about your social behavior, I have to trust you, and I cannot trust somebody who is evidently lying to me."

"Trust is earned."

His eyes were ablaze. His statement should have offended me because I shouldn't have been the one fighting to earn his trust. Yet, why was I suddenly under the compulsion to do exactly that?

ONE HOUR LATER, I FOLLOWED Isaac King into his obscenely huge office. The décor was pristinely white, from the paint on the walls to the furniture. It lacked in emotion just as the man that commanded the space.

"Charlotte, please do take a seat. Is there something I can help you with?"

Isaac King motioned me with practiced graciousness to a leather seat facing his enormous desk and watched me over his glasses. Even seated and behind his desk, the man exuded power and control, which he brought to disgraceful extremes.

"I wanted to discuss something with you, yes." I folded my hands in my lap and waited for him to offer me his full attention. I hated talking to someone who didn't pay me attention.

"My son, I suppose."

As always, a straightforward man. I respected that.

"Yes. I would have appreciated it if you had told me beforehand about his addition to my program."

"I apologize. That is, in fact, my fault, but you must understand, everything happened so fast." Isaac smiled apologetically, a restrained smile that didn't reach his eyes and didn't convince me. "He is my son. Regardless of our divergences, I do my best to help him. I admit I pulled some strings to get him into your program, but I knew for certain this would be a magnificent opportunity for him to rehabilitate himself."

"He doesn't seem a man in need of rehabilitation. He only seems…reckless."

It was best if Isaac didn't get the feeling that I was more on his son's side than on his.

"Indeed. Marcus is very reckless. I am worried about the

company he keeps, the actions they venture into, their habits and the outcomes."

"I understand."

"Forgive me. I am inconveniencing you with my concerns. He is a troubled young man, who needs a firm hand to control him and bring him on the right path. I trust we can accomplish that here, Charlotte. It is a favor I am asking you."

I nodded pensively. I decided not to contradict him if it wasn't essential. Marcus might have been his son, and Isaac might have had his own nefarious plans for him, but as long as he was under my tutelage, I was the one who presided over him, not his father. If he differed or attempted undermining my authority, he was going to meet a Charlotte that didn't resemble in the slightest the little girl he had seen growing up.

"I see." I nodded again, my face a hard mask that gave nothing away. "You do know I like to work with industrious people who try their hardest to achieve excellent results and expand their knowledge."

"I will make sure he understands that," Isaac interrupted me with a frantic nod of his head. I didn't like being interrupted either.

"So I hope *you* understand that I will not favor him, and I will not lessen his workload or responsibilities within the program. He has been admitted, now he will be like any other intern under *my* management."

"I sincerely counted on that."

"Good."

Without further ado, I rose to my feet and headed for the door. Isaac obligingly opened the door for me, and with a satisfied expression, he led me into the ample space that accommodated the reception area.

It was only when we shook hands in a very practical, unemotional manner that I saw Marcus. He was watching us stiffly with a huge stack of papers in his hands. His eyes traveled to our joined hands, and he scowled, displeasure evident at the familiarity between his father and me. Then he strode off, jaw set and eyes clouded, climbing the stairs two at the time.

I almost smiled. To some extent, it was amusing that Marcus, a bulky man with such a mysterious dark air about him, a man you'd rather see out in the open, exerting himself to exhaustion, was now enclosed in an office and had to clear a mountain of paperwork that not even our secretaries liked to sort out.

I smiled throughout the short three-floor ride. King Sr. was not a man easily fooled, as I suspected it was the case for King Jr., yet I believed I had put on an excellent performance to convince Isaac that I wasn't in particular support of his son. Then my big smile wavered. I had only made such a statement because Marcus had managed to breach my defenses, and I had let him.

I walked past the interns' office without glancing back although I knew that Marcus was in there. I could almost feel his gaze burning through the glass separating us and searing my skin. If I wanted to be credible, I needed to act as professionally and as coldly toward him as possible. The only thing I feared was that he would not let me.

The rest of the day passed in a haze, without any more interference from either of the King men. I knew, however, that I could not avoid Marcus forever, so I headed to the interns' office with a folder in my hands and a smirk on my face.

"M-Miss B-Burton," Phillip Foster stammered as he stumbled out of the office.

Excluding Marcus, I had picked all interns personally, and Phillip Foster was the one whose academic progress and endeavors impressed me the most. Behind his rectangular glasses and the nervous attitude that deepened whenever he came across me, there was a good-looking, gifted man with a potential I wished to develop to its best advantage. If only he acknowledged his own capacity. If only he were a little more confident.

"Mr. Foster. How is work going?"

"Good. Very good, Miss Burton."

"Good. Don't let me keep you."

I motioned him back to his business and stormed inside the vast office the interns occupied. All motion and activity ceased. Only Marcus continued typing on his computer, bored stiff and glowering at the screen.

Matt Russell sat behind his desk, almost drowning in all the files and papers littering its surface.

Victoria Brown clenched her teeth to prevent a glare. She was the only female candidate I had accepted, not because I didn't support the feminine endeavors, but because nobody had been convincing enough, yet Miss Brown failed to appreciate her luck. The fact that she was still a part of the program was due only to her surprisingly diligent work.

The one rendering the team incomplete was Adam Harris, but for the moment, I decided not to comment on his absence, which he must have known was unacceptable.

I threw the folder on Marcus's desk and waited for his reaction. His fingers stopped dancing across the keyboard immediately, but otherwise, he hardly moved. First, he picked up the folder between thumb and forefinger like it was an environmental hazard, then his eyes slowly traveled up my body until they met my own. The usual fire in his eyes had extinguished. Instead, an arctic stare locked on mine.

"So, Mr. King…" I sat in the chair in front of his small desk and couldn't help but bite my lower lip. Despite the frostiness he regarded me with, I felt aflame. "I will need your help with Ms. Hansen and Mr. McAlister's divorce."

"Who are you representing?" He flexed his jaw and his brow puckered as he stared down at the folder I had given him.

"Neither. They are both close friends of mine. I will need you to—reconcile the parties."

"I was under the impression they sent me here to do forced labor, not to help." His grumpiness was almost endearing, and I had to bite my lip once more not to grin. His eyes instantly fixed on my mouth, and an electric current ran down my spine, making my hair stand on end.

"You are under the correct impression, Mr. King, but helping me *is* doing forced labor."

He leaned against the back of his chair and pulled his legs forward under the table in an unceremonious gesture until they bumped against the tips of my shoes. Crossing his arms over his chest, his eyes shifted to the door before they returned to me. Absently, I registered Phillip sitting at his desk and the others staring at us every now and then.

The office, however, was big enough that nothing of our discussion had to be overheard if we didn't want it to be. But I wanted them to overhear, and I wanted them to have no reason to form suspicions that I favored Marcus.

"And you should also be under the impression that I will supervise and report your every move."

"Yes, ma'am."

"I have to warn you that Ms. Hansen and Mr. McAlister have a very dynamic and riotous relationship. Their rapport might vary from defending each other to the point of annoyance to scratching each other's eyes out. Since you will be in the middle, I expect you will deal appropriately with the situation.

"So I'll play marriage counselor. Fascinating."

"First and foremost, you will keep your opinions to yourself and try to reconcile the parties, just like I said."

I felt devious just picturing him in front of Rachel and Ethan, witnessing their heated arguments. They truly loved each other, but each time they disagreed on something, which was rather frequently, they wanted to divorce. I only hoped that the third time it would be less appealing to split up and more gratifying to actually enjoy their marriage.

"It seems to me I am only doing you a favor." Marcus lowered his voice and leaned in, turning from chilly to rapacious in a flash. My breath caught.

"As long as you do your job like I requested—" I trailed off indifferently. I was anything but indifferent.

"Don't you have another case? I don't like this."

"Oh. I'm sorry. You are not here to choose."

I stood, painfully aware of him inspecting my every move. He strained his muscles, forcing my attention to his enticing physique and his customary dark clothes.

"Utterly and unequivocally a nonconformist," I muttered.

"Always." And he finally managed a smile.

An hour after I returned to my office, Sofia stuck her curly head in and asked me if she could leave, which meant that almost everybody had already gone. I dismissed her tiredly and sighed.

Being the first to arrive and the last to leave should have offered me some degree of satisfaction. Instead, it only brought me frustration.

My aggravation amplified when all lights went out and the screen of my computer blanked before my eyes. Power outages weren't frequent in this part of the city, but when they did occur, it was unlikely that the problem would be solved soon.

Groaning, I gathered my purse and stood to leave. I simply hated darkness. I always had and perhaps always would. It didn't scare me out of my wits, but it produced a heavy, unpleasant tension spreading from my chest all the way to the pit of my stomach.

Outside my office, it was even darker. I groped my way to the reception area, anxious to get out of the building. The darkness combined with the deadly silence created an eerie effect.

"Did you plan to leave without your folder?" A languorous whisper coming from directly behind me rolled over my senses like honey. The incredible closeness, the abrupt disturbance of the quiet, and the shameless invasion of my personal space wrenched a loud shriek of panic from my chest.

"For God's sake," I breathed, my heart pounding against my ribcage.

"Easy," Marcus soothed, chasing the fright away.

He placed a hand on my stomach, steadying me. Suddenly, my back was pressed against his chest, and his breath was warming my cheek. He smelled of cologne, mint, and Marcus.

"What are you still doing here?" Although my voice came out cold and clipped, my trembling fingers settled on the hand he was keeping on my stomach. It was so warm.

"I work here now, remember?" He chuckled but didn't let go. It was then that I picked up on his mood change. He didn't seem upset anymore. Absurdly, the thought made me smile. "Besides, I don't understand why you are complaining. You are the one prowling about."

"I am not prowling about."

Affronted, I spun around in his one-armed embrace. I acknowledged my mistake as soon as he took advantage of my action and pulled me even closer. Through the darkness, I thought I saw him smile.

"What were you doing with my father, Charlotte?"

The abrupt change of topic made my head spin. I was glad I couldn't see his eyes properly. I was afraid of their intensity.

"I was having a civilized conversation."

"It looked like more than that."

"What are you implying?" I ground my teeth in mute protest and tried to back away, but he didn't budge. If anything, his breathing grew ragged and his hold even firmer.

"You looked like two people who had just made a deal."

"I don't make deals with your father, Marcus."

"Look, Charlotte. My father has always wanted to control me, and when he couldn't, he always made me feel like I lacked something essential. If you are on his side, let me know that from the start."

I was unexpectedly grateful for the darkness. "I wanted to determine his intentions concerning you," I whispered. "I also thought it would be best if he believed that your presence within my program was inconvenient to me and that I will not grant you any preferential treatment."

"Why would you go to such lengths for me?"

"Because if I can get Isaac out of your hair, implicitly, I'll get him out of mine. I was being practical."

I was lying.

"Undoubtedly," he mocked me.

"So I would appreciate it if you behaved professionally and kept your distance."

I tried once again to free myself from his firm hold but didn't achieve any more than I had earlier.

"Oh, Charlotte. That won't be possible."

His arm released me, and I took a much-needed step back. In the darkness, his eyes were the only light. When they dilated, I gasped. He fixed me with a dangerous gaze, making me feel unsteady. He enjoyed the nervousness he was building in me.

When I attempted another step back, Marcus growled. Without further warning, his hands secured my face, and his mouth slanted across mine in a rough kiss that stole my breath and offered me his. Marcus was pure male and raw passion, and his kiss did not betray his nature. His hand fisted in the hair at my nape to better position me for his wild onslaught.

He caught my bottom lip between his teeth and sucked greedily on the swollen flesh. His tongue coaxed me to respond just as fervently while his primal determination melted my restraint.

The warm, wet invasion devastated my senses and shook my whole body. Our tongues wrangled, but it was Marcus dominating the kiss, dominating me. I struggled to breathe, yet there was nothing I wanted to breathe more than his breath. There was nothing I wanted to taste more than him.

"Marcus," I panted. He leaned his forehead against mine and let his lips linger on my mouth in a chaste kiss.

"Why are you trembling, Charlotte?"

"You shouldn't have," I gasped.

I steeled myself, but by this point, there was little I could do. I could deny both him and myself. I could try once again to push him away. I could seek all the means to remove him from my life. But my heart never agreed with my mind, and sooner or later the inevitable was going to happen.

I shoved him away limply, and he flinched, hugging his left side. Involuntarily, my hand reached for the spot. Instead of walking away, I only walked closer.

"I told you my bruises are the least of my pains, but my ribs are still healing. Be gentle with me."

All roughness was gone. The ruthless creature that had tormented him was vanquished, and in its wake, Marcus was left a calm and gentle man. His fingers touched my hot cheek and settled on my trembling lips.

He was committing me to memory. He was burning his touch in my flesh. Once more he bent to seize my lips, this time in a quiet, soothing kiss that calmed the flames leaping in my blood.

"Don't—" I managed to pull away. "I told you that I do not mix business with pleasure."

"Yet, you enjoyed this as much as I did," he whispered and brushed my lips with his thumb. It frightened me because I didn't want him to stop. I didn't want him to let me think. "And you'll be thinking of me tonight."

I took a deep breath that didn't reach my lungs and sidestepped him. I wasn't habitually clumsy, but the way I bumped into the reception desk begged to differ. I groaned loudly.

My hip bone throbbed, and I hardly felt my leg. The clash was evidently going to leave a bruise. I winced at the thought as much as I did at the pain but aimed for the exit once more with characteristic stubbornness.

"Let me get you outside." Marcus wrapped his hand around my elbow and carefully steered me forward. His certain attitude and deep, commanding voice mollified me.

"Fine," I snapped, knowing it would be of no use to protest.

In the dim hallways, I swore I saw a flicker of a smile on his face. He didn't remove his hand from my arm until he was confident that I would manage walking on my own. When we reached the ground floor, I stormed out of the building, ignoring the doorkeeper, who saluted me dutifully. Marcus remained quiet, but he was right there behind me.

"Are you following me?" I inquired before I realized that he was probably heading for his motorcycle.

"Do you want me to follow you?"

My car beeped its welcome and so did the neighboring vehicle mere seconds later. It was an arctic seal gray Jaguar with blinding headlights and the unequivocal grace of a beast. Marcus pulled the door open, regarding me with a smug smile.

My gaze shifted confusedly from my so-called intern to the car he had just unlocked. My mouth hung open and my hands itched to touch the sleek animal.

"You like it?"

"I might." I was still thoroughly shaken. "But where is your motorcycle?"

"My baby is taking a break for now."

"Do you race with this too?"

"No." The firm negation pleased me. I honestly didn't like the thought of Marcus racing, regardless of his talents or competence.

"Good."

"Here is your file. I've made one for myself."

I nodded and struggled to swallow. Marcus stepped closer. I could get a clear glimpse of his eyes now, and they were fascinating—too blue, too wild, too intimate. When he started bowing closer, I recognized his intention and hurried to take shelter inside my car. He chuckled. With a smirk still playing across his lips, he slid into the driver seat, then the engine purred to life, and in a flash, he was gone.

Although the parking lot was almost empty, I took all the possible precautions and smoothly drove into the night. I rolled my window down, inhaling the sweet cold air, needing it to cool my senses. Then I heard a noise chasing me. It was the unmistakable roaring of a sports car.

In my peripheral vision, the Jaguar appeared lush and lissome like a big cat on the prowl. Marcus decreased his speed to match mine. With a single hand on the steering wheel and eyes brazenly inspecting my flushed complexion, he enjoyed having caught me off guard once again.

"I intend to be diligent in my work," he warned, and we both knew he didn't refer to professional work, but he kept teasing me nonetheless. "I hope I'll have good references from you, Miss Burton." I shook my head in disbelief at his audacity and persistence, expecting him to give up and speed away. But of course, he didn't.

"Be brave, Charlotte. Be daring."

I turned to meet his searing eyes. His seductively murmured words replayed in my head, making me unconsciously bite my lip. Marcus grinned wickedly, with a promise burning in that inciting stare of his. Then he stepped on the gas and disappeared with his eyes stuck on mine.

"God," I sighed both frustrated and amused.

What was he doing to me?

Chapter 13

Marcus

'Affaire, once so familiar and welcoming, seemed too loud and crowded all of a sudden. The waitress winked at me appreciatively as I slid into a booth and ordered four bottles of Guinness.

Mere moments later, Brayden and Bryson plopped noisily in their seats, taking large gulps of their beer without so much as a greeting. It was Kai, however, who drew my attention. He sat absentmindedly with an atypical scowl on his face. He was always surrounded by that eccentric and somewhat chaotic aura generously provided by his artistic side, so this withdrawn, dismayed attitude of his raised questions—and concern.

"What the hell is going on with you?" Bryson kicked the leg of my chair, catching my attention in the primitive fashion that characterized him. His expression was hostile and dangerous. Finally, the lecture I had been expecting ever since the ill-fated race was here.

"I was not aware that something was going on."

"What he's trying to say is that when you decide all of a sudden, without apparent reason to willingly go to jail, we'd like to give you a hand." Brayden's words might have sounded like a joke, but he was mirroring his brother's exact disposition. If their stares could have killed, well, I would have already been dead.

"What I'm trying to say," Bryson snapped, "is that I believed you knew you could count on us to have your back. Instead, you just disappeared for days."

"I do know you have my back and I do trust you. But I also know that both of you are a pair of hotheads that can't conform. That night I needed men who followed the plan Kai provided, and you would have likely jumped off your motorcycles and started knocking out any policeman in sight."

"You should have at least let us know."

"It would have been nice if you had at least asked."

Bryson and Brayden spoke in unison, basically expressing the same dissatisfaction. While I understood their displeasure, I also stuck to my own judgment. Neither one of them had been adequate to attend that night's race, and Kai had made the best decision regarding the crew. I clenched my teeth and willed my own displeasure to its tiny, secret cage.

"And you would have been at the race no matter what."

"Damn right, we would have," Bryson growled and hit the table with a white-knuckled fist.

"That's exactly what I am talking about. That race was about following a designed path, about me and me alone getting arrested. Not you two fools."

"I made the damn decisions." Kai's face was bleak and remote as he spoke in a tight voice. Something was certainly wrong with him. "I made the plan, and I didn't let you know. I already told you it was all on me, damn it."

"The fact that you trusted Samuel more than us speaks volumes," Bryson spat, his glare deepening.

Kai stood stiffly and strolled away, dismissing us with an angry sweep of his hand. I had been so absorbed the past few days that I had failed to check on him.

"Look, I get it." I met both Bryson's and Brayden's furious glares without blinking. At the moment, I was more worried about Kai's strange behavior than their displeasure. "I hurt your feelings. I'm sorry, babies."

"Don't make me punch you because God knows I want to."

Sometimes, Brayden's threats were the epitome of expressing his love. I laughed inwardly and watched him sternly. "Great. Tomorrow night works for you?"

"Tomorrow night."

With our scheduled fight already at the back of my mind, I stood and followed Kai. I found him outside, leaning against the wall of the building with a cigarette in his mouth. Kai only smoked when something truly bothered him. It was a habit of restlessness.

"It was you calling the police, wasn't it?"

His voice was low but unequivocally lethal. When I nodded my agreement, Kai clenched his fist and almost bared his teeth. He was usually a calm man, but when he got angry, he had the devastating force of a tempest.

"I asked you for this, Kai. Don't you dare have qualms of conscience."

He scoffed and rolled his eyes, irritation oozing out of him in waves.

"So you also planned your accident? Are you that stupid?"

"Of course not. I am not a damn masochist."

"Then are you insane?"

"I wanted Isaac to find out about the race."

Kai's glare grew deeper and colder. Had he not been younger and a little shorter than I was, had he not been the little cousin I had cared for almost my entire life, his menacing pose might have seemed threatening.

"Did you want him to get you arrested?

"I did, but I had a plan. I already told you."

"What kind of plan? To spend the next years in prison?"

"Your indignation on my behalf is heartrending but unnecessary."

My attempt at a joke only infuriated Kai further. Isaac's behavior had always enraged him, at times even more than it did me. He pushed a hand furiously through his shaggy hair and paced back and forth, only stopping from time to time to shoot daggers at me.

"Explain."

The truth tingled on my tongue, but in the end, I swallowed it. I explained the deal I had made with my father rather than confess what my actual plan had been about. It was neither the time nor the place to fill Kai in about my true intentions. I was not prepared yet for his questions and attempts at repressing my yearning.

"I had a deadline hanging over my head and no way out of my father's ploy. The least I deserve is to control the situation, so I met his schemes with my own."

When I finished telling him everything that had happened, he looked nowhere close to being appeased. His anger might have decreased a notch, but his indignation hadn't.

"How did you know about this internship?"

"Because I did my research," I lied. I'd had no idea about the internship program since my plan had only involved Charlotte getting me out of the mess I had made.

"Then why didn't you make a deal without offering him incriminating evidence?"

"Isaac is no fool. He'd never believe in my sudden change of heart unless he thought he had leverage on me. I intend to play his game until I can find a way to put an end to it altogether."

"How would you do that?"

"Still thinking about it."

He nodded distractedly and took a last smoke of his cigarette before tossing it to the ground and crushing it with the tip of his shoe. That peculiar despondency from earlier seemed all the starker now that anger and irritation dissipated.

"What's got you so wound up?"

I leaned next to him and observed him while he lit another cigarette and smoked on. I could see now that his affliction marred his heart more than his mind. I doubted it was just another fit of his artistic nature.

"Who," he mumbled. It was not a question.

"Who? Women problems?"

"Only one woman."

His jaw flexed before he opened his mouth to take another pull of his cigarette. His eyes were lost somewhere in the distance.

"You know you can talk to me if you need to."

"Yeah, I know." But he wasn't going to talk, and I respected his decision and his privacy as long as he didn't start doing reckless things. I nodded, ran a hand over my face, and straightened.

"Can I leave you alone? Are you going to be okay?"

"You want to babysit me?" he managed a chuckle, but the smile didn't reach his eyes.

"No, I don't." I laughed too, a short, strained sound.

"Then you can leave."

I turned to leave when his hand clamped on my shoulder. For such an innocent-looking man, he truly had a vicious grip.

"The talking part? It's valid for you too."

"I know," I said. If anybody was going to find out about the latest things occupying my thoughts and consuming my every waking moment, then that person was Kai.

ONE HOUR LATER, I WAS waiting in my car in front of Charlotte's apartment building, drumming my fingers against the steering wheel with undisguised unrest. A text message was all I had sent her.

'Be brave, Charlotte, be daring. I'll be waiting. 6 p.m.'

She hadn't answered, but I was still waiting. I believed in her courage even when she didn't.

Charlotte's mind was a vast and complicated place, filled with snares and fears that stifled her instincts. Her mind was singing a song of caution, while her body was a symphony on fire. Her body had told me everything her mind refused to.

I pressed my lips into a taut line, still feeling the texture of her mouth obediently receiving my kiss and yet wildly responding to it. Beneath her polished layer of aloofness, Charlotte was fire and wildness. I had to believe she was going to be *daring*.

Another half an hour later, the passenger door was pulled wide open, and the most beautiful, annoyed expression framed by glorious, brown curls appeared in my view. Charlotte glared at me, yet there was also amusement twinkling in her stare.

Between witnessing the battle on her face and embracing the electric current that snaked up and down my spine whenever she was close, I found myself grinning from ear to ear. She just rolled her eyes.

"Hello, sugar. I knew you'd make it."

"How many times do I have to explain to you that I do not like to be called—*that?*"

"Oh, Charlotte. I think you do." Her mouth puckered, and she swallowed heavily. The sight pleased me. "Get inside."

She finally complied, utterly displeased and adorably beautiful.

"I was serious, Marcus. We must have a professional relationship. You should be aware of this more than I am."

Her voice took on a pleading tone and her eyes a scared shade that pulled me to her like a magnet. I cupped her face in my hand, and when she nuzzled her cheek against my palm, my breath hitched.

"Look at me, Charlotte." She did so slowly, chewing on her lip nervously. How could I protect her when she stirred such basic instincts in me, when all I wanted was to ravish her? "I didn't accept my father's deal to have a professional relationship with you."

"Then why?"

"I want *you*, but I know I have to gain your trust first. This is my way of doing that."

She held her breath for so long that I feared she had forgotten how to breathe. Her cheeks colored, her pupils dilated, and finally, her lips parted, invading me with her sweet, sweet aroma.

I brushed my mouth against hers softly, tentatively, coaxing her to let go and give in. When her tongue traced the outline of my bottom lip, I groaned and seized her mouth in a deep, inescapable kiss.

"Question is, Charlotte," I continued, when our mouths parted, "are you daring enough to trust me?"

"I'm here, aren't I?"

Even her shy reticence was appealing. Like the first time I held her hand, she watched me stunned and slightly hesitant, with eyes full of hunger and an enticing mouth parted in awe.

"Fair enough."

I traced the seam of her lips, wanting to garner from her so much more than reticence, but at the moment, patience was crucial.

Charlotte and I functioned at different velocities. While I craved the swiftness of the unknown, she was satisfied with the slow pace of the familiar. She was the kind of woman I was willing to slow down for.

"So what now?"

"Since our horror movie date wasn't an actual date, according to you, I am asking you on a date."

Those beautiful chocolate eyes sparkled with remembrance, then a smirk lit her whole expression. I grabbed the wheel with one hand and the gearshift with the other. Otherwise, I would have simply kissed that teasing mouth until she was properly flushed and unable to sit still.

"I can say no."

"But you won't."

"You are very sure of yourself," she accused, the superior smirk fully on display.

"I am sure of you."

Taking by surprise a smart woman such as Charlotte was always a pleasure. As she fastened her seatbelt, her eyes sparkled, and her cheeks turned crimson. She was quiet for the most part of the ride, but eventually, she started kneading her hands in her lap and chewing nervously on the inside of her cheek.

I had always been unnaturally perceptive and attuned to people's emotions in a way that their disposition affected me as much as it touched them. With Charlotte, that awareness was even sharper. The closer I got to her, the more attuned I became.

"You seem impatient," I said.

"You wish." She managed a smile, but it didn't come naturally. "I am not."

"You know, I can feel you, and you are definitely impatient."

"And if you feel me so well, can you feel me starving?"

"I think I've just heard your stomach growl, yes."

Laughing, I decided to drop the inquiry, but for a relationship between us to work, we both needed to learn to communicate. I valued, almost craved, complete openness. I wasn't going to allow Charlotte to keep anything festering in her mind.

"Can I ask where we are going?"

"On a date. Dinner and a movie. The usual."

I retained control of myself, but I had my own nerves kneading me from the inside out. It wasn't going to be the usual—not for me. I rarely actually dated, and I had definitely never done with another woman what I was about to do with Charlotte.

"And we're going to dine on Mars?" Her attempt at a joke was as nervous as the glint in her eyes.

"Are you finally admitting that you're impatient?"

"Maybe I'm just hungry."

Evasion was never going to work with me. I placed my hand on Charlotte's knee and clutched it until I was sure I had her attention. "Talk to me, Charlotte."

She watched me briefly before resuming her fascinated view of the surrounding landscape. The edgy, bashful woman next to me was such a huge difference from the poised commandant at the office. I smiled encouragingly, and she sighed, defeated, even a little embarrassed.

"I haven't done this in a long while."

The confession momentarily staggered me. With big brown eyes that dug deep into my soul, Charlotte assessed my reaction.

"I can't say I regret it." I gave her my widest, most wicked smile.

It was so soon, and yet, I couldn't envision Charlotte with another man, his arms around her supple body, his lips caressing her smooth skin. I shuddered with disgust and barely contained rage.

By the time I finally parked the car in a glade at the back of the house, the sun was setting. I rounded the Jaguar, helped Charlotte out, then pulled her closer to me, pleased when her body softened into my side.

The house had been built by my grandfather in a clearing and was surrounded by countless different species of trees that formed a private ambit all around. A fantasy of leaves colored from shades of dark green to greenish yellow and stark red shaped one massive waltzing crown that spread far and wide.

Some feet away from the spot I had parked the car, there was a breach in the curtain of trees. I tugged on Charlotte's hand and led her there, enjoying immensely the surprise written on her face. We followed a short path through the trees that led to the manicured back lawn of my house.

I tensed slightly then took comfort in caressing her hand with my thumb. This was my most private space, my safest shelter. This was the place where, in its remoteness and loneliness, I had screamed my frustrations and reveled in my successes. So her reaction was nervously anticipated.

Charlotte stared at the two-story house in awe, having yet to speak. The wall facing us, which represented the backside of the house, was entirely made of glass. Inside, the lights were on just like I had left them, displaying the living room. Upstairs, bathed in orange spotlights was the bedroom with its adjacent bathroom and a small sitting area. It was a simple house yet sumptuous in its simplicity.

"Let's give you the tour," I whispered then kissed her temple.

I dragged her forward, and she moved like a puppet in my arms. Her eyes grew wider with confusion when, instead of inviting her inside, I guided her around the corner of the house. There was something more I wanted to show her, something that had a greater significance than the house itself.

When the artificial pond came into view, Charlotte gasped and covered her mouth with her tiny hand. The small lake was oval-shaped and the size of a tennis court, guarded by bushes of camellias. Between the purple red shades of the sunset and the wildly-colored camellias, the view held an intoxicating combination.

"Now I think it's time for you to say something." I smiled nervously.

"I—"

"Maybe you should eat first. I promise I won't poison you. I am a pretty good cook."

"It's beautiful. It's amazing."

She had trouble finding her words, and so did I. The pond was a monument to love itself, built by my grandfather for his wife as an homage to her devotion and dedication, a safe place where, no matter how big the quarrel, they buried the hatchet.

Charlotte didn't know it, but showing her this house was my

way of letting her in, of trusting her with a part of me I had never truly trusted anyone with before.

"I'm glad you like it. I thought it would be more special than a restaurant."

"It is," she agreed.

I walked to her until our chests brushed and nothing separated us. The look of total fascination in her molten eyes was my undoing. I bent and took her mouth in a slow, questing kiss.

When her hands cupped my face, and she moaned against my lips, I groaned and tightened my hold on her waist. My intentions had been limited to having dinner and spending a quiet, comfortable night together, but as usual, Charlotte was too much of a temptation. If she enticed me this way, I was not going to be held responsible for my actions.

"After you," I whispered in her ear. The way she trembled only excited me more.

It was chillier than usual for this time of year, so I showed Charlotte inside, my hand safely pressed against her lower back. Under the warm spotlights, in my home, with her big eyes peeking shyly at me, she was delicious.

The living room was dominated by a huge U-shaped sofa with a glass table in front, a fireplace on the far wall, and a big flat screen perched above it. I led Charlotte to the left side of the room where a rectangular table of six formed the dining space.

Pulling out her chair, I waited until she sat, then I disappeared into the kitchen to bring our food. As I set the table, her eyes skimmed me appreciatively.

I winked. She blushed.

"Tell me what you are thinking."

I sat to her left, pushing my chair close enough to become an extension of hers. When she didn't speak, my fingers enclosed her cold hand. Uncertainly, she glanced at me then took a sip of water as if hunting for courage.

"Charlotte, the fact that you came here doesn't mean we have to sleep together."

My in-depth scrutiny made her squirm in her seat. When my stern expression dissolved into a teeth-revealing grin, Charlotte relaxed as well.

Pouring us red wine, I handed her a glass then sipped from mine, watching her over the brim with the same shameless smile that I couldn't suppress.

"I only wish I had known I would pay you a visit." Her voice was low, feminine, and delectable.

"You mean to say that you wished you had known you would come into the wolf's lair?"

She finally managed a smile and started ever so slowly a soothing pattern of stroking my hand with her thumb. She didn't loosen up easily, and I suspected she didn't want to try that with everybody, which honored me even more, but when she did cast off her inhibitions, she transformed into a marvelously alluring woman. If she let me, I wanted to cast off all her inhibitions until none remained.

"Is this your house?" Her voice sounded suspicious, and her brows knit infinitesimally. "There's a completely different address in your folder."

"Yes, it's my house. My grandfather built it. Isaac sold it after he died, but I managed to repurchase it a few years ago."

"Your grandfather built it?"

"My maternal grandfather. He was an architect. He loved it here and had many dreams regarding the place. When he was alive, the house was always full of guests, but now, unfortunately, it is mostly empty."

"I bet you bring all your girlfriends here, so it can't be that empty."

She brought the wine glass to her lips and sipped slowly, her eyes firmly, stubbornly even, directed forward while mine burned holes through her skin.

She was fishing for information, but the uncertainty in her voice displeased me nonetheless. I leaned in until my lips almost glided across her cheek.

"I don't have a girlfriend, Charlotte. You are the first woman to come here since I bought the house."

"Oh..." she breathed and quickly looked away. "Isaac doesn't know about it, does he?"

"No, he doesn't."

I smiled at her brusque attempt to change the subject. I was a very persistent man, which she already knew. Nobody dodged me unless I allowed it.

"You're unbelievable. I wish I had the nerve to defy my father like this. I envy you."

"I promise I'll help you."

I gave her a wicked grin, just as innumerable questions flooded into my head. I wanted to know about her family and her childhood, about her dearest memories and worst fears. I wanted to know Charlotte Burton inside and out.

"But we are not going to talk about our fathers. I want to talk about us."

Evasion was definitely never going to be allowed between us. My fingers slowly traced the inside of her wrist until I reached the inside of her elbow. Under my touch, her temperature increased, and her breath caught.

My hand tightened around her forearm, and her eyes closed in capitulation—capitulation to her own yearning.

Chapter 14

Charlotte

I was afraid to open my eyes. I was afraid of what Marcus made me feel, of the reactions his touch triggered. When I finally dared to peel my eyelids open, Marcus was a breath away, his gaze searching me wildly, greedily, demolishing all my attempts to erect a protective barrier between us. With Marcus, there were going to be no barriers. It scared me. It made me crave it.

"I respect you, Charlotte."

In the depths of his eyes, there was a fire burning slowly, spreading even into his low, seductive voice. He was playing with my mind, conquering my senses, and defeating my resistance.

"I respect your professionalism. I respect your workplace, and I am humbled by your intention of protecting me from my father. I will comply with your rules at work, but I want you. I want you, and I am not willing to give you up."

"Why? Why me?"

Marcus smiled patiently, with an I-expected-your-question look. His lips were parted in invitation. His fingers still trailed patterns on the inside of my forearm, causing goosebumps to appear on my skin and a warm, frightening sensation in the pit of my stomach. I forced myself to glance at the fading bruise on his forehead, but he wasn't going to be deterred. He wanted my attention, and he made sure he had it.

"Charlotte," he called softly and waited until my eyes once again met his. He uttered my name in a way that made my insides clench and my heart flutter in my chest. I suspected he was acutely aware of his effect on me, while I had no idea if I had any effect on him at all. That was frustrating. "Why do we crave chocolate, for instance?"

"Because we like the taste."

"But I don't know how you taste. And I still want you."

His words and his voice made me lightheaded. I gripped the glass of wine a little too forcefully, and the liquid almost sloshed over the rim. I drank what was left, but the alcohol didn't provide any more courage than I'd had before.

Marcus King was an infuriatingly puzzling man. At times, he could be annoying, persistent, amusing, then he turned lethally determined and stunningly intimidating.

"Because it is a forbidden pleasure," I tried again, my voice trembling. Marcus grinned and almost nodded, but then he continued.

"There's no rational explanation, but we want it nonetheless. Maybe it is the taste, or maybe it is the dark, sensual promise it provides. Maybe it is its allure that entangles us, the sweet, rich aroma hidden beyond dark and impenetrable layers. Maybe it's the thrill of diving past those thick layers and discovering a unique taste, something nobody else can claim."

We both knew he wasn't talking about chocolate anymore. He eyed me with unconcealed ferocity, and instead of scaring me, it fascinated me. Nobody had looked at me in such a possessive manner before. I had never allowed anybody that close, not like Marcus seemed to want. His intensity almost flung me off a high cliff. I was afraid of the fall, of not being caught.

"I don't have a reason why I want you, or maybe I have thousands. I only know that I want to discover you. Will you let me, sugar?"

For once, his endearment didn't bother me. It was like an arrow that had been purposefully shot and had just met its target. I gasped and bit my lower lip while he waited expectantly. Anticipation made his eyes burn brighter—the predator in him was ready to seize the prey, but was I really prey if I was willingly yielding?

"Yes."

I was in his lap then, and his hands were all over me. With formality and politeness gone, Marcus was an unleashed primal creature. His right arm, wrapped around my waist, kept me still and pressed to his chest while his left hand was clenched in my hair, securing my head for his ceaseless ambush.

He kissed me with the turbulence of a storm and the heat of the scorching sun. Marcus *was* storm and fire combined, and I was ensnared by him. He gave me no escape, and I didn't want to find one. So I let myself be daring.

My tongue tangled with his, and my hands ducked beneath the collar of his shirt. Under my fingertips, his skin felt satiny and warm, and the hard muscles it protected were a masculine lure to feminine senses.

His previous words kept singing in my mind. *The fact that you came here doesn't mean we have to sleep together.* He hadn't excluded the prospect altogether. And suddenly, neither did I.

Instincts I had neglected for so long, desires I had stifled out of apprehension, came rushing to roaring life. The more I touched him, the more I wanted to continue. It was when my hands clasped his sides that he groaned and abruptly but reluctantly broke our kiss.

"Be gentle, Charlotte," he cautioned, but there was a smile lighting his expression.

"You keep saying that," I teased, but my tone quickly turned serious. "When I think, it should be me asking you to be gentle."

"I can go at your speed whenever you need me to."

"No." I shook my head adamantly, surprising us both. "I want to meet you halfway."

The wide, youthful smile he gave me was worth anything, even going against the shrilling voice in my head, warning me to be prudent.

"You are very brave, Charlotte." Gently, teasingly, he caught my earlobe between his teeth and tugged only enough to load my body with awareness, as if I could be anything but aware of him. "I am not worth your bravery, but I want you nonetheless. You are my temptation."

"Then maybe you should keep your distance. I wouldn't want to lead you into temptation."

He laughed gloriously at my little joke. It was Marcus who was leading me into temptation. I watched him, transfixed, as he grabbed the bottle of wine and refilled our glasses. The muscles in his forearm constricted, and the veins stood out in mouthwatering fashion.

"Please do."

He put the bottle back on the table with an audible clink, and his eyes flashed to me. Before his lips managed to encase mine yet again, I put my hands flat on his chest and stopped him. He had a heady effect on me, especially when he started kissing me so skillfully, but like him, I wasn't easily deterred. I arched an eyebrow and traced the left side of his body with my index finger, from the still visible bruise on his forehead to his hip.

"I want to know how badly you were injured. Evidently, you still live with the outcome of the accident."

"Oh my, are you asking me to undress for you, Miss Burton?"

I almost choked on my wine and flushed a darker red than the liquid in my glass.

Despite his delighted grin, he took pity on me and didn't prolong my embarrassment. Instead, he took my hand in his and carefully placed it under his shirt while slowly pulling the material up so it revealed wide stretches of brown, purple, and greenish bruises against appetizingly tanned skin. At the sight of his battered torso and obviously pained expression, I winced too. I had expected him to be a little bruised up, but underneath the abused flesh, there were actual injuries.

"This looks awful."

"Falling off a speeding motorcycle tends to do that. But it's healing now."

His smile didn't make me feel any better. This was an injury he would recover from, but what if it had been worse? I pressed my hand flat against his many bruises, hearing his nervous intake of breath, then I sighed.

"I'm alright now, Charlotte."

His arms went around my waist, but the thoughts whirling in my head and the danger his bruises represented didn't reassure me at all.

"What you do—is dangerous."

I couldn't ask him to stop. I couldn't ask him to give up something he truly loved, but every instinct in my body screamed exactly that. Could I let myself be involved with someone who deliberately put his life in danger?

"I know. But let's not think of it tonight. Dessert and a movie, Miss Burton?"

Marcus stood, dragging me up with him, wearing a mind-blowing smile that scattered all my previous thoughts into oblivion. When I didn't answer immediately, his fingers touched my face fondly as if I were made of glass. He looked stripped of his usual conceited confidence. He looked so young and almost vulnerable.

"Of course."

I put my hand in his, and for the night, I let worries and troubling thoughts fade into the background.

Marcus led me to the couch and turned off a set of headlights so that only a few lights shone behind us, creating a calming, enthralling dimness. Predictably, the movie became soon enough only a series of noises and images unfurling on the flat screen.

"We are terrible at watching movies," I commented. I didn't even know what movie he had chosen, and he didn't elaborate.

"Tell me about your family, about growing up, about you," Marcus urged. I felt a fuzzy warmth spreading in my blood, and I wasn't sure it was only because of the wine.

"Any questions specifically?"

"You don't get along well with your father, either."

"Oh, so we are back to fathers. And that is not a question."

I managed a smile that didn't quite reflect my sudden mood change. Marcus tugged me closer to his side, his arm tightening around my shoulders. I remembered how he had placed his arm on the backrest of my chair in the movie theater and how uneasy it had made me feel. Now, the proximity was natural, desirable.

"My father has always been rather strict, for my own good, he said. I never went against him. Never got the courage. After all, his demands weren't completely irrational. He does want the best for me, only we have different concepts of *the best*. Our relationship started deteriorating considerably ever since he ordered me to go to law school. It was the first time I didn't obey him. A foolish mistake."

"What did he do?"

Marcus's voice was strained and his eyes deeply serious. I just stared down at our linked hands. I wasn't exactly delighted to dig into the past when I had already resigned myself to the fact that I couldn't change it.

"I had just been admitted to New York's School of Visual Arts when my father made sure I got expelled. I had never comprehended the extent of his power and influence until then. Perhaps I hadn't comprehended it clearly until I bowed to it. So I went to Law School instead. It's been delightful ever since."

"What about your mother? Didn't she support you?"

"She did, in her own way." I hesitated. Talking about myself or my family was never easy, especially when I still had mixed feelings about all those issues. "She was there, encouraging me, listening to me and my problems when they appeared."

"But she never stood up to your father." He sounded harsh, and suddenly, his body stiffened. I suspected he hadn't had anybody to stand up for him either.

"She did, but James Burton is not an easy man to stand up to. In the end, she understood that and walked away."

There had never been violence in my family, but sometimes, the constant disagreements were a heavier burden than physical cruelty, so when my mother had had enough, she packed her bags and moved to another country altogether.

My father, although I suspected he still loved her, was too proud to admit he had been wrong. They were not divorced, but they hadn't lived under the same roof for years, and certainly, they hadn't spoken unless necessary.

"So she walked out on you."

"Things are not like that. I am very close to my mother, and she deserves her own happiness. I don't blame her for seeking it elsewhere than by my father's side."

"I know. But I still wish somebody had taken your side."

We leaned into each other, our lips brushing softly as we sought the comfort of intimacy. Kissing Marcus was always a potent experience, a perpetual oxymoron, where softness bordered on wildness and wildness became softness once more with a mere touch. He cupped my face and traced the line of my lips with his thumb, making me aware of the blood pounding frantically in my veins.

"Visual Arts. Which department?"

The sudden change of topic fused with the intense stare he kept trained on me was disorienting. When he looked at me with that single-minded intensity, he bared me. He watched me hungrily like he knew every part of my body.

"Mm—Photography," I said in a whisper.

My throat suddenly felt dry and his gaze much too hot on my skin. I took a hasty gulp of wine, but the sweet burn of the alcohol made the blood in my veins feel even more heated.

"It's not too late, sugar."

Marcus caressed my flushed cheek with the back of his hand. The touch was searing. It was delicious. It was nearly not enough. The sudden thought made me gasp, and he smiled. While I remained confused, he knew exactly what he was doing to me.

"Don't give a girl hope. Hope hurts more than admitting the truth, which is that my father has gotten what he wanted. I am a lawyer now."

"No, Charlotte. The worst is not having hope. The worst is not following what you truly love."

"For a person who is used to asking the questions, I'm certainly giving you too many answers."

I laughed nervously. A weird sensation was unfurling its long, thick tentacles within me, seizing my breath and making my insides boil. I stifled the impulse to unfasten one or two buttons on my shirt. Marcus licked his lips, and the gesture only made me want to be the one moistening them.

"What do you want to ask me, Charlotte?" he asked quietly, sensually, tucking a lock of my hair behind my ear and making sure that his fingers lingered long enough on my jaw to make me tremble.

"I like how you say my name." The words popped out of my mouth before I got the chance to filter them.

"That is not a question, either." He spoke patiently, mimicking my earlier response, but his eyes were blazing.

"What about your childhood, Marcus? I imagine it was difficult after your mother—"

My eyes widened at my own intrusiveness, then I glared at myself and at my complete lack of diplomacy. Isaac's wife had died when I was four, which meant that Marcus had been roughly seven years old. I didn't even want to imagine a little boy attending his first day of school without a mother to give him a reassuring kiss and a bright smile to scatter his fears or bask in his illusions.

I was increasingly intrigued by him. I wanted to know everything I had missed in his life, but the negligence I had approached the subject with was mortifying.

Marcus pulled my legs from beneath me and dragged them in his lap, starting a slow, cadenced stroking that made the skin under my jeans tingle. He didn't seem upset with my invasiveness. He only appeared—dismayed.

"I'd rather not talk about my mother, Charlotte."

His jaw flexed, his eyes closed, and I was afraid he would start crying. When he finally did open his eyes, they were blazing again, but this time there was an underlying sadness too.

"I'm sorry," I mumbled, frustration and embarrassment growing.

Marcus shook his head, but the air of sadness still enveloped him. He clutched my hands and brought them to his mouth, causing my lungs to stop working for a moment.

"You smell so good. Like tuberoses." He kissed my knuckles and inhaled deeply as if he could smell my very blood. The fascination he was kissing and caressing my hand with beguiled me in return.

"I—"

"Any other questions?" Marcus prompted.

His tongue darted out, licking tenderly between my index and middle finger. His stares were shameless and challenging. I gave a start and inhaled sharply, a breath I forgot to let out.

"What about high school, college..." I was close to stammering. And it was hot, too hot. "Were you just as rebellious?"

"I believe that courses through my blood. It was even worse then."

"I believe your rebelliousness is a defense mechanism."

Leaning against the backrest, with my hand under his curious, persistent mouth, I took another sip of wine and assessed his reaction. He didn't deny it.

"It might, or it might just be a failure of my character."

"Don't quote your father," I admonished gently and tugged my hand back.

He was not only tickling my skin. He made it burn, causing a longing I was afraid to acknowledge. Marcus's eyes snapped to mine, and it was difficult to say whether his reaction was caused by my mention of his father or because I had withdrawn my hand.

The answer became clear when his grip on my fingers tightened, and he continued examining my hand. It was that single part of my body that he touched, kissed, and occasionally nipped on, and yet, the sensations he triggered rushed through my whole body.

"Why was it worse?"

"Growing up was difficult. I was a very secluded kid. Being rebellious, I guess, was the only way I found to socialize. I broke a lot of rules, got frequently punished, and pissed a lot of people. Eventually, I found other ways of consuming my energy."

"Which are?"

Curiosity spiked, although with every passing moment I found it all the harder to concentrate. I took another swig of wine to calm my nerves.

"Tit for tat, Charlotte." He sounded almost cautionary. And he simply didn't stop touching me. If he could affect me this badly only by touching and kissing my hand, what would happen if he touched more? I felt dizzy all of a sudden. "How were you during high school, college..."

"I was—shy. Surprising, right?" I giggled. The sound came out shriller than I expected, and that made me giggle even more. "It was the reverse with me, I believe. When I was little, I was more open, more sociable. It was when I grew up, and all the insecurities kicked in that I became secluded and timid. It's actually an annoying fault."

"I don't think your timidity is a fault. I find it very appealing, in fact." He dragged his lips agonizingly slow from my knuckles to my wrist then upward, inch by inch, until he stopped at the inside of my elbow.

"So what other ways did you find to consume energy?"

"Sports," he murmured against my skin.

"You mentioned more than one way," I commented. I might have felt peculiarly dizzy, but I wasn't easily sidetracked.

"And girls," Marcus laughed, mischief in his eyes.

"Of course," I muttered dryly.

Earlier, I had been curious about his former love life, but right now that thought didn't sound as exciting. Right now, I felt dazed and warm, too warm. I also felt courageous and had an unexplainable urge to giggle again.

"How were boys for you?"

The question startled me as did his abrupt motion. He put his hands on my hips, and in one swift movement, he pulled me onto his lap. I laughed, drinking in his hot stare, then laughed again only because I liked the sound.

"Difficult to let in."

"But you did let in some." He sounded jealous. That amused me. I heard myself chortling again.

"Of course. I've been trained to become a lawyer, not a nun."

"Don't tease, Charlotte. Not with this. I don't like it."

Marcus actually growled. His nose nuzzled my throat, eliciting a low moan from my throat.

"Are you seducing me, Mr. King?"

"Yes, Charlotte, I am."

His admission came without hesitation, and once again, I couldn't help but think that he knew exactly what he was doing, how his touches and the proximity between us made me feel.

Before I gave it much thought, I jumped off his lap to my feet.

My knees wobbled, my breath left my lungs in a rush, and my head spun violently. I realized I had been falling when my chest suddenly crashed into Marcus and his arms enfolded me in a secure embrace.

"Oops," I giggled, looking up at him. He bowed his head so enticingly close that his minty breath fanned over my face. His lips looked a little swollen, tinted a glowing shade of red.

"I caught you," he murmured and kissed my forehead. "I'll always catch you."

"Mm…" I mumbled, relishing the feel of his powerful arms holding me tight.

"You should have warned me that you have no trace of alcohol tolerance," Marcus chided sternly, yet amusement flickered in the blue of his eyes.

"I'm very tolerant," I protested and struggled to find my balance. Within the protective circle of his arms, I didn't have to. "You're swaying."

I blinked twice, but my vision became blurred. A dull ache throbbed at the back of my head as if I had just bumped it against a hard surface. And he looked dreadfully concerned. I laughed, running my hand through his ruffled dark hair. It felt so soft.

"Of course, I am," Marcus spoke sardonically, his arms steadying me once again. It was difficult to discern whether or not he was truly amused. "I cannot let you go home, Charlotte. I need to make sure you will be all right."

"I am wonderful."

Those parted red lips of his were truly tempting. I rose on my tiptoes and caught his face between my hands, pressing my mouth to his in an exploring kiss. He might have blamed the wine, but the desire burning through me was exclusively because of him. Marcus was doing strange things to me, but whatever it was, I didn't want him to stop.

"I'm glad you say so, but I'd like you to kiss me consciously." His long fingers covered my shoulder and gently pushed me away so he could stare into my eyes. The movement, no matter its gentleness, still made me feel lightheaded and weak on my feet.

"Sit. I will bring you a coffee."

The severe look he gave me and his sudden commanding voice compelled me to obey. The coffee, however, never came.

WHEN I RESURFACED, IT WAS with an abrupt jerk, head pounding, heart beating violently in my chest, and sweat trickling down my spine, making me shudder. The nightmare felt so genuine, and its effect was so debilitating that I struggled for breath. I was sitting, my fists clenched and my jaw tightly set when I realized I was not alone. I almost shrieked.

"Charlotte, baby, it was just a bad dream. You're not alone." Marcus's voice sounded slightly disoriented and groggy from sleep.

He leaned backward, and a pleasant light came from a lamp nearby. I was lying between Marcus's outstretched legs, my stiff back pressed against his rising and falling chest. He tightened his arms around me and pressed a kiss to my hair.

It had only been a bad dream. Nothing was real. I rubbed my face and my temples furiously, but the dull ache pounding in my skull didn't evaporate so quickly. I couldn't understand why I kept having those nightmares.

"Do you have nightmares often?"

"I—I'm—"

"Hey, hey, come here. Don't cry, baby."

Wrapping me protectively in his arms, Marcus dragged me down so he was sprawled on his back and I was laying half on top of him, half pressed against the backrest of the couch.

I relished the warmth and tightness of his arms around me. I delighted in his calming fragrance. And I was relieved that he was with me and I didn't have to face the terror alone. I brought my hands to my face to find that I had been crying, perhaps a liberating, cleansing cry.

"I'm sorry," I apologized, wiping the tears away as I gazed into his troubled eyes.

"Tell me, Charlotte."

It was neither a request nor a command. Marcus brushed my lips with his thumb, parting and molding them to his touch, momentarily scattering my thoughts. Perhaps instinctually or perhaps because I was still under the evil spell of the dream, I decided I should tell him.

"It was rather short this time. I was alone in my apartment, and it was dark. The doorbell rang, and some people got inside following me. I closed myself in my room, but they kept knocking on the door and kicking, and their laughter, the sneers—they got so loud, and I had no way of getting out. I opened the window and struggled to climb down. It was such a long way down, but suddenly, I was outside, on the ground, my feet bare. I started running. They were so close behind me and—Then I woke up. And you were here."

I gingerly touched his stubble-covered cheek and hastily scraped my lips against his, my wordless attempt to thank him. But the laidback, comforting Marcus was gone. Instead, he had been replaced by a hard man, frowning up at the ceiling, his teeth clenched and his body suddenly cold. He swallowed heavily, and so did I, apprehensively waiting for his reaction.

"Do you have nightmares often?" he repeated his earlier question.

"Sometimes," I admitted. He looked down at me, a storm brewing in his eyes, and I knew then that he had connected the dots. He knew.

"The same or do they differ?"

"They differ."

Marcus rubbed his shut eyes with stiff fingers before he opened them and watched me intently, a little fearfully in fact. I was suddenly frustrated with myself that tonight of all nights I'd had a nightmare.

"It's because of Friday night, isn't it?" His glacial voice startled me, and my throat was suddenly dry.

"Yes."

"God, Charlotte." A combination between a sigh and a sob was wrenched from his chest, and he trembled under my weight. The storm in his eyes intensified and grew turbulent.

"I'm sorry."

I was sorry because he had to witness that. I was sorry because he had to know. I was sorry because I was not strong enough to eradicate that dormant fear from my subconscious.

"You have nothing to apologize for. Nothing." His sternness soothed and scared me. He wasn't mad at me, but he was mad nonetheless. "I should be the one—"

"No. You have nothing to apologize for either."

The determination in my voice was equally fervent. Taken aback, he blinked, then his brows furrowed slightly. Being so familiar with overthinking, I was able to sense the wheels turning in his head, spinning and reaching misplaced conclusions. I did not want him to take someone else's blame.

I just wanted him to—

"Please kiss me," I begged in a murmur.

With a reserved smile, Marcus complied, and neither of us could think anymore.

Chapter 15

Charlotte

lthough I sincerely wished he could, however big of a distraction Marcus was, he couldn't keep me from my duties forever. I stepped into the interrogation room, at first missing the young man perched on a metal file cabinet in the corner.

Commanding the whole room was Mayor Stewart himself. His gray eyes, so pale that they were frightening, looked at me, void of emotion, as I approached and stretched my hand for a handshake that raised goosebumps on my skin.

"Miss Burton, welcome to Washington. Please meet Cameron Drake."

Cameron Drake was famous both for his notorious cases and striking wins but also for the scandalous love life he flaunted. I could see the appeal. He was a relatively tall man, with dirty blonde hair that he kept perfectly trimmed, sharp features, and a penetrating stare that must have fascinated a fair share of women.

Yet, I could also see the sham. He might have looked like the scion of a Viking, but in the end, he was only a debauched man, with a questionable character, hiding in the perfect suit of a gentleman.

"And here is Vincent Cole."

The door opened to allow the third lawyer of Jack Stewart's defense team to enter.

Cole, unlike our other colleague, was by no means an attractive man. He was too muscular for his height. His round eyes seemed too round in an already round face. His mouth was crooked in an irksome smile, and the scowl between his brows made him look unapproachable and nearly frightening. It was an enigma how a man could smile and frown at the same time.

I shook both men's hands and took a seat next to Cole while Drake remained standing. He looked impeccable and supreme just like the mayor, and the sudden height difference almost made him smirk.

It became quite clear from the beginning that we weren't going to be a team, but two subordinates following Cameron Drake's orders. I might have lacked the dominating gene, but the thought most certainly didn't sit well with me.

"Jack, please join us."

Mitch Stewart sounded tired and just a tad displeased, but his son looked downright furious. He was quiet and isolated, both in body and in spirit, anger rolling off him in tangible waves.

Jack hopped off the metal file cabinet where he had been sitting with an intentionally loud thud and started pacing back and forth instead of taking a seat at the table. I had the feeling that the show of rebellion was fueled by more than innate obstinacy.

"Be quiet and move over here."

Jack's brows knit together, and his otherwise pleasant complexion turned into a disturbing sneer. He cracked his neck and squared his shoulders, but in the end, he slumped in the chair his father had been quietly pointing to.

"Give us a full recount of what happened the last night you were with Jennifer Gunnar," Drake instructed in a calm and slightly bored tone.

Jack's eyes were momentarily animated, but the flicker of emotion died down before he could be suspected of hurting at the sound of his late fiancée's name. Then defiance settled in once more.

"You mean the night she was killed?"

"Start talking, Jack," the mayor admonished and retreated to a corner where he listened and observed.

"Initially, I was supposed to go to Vegas for my bachelor party and Jen to Bali for her bridal shower. She said she was already too stressed with the wedding preparations to start preparing for a bridal shower as well, and she didn't want to leave that to her bridesmaids, so we decided to hold a single party before the wedding instead.

"I picked her up at eight in the evening from her parents' house. My father's driver, Karl, drove us to the Ritz-Carlton where we held the reception, then we received the guests. The party started with me and Jen dancing, then we had games, and it was practically a rehearsal for the wedding."

Jack halted and glared at the table, clenching and unclenching his fists. He was clearly frustrated, struggling to choose his words as if he was afraid of straying from a previously memorized speech.

"Look, I don't know what you expect me to tell you. I spent a lot of time with Jennifer that night but not all my time. I had my own friends to attend to. We drank, we talked, and we had fun, but neither of us sat down and wrote every damn detail in a notebook."

"Then let us help you," I said, and all eyes in the room pinned me with a mixture of disapproval and shock. "How would you describe your relationship with Jennifer Gunnar? If her clinging to you is any indication, she didn't seem to trust you much."

It might have been then the first time that Jack actually looked me in the eye. His stare was so void of emotion that it could have turned fire to frost. If that same gaze ever looked upon the jury, no juror would ever find him innocent.

"What relevance does that have? We were going to get married."

"It holds a lot of relevance, Mr. Stewart. A clingy, distrusting woman may become—let's say, irritating to a man. Your tolerance of such behavior might have run thin. It might be the motive for the murder."

The disapproval of my small audience turned into absolute outrage. Vincent Cole, however, leaned against the backrest of his chair and folded his arms over his chest with that half a smile of his tugging at the corner of his mouth.

Jack's eyes bulged, and his nostrils flared. Mayor Stewart finally stopped his irritating pacing, and the vein in his forehead inflated and turned an odd shade of purple. And finally, Cameron Drake's lips contorted into a sneer before he broke the tension and placed a hand on Jack's shoulder.

"What Ms. Burton is trying to say," Cameron Drake cut in with an awkward chortle, "is that you should consider rephrasing your discourse, Jack. You are the loving man who was about to get married and whose hopes and dreams are shattered. Don't portray yourself as the man who had grown tired of his own fiancée."

"I wasn't—" Jack swallowed his own words and resumed glaring at his clenched fists.

My focus was now on Drake's hand. Drake and the mayor had been good business partners ever since the latter joined the political scene. It wasn't a wild leap to assume they were even better friends and that Jack had grown up seeing Drake as an uncle.

But the way Drake kept his hand on Jack's shoulder, with his fingers almost tightened into a clutch, didn't seem cordial or affectionate in the slightest. It seemed censorious.

"We had just slept together. I wasn't tired of her. I was tired of all the pressure the wedding had generated, nothing else."

"You mentioned that the wedding preparations were making Jennifer uncommonly tense," I continued. "Had this tension generated a fight? Might there be any witnesses to such a fight?"

"Badgering, counselor," Drake snapped.

My voice might have been somewhat argumentative, and I might have raised it a notch, but we weren't in court yet to make objections. It was our responsibility to uncover every little detail about that night as well as prepare Jack for the same questions coming from the prosecutor. Drake's defensiveness was odd and uncalled-for.

I straightened in my seat and looked at Cameron Drake squarely. He could censure Jack, but he wasn't going to censure me.

"I'm not badgering," I said, struggling to appear friendlier than I felt.

I had come to Washington to look for answers of my own, for

any shred of proof that this was not an attempt to cover up a heinous murder, but thus far, I had more questions and suspicions than any answer whatsoever.

"We need to know all the facts and prepare Jack for a similar line of questioning in court. I doubt Leon Holden will take it easy on him. The clearer the facts, the harder will be for Holden to twist them."

"She's right," the mayor cut in, rubbed his eyebrows, then sighed. "Coddling him is not going to be helpful."

Jack threw a glance over his shoulder at his father. I could only see the side of his face, but I didn't miss the defiance and anger embedded in his features.

The two men seemed to lead a soundless, secret conversation that nobody else in the room was a part of.

"Then we should have an answer," Vincent Cole said and put his elbows on the table.

He studied Jack through authoritative eyes. They looked as if they were locked in a contest, neither of them looking away and neither wanting to capitulate. In the end, it was Jack who lost and finally squirmed in his seat, his show of arrogance slipping briefly.

"We didn't fight. We just had a conversation."

"The night of the party?" Cole clarified.

"Yes."

"Where?"

"Out in the garden. I was smoking, and she was talking."

Jack flashed a derisive grin like he had just told a secret joke and expected Cole to join in his misplaced amusement, but when the lawyer did not enable his behavior, Jack sighed and rolled his eyes, exasperated.

"What did you talk about?" Cole pressed on.

I was glad that Jack's wintry stare targeted Cole and not me. The question had evidently made him uncomfortable, but it was the mayor's defensive posture that surprised me. As if the conversation might have been about him.

"She was unhappy that a friend of mine was a guest. I explained to her that it was just a party and not the wedding itself, and that if she were so offended by his presence, he wouldn't be a guest at the wedding."

"Who was this friend and why didn't Jennifer like him?" I asked and momentarily related to the woman's aversion. I could easily think of some *friends* I did not like.

"It was Vinny Savidge. She said he was a bad influence on me. She was quick to judge sometimes."

"Jack, we need you to write down the names of every person who attended the party," Cole ordered and placed a pen and piece of paper in front of Jack.

Drake nodded but didn't seem very happy about how things unfolded. He had come into this meeting believing Cole and I would obey dutifully and follow orders like trained puppies, but he hadn't expected to have the power stripped from his hands.

"Please outline the name of anybody who might have witnessed this interaction between you and your fiancée."

Jack had a short moment of hesitation like he hadn't realized before that we were talking about his fiancée or that she was dead. Just when I was beginning to believe he might be suffering, cold arrogance took over his expression once again.

"There were no witnesses, I already told you," he sniffed. He nearly sounded proud of it, and the notion made my skin crawl.

We waited until Jack finished scribbling a list of over one hundred guests, and I wondered how he could remember all those names. He put the pen next to the sheet of paper and smirked at Cole, who took the list and added it to his folder.

"What happened after this conversation?" Drake questioned and finally took a seat beside Jack. It was ridiculous how they avoided the actual term for that *conversation*. They had had a fight, and the fact that it hadn't been witnessed by any of the guests didn't make it a simple discussion.

"Jennifer went back to the party. She danced and let herself be spoiled. Nobody realized we'd had a—conversation."

"When did you realize she was not at the party anymore?"

"She sent me a message on my phone to meet her upstairs, in our suite."

"When you got to your suite, what did you find?"

I all but shivered. Here came the grotesque part of the story.

Here came the end, and though it was his fiancée's end, Jack didn't even flinch as he delivered the last part.

"She was lying on the ground, and there was blood everywhere. At first, I thought she had done something stupid, but then I heard movement in the room. I wanted to call for help when I something hit me in the head. I don't remember anything else after that."

"There was a call placed from your phone around the time of her death," Cole noted while skimming through his folder. "That's good. It backs up your claim that you called for help."

Drake nodded, a smile finally etched on his face. But his contentment was short-lived.

I grabbed the phone out of my purse and dialed Drake's number. When his phone rang, he scowled but took the device out of his pocket and checked the caller ID.

"What is this, Ms. Burton?"

I hung up and placed my phone on the table. Drake and Cole seemed bewildered, Jack completely uninterested, and Mayor Stewart was impatiently supervising the whole scene.

"It's five thirty so around the time this meeting should end. I could call you to let you know that I took your notes by accident or that I cannot meet you for dinner or that something came up and I will be half an hour late for tomorrow's meeting. Whatever the purpose of this call, nobody can be sure of, and the fact that I placed the call is proof of nothing."

"If I had killed her, I wouldn't have called to report myself," Jack hissed and bumped his fist against the table.

I had made my point, so I refrained from telling him that he would have been neither the first nor the last to report his own crime to look innocent.

"You were the first witness, and you have no alibi to attest that by the time you got there, Jennifer was already dead. A phone call isn't going to win your case."

"That's true," Drake conceded and stood. That was the mayor's cue to stop pacing and walk purposefully to the door. Apparently, the meeting was indeed about to end. "But now that we have the facts, we should start by thinking how the prosecution will be thinking and counter their maneuvers. They don't have any actual proof that Jack committed the crime. All they have is circumstantial evidence, and like you said, Ms. Burton, Holden will try to twist the facts, so we must take the advantage out of his hands."

"And how the hell will you do that?"

Jack was not pleased to see the meeting end. His eyes flickered to his father then back to Drake, all the time ignoring Cole and me, ignoring us like he had done most of the time. He seemed increasingly impatient and a tad frightened that he was going to be left on his own.

"By looking for the actual killer, Jack."

Drake flashed that cocky smile again, apparently very proud of his judgment, but Jack shook his head and gnashed his teeth. His behavior was odd at best. One moment he was arrogantly confident, then a second later, he looked desperate and unbalanced and completely capable of killing. The thought made me sigh and clench my hand around my throat.

"So think long and hard who could have wanted Jennifer dead and most importantly why that person wanted you to look guilty." Drake instructed, and Jake's eyes widened incredulously.

"Maybe because he didn't want to take the blame?" he scoffed.

"Get ready, Jack. Your arraignment is in a week."

Mitch Stewart's fist connected with the metal door and I gave a start. As soon as the guardian unlocked the door, the mayor walked out without a glance to spare for his son.

"Father, get me out!"

It wasn't a plea or cry for help. It was a demand, so aggressive that it sounded like a threat.

Jack's furious shout still echoed in my ears after I left the penitentiary. That must have been why when someone called my name, I didn't initially hear him.

"Charlotte Burton," the voice called again, finally penetrating my eardrum.

I groaned. If the deep, gravelly voice belonged to whom I suspected it did, I was really in no mood to converse with the man. Now that the adrenaline rush I had experienced during the meeting was slowly dissipating, I felt bone-tired. I was also running out of boldness, and though I was pleased to have shocked Drake and the mayor, I feared I had no more resources for the day to impress yet another man who probably underestimated me.

"Charlotte Burton, I'm Leon Holden," the man said as I turned and he outstretched his hand.

Leon Holden was a tall man, whose light golden-brown hair and hazel eyes didn't make him look any less dangerous and commanding than he truly was. He was the prosecuting attorney on Jack's case, and he was known for being ruthless although fair.

"I know who you are, Holden," I answered and shook his hand, not leaving the impression that I was willing to participate in a cozy conversation.

"And I also know who *you* are. Imagine my surprise when I heard that a lawyer known for her charity work for the abused is now defending an abuser, a murderer nonetheless."

"Let's make something clear, Holden. My client is innocent, and you haven't proven yet he is otherwise, so I'd appreciate it if you didn't refer to him as one. Also, if you are trying to intimidate me, you are not the first, and you won't be the last, so let me tell you a little secret. It's not working."

"We'll see."

It wasn't clear if he referred to Jack's innocence or his ability to intimidate me. Holden grinned like a boy fond of mischief. I raised an eyebrow, but he added nothing to intimidate me or otherwise undermine my authority.

He had already told me enough—enough to raise more questions about my involvement in this case than I ever had.

"I'm looking forward to seeing you in court, Ms. Burton. I'd rather have had you on my side, but I welcome the challenge."

I slid into my car and left Leon Holden standing on the sidewalk. I hadn't defended Jack because I believed entirely in his innocence, but because as his acting attorney, it was my duty. After what I saw and heard today, I wasn't sure for how long I was going to find myself in that capacity.

Jack was so volatile that he could be capable of anything, but whether he was guilty or not, he wasn't the clueless victim he portrayed himself as. He was concealing information, and he was arrogant enough to believe he would get away with it.

The reality of what was truly happening remained like a bad dream lurking at the borders of his make-believe world, and the possibility of actually being convicted hadn't even crossed his mind.

But sooner or later the truth was going to come out.

Chapter 16

Marcus

J staggered against the punching bag, my arms going around it to steady myself. Sweat poured down my face and my back while my breath came out in a chest-quaking gasp. Between fulfilling the responsibilities of my own job and being part of an internship at a law firm, I was drained beyond imagination. And yet, there was a bad energy keeping me awake, not giving me peace.

It was perhaps the result of not having seen Charlotte in a week although we had been under the very same roof for half of that time. The plan to get under Charlotte's skin, which I had sacrificed my independence for in favor of my father's deepest wish, was not working as expected. That maddened me. It made me restless and vicious.

I shut my eyes and conjured Charlotte's charming face and contagious giggles, but instead of calming down, I became even more agitated. Question after question pounded in my head, creating a dire ache.

Why had Charlotte been so affected by Brayden's stupid assault? How frequently did she have those nightmares? Was she afraid of me? I groaned in frustration. Brayden's stupid behavior and

Bryson's stupid tendency to encourage him in all the stupid things he did made me feel wrathful.

Then a stinging hopelessness eclipsed the rage. Saturday night, while I had believed that the sweet, captivating flush animating her complexion, her ragged breath, or the heated nuance of her eyes were all symptoms induced by my seduction, they had only been the result of one too many glasses of wine.

In the silence of the exercise room, I growled loudly. Maybe I had no effect on her whatsoever. Maybe the attraction between us had been completely one-sided.

I hated feeling confused and being unable to do anything about it. But most of all, I hated that I couldn't get immediately in touch with her. Despite the confusion, I missed her, but she was in D.C., so all I could do was throw another punch and wait.

Turning off the lights and brushing my face with the towel draped around my neck, I locked the door of the exercise room and wearily made my way down the dark corridor to the living area. It was quiet, too quiet, and the quietness perturbed me.

"Dude, you stink." A voice spoke in the dark, making me jump and bare my teeth in a mute snarl.

Suddenly, light bathed the space, revealing Kai and Brayden sitting leisurely on my sofa and Bryson leaning against the wall with his hand on the switch. They erupted into copious laughter, while I glared and tried very hard not to retaliate violently. After all, I was foully mad at them.

"Look at him, scared like a little girl," Brayden mocked. "You need a pink tutu to complete the picture."

"Why are you here?" I snapped.

"Easy, don't get your panties in a twist."

Kai was the eternal peace-maker. I directed my glare to him and absently prayed that I wouldn't unleash my whole wrath on him. He had his part of the blame, but the responsible one for my fury, for Charlotte's fears, was Brayden.

"We figured we should pay you a visit if we want to see you. You've gone completely MIA."

Bryson moved from where he had been leaning against the wall and slumped negligently on the couch beside his brother. His face was, as usual, a combination of amusement and seriousness.

"I've been working, unlike others present."

I cast them all a displeased glance, and both Bryson and Brayden rolled their eyes simultaneously. They weren't brothers for nothing. Only Kai remained quiet and pensive in his corner, absently patting Kinga who napped serenely with her head in his lap. Apparently, whatever had ailed him a week ago, still did.

"Only working? Nothing else?" Brayden and Bryson both laughed and winked conspiratorially, but I chose to ignore them. I wished they weren't here so I wouldn't strain to remain patient.

"Have they tamed you already or are you up for a race tonight?"

I glanced up at Brayden, wondering if he truly was an idiot. I had recently staged a race, which had ended with multiple injuries, a nice view of a prison cell from behind bars, and a signed deal with my father. My bruises were finally fading, and my ribs had finally stopped hurting. No, I did not want to race. I wanted Charlotte and that made me groan, unmindful of my audience.

"Not necessarily to take part in it. Just to hang out," Bryson said.

He read me better than his reckless brother, so he cut in tentatively, cajoling, but ultimately, he failed to convince me.

"I have to stay legit for a while."

"You can stay legit on the sidelines," Brayden insisted. Once again, I ignored him.

"Are you racing?" I asked Kai.

He stared up, looking startled, then he nodded with a frown. "Why wouldn't I?"

"I don't think you're in the right frame of mind. You should stay on the sidelines tonight too."

"I'm a little old to be told what to do, don't you think?"

"I was not telling you what to do. I'm just worried about you."

Kai sighed and ran an impatient hand over his face then jumped to his feet, startling Kinga. Kicking a cushion, he walked to the window, brushing his jaw with furious fingers until a faint shade of red colored his skin. But through his unrest, he remained silent. I had never seen him this agitated or desolate.

"Well, can we all be worried on the road?"

My head snapped to Brayden with a scowl that I couldn't hide.

Thankfully, at that precise moment, the doorbell rang, and all our heads turned to the door. Kinga growled, preparing to bark, but fell silent once I fixed my scowl on her.

I padded slowly down the small corridor that led to the door and opened it with a resigned sigh. I had expected to be faced with somebody contributing further to my growing irritation, perhaps my father, but when I opened the door my breath caught.

"I know I might be trespassing or crossing a line, and I'm definitely abusing my power by showing up at your door unannounced, but I missed you. And I am on a mission."

"Charlotte."

She was on my doorstep, prattling while I stared at her like an idiot. She was really here. Her brown eyes shone with enthusiasm, and her fair skin glowed a charming shade of red. I itched to touch her skin, to feel the softness of her lips surrendering beneath mine, to have her lithe body writhing in my arms.

Then I remembered, with a frustration that simply did not want to vanish, that we were not alone. Inside, a thick silence had settled. I could only imagine Brayden, Bryson, and Kai, all straining to hear who I was talking to and especially what about. They were worse than gossiping women sometimes.

"I can leave."

Thrown between shock and frustration, I hadn't realized she would interpret my silence the wrong way. One moment, Charlotte was looking expectantly at me, then gradually her face fell, and her enthusiasm vanished.

"Come inside, Charlotte." My voice came out sharper and louder than I had intended. She jumped but quickly stilled and watched me warily. Her former girlish enthusiasm was definitely gone. "Please," I added and reached for her.

When she gingerly placed her small hand in mine, I exhaled in relief, only then realizing I had been holding my breath. I opened the door wider so she could come inside, and Charlotte stepped closer. Her warmth radiated off her cheeks and tipped me in a calming haze.

I cupped her face and let my thumb linger on her parted lips, absorbing the heat coming from the delicious depths of her mouth.

Then I stepped to the side, allowing her to come in.

Charlotte had hardly taken four steps inside when she halted abruptly, and I slammed right into her. My arm went instinctively around her waist to keep her from falling. Pressed tightly against my chest, I could almost feel her hectic heartbeat.

I followed the trail of her eyes and landed on the surprised faces of Kai, Bryson, and Brayden—the very same who had assaulted her, the very same who still haunted her dreams.

Damn it.

My first instinct was to throw the three of them out, but the rational part of me knew that I had to make Charlotte understand that they were only three immature men, who had hardly wanted to really harm her.

"I should go," she muttered under her breath.

Perhaps involuntarily, she pressed back into me, her instinct to flee back to her shell kicking in.

"No."

My hands curled around her shoulders, keeping her in place, while I fought the urge to put myself between her and the glares coming from Brayden and Bryson. Kai was the only one watching the scene impassively, curiously even.

"What is she doing here?" Brayden hissed and rose to his full height. In my one-arm embrace, Charlotte trembled and swallowed with difficulty.

"You shut up!"

"Who is she?"

"I'm Charlotte Burton."

She lifted her chin, and a spark of defiance settled in her fearful eyes. She had no confidence in her own strength, but she was stronger and braver than she knew. Inexplicably, I felt so proud of her.

"She is the reason you got into that firm? Are you a complete idiot?" Bryson's voice went through the roof, causing Charlotte to stiffen like a rock.

"Well, it's not a surprise. He has always been a complete idiot," Brayden spat, but I couldn't tell whether the disdain was directed at Charlotte or at me.

"I'll let you get back to your friends," she sneered quietly, and suddenly her impenetrable armor was up and tightly wrapped around herself. She backed away, both physically and emotionally, in a blink of an eye, and the beast within me roared furiously in protest.

"No," I said again and wrapped my hand around her elbow. She stilled. I tugged her back to me but refrained from enfolding her in my arms. "Charlotte, they won't hurt you. They are irresponsible but not criminals."

"Don't—" she snapped in a whisper. With her back to our audience, facing me, close but miles away, she quietly fumed and shuddered. She attempted sidestepping me, but when I didn't move, she began speaking through clenched teeth, in lethal, furious whispers. "You asked me not to defend your father to you. I ask you not to defend them to me."

I had little to counter that. I ran my hand over my face and through my hair, but for once, the gesture didn't help me calm down. In that precise moment, I was a breath away from spinning around and beating Brayden black and blue, like his own brother should have done long ago. Suddenly, a merciless headache threatened to make my head explode.

"You should all go," I snarled, and Charlotte gave a subtle start.

They were smart enough to not argue this time. Brayden brushed past us without sparing a glance, arrogance and defiance in his every move. Bryson, surprised and a tad annoyed, walked slowly, assessing Charlotte as if she were a rare, dangerous specimen before he joined his brother.

The last to go and the only one I felt regretful for having snarled at was Kai. With his shoulders drawn forward and a lost look in his eyes, he patted Kinga, who had hidden behind the couch, then strolled silently to the door. Just when I thought he would leave just as quietly, he stopped in front of Charlotte and watched us somberly.

"I'm glad for you if you're happy," he told me.

He sounded sincere and miserable at the same time. Charlotte looked up and apprehensively but intently perused him. The vehement tension that had coiled her whole body into a tight spring slowly dispersed. Apparently, she was quick to empathize with other's misery.

"So your awful disposition is still because of that woman."

Although Kai still concerned me, I allowed myself a breath of relief. At least, he wasn't involved in unhealthy affairs. Only his heart was at risk, a situation I knew painfully well.

"It is."

He nodded, and Charlotte's eyes narrowed in surprise, then her brows knit in confusion. She did empathize. Kai headed for the door, his arm grazing against Charlotte's. As if flames had swept over her skin, she jumped back, directly on my toe.

"Easy," I murmured against her hair and stroked her back reassuringly. Under my rhythmic touch, she slightly relaxed.

"Hey, I won't touch you," Kai said, raising his hands by his head. He was grave, embarrassed, and remorseful, but at the same time, mischief danced at the corner of his lips. "Some parts of my anatomy still regret deeply the first time I did."

"And only time," I punctuated with a low growl.

"Got that." Kai rolled his eyes, smiling. "Miss Burton, I am really sorry for our behavior. I don't expect you to understand or turn a blind eye."

When Charlotte's lips remained sealed, Kai sighed, nodded, and followed Brayden and Bryson outside. I made sure the door was locked then returned to Charlotte, who was standing rigidly at the edge of the living room, with her arms wrapped protectively around her torso.

"Welcome to my humble abode."

Wrapping my arms around her waist, I propped my chin on her left shoulder. She had come to me on her own initiative when I least expected it. Perhaps she had missed my company just as I had missed hers. The thought brought an unexpected warm feeling and a huge grin that I hid in the crook of her neck.

"You shouldn't have asked them to leave."

Her voice was soft and nervous, a whisper that cast its spell on me with each note. I spun her in a pirouette so our chests brushed together. She looked up at me as nervously as she had spoken.

"You should decide what you want, Charlotte."

"I don't think I am in the position to ask you to kick your friends out."

She licked her lips and looked away. Her emotions hit me like a big ball of tension. I was so deeply attuned to her that I could identify her facial changes when she was restless.

Her eyes crinkled just the slightest bit at the corners, and a crease appeared between her brows. Her mouth tightened and paled, and her gaze shifted from one spot to another. I itched to touch her, to kiss her. The unrest caused by her absence burned more avidly now that I fully realized what I had been missing.

Brayden had been right in a way. I was a complete idiot—because when I got attached, I poured my whole essence into that person until she became all I needed and all I craved. And while I let myself be consumed, I became possessive, overprotective, and suffocating. Or so I had been told.

I was too flawed to know how to love flawlessly.

"What was that about?" Charlotte asked. She nodded to the door, wearing an expression that was both puzzled and pensive. She clearly referred to Kai. "Does he expect me to press charges?"

"You should," I told her sternly, caressing her soft, flushed cheeks with both my hands. "If the incident affected you this badly, you should have."

She shook her head firmly and a little bit gloomily but commented no more on the subject. I just wanted to pick up from the instant I opened the door and she assaulted me with her enthusiasm. I wished I had been alone when she arrived.

"Smile for me, please."

Shyly, Charlotte looked up, thick, long lashes grazing against her cheeks. That blend of innocence and naughtiness of hers was my undoing. I bent and took her mouth in a slow, coaxing kiss that inevitably developed into an untamed crusade of tongues and lips and throaty moans. Then the strident sound of a bark interrupted the spell we had been under.

"Christ," Charlotte shrieked, and our teeth clinked together.

"Now you deign to appear, you poor excuse of a dog."

Kinga darted from behind the couch and inched tensely yet curiously toward us. Charlotte tensed too, and Kinga barked again, wagging her tail.

"Don't be scared. She's softer than a Chihuahua."

"Who is supposed to be on the list for most aggressive dogs."

I scoffed and suppressed a smile at Charlotte's cautious countenance. Despite being a scary-looking Cane Corso, Kinga was as docile as a puppy. Or so she behaved when she was treated with the same docility. I disentangled myself from Charlotte to her sudden trepidation and kneeled before Kinga.

"Kinga let's show Charlotte how aggressive you can be. Roll. Good girl."

The most beautiful sound echoed behind me. Charlotte giggled, and the brightest beam covered her lovely face. Oh no, she wasn't just lovely. She was breathtaking. And I wanted her to be mine. The realization stole my breath.

"So you do have a dog."

"I found her when she was little, after a race, in a box. She weighed less than a rabbit and had her paws frosted. By the time I nurtured her back to health, I couldn't just take her to a dog shelter."

"Quite the rescuer you are."

"Oh, Charlotte, I am far from that."

She shook her head with visible disbelief, but I was indeed far from being a rescuer. In the end, I was the one who abused his power. I stood abruptly, with a curt movement of my hand signaling for Kinga to sit, then I continued what she had interrupted. At that very moment, I felt like the worst hunter.

Charlotte gasped but met my assault without hesitation, without objection. I pillaged her mouth restlessly until neither of us could breathe. Our tongues stroked against each other in a feral, erotic dance. Her lips swelled under my inexorable plunder, but they kept molding firmly around mine.

There was a fierce passion within Charlotte that screamed to be unleashed. The more she received, the more she longed for, mirroring my hunger.

"I missed you too badly, Charlotte."

"You are not used to missing people," she stated. She was breathless and flushed, and she looked properly kissed. Good.

"No, I am not. And I think you are getting under my skin."

"Oh."

Taking advantage of her momentary surprise, I towed her to the couch and pulled her into my lap. Kinga's attention never strayed from us, but otherwise, she remained seated as I had instructed her.

Under my fascinated perusal, Charlotte fidgeted.

"What?" she asked, blushing.

"What mission were you talking about?" I asked instead of answering and began toying with a lock of her soft hair.

"Mm—"

She looked away, kneaded her hands, and blushed a deep crimson. Delectable.

"Don't get shy on me now." I grabbed her chin and lifted her face. I was too greedy to allow her any form of evasion.

"I think I should correct an assumption you have wrongly reached."

The mixture of shyness and determination as she looked at me with big doe eyes did strange things to me. It created chaos in the orderly emptiness inside me. I stroked her cheek, my fingers lingering on her lips. The more I touched, the less I wanted to stop.

"Yes…" I nodded encouragingly while she quietly chewed on her bottom lip. When her eyes met mine again, she blurted everything in one breath.

"I am attracted to you, Marcus. It was not the wine making me feel what I felt Saturday night. It was you."

Excitement, raw and potent, thrummed in my veins at her frank confession. I leaned into her, savoring the way her mouth parted, her breath caught in her throat, and her eyes turned dark. There was no wine affecting her reactions now.

"What did you feel?"

I hadn't misinterpreted our proximity then. I did affect her, just as she affected me. The notion released an exhilarating feeling inside me and my whole being pulsed with it. I stiffened all over when Charlotte turned in my lap then straddled me, locking her hands behind my neck. She was being daring. She was meeting me halfway.

"I think I was drunker on you than on the wine."

"So that's why you came once more into the wolf's lair. Willingly, now."

"I came willingly the last time too."

She mustered a delectably offended look, but in the end, she chuckled and so did I. She caressed the skin at the nape of my neck, occasionally twisting her fingers in my hair. I wondered if she realized how sensual that minimal contact could be or how much of a temptress she was.

"Why?" My voice was rougher now, tight and thick with desire. The primal part of Charlotte recognized my lust, and she gave out a strangled gasp.

With passionate resolve, Charlotte pressed into me, then her mouth was on mine. Her kiss was slow but firm, nervous but fiery. I met her halfway and let her be in charge, at her own pace. I enjoyed it even.

Her tongue explored the dark recesses of my mouth with voluptuous curiosity and innate talent. She tasted me, tormented me, ignited me as she slowly wiggled in my lap and found all the secrets my mouth could offer. *Or almost all of them*, I thought, smirking internally. Then her teeth closed around my bottom lip and her delicate nose nuzzled mine. For a change, it felt wonderful to be the one at the receiving end of a kiss.

"I wanted to kiss you. Consciously." She sounded breathless, but so was I.

"Oh, Charlotte, you are testing my power of restraint, darling."

"Maybe I don't want you to restrain yourself."

I groaned loudly, and Charlotte bit her lower lip to curb a sharp intake of breath. With eyes smoldering and cheeks blushing, she watched me expectantly. She didn't fully understand what she was requesting. Once I forsook restraint, I wasn't going to be willing to bow to it again.

There was an innocence about Charlotte, a certain lack of experience, that lit an even wilder fire inside me. Once I got a taste of her, I would never want to deny myself the pleasure of having her all over again.

"However, I'm still mad at you."

I changed topic entirely, only to calm the raging desire driving me slowly but surely mad. I was not sure yet if Charlotte was ready to meet the version of Marcus King with no holds barred.

"You're mad at me?"

I nodded and carefully slid her off my lap and next to me on the couch. With her so tightly pressed against my chest, straddling me, it was difficult to hide the evidence of my craving or its advanced development. Under her lazy stare, the air grew hotter and my determination weaker.

"Ms. Hansen and Mr. McAlister? They traumatized me."

When she regarded me with a serious, almost blank expression, I was afraid I had just crossed a line. After all, she had warned me that the cuckoo couple were close friends of hers. Then she erupted into copious laughter, taking me by complete surprise. She laughed so hard that she had to hug herself as tears trickled down her cheeks.

"Glad to amuse you," I bristled, but her laughter was heaven to my ears. "You did it on purpose, didn't you?"

"Well, it's only part of the duties specified by your internship." The laugh dwindled into amused chuckles until she pressed her lips into a taut line to prevent any sound from coming out. She was laughing at my expense, and instead of being offended, I wallowed in her amusement. "But yes, I did. Have they reached a conclusion?" And suddenly, amusement was replaced by concern.

"Did you expect them to?" I snorted, remembering the impossible meeting. I had never in my life met a pair of people more unstable or undecided. "They asked for a postponement. And next time, they want to meet with you. Coincidentally, I agree with them."

"Poor darling." Charlotte mocked me with another succession of melodious giggles.

She touched my cheek with a motherly gesture, enveloping me with her illicit fragrance of tuberoses. I buried my nose in her palm and nuzzled my cheek against her touch. When I lifted my head, Charlotte had stopped laughing. She was breathless and overpowered by deep, tantalizing yearning. My own longing responded fiercely to the luscious sight before me.

"When did you return?"

"In fact, I came from the airport," Charlotte admitted shyly, staring at the linked hands in her lap.

"Did you, now?" I was surprised, pleased, and newly enflamed.

"I told you I was on a mission. Besides, I missed you too."

"Oh, Charlotte…" I breathed heavily as the last remains of control vanished.

I leaned into her and she leaned back until she was sprawled on the couch and I hovered over her. With a visceral instinct that was deep-seated in her very nature, Charlotte inhaled loudly, absorbing my scent.

"It's complicated for me to tell where I meet your expectations and where I start taking advantage of you."

She rested her lukewarm fingers on my face, caressing and feeding a fire that she might have started the very first night we met. The low growl in my throat elicited a sweet moan from her swollen, red lips, and I was lost. I kissed her until she panted for breath, then something more.

"It's difficult for me to trust so easily and so quickly. But with you, I want to take a chance. I want you, Marcus."

Before her luminous, sincere eyes, I had to close my own. Her words thrilled me as much as they panicked me. They nearly hurt because it was clear now that our association was not a simple adventure. We were going to emerge victorious in each other's arms or leave the battlefield in pieces. There was no middle ground.

"I do," she reiterated, conviction etched on her face.

Her hands fisted in my shirt. Charlotte pulled me down to her and seized my mouth once more. Her resolve and her passion made me smile.

Between her fingers slipping beneath my shirt, exploring the skin from my nape to my lower back, and her delicious lips molding so perfectly with mine, it was difficult to concentrate on anything else.

I realized my phone was ringing in the pocket of my sweatpants only when Kinga barked in acknowledgment, causing Charlotte to shift underneath me. She was flushed and willing, and nothing could have prevented me from taking more of what she offered.

Then the phone rang again, a vicious blare ruining the sensual quietness we had been drowned in.

Liv.

A sudden chill chased the heat away.

"What is it?" The low, pained lamentations at the other end of the line froze me. "Where are you? I'm coming to get you."

Chapter 17

Charlotte

"Can I get you anything, Miss Burton?" Sofia asked before I even reached the reception area. Her green eyes looked tired behind the square glasses but just as kind.

"Coffee, please. Dark and strong. You're good to go afterward."

I massaged my temples as I strode to my office, willing away the ache that was an early indication of a future aggravated version of the same bothering pain. It was going to rain. I just knew it. A latent pain had been throbbing all day in my bones like a pest, but the physical pain was eclipsed by the heaviness in my chest.

The door of the interns' office was open, and Marcus was standing right in front of his desk, watching me. His hands were shoved into the pockets of his jeans and his eyes were serious and searing.

Faced with his intense perusal, my heart skipped a beat, but locking my jaw, I avoided his gaze. His perplexing behavior rendered me an irascible and unbalanced heap of nerves. So I just walked forward and took shelter inside my office.

I stopped only when I faced the gigantic glass wall that kept watch and ward over Central Park then took a deep breath in a failed attempt to settle myself. I didn't know what was happening to me when I was near Marcus. I wasn't typically so straightforward, but neither was I daring.

Marcus made me both straightforward and daring. He made me curious and willing and carefree. If he put his mind to it, he was capable of making me wild too. And I had the feeling he intended to do just that.

Then he was evasive and unfathomable and so frustrating. Saturday evening replayed in my mind, and the way it came to an end left a bitter taste in my system. The phone had rung and the warm, irresistible Marcus I hadn't been able to get enough of had turned into cold stone.

After hanging up, he had rubbed his face impatiently and had all but crushed the phone in his palm. Then he had donned a hoodie forgotten on the sofa, and mumbling an apology, he had stormed out of his apartment. He had just left me there alone.

Later that night he had called numerous times, but I had been too confused to answer.

Maybe what I needed was time, space. Or maybe I just needed him. The growing confusion and ache throbbing in my skull made me irritable.

I didn't like uncertainty. I didn't like chaos. And ironically, Marcus was both. The door clicked open, then the shuffling of feet disturbed the silence.

"You can leave the coffee on my desk. Thank you, Sofia."

"I am not Sofia."

I inhaled sharply but forgot how to exhale. Marcus's voice was quiet and slightly rough, a combination of a soft whisper and a menace.

I gasped.

Approaching footsteps alerted me of his advance, but I forbade myself to turn. If I met his eyes, I would fall under his spell again. What was it about him that made me want to forsake rationality and just give in?

"Charlotte..." he murmured, his breath caressing the back of my head. I suppressed a shiver.

"Here is your—" Sofia stopped abruptly when she realized I

had company.

"You can leave the coffee on my desk," I repeated, this time to the correct person.

"Is there anything else I can do for you, Miss Burton?"

"No, Sofia. Thank you."

When the door clicked shut, I knew I was alone with Marcus. Electricity sizzled off him and penetrated me like a raging fire. It had been cold, but it was unbearably hot now.

The heat stirred me, like I had been sleeping, and suddenly, I was awake. Marcus leaned into me, his chest flattened to my back and his cheek nuzzling against mine. A peace offering? An apology? A diversion?

"You shouldn't be in here," I finally told him and took a step to the side. Painfully aware of our closeness, I kept my gaze trained forward. Central Park looked dull and sullen. "I thought I had made myself clear."

"I need to talk to you, Charlotte. It's been half a week, and you won't answer my calls."

My brows dipped into a scowl, then I realized he was right. Lately, I had been growing irritable when I was away from Marcus for too long. I couldn't let him control my mood. I couldn't—but I was afraid it was already too late.

"Not here," I replied sternly and made to leave, but his hand promptly covered my elbow and stopped me in place, much too close to him. Despite my protest, I had known he wouldn't relent.

"God, Charlotte, look at me, please."

The concern merged with a deep, barely restrained frustration drew my attention. Marcus looked as exhausted as I felt. Wrinkles surrounded his eyes, his lips were pursed in a taut line, and tension matured his features beyond his years. *He hasn't been sleeping well*, I mused absently. And neither had I.

"You just left me there—" I awkwardly addressed the elephant in the room. A sob threatened to burst from my chest, not as a result of his action, but of how that action had made me feel. Lonely. Terribly lonely.

"I don't know how to apologize because I know that you shouldn't forgive me. I don't have an excuse for how I acted. I never do when I mess up, and I mess up frequently. But I never wanted to hurt your feelings, Charlotte. I never wanted you to doubt how I feel—"

"Why did you leave then?"

The fervor in his voice and his self-condemnation staggered and softened me in equal measure.

"It was a friend who needed my help. I had to go."

The words came out both as a wounded supplication and a sentence he stuck to fiercely. The mixture was dizzying, just like him. Marcus was a combination of combinations.

The only friends I knew were the same three men who had assaulted me and who still haunted my dreams. I wondered which friend he referred to and shuddered at the thought of what such friends would request of him.

His bad mood, however, created a resonating pang in my chest. The cocky, confident man became a lost boy, with fears, confusions, and problems that were beyond his ability to solve.

Marcus seemed fragile. My hands were cupping his face before I realized what I was doing. His eyes clouded with astonishment, but he received my wordless comfort with something akin to relief.

"Talk to me," I pleaded. There was something hidden behind that angst and powerlessness. Something was eating at him from the inside out.

"There are some things I am not ready to talk about yet."

Blue eyes begged me to understand, to not pursue the matter. The empathetic part of me decided not to push him or dig for answers. I experienced no eagerness to deepen his misery. The emotional part of me, however, still felt rejected and much too disconcerted. I was a mixture of emotions, and they were all jumbled inside me.

"Then if that is all, I have work to attend to." I sat at my desk, but I couldn't concentrate on work, and he knew it.

"No, it is not all." Marcus sighed. He gave me an exasperated look then rounded the desk and took a seat without waiting for an invitation.

"I'm listening." I started typing on my computer, grateful that Marcus couldn't see the screen and the incoherent words I was writing.

"I want you to meet with my friends."

"What?"

I had managed to reach a decent level of calmness, and all of a sudden, I had to strain not to shout. It was painfully obvious which friends he referred to, and the mere notion made my skin crawl. It must certainly have been a joke.

"I know you don't like them although you seemed quite appeased by Kai. Sometimes I don't like them either, but I want you to spend some more time with them."

"What?" I repeated, sounding stupid to my own ears. Whereas my displeasure escalated, he remained calm and assuaging.

"I want you to overcome your irrational fear, Charlotte."

"It isn't that irrational if you think about it," I retorted stiffly, my spine straightening.

"Hey," he sighed conciliatorily and pressed his hand to the desk, reaching out to me. His hand waited for mine, but I couldn't bring myself to touch him. It was easier to cling to anger than give in to anxiety. "I am neither underestimating your apprehension nor judging it. But I don't want you to be afraid. And I don't want you to have those nightmares anymore. The only way you'll see that they are not a danger to you is to get to know them. They are just a stupid pack with too much free time on their hands."

Astonishment efficiently shut my mouth. I had never looked at things from his perspective because I had never imagined I would have to see those men again. I couldn't deny he was right, but then vivid glimpses of my nightmares flashed before my eyes, and I knew I couldn't meet with *his friends* that easily.

With an unreadable expression, Marcus stood and headed for the door. There was a spark in his eyes, though, that assured me the conversation was not over and his intentions would not falter so easily.

"Charlotte, I'd rather you didn't drink coffee at these hours."

As soon as he walked out the door, I took a sip of the hot liquid out of mere defiance. Abruptly, the coffee didn't taste as appealing.

It was with surprise moments later that I lifted my eyes from the case files I was reading to see Marcus ambling in. He set a glass of orange juice in front of me and dropped a small pill beside it. *Advil.* I watched him, perplexed. How did he know I had a headache?

"Drink." It was not a request. "I will be waiting for you in my car."

Then he was gone. His commanding attitude outraged me, yet his promise filled me with traitorous delight.

Half an hour later, giving in to curiosity, I rode the elevator to the parking lot and walked to my car just to show him that I was also capable of defiance. But in front of my car, blocking it, was parked a menacing Jaguar.

I stopped right in front of his car, glaring at him through the windshield. Marcus was sitting behind the wheel with arms folded behind his neck. He winked, somehow sensing that my glare was purely for bravado, and nodded for me to climb in. I did so petulantly and slammed the door shut as a final touch to my little show of bad temper.

Without warning, the need to make peace with him blasted like fireworks in my blood. I wanted him to hold me to his chest where I could inhale his fragrance. I wanted him to do so much more than that. I knew I was blushing before he looked my way.

"If we are going to have an argument, we are going to have it by talking. I will not let you shut me out."

His brusqueness momentarily took me aback, and I almost recoiled in my seat, but the magnetism between us was too strong. I was inexorably drawn to him.

"What else will you not allow me, Marcus?" I mimicked him and involuntarily leaned closer.

"Do not provoke me, sugar."

His eyes twinkled with pure sin and lascivious challenge, causing the blood in my cheeks to burn feverishly.

He turned on the ignition, and in less than a minute, the car was flying down the road. The notion of him racing frightened me, yet here I was by his side comfortable with his speed.

He looked completely in control, a master taming a wild cat. It shocked me when abruptly, that mischievous air about him dissolved entirely and he blanched.

"What is it?"

"Is that why you didn't like me calling you *sugar*? Because of Brayden?"

"I don't think that's the reason." I just had to reassure him. Somehow, sometime, I also had to make him stop taking other's blame. "It only seemed you were taunting me."

"I was not. Not entirely." He offered a small smile, but the downcast appearance immediately returned. "Did you have any more nightmares?"

"One," I said in a small voice, gauging his reaction. His hands tightened around the steering wheel, the car suddenly moved faster, and he scowled in silence at the road ahead.

"Tell me."

"No. Marcus—I want you to understand that you have nothing to feel responsible for."

My attempts at reassuring him failed miserably. I doubted he had even heard me. Stubbornness was yet another trait on the endless list of Marcus's complex personality, but so was determination, and he was going to be relentless until he chased all my nightmares away.

I sighed and massaged the bridge of my nose, pondering his theory. Maybe not knowing his friends was the reason my mind overreacted. So I decided that I owed it to both of us to at least try to see those men through his eyes.

"I can't even put names to faces. Tell me about them. I promise to listen."

Marcus glanced at me doubtfully then acquiesced to my request and met me halfway, where I was waiting for him.

"When you came to my apartment, the second one who left was Bryson."

It was the blonde one who looked older, yet more affable than the other, although I still had my doubts if such a term was appropriate for a man like him. It was the blonde who had seemed to encourage the other one on that Friday night rather than take matters into his own hands.

"We met in college at a party. We bonded over subsequent debaucheries and improprieties. The first time I knew I could count on him for more than having fun and getting drunk was when he stood up to my father for me. Nobody had done that before.

"After that, his scholarship was withdrawn for mysterious reasons. He never cared. He never allowed my father to intimidate him."

"You feel like you owe him."

"I do, Charlotte. Not because he stood up to Isaac. I owe him for the countless times he put me back on my feet when I was at my lowest. I have a tendency to hit rock bottom."

Marcus smiled bitterly as if remembering something unpleasant. When he didn't find in my gaze the accusation he might have expected, his eyes narrowed, and he rubbed his chin with the back of his hand.

I didn't see him as a man who hit rock bottom frequently. I saw him as the man strong enough to pursue what he wanted.

"You met the side of him I disapprove of. You met the Bryson who encourages his brother when he should beat some sense into his thick skull. I have a mind to do that myself, though."

"Brayden is his brother?"

A sudden chill seized me by the throat and invaded my whole body. He was the protagonist of my nightmares.

"Yes."

The serenity of his eyes turned dark. Displeasure rolled off him in tangible waves. He appeared deep in thought before he pursed his lips and returned his attention to the road. What was going through his mind?

"I will not try to defend him," he started. "I do not tolerate his behavior any more than you had, but he has not always been like this. When Bryson and I were in college, Brayden used to be an incurable romantic."

"That's a little difficult to…imagine."

I knew I had just scoffed and rolled my eyes, but suddenly, I doubted we were thinking of the same nasty man.

"I don't like to disclose other's secrets or invade their privacy, but after what he did to you, after the way he scared you, I don't think he is in the position to make any complaints."

The surroundings that blurred past us slowly became familiar. Marcus was driving us to his secret house by the pond. The thought made me smile as anticipation built deep inside me. That house didn't feel just miles away from our real lives but in a whole different world—Marcus's private world.

"Brayden doesn't have a kidney. In brief, he donated his perfectly good kidney to the woman he was going to marry. I can't even come close to comprehending the amount of love and selfishness a man must possess to literally give up a part of himself. Brayden possessed all that love. I don't think I saw him happier than the day the doctor told him he was compatible for the donation, not even the day he got engaged.

"Then, seven months after the successful surgery, Brayden and Bryson went home for Thanksgiving. Brayden came back to New York early because he simply missed her. He—he found her in bed—their bed—with another man, screaming a foreign name in pleasure. The sweet Brayden we knew died that day, and a cruel misogynist took his place. That is why he behaves the way he does. His behavior, however, ceased to be excusable long ago."

My fingers involuntarily wrapped around my throat and absently massaged the flesh that was warm in spite of the coldness within. Beyond all expectations, I empathized, but I empathized with the ache and disillusionment of the man who had seen his life collapsing after a cruel betrayal not with the man he had become.

"Marcus, it never has."

"I know. And I am partly to blame for how Brayden still behaves."

His unrequited love with blame was becoming genuinely frustrating, but I decided against speaking my mind for the time being. Marcus watched me somberly, assessing more than my reaction. He weighed my frame of mind.

Seriousness was laced with the covert sensuality Marcus radiated, the very same that fanned the flames of my desire. I looked away, closing my eyes and discreetly biting my lip. What was he doing to me?

"I think you can identify Kai already," he continued in a steady voice.

I nodded, and the image of the tall brown-haired man returned to my mind. I was still somewhat stunned by how hopeless he had looked Saturday night before he left Marcus's apartment. It was difficult to reconcile the idea of him suffering for a woman and the amusement he drew out of scaring women in dark, empty allies.

"He is my cousin. He is three years younger than me. After—after my mom—"

Words abruptly failed him. Grabbing the wheel forcefully and shutting his eyes tightly, he poured his anger into the car he was driving way above the speed limit. By the time he refocused on me, he was struggling to slow down.

I believed I could understand, even for a little bit, why he raced. He sought the blankness that swallowed all the thoughts that tormented him. He sought the exhilaration and relief of not thinking.

"I used to live a lot with my mother's sister. Kai was very little at the time and awfully dependent. I think the more he annoyed me with his childish clinginess, the more I felt the need to protect him. I had never wanted a brother because I already had Kai. He is good, Charlotte. He is the best of us. I think you sensed that already."

"Does he race too?"

Marcus grinned. He had expected my question. "He does. He is much better than I am."

"God, is it a family trait?"

Marcus responded to my frustrated groan with a lighthearted laugh and placed his hand on my knee in quiet reassurance.

"He is an interior designer. He followed in our grandfather's footsteps. Of course, in his spare time, he is also a painter, troublemaker, and wounded puppy."

"So many talents."

He laughed again but didn't add anything else, which gave me time to ponder his request.

"I know you are right. I know that meeting with them might help me, but—give me a little time. Let me assimilate what you have told me."

"I am not pressuring you, Charlotte."

He was not pressuring me, but he was persuading me, which was so much worse because I blindly let him. Sighing, I shook my head to dispel the gloomy thoughts. Then I changed topic just like he was so fond of doing himself.

"What are *you* in your spare time?"

"Exquisite lover."

Heat invaded me, so powerful and merciless that it conquered me before I even thought of resisting it. Marcus licked his lips slowly, allowing me to see the tip of his tongue as it stroked and dampened every millimeter of his luring mouth.

"And exceedingly modest," I retorted.

Chapter 18

Charlotte

uring my first visit to Marcus's forest house, I had been too overwhelmed to pay much attention to the house itself. It was an impressive two-story house, reasonably small, yet it looked like an enormous beacon in the growing dark. Modern architecture merged with a pleasant rustic style. The simple exterior was almost somber, save for the high wall of glass that separated the inner living area from the outer porch.

It was, however, the upper floor attracting my attention as I looked at the house. A large balcony, the size of a whole room, with an ornate metal banister, extended in front of the glass wall that was bathed in amber light. I couldn't help but wonder if that was Marcus's bedroom, and the sudden curiosity brought a fierce blush to my cheeks.

"Walk with me."

Marcus brushed his lips against my temple and tightened his hold on my hand. Nodding, I followed his lead around the house and to the pond.

The air smelled of rain and Marcus. In his one-armed embrace, with his lips brushing every so often against my forehead and my cheek, the smoldering ache in my bones almost disappeared.

As the silence stretched, only the soft whistle of the wind and the rustle of leaves could be heard. In front of the small expanse of water with its belt of camellias, there was the wooden sculpture of a lion that served as a bench. Marcus sat and pulled me onto his lap, his arms closing naturally around my waist.

"Are you still mad at me?"

"I wasn't mad." He arched an eyebrow and tilted his head to the side. "I was disconcerted. You disconcert me."

"That can't be altogether bad." He smiled against my face and ran his hand through my hair making me shiver. I couldn't have remained mad at him even if I had tried.

"Easy for you to say," I sulked, but responded to his chaste kiss as soon as his lips touched mine.

"You disconcert me too, Charlotte. You have no idea."

"Tell me, then."

"Hm…" He laughed and shook his head. "I don't make a habit out of empowering women against me."

"How would you empower me against you?"

"Women control men without knowing how much they affect us. I don't want to imagine the amount of power a woman can wield once she is in possession of that knowledge."

"That can't be altogether bad," I replied, using his own words. We both laughed, but it was Marcus who stopped first.

The transition from laughing to tantalizingly serious was abrupt and staggering. With narrowed eyes, he pinned me in place, his gaze searing through me. My lips parted spontaneously, and Marcus responded with a throaty groan. When he leaned in, the first drops of rain finally sprinkled our foreheads.

I looked up, grateful for the cold drops cooling my flesh as they fell more and more frequently. Marcus took my mouth, capturing the raindrops that had gathered between my closed lips with one swift lick of his tongue. He ignited and appeased in equal measure a deep hunger in the pit of my stomach.

"You are so sweet, so tempting, Charlotte, and I can't stop myself from pulling you to the dark side. I don't want to taint you, but I always end up tainting what I love the most."

The loud cracking noise as my hand hit his cheek and brusquely pulled his head to the side stunned both of us. An unexpected anger and revolt boiled inside me, but it was anger merged with a fierce desire to shield him—shield him from himself.

"Don't. Talk. Like. That."

Each word distinct, spoken between clenched teeth. While he remained thunderstruck and I glared furiously at him, it had started raining in earnest.

"What was that for?" he hissed, but he was more surprised than mad.

"I do have my own volition. I don't need you to denigrate yourself to change my mind. I will not allow you to."

"Don't say I haven't warned you, dear Charlotte."

He stood with me in his arms, my legs tautly circling his waist and my hands twisted in his damp hair. He walked back to the house, not letting go of me, while a thick, incessant veil of water soaked us.

We didn't kiss, but the electrifying intensity of our locked stares made up for anything else. The water bathing our bodies was cold, but heat raged in our blood.

When he pushed the glass door open and strode inside with me in his arms, he was smiling. Disconcerting, to say the least. I frowned, and his grin widened, a boyish light reducing the tension in his features.

"What's so funny?" I snapped.

Marcus closed the door with his foot, but instead of putting me down, he gripped me tighter. It was dark, quiet, and intimate. I was aware that water dripped from our soaked clothes and that I was attached to him like a spider to a wall, but I couldn't bring myself to move either. With one hand still twisted in his wet hair and the other one resting against his heart, I found myself succumbing to the unique spell only Marcus could cast.

"Nobody has ever slapped me before for talking badly about myself."

"Get used to it then."

"Where you are concerned, there are a lot of things I need to get used to." He clasped the hand I was holding over his heart, and his eyes bore into mine with raw, quickening emotion. "For instance, this feeling that you brought to life right here."

With our joined hands, he massaged his chest. His breath was heavy and uneven, and drops of water were rolling down his face. Strong, furious thuds reverberated against my cold hands. In the perfect silence of the house, I could hear his every sound, and he could hear every pulsation of my blood.

Marcus bent to place me back on solid ground, but I tightened my legs around his hips and watched him boldly. He tried once more to disentangle me from his body and chuckled when he was acquainted with my stubborn resistance. I loved his laughter and the calm expression that settled on his face.

"You are really strong for such a little woman."

"I am not little," I hissed, offended, and punched him in his right shoulder.

"Of course not," he kept taunting me even as I jumped off him and shot him a glare.

Immediately, he pulled me back, closer to him. With him so tall, hovering over me and inspecting me, I did feel small, but I felt small in a bewilderingly pleasant and feminine way.

My breath hitched, and my heart started pounding faster with anticipation. It nearly hurt to be so close to him. I was afraid I couldn't stop the feelings that grew and conquered barriers that had been frozen in place for such a long time.

Towing me slightly to the side, Marcus reached somewhere behind me. "I think it's safer for you if the room is properly lit. Just in case."

"I can handle myself very well in the dark, thank you very much."

"Yeah, I've seen that." He raised an eyebrow mockingly, clearly reminding me about the incident at the office.

The soft click of the switch echoed before a blinding light spread around us, hurting my eyes. I blinked rapidly, trying to accustom my sight to the new illumination, but Marcus was quick to notice my discomfort. Flicking off the blinding lights, he switched on the amber spotlights.

"Better?" he demanded softly.

"Yes, thank you."

The atmosphere had suddenly become more intimate, more engaging. Magnetism revolved around us, drawing restricted desires to the surface and pulling us closer. Worrying my lip between my teeth, I wondered if he could feel the same heated electricity I felt when I was this close to him.

"Let's get you some fresh clothes."

His voice was tight and hardly controlled, but his eyes were blue wildfire. There was no shred of control in their depths, and I was categorically pleased.

"Marcus, what are you doing?" I screamed all of a sudden.

He scooped me up and threw me over his shoulder, laughing as I tried to kick, but he quickly immobilized my legs with his strapping arms.

Suddenly, he stopped, and so did my grunts and squirming. I expected him to drop me any minute now, but he only held me tighter.

"Marcus…" he mocked and started ascending wooden stairs, covered by a maroon carpet.

"It's your name, isn't it? Should I call you Mr. King? Put me down already."

"So bossy." Marcus laughed and, evidently, did not obey. "And no, I love how my name sounds on your lips."

Upstairs there were no doors and no hallways but an ample, almost unending space that was Marcus's bedroom. He put me down in the middle of the room, wearing a playful and elated expression. As soon as I shot him a glare, I understood that his intention had been to goad me.

I looked around, upon a room decorated in nuances of cream and mahogany. The entire floor was dominated by a King-sized bed with a garnet wooden headboard and a matching duvet. Huge pillows and cylindrical cushions were covered in cream silk and were perfectly arranged on top of the comforter.

In front of the bed, there was a low bench with dark velvet upholstery that contrasted with the light cream carpet covering the floor. The opposite wall was made of glass and it looked over the balcony. An ensemble, consisting of a small couch, two loveseats, and a carved tea table, was well-ordered in what represented a small sitting area.

Except for a few tall lamps strategically placed around the room and the impressive chandelier hanging from the ceiling, there were no other decorations. It was a clean, vast space that shrunk and became smaller with Marcus standing proud and tall within its confines.

"You're going to soak my carpets, and I bought them at an auction."

My eyes fluttered back to Marcus, and he owned my attention instantly. He greeted me with a quiet, wistful smile and a bone-penetrating gaze. I realized then that, although we were indeed soaking the carpets, he was only teasing. Bought at an auction or not, the space was too marvelous to be ruined.

"Fresh clothes are in there." Marcus pointed to our right, then he nodded behind me, somewhere past the gigantic bed. "And there, you can find the bathroom if you need anything."

It was the first time I realized that the floor was in fact divided. Where Marcus had pointed, there were walls made of smoked glass that cleared as soon as he pressed a button in the small square control panel, fixed in the wall by the stairs.

To the right, there was a simple but large dressing room, while behind us, the smoked glass separated the bedroom from a breathtaking bathroom that looked cut out of a home & design magazine.

"Choose whatever you like."

The problem was that I didn't want to choose anything but him. I grabbed the lapels of his drenched jacket and didn't let go. His eyes widened, then his pupils dilated, and blood rushed to his lips as they swelled in anticipation. His reaction was mirrored masterfully in every cell of my body.

"Maybe I don't want clothes to change into."

My throat felt dry, my heart trembled in my chest, and a shiver ran up and down my spine. Yet, the apprehension was not strong enough to stifle the desire.

"You are one infuriating woman," Marcus growled softly, his lips pressed to my temple and his hands fisted by his sides. "I told you, I don't know where I meet your expectations and where I start taking advantage of you."

"And I told you that I want you too." I took his hand and rubbed our linked hands against my chest, reflecting his earlier gesture. "The feeling that you stirred here is all-consuming. It burns, Marcus. It burns everywhere."

I had pulled the trigger, and nothing could stop the explosion now. I was in Marcus's arms, and his mouth was on me before I drew another breath. He was wild, relentless, and hotter than fire. His touch was equally gentle and rough—a man's deft, knowing touch. His actions came now in a restless rush of kisses, bites, and ardent caresses.

Then, to my complete panic, he stopped and took three steps back. Without him enveloping me in his heat, I froze.

"No." He was panting and hardly restraining himself, yet there he was away from me. "Not like this. I want to savor you, Charlotte. Every inch of skin, every little atom of your pleasure."

"Oh." Desire pulsed madly through my veins, and it left me breathless.

"I want to undress you, peel every garment off your body, and I want you to keep still. Can you do that for me?"

"No."

In spite of the predaceous concentration that had suddenly taken over his features, Marcus managed a small smile that hinted at his boyish side. He shook his head disapprovingly but did not come closer.

"You have lured me, built a fire inside me that wants to erupt," I said. "You cannot ask me to keep still."

My voice was strained, and so was my body. It had been so long since the last time I allowed myself to let my guard down. I hadn't felt an emptiness, a deficiency in my life, until Marcus started tempting me, driving me insane with emotions that terrified me.

When Carter and I split, my father supported me by keeping me engrossed in numerous projects that didn't give me the time to entertain carnal appetites. Once Carter was gone from my life, I felt disappointment and an emotional void instead of frustration at not having my needs met. I had all but forgotten about my deepest, primal wants until Marcus made sure to awaken them one by one.

"I want to appease that fire, Charlotte, but first, I want to ignite it to a firestorm. Do you trust me?"

"To kill me slowly? Yes, I do."

He smiled again, but this time he finally moved, taking one cruelly small step nearer. Dominating me with his eyes, he slowly removed his dark jacket and let it fall to the floor. Beneath the thin material of his shirt, his chest rose and fell in invitation.

"I will bring you back to life. I promise," he whispered, each syllable a tease to my senses. His lips skimmed across mine, but he didn't kiss me just yet.

"I trust you, Marcus."

"Good."

Blood pulsed feverishly through my veins. Straightened to his full height, Marcus inspected me through heavy-lidded eyes before his fingers started working deftly on the buttons of my blouse. He hooked his fingers under the collar and pushed the material back maddeningly slow, revealing one shoulder at a time.

My skin was wet from the rain, but my flesh grew hotter with each passing moment. Following the blouse down my back, his fingertips glided across my skin with tantalizing softness. He touched, discovered, and set on fire every inch of my body. I reached for him, but his hand locked around my wrist as soon as I moved.

"Keep still," he warned, his voice a rough commanding whisper of lust.

Marcus ignored my strangled groan and circled me, stopping right behind me. I wasn't exactly a novice at making love although I was certainly out of practice. Holding my breath, I expected him to release the clasp of my bra and bare me. Instead, he approached me leisurely, aligning his whole length against my back, making me aware of every inch of him before he purposefully touched me again.

His breath blew warmly against my cheek, and his tongue lapped at my earlobe. When he caught the sensitive flesh between his lips, I jolted and he chuckled softly. His hands settled on my hips, caressing my curves with his knuckles, then his talented fingers moved to the front of my suit pants and released the button.

Somewhere in a foreign place, where my mind could still function, I knew what he was doing. Teasing and suspending that inevitable moment of complete intimacy, Marcus was building my desire to a fever pitch.

"You won't be needing this."

He knelt and pushed the pants down my legs, making sure that his hands were always in contact with my skin. Then his moist lips followed the trail his hands were leaving.

I couldn't keep still.

He helped me step out of the drenched pants, then in a flash, he was back on his feet hovering over me from behind. Anticipation was both arousing and cruel.

His hand fisted in my hair and pulled my head back until it was inclined against his broad chest. Slowly, permitting me to observe every twist of his features and every thread of hair as it fell over his forehead, Marcus bent down and pressed his lips to the slope of my throat, trailing open-mouthed kisses all the way to my collarbone.

"Marcus, you're driving me insane," I complained but melted into his hard chest.

"So are you." He chuckled and met my supplicating eyes with a stare ravaged by desire. "It's curious that you are the one so rushed. I, on the other hand, enjoy the slowness."

I don't, I wanted to say, but that would have been a lie. The waiting was torturous, but it was equally scrumptious.

His mouth and hands moved on my body like a perfectly orchestrated dance. The clasp of my bra finally clicked open, and my breath hitched, both in anticipation and uneasiness. It was never comfortable to bare yourself, to make yourself vulnerable, but Marcus gave me the strength and confidence to try.

While his fingers peeled the straps off my shoulders, and the bra fell to my feet, he peppered kisses from my nape to the sensitive spot between my shoulder blades. My hypersensitive skin was wildly aware of his every touch, and so, I trembled.

His left hand caught my right, and for the briefest instant, he forgot all about slowness and whirled me in a pirouette. He steadied me with a hand splayed on my hip when I faced him. While I still tried to catch my breath, Marcus absorbed the sight of my bare chest, rising and falling frantically under his brazen inspection.

"You are a vision," he murmured breathlessly.

Despite the raging hunger that plagued me, insecurities threatened to take over. Before quite thinking through my gesture, I lifted my hands to cover my unprotected breasts. Marcus's fingers instantly wrapped around my wrists, and he pulled my hands back to my sides.

"Don't hide from me." His stare was scorching and invasive like he could see far beyond my naked flesh. "There's not a single part of you that you should be embarrassed to show me. You're so heartbreakingly beautiful, Charlotte."

My self-doubting mind disagreed, but the passion in his voice and the ravenousness in his stare were so authentic and so compelling that I could neither resist nor doubt him.

Marcus made me feel desirable. He made me uninhibited enough to gradually become comfortable with my nakedness.

"And you are distressingly clothed," I complained.

My gaze ran up and down his tall, muscular, and excitingly virile body, caressing him in all the places where my hands couldn't. Grinning widely, provocatively, he gathered me in his arms but placed me on the bed before I even managed to touch him properly. He rose, standing next to the bed, a dark, merciless torturer. My sweet torturer.

"We should rectify that then."

A lazy smile spread on his whole face, lighting his eyes. The same skilled fingers that had been tantalizing my flesh gripped each button of his shirt and unfastened them, then he let the sodden cloth fall to the carpet.

A battle of wills quietly unfurled in his eyes. He was torn between making each moment last and just ripping the clothes off and indulging in a frenzied congress. His actions, lacking more and more the deliberateness he had been clinging to, betrayed his waning control.

By the time he unzipped his jeans and quickly removed them, I was panting. Marcus was not only beautiful, but utterly fascinating.

Smooth, sun-kissed skin encased hard muscles. My eyes traveled over his broad chest, down his sculptured abdomen, and followed the happy trail that ended beneath the black material of his boxer briefs. Then I let myself gaze lower, over his well-built thighs and hair-sprinkled sinewy calves. His appeal was a combination of vintage elegance and mouthwatering roughness.

"If you keep staring at me like that, I will lose the last remnants of control I possess, Charlotte," Marcus growled and descended upon me with fiery determination.

"I want you to." My hands locked around his neck as he settled between my thighs, and his chest pressed against my swelling breasts. I couldn't keep still anymore.

"I want to be gentle. This once, I want to go slowly. Not miss a bit."

"I don't know how to do this slowly, Marcus. Once I'm in, I'm in."

It was a warning, and in his intent look I found empathy. I did not refer to the pace of our lovemaking but to the pace of my heart. I wasn't the type of woman to go to bed with a man only for pleasure's sake. My pleasure derived from deep-rooted feelings that once kindled did not go away easily.

Where matters of the heart were concerned, logic failed me entirely. It didn't matter how smart I was. In the end, my heart always had a way of fooling me. And this heart of mine already had a fondness for Marcus.

"Good. Because where you are concerned, Charlotte, I can't go slow either. For you, I am willing to slow down, but I'm damn happy I don't have to."

He did not refer to the pace of our lovemaking either. He was happy I had found the strength and trust to meet him halfway, and so was I.

His hands stroked down my sides and fisted in my panties, then they were off and so were his boxers. The closeness of bare skin meeting in a suffocating embrace made me throw my head back, gasp, and writhe under him. I had never been this lustful, this unrestrained, but Marcus was unleashing a side of me that seemed to have been waiting to be brought to light for far too long.

"Let go, Charlotte," he whispered against the skin of my throat.

"Leave restraint aside. It's just you and me in this bed."

"And the firestorm," I breathed.

"And the firestorm," he agreed, finally taking my mouth.

His tongue stroked past my lips and intoxicated me with his taste. Under his weight, I felt soft, warm, and aching in all the right places. He pressed into me enough to render me aware of his arousal lying against my hip but not too much to smother me.

I trembled in mixed expectancy and pleasure. I wanted him with a fierceness that wrecked my body. He had reduced me to a mass of simmering emotions.

I was the firestorm.

With our lips engaged in a sweet, torturous battle, his hands expertly grasping my hips, and my arms wrapped around his shoulders, Marcus thrust inside me agonizingly slow, allowing me to feel every exquisite inch of him as I struggled to accommodate his invasion.

Then he started moving, a lazy, carnal rhythm that slipped gradually into a frenzied bodily dance. I clung to his shoulders tightly as if I would fall if I let go. Under my tentative fingers, his back felt wiry, straining, and damp with perspiration. He was an excellent male specimen of unhindered passion.

"Oh, Charlotte, you undo me."

I kissed his jaw and licked the enticing shape of his lips before he granted me access inside for another breathtaking kiss. I gasped and thrashed against the cool duvet. Very deep in my stomach, a spiraling tension constricted my insides and gave way to a growing, aching pleasure.

Marcus buried his head in my throat. He inhaled my scent and groaned, a raw rumble that came from the depths of his chest, adding fuel to the fire consuming me. His hands caressed my hair, slithered along my sides, and cupped my bottom with a dominating flexion of his fingers, which brought him deeper inside me. The anticipation stole my breath away.

"Marcus—" I murmured weakly. So many things raced through my mind, but I was unable to voice a single coherent thought. Within me, the tension reached an unbearable peak. It was sensory overload.

Hardly managing to keep my eyes open, I was faced with the striking sight of his carved chest. I craned my neck and pressed an open-mouthed kiss to his right pectoral, smiling when the muscle jerked under my touch.

Only the sound of our flesh meeting and Marcus's sharp intake of breath could be heard. And our hearts—our raging, pounding hearts.

Linked together, we soared higher and higher, and it was then that I truly valued Marcus's desire to savor every moment, to make each instant last. This first time of complete and unrestricted intimacy, this first time of discovering each other in the barest and most vulnerable of manners, was never going to happen again. We only had a *first* and Marcus had made sure to make the best of it.

He sucked and licked the spot behind my ear where my pulse beat fast and strong, and suddenly, there was too much emotion stretched tight in my body. I couldn't contain it any longer.

I arched off the bed, my fingernails digging into his shoulders as I caught him in an unyielding grip. Marcus clasped my hip hard, power and passion oozing from his touch, and with his other arm, he supported my convulsing back.

For an indefinite moment, the firestorm encapsulated our whole world, then I came undone. A heartbeat later, Marcus joined me, his head falling on my chest.

Outside, it poured down with a vengeance, but here in the little cocoon we had created, only our ragged breathing and rampant heartbeats reverberated like a symphony of desire. Minutes passed by, but neither one of us let go of the other. Underneath Marcus's weight, it was blistering hot, headily dangerous, and yet, soothingly safe. Against his skin, I smiled.

"You are incandescent, Charlotte."

He watched me, mystified, as if he could hardly comprehend what had just happened, then he wrenched the duvet from underneath and rolled us so he was lying on his back, and I rested on his chest.

"You make me incandescent. You make me another woman."

Absentmindedly, I stroked his chest, the length of his throat, his stubble-covered cheek, and once in a while, my fingertips rested on his lips as he pressed soft kisses to my knuckles.

I wasn't the only one glowing in the room. He was too—brightly like fire. Marcus was fire. He could warm you, but he could always scorch you beyond repair.

"No, sugar. You are the same woman you have always been. I only try to bring forth the Charlotte you have locked inside yourself."

"You want to bare me beyond clothes." It wasn't a question, but a certainty.

"I do," he hummed and kissed the top of my head. I was terrified as well as intensely excited to let him discover me. Entirely.

In his arms, my eyes closed lazily, and my limbs suddenly felt so heavy that they almost melted into the mattress. I protested with a grunt and unsuccessfully tried to catch Marcus's arm when he slid from beneath me and climbed out of bed. He returned, wearing a gray pair of pajama pants and holding a white shirt and a hairdryer.

"I wasn't aware you owned anything that wasn't black," I giggled, feeling peculiarly giddy.

Marcus pushed me to a sitting position with unexpected care and gentleness. He smirked, but instead of arrogance, his face was filled with something akin to fascination. I lifted my head to kiss him, but after a chaste brush of our lips, he stilled me and helped me slip into his oversized shirt.

He sat on the edge of the bed, with his back to me. I kissed his shoulder enjoying his ensuing soft chuckle before he bent to plug in the dryer. By the time he straightened and turned to face me, I was already sprawled on the bed, legs pressed together to alleviate the lingering, pleasurable ache between my thighs, arms stretched askew, and a stupid grin on my face.

"You look beautiful. Especially since you are in my bed." I was too tired to open my eyes, but I could imagine the brooding quality of his smile.

"Hm…"

He switched on the dryer, and his fingers started massaging my scalp and playing with my damp hair. The tender stroking and warm air blowing over my skin combined with the raptness Marcus had breathed in my blood were a narcotic I couldn't resist. Before he finished drying my hair, I drifted off.

Through the noise of the dryer and the muddle of my dozing thoughts, I thought I heard a phone ringing.

Chapter 19

Marcus

I rejected the call and ran a hand over my face. Then the phone rang again. Liv was inexorable, and though her tenacity used to please me, tonight it was stifling. Frustrated and with an unsettling feeling of guilt, I switched the phone off and let it drop in the drawer of my nightstand.

I owed Liv more than I could ever repay, but tonight, my time and focus belonged to someone else. Charlotte was in my bed, flushed with rapture and languorous like a goddess in her resting pose. Tonight, everything apart from Charlotte and her warm, supple body lost in my arms was superfluous.

When her hair was satisfyingly dry, I slid beside her and gathered her to my chest. She was uniquely beautiful while asleep. Restrictions and inhibitions left aside, her face was serene, almost smiling, arranged into a peaceful, sated, and purely feminine expression.

"I'm pulling you to the dark side, sweet Charlotte," I sighed in the night. Like I had done time and time again with all the people I loved.

I held Charlotte tightly and brushed my lips across her forehead, wishing she were enough to make the remorse go away.

I always felt guilty and indebted when Liv called, and so, I always ran to her. It was nearly a compulsion, one that had already hurt Charlotte's feelings when, without so much as an explanation, I had left her alone in my apartment to save a girl who perhaps could never be saved.

THE TIRES SCREECHING ON THE *pavement and the booming of the engines amplified with each step I took, yet it was the pounding of my blood that I heard the loudest. Liv's scared, nearly pained cries echoed in my head until they became real. My head snapped forward, and all of a sudden, I saw red.*

In a crowd of drunken, jeering men, Liv was cowering like a defenseless little bird. Her sobs wafted in the night, and her fear dribbled like poison in the air. Of all people, Liv shouldn't be scared or aggrieved again.

"Take your filthy hands off her," I growled right before my fist connected with a jaw that quickly cracked.

I possessed the advantage of having surprised them, and I also possessed the rage they lacked. I pushed Liv behind me so fast and so forcefully that she almost collapsed.

A fuming gorilla with a bald head and an unkempt beard approached me, and I greeted him with a knee precisely placed to his gut. He howled and fell to the ground as another buddy came to the rescue.

The poor excuse of a man hit me in the chest, managing only to enrage me a little bit more. I caught his arm, pulled him forward, and elbowed him so hard that he staggered a few feet to the side, holding his jaw and whining like a puppy.

"Marcus, be careful."

Liv's soft-spoken warning came at the same time a brutal blow to my head caught me off guard and pushed me backward. I slammed into Liv's body, the impact affecting her balance. She dropped to the ground as I cupped my right ear, a terrible ringing deafening me shortly.

"All of you, cease this nonsense."

A motorcycle stopped next to us, casting a cloud of smoke. I looked up to see Kai climbing off, his furious countenance so unlike him. He jerked his chin, his eyes spat fire, and instantly, everybody except Liv and me scattered away.

Here, at the races, Kai was in command, but I was impressed to realize how influential he was.

"Where were you?" I spat, bending to help Liv to her feet.

Head bowed, hands powerlessly linked together, she was crying. I hated when she was crying. I hated the most that I could do nothing to make her tears disappear.

"She is not my responsibility." Kai walked to me, a stern, resolute expression on his face. "And neither is she yours."

Liv sobbed and sagged into me. My arms went around her naturally, knowing the shape of her soft, fragile body all too well.

When she was crying, when she was so weak and so painfully defenseless, she unraveled me. I pressed my lips to the top of her head, inhaling her scent and instead remembering how Charlotte had felt underneath me less than an hour ago.

Liv cried harder and wrapped her arms around my waist to steady herself. Guilt ate at me with a ferocious, merciless brutality that stole my breath. Here I was with Liv crying in my arms, and my thoughts were directed to another woman, my whole body remembering and needing that woman.

"She is not your responsibility anymore." Kai watched me fixedly, his jaw rolling at the sight of Liv in my arms.

He didn't understand. He couldn't understand that Liv was always going to be my responsibility. My debt to her was never going to be settled.

"That is enough, Kai."

I was much too quickly drained of energy. After days and days of restlessness, I finally felt tired, but then again, I always seemed to feel tired around Liv. I cradled her close and steered her to my car without casting another glance at my cousin.

"Why were you here, Olivia?"

Raw anger struck me like lightning. Nobody should have valued and pursued safety more than Liv herself. And yet, she didn't. Liv eyed me, startled, looking as if I had just slapped her.

Swallowing down my remorse, I went on. "What were you thinking, coming to a place filled with drunk people? Have you lost your mind?" Tears trickled down her pale face, inflaming the guilt and therefore the anger. Was she doing this to torment me? "Answer me, damn it."

"I—I—" Words failed her as she began crying in earnest.

"Stop crying," I snapped, then bumped my fist against the steering wheel.

Olivia Lambert generated many emotions in me: happiness, pleasure, affection, despondency, guilt, but most frequently anger. And most commonly, I didn't know whether I was mad at her or at myself.

"I was looking for you," she sobbed then looked out the passenger window.

I turned on the engine and stepped on the gas with an economy of movements that rendered me brusque and stiff. Liv covered her mouth with her tiny fist in a failed attempt to muffle her sobs.

"Why?" Despite my efforts to soften my voice, it still sounded angry and harsh, but I needed to know why I had left an excited Charlotte, without so much as an explanation, alone in my apartment.

"I have been calling. You never answered. You fought with Brayden, and I was so worried. And you never call or visit and—I was worried."

"You were worried about me fighting with Brayden? It was not a fight, Liv. We were blowing off some steam."

"Oh yes, because for you getting in fistfights is recreational."

Brayden and I had a long history of settling our issues in random boxing matches, but those could hardly be called fistfights. By the time the match was over, both of us would feel better and any problem would be forgotten. For us, it was a way to let go of bad energy, a method Liv had never understood nor approved of.

I ran a nervous hand through my hair then grabbed the steering wheel with unnecessary force. I had learned my lesson not to argue with Liv while I was driving, so I let the silence stretch and ignored her crying, inquisitive eyes.

We were close to Liv's apartment building when I realized it was the same building Charlotte lived in. I clenched my teeth and prayed with all my might for this night to not get even worse than it had already been.

"Talk to me, please." Liv leaned in and rested a hand on my knee that I couldn't help but glare at. It struck me all of a sudden that her touch didn't feel like it used to. Or I was the one who had stopped needing the intimacy?

By the time we reached the confines of her apartment without any casual encounters, I had yet to talk. I locked the door and strode to the window, my hands shoved in my pockets. With some degree of difficulty, Liv followed me, but hesitation radiated off her.

"Please, Marcus, don't be mad at me." It was so like her to drive me mad then sneak her way past my anger and appease me once again. This time it was not working. Not yet.

"Do you have the tiniest understanding of what you do to me, Olivia?"

"Don't call me that," she whimpered.

Slender arms wrapped around my waist, and she leaned her head against my rigid back. Her feminine touch reminded me of soft, tuberose-scented skin, heated cheeks, and brown eyes. It reminded me of everything that was amiss and could never be mended between us.

"Are you doing it on purpose?" I continued, ignoring her. *"Do you consciously put yourself in danger to torture me, to show me that I cannot protect you, to remind me that I never could?"*

"How can you say that? I would never try to hurt you."

She kissed my shoulder and nuzzled her cheek against my sweatshirt. The hands she kept locked around my waist started a journey of their own. While one hand traveled north, stroking my chest in a practiced, possessive gesture, the other one dived south, brazenly ducking past the waistband of my sweatpants. The gesture that once would have instantly ignited me, now did nothing more than leave me cold.

"No." I caught her wrists and pulled her hands away, letting them fall limply by her sides. When I turned around to face her, Liv was pale with shock.

"No?" Shock was replaced by a deep lack of comprehension.

"What we do is not healthy. It should stop. I think I should leave."

I was halfway to the door when her furious sobs stopped me.

"Of-of course. Y-you only come when you need me. N-never when I n-need you."

"Never when you need me? I always drop everything and come running to you when you need me, Olivia."

I whirled back around so fast and closed the space between us so wrathfully that her eyes widened in fear. She stumbled backward, and in a matter of seconds, she was on the ground, sagging and sobbing. Watching how she clasped her limp leg and gathered her knees to her chest as if she sought protection made me fist my hands in my hair and almost howl. I was torn between frustration and the need to be the one protecting her, but eventually, the latter prevailed.

"Liv, I'm sorry." I went to my knee, crouching over her, but stopped dead when she flinched away. It was so déjà vu.

"Don't. I don't want you near me."

"Then why do you call, Liv? Why do you keep drawing me back if you don't want me near you? You drive me insane."

"I-I need you. I d-don't know how to show you what I feel anymore."

Hurt in its purest, severest form oozed from her eyes. The tears never stopped pouring down her cheeks. Her eyes were red-rimmed, and her small nose looked just as red. The genuineness of her vulnerability called to me.

My protective instincts kicked in, and just like that, I was cradling Liv in my lap. She cowered and clung to me like a little girl. I watched her through eyes filled with pain of my own. She had once been my girl.

"I'm so sorry. I didn't mean to make you angry." She rocked back and forth in my arms, her trembling hands covering her eyes. "I was wrong in looking for you at the race. I was wrong—about everything—tonight."

Liv was a complete rollercoaster. One moment she was arguing and fighting, and the next she was apologizing, seeking my good graces with a persistence that made me believe her whole life depended on my approval.

"Hush, Liv. Stop crying."

"You were so violent tonight. Why must violence always be involved?"

Violence repulsed her not because of its primal brutality but because of its bloody outcome. Liv couldn't bear the sight of blood. When she shuddered, my arms automatically tightened around her.

"Liv, you called me. You asked me to be there. What did you expect? Besides, nothing would have happened if you had stayed home." Anger was barely contained behind a soft but stiff voice.

"I needed to see you. I needed to make sure you were alright. How could I reach you otherwise if you don't answer my calls?" A spark of anger leaked in her voice, but she quickly resumed her quiet, unstoppable sobbing.

"Let's make a deal. I answer when you call, and you stop doing this sort of stupidity. Does this sound like a fair deal?"

"Okay."

"Liv, I'm serious. Next time you willingly put yourself in danger I will not come to the rescue."

Liv gasped and gaped, noticing an adverse determination in me that hadn't existed before. I could feel the change too, and I also knew the change bore a name.

Charlotte.

WHEN I WOKE UP IN THE morning, the bed was empty. Only the outline of Charlotte's body in the rumpled sheet was proof of her having been there. I heard the shower running before I climbed off the bed, and an adolescent pleasure filled me at the idea of having Charlotte going through her morning routine under my roof.

I opened the glass door and strode into the steamy bathroom, leaning casually against the sink. With arms folded on my chest and desire-loaded eyes, I watched her silhouette behind the misty screen of the shower cabin.

My body recalled with stark accuracy her soft curves and supple legs wrapped around my hips, her swollen lips and pear-shaped breasts pressed against my chest, and her ever-present tuberose scent.

The shower door opened, and Charlotte emerged with excessive carefulness. Her hair was piled up on top of her head in a messy bun. A few brown curls disengaged from the sexily mussed updo and caressed her pale shoulders with the same softness I longed to touch her.

Her eyes lifted from the floor and lazily focused on me. She watched me with astonishment and longing of her own, then she gave a start that only fed my amusement.

"Marcus," Charlotte hissed.

"Charlotte," I chuckled.

Her hands hesitated in midair, then they went around herself to cover her breasts. I muffled the growl but couldn't disguise the disapproving look in my eyes.

She lost her balance, and I was instantly in front of her, wrapping my arms securely around her invitingly wet body.

"There's no point in hiding from me now."

I scooped her up into my arms and locked her legs around my waist. Only the inconsequential material of my pajama bottoms separated us. She bent, and my mouth naturally found hers, engaging in a fanatical dance of inflamed lips, searching tongues, and ragged breaths. By the time I placed her on the cold marble next to the sink, my response to her couldn't be concealed.

Charlotte gave a soft, shy moan and let her head fall back against the mirror behind her. I trailed kisses down her chin and her jaw, to the graceful column of her throat. With eyes tightly shut and lips parted to allow quick, panting breaths, Charlotte looked divine.

A mischievous grin lit my expression as I bent to kiss her throat again and gently bit on the flesh at its base. She gasped.

"We don't have time for this. I need to go home before work and change. My clothes aren't exactly useable."

Palms flat on my chest, she gave me a soft shove, stopping me. Every instinct in my body urged me to *stop her*, but I didn't want to be the cause of her drawbacks. I didn't want to give her reasons to turn from me.

"I will drive you—after you eat."

"I don't eat in the morning."

"You will now." My resolve initially surprised her, then she rolled her eyes but wisely chose not to protest.

Twenty minutes later, Charlotte descended the stairs to the living room, wearing one of my shirts and begging to be disheveled again. I bit down a smile and motioned her to take a seat at the table where a plate full of scrambled eggs, bacon, and waffles with maple syrup and berries was already waiting for her.

"You are going to eat too, right?" Her eyes widened as she gestured to her own plate.

"I would very much like to eat, but I wouldn't want to be the reason you are late, Miss Burton."

Then I couldn't restrain my smile anymore. She blushed with renewed shyness, which, as much as it fascinated me, had no place between us.

I pulled a chair next to her and sat so my knee brushed against hers, and each time I moved, our arms casually touched. I planned to make Charlotte completely aware of me on all levels. She took a bite of the waffles and gave an enticing moan that came from deep in her throat.

"How do you take your coffee?"

A loose curl escaped from her low ponytail, and my fingers quickly pushed it behind her ear. Once I touched her, my hand remained in permanent contact with her skin.

"Black."

I arched an eyebrow, rather surprised at her choice.

"What?"

Charlotte put up an affronted façade, but the rosiness in her cheeks and the way her eyes quickly looked away betrayed her coyness.

"It is not a common selection for women."

"I wasn't aware we drink our coffee depending on gender."

Smiling at her sassy reply, I poured her a generous cup of coffee, involuntarily remembering they day she crashed into me, spilling coffee all over herself. The sight of Charlotte angry was delightful, yet the sight of Charlotte unguarded and overwhelmed by pleasure was an image not likely to ever ebb from my mind.

"You never told me how your trip to D.C. was."

"Tiring," Charlotte answered in a small voice, after diligently chewing on her lip.

Her professional persona slipped in place. The tranquility of her features took on a stone-hard quality while her eyes grew vacant with recollections that made her press her lips in a straight line. But what worried me the most was the pallor that had suddenly chased away the color in her cheeks.

"Tell me," I encouraged, my hand wrapping around her small fist. Charlotte tilted her head to the side, studying me as she absently chewed on her waffles. I had almost resigned myself to her silence when she started speaking.

"It's tradition for an associate who is promoted to Junior Partner to receive a top-level case, one that offers as much exposure as possible. I've been expecting one, but I never imagined that my father would appoint me Jack Stewart's case."

During the past two weeks, Jack Stewart's story had been all over the news. From daily reports to the last editions of the most important newspapers, the prodigal son of Mayor Mitch Stewart had been ever-present. To top it off, not a day had passed at Burton & Associates without someone mentioning the troubling news.

Jack Stewart had been discovered unconscious in a hotel room, lying beside the corpse of his fiancée. At first glance, he seemed as much of a victim as the dead woman. Speculations, however, arose when the results of the preliminary investigations were received. The lethal weapon, a Beretta M9, was covered in a single set of fingerprints—Jack's.

The proof was indisputable, but insufficient for the prosecutors to close the case. Mitch Stewart's influence and money had quickly assembled the best legal team for his son from high-class firms around the country, including Burton & Associates.

I hated that Charlotte was involved in a case about murder, but what I hated the most was the idea of her having to swim in such troubled waters with such big and dangerous sharks. My concern and dislike, however, were firmly but very difficultly concealed.

"Your father assigns the cases?"

"It still is his firm, Marcus. I have my own clients, but if he chooses, he can assign any case he wants to anyone he wants." Charlotte gave me an exhausted, pleading look. In response, I only tightened my hold on her hand and pressed a delicate kiss to her knuckles.

"What if you decline a case?"

"I have. Jack Stewart's. The resultant hassle wasn't worth it."

"Are you afraid of your father, Charlotte?"

A slow-devouring rage built inside me and expanded when Charlotte's eyes widened with something akin to trepidation.

"In which way?"

Her voice trembled, but I assumed she was oblivious to the way she tensed each time the subject of her father came up.

"In the way that you do not dare to defy him. At all."

"I told you. I am not that daring." She smiled weakly and watched me over the rim of her cup of coffee.

"That is not true. You were daring enough to give me a chance, remember?"

The timid smile expanded, and her tongue darted out to lick coffee-coated lips. Admitting defeat to her charms, I leaned into her until I heard her breath hitch then took my time savoring her mouth.

"Continue, please."

"Kissing you?"

"Oh, sweet Charlotte, I'm corrupting you already."

"That is not true."

Despite her grin, her voice was censorious, which reminded me of her hard slap from the previous evening. While she struggled to put her thoughts in order, I struggled to wipe the growing smile off my face.

"I went to D.C. to meet Jack Stewart," she said. "I talked to his lawyers, to his father, to him, and the more I talked, the more I got the nagging feeling that something was wrong."

"A true Cancerian values her feelings," I muttered, distracted by her tongue as it glided lasciviously over her bottom lip.

"I do," she conceded, wearing a pensive expression. "I value my intuition and my capacity to read people. I also talked to the prosecuting attorney, and oddly, my discussion with him felt more honest than that with my client. There are things Jack is not saying, which I believe his father knows. His behavior is strange to say the least, erratic at times. Among other things, he is accused of second-degree murder. He should be revolted at the allegation and determined to prove the prosecutors wrong because he should want to discover the true murderer in this story. Most importantly, he should be suffering for his fiancée. He is and does none of what I would expect from an innocent man."

"You don't believe he is innocent."

It was a statement, plain and simple, and though Charlotte didn't verbally agree, her eyes spoke volumes. She placed her fork and knife on the half-empty plate and straightened in her seat.

"That is all I can divulge. Regardless of what I think, I owe him confidentiality."

"As usual the professional."

"I have to be," she murmured quietly. Her seductive voice reminded me of her uncontrolled moans as I was deeply sheathed in her hot, addictive body.

"I know. But I'm always here to listen when you need me to."

I kissed her briefly because I needed the physical reassurance but did not deepen the contact since I knew I would not be able to stop myself. The strange sensation that Charlotte shouldn't be a part of Jack Stewart's trial intensified. I valued my instincts too, and they rarely failed me.

"It would have been so much easier for both of us if you hadn't been a lawyer. But if you heard yourself talk, if you heard the dedication in your voice, you wouldn't doubt for a minute that you are marvelous at what you do. But then again, I believe you would be marvelous at anything you did. That worries me."

Charlotte blushed. "Why?"

"Because you'll eventually figure out that I am not good enough for you."

"You are such a fool. Once I'm in, I'm in, Marcus."

Repeating the words she had whispered to me the previous night was a comfort I didn't expect. Charlotte rose from her seat and climbed into my lap in one lissome movement. Her hands secured my face, and her mouth descended upon mine with firm delicacy.

Yet, her subtlety couldn't conceal the passionate woman inside. When we resurfaced for air, she eyed me intensely, chidingly. In the face of her fervor, I couldn't help but grin.

"When are you free this week?" I asked, tracing her lips with my thumb.

"I can make time Friday. Why?"

To my utter satisfaction, her curiosity immediately sparked. She prodded me with her fingers to offer the answer to her question, but before long, I discovered that a curious Charlotte was a sight I wasn't willing to get rid of too swiftly.

Chapter 20

Charlotte

The inside of a courtroom always raised goosebumps on my skin. There was something solemn and elegant in the air even with all the uproar and commotion. It was also terrifying. Once a trial started, any outcome was possible, and the fate of the defendant lay in the hands of some unknown, unpredictable jury.

Jack was brought by the bailiff and looked considerably different from the last time I saw him. He was clean-shaven and wore a black suit with a matching tie and a crisp white dress shirt. His hair was brushed to the side, and his eyes were cast obediently downward. He looked subdued and distracted but properly grieving. Apparently, Drake had prepared him well for today.

Jack passed me by to sit next to Drake, and I experienced the same shiver that made my hair stand on end, so when Vincent Cole flanked Jack's left side, I could only be grateful that I didn't have to be so close to the man.

Drake and Jack talked in hushed voices, Drake giving him last minute instructions, while Jack hissed his approval and fisted his hands under the table so harshly that the skin turned white. Maybe he wasn't that subdued after all.

"All rise," the bailiff announced, and my heart started thumping faster.

And so, it all began.

We all stood respectfully as Jack finally and unequivocally became aware of his situation. All of a sudden, his face turned ashen, and his feet didn't seem to support him properly.

From the audience, Mayor Stewart flashed him a warning glare, and his mother, Penelope, smiled encouragingly. She was perhaps the only one in their family who didn't carry that cold-blooded expression that made you suspect the worst of her.

"Are both parties ready to proceed with this arraignment?" Judge Norton asked once everybody sat except Holden, Drake, and Jack.

"Yes, Your Honor," both counselors answered.

"Mr. Stewart, you are charged with second-degree murder. If found guilty, the maximum sentence is incarceration for life. Do you understand the charges against you?"

"Yes, Your Honor."

"How do you plead?"

"Not guilty, Your Honor."

Jack's voice sounded unexpectedly stable and collected. Behind the prosecution's desk, Jennifer's mother muffled her sobs in her husband's neck, and Holden's words rang in my head.

What if I was on the wrong side of this case? What if, by defending Jack Stewart, I made a mockery out of a family's grief and a last abuse to a woman who had been unable to protect herself?

"Very well. Bail is set at 1.5 million dollars."

"Objection, Your Honor."

It was a pre-trial hearing, but Holden was already living up to the pit-bull image the media had crafted for him. As he almost shouted the words, he looked ferocious like an animal, all but baring his teeth in anger. Although I was shocked by his objection, since it was not common or advisable to challenge a judge's decision before the trial actually started, I was even more shocked that bail had been so quickly set.

Judge Norton raised his eyebrows in surprise and challenge of his own.

"Let me rectify, your Honor," Holden amended. "The prosecution respectfully asks that bail be denied."

"On what grounds, counselor?"

"On the grounds that Mr. Stewart is a class A felon, a danger to society, and a man with the resources to evade justice."

"Your Honor, there's no foundation for the prosecution's claim," Drake cut in, his tone tough as nails. "My client has no past criminal record, and there is no potential flight risk because it is in his best interest to face justice and be acquitted. In fact, the defense wants to present evidence of the prosecutor's habit of intimidating defendants."

Drake handed a folder to the bailiff, who handed it to the judge. In his corner, Holden fumed with hardly suppressed rage. There had been a case when Holden had argued against granting bail only to fail to prove the defendant's guilt in the end. The man had been innocent, and he had almost been killed in prison. Certainly, that case had been a grave lapse in judgment for Leon Holden, but I doubted he had a pattern of malicious prosecution.

Judge Norton skimmed through the files, dissatisfaction clear in his gaze.

"If what I am reading here, Mr. Holden, is true, then I might even consider removing you from the case."

Holden's chin went up, and his eyes turned stony. He didn't like to be backed up against a wall, and that was exactly where Drake had driven him.

"Do you have conclusive evidence to support your request, counselor?"

"Not at the moment, Your Honor," Holden said.

"Then I am forced to caution you, counselor, that I will not tolerate abuse of power in my courtroom. Jack Stewart is not a felon as he has not been convicted yet." Judge Norton's gaze was sharp and determined as it fixed Holden, leaving him speechless, then he zeroed in on Jack. "Mr. Stewart, you will have to report to this court throughout your trial. Otherwise, bail will be revoked, and you will be imprisoned."

"I understand, Your Honor," Jack answered distractedly after

Drake gripped his elbow with enough force to cause harm.

"Mr. Holden, if there are no other objections, is the prosecution prepared to begin trial?"

"Yes, Your Honor."

Holden was not pleased, that much was painfully evident when his eyes met mine. There was reproach there and maybe also regret, but we were on different sides as he had pointed out a week ago, and whatever my reticence or doubts, I defended Jack. If Holden was prepared, we had to be even more so.

"In that case, trial starts in six weeks."

The judge stood, and the hearing ended as quickly as it had started. Holden gathered his files then threw a venomous glare in our general direction and an especially disgusted one to Jack, then he left.

Jennifer's parents, huddled closely into each other's sides, followed him quickly afterward. The mother was devastated. The father was just numb, a statue going through the motions.

"Does this mean that I'm free?"

Jack was almost hopeful, although quite naïve. Drake rolled his eyes, looking irritated as one did after hearing the same question over and over again. To my right, Cole sketched a smile that he quickly shrouded behind a concentrated scowl.

"Not yet, but you'll sleep home tonight, Jack," Cole told him when nobody seemed willing to offer an answer.

However, the day was not over, and there was still much work to be done. After he was cleared, Jack left court with the mayor and his mother, while Drake and Cole drove together in Drake's Mercedes.

Although I had been invited to join them, I preferred to take the ride to Drake's firm alone, if only to revel in some quiet time on my own.

Drake Kendrix Zane occupied the top floors of a building that looked as pretentious and intimidating from the outside as it did from the inside. An assistant, with her blonde hair tucked in a ponytail and her perfect designer dress complimenting her curves, greeted me by the elevators and led me all the way to the conference room where Drake and Cole were hunched low over stacks of papers.

The room was graceful and somewhat intimate, resembling more a private living room than an official area in a law firm. The paneled walls matched the chestnut furniture to perfection while the beige tones of the upholstery and the lighting fixtures invigorated the space. The far wall had a wide window sill and was made nearly entirely by framed windows. I was thankful that some were already open.

"Please take a seat, Charlotte," Drake welcomed me with an unexpectedly warm smile. "Jack is supposed to arrive any minute."

I nodded although Jack's arrival didn't generate any particular excitement. By the time he did manage to arrive, we had gone over several defense strategies and looked over the papers that littered the conference desk.

"Finally," Drake muttered, but otherwise didn't even acknowledge Jack's arrival, and in his turn, Jack didn't acknowledge our presence either.

The mayor's son walked to the window, climbed on the window sill, stretching his legs, and lit a cigarette. It was, indeed, going to be a long day.

Drake stood, grabbed the half-smoked cigarette out of Jack's fingers, and threw it out the window with what I could tell was his customary glare.

"You had homework, Jack," Drake told him.

"Math, history? Oh no, let me guess. Philosophy?"

"Cut the idiocy. Who wanted Jennifer dead?"

Jack sighed loudly and banged his head against the window frame repeatedly. I couldn't be entirely sure whether his frustration stemmed from being unable to identify who had wanted his fiancée dead or from not finding the perfect culprit to pin his own crime on.

"She was a stunning woman. Other men might have wanted her, I guess, but—"

The door of the conference room burst open, and the high-pitched voice of the blonde mannequin of a secretary invaded the whole space. Unlike the still man standing in the doorway, she was too noisy and her gestures so erratic that she appeared somewhat crazy.

"Sir, you are not allowed here. You force me to call security," the woman kept saying, but nobody was paying her any attention.

The man advanced into the room while Jack slid off the window sill and froze. Drake stood, equally disturbed, and stepped in front of Jack, not to shield him from any danger but rather to defuse the pending explosion. Evidently, neither one of them had expected to come face to face with Jennifer Gunnar's father.

"Sir, please."

Drake found his bearings and made a curt gesture to his secretary. Immediately, she fell silent and left the room. Without her noises, the room was eerily quiet—the quiet before a storm.

"Mr. Gunnar," Drake finally addressed him, and the man's attention, which had been exclusively focused on Jack, shifted to his lawyer.

"Don't talk to me," Mr. Gunnar spat. His nostrils flared, his lips curled over his teeth, and loathing dripped from his stare. "I wanted to see with my own eyes how you are murdering my child all over again, how you drag her memory through the mud."

"Mr. Gunnar," Jack spoke and walked past Drake who failed to grab his shoulder by an inch. "I—I loved her. Maybe not like you wanted me to, maybe not like she deserved, but I did care for Jennifer."

Cole watched the whole scene just as stunned as I felt. This might have been the longest, most charged speech about Jennifer I had heard from Jack's mouth ever since we met. While he spoke, with eyes wide and full of sadness, and his body hunched and trembled, it was so easy to believe that he was nothing but an innocent man in agony.

"Don't you say her name. Don't you dare claim you ever loved my daughter. I warned her. I kept telling her that you were no good, that you would get rid of her first chance you've got. I never imagined you'd—"

"I was going to make her my wife," Jack bellowed, turning grief into anger like an expert.

"That's enough," Drake cut in. "We all understand this is a difficult time for you, Mr. Gunnar, but I will not stand for this behavior or the accusations you make. I will ask you to leave this office immediately."

Like clockwork, the security detail stepped in and gently motioned Mr. Gunnar outside, which made me believe they had been waiting for a cue all this time just outside the conference room.

"You are a disgrace. All of you are," Mr. Gunnar hissed and shoved at the grabbing hands of the two bodyguards. "I hope you rot in jail, you murderer. I hope you'll never see daylight again."

After security finally escorted Jennifer's father out, we remained silent. Jack returned to his seat on the window sill and smoked two cigarettes in quick succession. This time, Drake didn't bother to curb his behavior. It was Cole who eventually resumed our discourse.

"How did you get along with Jennifer's parents, Jack?"

Jack stopped in mid-smoke only to cast daggers at Cole. He seemed defensive, insulted, and dispassionate, all at the same time. Vincent watched through hawk's eyes the emotions playing on Jack's face, engaging in an already routine battle of wills. In the end, it was still Cole who won and Jack who caved.

"As you could see, they didn't approve. They didn't support us. Ever since we announced our engagement, her father tried to break us up. She had no relationship with her father, and she talked very little with her mother."

"That sounds drastic."

"Drastic was when he threatened to shoot me if I didn't leave Jennifer alone."

Cole looked disappointed. If he had intended to use Jennifer's parents to testify in favor of Jack and build him the image of an adoring fiancé, then his tactic had been short-lived.

"How would you explain this antagonism?" I asked him.

"I never got to know them too well, so I don't know what was on their mind. Maybe they just didn't want Jennifer to be happy."

I wondered how a jury would receive such a confession at trial. How was it possible that a man who claimed to be profoundly in love with a woman never found the time or common ground to get to know her parents?

"They didn't support you as a couple or just you, Jack?"

"Why does it matter?

"Because if they did not support you as a couple, that suggests they didn't encourage a relationship between a daughter they loved and a man who didn't deserve her. It doesn't mean they were bad parents just because they did not agree with Jennifer's choice. That raises more questions about you than about them, Jack."

"But if they did not like Jack, can that suggest that Jennifer's parents were prejudiced against him?"

My jaw clenched, and Drake's mouth quivered.

"Jack was their daughter's choice, and if they supported her like you say, Ms. Burton, shouldn't they have supported Jack as well?"

When you loved someone, you couldn't support the people set on ruining them. I didn't bother to explain that to Cameron Drake, who gifted me with a splendid Cheshire cat smile. I had been right, but Drake was skilled enough to turn the tables and paint a pair of grieving parents into two people hostile to their own daughter's dreams.

"But like you pointed out, they didn't like Jack at all, and they didn't get along with their daughter," Drake added. "In fact, they refused to attend the party, and they hadn't rsvp'd to the wedding invitation either, so we can only assume they didn't intend to participate. They were getting impatient, desperate even, that nothing they had done convinced Jennifer to end the engagement. So the correct question, I think, should be who wanted to incriminate and get rid of Jack? Nolan Gunnar seemed very interested in getting rid of Jack."

I wasn't entirely sure whether I gasped or stopped breathing altogether. When I realized that Jack looked just as dumbfounded as I felt, I almost gave in to hysterics. Then rage settled in, potent and destructive. I feared Jack's mood swings were rubbing off on me.

"I will not stand for you disparaging a father who is mourning her daughter, Drake."

"You might forget our client is Jack, Charlotte," Drake cajoled, but behind the sweetly spoken words, there stood a threat. "I deeply feel for their loss, but we are not grief counselors. Anything that helps Jack's case is fair game."

At first, Jack didn't seem to agree, but eventually, he turned his attention to whatever was happening beyond that window and back to another cigarette.

"Nolan Gunnar might have had motive to want Jack out of Jennifer's life, but he didn't have the motive to want his own daughter dead."

"Nolan Gunnar is a cop. He has connections, and clearly, he has people who owe him. I'm not trying to say he wanted his daughter killed. I'm trying to say he might have had a plan to get rid of Jack and it backfired."

"It's a theory as good as any," Cole agreed.

Glaring at both men, I understood I had built an aversion toward Drake only when Cole joined him. At that moment, I hated them both, but if this was how the trial would play out, I was going to hate myself immensely more for being a part of it.

In a show of impulsiveness, I stood, pulled my notes together, and shoved them in my bag, then I slung it over my shoulder, ready to leave. Drake seemed taken aback by my rashness as he jumped to his feet and rounded the table to block my way. Cole remained in his chair, looking over his files and wearing his trademark smile.

"We are not always going to agree, Charlotte," he began conciliatorily.

"I am aware of that, but at the moment, I think we've said everything there was to say."

He wasn't used to being conciliatory, let alone groveling, so when he came face to face with my staunch stance, he stepped aside, straightened, and walked back to his seat like a peacock.

"We should start gathering evidence that Jack was nowhere near the crime scene when it happened," Drake said, arching an eyebrow as he spoke as if he wanted to reiterate his earlier words. We were defending Jack, and everything was fair game. "And we should start doing so by deposing every person of importance that attended that party."

I nodded, but given that we weren't going to do that today, I didn't want to spend another minute in their company. I left Drake Kendrix Zane in a hurry, and by the time I shut the door of my hotel room, I felt drained, and my hands were trembling uncontrollably. Perhaps the correct questions had been all along: who benefited from Jennifer Gunnar's death and why?

My phone buzzed in my bag, and I all but ignored it. When it buzzed again, curiosity got the better of me. There were three messages from Marcus, telling me that he missed me, that he was looking forward to surprising me on Friday, and that he wanted me to call him when I was free because he wanted to make sure that I was alright.

His solicitousness and worry, even his name flashing on my screen, triggered conflicting emotions. I smiled, but I was also on the verge of tears.

I dialed his number and sighed with relief when he answered on the first ring.

"I miss you too," I told him and wished I could surrender in his arms and feel his lips pressed to my forehead.

"Look in your suitcase, Charlotte," Marcus instructed. His manner might have been brusque, but his voice was intense and thick with longing.

I walked over to the bed and flipped open my luggage. Tucked in the front shell, there was a package wrapped in silk paper with a note attached to it.

For when you miss me, was written in cursive letters that I recognized as Marcus's handwriting.

I removed the contents and laid them on the comforter, then I started giggling. He had packed the shirt he had been wearing three nights ago when we made love and a small bottle of his shower gel, which I had used the following morning.

"You're already much closer now," I chuckled as I brought his shirt to my nose. It smelled clean like it had been recently washed and ironed, but it still carried an undertone of Marcus's personal scent.

"You displayed a fondness for them, so I thought you'd like to have them with you."

"When did you slip them in my bag?"

"I have my ways," he replied cockily.

"Thank you," I sobbed and leaned against the pillow with

Marcus's shirt clasped to my chest. It wasn't as good as having him hold me, but it was the next best thing.

"For the shirt or the shower gel?"

"For giving me a reason to smile."

We didn't say anything more. We didn't need to. Marcus breathed evenly, and the little sounds he made calmed the storm in my head.

The knock at the door startled me, and for a tiny second I just hoped that I would open the door to find him leaning against the doorframe with a lopsided grin and utterly unorthodox intentions in his eyes.

"I have to go," I told him with regret. It wasn't Marcus knocking on my door but a mailman holding a yellow envelope.

In the envelope, there was an unlabeled DVD and a business card—Leon Holden's business card. I flipped it over just as I pushed the DVD in my laptop and read the message on the back of the card.

'Is this the man you want to defend?'

Holden's message became clearer once the DVD started playing. It was footage from the night Jennifer Gunnar was killed. I fast forwarded through the actual party and didn't fail to notice that some parts of the footage had been cut out.

It was unnerving to see a woman so full of life and joy and know that her existence had been nipped in the bud. She was stunning, as Jack had said, and had a sense of fashion that, although reasonably elegant, indicated that she might have been trying to compensate with luxurious clothing for other shortcomings. She flashed her engagement ring at everybody who asked, laughed, and attended to every guest.

On the other hand, Jack seemed to be mostly absorbed by a bald man wearing jeans and a gray shirt, whose face the cameras never managed to capture fully. Perhaps it was the Vinny Savidge, whom Jennifer didn't like. Perhaps it was another man altogether, but it was certainly someone who was giving Jack terrible news. His expression as he slammed a glass against the countertop of the bar was thunderous.

Then Jennifer was nowhere to be seen, and neither was Jack.

The footage was discontinued again, then there was a last image of Jack with his head bowed low and his body stiff, hurrying down a corridor. He left behind room after room, making it obvious that he was heading for room 311—Jennifer's suite.

I removed the DVD from my laptop and decided to pay Holden a visit. I wasn't entirely sure why he had sent me this footage, but whatever his reasons, I was certain he had ulterior motives. Unlike him, when I had a message to deliver, I had the courtesy to do it in person.

I was led to Holden's office by an assistant who wasn't very pleased to be forced to leave her desk, or chair for that matter. Holden stood and circled his desk, greeting me with a quizzical smile like he hadn't been waiting for me, but wasn't surprised to receive me either.

"Ms. Burton, what a surprise," he said, although we both knew it wasn't a surprise at all.

While he perused me, I swiped a glance over his neat office and nearly felt disappointed. I had expected some extravagance from the great Leon Holden or some particularity of his authoritative character to personalize his workplace.

The room was half the size of my New York office and empty save for a tremendously massive desk with a comfortable leather chair behind it and two smaller replicas in front of it. A coat rack was set to the left, two enormous file cabinets rested to the right, and nothing else. The monochrome theme and austerity of the space were somewhat depressing.

"I hoped we could talk."

"Please, take a seat. How may I help you?"

His practiced courtesy didn't deceive me. He watched me precisely like a buyer who, spotting an item of interest at an auction, was set to have it. Leon Holden was not inclined to help me but keen on exploiting me in order to help himself. Once I sat, he resumed his seat, unfastening the sole button of his jacket. I met his eyes unflinchingly, nearly defiantly. His mouth curved just a notch before he flattened his lips in a straight line.

"What is your angle?"

My straightforwardness seemed to take him by surprise, and I couldn't help but feel pleased. Holden recovered quickly and laughed, ultimately enjoying that I didn't beat around the bush.

"I have no angle. I'm looking for the truth, and I think you are a woman who appreciates it as much as I do."

"I do want to reveal the truth, Holden, but I believe you are underestimating me. If you think that I am easily manipulated, then perhaps you are not as sharp as the media portrays you to be."

"I wouldn't dare underestimate you. Actually, I'm counting on your instincts and abilities."

"What's that supposed to mean?"

He just smiled and massaged his closed mouth with his thumb. He had planted a seed and now was waiting to reap what he had sowed. I didn't want to give him the satisfaction, but regardless of my bravado, he had brought my skepticism about Jack Stewart's innocence to new extremes.

While Drake and Cole fought to defend him no matter the cost or the ethical breaches, I could not defend Jack if he did not deserve it.

When Holden didn't seem inclined to elaborate, I stood stiffly and flattened my palms over the soft material of my dress. His eyes followed my movements with tense concentration, small creases forming across his forehead. He didn't know what to make of me or of my responses, and that nearly made me smirk.

Keeping off-kilter a man of his type was key in successfully dealing with him. If I wanted to achieve my goal, I needed to maintain the upper hand.

"I'm not going to collude, counselor."

"It would be collusion if you used what I gave you in favor of your client, and there's no way in hell you could use that in his favor. Moreover, as of an hour ago, your team was notified that we have this footage."

I nodded though I was confused about my sudden sense of disappointment. For some reason, knowing that Drake had seen the footage didn't sit well with me, but Holden was right. We couldn't base our defense on the footage he had disclosed unless—unless Drake planned on using it to find someone to pin the murder on. My stomach turned, and bile rose in my throat. The idea didn't seem unlikely since he had already tried to implicate Nolan Gunnar in his own daughter's murder.

"Are you alright, Charlotte?" Holden asked, his sympathy either genuine or expertly counterfeited.

I waved his question like nothing was really happening and refrained from saying that it could also be collusion if I ended up helping him put Jack behind bars. There was no doubt in my mind now that before I moved forward with this case, I needed tangible proof of Jack's innocence.

I nearly gave in to another hysterical streak of laughter, thinking of Mitch Stewart and how he would react if he found out that a lawyer on his son's defense team searched for evidence that might incriminate him.

"I'm not your tool, Holden," I told him, my voice coming out more aggressive than I had intended. "Don't treat me as such."

I left his office with a strong feeling of nausea and a stronger wish to just go home, but for tonight, Marcus's shirt had to be enough to keep me warm and settled.

Chapter 21

Marcus

"Where are we going?" Charlotte's increasing curiosity and impatience brought to mind the countless text messages she had sent me the previous night, asking the very same question she was asking me now. I winked secretively, slid into my seat, and turned on the engine without offering her an answer.

"You did it to yourself, you know?" I told her when she pouted prettily. "I had no intention of making you curious, but the sight is too appealing to resist."

"You're cruel," she accused.

Sulking, Charlotte crossed her arms over her chest and looked away from me, her mouth set, her brows knit. Despite the façade, I knew she wasn't distraught.

"It's nothing out of the ordinary, Charlotte. I've been into your world. I want you to be in mine for a day."

Doubt produced an invisible heavy weight to press over my chest and block my airways until Charlotte placed her hand on my knee and squeezed gently.

"You like surprising me. Maybe I'd like surprising *you*."

"Oh, I'm truly looking forward to that." Winking, I gave her a sincere grin and received a timid roll of her eyes.

The drive to my office seemed shorter than I remembered. By the time I parked the car in the underground lot, Charlotte's eyes were gleaming with excitement and anticipation. Surprising such a smart woman was a delicate matter, I thought absently as I helped her out of the car and wrapped my arm around her waist.

The building was relatively small, housing only CKM Engineering. We took the elevator and rode to the third floor in silence. The doors of the elevator dinged open, and Charlotte walked out with my hand steadily placed on her lower back.

As I guided her past the reception area and down an empty corridor that led to my office, I couldn't help but think how different it felt to be with her here. While at Burton & Associates she was my handler and I a troublemaker, here neither of us had to hide or pretend. I was an engineer, she was a lawyer, and we were together. The thought put a stupid smile on my face.

"Welcome to my world, Charlotte Burton."

I pulled her into my office and closed the door behind us. She walked inside hesitantly, drinking in every element around her. Not tolerating the distance between us, I followed and drew her to me, burying my nose in her throat while still allowing her to familiarize herself with the space where I spent most of my time.

"This is…fabulous." The shine in her eyes humbled me.

"I wouldn't go to such lengths, but I am glad you approve."

Her eyes sparkled as she explored my workplace. My hands fell from her waist at the same time she took a step forward. A surge of exhilaration inundated me, the same kind of euphoria I had felt when I opened the door of my apartment to find her on the other side for the first time.

Ever since Charlotte and I met, control had been ripped from me, but now as she advanced into my office, a modicum of that power seemed to come back.

To a man who was naturally in control, the delight of being on familiar territory while his female dived out of her comfort zone was an aphrodisiac that spurred my desire to frenzied heights.

"That is the drawing table," I explained, my voice coming out gruffly.

Charlotte's eyes darted to me, recognizing the passion behind my words, before she returned her attention to the scrolls of paper lying on the table with an adorable splash of red in her cheeks. I trailed after her with my hands locked behind my back and my eyes fixed on her. She was a vision I couldn't get enough of.

"Did you draw this?"

Her fingers flew softly over provisional sketches that I had finished during the morning, and her eyes followed with awe the invisible traces left by her fingertips.

"Yes."

I wanted to offer her the space to explore at her own pace. I truly did, but ultimately, I failed. When my chest touched her silhouette, part of the unpleasant sting created by distance thankfully vanished.

"These are parts of a concept motorcycle we are working on."

I pointed to a few drawings, and she looked at them curiously. The honesty of her enthusiasm surprised and pleased me equally. Nobody had ever approved of, let alone showed interest in my work.

"So you do mix business with pleasure." Charlotte smiled pensively, then continued her exploration.

My office was considerably smaller than hers and definitely messier, but the room welcomed me each time I crossed its threshold with a warmth that could only be derived from a broad sense of accomplishment.

It was a practical workspace that harbored a drawing table to the left and a walnut L-shaped desk to the right, protected by a leather desk pad emblazoned with the company logo. An all-in-one system surfaced from mountains of files and binders, which I had neither the time nor the proper disposition to read through, and a Chesterfield executive chair was left waiting askew.

Facing my desk, there was a small sitting area comprised of a leather couch flanked by matching loveseats that remained, more often than not, unoccupied. Charlotte moseyed around, committing to memory the dark tones of the furniture and the contrasting light nuance of the upholstery.

"What do you do here?"

She licked her lips, momentarily distracting me. Her fingers drifted over the backrest of a loveseat while her eyes scanned me suggestively.

"What exactly are you asking, Charlotte?"

I closed the space between us before she drew in another breath. Charlotte was a marvelous actress when she wanted to be, but behind her unabashed attitude and blatant innuendo, insecurities whirled furiously.

"It's a lovely sitting area you have here. I was only curious."

She turned around, apparently moving about with indifference. My hand wrapped around her elbow, and my body aligned against her stiff back.

"I don't like guessing, Charlotte. I want you to ask me the actual question so I can answer properly."

"Have you ever taken advantage of this couch…with a woman?"

Her cheeks turned scarlet, and her whole expression was a combination of shyness and mortification. She tried walking away, but I quickly pivoted her in my arms until she faced me and was no more than a heartbeat away.

"No, sweet Charlotte."

She was blissfully flushed and flatteringly intrigued. As usual, I couldn't resist her. Her mouth was sweet and warm as my tongue licked and stroked incessantly depths and crevices that once reached made her moan and soften into me.

"I do not bring women to my office, mostly because I don't stick around for long enough to develop a relationship, let alone the desire to bring them to my world."

"Why would you want to be in a relationship with me?"

My burst of laughter earned me her offended frown, but I was not laughing at her. I was laughing at the way she was addressing the issue. It was I who should have asked her why she wanted to be in a relationship with a man like me because at the end of the day, it was I who did not deserve her.

"Sugar," I whispered, emphasizing the word. My hands cupped her face, pulling her close. Pleasure filled my system when she did not flinch at the endearment but took comfort in it. "Because you are not the kind of woman who deserves less, and I don't believe I could handle anything else with you."

"Such a charmer."

"It's the truth." I caught her lower lip between my teeth and bit and tugged on it hard enough to make her aware of the heat simmering between us. "And now that you mentioned the couch, are you going to leave me seduced and unsatisfied?"

"Behave, Marcus," she giggled and wriggled out of reach.

"It's hard around you."

Flustered but still giggling, Charlotte sauntered to my desk and slid elegantly into my beige leather chair. She touched with unnecessary delicacy the mock-ups of a car, a motorcycle, and a car engine that I kept on my desk, then she skimmed through the mess of papers. Her small frame cushioned by the tall chair was the highlight of my day.

"I suppose here is where you spend most of the time."

Her chocolat-au-lait eyes met mine and lured me in. I stopped only when I was right in front of her. I sat on the edge of the desk with my fists placed on the polished tabletop and my knees on either side of Charlotte's crossed legs. Finding herself suddenly cornered, her lips parted to accommodate ragged breaths.

"It is a tie between the desk and the drawing table."

"I want you to remember me when you'll sit again in this chair."

She smiled impishly yet with a dose of seduction that she was undoubtedly unaware of. Glimpses of her boldness were always fascinating to witness, but they left me thunderstruck nonetheless.

"You're cruel," I mimicked her earlier reply. "But from now on, I will remember you as soon as I cross the threshold."

The smile she granted me was stunning and too tantalizing to even begin to resist.

I bent closer and let my fingers slither across the bare skin of her knee then upward along the inside of her thigh. In a moment of uncontrolled rapture, Charlotte let her head fall back and her eyes close. She pressed her lips tightly together but couldn't muffle the moan that built from her chest and materialized into a carnal sound that called for a response just as primal. I groaned, my face inches from hers, and her eyes snapped open.

"Marcus, behave." She looked a little panicky but immensely aroused.

"I don't want to." I grabbed the armrest of the chair and pulled her brusquely toward me, eliciting an exquisite gasp from her delightfully red lips. "I want to do something about that *unsatisfied* part."

She squirmed in her seat and pressed her thighs together while the blood charged to her mouth and cheeks. A rush of sensations recapturing our night together made my blood heat and my skin tingle with renewed yearning, a reaction that was visibly mirrored in Charlotte's provocative posture and the unconscious undulations of her hips.

The lewd trance was abruptly broken when the door opened and Charlotte jumped in her seat, almost knocking her head against mine.

"Easy," I breathed without turning to our intruder.

"Mr. King, there's an emergency. If you could assist Mr. Caldwell—"

"Is Mr. Caldwell mentally incapacitated that he needs assistance?" I snapped and still did not turn to see the stunned expression of my assistant.

I focused on Charlotte's wide eyes and ran a hand over my face. If Weston Caldwell needed my assistance, it had to be something serious although it interrupted much more entertaining and pleasing activities.

"It's okay, Julia. I'll be down in a minute."

"I can wait here," Charlotte mouthed as Julia vanished out the door in total silence.

"No. Come with me, please."

Loud noises and hectic shouts greeted us long before we entered the workroom. I led Charlotte to a chair far from the pandemonium unfolding but close enough so she could see everything that happened. As I walked to Weston, I wondered how all the machines and devices looked to a woman who had nothing to do with engineering.

Weston assessed me, then glanced behind my shoulder and

chuckled when his eyes landed upon the exquisite vision that was Charlotte Burton.

"That never happened before," he commented.

"If we could work this out quicker, I am somewhat busy, as you can see."

"Of course."

He laughed but immediately adopted the business attitude that had helped him flourish from a reckless young man to a defined, efficacious businessman.

Weston and I worked on a project that was still in the pre-production stage. The engine we had in front of us looked more like a device from a science fiction movie than an actual functioning vehicle part, yet our hopes were high and our enthusiasm strong.

Since I had drawn the initial outline of the project, I was somewhat the figure the rest of the team looked up to and sought for advice. I listened patiently while Weston and our coworkers explained the difficulties they had stumbled upon and easily took charge.

Always aware of Charlotte's gaze absorbing each and every one of our movements, I sat on a backless chair and worked side by side with my team.

"Good work," Weston applauded, clamping my shoulder with a capable hand. He looked at the little piece he was holding then discarded it on the working table.

"We should revise some of our initial ideas." I looked at the piece Weston had carelessly dropped, not completely sure that we didn't need it anymore. Then I glanced over my shoulder and forgot to exhale. Charlotte's hungry stare sheltered a million thoughts. I wanted to strip bare each one of them. "And now, if you'll excuse me, I am busy."

"You are excused. As soon as you thank me for making you look like such an expert to your date."

"I *am* an expert," I retorted.

Laughter echoed behind me as my feet carried me back to Charlotte. She stood as soon as I approached and smiled bashfully. Since I wasn't a man who curbed his desire or postponed things he wanted to address straightaway, I secured her face between my hands and took her mouth in a demanding kiss. When she gasped, I smiled.

"What was that about?" Although her censorious eyes chided me, I knew she wasn't asking me about the kiss.

"Your lips just begged to be kissed." As expected and desired, she blushed a beautiful rosy hue.

"I didn't mean that." She squirmed, flushed, and worried her lips. "What was the trouble about?"

"We are projecting a new type of engine. They were ruining the smaller parts."

"Explanation for dummies."

Charlotte giggled, and I nearly leaned in for another kiss. Her eyes fluttered to my mouth as if sensing my thoughts, but a hoarse cough that rather disguised a laugh stopped us both. When we turned around, Weston was watching us with something close to bewildered appraisal.

"Charlotte, please meet Weston Caldwell. Weston, this magnificent woman is Charlotte Burton, my girlfriend."

Had she not been so tightly pressed to my side and had I not been completely attuned to her, I might have missed the sudden alteration to her mood. She shivered, and a soft puff left her lips in a rush. Wide eyes, filled with surprise and excitement, stared up at me. The dreamy, high-strung expression that fell over her face prompted to mind the delectable image of Charlotte sprawled and complacent under my body.

"Pleased to meet you," Charlotte murmured, extending her hand while frowning softly.

Weston gave her a wide smile as he shook her hand, tracing her knuckles with his thumb. "The pleasure is entirely mine."

Gray-eyed, a thin blade of a nose, full sculpted lips, and nearly aristocratic countenance, he was a man easy to love, who had broken lots of hearts and crushed lots of dreams.

In an unveiled possessive gesture, I wrapped my arm around Charlotte's shoulders and pulled her closer to my side. Weston's mouth curved to the side, and he shook his head, coaxing a smile of my own. Despite the possessiveness I displayed, I knew that Weston was thoroughly taken.

"I heard that you liked the ranch. I hope you will visit us again."

"Oh...that Weston," Charlotte breathed, looking from me to Weston as complete understanding dawned on her. The blush that colored her cheeks was so natural-looking that it was already a part of her.

"Yes, that Weston. Am I famous already?"

"Nearly." Charlotte smiled a reserved, gracious smile that I instantly wanted to be only mine. "The ranch and the surroundings are marvelous. I do hope to visit again."

"Soon." I nodded when Charlotte looked up at me for approval. "How is Marina?"

At the mention of Marina's name, Charlotte stiffened. My arm skated from her shoulder, down to her hip. Slowly, but with undeniable firmness, my fingers coiled around the soft curve, catching her attention. We exchanged a meaningful glance. I thought I had clarified her doubts already.

"Still mad at me, of course. I might need some help with that."

"I'd rather not interfere where couple problems and angry women are involved."

"Maybe I was asking for Charlotte's help," Weston retorted, looking as if he truly wanted to stick his tongue out in a complete childish gesture. I chuckled.

"Listen to her. And bring her chocolates. There's nothing that chocolate can't cure."

It was the first part of her counsel that caught my attention. It was important to Charlotte to be listened to, to receive as much as she offered, to be met halfway. That was a lesson I should never forget.

"I'll take that into consideration." Weston scowled absently, his thoughts momentarily drifting someplace else. I thought of him, of Kai, of Brayden, and I shuddered with a sort of apprehension I had never felt before. In each man's life, there was a woman who could bring him to his knees, who made him want to go to his knees for her. "Although that would require het to talk to me first."

"I'm sure you'll find a way."

"I hope so."

We said our goodbyes shortly after. Weston returned to work, and we left the workroom in a much quieter state than when we arrived. Hand in hand and leaning into each other, I was leading Charlotte to the elevator when Karl Johns, my mechanic, jogged to us.

"Mr. King, Miss—" he saluted us then trailed off when his eyes landed on Charlotte.

"Karl, is there a problem?"

There was definitely going to be if he continued looking at Charlotte below chin level.

"No. Actually, I wanted to let you know *the beast* is ready to go."

"Very punctual, as usual. Thank you." I nodded in thanks and he nodded in acknowledgment then took his leave without further ado.

"The beast?" Charlotte asked as we fell into step again. The puckered brow and hardly suppressed disapproval written on her face betrayed that she already had the answer.

"My motorcycle. You didn't expect her to get out of our up close and personal meeting with the asphalt any better than I did, right?"

"I expected you not to get on it again this soon." She pouted with the perfect combination of childish pique and womanly charm. I couldn't help but bend and kiss the top of her head.

"The accident was staged. Nothing changed from the last time we rode together until now."

My thumb brushed across her knuckles, urging her to speak, but she continued walking somewhat stiffly while stubbornly looking ahead. Her worry flattered me.

"I can be good, Charlotte." It was a reassurance as much as it was a promise.

"Can you?"

She regarded me with a frustrated look on her face that deepened when I grinned. I loved that she was concerned about me as much as I hated to worry her.

"If you ask me—nicely."

She groaned, a primal sound coming from deep in her throat, and regaled me with a splendid glare. I bowed to take her mouth in a chaste kiss, and she opened like a flower, willing and sweet, even when she wasn't exactly pleased with the man caressing her.

"Can you ask me nicely?" I asked softly, against her parted lips. She breathed unevenly, and I swallowed her breath, absorbing her very essence in a gentle but indisputably claiming kiss.

"Please be careful, Marcus."

Even as I allowed her to read the answer in my eyes, I was afraid she could see too deep and too far past my own protective armor. I was afraid she already knew that there was nothing I wouldn't do if she asked.

When I was in, I was in. Just like her. And with Charlotte, I was completely, irrefutably, and helplessly in.

My phone vibrated in the pocket of my jeans, and the spell was momentarily broken. I straightened, and so did Charlotte, running a hand through her hair, although her brown mane was in perfect order.

"Kai?" I answered, but my eyes were stuck on Charlotte.

The call was short and to the point. After days of atypical silence, Kai finally sounded like himself.

"If you are busy—" Charlotte trailed off hesitantly after I placed the phone back in my pocket.

"No. I promised Kai I'd pick some parts for his motorcycle and drop them by, but that can wait."

In the middle of the hallway, unmindful of who could see us, I took her in my arms and sealed my mouth over hers again, swallowing her stunned intake of breath and stilling her protesting hands. Before I was done kissing her properly, my body caged her against the wall.

"I seem to get so little of your time. Do you think I will trade it for anything else?"

"We'll make more time," she panted, leaning her head against the wall for support.

"I'm afraid it will still not be enough."

This time, when I sought her mouth, she didn't offer any form of resistance. She kissed me as much as she let herself be kissed. Her hands dipped beneath my jacket, molded on my hips, then crawled up my torso until they settled flat on my chest. Charlotte pulled herself to me with a gentleness that appeased the fiery need growing inside me. Instantly, my arms folded tighter around her.

"Can I help?" she asked tentatively. When my eyebrows arched, she clarified. "With your cousin."

"You're willing to pay him a visit." I wasn't sure whether it was a question or a statement. Doubt echoed even in the resulting silence.

"Little by little, remember?"

"You're soon going to fall for Kai's charms. I don't take kindly to jealousy." It was a joke, but not entirely.

"Don't be ridiculous."

Rolling her eyes and slapping at my chest, Charlotte laughed and sidestepped me. I caught her by the waist in a steely grasp before she took her second step and rapaciously pressed my mouth to her ear.

"I mean it."

I led Charlotte to a room on the second floor where I had stored the motorcycle parts I had created for Kai and put them in a big box, then we returned to the car in companionable silence and hit the road just as the sun was going down over the horizon.

"So I am your girlfriend. Does that make you my boyfriend?"

There was a complete discrepancy between the amused twinkle in Charlotte's eyes and the nervous way she kept kneading her hands while she threw me expectant glances.

"*Girlfriend* is too much of an understatement of what you are to me, Charlotte. But yes, I am yours and you are mine. Which reminds me of a discussion I wanted to have with you."

"Yes?" She seemed breathless, which pleased the animal lurking within me.

"I am a very possessive man, sometimes irrationally so. I mess up a lot and act on a whim. I am flawed beyond repair, but despite all my failings, I am loyal to a fault. I cannot tolerate anything less than complete exclusiveness. This is the only thing I am not willing to negotiate."

"I never considered anything else."

"Good," I nearly growled.

Stopping at a traffic light, I unfastened my seatbelt and leaned so close to Charlotte that I almost straddled her. I watched her raptly, with unleashed wildness before my mouth descended upon her and muffled the guttural whimper erupting from her throat.

A loud honk had me dropping back in my seat with a soft chuckle. I fastened my seatbelt and stepped firmly on the gas. Charlotte glanced back, mortification etched on her face. She was a full-grown woman, with a charisma that at times she was utterly unaware of, and yet, she could portray perfectly a young girl embarrassed at having been caught sharing her first kiss.

"Can you negotiate behavior?"

Her gracious fingers wrapped around her throat as if she wanted to tame the fire burning from within. The scolding glance she gave me lost its authority when confronted with the patent arousal I could smell in the air. I affected her just as badly as she affected me, and the notion alleviated a deep aching need I hadn't known existed.

"Behave, for God's sake."

"I can negotiate. But I won't be the one losing."

I smirked deviously, provoking her even as I provoked myself. Charlotte rolled her eyes and shook her head. She faced away from me, yet the smile that tugged at the corners of her lips didn't remain concealed.

It was late in the evening when I parked in front of Kai's workshop. When he didn't make a mess out of his apartment, he deigned to use the actual allotted space for his creative craze.

I climbed out of the car, collected the box I had stored in the trunk, then helped Charlotte out, linking our hands together as we treaded forward.

"I don't want you to ever be afraid, Charlotte," I whispered against her ear before we walked inside, and the pungent smell of solvent assaulted our nostrils. The reek was almost suffocating which made me wonder how Kai survived it.

"Finally, you arrive. I've been hot and ready for you all day, baby." Kai droned on without turning, clearly mistaking our arrival for someone else's. I dropped the box I was holding, causing an intentional too loud noise, then wrapped both my arms around Charlotte, pulling her in front of my body.

"If you would so kindly spare us the horrid details."

Kai whirled around, knocking to the ground a jar filled with orange goo and almost dropping the thick brush he was holding. His surprised expression morphed into a glare then returned to confusion as his eyes settled on Charlotte.

"Oh, *mon Dieu*, I startled you," I mocked him, earning a satisfyingly deep glare. To his growing frustration, even Charlotte giggled softly.

"Miss Burton, my beloved, idiotic cousin," he welcomed us then returned to his painting in that typical absent-minded way of his.

"Call me Charlotte."

Kai, wide-eyed and stunned, turned to study her, yet her reply did not amaze me. Although she didn't quite know it yet, she had already started liking Kai. He possessed a covert charm that made you like him even when you wanted to hate him the most.

"Charlotte," he said as if he weighed the word, then a nearly imperceptible guilty frown distorted his features. "It's a pleasure you are here."

"Thank you."

"Although it would have been a greater pleasure if somebody else visited you. Who are you waiting for?" His mood was definitely lighter compared to the past days.

"That's none of your business."

Kai glared, and I frowned back, while Charlotte ignored us and examined the workshop. The place was simple and a total mess as was the apartment where Kai lived, worked, and fornicated.

His easel was placed in the middle of the room, under a bright spotlight facing a tall platform covered in white satin sheets. The walls were lined with paintings in all forms and sizes, which Kai kept religiously covered. Few people had, in fact, the honor of seeing his canvas before an organized exhibition. Kai was all about planning things, and nothing happened before he thought it proper to do so.

"Do you exhibit?" Charlotte asked, deploying the same polite voice she reserved for subordinates and strangers. If she had yet to feel comfortable around Kai, there was a long way until she would feel anything else than tense around Brayden and Bryson, but she was daring enough to try.

"Yes." Kai turned once more to face us, gazing at Charlotte with the same dumbfounded look in his eyes. "But I am very possessive of my paintings. I have only the time before an exhibition to keep the paintings only to myself, then they will be exposed for everybody to see."

"I think I can understand that."

"Rarely somebody does," Kai laughed, coaxing Charlotte to laugh too, and in the end, I joined them.

My grin, however, disappeared altogether when the shrill, unpleasant voice of a woman caught us by surprise. Joleen Stone, also known as The Fox, waltzed inside Kai's workshop as if she owned the place.

With blood-red tipped blonde hair, pale skin, and light amber eyes that sometimes glowed yellow, Joleen looked surreal. The perfectly proportioned red lips, small nose, and high cheekbones gave her a beautiful appearance that was complemented by her willowy figure, which at times made her look vulnerable. Yet, I knew better. Joleen was anything but helpless. She was sly and treacherous.

"Baby," Kai greeted her with a stupid grin that I recognized and had lately seen in the mirror—the same smile that Charlotte put on my face.

"Marcus, it's such a delight," she purred after thoroughly kissing a more than eager Kai.

I held on to Charlotte. Her warmth and presence carried me to a peaceful place that settled raging violence and unwise impulses.

"I wish I could say the same."

She met my critical scowl with an insolent smile that spread on her whole face.

She was a fox. She was a cold, calculated woman, who pursued her personal interests and walked away when the going got though.

She was everything that Kai did not need. But as she leaned into him and they kissed again, he looked as if she was everything he wanted.

Chapter 22

Charlotte

The week never progressed well when it started with a thorough fight with James Burton. From behind his desk, my father watched me through narrowed eyes. His mouth was set in a displeased line, and his chin was lifted so that he looked down at me even though he was sitting.

"I cannot represent someone I don't believe in."

I was pacing back and forth with my hands held tautly by my side, while my father's disposition was perfectly controlled and even. The contrast rendered me nearly hysterical.

"Lawyers don't ask their clients if they are innocent, and they don't care. They do their job. So, do yours, Charlotte."

"Numerous other lawyers can represent Jack Stewart, Father. It doesn't have to necessarily be me. In fact, we both know that Isaac King would be a better fit than I am."

Isaac King was a beast on the loose when he set his mind on achieving a goal. I considered his own son's case, and a wave of anger and revulsion washed over me.

He was an ambitious man, who cared more about winning than ethics. As long as he won the case and was rewarded with praise, he wouldn't care whether or not his client had actually been innocent. I, on the other hand, did care.

"He might be a better fit than you, but it is not a case he needs," my father responded calmly. He rested his chin on his linked hands, watching me with the sort of steady stare that told me I was testing his patience. "You, however, could benefit from the insane coverage this case has. If Jack Stewart is cleared of all charges, you will be part of the winning team. You will build a reputation, Charlotte. If you weren't so stubborn and set on defying me, you would see that for yourself."

"If, Father, if…"

I remembered Jack's washed-out eyes, and a chill ran down my spine. The tingle of dislike had gotten under my skin from the very first moment I met him, so maybe I was irrational. Maybe I was not objective.

No matter how hard I tried to convince myself of his innocence, my gut screamed a different theory. Even in submission, Jake Stewart had looked like a dangerous man—a man who couldn't be completely innocent.

"Let me rephrase, then. *When*. With such an army of lawyers to back him up, there is no chance that Jake Stewart will be convicted."

"And isn't that a little too conspicuous? Why would a man who claims to be innocent need three renowned law firms to back him up?"

I raised my arms in frustration, feeling a deep exhaustion settle in my bones. The fact that I had been working the entire weekend and hardly managed to see Marcus had me even more restless and irritable.

My father fixed me with a stern glare, exasperation slipping past his otherwise calm mask.

"It has nothing to do with innocence or guilt. He is the son of a powerful man, who has his fair share of enemies. There is no better way to get to a man and diminish his strength than through his children. Somebody is trying to sabotage Mayor Stewart. You should focus on that."

That was indeed one of the theories that Jack's team had

presented and was trying to develop. The argument might have been valid, but not to me. And it was a theory that couldn't be backed up, so it wasn't going to stand up in court. My father knew that, and the fact that he was urging me to pursue a dead end angered me as much as his dismissive approach.

"Why don't *you* take up the case?" I seethed and bit my bottom lip to keep from saying more. "You control every move and every decision I make. I'm not in charge. You are, so you could very well take charge officially."

James Burton rose to his full height, fastened the second button of his suit jacket, and rounded the desk with menacing grace. I swallowed nervously, and somewhere in the back of my mind, I noted how I put several feet of space between us when he approached me. In his repeated efforts to train me to become the perfect daughter, he had become a stranger.

"Better tell me what happened in Washington and what your strategy is," he demanded, leaning against the edge of his desk with arms crossed over his chest. I let out an uneven, frustrated breath and steeled myself.

"Since, apparently, I haven't managed to convince you to let me drop the case, any communication between my client and me is privileged. So if you'll excuse me..." I turned to leave, determined to storm out when his low, warning voice halted me.

"Tread carefully, Charlotte. You wouldn't want to make enemies this early in your career." Both a concerned counsel and ominous warning, Mr. Burton's words were always a double-edged sword. Only the fleeting emotion that sparked in his eyes told me it was my father speaking and not my boss. "Just do your job and defend the man. It will soon be over."

The inevitable end he was talking about eluded me. When I reached for the door handle, the door opened wide, and Isaac King filled the space with authoritative superiority akin to that of his business partner. I sidestepped him as soon as possible, not missing the insulted glance he gave me. I predicted another discussion with him about Marcus, and today was the worst day to have it.

I made a beeline for the elevator and stabbed tetchily at the button until the doors slid open. Since few people had access to the top floor, the car was empty. As soon as the doors closed, I leaned against the wall, covering my face with my hands.

When the car stopped on my floor and the doors opened with a ding, I walked out with an ill-tempered mood that had the large group of people waiting for the elevator splitting and hastily making way for me to pass.

I marched past the reception area, ignoring Sofia when she stood to report the latest critical news. She took a step toward me then stopped abruptly when she correctly gauged my mood.

I almost smiled, but then all air left my lungs. In front of the interns' office, Marcus was talking with an average-looking man I had never seen in my life, but that was not the reason my blood heated.

Dressed in a slate gray two-piece-suit, impeccable white dress shirt, and a dark blue tie that matched his eyes, Marcus observed me with ravenous intensity. Leaning against the doorframe, with a hand shoved casually in his pants pocket, his eyes glimmered with amusement and a covetousness that was both inappropriate and dangerous to display within this building.

He nodded absently to the man, his eyes never leaving me as the stranger scurried away and I walked to him. With every step I took, my heart thumped faster, and my blood grew hotter. A fine tingle revived my senses and made me acutely aware of Marcus's lethal masculinity.

"What are you doing?" I hissed as I got in his face.

My bravado, however, was a flimsy façade wrapped around the violent burst of excitement pounding at the walls of my resistance. He could see right through me. He could see how the sight of him affected me, and with a smirk, he stepped closer, exploiting my weakness shamelessly.

"Mm...Working."

Amusement danced in his eyes. His muscles hardened under his jacket, which made the sight of him in a suit absolutely jaw-dropping. His rough, desire-laced voice enveloped me. I nearly sighed.

"What are you doing dressed like this?" I snapped and bypassed him.

"Proving that I own more than black clothes. Do you like it?"

A part of me enjoyed his playfulness and unmerciful teasing, but the more substantial part of me was worried at the thought of having Isaac King discover that his son and I shared more than just a professional relationship. The only way I could be his handler and thus protect him from his father's influence was to keep the nature of our relationship hidden. I censored him with a stern look, and part of his amusement faded.

"Miss Burton, if you could verify the data I have just attached to the Williams file." The shrill voice that quickly materialized in Victoria Brown's grating figure startled and released me from Marcus's spell. "I think Sofia has already informed you—"

"I am not here for your personal benefit, Miss Brown, nor inclined to carry out your duties," I snapped and walked away stiffly, hearing her high-pitched whisper even as I left her behind.

"Oh, she is particularly bitchy today," she muttered resentfully. Marcus didn't say a thing.

Once in my office and far from prying eyes, I sat at my desk and rested my head against my folded arms, concentrating on taking deep calming breaths. I experienced a sudden urge to cry. The negative energy pulsing in me was going to give me a headache soon, and I needed to find a way to eliminate the tension. Before long, the distinct sound of the door opening got my attention.

Marcus strolled inside as if he owned the place. He looked elegant and yet profoundly savage. Our stares locked and the air sizzled. The lustful glint in his eyes and the purposeful quality of his stride as he approached me betrayed a ravenous eroticism that had me panting and softening for him before he even touched me.

I stood and hid behind my chair. If he touched me, I wasn't going to be able to resist him.

"Not here, Marcus. I thought we settled this." My voice was so weak that it almost sounded pleading. Yet it begged for something entirely different than what my words had conveyed. Was it so absurd to miss him?

"Come here, Charlotte."

He opened his arms and waited in front of my desk. I literally shook with the need to surrender in his arms, and eventually, I did exactly that. I circled the desk, and in three long strides, I collided with his chest, sobbing with relief. He wrapped his arms around my shoulders, holding me tightly, and I caught him by the waist, pulling him closer. The proximity and unrestrained intimacy soothed my raging nerves.

Tears leaked from the corners of my eyes, and I couldn't stop them. When my cheeks felt seriously wet, part of my bad mood morphed into much-needed tranquility. Or was that the effect of being in Marcus's arms? Despite his wild, rebellious nature, he settled me.

"What happened, sugar? Tell me." He kissed the top of my head and gently stroked my hair. I only held him tighter.

"I don't seem to see eye to eye with my father."

"About Jake Stewart's case?"

"Yes. How did you know?" I pushed away just enough so I could look up at him.

Observing me with undivided concentration, Marcus wiped the stray tears on my cheeks with his calloused thumbs but did not comment on my weak outburst. If anything, his eyes were filled with silent approval. I had needed to shed those tears, and he seemed to understand that.

"I don't think you have any other case on your plate at the moment that consumes you like this."

I nodded and placed my head back on his chest. His heartbeat was a steady musical refrain that lulled the brewing storm inside me to a quiet, pleasant breeze. Forgetting where I was and why I shouldn't do what I was about to do, I lifted my hand to Marcus's lips then twisted my fingers in his hair and pulled him to me.

"Not here, Charlotte. I thought we settled this." Famished blue eyes looked down at me with delight.

"Don't mock me." I smacked his shoulder, earning a full laugh that I quickly joined with low chuckles of my own.

Marcus bent to kiss me, his large hands securing my face for his relentless plundering of my lips. I was breathless, but I needed more. I felt exhausted, yet he reinvigorated me. His hands traveled up and down my torso, occasionally fisting in my clothes and gripping my hips to outline his own unstoppable desire.

"Next time you go to D.C., I am coming with you. It is not a request."

He rested his forehead against mine, and his eyes burned through me, not accepting objection.

It was too soon. It was too much, but Marcus tossed me into a whirlwind of emotions that couldn't be slowed or stopped.

"And he already has boyfriend demands."

"Call it what you want."

As if he knew how his touch calmed me, Marcus never stopped stroking my skin. For what felt like endless minutes, we just stood there, feeling each other and making up for the weekend we had spent apart. Now and again, my eyes roamed his appetizing body, and each time, the sight of him made me inhale deeply and forget how to exhale.

"I dressed up for you, and you didn't even say if you liked it or not."

He took a step back, offering me a better view of himself, and faked a look of hurt disappointment that had me giggling. Marcus pouting was a sight to behold.

"You did it to taunt me," I accused.

"I did not dress like this to taunt you," he retorted, but the air was suddenly charged.

"Then why?"

"I wanted to show you that from time to time I can conform. For the right person."

"It suits you. Very much."

I gave him a once-over and found myself thinking how I wanted to grab him by his tie and ruffle his flawless exterior.

"How am I taunting you, sweet Charlotte?"

I swallowed, suddenly overwhelmed by the fervency he projected. Taking a deep breath and licking my lips, I filled my nostrils with his scent.

"You know exactly how."

I was unable to look into his eyes anymore. The eye contact was as powerful and arousing as his touch.

"I want you to tell me."

Without warning, every trace of the playful, easygoing Marcus vanished. In his stead stood six feet and two inches of severely alert alpha male. Untamed blue eyes and a hoarse voice assaulted me with passion and made me tremble in anticipation.

"You make me think of the undomesticated man beneath the sophisticated clothes. You make me itch for your touch while you wear this suit. You make me feel highly inappropriate under the circumstances."

I looked around us to emphasize my words, but Marcus was not affected by the unsuitableness of our surroundings. He pressed his body against mine so there was not a single inch of us that did not touch. Being this close, I had to tilt my head back to see him. The hunger I saw was more than desire, more than what I was accustomed to.

"I did come only to hold you, but that is never enough with you. It's *you* who are taunting me."

His eyes burned as he bent and caught me by the knees. I was in his arms and on my desk before I could properly measure his intentions. Pencils and books fell to the ground. Even Newton's cradle which I always played with when I was bored or edgy tumbled down, but neither of us stopped. Marcus's mouth was on mine, moving with harsh fervor. His body pinned me down, alerting me of the uninhibited male possessing me.

"God, Marcus," I sobbed, throwing my head back, allowing him to nip and lick at the sensitive skin of my throat.

I reached for his tie, but his hand caught my wrist and pressed it to the cold surface of the desk. His amused yet warning smile had me writhing and groaning in protest. When he overwhelmed my senses so thoroughly and induced a haze that took over me, it was difficult to remember that we had appearances to keep up.

"I don't like missing someone," Marcus spoke against the skin of my breasts, which he had just exposed, making my body tingle all over. "And I missed you all weekend, Charlotte. I need you. I need to hold you when I sleep. I need to make love to you before I do."

"It's too soon—to feel like this."

I realized I had spoken out loud when he lifted his head. His face was inscrutable, then he nodded in agreement. It was too soon, yet neither of us knew how to slow down. Neither of us wanted to.

Keeping his eyes locked on mine, knowing how deeply the connection affected me, Marcus lowered his head once more and licked between my breasts, making me shiver.

Nobody had ever made me stop thinking the way Marcus did. When the phone on my desk rang, the piercing chime startled me so aggressively that I arched off the desk, sending Marcus a few feet backward. The momentary distance didn't dampen down the electrical desire surging through us but merely diverted the animal beneath the polished exterior.

"Yes?" I picked up with trembling hands, hardly schooling my voice into a calm tone.

Eyes twinkling and mouth parted to allow a wicked tongue to dart out over enticing lips, Marcus closed the space between us and came at me again, ignoring completely the fact that I was talking on the phone.

"Stop," I mouthed horrified as Sofia announced my twelve o'clock appointment.

He pressed wet lips to the spot where my pulse beat frantically and suckled until I nearly moaned. When Sofia finished talking, I shoved the handset in its cradle unceremoniously and fisted my hands in Marcus's hair for a deep, blood-stirring kiss that was going to galvanize me for the remainder of the day.

Reluctantly pushing him away, I hopped off the desk and hastily tried to tidy up my shirt and pencil skirt. It was a challenging task since Marcus's hands never left my body and never ceased tantalizing me.

"Spend the night with me, Charlotte. I'll be on my best behavior. I promise."

His sexily rasping voice altered into a jesting tone. I couldn't imagine Marcus King behaving behind closed doors when he had trouble doing so in such an inappropriate place as his handler's office.

"Go, Marcus, please."

I bent to retrieve the items that had fallen earlier then straightened my outfit again. He had yet to move. My eyes repeated with alarm what I had just told him.

"I'll be waiting."

He cupped my face and watched me almost imploringly. He didn't need to. I missed and needed him just as badly.

"I'll bring dinner," I consented while staring anxiously behind his shoulder at the still locked door.

A brief, chaste kiss was our silent goodbye before Marcus finally obeyed and turned to leave, looking fresh and immaculate, while I was still stunned and flustered. Taking a nice, long view of his back, I returned to my seat then called his name. If I was this provoked and needy, he might as well be.

"Marcus?"

"Yes, Miss Burton?"

"I don't want you to be on your best behavior."

His pupils dilated, and his jaw tensed, rolling back and forth. I winked at him, pleased to witness the fire that erupted in his gaze, knowing I was the cause of the flames that seared him.

The day dragged on dully, and there was so much work to be done that I rarely left my office and only when it was unavoidable. I honored two more appointments and held a two-hour long video conference with Jack Stewart's legal team that drained me more than a whole week of work.

By the time four o'clock rolled around, I became aware that Ms. Victoria Brown hadn't completed and provided me the Williams brief I had been requesting since Friday evening. Despite my best efforts to maintain an impartial attitude toward her, the insubordination she displayed so defiantly urged me otherwise.

The argument, whose topic I was altogether disinterested in, ceased as soon as I walked inside the interns' office. Marcus looked up and locked eyes with me before I could glance away.

"Miss Brown, I would have appreciated it if you had finished the brief I requested and delivered it to me."

She flashed a cheeky smile before she disciplined her expression into a forcedly polite mask. Immediately, she stood and began rummaging through the pile of papers on her desk but didn't seem to produce anything helpful.

Impatiently, I tapped my foot against the marble floor, engendering an irritating thumping sound that was only muted by

Ms. Brown's increasingly anxious digging.

Fabricating undertakings such as ordering the pens in their holder and moving items from one side to another, Marcus rounded the desk and stopped only when he was almost close enough to be touched. His eyes drifted to his colleague, and amusement flared up the ocean blue of his eyes.

"It was here. I left it here—" Victoria Brown muttered crossly, under the watchful and slightly appalled eyes of her coworkers.

My eyes, though, were fixed on Marcus. It suddenly struck me that he looked much too pleased to not be involved in the mysterious disappearance of the Williams file from Ms. Brown's well-guarded desk.

"What have you done? We need that folder," I hissed under my breath. His smile never faltered.

"She needs to work more and talk less. The folder is already in your office."

"Oh."

I had to look down to hide my own growing beam when I understood that he had, in fact, reacted to Victoria Brown's earlier disrespectful words even if he hadn't done it verbally. I might have been somewhat petty, but the knowledge brought me a silly form of satisfaction.

"I'm sabotaging her not you."

I folded my arms over my chest and decided to play the game he had initiated. Noting my irritation, although it was pretty much faked now, Phillip Foster stood dutifully to help Victoria. A curt flick of my wrist stopped him cold in midstride.

"Return to your work, Mr. Foster. If Ms. Brown is not capable of carrying out a simple task, then maybe I should reconsider her position. I want that file first thing in the morning."

I strode out decisively, shaking my head in what should have looked like a disapproving gesture, when in fact, I couldn't believe Marcus's schemes. I smiled widely, the idea of making Victoria Brown's life difficult not troubling me in the least. I was definitely petty.

As promised, the file was indeed on my desk. Marcus must have dropped it by on one of the rare occasions I had left my office. His thoughtfulness, although severely malicious, kept me warm and gratified for what remained of my workday. When I grabbed my purse and almost left the office, consumed by a sweltering eagerness to get to Marcus, the phone rang loudly.

"Charlotte Burton's office. How can I help you?" I answered, knowing that Sofia had already left, and the call was automatically directed to me. There was silence at the other end of the line except a subdued panting. "Hello?" I tried again but to no avail.

The soft, slightly fearful noises the person emitted made me believe it was a woman. I was about to ask who she was looking for when the call ended. I looked dubiously at the phone but shrugged off the occurrence before I even left the building.

My office received calls from abused women rather frequently since every paper in the city had written about my pro bono program. Being able to defend those who couldn't defend themselves was the benefit and at times the best part of being a lawyer. Sofia must have dealt with these types of situations all the time without my knowing.

AFTER I WENT HOME TO TAKE a shower and change my work outfit in something that was both comfortable and sexy, I headed for my favorite Japanese restaurant to get dinner just as I had promised.

It was getting seriously dark when I neared Marcus's apartment building. Absently, I recognized that this was the first time I walked somewhere on foot since that Friday night.

A shiver chilled me. From the parking lot, raucous laughter echoed, making me stagger in midstride, before I recognized the voice that responded just as loudly. *Marcus.* Although I couldn't see him, nor whoever was accompanying him, the more I concentrated, the easier it became to follow where his voice and the endless laughter led.

"Dude, you should have seen her. She was completely wasted, and she proposed to him. I wasn't sure whether he wanted to disappear off the face of the earth or kill her first. He eventually said yes only to get rid of her and hoping that she was drunk enough to not remember the next day."

"But of course, she did," Marcus laughed. Although I could see his cousin, Kai, leaning against a foreign car, his hands propped against the hood and his legs crossed at the ankles, there seemed to be no evidence of Marcus's presence save for his voice.

"Exactly."

"Good evening, gentlemen."

When I stopped in their shadows, I got a beautiful view of both Kai and Marcus. While Kai was leisurely watching his cousin, Marcus was sprawled under the massive frame of a black and red motorcycle, his hands working quickly and efficiently even while his eyes found me, and he gifted me with a grin.

Lying there on the ground, with a head flashlight on his forehead and greasy smears on his face, Marcus looked so coarsely beautiful that my heart skipped a beat and my throat instantly went dry.

"Hi, Charlotte," Kai greeted me with a genuine smile.

He seemed a different man. His intense stare analyzed me from head to toe, and I looked away awkwardly. Kai had the same penetrating gaze as his cousin although it didn't affect me the way Marcus's did.

"On foot?" Marcus slid from beneath the parked motorcycle and effortlessly rose to his feet.

He approached me with burning eyes and calculated movements. His features were arranged in a guise somewhere between suspicion and concern.

"A woman has to stay fit," I replied, looking away, embarrassed at the feeling of being scolded.

"You shouldn't walk on foot at night if you can help it."

Laughter left Kai as remorse returned. He clenched his jaw, shoved a hand through his hair, and eventually looked down to his feet. I understood then, as his exaggerated repentance hit me, that I might have never been resentful of him.

Placing a hand on his shoulder, I smiled reassuringly when his eyes went wide, and his jaw dropped. I hoped the friendly gesture was enough to appease his guilt.

"Getting ready for something?" I asked both men, nodding

toward the two-wheeled vehicle now behind us.

"Kai is racing Friday night," Marcus answered simply as if it were the most natural thing to do for a man their age.

"Dude." Kai's head snapped up, an admonishing glare screwing his features into a scandalized expression. I had to bite the inside of my cheek to keep from laughing. "Do you want her to have me arrested? I'm not sure she—you know, forgave me."

"I won't have you arrested. And yes, I forgave you."

"I trust her, Kai."

Between the ridiculously joyful smile that Kai gifted me with and Marcus's unshakeable reply, I felt my knees become too weak to sustain my own weight. Marcus was right behind me before I consciously decided to lean into him as if he had read my emotions; as if he could feel me. He brushed his lips against my hair and curled his arm around my waist, draping me across his chest like I was an extension of his body.

We settled into a pleasant conversation about Japanese food, martial arts, and favorite pastimes. It came completely out of nowhere when Marcus pressed his mouth to my ear and whispered huskily, "I don't want to be on my best behavior, either."

To his sheer amusement, I blushed a deep red, which Kai politely ignored. I suspected that was because he didn't want to upset me so soon after I admitted that I had forgiven him for the Friday night incident.

I looked up at Marcus and took in a deep breath that once again I forgot to let out. I believed him.

Kai took his leave soon after, perhaps recognizing from experience the signs of arousal that were painfully evident in both his cousin and me. Marcus wrapped his clean hand around mine and led me in charged silence from the parking lot to the lobby of his apartment building and finally to the elevator.

"Are you going to race too?" I didn't want to be the woman who forbade him doing the things he loved, yet I didn't want to be the woman who waited home terrified, not knowing if or how her man would come back to her.

"No."

He caged me between the elevator wall and his rock hard body, placing both hands on either side of my head. There was no escape from him or his indiscreet eyes. His body wasn't making love to me yet, but his eyes already were.

"Good," I panted. I was pretty sure I had wanted to add something else, but that mischievous mouth hovering over mine was too distracting to be able to concentrate.

"There's fun in the races too."

"I can imagine." Under his scolding stare, I laughed sarcastically.

"Let me show you."

Then his mouth was showing me—a passion that set me on fire.

Chapter 23

Marcus

"Marcus, they will lynch me. I am a lawyer among—"

"Among rascals?"

"I didn't mean to say that."

"Yes, you did. And you'd be right. Mostly." I let out a laugh that contrasted with Charlotte's strained frame of mind. "Besides, nobody knows you are a lawyer. Relax."

"Your friends do."

The thought of Brayden and Bryson, but especially of the former, still caused her hair to stand on end. She masked her emotions well, still not well enough for me not to read them.

"My friends will never endanger you again."

The angry quality of my voice startled her. It was gentleness, however, that mollified Charlotte. My fingers gripped her knee in a calming caress, and my lips brushed against hers just enough to have her wishing for more.

"Relax." I parked the Jaguar reasonably close to the meeting spot and turned to face Charlotte. "You are with me. I wouldn't take you to a place if I knew you could be in danger."

"I know that."

She sighed and sneaked her hands underneath mine, craving my warmth and the physical contact. It wasn't fear for her safety she felt. "Then what is the problem?" I asked although I knew the answer. I brushed the hair out of her face and casually fisted my fingers behind her head.

"I guess I don't want you to realize that I don't fit."

"You fit with me. That is enough."

We walked hand in hand to a place I knew by heart, crammed with people that Charlotte might have never socialized with under different circumstances. I was still dazed that she had eventually agreed to join me at the race although she seemed prematurely convinced that she would hate every moment of the night. She had been convinced to give it a try when I had promised I wouldn't be racing myself, but I suspected her concession was her way of pleasing me. And she succeeded.

I spotted Bryson first, then Brayden. Sending each of them warning glares, I directed Charlotte forward, right into the middle of the crowd. She glanced around, absorbing the symphony of shades and sounds and the amalgam of faces. No trace of judgment animated her features, and the ease with which she blended in humbled me. Because she was doing it for me.

"Do you normally hang around with these people?"

"There are a few I see outside racing nights, but they are mostly Kai's friends."

Thick, white smoke curled in the air. Biting noises penetrated our ears. The chaos of the races had been my natural habitat, but now something felt amiss. Charlotte had taught me to go slow. While I had always moved through life like a bullet, she had made me crave the deliberateness of enjoying each little instant. Of enjoying her.

I knew the exact moment when Charlotte caught sight of Brayden. She stiffened, missed a step, and turned from curious to increasingly agitated in a blink of an eye. My right arm banded around her waist in an iron grip.

Pulling her into my side, I buried my face in her hair to calm us both. I was still debating whether I should properly mop up the floors with Brayden.

"Can I suggest something, Miss Burton?" I hoped teasing would take her mind off her memories, and she would go back to relaxing and enjoying herself.

"What is that, Mr. King?"

"Just kick the idiot in the gut." I pointed to Brayden, earning his immediate glower, which I dismissed nonchalantly. "I promise to hold him still for you."

"How do you know I can't kick him all by myself?"

She regaled me with a smile that didn't reach her eyes, but I appreciated the effort, then she was the one to pull us into motion again. Kai came our way and wrapped me in an uncharacteristically warm hug, then he awkwardly embraced Charlotte, making me seriously wonder whether he was already drunk. His evident happiness pleased me, though, no matter its source. I only hoped it would last.

"I'd tell you to set your bet, but I don't think that is something you'd like to do," Kai told Charlotte with a shy hesitance that women loved.

"I might not approve of what is happening here, but let's say that tonight I forget about right and wrong, and I'll root for you to win."

"Oh, my... Thank you."

Charlotte was definitely falling for the scoundrel's charms.

My own smile dispersed a shade when Brayden passed by us, glaring and all but spitting our way. Gratuitous rage and dim-witted arrogance rolled off him in poignant waves. He was off with an earsplitting roar of his engine.

Bryson, on the other hand, still lurked around. He neither took off in Brayden's drama queen fashion nor dared to come too close. He didn't ask for forgiveness obsessively like Kai had, and I doubted he ever would, but he had the grace to frown upon his little brother's stupid and misplaced arrogance.

I nodded my salute to him, and he nodded back, his eyes settling questioningly on Charlotte. There was one simple thing they had to grasp. They were going to respect her.

"Of course, you can root for him, but it won't be him who wins." Joleen Stone, dressed in a red leather race suit, tiptoed her way to us and leisurely rested her elbow on Kai's shoulder. "We were never properly introduced. I'm Joleen."

"Charlotte."

She shook Joleen's hand, throwing me a questioning glance. We hadn't discussed Joleen or my dislike of her after the encounter at Kai's workshop, yet Charlotte was smart enough to notice my displeasure.

"You want to bet on that?" Kai sneered at Joleen. His voice was defensive bordering on aggression. His eyes, though, were undressing her in a million different ways. I felt nauseous.

"Darling, I bet when the odds are even. I don't want to slaughter your dreams." Joleen smacked a kiss on Kai's waiting mouth, then she returned her attention to Charlotte, making me glower. "Can I show you around, Charlotte?"

"She is with me. I'll show her around."

"When Caveman King relents, join me for a girl talk."

Joleen made her retreat stealthily and cunningly like a fox, shooting a luring smile Kai's way. Her red suit stood out even in the midst of the gathering crowd. I wasn't going to change my mind though. I didn't like her company for Kai, let alone for Charlotte.

I stroked Charlotte's cheek and felt warmth spreading inside me when she gifted me with a grin. If she thought I was a caveman, she didn't seem too bothered by the idea. Not yet, at least.

"That was uncalled-for," Kai grumbled.

"Kai," I warned with a glare fixed on Joleen's back.

"I trust her, Marcus."

Faced with my own words, I remained speechless. Consciously, I knew that Joleen wasn't necessarily an evil woman. What I didn't trust about her was her ability to take care of Kai's heart.

"He has a point," Charlotte whispered, yet both Kai and I heard her clearly.

With a smile and a wink, Kai returned to his motorcycle. Suddenly, he was lethally focused and savagely determined.

"Aren't you going to show me around?"

I didn't tell her that Kai and maybe even Joleen were the most suitable to show her the ins and outs of the races. While I introduced her to the people who were worth knowing and explained a few technicalities about motorcycles, speed, and racing rules, I reached the understanding that I was almost as much of an outsider as Charlotte. I had only come to the races the same way somebody went to the pool for a swim. While I had always been in transit, there were others who had built a lifestyle here.

A few women approached me boldly, although they probably didn't even know my name. I was mildly surprised to catch Charlotte glaring coldly at a petite blonde ogling me shamelessly. My hand twisted in her hair to dip her head back. Before I kissed the living daylights out of her, I watched her proudly, hotly. I enjoyed owning a woman as much as I enjoyed being owned.

"The things you do to me..." I whispered against her glistening lips. "The things I want to do to *you*."

I heard the air wheezing through her teeth as she inhaled and felt the temperature of her body rising.

"Are you a thing now?"

This time, her sharp intake of breath was not caused by my wicked promises but by Bryson's hostile voice.

"Yes, we are."

My fingers tightened around Charlotte's hand, but my eyes never left Bryson. I saw when acceptance settled in his gaze, and his opinion of Charlotte changed. He knew me well enough to realize that if forced, I would always choose the woman by my side.

"I hope we can start fresh," he told Charlotte, but endless pride prevented him from doing anything more.

"I hope," Charlotte answered warily. She didn't mask her displeased expression.

The music started then, so loud that it was obnoxious. Bryson headed for his motorcycle and straddled it smugly.

Tires screeched on the pavement, a useless display of brutality and wildness, yet a component that fused perfectly with everything else about the illicit circumstance. I pulled Charlotte into me, intentionally startling her out of her controlled calm. When I pressed my mouth to her ear, I felt her moan rather than heard it.

"Here comes the fun part." For someone who condemned such illegal affairs, she was looking around quite enthusiastically. "Careful, sugar. You look like you're enjoying yourself."

"I'm enjoying *you*."

"Are you sure you want to provoke me, Charlotte?"

I gripped her hips and pulled her against my front so tightly that there was no escape. Against my hard, awakened body, she squirmed. I pulled her hair back and buried my head in her throat, smelling her deeply, until she was etched in my very lungs. I kissed her throat and suckled on the soft skin above her collarbone.

"Marcus." It was a plea for mercy. It was a plea for more. Both her hands covered the hand I was resting on her belly and clung tightly for support.

Kai brought his Kawasaki to a standstill and watched us with quiet amusement. He folded his arms over the handlebar and leaned closer, his eyes fixed on Charlotte, who fidgeted adorably.

"Public lewdness—I did not expect that of you, Miss Burton."

Throwing my head back, I released a strident laugh. Charlotte elbowed me with a glare that she divided between Kai and me. I only held on tighter to her delicate hips.

Bryson inched closer to the starting line, followed by The Fox, Brayden, and Samuel, Kai's friend. All participants were ready and eager as the music raged on, and I felt a distant desire to be atop my motorcycle, with adrenaline pumping in my veins and freedom on the horizon. I could fool myself that I was content to simply hang around, but the truth was that I wanted to race. I missed the exhilaration.

"I'd like to paint you." The look Kai gave Charlotte was the perfect blend between analytical coldness and artistic interest. "Maybe on Marcus's motorcycle."

"Don't you even dare think about it."

"Oh, but that would be—out of the ordinary." Charlotte chuckled nervously. Her smile was expectant and genuinely excited.

"Charlotte, he paints nudes."

"They are works of fine art." Kai winked, his expression somewhere between challenging and inviting. I took a menacing step toward him, but he was already speeding to the lineup. "Think about it," he called to Charlotte, knowing that persistence on the topic was the perfect way to goad my temper.

An earsplitting boom made Charlotte jump in my arms, then a

second boom signaled the beginning of the race. All contestants took off in a fury, casting an asphyxiating smoke behind them. They were racing on a circular course, so they were supposed to return where they had left from. As soon as the motorcycles became blurs in the distance, the crowd shifted to face the finish line. Then the excitement and the noise mounted to epic proportions.

"Imagine me being caught here by the police and my father bailing me out of jail," Charlotte shouted.

She laughed, a sound deep and sincere, one that hinted at freedom. I realized then that being here might have been the most unconventional thing Charlotte had ever done. I pillaged her mouth but trusted she could read the gentleness in my wildness.

"You have never done anything forbidden, have you? Why did you take the risk with me?"

"Because I trust you."

In the hollows of my chest, I felt an all-consuming fire expanding, seeking, finding, and conquering. It was a fire that Charlotte had unleashed and only she could tame. That fire was Charlotte herself.

She came into my arms before I reached for her, filling a place in my life that just now I comprehended how badly I needed to have filled.

Spinning in my embrace so she faced the boisterous crowd surrounding us, Charlotte perused the couples dancing without inhibitions, grinding against each other. Women clapped their hands and jumped animatedly, waiting for the ones they cheered for. Men placed outrageous bets and engaged in good-natured arguments. During it all, I watched her. In the dark, illicit night, she was the light.

"See? People are having a great time. It's not about breaking the law. That is only the drawback to the experience."

I propped my chin on her shoulder and pressed my cheek against hers. While I had neither strived to make my father understand what the races could offer nor cared much about his opinion, I wanted Charlotte to understand. I wanted her to see and listen before she judged me.

"You'd really want to race, wouldn't you?"

She surveyed me from beneath sensually sluggish eyelashes. She could understand the fascination the races held, but I doubted she could ever accept them.

"Yes. But this time, I think I'd find the experience lacking."

"Lacking what?"

"You behind me, your arms wrapped around my waist and your hot, tantalizing breath against my back."

I really, really missed the sensation, even more so than the racing itself. Charlotte pressed into me, her weight a warming comfort as well as a harsh temptation.

"Look," she squealed, definitely excited. "They are getting back."

Indeed, some of them were getting back and furiously fast. A flash of green shattered the black of the night and raced against a white blur, topped by a red silhouette. Yet, it was Kai's dark and red motorcycle leading the way, flying over the road like a weightless spirit. Despite the distance that separated us, his control was clear.

"Kai and Joleen are racing for first place now," I explained, pointing to the two motorcycles that approached us vengefully. Distantly, Brayden let out an enraged shout, slicing the already thunderous atmosphere.

"Who are you betting on?" Rising on tiptoes, she struggled to see past the gathering throng.

I guided her forward with an arm coiled around her waist and the other pushing people aside. Ignoring groans and protests, we managed to get to the first line just in time to watch Kai claim leadership once more.

"Kai, of course."

"Because he's leading or because you cannot stand Joleen?"

"It's not about being a misogynist."

"Nor jealous," she supplied. If I hadn't held her in my arms, I wouldn't have detected how her spine straightened up.

"Charlotte." My low growl was authoritative enough to compel her to face me. "I am not jealous. I am protective of my little cousin and his stupid artist heart."

I knew her suspicion wasn't deep-rooted when she replied with a satisfied beam and leaned once more into me. The bikes arrowed toward us until they got so close that we could see their incensed faces. Joleen's upper lip was curled over her teeth, and her eyes and lips had a defiant set. Kai was crouched over his speeding motorcycle like a panther about to pounce, confident and conceitedly satisfied.

"Poor bastard," I laughed when Kai hopped triumphantly off his bike. He might have won, but a woman like The Fox certainly had limitless methods to make him regret his victory.

A group of excited females came rushing toward Kai but stopped abruptly when Joleen climbed off her motorcycle and shot them a deadly glare. They knew better than to get on her bad side.

Charlotte congratulated him while Kai embraced her on a whim. "What about that painting?" he giggled.

I took advantage of their discussion to tackle Brayden. He finished fifth, behind Bryson and Samuel. Climbing off his bike, he wrenched the leather gloves off his hands and pushed them into his back pocket. As soon as his feet touched the ground, he careened unsteadily to a blonde who offered him a cheap bottle of beer.

"Do you want to kill yourself?" I shouted at him. He merely took another swig of his beer. "You're drunk."

"Leave me the hell alone," he spat and shoved me with a force that momentarily caught me off guard then teetered away.

"Hey," I bellowed as I caught him by his collar and forced him back to face me. "Your behavior has long ago ceased being cute. One of these days you'll end up a pile of flesh and bones, and it won't be pretty. If you don't care about yourself anymore, then care about your family. You're killing them."

"He got the point, Marcus. Cut him some slack." My gaze cut to Bryson. His constant coddling wasn't helping his brother either.

"If *you* keep cutting him some slack, you'll end up picking his body from the morgue."

"What's your damn problem?" Brayden spat again.

The leggy blonde produced a second bottle of beer and pushed it in Brayden's hands with a wide smile. Her arms snaked around his neck, and her mouth found his although they were no more than strangers. He ended the coarseness when I grabbed his bottle and crushed it to the ground.

A growl was my only warning before his fisted hands hit me in the chest and pushed me backward. He was starting to get on my nerves.

"Aren't you getting enough of that split-tail? You're too cranky and noisy for one who should be actively banging."

"Hey," I snarled, my hands automatically fisting in his jacket. "You respect her!"

"Or what?"

"Come on, Brayden. Let's go home. The race is over." Bryson's peacemaking words remained noises in the background.

"And the fun apparently."

I glared at him and concentrated on restraining my own anger. Yet there was still a part of me that worried about him, that hated the state he was in, that wished his life was different.

"Dude, keep your hands off."

Kai's sharp, commanding voice reverberated louder than all lingering noises.

I turned and saw Charlotte standing still, her arms wrapped around her body as if to protect herself. Her eyes were tense; her mouth was set in a pale line; and her jaw was clenched tight. She watched me mutely, nearly reproachfully.

Only when my eyes darted past her shoulder to Kai and the leather-clad rider he was holding back, did I figure out Charlotte's reaction. She was afraid, and I had promised she would never be frightened again.

With a growl, I gunned for the man Kai was nearly blocking from view. No questions asked, no instant of hesitation, my fist connected with the idiot's jaw as soon as I stopped in front of him.

I wasn't in the mood for a fight, so I cut it short. He stumbled back, the stench of alcohol greeting me as he huffed and dropped to one knee. I caught him by the throat and grabbed his right arm, pulling it back. The satisfying crunch of dislocating bones echoed right before the man howled and collapsed to his side.

"Don't come near her again."

I panted for breath and massaged the suffocating ache in my chest while my eyes remained angrily fixed on the man's retreating back. When I couldn't turn, when I didn't dare face Charlotte, I came to comprehend that with my sudden burst of anger, I had just ruined the entire night all by myself. I had shown her the dark side of me that I had never wanted her to see. I had demonstrated just how utterly unfit for her I was.

Charlotte was unnaturally still and absolutely silent when I eventually turned to her. The warmth of her eyes turned cold and glassy, and though her gaze was pinned on me, she was looking everywhere but in my eyes. There was suddenly a bottomless chasm that spread between us.

"Charlotte," I called, my voice coming out tartly. But I was pleading.

The instant she turned around and started walking away from me, a sense of dread paralyzed my judgment. I hurried after her, but when she sensed me following, she walked faster, farther, as if she couldn't stand my very presence. I growled in frustration, and I could swear that she shivered.

Charlotte ran a hand through her long, curly hair then rested her fingers around her throat. My hand caught her elbow, and I hauled her into me. The muffled shriek she let out sliced at me. The scared glimmer in her eyes drove me mad. It was a glimmer I had seen all too often in Liv's eyes. Was it my destiny to always ruin everything?

"Don't look at me like that," I snapped. But I didn't want to snap. I wanted to implore her to give me another chance, to not give up on me just yet. As usual, though, everything came out wrong, so very wrong. "Please, Charlotte. I didn't mean to scare you. I didn't want you to see this—side of me. Please—"

"I just want to leave."

"No," I almost shouted. My hands cupped her shoulders and squeezed hard. She couldn't leave me. Not for this stupidity.

"I won't stay here any longer, Marcus," she stated curtly. "You can either remain here or join me."

She shrugged my hands off and started walking again. I allowed myself a breath of relief before I went after her. She wasn't leaving me, not yet, and that was all I needed for the moment. I held the door of my car for her, gritting my teeth as she climbed in, painfully careful not to make any contact with me.

I joined her in the car because sticking in a place without her was no longer an option. I turned in my seat, so I half faced her, but her eyes were shut and her demeanor guarded and aloof.

"Charlotte—" I began.

I kept myself in place by gripping the steering wheel with one hand, so tightly that my knuckles turned white. It was all I could do not to clutch her by the waist and pull her into my lap.

"Just drive."

I bumped my fist against the steering wheel before I turned on the ignition. It was the distress in her eyes that made my blood boil. The anger, directed all at myself, gathered like the bad blood beneath a bruise, like the puss in a bubble. It threatened to burst and spread through my whole system.

"Slow down," she ordered, her voice low but steady. I hadn't even realized how fast I was driving.

I snapped to attention, scowling and stiffening. Charlotte looked away, her gaze trained on the buildings we left behind. Although I wanted so badly to see her eyes, I didn't need the visual contact to gauge her feelings. She practically oozed disappointment.

"Damn it, Charlotte. Once I get mad, I can't think properly."

"So what?" she finally snapped. Oddly, her outburst calmed my raging nerves. As long as we fought, it meant we were worth fighting for. It had to get worse before it got better. "I'm supposed to treat you with kid gloves, always afraid of doing something that might make you *mad*?"

"No. I don't want you to be afraid of me."

"I'm not—argh—just stop talking, Marcus."

"I don't want to stop talking. I want to sort this out. The moment I stop talking, things will remain unsettled, and eventually, you'll turn away and leave. I cannot let that happen."

"That much confidence you have in me? That's refreshing."

"Charlotte," I said, a plea that came out through gritted teeth.

"Don't Charlotte me. I'm mad right now. The more you talk, the angrier I get. I want you to shut up for a minute. Is that too much to ask?"

It was impossibly much to ask, especially when I knew from experience that the quieter it became, the farther apart we would drift.

I rubbed at the chill that had settled in my chest and complied. It must have taken me another fifteen minutes to get home, but it felt like an eternity. By the time I parked in my usual lot, the tension had grown so dense and unpleasant that it became choking.

"Come upstairs." I studied her fearfully. My fingers itched to touch her, but I knew she wouldn't welcome the gesture.

"It doesn't seem I have a choice." She looked up at my apartment building, clearly wishing I had driven her home instead.

When we entered the building, the doorman watched me somewhat panicked, then he saluted us respectfully. If he had noticed any hostility between Charlotte and me, he remained stoically quiet. Rather than leading, I followed her to the elevators in complete unnerving silence.

She strolled inside as soon as the doors opened, taking refuge in the farthest corner. She was still, with her arms wrapped around her torso and a chilly disposition that expanded the gap between us beyond the physical distance.

Groaning, I got in behind her and watched her rigid back with that growing chill in my chest. When the doors closed, and the car began its ascent, I placed a hand on her hip and my mouth to her cheek. Charlotte breathed sharply but otherwise remained quiet.

I knew something was off the minute we walked inside my apartment. Kinga, who always barked when I got home, didn't let out a sound. The lights, which I had switched off before leaving, were now blindingly on.

The knee-jerk reaction was to think of my father, then a subtle floral fragrance penetrated my nostrils. It was a perfume I recognized, one I had smelled often and intimately.

"Marcus, where have you been?" Liv came limping from the kitchen with Kinga happily padding after her.

"Why are you here?" I nearly hissed, regretting my tone instantly. Liv winced. Charlotte withdrew even more into her shell.

"I didn't know I would be intruding. You never told me that—

"

I hadn't imagined my anger and frustration could escalate any further. Liv and Charlotte stood facing each other, the past meeting the present. I rubbed my face with both hands and bit my tongue to stifle the groan that wanted to erupt from my throat. I had never wanted them to meet, let alone under such circumstances.

Before I did something I would regret, I turned to Charlotte, not quite meeting her questioning gaze.

"Please, give us a moment."

Her eyes widened in disbelief, and I could swear she would just leave. Jaw clenched and eyes wounded, Charlotte granted my request when all her instincts certainly told her to run and save herself the heartache. I felt her insecurities and almost heard the questions buzzing in her head. But everything she imagined was false.

"Why are you here?" I repeated, harsher than before and suddenly not quite caring how Liv felt about that.

"Who is she?"

She walked closer, hurt and irritation blending on her face.

"You are not allowed to play that card with me, Olivia. Not anymore."

The only response to my low-spoken, menacing words was an incredulous gasp. I still cared about Liv, in a way that had nothing to do with the past. I didn't want to take radical measures as far as our relationship was concerned because I owed her affection and care. But sometimes, she tempted me terribly to do just that.

"It seems I am not welcome in your life anymore. The only way I can get a hold of you is to harass you, and when I finally reach you, I get hissed at." Tears glistened in her eyes and fell promptly down her pale cheeks.

"You are always welcome in my life, Liv." By dint of great effort, I managed to rein in my temper. "Tonight is not the best time, though."

"It's never the best time, Marcus." She shoved past me, but even as she headed for the door, she expected me to catch and stop her. I didn't. "Don't get in too deep, Marcus. She'll hurt you."

After Liv left, I stared down the hallway that led to my room where Charlotte was waiting. Mere feet separated us, but the emotional distance pushed us worlds apart.

Liv's warning came much too late. I already was so involved that I was unable to stop being involved. Charlotte was going to leave, and I was going to hurt.

My mind disconnected from my body. Shards of glass fell clinking to the ground, and a sharp stinging burned my knuckles. I watched my bleeding hand and the broken mirror hanging in the hallway with a bizarre sense of detachment. It was Charlotte's alarmed voice that dragged me out of my stupor. Instead of making it better, I was messing up all the worse.

"Oh, my God, Marcus, what have you done?" she choked.

"It's nothing," I lied.

While I could see her rushing to me and feel her hands as she cradled my wounded right hand, I was unable to react. It was as if I watched my own body from afar.

"Let me see," she ordered.

With controlled gentleness, she inspected the damage. Her brows knitted so tightly together that they formed a single brown line.

"It's nothing."

She looked up at me, her eyes penetrating so deeply that I felt her searching my very soul. She gauged my disposition just as well as I could determine hers. And she knew that something was wrong with me, inside me, even when I didn't.

"What's wrong, Marcus?"

Charlotte cupped my cheek with her free hand and rested her forehead against mine. I breathed deeply, her tuberose perfume filling my nostrils. It was the warmth in her voice that pulled me from the dark places I had sunk into.

"Don't let me mess it all up, Charlotte."

"Why did you break the mirror?"

She glanced from my face to the broken glass then to the bleeding hand she was still holding carefully. I heard the questions in her head as loudly and clearly as if she had spoken them out loud. And I couldn't tolerate another second without her in my arms. Ignoring the stinging ache in my hand, I cuddled her to my chest so tightly that her heart pounded against mine.

"What you're thinking—" My lips hovered over hers, but Charlotte closed her eyes, not welcoming the intimacy of a kiss. "Nothing of it is true, Charlotte."

"Is she the friend who needed your assistance when you ran out of your apartment?"

"Let's not go there. Not tonight."

Her hand dropped from my face, and she pulled away, skirting me and the shards on the floor. She was slipping through my fingers.

"Why not? What is she to you, Marcus?" Her eyes burned, but her voice was low and ice-cold. *She* was someone I couldn't discuss, not with Charlotte.

"Are you picking a fight?"

"If stopping you from insulting my intelligence is picking a fight, then yes, I am. I don't think she is just a friend."

"Charlotte, not tonight."

"A simple friend doesn't look at you the way she did. A simple friend doesn't shoot daggers through her eyes because she caught you with another woman."

She took a step farther from me, pulling her jacket around herself like a shield. I moved forward, catching her by the waist when she kept backing away. Immediately, her hands covered mine and shoved at my steely grip.

"Stop," I ordered and pressed my mouth against her temple. "Don't fight me."

The way she made me feel turned me inside out. I didn't know how to deal with the avalanche of feelings inside me. I didn't know how to react to her rejection. I only knew I wanted to mend what I had ruined tonight. So I did what came most naturally. I sought the intimacy of the flesh and bent to cover her mouth with mine.

"Don't." That single word stopped me just as efficiently as the fingers she pressed on my parted mouth. "Don't use my need for you against me."

"Charlotte, please. Let me fix this."

"It's late, and I'm tired…"

Each step she took away from me, I took toward her. Yet, I

couldn't force her to stay.

"Don't leave. Please."

"I can't stay with you tonight. I can't get rid this easily of how you have just made me feel. I thought exclusiveness went both ways."

"Charlotte—For God's sake. It does."

"You made me feel like I am the other woman, Marcus, and I want to be the only one."

With tears shining in her eyes, Charlotte let the door close behind her.

Chapter 24

Charlotte

"**A**re you sure you want to do this? You don't have to if you're not up for it."

Christina watched me with heartfelt concern. Ever since she crossed the threshold of my apartment, she had known something was wrong with me.

In a moment of weakness, I had let out everything in a rush from the circumstances under which I met Marcus to last night's events. Christina had listened to everything I said until no detail and no thought remained unspoken.

She didn't assault me with invasive questions or outraged alarm. She didn't prod for details and didn't expect more than I had shared. Her quietly patient demeanor, however, didn't veil her concern or displeasure. She was a very protective sister, and right now, Marcus King was not in her good graces.

"I'm always up for taking care of my little niece. Marie and I will spend some quality time this weekend, won't we, sweetie?"

Marie gurgled happily and rolled on the bed. I tickled her belly, and she thrust her small fists in the air in that adorable way only babies pulled off. Her ingenuous chortles put a sincere smile on my face, the first since last night.

"Where does *he* fit in all this quality time?" Christina asked, continuing to apply her makeup.

In a pine green bandage dress, with black straps covering her shoulders and a half scooped back that displayed her tanned skin, Christina looked ravishing. Diamond stud earrings sparkled in her ears while marquise-shaped diamonds set in white gold adorned her right wrist. Her naturally feminine beauty was all the better highlighted by her dark hair, cascading in perfect curls down her shoulders.

"I'm not sure where *I* fit in *his* time."

I met her troubled look in the mirror, and for a while, we were grave and thoughtful, then we both started laughing. With one eye already wearing makeup and the other bare of any cosmetics, she looked hilarious.

"Don't laugh at me," she complained, throwing a makeup brush in my direction. She sobered much too quickly. "It should be him trying to fit into your time, Charlotte. Never the other way around."

I chose not to contradict her, not when she was so utterly determined to protect my interests. I didn't want to give Marcus scraps of my time any more than I wanted to receive the same in return.

I wanted the middle ground. I wanted that exclusiveness he had talked about, the same exclusiveness I wasn't so sure he respected. Although relationships were never simple or easy, I wanted the simplicity of just being together.

Christina arched an eyebrow at me when my phone rang for the umpteenth time. I knew who was calling before I checked the screen.

Marcus had called incessantly ever since I left his apartment. When I didn't answer, he started texting. I was pretty sure that my voicemail was also full, but I forced myself to reject his calls, ignore his texts, and fight the temptation to listen to his voice. I needed the distance to clear my head.

"Are you going to get that?" I shook my head, although I itched to press the answer button. "Good. Let him stew."

"I don't want him to stew."

I threw myself against the pillows, and Marie immediately

climbed on my stomach, her curious fingers playing with the flowers adorning my blouse. I didn't know what I wanted, but without a doubt, my retreat had nothing to do with tormenting him.

"I do," Christina snapped, angry on my behalf. I had been angry too.

In fact, in one evening I experienced an extensive palette of emotions.

Concern—when Marcus fought with Brayden. The authority in his eyes commanded obedience, and I couldn't imagine anyone, regardless their recklessness, going against such feral willpower. Anybody who was wise would avoid getting on Marcus's bad side, but Brayden had been hardly conscious, let alone wise.

Disgust—when that man, nearly naked and covered in tattoos, caught me in his arms and licked my throat. Kai intervened promptly, with such supremacy that it left me stunned. I wasn't sure what to think about Brayden and Bryson, but Kai behaved completely differently from how he had that Friday night.

Then anxiety and disgust morphed into downright panic. Turning around, Marcus spotted Kai and the bald man he was pushing away from me. I sensed the violence rattling inside him, but it still shook me to the core when Marcus exploded.

His fists clenched, his knuckles turned white, then he pounced on the man. Unleashed brutality made of Marcus a terrifying man. And none of it would have happened if we hadn't been there.

How did he expect me to approve of an environment and a pastime that goaded him into becoming beast instead of man?

I would have turned a blind eye to all that. But to a woman waiting for him in his apartment like she owned the place? I couldn't. Shock gave way to anger when he practically sent me away to deal with her, and eventually, disappointment settled in.

When the familiar throbbing made my chest feel heavy and breathing became difficult, I knew that attraction had altered into something much deeper and more dangerous.

"You're going to give Logan a heart attack. You are marvelous."

I pushed my thoughts aside and appreciated Christina with sisterly pride. She put on her gold Jimmy Choo heels and came strolling to the bed, her hips swaying with natural sensuality.

"I'd rather give him something else," she said, winking.

"You're so mean," I laughed, and she did too. It wasn't beneath her to tease poor Logan all through dinner and make him suffer until they would finally be alone.

"Consider it my gift to him."

Despite her concern for me and the little jokes at her husband's expense, Christina was nervous. She was leaving for the weekend with Logan, celebrating five years of marriage, and she wanted everything to be perfect.

Marie crawled into her mommy's lap, and Christina pressed a quick, loving kiss to her dark honey hair. Although she was tremendously excited to spend time alone with her husband, I expected she would call every two hours to ask how her daughter and I were doing.

"You look awful." She cupped my cheek and inspected my red-rimmed eyes.

"Thanks."

"No, Charlotte. You really do look awful. I'm worried about you."

"Marcus and I will sort things out. I just need some space and time to think."

"You don't have to brave it out. I'm supposed to listen to you crying and kvetching. I'm supposed to be your support and counsel. I'm your sister, Charlotte. I want to be there for you when you need me."

Tears gathered in my eyes, but I didn't want to cry in front of her and spoil her night.

"I am not trying to put up a brave façade. We have to sort things out." Christina's eyes grew big with surprise and understanding. "I am falling for him. I'm falling hard."

"I'd like to talk to him."

"What? Why?"

"To give him the threatening sisterly speech, obviously."

"Ah, that," I laughed, remembering I had done the same with Logan when I was too young to be credible. "It's not necessary, Chris."

"Of course, it is. He needs to know that I will literally cut his pride and feed it to the goats if he hurts my sister."

"Poor guy," Logan muttered, filling the doorway. Dressed in a dark suit, paired with a pale blue shirt and a fancy bowtie, he looked dashing. I smiled at him, and his fleeting masculine empathy vanished. "He'd better treat you like a queen. Otherwise, he'll have to deal with me."

I hugged and kissed them both, and they left soon after. I took Marie to the living room and played with her until she was thoroughly hungry and exhausted.

It was my cue to feed her when she started sucking on her thumb, watching me sleepily. Afterwards, I gave her a quick bath, daubed her skin with the baby oil that Christina had brought, and tucked her in my bed, surrounding her small body with pillows so she wouldn't roll and fall.

Unfortunately, I wasn't as exhausted as Marie. I sat on the sofa, pulling my legs underneath me, and sipped quietly at a glass of red wine.

My phone rested silently, too silently, on the glass tea table. I almost reached for it when the doorbell jolted me to my feet. I hissed in frustration, expecting Marie to start crying at any moment, but seemingly, she was too tired to be bothered by the intrusive noise.

My heart thudded almost violently in my chest, and my breath caught in my throat as I crossed the small space to the door. I already knew it was Marcus on the other side of the door.

Pressing my hands to the wooden frame, I struggled to control my ragged breath. I felt childish for not opening up, but the moment I saw him, I would cave in. I couldn't yield to a relationship where I felt betrayed from the beginning.

"Please, Charlotte. I know you are home."

I slid down to the floor, my back stiff against the wall. Could he hear my panting breaths or my savage heartbeats? Could he feel the misery and uncertainties warring inside me? Could he read the questions going on a rampage in my head?

"She is not who you think she is. She is the past, Charlotte. I cannot erase it, and I cannot repair it. Please don't cut me out."

The seafoam green eyes of the unknown woman haunted me. Her expression, although paling with anger when she found me by Marcus's side, hadn't lost its natural doll-like beauty. She seemed the type of woman that, through her mystery, drove men wild.

Despite the silence, I knew Marcus hadn't left yet. I rubbed my bare arms with robotic movements, but no matter how much warmth I struggled to infuse into my flesh, I still felt oddly cold. The feeling that I was the intruder returned to me like a punishment. That was exactly how the red-haired woman had glared at me—with crisp, pitiless reprimand in her eyes, punishing me for claiming what was hers. I shuddered and covered my mouth to smother a sob.

"I will explain. I promise. But give me time."

Time for what? Time to forget her? Time to turn me upside down?

Amidst all the confusion, something was painfully clear. Whoever that woman was, she embodied a past that Marcus wasn't ready to discard yet. The way his voice softened when he talked about her epitomized feelings that hadn't quite subsided.

Sobbing, I let the tears pour. Sometimes the only thing I needed to calm down was to cry.

I WOKE WITH A JERK OUT OF a sickening nightmare that exposed Brayden in a darker light than ever before. I was lying in front of the door in a tense fetal position.

Ever since the nightmares started, they had been variations of the same dream: a blonde man attacking me until somebody came to my rescue. Sometimes I could see their faces, sometimes I only intuited.

This time something had shifted.

I had just dreamt of Brayden, and nobody had come to the rescue. It seemed that the bad dreams returned with a vengeance when Marcus and I walked on shaky ground.

It was still dark outside when I returned to my bedroom to check on Marie, who was sleeping soundly. I wrapped a blanket around myself and crashed on the sofa by the window, succumbing to a restless sleep.

SUNDAY DAWNED EARLY WITH Marie's piercing cry. As soon as I picked her up and took her to the kitchen for her morning bottle, she recovered the previous night's bright mood. Her cute giggles and innocent eyes warmed me to the bone.

Christina called for the second time close to midday, saying that they would be back Monday before I left for work, as promised.

Although it was a splendid sunny day, my enthusiasm lacked as I ventured out of my apartment building, pushing Marie's fuchsia stroller down the busy street. I chose walking instead of driving to the restaurant Rachel had picked for our lunch as a substitute for my usual runs in Central Park, which I hadn't been able to enjoy lately.

Her copper blonde hair was perfectly coiffed as usual. She stood out as we entered the outdoor restaurant. When she sighted us, she waved so graciously that she could have been mistaken for royalty.

"Hey, you two beautiful girls," Rachel greeted us with a huge grin, standing to give me a hug and blow kisses to Marie, who had already fallen asleep. "I've missed you."

"Me too. You have no idea."

We exchanged long, meaningful glances as the waiter took our orders then vanished dutifully.

Rachel and I led agitated lives. While I was suffocated by the cases my father was throwing on my plate, she was holed up at the hospital where she worked as a nutrition specialist. Between our chaotic professional lives and personal drama, we saw each other less frequently than we once used to, but our friendship was appropriately nurtured and still thrived.

"So how are you and Ethan getting along?" I started without any further ado.

At the sound of her husband's name, her eyes sparkled then clouded. I related more than ever to her fluctuating emotions.

Her slender fingers, tipped by blood-red nails that matched her sleeveless blouse to perfection, started drumming on the tabletop.

"We're still getting a divorce."

Rachel had that soft kind of voice that curled around your senses like warm caramel even when it came out like a rasp tinted by desolation.

"So should I buy a fancy dress for your next wedding?" I asked, pointing to her ring finger. She was still wearing her wedding band.

She fixed me with knowing blue eyes, and I couldn't help but think of another pair of blue eyes watching me intently, shamelessly. I missed those eyes even when seeing them would have hurt.

Rachel's lips twitched with a barely contained smile, but the gesture didn't reach her eyes.

"It won't happen again. I'm done."

I was far from trusting her statement, but I supported her nonetheless. She and Ethan had been through many fights. This lunch and my discussion with Rachel felt too much like déjà vu to believe her completely when she said she was done. Sometimes, no matter how badly you wanted to be done, you still needed to continue.

"You can't be done with him, Rachel. You've tried, but you can't function without Ethan. You'll just go back to him."

"I know," she sighed.

She patted her hair although not a single lock was out of place. It was a gesture betraying her nervousness and her longing for Ethan. When she was away from him for too long, she grew impatient, irritable, and eventually flatly downcast. She always realized that as soon as the divorce papers were signed and the longing for her former husband became intolerable.

The waiter brought us the salads we had ordered, which offered me more time to study her. She looked radiant, although miserable, but then again, that was her factory setting. There was something in her eyes, though, that I couldn't quite pinpoint, yet it gave her a new sort of beauty and vigor. She seemed rejuvenated.

"You already did, didn't you?" I gasped and covered my mouth to tone down my voice.

I laughed, and Rachel scowled magnificently, the glare turning into a delightful childish look that made me laugh all the harder. She and her patterns were incorrigible.

"I slept with him," she admitted in a rushed whisper. Gripping tightly her fork and napkin and leaning in so nobody would hear her speaking, she looked as if she had just confessed having committed murder. "I slept with my husband, and it felt like I was with a lover, doing something illicit. Something that felt so good."

"That's not bad, Rach."

"Of course, it is. I've practically cheated on my husband with himself."

"That doesn't make sense. Not even for you."

She sighed overdramatically, but in the end, the smile that covered her face was dazzling. The reason for her newfound vitality was the affair she had with her husband.

I smiled, widely and sincerely. Whatever their problems, I trusted they would solve them, and Rachel seemed to believe that too, regardless her proclamation that she was done.

"You don't seem your usual exultant self."

Rachel scrutinized me as she slowly sipped her margarita. Squirming and looking away, I realized I wasn't prepared to discuss Marcus, but I didn't want to lie to Rachel either. Despite her tumultuous love life, she always offered me insightful perspective that helped me deal with my problems. Her inquisitive stare propelled me to answer.

"You met Marcus King," I stated with controlled calm. My blood simmered at the mere mention of his name. "He's giving me headaches."

"Headaches as in sleepless-nights-headaches or you're-incompetent-headaches?"

"Headaches as in I-don't-think-I'm-the-only-woman-in-your-life-headaches."

"Lottie," Rachel sighed and covered my hand with hers in a comforting gesture.

It wasn't pity she felt for me but empathy. When she met Ethan, she had just gotten out of a long, painful relationship that ended with the man's crude betrayal. It didn't mean it had been completely wiped from her mind just because that episode seemed so far away.

I frequently suspected that she feared Ethan would cheat on her, but she loved him so deeply that she trusted him with her heart despite her fears. I didn't know Marcus enough to trust him so blindly.

"Have you talked to him?"

"Not exactly. He called, though."

"How many times?"

I slid the phone across the table, and she picked it up, switching to my call log. There were seventeen missed calls from Marcus King. Rachel's mouth dropped open, and her eyes grew as big as onions.

"Persistent, I know. He also came by last night, but I didn't open the door. If I had, he would have just convinced me that everything was okay. And it isn't."

"Maybe you want to believe that everything is not okay because everything is happening much too fast?" Rachel suggested, her eyes kind but admonishing. I shook my head but couldn't bring myself to verbally deny. She might have been right. "Seventeen missed calls can't be the sign of someone who is interested in cheating on you."

"They can also be the sign of someone who has too much apologizing to do."

"I don't know him well enough to defend him, but I think you owe it to yourself to hear him out."

"Ha." I managed an honest laugh. For once, she had the opportunity to give me my own line. She enjoyed it, and she showed it with a big smile of her own.

When Marie stirred, Rachel clapped her hands then cradled her to her chest, cooing over the baby as if she were her own. One day, perhaps soon, Rachel was going to be a spectacular mother.

We spent the following hour talking about Marie, my sister, Logan, and celebrations of all kinds. When we said our goodbyes, both of us felt a little better.

A taxi passed me by, but I chose to walk back home, knowing that the excess of physical activity wouldn't do me any harm. It was still warm and pleasant outside, but the sun didn't burn as it had earlier.

I pulled back the canopy of Marie's stroller and reclined the seat so she could sit and play with her little Minnie Mouse toy. I was making funny faces at her when her uncontrolled giggles were drowned out by the most familiar voice echoing right in my ear.

"Stalking seems to be necessary with you, sweet Charlotte."

I jerked and came to a halt.

It had been less than two days since we parted on precarious terms, but the separation felt longer and more scathing than that. Marcus was close enough that his arm brushed against mine, the contact making me tremble.

I looked back at Marie, who was ogling and pointing curiously to Marcus, and forced myself to ignore what the sight of him did to me even when I was mad and hurt.

Dressed in gray slacks and white shirt, smelling of clean soap and man, exuding his characteristic quiet dominance, he demanded my attention without speaking. He was a magnet I had to respond to.

"Who is she?"

He stared at Marie just as curiously and suspiciously as she was staring back. It was refreshing to see that there was someone who didn't feel intimidated at the sight of him even if that someone was a baby girl, unaware of the power a man could wield.

I faced him and arched a challenging eyebrow. He couldn't honestly expect to receive answers while I didn't.

"You should have waited until Monday," I responded instead.

"Why? So you could keep avoiding me?"

"I'm not avoiding you, Marcus."

But I was.

He growled so low and deep that the sound reverberated in my whole being. In the middle of the street, surrounded by strangers, I was acutely aware of the male standing a breath away from me. I anticipated his touch as much as I feared it. I didn't want to surrender to him unless I was sure he was worth surrendering to.

"No? Then how do you explain not answering my calls or my texts, not opening your door when you were clearly home?"

His anger was barely concealed, but there was also that look in his eyes that told me he hadn't expected otherwise.

"I'm entitled to be upset. I'm also entitled to an explanation. I don't care about your outburst at the race. I didn't like it, and I don't like the idea of you being a part of that scene, but I can overlook it. I can't say the same for what happened in your apartment."

"Charlotte, I need you to trust me."

There were several good responses he could have given. He could have apologized. He could have explained although I might not have liked the explanation.

Evading wasn't a reply I would tolerate.

I grabbed the handle of the stroller and pushed forward, my gaze stubbornly trained ahead. He followed, or rather, stalked.

"Would you trust me so easily if you found a man waiting for me in my apartment?"

"I would probably murder him, but I would trust you." There was no hesitation in his voice, no hint of concession.

"Murder wouldn't be a sign of trust."

When I walked faster and refused to look at him, I considered that Rachel might have been right, that I was purposefully making a mountain out of a molehill.

Then, the image of that woman returned in my mind. The fact that Marcus declined to explain who she was proved she had a place in his life, one that I might have wrongfully occupied.

"Charlotte, please. I upset you, and you made your point, but don't leave me hanging like this. I can't stand it."

"You're doing the same, Marcus. I'll see you tomorrow."

The wounded, frustrated groan he emitted in my wake accompanied me throughout the night and most of the following morning.

The week started with a call from Jack Stewart's team summoning me urgently to Washington. By midday, I felt irritable and restless.

Nothing worked out well when Marcus and I did not work out well. That was why I didn't like mixing business with pleasure. If something went wrong on a personal level, it affected everything else.

"Miss Burton?"

Sofia stepped cautiously inside my office, assessing my mood correctly as usual and avoiding getting in my way when I was already touchy. I looked up from my notebook screen, and she got the cue to continue.

"I booked your flight for tonight at eight o'clock and made reservations at Willard Intercontinental. Is that alright?"

My temper got worse when I thought that I might have to remain in D.C. until my client was exonerated or convicted. As his lawyer, I should have believed in the former, but my heart was leaning toward the latter.

That was my chance right there to be vindictive. Marcus had demanded that he come with me the next time I went to D.C., and the opportunity presented itself sooner than we expected. Since we had fought, and I was rightfully upset with him, I could have simply left and let him mind his own business. But that was not the way I was built.

"Book two rooms, please. Let Mr. King know I need to have a word with him."

"Senior?"

"No. Junior."

Sofia arched an eyebrow but otherwise made no comment.

"Will that be all?"

"Yes."

Less than ten minutes later my door opened and closed without a sound. I knew it was Marcus before I looked up to confirm what my body had already acknowledged.

I stood up immediately but remained behind my desk. My stilettos did not boost my height enough to tower over him, but it made me tall enough to feel a little less vulnerable before his stately pose. He marched inside with purpose stamped in his gaze, making my heart skip a beat.

"You should knock."

"I am not accustomed to knocking."

His nonchalant voice was warm even when irritating. And he marched on—to me.

"I am flying to Washington tonight. I just wanted to let you know."

I took two steps back when he rounded the desk and continued decisively to me. The only sign that he had acknowledged my words was a curt nod of his head, then he was on me.

He pushed me against the metal frame of the window and fisted his hands in my hair at the same time his mouth sealed over mine.

He kissed me wildly, taming my tongue and bruising my lips without apology. He kissed me ruthlessly, lavishing me with his taste and scent and making up for all the hours we hadn't touched. In the end, when my lips felt so swollen that I thought all my blood had gathered there, I wanted him to start all over again. And he did.

"Good. Should I pack light?" he asked eventually.

"Are you coming? You might be needed by somebody else."

"Charlotte."

His voice was low and rough and tingling my senses in ways that almost made me moan. Resisting him was not an easy job. He tightened his hold on the nape of my neck and rested his forehead against mine.

"You can keep being mad at me, but I will not allow you to push me away any longer. A damn weekend is all I can give you. I am not needed by anybody else. I am coming with you, and that's not up for discussion."

"Pack for an unlimited period then."

Trying to move out of his arms, I only managed to be trapped in a tighter and more irresistible snare.

"What did I just tell you?" he murmured in my ear, catching my earlobe and tugging punishingly. "Stop pushing me away."

"I cannot think when you hold me like this."

"I don't want you to think."

"But I do."

Thinking was my last grasp of control but also my greatest flaw. Keeping the perfect balance between thinking and overthinking was a trying endeavor when Marcus kept urging me with everything he had, from his actions to his words, to quit doing it altogether.

"Tell me what you feel, Charlotte. What does your instinct tell you? Have I betrayed you like you think I have?" His abrupt straightforwardness had my head spinning.

I watched his darkening blue eyes and absorbed the warmth of his touch. All weekend, I had been thinking, suspecting, and creating scenarios that might not exist, but I had refused to feel.

Despite my suspicions and insecurities, he didn't strike me as the sort of man who cheated. He was too blunt to bother with the complications of leading a double life.

"No."

A soul-deep, cleansing sigh left my body and the weight that had pressed over my chest ever since I stepped out of Marcus's apartment slowly dissipated.

I hadn't decided yet whether he was worth surrendering to or not, but I owed it to myself to give our relationship a chance.

Chapter 25

Marcus

We landed in Washington roughly an hour after we took off from New York. I had hoped to use the duration of the flight to close the still hostile gap between Charlotte and me, but as soon as we boarded, she took refuge in her work, erecting a chilly barrier I didn't dare disturb. For the moment.

At the airport, she was greeted by a small crew consisting of a driver and two lawyers, whose names I didn't bother to remember, although Charlotte dutifully made introductions. They watched me dubiously, but by the time we climbed in the black sedan waiting for us, they had already monopolized Charlotte's attention and were absorbed in a tense discussion revolving around their client's case.

The straw that broke the camel's back, however, was when the receptionist of the Willard Intercontinental offered us two separate keys for two separate rooms. I glared at Charlotte throughout our ride to the eighth floor but otherwise remained silent. My silence unsettled her. Good.

Liv's presence in my apartment had been unacceptable and something that would not happen again, but while I deserved her reserve and respected her hurt feelings, I also couldn't tolerate the emotional distance she was stubbornly exhibiting.

Back in her New York office, where it had been only us, where I'd had her cornered between the window and my body, she had relented. She had let herself feel and she had felt right. I was not unfaithful. I could not conceive disloyalty. Her heart knew the truth although her mind still doubted it.

Liv and I had a long, tumultuous history that had gone on even when everything between us ended. The moment Charlotte and I had turned from acquaintances to lovers, whatever I had had with Liv ceased. Yet, I was not prepared to let Charlotte in on the gruesome past I shared with her, or on my many faults and bad decisions. I wasn't ready to watch her turn from me because of that history.

We stepped outside the elevator, still accompanied by the two lawyers. Gritting my teeth, I delivered a hurried good night then strode off to my room without another glance for Miss Burton. If she demonstrated her displeasure through silent coldness, I could adopt the same tactic since at the moment, I was very displeased with her. Those chocolate eyes of hers burned through me as I retired.

I wasn't quite sure if the displeasure pumping viciously in my veins was directed at Charlotte or at myself. After the emptiness her absence had caused and the fear that I might have lost her, I knew I couldn't settle for scraps.

I didn't only want Charlotte's body. I wanted her soul. I wanted all of her. Although finally feeling was riveting, what Charlotte Burton forced me to feel was terrifying.

It was almost midnight when I knocked on her door. She opened with the immediacy that betrayed her impatience. She had been waiting for me. The idea put a smile on my face as I leaned against the doorframe and watched her reddened cheeks and parted lips.

Covered by a silk robe and wearing matching white slippers, her skin looked contrastingly rosy. Her long hair was pulled back in a ponytail, but a few wavy threads still hung damply around her face. I almost groaned with the desire to taste the water droplets on her throat.

"Hi."

Unable to resist, I raised my free hand and touched the pinkness in her cheek, absorbing the delicious warmth.

"Hi," she responded quietly, licking her lips. Greedy eyes raked me from head to toe as she pressed her legs together. My smile grew bigger.

"I brought a peace offering." I lifted the bottle of Moët & Chandon that I had ordered earlier and imagined how the champagne would taste off her voluptuous lips.

"Come in."

Charlotte opened the door wide and stepped to the side so I could walk inside. I sensed her fidgeting as I paced to the breakfast bar dominating the kitchenette. I chose two flutes from a glass case and filled them with the sparkling liquid, painfully aware of the electricity drawing Charlotte and me together.

She watched me, her fingers playing with her hair and her teeth playing with her lips, as I pulled ice from the freezer and placed the bottle in a bucket. When I approached her, flutes in hand and a wicked smile on my face, her tension-etched features caught shades of impetuosity. Then she burst.

"I wasn't trying to be petty when I asked for two rooms. I wasn't trying to get back at you or put distance between us, but you are certainly aware that your father has eyes everywhere. He will find out if we sleep in the same room. I created the reason for you coming to D.C. with me. I had to create the proper setting too."

"I wasn't asking you for an explanation," I muttered quietly, handing her the flute and urging her with my eyes to drink. She took it hesitantly and led the way back to the sitting area, now and then glancing back to assess my mood.

I was on the prowl.

"I wanted you to know I wasn't trying to take revenge—"

"I knew."

"But you were upset."

"I was. But I still knew."

A muscle in her jaw jumped. She got my allusion, and remorse momentarily misted her gaze. Immediately, my own guilt mirrored hers. It brought me no satisfaction to upset her. I followed her until she bumped against a writing desk littered with papers, and her hands curled around the edges.

"This was your only get-out," I told her bluntly, my voice intentionally turning low and rough.

I bowed closer. Our lips nearly touched but not really. Teasing a woman until every pore of her being desired me was part of the thrill. Seducing Charlotte gave me as much pleasure as that final moment of exquisite release.

"I told you I mess up a lot, but the next time I do, don't expect me to let you go again."

"I'd rather you didn't mess up."

"I'll try not to."

It was a promise, but my eyes showed the lack of confidence I had in my own words. Whether I wanted or not, I always ended up failing. My father's smirk flashed triumphantly before my eyes. Clenching my jaw and cracking my neck, I looked away with a frustrated groan.

Charlotte took my head in her hands and slowly stroked the sides of my face with her thumbs. Her stare was all-pervading, her scrutiny invasive, her tenacity to read my very soul devastating.

As she dragged me lower, her slender fingers searched my face as if she were touching me for the first time. When her fingers settled on my mouth, I took the half-empty flute from her hand and placed it together with mine on a stand nearby.

"You have tempted me several times now, sweet Charlotte. I plan on collecting."

"I have done no such thing." The playful smile coloring her eyes incited me.

"In my office," I explained, remembering how deeply she had roused my desire with her jealous curiosity when she wondered whether I had been with another woman in my workplace. "In your office," I continued and nudged her backward until she was forced to climb on the desk. We had shared a similar position in her office, but on that occasion, things had not concluded like I wanted. "In the hallways, when you pass me by. At the cafeteria. You tempt me every minute you are around me."

"You get tempted too easily then."

"You enjoy my torment too much, sugar."

I gripped her hips and pulled her against me with one ruthless movement. Charlotte gave a delightfully loud yelp. Come dawn, the entire hotel would know that we hadn't slept in separate rooms.

"That is not advisable."

"No?" she teased as her hands twisted in my shirt and drew me closer.

"I guess you'll have to find out."

And she was going to find out when she would toss and turn underneath me, begging for release. I leaned forward until she was sprawled on the desk and my hips were comfortably cradled by her thighs.

Kissing her, I untied the knot securing her robe and freed it brusquely, seeking the warmth of her bare skin. When the white fabric fell beside the desk, and Charlotte remained naked and ready for my touch, she coiled around my body, licking the notch at the base of my throat.

"I'm completely in, Charlotte."

Her rhythm faltered, and her eyes found mine with blazing intensity. She started working on the buttons of my shirt, never releasing me from the spell her brown eyes cast. I bent again to take her mouth, crazy to be touching her, but she stopped me with a firm hand placed over my heart.

"Undress," she ordered, unfastening the button of my jeans.

"Undress me," I challenged.

She hopped off the desk and circled me. With a smile, I understood what she was doing—what I had done the very first time we made love. She was taking her time, teasing me until both of us would be on the point of combusting.

Grabbing the open sides of my shirt, she tugged it back and dropped it to the ground on top of her robe. Her hot mouth closed over my left scapula where an irregular scar marred my skin. My body was a living testimony of the turmoil rattling within me. I had scars to remind me of disasters that couldn't be erased. Unknowingly, Charlotte worshiped them all.

She dipped her thumbs beneath my waistband and crouched to

release me from the confinement of my jeans. When she stood, her fingers trailed patterns up and down my spine making me shiver. I spun around so fast that she staggered back a step. But she was in my arms and pressed against the paper-littered desk before she could draw another breath.

"Witch."

A delicious smile took over her delicate face. Her legs locked around my hips, pulling me closer, urging me to take what I so desperately craved. I moved slowly, savoring every inch of her heated depths, our chests smacking together with each slide back in. We had gone slow our first time and the times that followed, but now, both of us needed the purge only wildness could provide.

I bit on her lip and sucked on her tongue until breath left her lungs, and her nails dug deep crescent marks in my shoulders. The slow pace maddened her as much as it maddened me. Settling her hands on my waist, she attempted to move faster, but I intentionally denied her.

"Wasn't slow your pace, sweet Charlotte?" I crooned against her ear, licking the delicate shell with my tongue.

"No, not tonight," she pleaded.

I studied her, ceasing all movement. Through my insistent stare, I transmitted what my tongue didn't verbally express. Once I started, once I drowned in my passion and let myself be caught by hers, I wouldn't stop, not even if the ceiling fell on my head.

Stripped of slowness and caution, I spread her thighs and thrust without delicacy, without restraint. Charlotte wailed her pleasure while her back arched and her arms went around my shoulders, clinging tight. Anchored to one another, we met halfway in perfect synchronization.

The need mounted and pulsed in every cell of my body. My blood grew hotter with the abandoned desire to possess her, to have her only to myself. I caught her wrists and forced her back on the desk. Naked and on display for my pleasure, Charlotte was a true living temptation. And I did not hold back.

When the first climax quaked her body, her eyes lost focus and her arms stilled by her sides. Words were not enough to describe the ravishing beauty Charlotte radiated in those moments of unrestrained pleasure. In the slackness of her sated body and the glint in her unfocused eyes, there was peace.

"Do you know what you're doing to me?" Her voice was rough from moaning so loudly and still supremely sensual.

Charlotte reached to touch my sweat-coated chest, and I hunched lower, hungry for her stroking hands. At first, she caressed my left side, her eyes meeting mine before she returned her attention to the line of scars trailing from my midsection to my right hip. Those were the marks that went deeper than flesh.

It was the crescent sign resting between my collarbones that she preferred above all others. Pushing her weight on her elbows, she pressed her burning lips against the unpleasant disfigurement and sucked gently, replacing the remembered pain with much too vivid pleasure.

Charlotte could do that to me. She could heal me. But she could also mess me up more than anybody else.

"I know. It's exactly what you're doing to me."

I caught her face and willed her to understand, to see beyond my rough edges and countless mistakes. Her eyes glowed with understanding. Her whole body did. We were still linked, still unfinished, still eager for more. I flexed my hips and succumbed to an unyielding rhythm, enjoying every helpless moan she gave and every shudder of her body.

"Stop tormenting me," she complained eventually, thrashing under the exquisite pressure I exerted over her body. My spine tingled with the need to surrender, but for another moment I found the strength to deny us both.

"It's not advisable to torment *me*," I murmured in her ear.

It was a warning as much as it was a plea. She laughed frustrated and pounded her small fists against my heaving chest. I relished her whimpers and the way she threw her head back. I lavished her throat with wet kisses and seized her mouth in an embrace of lips and tangle of tongues that equally scorched and soothed. Then I carried us both to our intimate personal nirvana.

"We are not going to sleep in separate rooms, Charlotte," I told her after I laid her on the bed, hovering over her delightfully sleepy frame.

"No, we are not," she agreed with a drowsy giggle then dragged me to bed, by her side.

My arms wrapped automatically around her body, nestling her into my side, where nothing and nobody could take her from me. I had learned that this state of peace and soul-deep satisfaction didn't last for long, so I intended to enjoy it while it did.

Charlotte falling asleep in my arms, trusting me when she was most vulnerable, brought me the kind of gratification that put my demons to rest.

THE NEXT DAY I IDLED on my own. After Charlotte joined Jack Stewart's team, I slipped into my room to give it a satisfactory lived-in nuance. At lunch, she called to postpone our date but promised we would have dinner instead. At six o'clock, I contacted her to let her know that I would pick her up whether or not she still had things to deal with.

I valued her work, but I valued her sanity more. She didn't even protest. The sigh she gave before I hung up showed she was grateful although her sense of responsibility prevented her from admitting it out loud.

Dressed casually and wearing a pair of aviators, I leaned against the black Mercedes I had rented and waited with barely controlled impatience. Charlotte went through the glass revolving doors of Drake Kendrix Zane, then she exited into the warm summer day with a stiff, somber expression that didn't suit her. She spotted me, and her delighted expression warmed my heart.

"I need you," she whispered as soon as she came within earshot.

She gripped my biceps, rose on tiptoes, and quickly brushed her lips against mine, then she carefully stepped aside, acting detached. If we kept our relationship private, my father wouldn't have any more leverage on me, yet I wasn't wholly convinced I wanted to hide it any longer. What Charlotte and I had shouldn't remain in the dark. She was radiant, and she deserved the limelight.

"You have me. Any way you want."

We rode in silence, my hand resting on Charlotte's knee and her hands playing absently with my fingers. Her thoughts were still directed to the case she was working on, but I didn't intend to let her dwell on it for much longer.

We dined early at the Bourbon Steak, and when I was satisfied with the change in her mood, I intertwined my fingers with hers and escorted her back to the car for our ride to the hotel.

Charlotte watched me, puzzled and visibly hurt, despite her efforts to hide it, when I brushed my fingers across her cheeks and left for my room. The shy smile that greeted me half an hour later as she opened the door of her own room caused a warm throbbing in my chest. I kissed her deeply even as I absently rubbed at the heaviness in my chest.

"Care to join me for an evening stroll?"

"I thought..."

"No assumptions, Charlotte," I interrupted her, pushing my way into the room with her tightly in my arms. "When you need to know something, ask me. I'll try my best to answer." She nodded pensively, knowing I meant more than just tonight.

I held up the little package I had brought and assessed her surprised reaction with a barely suppressed grin. Her attention traveled between me and the box as she deftly ripped the gift paper to reveal the sports outfit I had picked that morning. Her momentary interest turned immediately into a disconcerted scowl.

"Is this your subtle way of telling me that I should lose weight?"

When I understood her question was not a joke, I growled. Loudly.

"No. Get dressed and meet me downstairs in ten minutes."

"Yes, Sir," she replied, giving me a mock salute.

"Oh, Charlotte," I sighed, shaking my head. "Tempt me like this, and I will not be accountable for my actions." I slipped out of her room to the sound of youthful laughter.

BY THE TIME WE WALKED hand in hand past the gates of Rock Creek Park, Charlotte hadn't figured out my plan. However, when I rented a bicycle, she paled like a marble statue.

"Are you planning on killing me?" she demanded, horrified, stepping away from the bike as if it was a venomous creature ready to strike.

"I'm planning on teaching you how to ride a bike."

"I'm content when you ride your *bike,* and I'm behind you. That is when you drive within the speed limit and don't race—"

"Charlotte, calm down." I cupped her face and kissed her, uninterested in who might see us. "What are you afraid of?"

"Falling, evidently." But that was not all. Her agitation was too wild.

"And?" Hesitating, she looked at the bike doubtfully.

"I don't want to make a fool of myself."

Her voice was so soft and vulnerable that all amusement left me in an instant. I enveloped her in my arms and kissed her hair.

"You are not going to fall. I'm not going to let you."

I lowered the seat, watching her reluctantly sling a leg over the bike and clasp the handlebars more firmly than was required. Her jaw was set and her brown gaze intensely focused. Although I couldn't hear her heart beating, I could guarantee it was pounding frantically.

"Here are the brakes," I told her, pointing to the handlebar. "And here are the pedals." I touched them with the tip of my shoes. Charlotte rolled her eyes, exasperated, but her mouth curved at the corner as she slowly loosened up.

"The point is to never stop pedaling. I know the theory."

"First, practice your balance. Straddle the seat, and let's walk a little. You should get the feel of how the bike moves and how you should steer it."

I placed a hand at the small of her back and walked beside her, giving her the confidence she needed while making sure she was completely safe at all times.

Charlotte moved with the caution of a little girl and wore the most innocent look on her face, but the body flexing and tensing under my touch was pure, tantalizing woman.

"Am I doing it right, coach?"

I hummed my approval and bent to suck at the soft skin behind her ear. Charlotte moaned, leaned into me, and briefly lost control of her bike.

"Yes."

My hand shot out to grab the handlebar. Straightening, I chuckled as I brushed her heated cheeks. I had never imagined she would look so irresistible on a skinny little bicycle.

"Let's move a little faster."

"But—"

"On a bike, moving slow and hesitating is what gets you face down on the ground."

She obeyed and pushed herself against the flat concrete faster, but her former, difficultly-acquired relaxation vanished. She squared her shoulders, stiffened her spine, and scowled, concentrating on the road ahead.

Charlotte and I were alike in many respects. Neither of us enjoyed when we were put in situations that we couldn't control, yet we enjoyed challenges and didn't back down.

Always in contact with her body in one way or another, I helped her steer the bike with her hands, take turns, and move with the help of her body until I was utterly satisfied that she could take her feet off the ground.

"Let's raise the seat a little bit."

"It's okay like this."

I gave her a wicked wink and pinched her chin. "You're going to ride now, Charlotte."

Her lips parted on a gasp, and that enticing tongue of hers darted out to curl around her lower lip as her pearly teeth sank in the flesh. She read my thoughts as clearly as if I had spoken them out loud. At that moment, as her pupils dilated to dark points, the only thing I wanted her to ride was me.

"Um, okay."

I held the bike with both hands, steadying it for her. Between me flustering her and suddenly not having the ground underneath her feet, Charlotte momentarily lost her balance. Impulsively, her right arm wrapped around my shoulders and clung tightly.

"Hands on the handlebars, Charlotte," I instructed, my voice coming a little rougher than I had intended. "Start pedaling."

I did not remove my hands from the bike, and when she started pedaling, the bike didn't budge an inch. Uncomprehending, Charlotte cast me a puzzled look, but I urged her to continue.

When she became sufficiently confident in her skill, I removed my hands from the handlebars and allowed her to pedal down the trail. My left hand, however, never stopped gripping the leather seat of her bike.

"Faster. And don't stop pedaling."

Soon, I had to jog to keep up with her, but her ecstatic grin and the way she enjoyed herself like a child made it worth the effort.

When we met, I had been afraid of what Charlotte made me feel. Now the feelings were too powerful to deny. Charlotte Burton had gotten under my skin, and she was going nowhere.

"Excellent, sugar. Now, I'm going to take my hand off."

"I'm not sure I can…"

"You can, Charlotte. Keep pedaling."

I released the bicycle and allowed her to pedal freely. I was never too far behind, but I didn't go too close either. If she relied on my presence to feel safe while riding the bike, she would never trust doing it on her on.

For another couple of minutes, while I jogged behind her, Charlotte continued pedaling, then her sudden shriek startled even the birds in the trees.

"Marcus!" As soon as she cried out, my arms wrapped tightly around her waist and caught her before she even began falling.

"I've got you."

The blistering look she gave me was enough to make me groan and hug her tighter. Families with children and smitten couples walked past us, but the center of my existence and the only one holding my interest was Charlotte. I cupped her cheek and met her halfway for a sweltering kiss.

"You have a riding fixation. Motorcycles, horses, and now bicycles? What's next?" Charlotte demanded while we made our way back to the rented car.

Darkness had fallen, and Charlotte sagged happily against my side. I hated that tomorrow she would resume the stressful work that brought her no satisfaction.

"Unicycle, perhaps?"

"Very funny."

"And you look delicious on every one of them. I'd take Kai's suggestion into consideration if I were able to paint you myself. The image of you spread naked on my motorcycle, watching me as my eyes caress every inch of your body, makes me wild and desperately in need of you."

"Then drive faster," she teased.

I could only oblige.

THE FOLLOWING TWO DAYS I hardly saw anything of Charlotte. She left the hotel early and returned long after dinner time, which allowed me to complete a few tasks that Weston Caldwell had emailed me, yet her absence and especially the way she had to exhaust herself over a case she did not believe in didn't warm me up to her father or to her client's cause.

Friday evening, we dined in my room, only to mess the place enough that the cleaning staff wouldn't wonder whether the room was occupied or not.

I took Charlotte to bed well before midnight and was pleasantly assaulted by an exhausted but thoroughly aroused handful of woman, who practiced her riding skills and nearly made me lose my mind.

Saturday, she holed up in a conference room at Drake Kendrix Zane with the whole legal team and Mitch Stewart himself. When she returned to her hotel room, where I was already waiting for her, she rushed into my open arms and started crying—not a quiet cry, with tears trickling down her cheeks, but a cry with uncontrolled sobs that made her body shake.

I gritted my teeth until my jaw hurt, but I held her in silence and stroked the tears away.

By Sunday noon, I managed to boost her mood enough that the notion of a walk to Constitution Gardens piqued her interest. If the only way I could help ease her mind was to keep it occupied with something other than that damned case, then I would sure as hell do it.

"Do you own a professional camera?" I asked her out of the blue.

Sitting cross-legged in the middle of her bed, dressed casually and wearing no makeup, Charlotte finally looked her age. When stress and worry didn't mar her expression, she radiated a different kind of beauty, an irresistible charm. She threw me a puzzled glance and drew her lower lip between her teeth.

"Mm, yes," she replied uncertainly. "Are you going to tell my father?"

My enthusiasm momentarily faltered, and the surprise I had prepared for her didn't seem as inspired as it had when I came up with the idea.

"Do you, by any chance, still use it?" I pressed on.

"What's with the inquisition?" An adorable frown knit her brows together, and to her immediate dismay, I chuckled.

"Yes or no?"

"Sometimes, yes," she let out exasperated. "But it's old and a pain in the behind."

I grunted and winked satisfied then took her hand and led her to the adjacent sitting area of her room. On the coffee table, there were three gift boxes wrapped in glossy red and white paper with a huge bow on top of the middle box.

"You didn't."

Charlotte grinned and squealed and darted for her gifts, ripping the paper and digging through the boxes like a child on Christmas morning.

I knew nothing about photography or DSLR cameras, but the saleswoman had sworn that the brand, as well as the model, was top-notch.

Additionally, I had bought a tripod and an empty picture frame the size of a drawing block, hoping that Charlotte would use it for one of her masterpieces.

"Is it any good?" I asked and leaned my hip against a loveseat, crossing my arms over my chest and enjoying Charlotte's cheerfulness.

"Yeah, Marcus, it's—" she trailed off and put the camera back on the table. "I'm not used to receiving expensive gifts."

"That's nothing," I said and walked over to her to smooth the worry lines between her brows. "From now on, you'd better get used to it."

I brushed my lips against hers and swallowed the little moan she gave. If I kept touching her, she would never finish unpacking her gifts, so I went back to the loveseat and let her explore.

Next, she revealed the tripod and commented on its sturdiness then opened the box with the picture frame and looked it over carefully.

"What's this for?"

"Kai offered to paint you, but what about framing your own work?" She glowed, a thousand dreams waltzing in her eyes. It wasn't the first time she considered the possibility. "I hope you'll use this to frame one of your dearest pictures."

A couple of hours later, in Constitution Gardens, Charlotte was practically bouncing while I lay quietly on the ground, admiring her. With the Canon held adroitly in her hands, she knelt and rotated, capturing the lake and the trees from all angles.

"You should be doing this more frequently," I told her, nodding to the camera she was holding reverently between her hands.

I didn't need her to tell me that she hadn't indulged in her passion for a very long time. The joy in her eyes and the enthusiasm that she couldn't curb were proof enough.

"Indeed," she agreed and snapped several photos of me in quick succession, grinning broadly when she eventually came to settle in my arms, the camera resting on the grass next to us. "I missed this. Thank you."

"There's nothing to thank me for. I want you to be happy. I'm especially happy myself when I am the cause for your happiness or at least part of it."

She craned her neck and caught my lower lip between sharp, demanding teeth. I was used to leading in a relationship. Hell, I was always used to leading in my life. Yet, Charlotte taught me it was equally rewarding to be led, to surrender, and simply be the recipient of someone's attention.

"What happened the night of the movie?" I asked all of a sudden.

Charlotte stared at me, then her mouth curved, and her expression turned sultry at the memory. Against all rational thought, she had enjoyed my attention even then.

"Your sister and her husband were worried," I supplied.

"You remember…"

"I remember a lot of things. Like how delighted you were when I showed up."

"Oh please, don't get cocky," she scoffed and rolled her eyes.

I picked the camera off the ground and snapped a quick picture of her, lying there in my arms, looking cheerful, albeit cheeky. Charlotte giggled then sighed contentedly, and I couldn't help but notice how different she looked in that moment from the commanding lawyer.

"My niece had a fever. You met her last Sunday."

I remembered the wide-eyed baby girl, sitting in her fuchsia stroller. And I also remembered the near heart attack she had given me. The little girl was basically mini-Charlotte. For a tiny, dreadful moment, I had wondered if she was her daughter.

"I'd like to meet her again, get fully and properly introduced."

"Christina might not like you much." Shyly, almost repentantly, Charlotte looked up at me from beneath thick lashes. "But she does want to meet you too. Get fully and properly introduced."

"I deserve that. I do hope her sister still likes me, even a little."

"That's an understatement of how I feel."

Charlotte's eyes were loaded with too much emotion. My chest hurt, and my lungs burned from lack of air. It should have been simple, two people falling for each other, but nothing worth having was simple.

Stroking Charlotte's face, I sighed and let my head drop in the grass. I always failed when I needed the most to succeed.

"Don't let me fail you, Charlotte," I pleaded.

Chapter 26

Charlotte

*D*espite Marcus's desire to spend all his time in Washington with me, playing the role of an unpaid bodyguard and excessively skilled lover, he had his own job to return to.

I awakened to an empty bed and a displeased call from the almighty James Burton, then I went through my morning routine swiftly but with a restlessness that made me jittery and quite gloomy. I didn't realize I had been feeling safer knowing Marcus was around until I knew he wasn't there anymore.

At nine o'clock sharp, Vincent Cole knocked on my door. With a resigned sigh, I opened to find him leaning against the doorframe, holding two tall paper cups, emanating the delicious scent of dark coffee. When he saw me dressed in a dark blue sheath dress, he greeted me with a crooked smile that mitigated the severity of his features.

During the past weeks, I had fluctuated from disliking him as much as I hated Drake to actually appreciating his opinions and work ethic. Once you got to know him, he seemed an honest man, with a staggering drive for work, who pursued his goals with sharp ruthlessness.

Still, I suspected him of being stealthily ambitious, but for the moment, I chose to ignore that trait of his personality. Lately, it seemed he had as many reservations about Jack as I did.

"Thank you," I said, accepting the cup of coffee and falling into step beside him.

"Have you had breakfast? I'd like to discuss something with you."

"Sure. I was just heading out."

"Perfect."

We didn't bother chatting on our way to the French bistro downstairs and remained in companionable silence for the first part of our breakfast. Cole was the kind of man who didn't tolerate small talk, and strangely, his attitude did not offend me. After all, talking anything but business would have made us both feel awkward.

"I'll be forthright," he said out of the blue, placing the napkin beside his plate and straightening in his seat. The look in his eyes was as stern as his voice. "Has Mayor Stewart threatened you?"

"No? Why would you think that?"

His grave stare turned graver still, if that was possible. He looked around nervously as if somebody might be keeping an eye on us, and maybe his prudence was not entirely misplaced. The thought chilled me and made me miss Marcus all the more.

"Maybe I should not have mentioned it—"

He cast another glance around us, making me feel as suspicious as he seemed to be. Tension seized me more fiercely with each passing moment, and the ache in my bones amplified. It was clear that Vincent Cole was a man fearing for his safety, a man who had been threatened.

"If Mitch Stewart threatened you, that is very serious."

The confession struck me as odd. As far as I knew, Vincent Cole and Mitch Stewart had never met alone, but apparently, I didn't know everything.

"I'd say that is significant," he corrected me, the former fear I had sensed in him completely gone.

"Clearly. But aren't you afraid? For your safety, I mean."

"I wouldn't have gotten where I am if I had been afraid,

Charlotte." He grinned, a teeth-showing smile that looked awkward on his face. "I can call you by your first name, can't I?"

"Of course."

I experienced a sudden appreciation for the man, and a connection formed between us that hadn't been there before. The smile I gave him was small but sincere.

"What I wanted to discuss with you is not exactly Mitch Stewart's threat to my person, but what it implied. Why would a father threaten his son's lawyer to tread carefully if his son didn't have anything to hide? I believe you share my doubts about Jack's character and his actions, Charlotte. Am I right?"

"You are." I trusted my instincts and decided that Vincent Cole was a man I could place my faith in. "I don't think Jack is entirely innocent, if at all."

"I have a lead I'd like to pursue, but I didn't trust Drake to discuss it openly. Care to join me for an unscheduled interview?"

"Sure."

Maybe because I had gotten used to Drake's extravagance and his blatant tendency of showing his wealth, I didn't expect Cole to own a luxury car. He opened the door of his Bentley and brought it to life with economical movements. The interior was opulent and made of cream leather and wooden veneers. It looked starkly new, but I suspected that was only due to diligent maintenance driven to paranoid heights. *Men and their toys*, I thought and couldn't help a smile.

"Drake is furious," Cole said.

I gave a start. Thinking about Marcus and his own love for his toys, I had all but forgotten that he was not the driver but Cole.

"Why is that?" I asked although I wasn't quite interested.

"He filed a motion to dismiss. The judge denied it."

That caught my attention, not only because once he filed a motion to throw out a case, submitting it again to the same judge would probably not yield different results, but because I had never been informed about his decision. Apparently, in Drake's vocabulary, being lead counsel meant being the only counselor, which reminded me that I was part of this team only because I scored them image points.

"Did you know about it before he filed?"

"Nope," Cole made a popping sound and smirked, then he regained his seriousness. "I wanted to show you something too. It's in the glove compartment."

I pulled out a set of photographs that I recognized as screenshots from the footage that Holden had sent. It was Jennifer standing at the edge of the dance-floor in deep conversation with two other women. I held the pictures and arched an eyebrow at Cole. I had seen the footage, but of all people Jennifer had talked to, why were these two girls special?

"Jack never put their names on the guest list although they were evidently present," Vincent explained. "So I did some digging. The blonde girl, to Jennifer's left, is Elana Beckham. The other one is Rheya Larsson. I understand they knew one another since elementary school and were very close friends."

"Why would Jack not mention them?" I thought out loud, and Cole nodded, the same suspicion reflected on his face. "And wouldn't Drake want to depose them? If we know about them, then Leon Holden certainly does and has already taken their statements."

The communication between Jack and Drake was more open, so it was very difficult to believe that Drake hadn't known about Jack's little omission.

In an exaggerated show of zeal, Drake had started deposing every person who had attended the party. He explained his desperation to learn what every potential witness knew and might say at trial as a quest to find the truth. To me, it looked more and more like a quest to bury it.

"Exactly, but who understands Drake? Which brings me to the next matter."

He stopped the car at a traffic light, took his phone from the inner pocket of his jacket, and handed it to me after quickly typing the security code. I was uncertain at first, but he encouraged me to play the only video in his media gallery.

It was only a few seconds long, and it showed a man who was too skinny for his impressive height. He hurried down a corridor with walls coated in gold and beige wallpaper and parquet flooring covered in red velvet. It was a corridor like the one at the Ritz-Carlton Hotel where Jack and Jennifer's pre-wedding party had taken place, like the one where Jack had been caught on camera before Jennifer was killed.

"There's another picture in there," Vincent told me, nodding again to the glove compartment that was still open.

Sure enough, there was a screenshot of Jack on that same corridor, but while Jack walked forward, the thin man seemed to be leaving.

"This wasn't in the footage Holden sent. How do you have it?"

"It was on Drake's computer."

Cole looked ashamed like one does after being caught with his hand in the cookie jar, but then, he shrugged and continued driving without really caring what I thought of him going through Drake's computer, evidently without his knowledge or permission.

"That's Jase Parker," Cole explained. "And that's the hallway that led to Jennifer Gunnar's suite. Look at the vase."

Right in the middle of the hallway, there was a high table placed against the wall with a vase on top and fresh flowers. For every floor, the vase was different as though the interior designer had meant to set a different theme for each level of the hotel. On the floor where Jennifer's suite had been located, the vase was lilac, and that night, it had been filled with white lisianthus.

I stopped the video right as the thin man was passing by that table and compared it with the screenshot showing Jack. In both images, there was a tall lilac vase with white flowers.

"Only the timestamp on Jack's footage writes 2:10 a.m., and the timestamp on this video is 2:15."

"Curious, isn't it?"

It was definitely curious, but it was more curious still how this footage had resurfaced out of nowhere and how only Drake seemed to know about it. Replaying the footage and comparing it for the fourth time with the picture of Jack, I started questioning two things.

One, had Jennifer had an affair with this mysterious man while still planning to marry Jack? If that were the case, it meant both men felt differently but equally scorned, so both had motive to kill.

And two, had Drake doctored the real footage by planting this video of the blonde, curly-haired man to absolve Jack of any suspicion?

We drove to the main campus of the American University, looking for Jase Parker, who was not an easy man to find. When we finally spotted him, he was scurrying to the cafeteria. His hands were shoved into the pockets of his trousers, his dirty blonde hair seemed disheveled, and his eyes haunted.

"Mr. Parker," Cole stopped him, his tone friendly, his posture ominous. "Can we have a word, please? We won't take much of your time."

I could swear the air froze in his lungs. Jase Parker stiffened, and his eyes widened as his jaw set. The vein in his forehead throbbed, and his white skin turned whiter still.

"Who are you?" he managed through thin lips.

"I'm Vincent Cole. This is Charlotte Burton. We are Jack Stewart's lawyers."

"Isn't Cameron Drake his lawyer?" Jase asked and looked over his shoulder like he expected to find someone watching.

"Yes, he is," I told him and presented him with my most cordial smile. "But we are part of his team too and hoped you could answer a few questions. Come on, brunch is on us."

He hesitated, but after scanning his surroundings and glancing one more time at Cole, who fixed him with that spine-chilling stare of his, Jase walked into the cafeteria. We encouraged him to order anything he wanted to eat or drink, but he refused and hid inside a booth. Neither Cole nor I missed that Jase had chosen the farthest possible table from the windows.

"The night of June 30th you were at the Ritz Carlton, attending Jennifer and Jack's party. Is that correct?" Cole started and folded his hands on the table.

"Yes."

Jase's gestures fluctuated between drumming his fingers on the tabletop and cracking his joints to moving his legs restlessly under the table and glancing almost obsessively at the door. He was edgy, and every time he glanced at Cole, he became downright frightened.

"Can you tell us, to the best of your knowledge, what happened?" I asked and cautioned Cole with a glance to back off.

We wanted Jase scared enough to spill out any information he might be in possession of, but not so scared as to not speak at all. Vincent leaned against the backrest and pretended he was inspecting the cafeteria while I took the reins of the questioning.

Jase recited a story of happiness and love that sounded too much like a survival protocol, something arranged beforehand. Just like Jack, he painted the perfect night, the most fascinating of celebrations, but the fairy tale had ended with a murder.

"I understand. You are trying to say that prior to the murder, there wasn't any obvious cause for hostility between the two."

"They were in love. There was no hostility," he said in a clipped voice then shoved a hand through his hair, sending his curls in all directions.

"But was there any hostility between you and Jennifer? Perhaps between you and Jack?"

That gave him pause. It finally dawned on him that my open-arms attitude coupled with the warm smile did not imply that I was a pushover. His brows furrowed, and the blood drained from his lips.

"I don't understand," he muttered dryly.

"Then let me rephrase. Were you involved with Jennifer, and Jack found out, or were you fighting with her because she didn't want to tell him about your affair?"

"I have a girlfriend," he answered outraged. Jase Parker didn't strike me as a particularly mercurial person, but at the moment, he was switching from one emotion to another. He was restless.

"That does not answer my question."

"I was not involved with Jennifer, and if you are trying to suggest that I killed her, I think you should be talking to my lawyer."

Cole ran a hand over his face to hide his grin. Jase knew his rights, and if he decided to not talk, we had no authority to make him, not without his lawyer present. Leaving this meeting without answers was not even remotely close to amusing.

"Look, Jase, we don't believe you killed anybody, we just have to get your testimony," I struggled to assuage his rising temper. "At trial, the prosecutor will be much harder on you or any other witness."

"So you have to be prepared, right?"

"Right," I agreed and wondered if he had already been prepared for testimony by another lawyer. "So how close are you to Jack?"

"We're like brothers."

"Would you say you are close enough to him that you would lie to protect him?"

"I am not lying. This is the only truth there is."

"I didn't say you were lying. I only asked if you were willing to lie, by omission or otherwise, in order to protect your friend?"

"No. Not if murder was involved."

He was lying. It was right there in his frantic eyes and the tight line of his lips. He was lying, and he was afraid.

"Just one more question, Jase. Can you tell us where you were that night between 2 o'clock and 2:30 a.m.?"

Jase Parker blanched.

"At the party, evidently."

"More specifically," Cole cut in.

If I had been on the other side of the table, and Cole had been the one examining me, perhaps I would have looked just as high-strung and short-winded as Jase.

"I don't know," Jase snapped. "I never thought I would have to account for my whereabouts."

"We have proof that you left the floor of Jennifer's suite at exactly 2:15 a.m. Jack got there at 2:10 a.m. That means there are 5 minutes you spent in that suite with Jennifer and Jack."

In point of fact, we didn't have proof that Jase Parker had ever been in Jennifer's room. Up to that moment, we hadn't even been sure that the footage of him leaving the floor was real.

"I've never gone in that room," he hissed.

He was too quick to defend himself and his voice too shaky and loud. People looked at us and gossiped quietly, which appeared to stress Jase out even more. He licked his lips and played with the black leather bracelet on his left wrist. Under the table, he shuffled his feet, getting ready to flee.

"But you were on that floor. Why?"

Parker's eyes shifted around the place as if he was looking for inspiration or rather salvation. Tiny dots of perspiration coated his forehead, and he oscillated from glancing away to staring too intently at Cole and me.

"I received a call. I was supposed to meet a business partner."

"Funny," Cole chuckled and focused his gaze on Jase. "When I have an appointment, I tend to know at what time it is."

"I was at a party. I didn't keep track of time."

"Who is your business partner?" Cole went on dully.

"Vinny Savidge."

I did not hide my surprise, and as my eyebrows arched and my body jumped just a little in my chair, Jase realized the huge mistake he had just made.

"Then you won't mind if we ask him to corroborate your statement."

"Look, I have classes," Jase replied and stood on wobbly legs. "If that would be all…"

"It is. Thank you for your time, Mr. Parker," Cole told him, displaying something akin to a triumphant smirk.

He hadn't given us any clear-cut answers, but like Marcus had once noted, I valued my instincts, and they were telling me that Jase Parker knew more about that night than he was letting on.

"Jase," I called. He looked over his shoulder, hesitating. "Are you afraid?"

"What kind of stupid question is that?"

"Has someone threatened you?"

He didn't reply, but the answer was in his eyes.

"No," he lied.

"Good," I smiled. "What did you say you were studying?"

"Computer science."

"I thought you were a guy of the arts, but I suppose science would fit you better." He frowned and eyed me like I were crazy. "You'd make a terrible actor."

Jase turned green like he was going to be sick. He knew I knew he was lying. He spun, and half-stumbling half-running, he fled from the cafeteria.

On our way back to the car, neither Cole nor I spoke. It was clear now that Drake had found his scapegoat. If there was no evidence, no credible witness to point at Jack, and suddenly a new suspect surfaced, then Drake really had a chance at winning.

Vincent's phone rang, and whoever called didn't give him good news. At first, he looked stunned, then he turned forlorn. The call was short and succinct, and after he hung up and faced me, his appearance was grave and slightly pale.

"It was my PI. Rheya Larsson has been found dead."

Chapter 27

Charlotte

*E*lana Beckham was in danger.

I watched the footage for the tenth time since Cole left to meet with his private investigator, and for the tenth time, I hissed and slammed my fists against the table. If only I could decipher what Jennifer had been telling Elana and Rheya. Evidently, whatever Jennifer had known was worth killing for—again.

Elana Beckham was the last of the three friends to really know what happened that night. She was the last link to a secret that Jennifer had been in possession of, a secret that was so dangerous that it had to be silenced.

On a whim, I gathered my purse and drove to Jack's apartment. The tracking anklet he was wearing was his alibi. He couldn't be blamed for Rheya Larsson's death, so if Drake could prove that there was a link between Jennifer's death and Rheya's, then he could create reasonable doubt. Since Jack didn't kill Rheya, he had no motive to kill Jennifer either.

I did believe the two murders where related, but I did not think they were not connected to Jack. In fact, I was convinced that the only reason Rheya had been killed was to take to the grave the secret Jennifer Gunnar had confided in her.

At half-past two in the afternoon, Jack was sleeping. The cleaning lady showed me to a surprisingly tasteful living room and told me to make myself comfortable until she woke Jack up. From the way she rolled her eyes, it was obvious it would take a while.

I was too agitated to sit, so I walked to the window while marveling at the beauty of Jack's apartment and wondering whether Jennifer had decorated it herself.

Unlike the man who inhabited it, the space was welcoming and classy, in shades of gray and purple, a perfect mix of male practicality and ladylike finesse. Despite the lush decor, the apartment seemed impersonal. There were no framed pictures on the mantelpiece or souvenirs in the showcase. There was nothing to make it look like home.

"To what do I owe the pleasure?"

I flinched. Jack strolled through an archway that must have connected the living area to his bedroom, wearing nothing but gray sweatpants that hung obnoxiously low on his hips. His face bore the creases of his sheets, and his hair was in utter disarray. He looked annoyed at having been disturbed but not remotely worried. If he knew about Rheya's death, he didn't seem affected in the least.

"What can you tell me about Elana Beckham, Jack?"

The muscle in his jaw ticked. His eyes darkened, and his laidback disposition changed abruptly. With a grunt, Jack slumped in an armchair and crossed his legs at the ankles.

"She was Jennifer's friend," he replied shortly and fumbled for his cigarettes.

"She was at the party on June 30th, wasn't she?"

Out of nowhere, the maid appeared with an unopened pack of cigarettes and an ashtray that she placed on the table next to Jack. He shrugged and started smoking while glancing into the distance.

"You never included her on the guest list. Why?"

"I must have forgotten about her. There were a lot of people."

"You are a smart man, Jack. You do realize that by concealing her name, it looks suspicious. Why did you leave her name off of the guest list?"

I didn't mention that he had also forgotten about Rheya Larsson but waited patiently for his reaction. He extinguished his half-smoked cigarette and jumped to his feet, walking to the crystal bar in the corner where he poured a generous glass of brandy. It seemed his nerves needed more than just tobacco to be soothed.

"It just slipped my mind," he insisted and gulped down the second glass of alcohol.

"You know what I think? That it slipped your mind exactly because she was Jennifer's friend."

My instincts had not been wrong. Jennifer had told something of importance to her friends, and now, only Elana Beckham was aware of that information. Luckily, she could be a substantial pawn in the elucidation of Jennifer Gunnar's murder, but until all the cards were on the table, she risked the same horrible fate as her deceased friends.

"You know what I think?" he shot back, his tone menacing, his eyes cruel. "That you are my lawyer, and as my lawyer, you are doing a very lousy job."

"I have your best interest at heart," I lied but tried to appear serene nonetheless. Unlike other lawyers, I was naïve enough to side with the truth. I was naïve enough to want justice to prevail. "She might be a valuable witness. We should depose her, don't you agree?"

Jack looked incredulous. His eyebrows nearly united with his hairline, and his jaw turned slack before he composed himself.

"She has nothing to say that the other guests haven't already said," he muttered, but his fingers trembled around his tumbler as he lifted it to his lips.

"Let's hope she has more to say than Rheya Larsson."

The glass fell through Jack's fingers and shattered in tiny pieces as it hit the ground. He pinned me with a glare so full of hatred and contempt that the blood turned cold in my veins. I grabbed my purse and headed for the door. Just like Jase Parker, Jack hadn't verbally supplied anything of significance, but his attitude and the dread in his eyes divulged all I needed to know. I was close to the truth.

"You know what's funny, Jack?" I asked, glancing over my shoulder. He sighed heavily and didn't seem remotely interested.

"People from that party keep dying, and the question is: why would someone go so far to silence them?"

I turned and left, but as I exited Jack's apartment, I thought that his expression right at the end looked even funnier. He looked surprised like he truly didn't know the answer to my question.

A crew was working on the elevator and politely directed me to take the stairs, but as I headed to the other end of the hallway, Vincent Cole came jogging up the stairs and quickly disappeared inside an apartment.

I followed him as if in a daze. At first, drowned out by the blows and crunches and loud voices of the workers, I missed the sound of approaching footsteps coming from an adjacent hallway. At the very last minute, urged by pure instinct, I whirled back and hid around the corner. Mayor Stewart pulled a key from his pocket and opened the door of apartment 13, the same apartment where only moments ago Vincent Cole had entered.

"Finally," he snapped, not stepping inside just yet. "I've been looking for you all day. Where were you?"

I could see his profile, but Cole remained inside, his voice not carrying to my little shelter behind the wall. The mayor was distraught and furious, and while he spoke, he gestured angrily, much like his son did.

He hesitated in the doorway, glancing my way. I shrank in my refuge and tightened my fingers around the handle of my purse. I was breathing raggedly, and my heart was thumping crazily in my chest. It would have taken the mayor less than ten steps to find me, and then...

"This is getting out of hand," he continued, and I let out a breath of relief. "I expected you to have dealt with it by now. If they keep digging—"

That piqued my interest. He was worried, and the emotion felt alien to a man who wielded his power as a weapon. Whatever hadn't been dealt with could cause him serious trouble.

"I'm doing my part, now do yours," the mayor threatened then paused.

I strained to hear Cole's reply, but nothing came, not from what I could hear. A worker spotted me standing there around the corner and eyed me suspiciously, then he glanced at the mayor. I smiled and rummaged through my purse, faking clumsiness until the workman lost interest and returned to his business.

"And take care of that—girl. She's causing more trouble than she's worth."

With that, Mitch Stewart stepped inside the apartment and shut the door with a bang. Frustration crawled up my skin like a swarm of ants. Who was *that girl* and what was the mayor afraid could be found if *they kept digging*?

It must have been less than five minutes when Cole emerged from the apartment, looking like a burglar afraid to get caught. He walked down the adjacent hallway where the mayor had come from, holding his phone close to his chest.

Eventually, I mustered the courage and strength to move from my hiding spot and leave the building. My legs were trembling, and my palms were sweaty, but worst of all were my muddled thoughts.

My head ached with questions and doubts. When Cole excused himself earlier on, he looked odd and a tad too rushed, but I had never imagined his urgency had anything to do with stealthily meeting the mayor.

Just when I thought I had a grasp on things, everything turned upside down. Just when I thought I had placed my trust in the right people, new suspicions dismantled all I had believed.

Maybe Cole was not the man I believed him to be. Maybe the one covering things up for the Stewarts had never been Drake.

I returned to my hotel room and continued working, struggling to extract the truth from the spider web that had been woven around Jack Stewart. Sometime after four in the afternoon, a knock at the door interrupted my work process.

A young man wearing the hotel's uniform politely handed me a single coral pink rose with a red ribbon tied in a pretty bow around the long stem. I accepted the flower and the enveloped card and remained dumbfounded in the doorway long after the valet left.

"Let me gaze upon your shadow,
And kiss the soft contour of your shape

In waves of emerald and cotton
As it spreads and trembles
And in the end, it breaks."

I looked at the white card and the black written lines with a stupidly giant smile on my face. If I hadn't recognized the writing, I might have even felt offended, but I knew who had sent the rose and written the note. *Marcus,* I thought with a sudden warm feeling in my chest.

Roughly an hour later, silence was disrupted again by the same controlled knock. When I opened the door, the same young man greeted me with a warm, conspiratorial smile and handed me a peach-colored camellia in a transparent plastic case. Another note was tied to the case by the same red satin ribbon.

"Let me find shelter under your wings of fire,
And stroke the softness of your heart
For you are light and I am dark
And as your flames leap and conquer
To you, my lady, I will bow."

Marcus was not here with me, but I could swear I felt his breath fanning across my skin while he sensually recited the words. From miles away, he managed to make my blood hot and my flesh burn for his touch. With his attentive gestures and well-planned scheme, he surprised and seduced me.

Sometime close to six o'clock, I realized I was actually expecting another knock at the door, and eagerly so. When it finally came, I almost darted to wrench the door open, a giggle escaping me right before my eyes stumbled upon—nothing.

Nobody was waiting in the hallway, but there was a single white envelope forgotten on the ground. I went back into the room and grabbed a napkin, then I used it to pick up the envelope and retrieve the folded card inside.

DON'T give up!

The cryptic message left me speechless, but my thoughts were roaring. Who had written the note, and what shouldn't I give up on? Was this a stupid joke or just a test?

When another knock echoed timidly, I hurled the door open with visible irritation, expecting the mysterious messenger from earlier to finally make an appearance, when in fact my flower valet waited patiently and slightly amused in front of my door.

"Oh, I'm sorry," I muttered, schooling my expression in an amicable one.

"For you," he said simply, pushing forward a sophisticated crystal vase with tuberoses, a red ribbon, and a safely tucked note beneath the satin bow.

"Let me love a love that sheds its armor,
And feast on lips of silk and velvet
For I am storm and you are fire,
And as for you I thirst and hunger
Together, my little lady, we shall ignite."

I brought the note to my lips and kissed it. I had never been particularly fond of poetry because I had never been overwhelmed by emotions enough to understand it. Now, laid on paper in Marcus's crisp handwriting, almost coming to life in his voice, the lyrics made me feel giddy and desperately in need of being touched, of slowly becoming complacent under his deft caress.

The thought that Marcus had planned this before he departed, leaving strict instructions to the hotel staff for when and how to deliver his gifts had me basking in a pleasant, calming joy. I wasn't the only one starting to care.

Setting the tuberoses in the living room next to the rose and the encased camellia, I allowed myself another moment of admiring the beauty of the flowers and rejoicing in the feeling that made my heart thump faster, then I returned to work.

I ordered dinner and finally switched my laptop off sometime after ten o'clock. I felt tired, but even more so in Marcus's absence. I considered calling him, but hearing his voice and not having him beside me would have been like pouring salt over fresh wounds.

Eventually, I slipped inside the steamy shower, letting the hot drops pour down over me like rain. I stood there, with my head bowed, my forehead pressed against the tiled wall, and a hand gripping my throat until the torrents of water battered the restlessness pulsing in my muscles.

When I finished, I returned to the bedroom, my eyes appreciating the comforting darkness. I climbed into bed with my back to the windows and to Marcus's side of the bed. Enveloped by the sheets that only a night ago had been tangled around our clammy bodies, his scent was so strong that I could almost taste it on my tongue.

I closed my eyes, and his beaming, seductive face appeared effortlessly behind my eyelids. I thought I could feel his warmth, his breath caressing the nape of my neck, his touch warming my shoulder, making my skin tingle in anticipation.

"The poem, did you like it?"

Although I recognized his voice, I twisted under the covers and let out an impulsive, earsplitting scream. A hand came over my mouth, stifling the distressed sounds, and an easy amused laughter mingled with my scared shrieks.

"Easy, sugar."

"Marcus," I breathed, thinking in a corner of my mind how tired he sounded. "You are here."

I reached for the lamp on my nightstand and flooded the room with an amber light. I was sure I looked just as shaken as I sounded. Marcus was lying on his side, supporting his head in his left hand. A sleepily amused grin twitched his lips upward, and a lustful look settled in his ocean-blue eyes. He was here with me, and I was sufficiently selfish to luxuriate in the joy and comfort his presence brought me.

"Where else would I be?"

"New York," I muttered, knowing he had his own responsibilities and deadlines at the engineering company he worked for.

He shook his head, a listless movement that gave away his exhaustion. I secured his face between my hands and brushed my lips across his. The kiss was short and chaste, yet full of emotion.

The smile he regaled me with almost stopped my heart.

"You expected me not to come back? It makes me edgy when you are away from me. It makes me desperate when I am not certain that you are safe. I'll be coming back to D.C. for as long as you are here."

"And it's not up for discussion," I said, mimicking his voice as well as I could. We looked at each other in silence, then we both started laughing. He clasped my shoulders and pulled me to his chest, where nothing could touch me but him.

"The day is too long without you."

"I know the feeling."

Lying on top of him with his arms like bands of steel around my waist, I writhed just enough to be aware of his presence, of his hot body underneath me. I stroked his face with gentle fingers and lingered on his sleepy eyes and parted mouth. No touch, no kiss, not even a breath was hurried.

The transition between innocent touches and frantic, purposeful thrashing happened smoothly like we didn't care about anything else in the world but simply being together. With Marcus, it was never about the race to the glorious mind-blowing pinnacle, but about the journey that led to it. It was about the firestorm that consumed and united us.

"Thank you for coming back. You center me. You keep me anchored. You keep me safe."

"Always."

Marcus nestled my body tightly against his chest, refusing to allow any modicum of distance between us. I kissed him one more time and stared at him until my eyes closed, and I drifted. I knew he wouldn't be by my side in the morning.

THE NEXT DAY, VINCENT COLE waited for me in the reception area, and we drove to Drake Kendrix Zane together. It was difficult to keep my cool and not let my suspicions show, but eventually, I managed to put on a collected smile on my face.

At the firm, Drake wanted to prepare Jack for testifying during trial. If the jury saw his pain and heard his side of the story, they would be less inclined to convict him, Drake claimed.

Jack was particularly irritable, so I chose not to interact directly with him if possible. He wasn't as sarcastic as usual and listened to all the suggestions that Cole and Drake were giving him, but his heart wasn't in the testimony they were forging.

Sometime during the meeting, my phone chimed with a text from Marcus. *Have lunch,* he wrote. I nearly chuckled. He knew I wouldn't get the chance to eat, but it was nice nonetheless that he had thought of it. After that, my attention took a more enjoyable path.

I thought of Marcus and how delicately he had kissed me early in the morning before he returned to New York. I thought of the many ways he had surprised me over the little time we had been together and how badly I wanted to reciprocate. For the remainder of the day, I considered all possibilities and produced all sorts of scenarios, but because I was not as impulsive as Marcus, it was harder to think of ways to surprise him.

By ten in the evening, I was already expecting him. I knew the journey back and forth, the long workday, and the distance between us would drain him. I also knew that a man like him didn't frequently take bubble baths with calming salts, champagne, and chocolates to complement the mood. It wasn't something out of the ordinary, but it was my way of showing him that I cared for him and that I appreciated the effort and the time he put into our relationship.

Disappointment gripped me as the minutes rolled by, and Marcus didn't come back. It was well past eleven, and there was no sign of him. I nearly took the bath alone, but doing so would have only stressed even more harshly his absence.

Sitting on the edge of the Jacuzzi, I dipped my fingers in the water, feeling the soft texture of the foam. It was getting chilly.

I turned on the heating system and kept waiting for Marcus as the water warmed up again. Wearing a white satin robe and nothing underneath, I strolled to the living area and finally worked on something other than Jack's case. I did something I hadn't done in a tremendously long time.

I downloaded the pictures I had taken in Constitution Gardens and started editing them until they looked like stills from a movie. The work kept me busy and the disappointment at bay.

"Charlotte?"

It didn't matter how late it was or how long I had waited for him. I leaped off my seat and dashed to the door, jumping into his arms and locking my hands around his neck as soon as I reached him. I slammed my mouth against his with an exultant giggle and only released him when neither of us could breathe anymore.

"What's this for?"

Those gorgeous eyes of his looked as tired as they had the previous night, but they regarded me with desire and delight.

"I..." the words got stuck in my throat and the notion of what I had been about to say made me flush and look away. Marcus had gotten too quickly and too deeply behind my barriers, but I wasn't ready yet to let him know just how deeply. "You kept me waiting, Mr. King."

I slid off him and struggled not to beam when his hands didn't leave my body. I gently pushed his hands aside and slowly walked backward to the open door of the bathroom.

Grabbing the knot of my sash, I untied it without releasing his sultry gaze. A low rumble came from deep within his chest, and his Adam's apple convulsed in his throat. His former hungry stare was voracious now.

Taking another step closer to the bathroom, I pushed the robe off my shoulders and let it pool at my feet while Marcus drank me in. I was by no means so courageous as to not feel self-conscious, but I steeled myself and stomped over my insecurities. I had planned to seduce him, and I wasn't going to back down now.

Marcus inhaled sharply, taking one tentative step toward me. I winked and gave him a provocative smile, then I turned around and proceeded to the dim-lit bathroom, aware of my complete nakedness and the way the warm, perfumed air caressed my skin.

My heartbeat echoed a raging rhythm in my ears, but I knew Marcus was following. Slipping a foot into the hot water, I focused on my toes as they disappeared under the white foam, rather than on my nudity. I glanced over my shoulder and found Marcus standing mere feet away. His fingers were working quickly on the buttons of his shirt.

My gaze slid downward, caressing the length of his body, and halted on the firm bulge that the material of his trousers couldn't conceal. He was just as aroused as I was.

"Join me," I whispered and sank into the water all the way to my chin.

Chapter 28

Marcus

The office in Charlotte's absence was a complete nightmare. Had she not asked me to pick up some necessary papers she had ordered from Sofia, I wouldn't have even gone near the building.

I strode into the interns' office, and the buzz of conversation ceased as four pairs of eyes turned to me. Unaffected, I went to my desk and started typing an email to Charlotte while I waited for her assistant to give me the documents I needed.

I saluted my so-called colleagues but otherwise made no attempt to join their discussion. I did not doubt Charlotte's judgment, but by God, the interns she had picked were insufferable.

Matt Russell and Adam Harris were best buddies and equally arrogant. Despite the camaraderie they boasted, I knew for a fact that both of them were stabbing each other in the back.

Victoria Brown, although she had the beautiful face of a supermodel and a matching body, was the queen of vanity. Her inner ugliness eclipsed her physical beauty, rendering her dull and uninteresting.

The only decent person in the room was Phillip Foster, who I liked although I hadn't had much contact with him, and his affinity for Charlotte irked my possessive side a bit.

"Mm—are you free this evening?"

I looked up to find Victoria Brown leaning against my desk. Fidgeting with the hem of her red jacket, she cast me unappealing, flirtatious stares that weren't by far as subtle as she imagined.

"I'm afraid I am not." The chill in my voice stunned her, and her mouth hung open.

"Oh, come on," she insisted, recovering quickly. "We are all going to a bar nearby. It's called *L'Affaire*. Do you know it?"

"I do know it. I also know it's not the proper environment for a group of lawyers." My disdain was hardly concealed. Ms. Brown frowned before a plastic smile spread on her face, trying to lure a man who had already been lured by another.

"We are not going as lawyers but as friends. Think about it. It will be fun."

"Maybe I will drop by with my date."

I knew that wouldn't happen, but I just couldn't help myself. Her kittenish expression turned suddenly into a venomous, strained look that killed the last remnants of her appeal. She was a woman who had visibly never been faced with rejection. Being the one who acquainted her with it was a pleasure in itself.

"Mr. King, your presence is required upstairs." Sofia appeared in the doorway with her glasses hanging around her neck and her hands struggling to contain a frightening amount of papers.

I sent my email, turned off the computer, then followed the kind-eyed woman without casting another glance at the frozen harpy by my desk.

"My father?" I asked between gritted teeth once we stepped outside. Her abrupt but sympathetic nod was my only answer.

By the elevators, my father's assistant waited for me with a huge smile that rivaled Ms. Brown's. I had to clench my teeth to swallow the bitter words that wanted to rush out.

The lady sported platinum hair, perfect, long legs, and big, luscious breasts that were too large for her slender figure. Her gray eyes roamed almost hungrily over my body, the kindness as fake as her plump, red-tinted lips. I knew what she was doing—she was comparing me to my father. And I knew who she was—his whore.

"Mr. King is waiting for you," she said and led me to a conference room.

Isaac King was standing tall and stiff, looking out the window and facing what he hoped one day would become his kingdom. Even still and silent, the man looked authoritative. I braced myself for another pointless lecture and stepped inside.

"Anything else I can help you with, Mr. King?"

Of course, darling, just not right now, I thought scornfully, glowering at my father's rigid back.

"You may retire, Tessa."

The frosty dismissal didn't affect her in the slightest, or if it did, she had learned to hide her disgruntlement perfectly.

I debated whether to sit or stand, not because my father intimidated me, but because I wanted to leave as soon as possible. He turned and took the seat at the head of the conference table in one fluid movement then gestured to me with a bored air to do the same. Surprising him, I sat, but that didn't mean I had become compliant.

"You're doing a magnificent job here, Son."

"It doesn't suit you to compliment me, Father."

Merciless eyes regarded me coolly. The kind preamble was a useless postponement of Isaac's actual intent. His niceties disturbed me more than his insults because I knew that a stealthy man was to be feared more than one who attacked you boldly.

For a fraction of a second, I wondered if the unscheduled meeting was because of my relationship with Charlotte. In the short-lived silence, I realized that I couldn't care less if my father found out or not.

"You seem to have gained Charlotte's trust, maybe even her esteem, I might add. That is a good thing, Son. You are making progress."

"What is this about, Father?"

"Are you in a hurry?" he questioned, the same disgustingly benevolent smile curving his mouth but not reaching his eyes. "Then I shall not keep you for long. In fact, I did not bring you here to meet with me. I brought you here to meet someone."

"And who is that?"

"Meet Julian Hudson."

Right on cue, the door of the conference room opened, and a gawky man staggered inside. Holding a stack of papers, he struggled to keep his balance. Alarmed, gunmetal gray eyes, thickly laced by long, dark lashes, looked up to meet mine. With my arms folded across my chest, an arched eyebrow, and implacable expression, I analyzed the man, and he squirmed.

Relatively tall and rather leaner than muscular, his body projected a dormant vitality that was in complete opposition to the way he presented himself. Stumbling his way to the seat across from me, he pushed rectangular glasses up a small, sculpted nose.

He was too beautiful for a man, lacking the ruggedness I was accustomed to seeing in the mirror each morning. He had the sort of face that appeared on magazines and compelled you to do as he ordered.

He placed the stack of papers to his left then steepled his fingers on the tabletop. Suddenly, he was the one analyzing me. He took off his eyeglasses and placed them carefully in front of him on the table. He straightened the knot of his tie and smoothened his hands over his suit jacket.

He made a show out of every movement, every breath, and every changing plane of his face. Little by little, his expression turned hard and dangerous until eventually, the man who sat across from me was no longer the same jumbled man who had entered the room but an impressively confident person who commanded the room with a mere glance.

"Now we can get properly acquainted. I am Julian Hudson. The one who entered the room was Ian Quinn."

"Beg your pardon?"

Julian Hudson's, or Ian Quinn's, or God knew whose eyes swept to my father questioningly. Isaac shook his head then leaned in, wearing the same expression he had worn the night he told me he had been a fraud for almost his entire life. And suddenly, I knew who the man across from me was—the man in charge, the man who wanted to recruit me. I directed my glare at him, but he merely smiled and made himself more comfortable in his seat.

"I suppose there is no need to explain who I am or why I am here. That's good. I disclosed one of my identities as a sign of trust, Marcus. I can't expect you to trust me if I don't offer you the same in return. I chose to make the first move, and I hope to not be wrong about you."

"Yes, you are here to recruit me, but you know nothing about me. If you had, you wouldn't make me this offer in the first place," I spat and struggled not to slam my fist against the table.

"I admit you are not my first choice. In fact, you weren't an option at all until your father convinced me. Since we are running out of time, we are willing to negotiate and accommodate any requirements you may have."

"My only requirement is to stay the hell out of my life."

Hudson's assessing eyes lingered on me before he glanced at Isaac, who answered an unspoken question by stiffly shaking his head. Being clueless irked me and didn't help any in the frail attempt to control my temper.

Displeased for reasons outside of my comprehension, Hudson drummed his fingers on the table, his gaze stuck on the mount of papers he had brought with him. Suddenly, I doubted they had been brought only for artistic effect.

"I see." Somber eyes locked on mine as he slid across the table a relatively thin folder labeled with my name.

Taking the dossier and skimming through it meant I would play their game, and I definitely didn't want to offer that kind of satisfaction to my father, but in the end, curiosity got the best of me.

I was horrified to see a detailed chronology of my academic history, including marks and the original notes of my teachers, copies of my birth certificate, identity card, passport, all my diplomas, and all the contracts I had ever signed.

Then, as if I hadn't already reached the pinnacle of a horrible nightmare, I turned the page to stumble upon a series of pictures of me, starting from my very first year of college up to the present day. Pictures of my graduation, of countless races, of late-night parties at *L'Affaire*, of Liv and me, of me entering the building of CKM Engineering, then there were a few blank pages as if some images had been pulled out, and eventually, there were a few snapshots of me at the airport. Each picture had a note stuck to it, and each picture meant a grave infringement of my privacy.

"You had me followed?" I roared, jumping to my feet. My ominous scowl and my white-knuckled fists slammed against the clear evidence of their scrutiny didn't bother or surprise them in the slightest.

"I had you checked up on, and you passed," Hudson explained matter-of-factly. I wasn't completely sure who made me angrier— the utter stranger who seemed to have taken the liberty of putting me under a microscope like I was a damn guinea pig or the stranger who was my father. "I need to know exactly who I am working with. As you can see, I know more about you than you think."

Through the searing rage and the cutting feeling of betrayal, my mind focused on the blank pages and the missing pictures. I found Hudson's unwavering eyes and saw the knowledge in them. He did know everything about me, and I suspected he knew things he didn't want to share with my father. For instance, what Charlotte and I had.

Isaac glowered and raised his hand to caution me to lower my voice, but I was hardly able to focus on my breathing, let alone control myself. I felt violent, truly irrevocably furious. He leaned in, about to speak, when Hudson cut him off with a decisive motion of his index finger.

Almost gaping, I realized that this man, who was not much older than me, controlled the great Isaac King. Then I started laughing hysterically until my stomach hurt and my eyes stung with tears. This imposter I had for a father was the person my mother had loved the most and the person who had deceived her the worst.

"Are you done?" Hudson demanded coldly.

"You are his boss, aren't you?"

Isaac's jaw flexed, and his eyes darkened. For a man who claimed to be his own boss, he had painfully too many people to answer to.

"I am. And I will be yours too when you accept my offer."

"That will not happen, Mr. Hudson."

I turned to leave, my spine tingling with hardly contained fury.

Hudson's deceptively soft words halted me with my hand on the door handle.

"Are you sure, Mr. King? You haven't even heard the offer I have for you."

I faced Hudson, who stood and fastened the single button of his jacket. My gaze slid defiantly from him to my father. For once, Isaac didn't look goaded by my attitude.

Sighing and burrowing his hands in his pockets, he appeared much older than his age. His naturally smooth forehead was crisscrossed by wrinkles. His lips were bloodless and his eyes too grave and too dark.

"I am not interested in any plans my father has designed and you are now delivering."

The only indication of Hudson's growing impatience was an unnaturally stiff jaw and the hard set of his eyes. He nodded to himself then glanced at my father, who nodded in return. They acted as a well-oiled machine, which did not need the use of words to function. Understanding his younger superior's command, my father slipped out of the room, his attention entirely someplace else.

"It's just us now." Hudson motioned me to return to my seat only by raising his eyebrows in its direction. He was making a command and expecting me to conform. The idea didn't sit well with me. "I'd like to make something clear before we go any further with our discussion—"

"I never agreed I would go any further."

"I'd like to not be interrupted." The man did not glare but cast me a critical look that efficiently shut me up. For the moment, at least. "As I was saying, I'd like to be clear from the start. I am the one recruiting agents and making the decisions, not your father. He is a mere pawn in a larger scheme that I coordinate."

"Who are you, exactly?"

Hudson gritted his teeth and stared at me with the same critical look on his face that I was starting to learn suited him best. His eyes narrowed, and his mouth thinned in an irritated line. He didn't like to be interrupted. Deeply fascinating. Completely uninteresting.

"I am Special Agent in Charge of the Criminal Division of the Washington field office, Mr. King, and I want you to work for me."

"Why? My academic training doesn't qualify me as an undercover agent or any other agent, for that matter. If you are not helping my father put into practice his schemes, why would you be interested in me?"

"Your father's input has been truly substantial, but he doesn't have the final word."

"You do, right," I scoffed and plopped back in my seat, exasperated.

"Exactly."

"So why me? What do you think I can accomplish that somebody else can't?"

He covered his chin with his right hand and studied me. It was that perfectly confident countenance of his that made me feel uncomfortable, but I was also confident enough not to give him the satisfaction of showing it.

My eyes fell over the still scattered papers on the desk, and I couldn't hold back a frown. What else had this man found out about me?

"I see potential in you. I also see a resourceful man and the ability to adjust to completely different environments. For instance, who would believe an engineer spent his nights taking part in illegal races?"

"And everything revolves around the damn races," I hissed and shook my head.

"It revolves around your chameleonic nature, Mr. King. Don't you think that's key for an undercover agent? Just think about all the different operations you can be a part of. There's a level of danger and adrenaline that I believe you'd both enjoy and be able to handle."

"You read people, I get that, but do not use psychology against me."

Hudson laughed and made an appreciative gesture with his hand. Showing him that I wasn't easily fooled or controlled might have just made him all the more determined to have me on board with whatever plans he had. I stifled a groan.

"My offer is simple. I know for a fact that Mitch Stewart is a corrupt man and his son a murderer and a drug dealer. I think you can infiltrate his circles and get me the proof I need to prove their crimes. Work for me on this operation. Finish it successfully, get me what I need, and you will never have to worry about your father and his demands again."

"That simple?" I asked even as my heart lurched in my chest. If Mitch Stewart was the corrupt man that Hudson claimed he was, then Charlotte had landed in a bigger mess than she imagined.

"Oh, it will not be simple at all. You will be dealing with drug dealers and ruthless criminals. You'd have to gain their trust in order to get in their midst. But, give me the results I expect, and I will keep my end of the bargain."

"Otherwise there's no deal."

"See? We understand each other, Marcus."

"I have issues complying. I really don't think I am the man for your position."

"I don't need a man who complies. I need a man who takes action. Think about my offer. I will expect an answer by the end of this week."

I left with the nagging sensation that I didn't have an option at all, that my fate had already been sealed.

EVENING FOUND ME AT *L'Affaire* although I didn't plan on staying for too long. I missed and needed Charlotte with a fervor that bordered on pain.

It was Bryson and Brayden's birthdays, which meant that the place was crammed with people, raucous beyond bearing. Although born at a difference of two years, they shared the same day of birth, which as inconsequential as it was to others, to them it was yet another thing binding them as brothers.

It was karaoke night, and a tipsy girl, barely out of high school, tormented everyone who was within hearing distance. She had the spectacular type of voice that made babies cry, windows shatter, and puppies whine in agony. As I waded my way to our usual table, I simply wished somebody had taped her mouth shut.

Bearing no gifts but a rather dangerous strategy that involved Brayden, I took a seat, making no fuss about my arrival. Kai, who was cradling The Fox in his lap, shook my hand vigorously, and Bryson eyed me, nodding in resignation. It hadn't been easy to convince him of what we were going to do, but he realized it was time to take action. It was when Brayden caught sight of me that all conversation ceased.

"Am I still welcome?"

"Why wouldn't you be?" Brayden snapped. "It's not my problem who you choose to bang."

I bit my tongue to stifle the words. I didn't want to take his bait. I didn't want to give him the satisfaction of lashing out because, in the end, this was not the true Brayden talking but a ghost of the man he had once been.

I merely smiled, earning his disgusted frown. Then he returned to his friends, throwing himself with a violence in the whirlpool of dirty conversation and unhealthy habits.

"Are you really going to do it?" Kai asked, raising his chin in Brayden's direction.

"It's time. If we don't, I'm afraid he'll get himself killed."

"He'll hate us for this."

"I'd hate us for this if I were in his position. But I'd hate you worse if you just stood by and watched me waste away."

"I hope he'll see that too. Eventually. I hope Bryson sees it."

I scanned Kai's atypically stern expression then glanced at Bryson. He had agreed to my suggestion. He had even added his own ideas and hopes to the plan, but he hadn't put his heart in it. After all, how could he act willingly against his own brother, even if it were for his own good?

While Brayden drank himself unconscious, flirted obscenely with women coming and going, and made a poor joke of himself up on the stage, Bryson remained relatively quiet and brooding. It took me off guard when a red-nailed hand curled around my shoulder.

"Liv?"

"Oh, boy," I heard Joleen sigh dramatically, and for a fraction of a second, Liv glared her way.

Immediately, she returned her imploring eyes to me. Seeing her reminded me just how mad I was at her. I rose to my feet, and she limped a step back, whimpering low in her throat. Once, the sound had amused me. It had even ignited my desire. Now, it was only making me angrier because Olivia Lambert knew which buttons to push. She knew how to handle me to bring me to heel.

"What are you doing here?" I snapped, grabbing her elbow and steering her away.

"What? Should I bar myself inside my apartment and never get out? That much you hate me now, Marcus?"

"Don't play that card with me, Liv. I am not in the mood."

I dragged her in an isolated corner and turned her around so she faced me. She staggered on her feet and collided with me, more because she knew I would catch her than out of necessity. As soon as I steadied her, I put a decent distance between us.

Liv noticed and frowned. There was genuine hurt in her eyes when she reached for me and I blocked her advance.

"No, Liv. I don't mean to hurt you, but this has to stop." I waved my hand between the two of us, but she hardly registered. She might have not even been listening to me. Her mouth shaped in a surprised O and her eyes reddened instantly. "You have to stop depending on me. You have to move on and find your own purpose."

"I do not depend on you," she hissed. As usual, she refused to accept a truth that was beyond evident. "I just trust you the most. I need you in my life, Marcus."

"We are toxic together. We are toxic to each other, Liv. We have always been."

"What are you trying to say to me?" She was positively shaking, and she wasn't far from crying either.

"I think it would be better to not see each other for a time. I care for you deeply, Liv. I will never stop, but it's time for a change. It's time for us to build a life with other people."

"Like Charlotte Burton?"

My face fell, but my eyes were blazing. "Don't go there," I cautioned. I could have said nothing for all the good it did.

"She is pretty, whole—" she trailed off, scowling at her left leg.

"She is also your father's colleague. She is making a puppet out of you, Marcus. Why didn't you tell me you have taken an internship at your father's firm? Is she not letting you?"

"She does not command me."

"She is your handler, though."

Liv's voice went up an octave, and her face turned red. It was beyond me how such a fragile-looking woman could exude so much violence.

"I will not even dwell on the fact that you know things you shouldn't—"

"Because you don't tell me," she accused.

"If *I* don't tell you, you do not have the right to investigate behind my back, Olivia."

My sharp retort had the same effect of a slap. Liv leaned against the wall, and anger gave way once more to genuine hurt. She looked away and kneaded her hands together in front of herself. I could already *hear* the tears coming.

Cupping her right shoulder, I used my other hand to tip her chin up. When she looked at me, I saw glimpses of the scared little girl I didn't have the heart to chastise or cut out of my life.

"You are a gorgeous, brilliant woman, Liv. You can have anyone you want."

"No, I can't, and you know it."

"That is not true," I sighed, knowing I could not convince her of something she refused to accept. "It is you who are denying yourself the chance to try again. It is you condemning yourself."

She laughed bitterly and shoved my hands aside. It was so confusing and so frustrating trying to understand her. She fought to keep me in her life as much as she pushed me away, and the combination was simply tiring.

"Tell me about her." An abrupt change of topic. Typical Liv. "She has already stolen you all for herself."

"No, for Christ's sake, Olivia." Sighing around her was customary. She glared at the sound of her full name, which was also customary. "I told you I don't mean to hurt you. I am not going to chitchat with you about Charlotte."

Not hurting her was part of the reason, but refusing to talk with

Liv about Charlotte was mainly because I wanted to keep my relationship uncontaminated by the gruesome past and the dark side of my life that I hoped would never touch Charlotte. In the end, it was a selfish motivation.

"Then maybe I should talk to her myself. Maybe she will be more forthcoming."

"Don't you dare. Just don't."

"What would be the problem? You haven't told her about me, have you?"

The way my face hardened and my eyes welled up with guilt was answer enough. I truly didn't want to have this discussion with Liv any more than I wanted to talk to Charlotte about her. Although I tried hard to keep the two women in separate worlds, I knew it would not last forever.

"Marcus?" Kai called, and I sighed. "I think it's time."

He looked worried, an expression that appeared on his face only when something was deeply wrong. I glanced past his shoulder at our table to find it almost empty. Brayden was gone, and so was Bryson.

"Go home, Liv. Think about what I said. Try." I didn't linger to hear her reply.

Kai led me outside to the parking lot. The night air flapped coldly across my skin, soothing the chaos unfurling inside me. The meeting with Julian Hudson had given me much to think about, and it had unsettled me in a near brutal manner, but it was Liv who had drained me.

I hoped whatever energy I still owned would be enough to deal with Brayden.

There was a line of people blocking my view, but the garish laughter mingled with angry shouts and a woman's whimpers painted clearly the image of what I was about to see.

As we approached, Brayden's exceedingly idiotic friends jumped to the side to make way. Across the hood of a red car, Brayden had a woman splayed and pinned under his weight while Bryson tried unsuccessfully to drag him off. I ordered myself not to let my own resentment get in the way.

"She had been purposefully making my mouth water all night.

She wants this."

"I wanted you until you turned out to be a jerk," the woman protested and shoved at his chest.

"Come on, pretty boy. We're going on a journey."

Catching Brayden in a chokehold, I effectively pulled him back. I threw a glare at Bryson and shook my head, exasperated. He should have understood by now that Brayden was well past the point of pleading with.

"Take your damn hands off me," Brayden snarled while Kai made sure the damsel in distress was unharmed and silently made her disappear.

Calloused hands grabbed my shoulders just as a man's slurred voice ordered me to get lost and not spoil their fun. Had I owned an adjacent pair of hands, I would have hit him bloody. Bryson hit him for me, though, and growled his frustration as he pushed the idiot away. Displaying unrequested solidarity, the others joined in, poised for a fight.

"Mind your own business," Kai shouted and planted himself in front of the enraged crowd.

They mumbled their disagreement but did not go against the command that had been given. Sometimes it was difficult to understand how or why Kai commanded these people, but the point was he did.

Within minutes, they all scattered away, leaving behind an uncontrolled Brayden, a powerless Bryson, a stern Kai, and me, literally taking the worst of the situation.

"I said take your hands off me."

Brayden pushed his shoulder into my chest, forcing me to stagger back. He usually had better fighting skills than me, and boosted by his drunken anger, his power was too raw and unexpected to compete against.

He struck right at the base of my throat, then in quick succession, he hit me in my liver and kicked me in the knees. Doubling over and clasping at the battered spots, I fought for breath. The bastard could fight, alright.

"That's enough, Brayden. For God's sake that's enough."

"Says who? You? Oh, please," Brayden spat, and Bryson

flinched, the hurt he felt evident to us all, save for his brother. "I'm going to go back in there, and none of you will follow. It's my birthday. If you want to ruin my night, then I don't need you here at all."

"You are not going anywhere."

Bryson's words came out too softly to catch Brayden's attention.

I scrambled to my feet and connected my fist with his gut, making him hiss and curse and hit me back. I laughed. This was how Brayden and I rationalized, and in our brutish way, it always worked out.

"Can't you just pack him up and send him on his merry way?" Kai asked, leaning against a wine-red SUV. With arms folded on his chest and a bored expression on his face, one would have thought he was witnessing the most ordinary of happenings. "The result would be the same but quicker—and less brutal."

"Oh no, the result would not be the same." I ducked a fist aimed at my face and slammed my own against his jaw. "He needs a quick, efficient beating."

"I need you to get the hell out of here."

A mean blow to my stomach had me stumbling back. He didn't hit to blow off some steam but to cause damage. I was going to bruise, but so was he.

He hesitated, debating whether to walk away or fight me some more, and that was all I needed. I gripped him in another viselike hold while he struggled futilely. After what seemed an eternity, Bryson planted himself in front of his wayward brother and took a stand.

"What you need is help. Enough is enough, Brayden."

"What the hell are you talking about?"

"You are a man who has one kidney and is on the brink of becoming an alcoholic."

"How I live my life is my own freaking problem. Get off me."

He elbowed me and kept struggling, but I held tight. He was going to hate me for fighting him, Kai for just watching, his brother for not coddling him, but in the end, I hoped he would understand and get better.

"Charlotte has nightmares because of you, you idiot," I snarled and planted a fist to his side. "And you scare countless other girls like this. I get it. Harper betrayed you, hurt you, messed you up really good, but that is no excuse for what you do to women who never wronged you."

"You are depressed and not a moody one. You attack people, Bray," his brother continued. "You hurt them. Man, somewhere inside you, you have to realize how wrong that is."

"Are you going to stand with him on this? People hurt each other. It's what we do. Why should I be the only one condemned for it?"

"He's right, Brayden. I think I have encouraged you for far too long in activities far too wrong."

"We are not condemning you," I cut in, softening as misery flashed in his eyes. I was furious with him, but he was still my friend, and even if there was only a small trace of the man he had once been, he deserved to be salvaged. "There's more to life than just hurting, Brayden. You deserve more than this miserable life you keep up. We are trying to get you help because we care about you."

"I don't need help," he spat, but he wasn't struggling as badly as before. His drunkenness had given him power, but not stamina.

"Yes, you do." Bryson caught Brayden's collar and forced him to focus, to listen. "There's a facility just outside the city. They have the best program and the best doctors, I promise. They deal with people—like you—who have problems like you do. They can help."

"You want me to see a shrink?" Brayden's outraged shout quickly morphed into uncontrolled laughter.

I released him when he completely stopped struggling, and as soon as I did, he nearly fell to the ground. Bryson and I caught him and threw his arms over our shoulders, supporting his weight.

"I want you to live there. Get away from here. Clear your mind."

"You are not joking. You are serious." Brayden was utterly appalled and entirely against our suggestion.

"It will be like living on campus," Bryson went on with an enthusiasm that he didn't truly feel. "You'll get help and have nothing to worry about. See it as a trip out of crazy. Yes?"

"No. Hell no. I am not going to prison. NO."

"Brayden, please, Son."

We all turned to see Lydia Morton crying. Brayden and Bryson's mother was a petite natural blonde, with hair so long and shiny that looked sophisticated even in her simple braid. With her youth behind her, she was still fresh and amazingly beautiful.

My eyes stung with a craving I had always had. Wounds caused by my mother's absence felt raw and throbbing at the sight of Mrs. Morton's approaching figure.

"Please, Brayden," she urged, opening her arms. My eyes slid to Kai who watched the scene somberly but relieved. Apparently, while we had been fighting, he had done something far more efficient.

"Mom."

Like a little boy, Brayden crumbled in his mother's arms, and though come morning, he would start his objections again, tonight he was going to comply.

I left, tired beyond imagination. I needed Charlotte. I needed her warmth and her quiet.

Chapter 29

Charlotte

J climbed out of bed and stretched my arms above my head, relishing the delicious feeling of being away from Washington and Jack Stewart. The bliss was going to be fleeting, and I intended to enjoy it to the fullest.

The soreness between my thighs reminded me of last night's wild, repeated activities, and I found myself grinning as I passed by the smoky glass that hid the bathroom.

Winking, I mimicked a kiss. Although I couldn't see him, I knew Marcus could see me. The notion that he had been watching me while taking a shower made my flesh burn even hotter.

Wearing nothing but his black shirt, I hurried outside to the balcony where the crisp morning air blew pleasantly across my flushed skin. The glass wall that separated the room from the deck outside had some fancy sensors that allowed the doors to slide open when you approached. I stepped onto the balcony, which was as long as the room itself, and was immediately enthralled by the view of the forest surrounding the house.

I leaned against the handrail but avoided touching the glass fence encased between the metallic frame and the wooden floor.

My eyes soared over the fairy-like pond and its white and pink camellias before I glanced over my shoulder at the ruffled bed and rumpled clothes still lying on the ground.

It was odd that with all the chaotic emotions swirling inside me, I thought about how utterly different this house looked from Marcus's apartment. While his apartment was clearly a man's space, the house had a rather welcoming quality, a peace that created a protective bubble between its inhabitants and the outer world.

It was a family home. I could nearly picture a throng of kids running around with Kinga's puppies after them, laughter and noise drifting in the air. The image brought a nostalgic smile to my lips, then it chilled me. I couldn't entertain such thoughts.

"What is going on in that beautiful head of yours?"

Marcus's arms wrapped around my waist, and he pulled me flush against his chest, nuzzling his nose against the skin of my throat. He smelled of aftershave and man.

I rested my head against his shoulder and let out an involuntary moan. His hands ducking beneath the hem of the shirt and traveling up my thighs to my quivering belly felt too good for me to concentrate. He kissed my temple then brought a hand to massage my scalp. I almost purred.

He acted so strangely. While last night he had fluctuated from wildly aroused and somewhat edgy to tenderly caring and downright exhausted, he seemed calmer now, more settled. Yet, it was this alteration to his mood, within such a short timeframe, that confused me. He had warned me he was chaos embodied, but I hadn't witnessed its manifestation so openly before.

"You are not alright," I heard myself muttering. He stiffened, and though his arms remained around me, his eyes were directed far into the distance and his focus farther still.

"I guess, I'm not."

"Tell me."

"It worries me that you are involved in Jack Stewart's case. It annoys me that my father is still able to affect me. It upsets me that Brayden doesn't see reason. Everything is changing too fast, too soon. It's been a long week, and it's not over yet."

He offered me a forced smile that did not manage to comfort

me. There was something he wasn't telling me. I just knew. Pulling me tighter to him and sighing heavily, he propped his chin on my shoulder and looked out upon the lake. It seemed to calm him.

"I wanted you to see this." His voice almost bore a dose of reverence.

"It has a story, doesn't it?"

"The lake is the wedding gift my grandfather gave to my grandmother. They had a history with lakes. He met her for the first time at a lake party and became instantly smitten with her. He followed her everywhere until she accepted his invitation for a tea date."

"So stalking runs in the family." It was a double-edged joke, but Marcus received it good-naturedly and chuckled.

"Seems like it. He proposed during a boat ride on the same lake where they had met, and judging by tidbits Kai and I had involuntarily gathered, they had done much more on lake shores. An adventurous pair they were. Their history gives a man some ideas he can borrow."

"Oh." My skin grew hot again. "What kind of ideas?"

"See that patch of grass right there to the left of the lake? I'd like to take you there, Charlotte, feel you bare underneath me with nothing beneath us. Just you and me. I'd like to hear your moans mingling with the soft rippling of the lake."

"Mm—what about the camellias?"

My evasion earned Marcus's hearty laugh, and I turned to smack his chest, a small punishment for making me burn again. When he flinched, I was immediately remorseful for my action. Knowing he had been fighting with Brayden did not warm me up to his friend.

"They had been in my grandmother's bridal bouquet. She loved them above all flowers, so they had to be close to the lake too. It's like a big monument to their memory."

"It's beautiful."

Tears gathered in my eyes for a pair I hadn't even met and never would, for the beauty of their story, and for how badly I wanted to find the same love and devotion they had shared. Marcus kissed my temple again then whirled me in a pirouette and slammed me against his chest, no apologies and no warning. His mood had changed once again.

"Wicked man, leave me alone. I need time to recover," I protested when I saw the lustful gleam in his gaze. At the moment, I felt deliciously sore, but from that to walking-funny-sore, there was only one tiny step.

"Do you, now? Because I clearly remember how you begged me last night not to stop."

His lips hovered over mine, tempting me when I knew my body couldn't deal with more. Pushing my hands flat on his chest, I jumped out of the circle of his arms. The man was not only convincing when he wanted to be but incredibly tenacious. He strode to me, reaching for my hand.

"No," I objected and walked back inside the bedroom.

"Yes," he urged, winking and smiling mischievously, enticingly.

"Marcus, no," I screamed and ran for the stairs.

He followed, effortlessly keeping up with me. While I sprinted downstairs, I groaned, laughed, and yelled at him to stop. Before I reached the ground floor, his arm banded around my torso, beneath my breasts, and lifted me up, making me squeal and kick. I only hit thin air.

"I only want to feed you breakfast, for God's sake."

"Oh, sure," I scoffed and struggled against his firm hold.

"It's you who are corrupting me and not letting me rest. Please, Charlotte, you're insatiable. You wear me out."

Marcus pulled me down and covered the stone planes of his stomach while he shook with laughter. I had seen his bruises and knew he was hurting, but I couldn't stop from smacking his shoulder. He dodged my strike and laughed harder.

"Don't play the innocent," I cried and bit my lower lip in a weak attempt to look stern. Evidently, I failed.

We did have breakfast, kissing and teasing each other between bites of food, and eventually, we did make love again, on the cream sofa in the living room, slowly and never breaking eye contact. When the time came to leave the bubble and return to our New York life, I felt a pang of regret.

SOPHIA WAS SURPRISED BUT still happy to see me. I stopped by her desk and let her get me up to speed with what had happened in my absence. The more she talked, the more disconnected I felt from the day to day reality of the firm. She cast me a knowing glance but said nothing about Jack Stewart or how his case drained me of energy.

"May I speak freely, Ms. Burton?" she asked at some point.

I rolled my eyes. As much as I appreciated her manners and ever-present professionalism, we had worked together for long enough to quit the formalities.

"You know you can, Sophia."

"You don't have to work alone, Charlotte."

Sophia nodded toward Philip Foster, who was emerging from the interns' office. He was relatively timid but loyal and diligent. He was a terrific researcher and utterly determined to find solutions for all the loopholes and issues of a case. Of all the interns, he was the only one who really excelled, the only one I was going to hire.

"Maybe you are right," I said and pondered precisely how Philip could be of assistance, then I decided he was worth taking a chance on.

I went to him, and the way his eyes widened and his cheeks reddened just a bit was endearing. I motioned him to my office, and we walked in perfect silence. Sophia grinned encouragingly, Philip flushed and fidgeted, looking a little panicky, and I marched forward, enjoying the sight of my office, after all the time I spent in D.C.

"Please, take a seat, Philip."

He looked around my office like a kid in a candy store, and it struck me that he had never been there before. Panic shifted into discomfort as he realized that I was studying him, and finally, he grew confused.

I told him about Jack's case, which he was mostly familiar with already, then I shared my own uncertainties, but Philip was not entirely shocked to hear them. I told him about the urgency of locating Elana and doing it as quietly as possible. I stressed the importance of his full confidentiality with a sharpness that nearly offended him.

After realizing that I had been wrong about Cole, it was difficult to put my trust in somebody else, but Sophia had been right. I couldn't work on my own, and I needed help.

"This is my guy," I said, handing him a business card.

Reid Tanner was a college dropout, but a magnificent private investigator and tech-savvy. In fact, he was so slick that I suspected he was an undercover hacker, but where he was concerned, I preferred not to ask questions whose answers I wasn't going to like.

"Tanner is frequently brusque, but tremendously competent, so don't let him scare you. You could call him in the middle of the night, and he'd still get the job done."

"I don't think I should really do that," Philip replied, faking terror, then he smiled coyly.

"You're probably right," I agreed and smiled too. Philip could also be funny—that was a new side of him, and I liked it.

"I need you to contact him and find where Elana Beckham is. It's important that all communication between you and him remains private and completely unrelated to me. I suspect I am being monitored, so when you have any results, I would ask that we meet somewhere else, somewhere secure."

"But shouldn't that secure place be here, at the firm? Unless you think your office has been bugged," Philip trailed off and looked around suspiciously.

"Truth be told, I'm not sure of anything at this point. Even what we're saying now may be overheard, in which case, Elana is in more danger than we think."

"If your office is tapped," he whispered, "you could be accused of colluding with the prosecution and breaking attorney-client privilege."

"I haven't broken any privileges, but if Jack Stewart is guilty, I cannot be part of this charade."

I didn't add that embarking on this journey I had more to fear than an accusation of colluding with the prosecutor. Whoever looked for Jennifer's secret was in as much danger as the one who still possessed it.

"Yet."

"Philip, I know what I am asking is very difficult and potentially dangerous. I won't hold it against you if you refuse."

"I want to help," he said, his eyes blazing with determination.

"Good," I nodded and stood, stretching my hand out to him. His handshake was firm and cordial. "Then find Elana Beckham, but keep in mind that if we find her and we are not careful, we might put her in more danger than she's already in."

"Because we could lead the killer directly to her doorstep."

"Exactly."

Philip threw me another somber look although I suspected he was secretly excited about the whole ordeal, then he made to leave.

"Also," I stopped him, "you should give him this."

I pulled out of my purse a clear zipper bag that contained the note I had received in D.C. with the cryptic message. Philip studied it with an arched brow. In his confusion, with his locks covering his forehead, he looked younger than his years. I found myself smiling and nearly stroking the hair out of his face. If I'd had a little brother, I imagined he would have looked just like Philip.

"Have Tanner run the card for fingerprints. Someone left it in front of my hotel room in D.C."

By the time I left the firm, Philip's desk was empty, and Sophia rolled her eyes in a way that indicated he had been gone a while. He must have already been handling his secret assignment.

I WENT HOME EARLY TO PREPARE for dinner with Christina and Logan. At seven o'clock sharp, a knock had me sprinting to the door with an excited grin on my lips. The smile faded some when I found nobody waiting in the hallway, but it grew enormous once my eyes stumbled on an adorable teddy bear with a heart of pink and white roses between its paws. In the middle of the heart, there was tucked a note that simply said:

On the roof

Marcus was leaning on his elbows against the edge of the building, with his legs crossed at the ankles and a distant look in his eyes. His handsome profile with the sky on fire as the background created a glorious canvas, one that I wished to hang on my wall and never look away from.

I wished I had grabbed the camera he had bought me, but instead, I pulled out my phone and snapped three quick shots, then I put it back in my pocket and walked over to him.

I felt peaceful, settled, just by having him close. Wrapping my arms around him from behind, I settled my palms against the steady pounding of his heart. He straightened, covered my hands, then brought them to his mouth to pepper soft kisses on my knuckles.

"What's happening in that beautiful mind of yours?" I asked.

Marcus spun me in a pirouette then nestled me against his chest. "I wanted to show you this," he murmured and glanced around at the flaming sky and the bruised-looking clouds. "It's peaceful up here, almost another world."

I caressed his cheek and rose on tiptoes to meet his mouth. There was nothing sexual in the gentle sliding of our lips but a slow, sweet encounter of two souls that needed each other to breathe.

"When I was younger, I used to go up to the roofs of random buildings. It seemed the higher the building, the closer to the sky I was. Sometimes I thought that if I reached out, I could stroke the clouds, feel them under my fingertips."

I thought of his mother and how he had lost her while he was merely a boy. I thought of the little boy who in her absence still loved her and of the man who had grown to hate missing the people he loved.

The landscape was breathtaking, but that moment was not about the sunset or the beauty of New York as it prepared for sleep. That moment was about Marcus letting me in and showing me a part of him I hadn't seen before. He was vulnerable.

"You spoil me, Mr. King."

I looked up at him from under my eyelashes and pressed a kiss to his chest. Marcus smiled, innocently happy and just a tad proud.

"You deserve to be spoiled," he whispered and kissed the top of my head.

Although my head hardly reached his shoulder, at that moment, with the sunset light reflected in his eyes, his arms tightly wrapped around me, and his lips sketching patterns on my face, I felt as tall as a mountain.

"Plus," he added, mischief entering his gaze. "I thought I should give you the chocolates myself."

There was a bench close to the parapet that had been strategically placed by some of my neighbors to face the fabulous view. Marcus bent to retrieve a box of Swiss gourmet chocolates, the kind that combined exquisite pleasure with the velvet texture of sin.

Sheepish, but not exactly repentant, I dug in, and by the time we made it to dinner, I had finished half the box. Marcus winked, promising a different kind of sinful pleasure, and took my hand in his. He knocked on my sister's door while holding my hand tightly, a little too tightly.

His magnificent body was encased in a gray suit paired with a black V-neck shirt and black shoes. His hair was brushed back, and his cologne gave him the dangerously seductive air that he never lacked. Knowing he had truly prepared for officially meeting my sister, my brother-in-law, and my niece made me smile and soften up a little bit more.

"You're really set on impressing her, aren't you?"

"I'm really set on impressing *you*, but since she is your sister and her opinion matters to you, I want her to approve of me, of us."

I touched his cheek, and Marcus shut his eyes, nuzzling the palm of my hand. I wanted to kiss him, but instead, I only licked my lips, feeling his taste still lingering there.

"She will," I promised.

It was Logan who opened the door and ushered us inside, a reserved but polite smile on his face. Dressed in dark blue jeans and a white shirt, which I knew Christina had a particular liking for, with his sleeves rolled up to his elbows and the first two buttons left open, Logan seemed fairly casual, except for the tension around his eyes.

Neither Christina nor Marie was in sight, but if Marie's gurgled chuckles were any indication, they weren't far off. Logan pulled me into a warm big-brother hug, kissed the top of my head, then released me to inspect Marcus.

"Nice to finally properly meet you," Logan said, extending his hand and shaking Marcus's in that firm, painful-looking way men had.

"Likewise," Marcus answered. "It's a relief to actually stop stalking Charlotte and finally get an invitation."

All three of us thought of that night when Marcus had obnoxiously assumed he could join us for a movie. I glared at him and was surprised to hear Logan laugh. That night, he had acted like a stalker, but he was right. It was a relief that now things stood differently.

"I'll get that," Logan offered, glancing at the bottle of red wine that Marcus had insisted on buying.

Marcus handed over the bottle, his hip skimming against mine. He was dreadfully civilized, completely cordial, and just a bit distant. I supposed the latter was because he truly felt nervous and didn't want to do anything that could seem improper to my family. Yet, the heat between us was undeniable each time his body brushed against mine or his fingers encountered my skin.

We followed Logan to the living room, an ample rectangular space, elegantly separated into two sections. The first section consisted of a sitting area colored in shades of powder pink and burgundy. Two identical sofas faced each other, with a glass tea table between them, while two burgundy loveseats, placed perpendicular to the couches, faced the opposite wall where a huge flat screen hung above a contemporary fireplace. Ridiculously, what I loved the most about the room was the fluffy cream carpet underneath the low table.

The second section was a continuation of the first. Separated by an archway, the sitting area expanded into a stylish and very intimate dining room. A mahogany table for six dominated the space. The cream upholstery was still immaculate although I had been witness countless times to Marie's adventures with her sticky little hands staining the fabric.

The table was set for four, and the spotlights cast a pleasantly dim light. I was humbled to realize that Christina and Logan had taken as much care in preparing for our evening as Marcus had. And little by little, I was growing nervous too.

"Good evening."

Christina emerged from the kitchen, Marie cradled on her left hip, pulling excitedly at the straps of her black dress. Yet, Christina even in a modest, colorless outfit looked spectacular. I walked to kiss her cheek and retrieve Marie, who started burbling happily as soon as she took notice of our presence. She loved having guests.

"Hi," Marcus replied hesitantly. He was never hesitant. He was never uncertain of how he should approach somebody. "These are for you. I hope you like gerberas."

"They are gorgeous. Thank you."

Christina received the multicolored flower arrangement, smiled with that innate sensuality of hers, and rose to her tiptoes to press a chaste kiss to Marcus's cheek.

"Please, take a seat," Logan said. "I'm famished."

We laughed and complied without any further ado. Marcus sagged next to me, and I could swear I heard him let out a soft breath of relief. After warning him that my sister was a tad displeased with him, he had certainly not expected to be welcomed and accepted so easily. I had to bite my tongue to muffle a chuckle. Had he imagined they would chop his head off?

"It seems there is someone I hadn't been formally introduced to," Marcus cooed and bent to get a better glimpse of Marie, who had decided all of a sudden that she wanted to play the bashful card.

"Oh, Mr. King, may I introduce my niece, Marie Barrett? Marie, this is your aunt's very formal escort, Marcus King."

We all erupted into laughter, and Marcus joined us, but he looked at me with a tense expression that warned me not to mock him. He wanted to make everything right tonight, and I respected his devotion. Yet, I also wanted him to enjoy himself. Neither Christina nor Logan would judge him or disapprove of him as long as he didn't hurt me.

"Can I hold her?" he asked, glancing at Christina rather than at me who I was holding her.

"Of course. She might ruin your clothes, though." And that Marie frequently did.

Despite her newfound shyness, Marie went willingly to Marcus when he held out his arms. She started playing at once with the buttons of his suit jacket, and encouraged by Marcus's unexpectedly soft cooing, she took shameless advantage of him.

"She will end up a thief," I complained, shaking my head when Marie's little hands dipped into Marcus's pockets, searching for small souvenirs. As if delighted by her mischief, he smiled brightly, stroking her soothingly on the back.

"She'll have her aunt to bail her out of jail," my sister said.

There was nothing Christina refused her daughter, and she had a tough time reprimanding her, even when her little gestures, cute and innocent as they were, bordered on discourtesy.

Marie looked up at Marcus and stunned him with her megawatt smile that would one day break hearts. It didn't surprise me that she fell so soon in love with him. Her aunt had done just the same, I thought as my heart skipped a beat.

"Charlotte, would you give me a hand?" Christina asked, stepping away from the table and to the kitchen.

"Before she burns down the kitchen," Logan teased her.

"Ha. Don't irritate the cook, mister."

I recognized their intention. Christina wanted to corner me alone while Logan did the same with Marcus. I watched him doubtfully, not wishing to submit him to a big-brother speech, but he winked reassuringly then urged me with a nod to follow my sister. The big-brother speech, written beforehand by Christina herself, was inevitable.

"So what are you making Logan grill Marcus about?" I asked once we were in the kitchen, which was a complete and undisputable disaster.

"Nothing that he doesn't deserve." she smiled brightly and turned to the four empty plates set on the countertop.

"Christina," I warned, but she remained unaffected by my hard, cautioning tone as she often did when my wellbeing was concerned.

"He can handle himself. It's you I wanted to talk to."

"I imagined."

"How are you?"

She was fairly unskilled where the culinary arts were concerned, but she made up for it with her determination to set things as close to perfection as possible. However, the food was doubtless catered if she planned on feeding us without sending someone to the ER with a grave case of food poisoning. I focused on her hasty movements instead of searching for a truthful answer.

"Charlotte?" she prodded.

"I'm fine." I knew it was a lie as soon as her knowing eyes roamed all over my face.

"That is not completely true."

I let out a sigh and leaned against an open cabinet that held clean plates. I was fine and happy and scared, all gathered in one bubble of chaotic emotions.

"Two months ago, we didn't even know each other and now—" I trailed off, rubbing my face and sighing heavily. "He can settle me and turn me upside down just as quickly. He's gotten under my skin, Chris, and I don't think I can get him out."

"Charlotte," she spoke softly, almost like she did to Marie.

"I'm scared of his power over me, of myself when I'm without him, of us."

"Charlotte, darling," she interrupted me and wiped the single tear that was coursing down my cheek. "You are afraid of what may happen if there isn't an *us*, but you're not there and may never be."

"You don't know that," I sobbed.

"Love is the hardest, most challenging form of war" she continued. "You fight against fears, doubts, yourself at times, and maybe even ghosts from the past. In the end, you should decide if the prize is worth fighting for. If Marcus is worth it, fight for what you have. If he is not, don't put your heart at stake."

"How do I know if he is worth the fight?" My eyes stung, and my lower lip trembled.

"You don't know, not rationally. You feel it. When he gets into your system so profoundly that he courses through your veins, and he carves a little spot inside you that feels empty when he is not around, you'll know."

Christina told me what I had already known. Marcus was worth the fight, the struggle, and the affection.

The very instant we returned to the dining room, each of us holding two plates loaded with food, Marcus smelled the change in my disposition. I offered him and Marie a warm smile and was grateful when he didn't make any inquiries. His eyes, however, lingered on Christina before his attention returned to me, and he covered my hand with his. The warmth of his body settled me. It comforted me.

Marie grudgingly left Marcus's lap when Christina came to retrieve and place her in her high chair where she played with the penguin toy I had gifted her a couple of weeks ago. In her absence, Marcus drew closer to me, our bodies in even tighter contact than before.

Batting my eyelashes, I looked between Logan and Marcus. "What have you two gentlemen been talking about?"

"Lawyers, out-of-order motorcycles, illegal races—" Marcus muttered, and I knew he was referring to him and me and our unanticipated relationship.

"Dangerous getaways," Logan added, casting a conspiratorial glance at Marcus, and they started laughing while both Christina and I watched them puzzled. They were getting along well, apparently.

"What have you two lovely ladies been talking about?" Marcus mirrored my question with a playful smile tugging at his lips.

"The art of war," Christina giggled while displaying an intoxicating smile. Had I not known her so well, I might have missed the coolness behind the dazzling beam.

Marcus smiled in response, but under the table, his fingers tightened around my hand. He knew he wouldn't win Christina over with only his charming smiles and polished speech.

The dinner progressed pleasantly despite the short-lived tension, and Marcus answered dutifully all the questions he was asked. I had been wrong in assuming that Logan had been assigned to grill Marcus. Christina was carrying out the task triumphantly on her own, albeit very charmingly and utterly gracious.

"Have you lived long in New York?"

"Born and bred here. After finally getting used to the city, it's difficult to think of living any place else."

"It's a little odd that you and Charlotte had never met before since your father and James are in business together." Christina's sharp eyes, although perfectly schooled into a friendly gaze, didn't miss a single reaction.

"I lived with my aunt most of my childhood and adolescence. Afterwards, my father and I didn't quite see eye to eye, and we rarely attended family gatherings together or visited with friends."

"Your mother's sister?" Christina pressed, and my heart skipped a beat.

"Yes."

Instinctively, I tightened my hold on Marcus's hand, and he turned to me, his mouth quaking and his eyes warming up. I knew his mother was a sore topic, and I had never dared to mention her. His anguished look validated my thoughts. He still hurt over her absence.

"Charlotte mentioned a very charming cousin. Are you two close?"

"Kai is like a brother to me. He has his faults, indeed, but then, we all do."

The cutting edge of Christina's inquiry did not remain unnoticed by Marcus. He could read the subtle meaning in Christina's questions effortlessly. Logan and I smiled over the rims of our wine glasses.

The risotto and herb-crusted salmon were exquisite, but we hardly enjoyed the food or the wine we sipped regularly. I ate although my stomach was churning, and so did Marcus, yet the rigid set of his shoulders and the detached look in his eyes told me he was more concentrated on gaining Christina's trust than enjoying the food she had served us.

"Are you interested in a stable relationship, Marcus?"

"I am. I don't commit easily, but when I do, I don't turn back."

I was growing more and more nervous and mortified. Despite the personal nature of the questions my sister was asking, Marcus never seemed put out by her intrusiveness. In fact, he was more solicitous and prepared to offer her answers than he was with me. Sometimes, I wanted to be more like her. She had always had a unique capacity to gain the reactions and the answers she looked for.

"What about your hobbies?" my sister continued, looking fairly innocent while firing treacherous questions.

"You mean racing?" Marcus grinned and relaxed in his seat.

Noticing the change in his demeanor, I gaped at him in disbelief. Then I understood. He was changing tactics. While up to that point he had been the groomed, civilized man any sister would like for her sibling, he was finally letting her meet the true Marcus, sometimes lethally charming, sometimes dreadfully dangerous. I stifled a smile, but Christina didn't bother to. She also recognized the sudden alteration to Marcus's approach, and she liked it.

"Yes. Do you still race?"

"I haven't in a while."

"But you'd like to?"

"Sometimes," Marcus admitted, and an unpleasant chill crept down my spine. "It is not a hobby, though, as much as it is a form of de-stressing."

"A rather dangerous form."

"A liberating one. Charlotte can attest to that." He turned to wink at me suggestively, and my heart stopped in my chest. That was probably not something that Christina needed to know.

"What?" Somehow, she managed to drag that little word into three different syllables.

"We—rode together a few times. It was liberating indeed."

"Charlotte," she gasped outraged while Logan fought to keep a straight face.

"I will always keep her safe," Marcus cut in, his voice stern and decisive.

"You do that." Her retort came quickly and just as sternly. I sighed. Maybe, just maybe, the strict interview had reached its end.

"Have you finished the inquisition now?" I asked, long after our plates had been emptied and forgotten on the table.

"We were only getting acquainted," she explained innocently, and all four of us started laughing at the absurdity of her proclamation. If that hadn't been an inquisition, I didn't know what was.

"Have I been cleared?" Marcus chuckled. It took a real knowledge of his character and his mood swings to be aware of the tension simmering at the surface while he waited for Christina's answer.

"For now."

At a very long last, Christina gifted us with a sincere smile. The charged air dissolved, and the indiscreet questions were replaced by good-natured jokes and intimate testimonies about Logan and Christina's wedding anniversary.

"So who's up for a poker game?" Logan asked after he helped Christina clear the table.

"I'm a lawyer. I do not condone such activities." I made an outraged face and faked insult to my very deeply embedded legal ethics.

"Let me put Marie to sleep," Christina said and leapt out of her chair.

"Christina," I protested.

I didn't feel like I was breaching any moral law by playing poker, so I wasn't actually against it, but my sister's enthusiasm made me all the more adamant. She knew I had no inclination whatsoever toward games of chance.

She picked up little Marie, who had long ago lost interest in her toy and had dozed off. Molding into her mother's arms perfectly, she sighed and rested her small head against Christina's breast.

"Texas Hold 'em?" Marcus asked, eying the deck of cards that Logan had retrieved from a drawer.

"Always."

Less than fifteen minutes later, Christina rejoined us at the table, almost bouncing and clapping her hands with unrestrained enthusiasm. I scowled but couldn't get mad at her small betrayal when she was so happy. When *I* was so happy.

I looked at Marcus, and he winked at me, the mischievous glint in his eyes unmistakable. I was so going to lose, but while doing it, I was going to have a time to remember.

"So what is at stake?" Christina demanded eagerly after Logan dealt the cards.

"Oh, yes, indeed."

Logan looked pensive, yet the roguish look he cast my sister promised all sorts of shocking things I wished I hadn't witnessed. It was when I lifted my head and met Marcus's scorching eyes that I realized he was watching me with the same naughty expression. *Men*, I thought rolling my eyes. But the thrill running up and down my skin made me suddenly feel feverish and expectant.

"May I suggest shots?" Marcus asked politely, but there was no politeness in the wicked fashion with which his eyes sparkled.

"No," I groaned, knowing it wouldn't be pleasant whatever he was planning.

"Yep," Christina chimed, clapping her hands. "Tequila, lime, and salt."

"No. I get to prepare the drinks," Marcus said. "After all, whoever loses should experience the loss a little."

Christina looked downright inconsolable at being denied her customary college drink, and she pouted sadly. Logan appeared surprised but recovered quickly. And I—well, I looked resigned. I was going to experience the loss full force.

When Logan and Marcus returned from the kitchen, Logan was holding four shot glasses, and Marcus brought a decanter with a brownish liquid that smelled even more dubious than it looked. Both men sat in silence, looking tremendously pleased with themselves.

"Is that even digestible?" I asked, afraid of the answer.

"Lose, and you'll find out," Marcus laughed.

"I'd rather not."

I was not used to drinking alcohol, yet when I did, I had a little more refined taste than that ugly-looking, nasty-smelling drink in the crystal decanter between us. Marcus leaned into me, his mouth brushing against my ear. Abruptly, I forgot all about the peculiar liquid and found myself absorbed by Marcus King.

"Yet, if you do lose," he whispered softly, "I want something which I will collect in due time."

"What is that?" I was flushed and breathless.

"Don't be impatient, sweet Charlotte," he teased. "I will collect when it is just you and me in our bed."

"Oh…" I was definitely going to lose.

If earlier I had considered myself a terrible gambler, now not even focus was on my side. I felt hot and achy in all the wrong places and completely disorientated. What was he going to collect?

"Shall we begin?" Logan demanded.

Christina won the first game. She tossed her arms in the air, clapped her hands, and made a sensual little dance in her seat that triggered a smoldering look in Logan's eyes. I looked away, blushing and very carefully avoiding Marcus's gaze. I knew he was watching me too.

"They let you win," I grumbled and scowled at the cards.

"Drink up, little sister," she ordered, grinning widely like a fool.

Marcus poured three shots, for Logan, himself, and me, then he proceeded to down his own dose of the nasty liquid. He didn't even flinch. I gripped my glass uncertainly and pinched my nostrils together before I found the courage to swallow the drink.

Saltiness hit my taste buds with a vengeance. The fluid felt warm and velvety against my tongue. It was utterly and undeniably disgusting. It tasted of milk, cheese, apple vinegar, and alcohol, probably rum. It was for sure the single most revolting thing I had ever had to swallow.

"Dude, how did you come up with this?" Logan coughed and made a disgusted face, then slammed the glass against the table and wiped his mouth. "It tastes like something Satan would serve at his birthday party."

"I've had worse than this, believe me." Marcus looked completely unaffected while Christina and I cast him a half-shocked, half-repulsed glance.

The second game was once more won by Christina, who faked a swoon and clapped her hands again, while the three of us gulped down another shot. Then the boys finally brought in the heavy artillery.

Marcus won three games in a row, looking as natural and composed as if he were merely taking a walk in the park.

He was frustratingly gorgeous. With his suit jacket resting on the back of his chair, his black V-neck shirt hugged his muscles in a way that had me fantasizing about licking the sublime planes of his chest and stomach. My breath hitched each time he stole glances at me or when he brushed his forearm against mine, supposedly by mistake.

Completely at ease, with the hand he used to hold his cards resting on the table and the other arm draped against the backrest of my chair, Marcus smirked. He was aware of the arousing image he was generating and was completely unashamed of it.

"I'm going to throw up," Christina complained after Logan won a game.

"Are you giving in, darling?" Logan challenged but eyed the half-empty decanter hesitantly.

"Hell no!"

We played another few games, which obviously, I lost. My attention drifted obstinately back to Marcus's earlier promise. *I want something which I will collect in due time.* I was infuriatingly curious and inexplicably provoked by the wicked nuance I had read in his eyes. My skin tingled with electricity, and my blood ran hotter with each game I lost. Somehow, I knew the more I lost, the more he would want to collect.

It was well past midnight when we took our leave. My stomach rolled, and my vision blurred a little, but Marcus was in perfect, annoying order. He wrapped his jacket around my body and pushed yet another bottle of water in my hands, urging me to drink.

Christina stopped into the doorway, watching us somewhat blearily as we made our way to the elevators. "Marcus?" she called, the pleasant smile she had been wearing all night disappearing completely. "Don't dare to hurt my sister."

Chapter 30

Marcus

My father's residence was an obnoxiously expensive penthouse that overlooked the south side of Central Park. The classical apartment, decorated in shades of beige, gray, and dark brown, was not necessarily huge, yet the luxurious furniture and decorations, the rare paintings hanging on the walls, and one-of-a-kind sculptures scattered around the apartment, or the landscaped private terrace made it stand out ostentatiously.

To all the luxury of the entire apartment, I remained completely oblivious. Rolling a glass of my father's finest cognac between my fingers, I sat quietly in an armchair and waited. Darkness swallowed me in the farthest corner of the living room as I enjoyed the burn of the alcohol.

The rustling of clothes, the jingle of keys, and feminine laughter alerted me that I wasn't alone anymore. Bile rose in my throat with its bitter taste as the shrill sound continued and became louder. Suddenly, the living room was bathed in blinding light, and my father stood entangled with his assistant, his greedy hand ducked beneath the hem of her short dress.

I coughed or rather growled, and like an experienced felon, my father disentangled himself instantly from his companion. He regarded me with a disapproving look on his face while the woman seemed to have a hard time recovering. She was flushed and winded, and if her ruffled state was any indication, absolutely ready to fornicate. I was repulsed.

"How many times did my mother witness this type of scene?" I demanded, pointing the hand holding the now half-empty glass of cognac between the blonde and my father.

"It does not concern you," Isaac replied coolly, his blue eyes turning colder still.

He stepped aside and wasted no more attention on his assistant. Stunned, she lingered uncertainly in the entryway.

I pitied her for being put in that offensive position, but I pitied her more for my pitying her in the first place. Pity was the most demeaning feeling a person could inspire.

"Leave us, Tessa."

"I—mm—"

"Now," Isaac snapped. "I will be with you shortly."

"You will use her shortly, you mean," I muttered once Tessa disappeared from view. Isaac sat across from me on the sofa, quiet and expressionless. It was his complete composure and detached manner that enraged me.

"I will not even begin wondering how you managed to get inside, but is there a reason for your unannounced visit?"

"It seems I don't know my own father," I scoffed acidly, looking at the spot where mere moments ago my father's lover had wiggled in his arms, a vulgar insult to my mother's memory. Isaac followed my gaze, and for the shortest of instants, emotion entered his stony stare. "I won't accept the deal unless I know everything."

It was finally the end of the week, and Hudson still expected an answer I hadn't given. He struck me as the type of man who would not present his offer again if I didn't let him know my answer by the time he had established. My father seemed to think the same. Interest and determination suddenly transformed his features into a warmer and more attentive expression.

"What do you need to know?"

"Everything, from the moment you started until today. Don't

bother with lies. I can easily walk."

He pinched the bridge of his nose and clenched his teeth. Whatever he was about to say would not be pleasant for either of us. But I needed to know. It wasn't even because I was curious. It was because I needed to know how the job Julian Hudson offered would affect me, and implicitly, Charlotte.

"You are not going to like what I have to tell you, Son."

"Try me."

"Very well then," he muttered to himself, strolling absentmindedly to the wet bar to pour himself a serious dose of liquid courage. I was momentarily taken aback when he slammed the decanter back in its place and fixed me with a stern look that resembled a glare. "I've been working with them ever since I was nineteen years old, before I became a lawyer, before I even met your mother. In fact, I became a lawyer to better serve my undercover duties. Your grandparents never found out that I was an FBI agent, so you may quit acting like a disgruntled child. You were not the only one kept in the dark."

"Have you ever told Mom?"

I couldn't keep my tone even. I had always been aware that Isaac had deeply hurt my mother, but suddenly, I felt like I was still oblivious to the extent of that hurt.

"She found out all on her own."

Regret filtered into his chilly stare, then he was once more the cold-hearted man who had become a father by mistake. With a full glass of liquor in his hand, Isaac sat on the sofa and resumed his speech without glancing my way.

"I have told you several times that I do understand your instinctive rebellion. I have experienced it too, yet not for the same reasons. I rebelled against the meager condition of my family and the grim circumstances that I was raised under.

"I do not come from a rich family of lawyers. Your grandfather was a cheap plumber who often returned home empty-handed, reeking of alcohol, and your grandmother was unable to keep a job because of her locomotor disability and because she needed to raise two children by herself. So you see, I rebelled against poverty because I despised it and was ashamed of it. I left that house before

I became of age."

"You were ashamed of your own family, Father. At least have the decency to admit that."

I had a bitter taste in my mouth, and it had nothing to do with the alcohol I had just drunk. I had known close to nothing about my father's family, but I had never expected this cruel depth to his story. I had never expected he had turned his back on a mother who had struggled to raise him and clearly needed her son's help. I had never expected my disgust for my own father to grow.

"I had recently graduated from high school when Agent White approached me and offered me a job. No, he didn't offer me a job. He offered me a life. He was going to fund my academic education and all necessary expenditures.

"Moreover, he was going to provide me with a decent salary and the possibility of climbing up the ladder. The only thing I had to do was befriend a certain elitist student, whose father was a remarkable businessman. He laundered money for the mob. I had to befriend the son, infiltrate into his home, eventually gain his father's confidence, and get proof of his criminal activities.

"That seemed a small price to pay for everything I received in return, so I accepted White's offer. I didn't care that he forced me to study something that I didn't necessarily liked. I didn't care about the danger. I only cared that I would never return to poverty. That was my first mission, and when I successfully completed it four years later, I was ecstatic, and I craved more.

"By the time I finished college and a few other operations, I realized I was truly cut for being an undercover agent. Being a lawyer only happened to be a truly fitting persona that provided me with lots of useful contacts."

"When did you meet my mother?"

"I met her accidentally. If I had gotten to the hospital half an hour later that night, we would have never met, she would have had a happy life, and you would have never been born."

My heart constricted painfully, longing for what it never had. In the absence of my mother, I had grown to love her so greatly that idols paled in comparison. She was the figure I worshiped, the woman I loved so desperately that if my nonexistence had spared her the heartache and misery she had been submitted to, I would have gladly chosen a world where she never met my father.

"That night the mission had gone from bad to worse, and I arrived at the ER with a serious laceration between my ribs. I still bear the marks of that night." My heart was in my throat as he fell silent and squeezed his eyes shut. "Your mother had a nasty sprain, and she was treated in the cubicle next to mine. By the time the attending on-call came to check on me, your mother had worked herself into a state of worry, so she stuck around until I got out of surgery. She was that kind and that caring. The next morning, she visited me, and it was all it took to infect me with an obsession that spread like a virus through my system.

"I know you are unable to believe it, but I loved your mother. I also hated her for making me love her so wildly. Until I met her, I never imagined there could be something or someone who could deter me from achieving my goals. Then she came around, and I was suddenly unable to concentrate on my missions like I used to or fulfill my duties like I was supposed to."

"How did she find out about who you truly were?" I hissed.

Although how his hidden life had affected my mother interested me the most because it was a clear reference point of how it might affect Charlotte in the future if I accepted Hudson's offer, hearing Isaac speak about my mother hurt more than I expected.

"You got your impulsiveness from your mother," he replied then sighed when he saw me frown in confusion. "She found out who I truly was because of her foolish impulsiveness.

"I was having dinner with a woman. She had a statuesque figure and was about ten years older than me but fascinating nonetheless. What fascinated me, and your mother failed to understand, was her involvement with the prime suspect in a case with multiple murders. Your mother showed up at the restaurant and threatened to ruin the connection I had managed to build with my target.

"So I chose what, at the time, seemed the lesser of two evils. I told your mother the truth. I explained to her that the wonderful blonde waiting for me at the table was only wonderful because she served a purpose. She was too angry to see reason. She said she couldn't share me. She was irrational."

"But she chose to remain married to you?"

"We went through a—tough period, but we eventually sorted out our differences," he retorted, tight-lipped. Anger rose in me like a wild flame.

"Do you mean you forced her to stay in a marriage she stopped desiring while you had your fun with countless other women?"

"Like I said, I loved your mother. It was she who refused me, who put a wall between us, who didn't want to accept that my missions did not affect the feelings I had for her. But I still wanted her, and most of all, I wanted her to be safe. Divorcing me wasn't going to accomplish that, so I opted to keep her where I could protect her."

"But you failed, didn't you? For someone who accuses his son of being a failure, you failed at what should have been your greatest mission."

"Yes, I failed," Isaac shouted, catching me off-guard as he jumped to his feet. His eyes were glazed, almost demented. "But it was her damn fault as well. She should have never gone against my orders."

"She was not your property to order around. She was a woman who you neglected for most of your marriage."

"She was my wife. She was supposed to listen to me."

He grabbed a handful of his hair then downed the contents of his glass in a single gulp. I hurt for my mother, for the loneliness and emptiness she might have felt next to a man who had yet to understand how much damage he had done.

"I was in Dallas, under a different identity, carrying out the plan White and I had crafted. You see, when you work with drug dealers and the worst of criminals, you cannot afford to deviate from your plan. But of course, your mother had a different opinion about that.

"She followed me to Dallas, expecting to catch me while I cheated on her. What she actually got herself into was an armed exchange between rival bands of drug dealers. I tried to protect her, to drag her out of there, but it was too late. They had seen her, and that would have been enough for them to discover her identity. They would have realized that I wasn't a foreign businessman, willing to invest in their illicit affairs if I hadn't introduced her as my mistress.

"Ironic, don't you think? She thought the same, and she was furious. But no decent mobster would have tolerated the involvement of a wife in their business. They are oddly built. While they run a cruel, unlawful business that results in countless deaths, they are religiously protective of their families and never involve them in this aspect of their lives. A mistress, on the other hand, seemed innocuous enough. That served a double purpose. For one, they didn't have reason to suspect and dig farther about us. Then, since a mistress was replaceable, they didn't have reason to believe that I was too attached to her, hence your mother remained protected."

"You involved her in your affairs, you bastard!" I grabbed the lapels of his jacket and shoved him forcefully onto the couch. A gasp left his lips, but otherwise, he didn't say or do anything to defend himself.

"She involved herself," he finally growled, the blue of his eyes darkening to pitch black.

"The instant she set foot in Dallas, you should have pulled the plug on your mission. You should have taken her home and never allowed her to get involved with mobsters. That's how you should have protected her."

"I couldn't step out. There was the mission involved and—"

"And you failed *her*," I shouted. I understood right there and then that I would never be able to choose a mission over Charlotte. "Is the story about her accident true?"

"Yes. It happened a week later."

"You are to blame. You are the only one to blame, Father," I spat disgusted, aching to my core.

I felt so repulsed, so raw and unbalanced that I couldn't tolerate another second of seeing his hard face and cold stare. I marched to the door but found myself halting in midstride. A mundane curiosity unexplainably stopped me.

"Are you working on an operation at the moment?"

"Yes."

"Which is?"

"I am not at liberty to discuss that with you. If you are remotely considering accepting Hudson's offer, you should understand that."

Then I was gone.

As I rode the elevator to the subterranean parking lot, I experienced a poignant need to straddle my motorcycle, to throw myself into a mindless race, but for now, the Jaguar had to do. The car purred to life, then it became a ghost down the streets.

I had stopped at a traffic light when I grabbed my phone and dialed a number I didn't expect I would dial.

"I was beginning to think you would never call," Hudson answered, his voice formal yet quietly pleased.

"I know that you know about Charlotte and me," I stated bluntly. At the other end of the line, I heard a soft chuckle then silence. "If you wanted to use this information against me, you'd have done it already, so you don't have any leverage on me."

"If you are trying to imply that I wanted to blackmail you into accepting my offer, you are mistaken. On my team, I want people who are loyal, not afraid or coerced."

"Then you'll take my answer better than I thought. You see, Hudson, to be loyal, I need to trust you, and just yet, you have done nothing to earn my trust, so my answer is no. I can't accept your offer."

I didn't add that the actual reason was my fear and not the lack of trust. I feared that I would put Charlotte in danger just like Isaac had done with my mother. I feared history would repeat itself.

Charlotte was already much too involved in Mayor Stewart's business, so I wasn't going to tempt fate and hurl her into the dark side of the world, where the only way out was dead and cold. What I was going to do was stick to her side until all this madness with Jack Stewart came to an end, then we were going to forget all about them.

"Look, Marcus," Hudson sighed heavily. He sounded like he was straining to remain calm. "We are running out of options, and we're definitely running out of time. If Jack Stewart is acquitted before we can find proof and a link between his father and his business, we won't have a leg to stand on. Mitch Stewart will walk free."

"I cannot accept an offer that will put Charlotte in danger, and don't bother to tell me it won't because we both know that it will."

He paused. I appreciated that he had the decency not to contradict me. Reluctantly, I liked him a little for that.

"You said you don't trust me and I guess that's fair," he continued with the resolve of a man who was not used to giving up or being denied. "What do you say I do you a favor and we'll revisit this discussion in a couple of weeks?"

"I don't need you to do me a favor so you can call it in later."

"You are a smart man, Marcus," he chuckled. "But I'll do this whether you accept my offer or not. The final decision is up to you. Tomorrow you'll receive a package from me. Have a good night."

With thoughts about my mother and my miserable childhood racing in my head, about how my father had hurt us repeatedly and how all the hurt could have been avoided, I hardly knew how I got there. Roughly an hour later, I was knocking on Charlotte's door, breathing heavily, feeling an immeasurable tension pounding in my veins.

I knocked again, unable to get rid of my growing impatience. Behind the door, soft footsteps approached. Half of me didn't want her to see me in this unstable state, but my only choices were coming to her or going racing, and somehow, I just knew she would not be pleased by the latter.

"Marcus?" Charlotte breathed as she opened the door and watched me uncertainly.

Still leaning against the doorframe, I took in her appearance, and as usual, the sight of her left me mute and breathless, but for once, her light failed to disperse the darkness inside me.

She was wearing my black shirt, which she had developed a fondness for lately, mainly when we were not together. The crisp material hugged her curves, and the creamy skin of her bare, supple legs stood out against the dark fabric.

My attention lingered on the shape of her breasts and the mouthwatering cleavage I could peek behind the parted collar. When I realized I could hardly meet her eyes, I ground my teeth in frustration.

She padded closer and placed her small warm hands on my hips, ushering me inside her apartment. "Marcus? Are you alright?"

I knew I had to settle down before I exploded like a firebomb. Charlotte was the last person I wanted to witness my wild side, but my grip on control was running so thin that only letting go could appease the fire burning inside me.

"No, I'm not," I mumbled.

"What's wrong, baby?"

Her voice was so soft and soothing that it nearly hurt. She framed my face between her hands and nudged my head upward until I had no other choice but to meet those searching, chocolate gemstones. There was no escape from her stare, and suddenly, I didn't want one. I was compelled to drown in the depths of her gaze. I was compelled to let go.

When I groaned, an unexpected primitive sound that reverberated across the room, Charlotte's eyes widened, and her mouth parted. Then I surrendered to my desperate craving for affection, and she surrendered to me—a small, fragile bird caught between the greedy claws of a scorpion.

I fisted my hands in her hair and took her mouth roughly, knowing her lips would be swollen and bruised by the time I had my fill, which was unlikely to happen any time soon. She moaned in surprise, but neither rejected me nor scolded me for my uncontrolled roughness. If anything, she responded warmly, comforting without a word as she wrapped her arms around my body and held me tightly. And I went on, pillaging her mouth and absorbing the sweetness of her taste until our blood started boiling.

We were burning.

"The firestorm," Charlotte murmured breathlessly, and both of us remembered our first night together, our first firestorm. But unlike that first time, tonight I was far from being gentle. Tonight, wildness raged through my veins, demanding to be set free.

"It's going to be much more than that, Charlotte," I told her, my voice hardly a whisper, oddly controlled given my chaotic disposition. "It's going to be a raging and rapidly spreading conflagration."

"Oh..." she panted and blushed fiercely

It was ridiculous that I had ever needed a stupid race to

consume my rage and disappointments. There was nothing that could compare to Charlotte. There was nobody who could quiet me down more effectively than she could. But first, both of us had to walk through fire. And in the end, I hoped, we would walk out cleansed and fortified—together.

"I will understand if you ask me to leave." I caressed her cheeks and let my head rest against her forehead. "But if you don't, know that I won't be sweet or gentle. I can't tonight."

"I would never ask you to leave."

She brushed her lips against mine with heartbreaking gentleness as if she wanted to fight off my dark side with her tender, incandescent power. Yet, her body gave her away. My hands gripped her arms, and she jerked abruptly, shivering as my eyes found hers.

"Don't fear me," I pleaded, massaging her flesh while I aligned my body against her. "Even blinded by rage and utterly uncontrolled, I could never hurt you, sweet Charlotte."

"I know. We are here tonight because I trust you. I trust you even when you are blinded by rage and utterly uncontrolled."

I flashed her a grateful smile, and she beamed back, hunger suddenly entering her hot gaze. Then I took a step back, appreciating her half-naked figure. She was soft and tempting, and she owed me something.

"You remember my prize, love? I'd like to collect it."

Charlotte gasped in disbelief, or was anticipation that made the elegant column of her neck convulse as she swallowed heavily? Under my fingertips, her skin burned hotter, and her big eyes regarded me expectantly, nervously. I brushed my fingers against her lips, a last gentle gesture before madness seized me, then I stepped back until a safe distance separated us.

At the sudden separation of our bodies, Charlotte blinked stunned, reaching for me before she dropped her hand and looked uncertainly around herself. Mixed feelings merged inside me. While I always wanted her to be absolutely comfortable with me, I enjoyed immensely the confusion and nervousness I caused her.

And I planned on exploiting that nervous anticipation that made her shiver under my penetrating stare. I was going to use her uncertainty as an aphrodisiac until she would detonate underneath me, and her fire would become my own, until we would be both consumed by it.

"Undress, please." She hesitated and cast her eyes downward as if she was embarrassed, but between us, there were going to be no barriers and no embarrassment. "Charlotte?" I pressed. She gave a light start that had me frowning in response.

My fingers itched to undress her myself, but if I touched her, I would take her like a savage before she was even suitably undressed. So I focused on my breathing and watched her as she brought trembling hands to the collar of my shirt and unfastened the buttons.

She was brave and beautiful, and her eyes were kind and loving as they watched me without blinking. Chewing on her lips and breathing raggedly, Charlotte pushed the shirt open with a feather-like touch that I almost felt on my own body. When the shirt dropped to the ground, I realized with increasing enthusiasm that she was bare save for her panties.

"Leave them," I ordered hurriedly when she dipped her thumbs beneath the lace. My voice came out coarse and harsher than intended. I wanted to pull those panties off her myself, with my mouth, while she wriggled under the intimate caress.

I looked over my shoulder at the hallstand where a beige trench coat, a denim jacket, and a handful of scarves were hung. I smiled wickedly to Charlotte's visible puzzlement, then I headed for the rack and pulled free the sash of the trench coat. The strap felt smooth and harmless enough under my fingertips but completely unyielding just as I wanted.

"What's that for?" Charlotte asked in a whisper, her chest rising and falling with erratic breaths that had the sanctuary of her mouth open in invitation. I groaned.

I could feel her emotions as if they were my own. She eyed the sash skeptically, but I was glad that fear did not taint her eagerness. I stalked toward her until the peaks of her breasts skimmed against the front of my shirt, then I let my forefingers graze the inside of her arms. The moan she let out was a sweet, seductive lullaby.

"Do you know how hard it is to keep my hands off you?" I

stroked her feverish lips with my thumbs, and instinctively, she leaned into my touch, craving more. Always more. I cupped her face in my hands and kissed her forehead before lifting her head to face me. "I want to tie you up, and then I want to set your body on fire. I need you to be still for what I have in mind for you."

"I want to set you on fire too."

"You do, baby. You've had me in flames ever since that Friday night. I couldn't stop thinking about you, and believe me, I've tried."

I stroked her forearms, from her elbows to her wrists, making her nibble on her lower lip and shift from one foot to another. She inhaled harshly as I brought her hands in front of herself, circled her wrists, and tightened my hold enough to make her aware of her defenselessness. I wanted her open, exposed, and completely at the mercy of the passion that devoured us from the quiver of our flesh to the depths of our very souls.

"Trust me," I urged, kissing each knuckle in turn before wrapping the sash around her wrists and binding them together. I clutched her hips and steered her backward to the glass-topped tea table in front of the couch. When Charlotte understood my intention, she started shaking her head frantically. "Lie down," I whispered, intentionally low and husky.

"Marcus, it will break."

"It will hold. And soon enough you'll enjoy the coolness of the glass."

Hesitating but visibly intrigued, Charlotte lowered herself to the cold smoked glass with the unthinking grace of a queen. My gaze stuck on her breasts and the mouthwatering manner they bounced as she moved.

I circled the table as she ever so slowly lay down and regarded me with hooded eyes, then I kneeled beside her head and quickly tied both ends of the sash to the wooden legs of the table. The almost naked sight of her took my breath away. She was bound and vulnerable, and yet, *I* was her slave.

"How does it feel?"

"Tight. Inescapable."

"Don't be afraid," I pleaded when I noticed the breathless

nature of her voice but couldn't contain a smile. She shook her head and moaned. "I'll be right back."

"Marcus, don't leave, please." Her head snapped up, and her eyes turned huge in her skull.

"I am not leaving. No man in his right mind would ever leave you, let alone like this. Do you trust me?"

"Yes."

"Oh, Charlotte..."

Three words scalded my tongue and tingled my lips. I was afraid of what she could do once in possession of the knowledge those words would bring, but I was terrified that the feelings I had for her might not be enough to keep her.

I padded to the kitchen and returned before Charlotte even had time to get properly accustomed to her bindings. Curiously, she watched me place two large bowls by the table and struggled to crane her neck to see their contents.

"Curious, love?" I winked teasingly but did not let her see the hot melted chocolate or the contents of the other bowl which were colder and less fragrant.

"No. It's chocolate and cinnamon," she beamed cockily, looking as if all her nervousness had disappeared.

I faked a displeased frown but couldn't suppress a satisfied grin of my own as I looked at the second bowl. She was never going to guess what it held.

"I don't appreciate that you ruined my surprise, but I promise to give you a reward if you guess what it is in the second bowl."

"Clue?" she asked after inhaling several times and smelling nothing.

"No clue."

"Raspberries, maybe?"

"No. Last chance, Charlotte."

Her brows knit in concentration and soon enough in frustration. It was a little mean making her guess something I knew she would never be able to.

"I don't know," she whined.

"Then no reward, sugar."

I straddled the table and Charlotte's body, then I assaulted her mouth without kindness or restraint. She strained against the sash and arched upward so her breasts pressed against my chest, taunting me.

I was a fool for ever thinking that I could tame her. She was a prime specimen of female wildness.

"You are so sweet, so intoxicating."

Reluctantly, I disentangled my lips from her and straightened enough to whip my sweater off. Charlotte's greedy eyes roamed my bare chest, then she drew her wet, rosy tongue along her inflamed lips. She was making me burn, and I intended to extend the same courtesy.

I climbed off her, licking my way down her body, past her ribcage, and around her navel until my mouth reached the band of her panties. I glanced at her from beneath my eyelashes, chuckling at her shocked, dazed expression, then lewdly traced my tongue against the sensitive skin that bordered the black lace of her panties.

"Marcus—" she moaned low in her throat and threw her head back against the glass top. She writhed and started burning slowly, brilliantly.

"Look at me," I rasped, making her moan again and press her legs together.

As she obeyed, her pupils dilated, and the delicious cinnamon of her eyes caught the shade of dark chocolate. I grasped her knees and pulled them apart, not granting her the relief she sought, then I clenched my teeth around the flimsy material of her undergarments and tore.

"I intended to blindfold you, but I believe I prefer you to watch everything."

"Everything?"

"Yes." I nodded slowly, assessing her reaction. She was breathless, and the flames were merciless as they embraced her, offering her no rest, no peace.

I straddled her waist again, my feet firmly planted on each side of the table and my gaze shamelessly studying her, learning her. Then I finally picked up the chocolate bowl and dipped my finger in the warm, viscous substance.

"Want to taste?" I asked her, showing her my chocolate-coated finger. When the first drop of chocolate fell on Charlotte's belly, she jerked forward.

"Mm—yes."

"Mm—but you didn't guess what's in the second bowl, so no reward for you," I teased and dipped my finger into my own mouth sucking it clean. Her cheeks turned crimson, matching the superb hue of her nipples.

I bent and flattened my mouth against her neck, pursuing the spot where her pulse pounded furiously, leaving chocolate stains in the wake of my kisses. She wriggled underneath me, but her movements were not born out of the desire to evade me but to attain more pressure against her fevered flesh. So I obliged her.

Dipping my fingers into the chocolate bowl, I coated my hands up to my wrists with the sinful liquid and placed them on Charlotte's body.

Then I really touched her.

I caressed her neck and traced the sublime contour of her shoulders and collarbone. Peppering kisses over her quivering mouth, I dragged my hands down to the full shape of her breasts, groaning as a whimper rolled from the depths of her throat.

The rosy peaks of her breasts were especially sensitive. They stood out brazenly against the dark chocolate, inviting me to roll and tease them between my fingers. She moaned loudly, her breath hitching and her eyes rolling in their sockets as her uninhibited body thrashed and sought the coldness of the table's glass top.

It was her body guiding me, asking me for more, instructing me which patterns to create across her supremely exposed flesh. I stroked the underside of her breasts and placed feather-like touches along her ribs only to return and mold her breasts between clenching, ravenous fingers.

"It's too much," she pleaded, her eyes wild in her face. She pushed her thighs upward, putting pressure on my overly sensitive shaft.

"Not enough," I warned her and thrust her legs back onto the glass tabletop.

As I lowered my mouth to hers, my eyes never left her. If she could only understand what she was doing to me. If only my dark, turbulent feelings were enough for her.

My tongue stroked insatiably inside her mouth until the only taste filling me was purely Charlotte. I nibbled on her lower lip, leaving her breathless. Facing away, she granted me access to her marvelously stained neck. I licked at her flesh furiously, cleaning the chocolate stains and feeding her tiny melted bits between voracious kisses.

I was slowly reaching the point where my control would shatter and teasing wouldn't be enough. I caught her stiff nipple between my lips, stroking, licking, and sucking it clean until it turned into a round pebble in my mouth.

"You are the perfect dessert now. What should I do to you?"

With my mouth open, still hovering over her naked breast, I looked up to witness the most breathtaking expression a woman could have.

She was flushed, somewhat ravaged, and profoundly entranced. Her eyes mirrored flames, and her jagged breaths spoke the words she was too overwhelmed to utter. She was prey to the conflagration we were creating. She was beautiful, and she was mine.

"Tell me, Charlotte."

"Lose control," she replied, her voice so soft that it felt like a dream.

And it was time I did exactly that.

Chapter 31

Charlotte

H is politeness did not deceive me. He was on the brink of an all-consuming explosion. Roughness radiated from his very pores and shone like wildfire in his eyes. Once he truly let loose the beast within him, there was going to be no politeness and no chivalry.

Placed between my parted legs, Marcus stretched to unbind the sash from around the wooden legs of the tea table while still leaving my hands tied together. He curled his hands around my hips, gripping just enough to make me aware of his power, then circled my waist, plastering me against his heaving chest. In a single fluent movement, he removed me from the table and pushed me on the couch, nestling my body between the cushions.

"Keep your hands above your head," he instructed sternly, his voice bare of control.

I was imprisoned by his intensely focused gaze, controlled as if I were a marionette and he was the master puppeteer, pulling my strings and bending me to his will. With eyes locked on mine and a tongue that could drive a woman insane dancing across his lips, Marcus caressed my naked body and shaped my legs with his tough-skinned hands. Then the touch was gone, making me whimper in protest and twist my body in search of the glorious feeling of his skilled fingers.

Marcus leaned away and pushed his hand into a bowl, producing a sharp, clicking noise, then he slipped his hand between my closed thighs, making me yelp in surprise. Contrasting with the molten chocolate that had brought my body to a fever pitch, his touch was freezing cold now, and his crooked grin was obnoxiously pleased.

"Ice," I gasped. "The second bowl—it's ice."

"To cool you down," he murmured, still grinning mischievously.

"No, Marcus, don't—"

He dipped his hands in the ice bowl once more, this time picking up shards of ice and caressing my squirming body with the ice in the palms of his hands. It was so unexpected, so cold, and yet, it wasn't cold at all. In fact, his touch scorched me as if my body was malfunctioning, unable to correctly identify each stimulus.

Marcus unzipped his jeans, gazing into my eyes as he pushed his boxers down to his knees. He knew what he was doing to me, and he was doing it with a vengeance. His fingers locked around my ankles, and he draped my legs over his shoulders. Then his hands were on my hips, and he shoved forcefully into me, pushing me backward on the sofa.

"I want you undone, Charlotte. I want you as out of control as I am."

Marcus pressed a freezing finger between my thighs and picked up a senseless rhythm that had me wailing in abandoned release and thrashing between the scratchy material of the sofa and his untamed body. I felt boneless, robbed of strength, but not remotely appeased. The fire within me could only be placated once the flames leaping high and wild in Marcus would quiet down too.

"I am not done," he rasped and went on even wilder than before.

"I know," I whispered, and though he had ordered me to keep my hands above my head, I disobeyed.

As I placed my tied hands on his chest, feeling his raging heart,

Marcus didn't protest. He watched me transfixed, almost tortured as he pummeled inside me with a ferocity that should have terrified me. And yet, the wilder he grew, the more he assuaged a deep-rooted need inside me. While our desperate exchange continued, I connected with him on a level that united us beyond our carnal joining. I could be for him a refuge in the storm and chaos of his world. I could be the solace he frenziedly strived for when nothing else comforted him. And he could be the strength that I lacked. He could be the pillar that supported my world.

Even my legs were sensitive. When Marcus turned his head and grazed his teeth against my calf, I gave a start, which made me all the more aware of his possessive flesh sliding against me. He scattered open-mouthed kisses on my knee, the length of my calves, the soles of my feet, then bent, taking my mouth just as madly as he was taking my body.

I threw my head back, powerless before him and the sensations escalating within me. I felt his tongue on my throat and his lips trembling on my skin, then his teeth dug into my flesh. I heard his smug laughter as he assessed the mark he had put on me. The bite of pain, as well as the unexpected sensation, triggered another explosion that made my body quiver uncontrollably and a moan lodge in my throat.

Marcus couldn't hold back much longer, either. I clasped his face between my hands and urged him down, where my lips nursed him through his tempest. Panting, he rested his head on my chest and shut his eyes. He released my hands and kissed each one in turn. In the end, we fell in a sweaty, exhausted pile on the floor.

"Will you talk to me?" I whispered after a while, relishing the warmth of his embrace. "Please, meet me halfway."

"It's my father, Charlotte. He hurt my mother so badly in every manner possible and—I'm afraid I'm becoming just like him. I don't want to hurt you. Ever."

He shed no tears, but that didn't mean he wasn't crying. Desperation still clung to him, and he was afraid of being a man he could never become. Marcus couldn't be any more different than his father. In all respects, he was a better man.

"You are nothing like your father." He shook his head and looked away as if he were too ashamed to meet my eyes. "Look at me. You might not be a perfect man, and someday you might hurt me, but you are perfect for me. You are the man I am willing to risk everything for."

"Sweet Charlotte," he sobbed and crushed me to his chest until the air left my lungs, but I did not protest. I loved being in his arms. I loved him.

He stroked the red marks around my wrist absently like he wanted to contradict my statement through his touch, but although the marks adorned my skin for days to come, he had not hurt me.

THE NEXT MORNING, I WOKE UP to find Marcus setting the breakfast table on my balcony. For a rebel, he was a pretty damn good cook and a very observant one. He had noted that I preferred a sweet breakfast, and he had made waffles with some sort of chocolate mousse and fresh berries, completed by ice-cold strawberry lemonade and a steaming pot of coffee.

I ambled to the table, wearing his shirt, while he was only wearing his jeans and nothing else to cover his delectable chest. When he saw me, he put the newspaper he had been reading on the table and opened his arms, waiting for me to fill the emptiness.

"I thought you said you don't know how to be romantic," I teased and sat on his lap.

One late night after he took me in the most primal of manners, a dirty, bumpy ride that had me panting for breath and losing my mind, Marcus was lying on his back with an arm under his head and his eyes closed, hugging me to his chest. He had never stopped touching and stroking my body, keeping me warm and sated, but something had shifted in him and turned cold and aloof.

Then he had started speaking, telling me that he did not deserve me, that he had done things he could never take back, that he was terrified of doing those things to me. He had said that most of the time he felt too possessive, just like a beast lacking logic, that he was unable to properly court and romance a woman. He had said that, despite all appearances, he was an undeserving wreck and that he was terrified of the moment I would realize that.

I had all but slapped him for talking poorly about himself—again. Instead, we had ended up making love again, sluggishly like we could never get enough of each other. We both had fears we needed to overcome, but as long as we were together, they seemed to dissipate.

"I'm only feeding you," he replied and bit my lower lip while we kissed.

"In that case, I'd better move a little farther from you."

I stood, walking to the seat across from him, and chuckled as Marcus growled and stretched his hand to catch my wrist. His fingers closed around thin air.

"Now, now," I cautioned. "Behave."

He resumed reading his paper, and I couldn't stop cracking a smile at the sight of him. He looked focused, sensual, and just as delicious as the breakfast he had prepared.

Our little bubble burst once my phone chimed the arrival of a message. Marcus covered my hand, caressing my knuckles with his thumb before I even finished reading the words. When I lifted my eyes, he was studying me intently.

"Something wrong?" he asked.

I remembered Sophia's words that I should not be carrying the burden of Jack's case alone. In the past, I had never mixed business with pleasure, but Marcus was different. *I* was different with him, and I trusted him. I trusted him to listen and offer me his unbiased opinion.

"I asked Philip Foster to contact my PI and find someone related to Jack's case. She was Jennifer Gunnar's friend, and I think she might know what really happened that night."

He nodded, but suddenly he was rigid in his chair. He didn't look pleased.

"Charlotte, I'm going to ask you something that you might not like. Have you considered pulling out of this case?"

"I can't," I said and leaned over the table. It was I covering his hand now and trying to comfort him. "I'm too involved now anyway. I need to get to the bottom of all of this."

"And if Jack is the killer? What then?"

"I will not defend a killer or let them use me as a shield for their cover-up."

"And after that? What then?" Marcus continued and cocked his head to the side. He was frowning.

"What then?" I mimicked, not understanding what he was getting at.

"Charlotte, can't you see? You are delving into a world there's no getting out of. You are not only looking for the truth. You are looking for danger."

He was upset, and to some extent, his concern flattered me. I went and sat on his lap again, framing his face between my hands. His brows remained furrowed, but his arms went around my waist and pulled me closer.

"I need to do this. It's not just about finding out if Jack is a murderer anymore. If my theories are correct, Elana Beckham might be killed, just like Jennifer and Rheya Larsson. I need to find her and warn her. Please understand, Marcus, please."

Marcus sighed and rubbed at the bridge of his nose.

"You need to be careful."

"I will," I promised and brushed my lips against his. "As a matter of fact, I told Philip I'd prefer to meet somewhere secure, someplace that has nothing to do with the firm. Just to be careful."

Marcus smiled a little at the end and nodded his approval. "I think I have the perfect place," he smirked.

"Oh, really?"

"Mhm. Kai's workshop."

KAI'S WORKSHOP WAS WORSE of a mess than the first time I visited it. I expected him to be indignant at our rude invasion of his space, but when he saw us, he came dashing with open arms and only became more thrilled once Marcus told him why we stopped by.

"He's bipolar," Marcus whispered when Kai didn't notice and winked secretly. I smiled awkwardly and really hoped he was joking.

Philip arrived less than ten minutes after we did. He had a full report on Elana, including her address and habits, which seemed to have changed dramatically over the last couple of weeks. I arched an eyebrow, and Philip nodded, indicating his own suspicions regarding such a drastic behavioral change.

"She's completely in the wind," Philip said with a generous amount of frustration. "No one could account for her whereabouts. No one has seen her in days."

"Or maybe she's hiding," I muttered. If Elana was smart, as I suspected she was, then she knew she was in danger.

"And there's more," Philip added and glanced over his shoulder where Marcus and Kai were talking in hushed voices in a corner.

"You can speak freely, Philip. I trust them."

Philip hesitated, then as if he had connected the dots, he shrugged and handed me a piece of paper—the fingerprints results.

"The fingerprints are Elana's," he confirmed. "She has been looking for you too."

AFTER ALMOST TWO DAYS OF puzzling over the information Philip had given me, I decided there was only one way to put an end to the mystery and find answers to my questions.

Had Elana been following me? Did she want to confess what she knew, but no one was willing to listen? Where was she hiding, and what did she know that was so important that her life was at stake?

I drove to the woman's small house, just outside Washington D.C. Usually, at this time she would have returned from the animal shelter where she volunteered each Wednesday and Friday, but in Philip's report, it stated clearly that she hadn't been there in weeks.

My chances to find her were slim, but I had to try. Elana had to know that I was looking for her too. She had to come out of hiding and talk to me.

I was halfway to my destination when I heard tires screeching and the unpleasant reek of exhaust fumes hit my nostrils. Flashes of almost forgotten nightmares unfolded before my eyes.

A glossy black Ranger Rover appeared in my side mirror, then it sped by, all but scratching the paint off my car. Just like a speeding snake, it veered right and cut me off. I shoved my foot on the brake, surging forward, as my own car came to an abrupt halt.

Though there was nowhere to go, my hands remained tightly clenched around the steering wheel and my eyes were wide and stuck straight ahead. The passenger door of the Range Rover opened, allowing a bald, black-suited man to step out. His movements were deliberately slow, as if every gesture was meant to incite fear in whoever was in his presence.

From a distance, I couldn't determine if his eyes were light blue or just a bizarre shade of gray, yet they were lethally fixed on me as he reached for the back door and opened it.

As soon as a shiny black shoe connected with the asphalt, I knew it was Mitch Stewart who would come out of that car. And I wasn't mistaken. Yet, as he fastened his coat and walked determinedly to my car with the leisure of a man taking a stroll in the park, I remained numbly fascinated by the bald man lingering behind. He gave me the impression that he was more than just the mayor's bodyguard.

The sharp knock at the window echoed like a grenade that went off. I jerked and swallowed heavily before gathering the courage to roll down the window and face Mitch Stewart's hostile expression.

"I will not inconvenience you for too long, Ms. Burton," he spoke calmly, a little too calmly. "I am paying you to defend my son. Make sure you do that."

"I am doing my job."

"Your job is to protect him," he reiterated, almost growling. His usual composed countenance slipped for the shortest moment, revealing a scarier man than the one I already knew.

"I am not sure I like the tone of this conversation, Mr. Stewart," I replied coolly, with a firmness and detachment I didn't quite feel.

"Believe me, Ms. Burton, I have been only polite and patient with you. Let's keep it that way, shall we?"

And I did believe him. I firmly believed that Mitch Stewart was capable of much worse in order to protect his son and his muddy affairs. After another moment of dominating me with those frighteningly impenetrable eyes of his, he turned to leave.

"What are you trying to tell me, Mr. Stewart?"

The man was too versed and calculated to reveal outright that he was delivering a threat, yet I experienced the foolish need to push him to the point he would admit exactly that.

His steps never faltered as he threw over his shoulder a dry retort. "I do not tolerate liabilities, Ms. Burton. Especially when family is involved."

They were gone swifter than they had appeared, and I was left there, in the middle of the road, struggling to catch my breath. The event was too fresh and the resulting emotions too chaotic to sort them out. I had just been threatened, and yet, when I convinced my body to react, my fingers curled around the gearshift, and my foot pressed on the gas, driving toward the same destination I had been set on before Mayor Stewart stopped me.

For some reason, Elana's modest-looking house took me aback. Seeing that she was a simple girl, living in a simple house in a simple neighborhood only strengthened my suspicion that she had been drawn into Jennifer's circle and didn't walk out empty-handed. If only she were brave enough to divulge the information she certainly possessed.

My clenched fist connected with the dusty wood of her front door several times before I pressed the doorbell impatiently. The profound silence cloaking the house was discouraging, and it made me question my decision to pay her a visit. If she were hiding, would she remain home where she could be so easily found and potentially killed?

Then I caught a glimpse of a curtain moving and a shadow near the window right by the door.

"Elana, I know you are home," I called, loud enough to be heard and feeling just a little foolish for talking to a closed door. "My name is Charlotte Burton, and I'm a lawyer, but I think you know that already. I'd like to ask you a few questions about your friend, Jennifer Gunnar. I promise whatever you tell me will not put you in danger. Please, can you open the door?"

Minutes ticked by, and only the wind foreshadowing a storm disrupted the eerie silence. The longer I stayed there, facing the closed door, the more confident I was that Elana was right behind that door, listening and perhaps too scared to come out of her shell. I was acquainted with fear and the comfort of a protective shell more than anybody else, so I understood her reluctance. It was unwise and potentially dangerous to trust strangers, so to some extent, I even appreciated her reserve.

"I know you have no reason to trust me, Elana," I spoke quietly as if I was confiding in a friend. I uttered each word deliberately, seeking to offer her the relief she needed to open up and take a tiny step out of her shell. "But I have a suspicion about you, which might be wrong, but if it isn't, I need you to be brave enough to admit it. I know you were friends with Jennifer and Rheya. You met when you were in kindergarten. I think you were very close, and the night of the party, Jennifer confided something in you and Rheya. Jennifer found out something she shouldn't have, and for that, she was murdered. Then, after her death, I think Rheya was willing to talk, so whoever killed Jennifer took care of Rheya as well, and now, you are hiding to protect yourself, am I right?"

I walked to the window and peered inside, but there was no other sign of movement, and no noise came from the house. I sighed heavily, waiting for any sign of her presence, but it never came. Whether I was crazy for having spent the last minutes talking to myself, or she was more terrified of getting involved than I had imagined. When nothing else came to mind to earn her trust, I returned to the door and slipped my business card inside.

"But I also think that you want the truth to come to light," I continued. "You have the information that will help me connect the dots. My private phone number is on the back of the card. Please, Elana, you told me not to give up. Now help me continue searching for the truth. Be brave. Be daring," I finished, by uttering Marcus's words and hoped they would motivate her just as they had motivated me.

I hurried to my car as the first drops of water sprinkled my skin. Having uttered my whole theory about Elana's involvement in Jack's case made me let out a gasp as the oppressive tension that had seized my lungs for days lifted and allowed me to breathe properly. I might have committed the stupidest of errors by divulging such a dangerous theory to someone who might not even be inclined to help me, but somehow, I hoped that would not be Elana's case.

A thick veil of pouring water was shrouding the hotel by the time I drove past the barrier and into the subterranean parking lot. I struggled to force all thoughts of murder, suspects, and criminals out of my head as I climbed out of the car, only to realize that I was returning to an empty hotel room, still bearing the dizzying scent of a male who had undeniably gotten under my skin.

Pulling out my phone and dialing Marcus's number, a small smile curved my lips. I needed to hear him. I needed his low, husky voice to soothe my nerves and carry me to a whole other realm, to a place where I felt strong and cherished and his. I needed to hear him call my name with that special cadence only he managed to inflect to a simple little word.

But the call never connected.

I felt a brutal pain in my thighs and lower back before I saw my phone skidding across the concrete. In the distance, the sound of the rainstorm disappeared, replaced by an inhumane screech and a loud thud. Only when I came face down onto the gasoline-soiled ground and glimpsed the flashing lights of a vehicle, did I realize that the thud had been produced by my body as it collided with the metal frame of the car.

My knees burned, and I felt blood soaking my pants before I checked and saw that the material was ripped and stained. It wasn't the pain in my legs preventing me from standing, though, but my faulty spine and the unbearable ache in my lower back. I could hardly breathe, and somehow, I knew I didn't have long to get out of there.

"Hey, bimbo, where are you going?"

"Come on, hon, don't run away."

"You'll make us think you're a frigid little one and nobody likes that."

"We just want to have a chat with you."

"Now, you're downright rude—"

It was déjà-vu. I gasped and whimpered in rising fear. Crawling away, I groped for the phone that was nowhere in sight. I almost expected a massive blonde man to come in pursuit. I nearly saw clear, beautiful eyes grow dark, angry, and vicious as he turned into a pitiless attacker. But it wasn't Brayden attacking me this time. It was a faceless man, all covered in black, tall and relatively muscular.

He stalked in my direction and reached for me.

A piercing scream left my lungs the very instant some hidden survival instincts kicked in. Adrenaline numbed the pain in my body as I put all my energy into crawling as fast and as far away as possible from the man hunting me. But I wasn't fast enough.

Fingers grasped my hair and shoved me back ruthlessly, making my scalp burn in sympathy with the cuts on my knees. I cried in shock and pain, but I could hardly hear my own voice. I could only hear the staccato of my wild heartbeats and the sickening panting of the man behind me.

"Help," I managed to scream, knowing it would be of no use to plead with him to let me go.

The man hissed furiously and locked a surprisingly powerful arm around my throat, blocking my airway. I panicked, struggling against his tight hold and kicking in vain. Somewhere beyond my fear, I reached a catatonic place where I assessed my attacker.

He was visibly fit and strong and determined to hurt me, which showed the attack wasn't random but carefully plotted. Yet, he didn't seem to be confident in his ability to carry out his game plan. His motions were rash and his gestures agitated. He looked around every so often, which proved that he hadn't secured the perimeter before he decided to assault me.

I opened my mouth and bit my teeth into the flesh of his forearm as I would have into a piece of meat, keen on drawing blood. My attacker howled, a frightening sound echoing in the parking lot, then he slapped me hard, sending me once more face down to the ground in one pile of aching bones.

"You nosy cow," he snarled and aimed at me once more, striking me so hard that my teeth clinked together and my temples throbbed. His voice sounded distorted, but there was something familiar about it.

Then he hit me again with a fury that could only be fueled by frustration. My head bumped against the ground, and merciful darkness swallowed me just as I felt the repulsive fingers of my attacker leave my body. It was dark, warm, and painless, and I couldn't help but succumb deeper to the mind-altering sleep claiming me.

WHEN I WAS CAPABLE OF feeling again, I sensed warm hands encasing my shoulders. The sensation was not unpleasant, but it made me tense and struggle against it nonetheless. A sound of protest and panic left my throat as my eyes flew open. Blinding lights stabbed me violently, and the pain was so abrupt and searing that I felt its sharp edge making cuts in my brain. "It's okay. It's okay. You're okay, young lady," someone soothed in a carefully low voice.

I blinked several times before my eyes adjusted to the light and focused on a chubby cinnamon-haired woman, watching me through her rimless glasses with a kind smile. Her green eyes shimmered with sympathy as she stroked a thread of hair away from my clammy forehead.

"Can I do anything for you?" she asked. She must have been a doctor.

"Water—" I croaked. My mouth was parched, and my throat stung.

I attempted to move, but my bones immediately protested. My back ached as if a chainsaw was cutting every nerve in my spine, and my legs throbbed incessantly. The choked noise that spilled from my mouth sounded pained and alien to my own ears. And the sense of apprehension expanding in my chest rendered me cold and oversensitive.

"It would be wise to take it easy, young lady," the woman instructed, her kind face slipping, replaced by a stern expression that didn't allow any comments. "I'm Doctor Stephens. You were brought unconscious to George Washington University Hospital three hours ago."

Doctor Stephens took a cup of water from a nearby tray and placed a pink straw to my lips, smiling gently as I sucked on it and nearly choked. When I finished, my thirst wasn't anywhere close to being appeased, but I assumed that was due to the medicine I had been given. Before I could move again, the doctor's hand pressed carefully, yet steadfastly on my shoulder, halting my motions.

It was in that instant that the nagging apprehension exploded into full-blown terror. My jaw stiffened, my hands balled into fists, my chest ached with fear, and my body shivered almost uncontrollably. Through the turmoil of my panicky emotions, I managed a curt nod.

I remembered. I remembered the painful collision with a car, the fear, and the growing pain as I was hurled to my knees, my attacker's stale breath as he immobilized and beat me. But most of all, I remembered how I had despised the feeling of being so defenseless, so dependent on another's man will.

"You have been bruised up a little, but nothing that will not heal. We patched you up and gave you some painkillers. You've been sleeping for a couple of hours and might still feel groggy, but otherwise, there's no cause for worry."

"Can I ask you a favor, doctor?"

"Certainly. How can I help you?"

"I need to make a call," I muttered, stressing every word even as my voice broke and my treacherous eyes mirrored my turbulence.

A tingling filled my nostrils right before the corner of my eyes began to sting. I wasn't exactly sure why I started crying, but tears slowly trickled down my cheeks. I was scared, lonely, and so emotionally tested that I simply needed to let it all out. What I didn't expect, though, was the irrepressible trembling that threatened to take hold of me altogether.

Doctor Stephens hesitated, my display of emotion momentarily staggering her before she schooled her sympathetic expression in a neutral one and produced from the right pocket of her smock a gray device. She pushed the phone in my trembling hand and offered me another small smile as if she could empathize with what I was going through.

Her kindness rendered me all the more emotional. I was about to ask her if she could offer me a moment of privacy when hushed voices drifted from the corridor. The doctor glanced at the closed door, sighed, then looked back at me.

I stiffened. I knew the procedure. I knew I had to talk to the police, yet I couldn't bring myself to do it.

"You might want to talk to them first. They have been waiting."

"I need *this* first, please."

I clasped the phone to my chest, my eyes pleading. I needed to make that phone call. I needed to hear that soothing voice at the end of the line. Doctor Stephens eventually nodded and walked silently to the door.

"Of course. I'll hold them off for a few minutes."

"Thank you."

I imagined that as soon as the doctor walked out the door I would connect the call, but roughly ten minutes later, I was still lying there with the phone clasped to my chest and my tears trickling down my face. I was numb, and that meant I wasn't nearly close to purging the chaos inside me.

"Marcus?"

He answered after the first ring, not giving me the opportunity to get used to the idea that I was finally truly calling him. I couldn't convince myself to sound calm. I couldn't train my emotions into impassivity. I felt like a wreck, and I showed it.

"Charlotte," Marcus spoke, his voice thickly loaded with emotions of his own as if he wasn't exactly alright either.

That was my undoing. Tears came pouring like the rain outside, and my body trembled wildly under the thin hospital sheet. I didn't cry elegantly—I never did. I cried until I couldn't breathe properly. I cried until I choked for breath and my chest heaved violently with unsuppressed sobs. I clamped a hand over my mouth in a poor attempt to hold back the sobbing, but if anything, I cried all the harder.

"I—I—can't—" But no coherent words passed my lips.

"Charlotte," he repeated, almost growling. "Please, sugar, don't do this to me. I'm going crazy. I can hardly handle it as it is."

"You know—you know," I gasped. "How?"

In the haze of ice-cold fears and fire-burning tears, I wondered if Marcus knew more than I did. Somehow, sometime, he had been notified of my accident in detail. I wanted to ask him how he had found out or who had let him know, but I lacked the energy. It was strenuous enough trying to rein in my emotions.

"It doesn't matter. I'm coming to you, sugar. Wait for me." He sounded strained, so much that he almost seemed too cool to bear which foolishly made me cry some more.

"Marcus—" I sighed.

Those three words were just there, about to spill like a cleansing out of my mouth. I wanted to tell him. I wanted to hear him say those words back to me. I wanted the comfort they would give me and yet...

"I know," he stopped me, sounding clipped and tense as if he struggled to control himself. "I know. Wait for me, sweet Charlotte."

After he hung up, I remained listening to nothing in particular, trying to uproot the somber feelings that soared in my heart. Doctor Stephens reappeared sometimes later asking me if I was ready to talk to the two police officers waiting by my door. I wasn't, especially not now when the one I had sought comfort in had seemed so odd and aloof. Resigning myself, I nodded and watched Agent Ella Foreman and Agent Richard Coulter walk resolutely to my bed, followed by—Vincent Cole.

My eyes widened, and I was quite certain that my mouth was hanging open. The somber, always composed Vincent Cole looked away and blushed while I kept studying him, doing little to disguise my shock. After a few awkward moments, he sidestepped the police officers and perched on the edge of my bed as if we were alone.

"I found you in the parking lot, Charlotte. You gave me a terrible scare. I thought—"

His jaw clenched so hard that I wondered why he didn't wince in pain. He looked more troubled than a simple work colleague should. In fact, I had never seen him looking so disheveled.

He wore no tie and no suit jacket. His white shirt was crumpled and hanging out of his pants. His hair was a mess sticking in all directions, and his eyes looked awfully tired. Running a hand over his face, he continued tersely.

"I called the ambulance, but I had to stay back at the hotel—" Cole's eyes wandered to the two agents, who promptly stepped in, a mask of considerate detachment on their faces.

"Did you see your attacker, Ms. Burton? Could you describe him?" Agent Foreman eyed me patiently, delivering the usual questions for such cases. Perhaps she foresaw my answer before I voiced it out loud.

Cole raised an eyebrow and looked breathless like something vital depended on my answer.

"No. He wore a balaclava, but he is muscular and of average height. I bit his forearm hard, so he should have a mark there for a couple of days. There's not much else I can help you with, I'm sorry."

Agent Foreman exchanged a secretly knowing look with the two men, instantly putting me on the defensive. Neither of them seemed surprised by my description. If anything, they looked nearly relieved.

"We found a man of your description lying unconscious a few feet away from you. Did you, by any chance, put down your attacker before you lost consciousness?" Agent Coulter asked, hopefulness and skepticism equal in his voice.

I just shook my head, stunned. The last thing I remembered was the aggressiveness of his blows as they connected incessantly with my flesh. In fact, the concept of inflicting any harm on the man who had reduced me to a bruised aching mess was so ridiculous that I would have burst out laughing if I hadn't been so shocked.

"You were found in front of an abandoned car. It looked like you had been hit, which your physician has already confirmed. Can you confirm that as well?"

"Yes."

"Is this the plate of the car?"

Agent Coulter pulled a letter-sized image in my hands with the license plate of a car. It seemed familiar, but my thoughts were too mixed-up to be certain of anything.

"Yes, I think so."

"You think? You are not sure?" Agent Foreman asked, arching a brow.

I hated when police officers treated victims as if they were too traumatized or flooded by painkillers to know what they were saying. I had to bite my lip harshly to stop from snapping.

"She was hit by a car and put in a hospital bed. Do you think her worry was to catch the license number?" Vincent Cole snapped in my stead. I glanced at him, deadpan, and wondered once more why he looked so unkempt and utterly upset.

"The car was not abandoned. The man who assaulted me was driving it," I supplied, although I supposed they had already intuited that.

Agent Foreman nodded silently while Agent Coulter wrote something down in the notebook he was carrying. They watched me with secretly knowing eyes that immediately unsettled me.

Vincent's cool, ashen expression didn't give anything away either. In those moments of not knowing, while my fears grew, and my heart pounded from impossibly fast to achingly slow, I missed Marcus and the safe comfort of his embrace the most.

"That is not all, is it?"

I hated how my voice trembled. I hated that I was alone in a hospital bed, and I hated that I had been put in such a position. I couldn't help but think that if my father hadn't forced me to accept Jack's case, I might have never been here.

"Do you have any suspicions who might want to harm you and why, Ms. Burton?"

"No."

"Have you ever used drugs or been involved with people who used or dealt drugs?"

"What kind of question is that?" I finally snapped, glaring at Ms. Foreman who at least looked sheepish and blushed profusely. My integrity was not something I was willing to have questioned. "No, of course not. I have medical records that can confirm that."

"We are not trying to insult you. We are trying to gather all the facts."

"I don't understand—"

Agent Coulter pressed another picture in my hands, watching for my reaction like a hawk. I stared dumbfounded at the image of a half-full syringe lying forgotten on the pavement. My eyes traveled slowly from the picture I was holding to each of my visitors, silently demanding explanations. But as I returned my attention to that eerie image, realization dawned abruptly, and my heart tightened.

"We found this next to your body," Agent Coulter finally spoke.

"It's been already tested. It is evident your attacker meant to inject you with an overdose."

"Are you sure you have no idea who it might be?"

I did have an idea, but I couldn't confess it to the two officers and make an accusation that concerned Mayor Stewart. Nobody would have believed me without concrete proof, so I chose to play the oblivious card.

"I do have an idea about who assaulted me. It was a man, wearing a balaclava. I already told you that. Have you not arrested him?" I sounded harsh and impatient, momentarily startling all three of my visitors.

"The man found unconscious in the parking lot has already been arrested," Agent Foreman confirmed coolly, her thick brows furrowing. "We need you to personally identify him before we can move forward with the investigation. We know that you didn't see his face, but something might catch your attention, which can help our investigation."

I nodded, although I was far from willing or able to identify a man who, faceless as he had been, would most likely haunt my nightmares.

When the door swung open and Doctor Stephens strolled inside, I was so relieved to see her that I audibly sighed and closed my eyes, fighting the urge to hide beneath the hospital sheets.

"Officers, if I may check on my patient now."

The two detectives left after quickly saying their goodbyes. Half of my tension eased once they departed, but my emotional state didn't completely abate. If anything, I felt even more vulnerable now that I was aware of the sordid details of my assault.

"Charlotte," Vincent Cole said. My eyes opened and focused warily on his massive body, hesitating in the entryway. "I hope you don't mind that I called your intern—Marcus King."

Cole fidgeted with his hands as I looked at him in astonishment. He cleared his throat, making me snap out of my shock, and nod thankfully. The man was intuitive, and my relationship with Marcus was due at some point to cease being a secret. At the moment, I was too shattered to care about the consequences.

It was late evening when I eventually convinced Doctor

Stephens that I was ready to be discharged and that I was going to call her if my condition worsened. My body still hurt so badly that breathing was difficult at times, yet it didn't hurt badly enough to convince me to spend the night in a hospital bed.

To my sheer irritation, the head nurse, a stubborn, severe-looking woman, insisted she drive me outside the hospital gates in an ugly, uncomfortable wheelchair. I stood as soon as the fresh air bathed my face, earning her disapproving scowl and an exasperated roll of her eyes. The darkness made me feel edgier and all the more impatient to get to safety.

"May I escort you to the hotel, Charlotte?"

I was jolted so violently by the unexpected voice coming from right behind me that I struggled to tame the wild beating of my heart.

"Don't do that," I hissed, unable to stop myself.

Vincent Cole stood from the bench where he had been sitting, crushing a half-smoked cigarette under his black shoe. He didn't look any more rested than he had a few hours ago, which made me feel all the more regretful for my reaction and wonder why he felt the need to look after me.

"I apologize," he sighed. "I wasn't thinking."

"I'm—I'm sorry. It's been a long day."

I couldn't get rid of the feeling that something was wrong with Cole, then a thought crossed my mind.

At the time of my attack, the aggressor had seemed taller, but what if fear had influenced my capacity to discern such details? What if my attacker looked tall only because I had been desperate and on my knees? What if Cole had never found me unconscious but rendered me so himself?

I stumbled on purpose, and his arm shot around my waist.

"Thank you," I muttered and gripped his forearm for support, exactly where I had bitten my attacker.

Cole flinched and removed his arm from my grasp.

I froze.

I didn't know whether he felt the temperature dropping or noticed my dramatic change of disposition. I stepped back and pulled my hand around my throat, rubbing absently at the flesh. My mouth was dry, and my palms were turning clammy.

"I think I will catch a cab. Thank you."

I could swear Cole looked relieved.

"If that's what you want," he agreed but stepped closer, blocking my way.

I prepared to scream. A sob left my lips when he buried his hand in the inside pocket of his jacket. I expected him to retrieve a weapon when instead, he pulled out my shattered phone.

"I thought you'd want it back," he said and handed it to me.

I couldn't bring myself to talk. I nodded stiffly, took the damaged phone and went closer to the cab waiting at the curb.

"Charlotte?" Cole pressed on. "I took the liberty of buying you a new one. It's on the mayor's tab."

He winked, but I remained impassive. I slid into the cab before giving Cole the satisfaction of collapsing. In the back seat of the car, I leaned my forehead against the cold window, appreciating the quiet as much as I despised it. It comforted me, but it also offered me too much time to think—to torment myself.

The image of that syringe kept returning to my mind, taunting me, frightening me. Then my suspicion that Cole had attacked me was like a punch to the gut. It left me dazed and breathless. But if that was true, who was the man the police had found unconscious next to me?

I remembered hands finally leaving my battered body as if I were stealing glimpses from behind a veil. Foggy eyes that had succumbed to the quietness of oblivion had caught a peculiar sight—somebody assaulting my assailant. What if somebody had saved me?

The hotel room, my empty Marcus-scented room, was irksomely quiet when I arrived. I felt fresh tears stinging my eyes, but thankfully, I managed to hold them back.

Soundlessly making my way to the bathroom, I changed into Marcus's black shirt. I leaned against the vanity and hugged myself, shivering for once without tears. I hated loneliness and right now, it was my only companion.

"Charlotte?"

It hurt to make the effort to run, but I bolted as soon as the familiar voice of rough velvet reached my ears. By the time the door slammed shut I was already halfway across the room, the liberation I felt filling me with joy to the bursting point. Marcus closed the distance stiffly, snatching me to his chest with one arm even as my chest collided with his body.

I buried my face in his neck and wrapped my arms tightly around his broad shoulders, unmindful of the pain the effort triggered. A sob of his own tore from his chest as his hands gently caressed my calves then linked my legs around his waist, holding me like I was a child. I felt weightless, sheltered, and finally safe.

"I love you," he breathed roughly, brushing his lips incessantly against the side of my face. He fisted his hands in my hair, managing to melt down a rough gesture into a gentle caress. "I love you so much that I feel like I'm going crazy. I feel murderous, Charlotte."

Choked by emotions, I remained speechless, and Marcus was content just to hold me. I experienced a harsh sense of panic when he attempted to pull away, and I clung even harder to him, begging him through my gestures when my words failed me to never let me go.

"Easy, sweet Charlotte, I am not going anywhere, and neither are you."

He slid me down his body and cupped my face between his warm hands. They were trembling.

"I'm fine now. I truly am."

His eyes narrowed infinitesimally, just enough to let me know that he didn't believe a word I was saying. But I was telling the truth. Finally, my emotions were settled and the apprehension in my heart appeased.

I rested my head against his chest and closed my eyes, relishing the comfort he gave me even as it frightened me. He had conquered my defenses and invaded my existence so completely that his mere presence was an invaluable comfort, a beacon of light in the darkness of the unknown.

"Let me see," he asked, pushing me two steps backward despite my groan of protest.

"I am fine now, Marcus." I tried to dodge and hide from his

reaching hands, but the harsh intake of breath and the threatening way his nostrils flared canceled every intention I might have had of stopping him. He was going to see the damage eventually anyway. Marcus assessed me carefully. His deft fingers unfastened the buttons of his black shirt that I had developed a fondness for and was wearing in his absence. He parted the sides without baring me completely. His eyes drifted to every bruise without hesitation as if they already knew where my flesh had been abused the most.

"That bastard," he growled under his breath, the glint in his eyes completely, uncontrollably wrathful.

I started trembling, almost convulsing as if I couldn't get enough of his warmth and comfort, but this time it was not with fear. The relief I felt was so intense that my whole body shook.

"Go to bed," he whispered, stroking my cheek with the back of his hand.

"I don't think I can sleep right now."

"I wasn't thinking about sleeping. Discard the shirt, please."

I gasped and knew by the abrupt heat in my cheeks that I was blushing. I didn't think I could do more than sleep, either, but I chose not to comment on it. I felt stiff all over, and the pain in my spine was shooting daggers through my whole body. Yet, that wasn't reason enough to refuse the solace and elation I would draw from the slow glide of Marcus's body against mine, from his mouth sketching patterns on my skin, or from his nimble hands worshipping me even when I was at my worst.

He disappeared into the bathroom and returned a minute later wearing only a pair of black boxers. Every step he took brought him closer to me, eliciting a thrill that deepened the flush on my face and ignited a heated rosiness all over my body.

"The shirt. Off."

He pointed to me then to the ground, and I finally obeyed his instruction, unable to take my eyes off him. When he stopped in front of me, he touched me reverently from the balls of my shoulders to the curves of my hips then bent low enough to softly kiss my lips.

"You scared me today."

"You don't like that," I breathed, my throat unexpectedly

barren.

"No, I don't. And it won't happen again."

I placed my hands on his shoulders, feeling the controlled rage in the slight tremor of his muscles. He was tense and furious although he masked those emotions well. It was when he touched my spine with the tip of his fingers, and I quivered at the teasing contact, that the frown on his face slowly dissipated.

"Lie on your stomach."

When I gave him a puzzled look, he smiled encouragingly and guided me into the requested position with firm but gentle hands. A soft whimper escaped my lips, and a low growl of his own was his only response.

He straddled my hips, and I almost yelped in surprise, but he never pressed his weight on my body and never inflicted an ounce of pain on my already pained limbs.

The mattress dipped under our combined weight, and Marcus was suddenly crouched over me, breathing roughly against my ear. I felt the renewed urge to cry when he pressed his cheek against mine and rubbed his one-day worth of stubble against my face, sighing.

"I want you to relax, sugar. Can you do that?"

His voice washed over me, and slowly, the knots in my muscles loosened. I nodded, mumbling my agreement, and he kissed my cheek, letting his lips wander until they found my earlobe. He bit gently into the flesh, and I moaned, the only encouragement he needed. He licked his way to my nape and kissed me there until I couldn't stay still.

"Is there a problem?" he asked against my skin, not deigning to stop.

"You are not helping me relax."

"Am I arousing you, sweet Charlotte?"

I wanted to convince myself that his cheekiness was the only thing that caused me to gasp, but I knew better, and so did he. That shameless tongue of his continued its journey down my spine until he reached my lower back, and he covered the bruises with healing kisses. I moaned again, but this time in contentment at having him cherish me so carefully.

Then he straightened, and a gust of cold air covered my back before his caring hands splayed again on my skin and stroked me from my shoulders to my abused lower back. The sensation was so soothing and delightful that initially I entirely missed the sleek quality of his gliding fingers and the citrus perfume of what I later recognized as my body oil.

"Are you giving me a massage?" I chuckled, feeling inexplicably shy.

"Indeed I am. Does that disappoint you?"

I could hear the laughter in his tone, and I smiled against the cool sheets. We both needed to relax, and perhaps this was not only a way to help me feel better but also his method of letting go of his own anxiety.

"No. Thank you."

Right then, I wanted to kiss him so badly that when he bent and took my mouth, I thought he might have heard my desire. He sucked gently on my lower lip, creating an ache that had nothing to do with my split lip or my bruised form. My body understood his distraction tactic, and it reacted of its own accord.

"Do your joints hurt?" Marcus asked so matter-of-factly like he hadn't just made love to my mouth. "The bad weather makes you particularly achy."

"You noticed—"

"I notice everything, sugar," he whispered proudly.

"My back hurts too much to be able to focus on any other pain," I admitted on a moan. The feel of his fingers kneading my flesh was divine.

Marcus growled under his breath but never stopped his soothing ministrations. His hands stroked gently yet applied the exact amount of pressure to turn my whole body to mush. I moaned in pleasure when his fingers absently touched the undersides of my breasts or when they performed a particularly delightful kneading of my tired flesh and whimpered when he reached my bruises.

Unspeaking, he bowed to scatter countless kisses, covering the hurting spots with the heat of his mouth. It didn't surprise me how wonderful he made me feel.

Before long, I found it difficult to keep my eyes open. I was well on my way to falling asleep when the shrill sound of my new phone made me jolt so hard that I bumped against Marcus's bent body.

My fingers closed around the disturbing device, and Marcus growled in warning when I answered. It was Christina, and I had a feeling she was not calling at this hour to wish me pleasant dreams.

"Why do I have to find out from James that you have been attacked and hospitalized?"

I shut my eyes and sighed tiredly, not even caring how my father had gotten hold of that information. But I did care that he had known all along and hadn't even bothered to get in touch with his daughter. My eyes stung again, but this time it was easier to control myself.

"I'm sorry, Chris. There was no time to call anyone, but I am fine now. I promise."

"You are not fine, Charlotte. You were attacked, for Christ's sake. You could have—God."

Her voice thinned and finally broke. I knew my sister well. She was crying. She neither sobbed nor sniffled, but she was crying, that silent, tormented type of crying that broke my heart and didn't help me one bit to rein in my own emotions.

"Please, Chris, don't cry. Marcus is here now. Nothing else will happen to me."

"How do you feel?" she asked after a while. She sounded calm now, but she wasn't fooling me. She was still crying.

And Marcus was still massaging me, the sensation so unbearably perfect that I could hardly keep quiet. One hand rolled over my skin, never losing its rhythm while the other was clenched in a fist and pressing deftly where it hurt the most, bursting each bubble of tension until all I felt was bliss.

"A little bruised up, but a lot taken care of—aah—"

I sank my face into the mattress, stifling my gasp a little too late, and batted entirely too ineffectively at the obnoxious man crouching over me. Marcus licked my nape then bit playfully, chuckling even as he groaned in protest. His hand curled over my phone, then he straightened, and the phone was gone.

"What on earth are you doing?" was the last thing I heard

Christina say.

"Hello, Christina. It's so nice to hear from you again. I am currently giving your sister a massage, and you just ruined my work by making her tense up again. We will be back in New York tomorrow. I'll make sure Charlotte pays a visit if that is okay with you."

I tried to roll over, but as soon as I moved, Marcus placed his hand on my back, a gentle but steady pressure that prevented any other movement. He paused and listened to whatever Christina was saying, and so did I, but in the end, I failed to hear anything. It wasn't difficult though to imagine the lecture she was giving him.

"Not when it happened," he said then paused. "I'm not trying to excuse myself." Another pause, another line he stroked down my back. "Yes, I did, and I will," he finally added, almost angrily.

The sound of his voice propelled me to look over my shoulder, but once more, his free hand prevented me from moving. When he slowly pushed my head back down against the mattress, I did not fight him. I was so tired that I hadn't even realized when the conversation between Marcus and my sister ended.

"We can't go back to New York," I murmured sleepily although being home and leaving Jack Stewart's entire mess behind was all I wanted. But I couldn't, and Marcus had to know that.

"We can, and that is not up for discussion." He sounded harsh and infinitely determined. I sighed, knowing an argument was inevitable. "If you are under the impression that I will leave you on your own in this damn city for even an hour, you are either sorely mistaken or you have no idea who you are up against."

"I don't want to fight, please."

"We aren't."

He rolled me over and covered my body with his, like a shield that wouldn't let anything get past it, then he took my mouth in earnest. His gentleness and thoughtful gestures could not conceal the fire in his eyes or the heat in his touch.

Marcus kissed me, and soon, I felt so dizzy that my mind failed to produce any coherent thoughts. He kissed me with no intention of stopping, but this endless kiss was for him. He had appeased my fears, and now he was appeasing his.

"You are safe now," he sighed and snuggled me close to his chest.

I believed him.

Chapter 32

Marcus

My hand reached to find the warm softness of Charlotte's body, but instead, it only fondled cold, empty sheets. The realization of her absence jolted me awake and sent my heart on a rollercoaster. *Gone.* She couldn't be gone.

I was almost sitting by the time I realized that she was leaning against the headboard, her knees to her chest and her arms locked around her bent legs. Her chocolate eyes looked upon me affectionately, yet they were markedly sad. I knew instantly that something was wrong, and though my heart had settled at the sight of her, it started beating erratically once more.

"Charlotte, what's wrong?" I asked, cupping her cheek with an uncertain hand.

Charlotte leaned into my touch, warming my heart even as my worry grew. She shook her head, a soft movement that spoke of hopelessness, and her lips flattened into a thin line. She was holding back tears.

I pulled her into my lap, securing her head between my shoulder and my chin. It was then that she finally sobbed, a solitary sound that tore my heart out. She must have still been afraid, and that threw me once again in a rage that I could hardly subdue.

"Did you only say it because you were scared? Because I had been in danger?"

She pulled away as far as my arms allowed, which wasn't farther than a few inches, but the distance felt as endless as a desert. I pulled her back to my chest, and when she wouldn't meet my eyes, I gripped her chin and forced her head out of its hiding.

I had believed she was afraid for her safety, whereas she doubted my feelings. That triggered a whole other type of anger.

My dread might have been the cause of finally accepting my feelings for Charlotte, but it certainly hadn't been the reason for their existence.

Seeing her vulnerable and in danger, every drop of blood in my body had been contaminated by the fear of losing her. Because I loved her, and that love had been cemented each hour and each day since I met her. That love was the purest feeling in my heart, and having it questioned precisely by the woman it had been born for, enraged me as much as it hurt me.

"Listen to me and listen carefully," I growled. Clasping her shoulders, I kept her immobile and completely focused on me. There were millions of things she could doubt about me, but she could not doubt my heart. "Yes, I was scared. I still am, now that it's painfully clear the danger you are in. But why would I be scared in the first place if I didn't love you? I meant every word I said last night, but let me repeat it, so there are no misunderstandings. I love you, Charlotte Burton. Doubt that again, and you will make me really mad."

She was surprised by my outburst, but skepticism remained. Although I knew that Charlotte was not a woman to be convinced by mere words, it infuriated me that she could doubt something that ran so deep and uncontrollable inside me, something so pure and beautiful that words could never do it justice, something that I showed her each time I had her in my arms.

"Charlotte," I warned even as I tossed her onto her back and crafted a tight snare for her that had her back flat against the mattress and her heaving breasts pushed against my chest. "You are not leaving this bed until you understand. I never speak words

I don't mean."

"I really want to believe you, but what if you change your mind?"

"You are so wrong. You have trapped *me*. Completely. I'm past the point of being able to change my mind."

She locked her arms around my neck and sifted her hands through my hair as if she was exploring me, as if she was storing my image in her memories for a future without me in it, without *us*. The thought made me desperate, brutal even. I pressed my body against her until we were perfectly aligned, and she felt the heaviness of my weight.

I swallowed her gasp with a punishing kiss, relishing her submission. Despite her fear of trusting, of hoping, she understood my need for her on a primal level and never even attempted to push me away. If anything, her arms tightened around my shoulders, and her lips met my fierce plunder with a hunger of her own.

By the time neither of us had any air left in our lungs, her new phone blared from the nightstand. I stood, enjoying her moans of complaint as much as I had enjoyed her soft body underneath me.

Charlotte answered with an impatient tone she rarely used, all the while keeping her eyes focused on me. And I couldn't help myself. I rubbed my lower lip with the pad of my thumb then licked my lips slowly, teasing her shamelessly. She blushed and stammered, momentarily forgetting about whoever she was talking to.

I touched my neck, where she loved to kiss me, and rubbed my chest, where my heart beat hungrily for her, then, ever so slowly, I let my hands follow the trail that led to the drawstrings of my pajama bottoms.

Those huge almond eyes of hers followed my every move, and as soon as she understood my intention, they grew wide and delectable then turned panicked and censorious.

"Don't," she mouthed, shaking her head sternly, almost hyperventilating.

But I did. I untied the knot that kept my pants secure around my hips and let them fall to the ground without a sound. She inhaled sharply, the pinkness in her cheeks deepening to an adorable red.

"Yes, yes, I am fine," she was saying. As I crouched once more over her, Charlotte took cover beneath the duvet, groaning as I ripped it from her fingers and threw it to the ground.

I pounced like a jaguar on its prey. She stuttered, hardly paying any attention to her caller, and licked her lips, tempting me even when she wanted to contain me. My lips closed around the sensitive spot where her pulse beat chaotically, and I sucked and nibbled until my mark was starkly imprinted on her beautiful skin.

"No hiding allowed," I warned her, trailing wet kisses on her quivering flesh until I reached a half-exposed breast and lavished it with attention.

Her fist clenched in my hair, pushing me away even as she pulled me closer. The low moan that trembled in her throat elicited a groan of my own. I was close to losing control, when my intention had merely been to tease her, to lure her like she always lured me.

"One day, there will be no doubt in your mind about how I feel for you, Charlotte."

"Nothing, you must have heard wrong."

Only to test her reaction, I caressed her hips and let my hands dip south, seeking the blatant evidence of her arousal. She hissed and shot out of bed, grabbing the duvet and wrapping it around her body.

"I am busy at the moment," she excused herself as she faced the window. I threw my head back and laughed, which earned me an adorable glare and a pointed finger that guaranteed retribution. "I will make sure to visit as soon as possible, I promise."

"Bring it on, baby," I dared her then finally headed for the bathroom, leaving her to her caller, who most probably was her sister.

When I emerged from the shower, she was still on the phone, but I instantly got the impression she was not talking to the same person as before. Her features were drawn into a frown, and her hands were trembling by her sides. I pulled her into my arms and pressed a kiss to the top of her head, keeping both of us calm and collected.

Charlotte softened promptly and let out a sigh of resignation. "I will be there, but there is not much I can help you with, detective," she spoke curtly, then hung up, rubbing her face in frustration. I already knew where she needed to go and why.

"You are safe, Charlotte. You are not going alone."

She watched me hesitantly, but equally hopeful. I knew her reticence about being seen with me in public was prompted by her wish to protect me from my father's prying eyes. Given the latest events, that was so far out of my mind that I couldn't even bring myself to care. I kissed her breathless and chuckled when she swayed a little.

It was when she saw my positively brazen and totally amused grin that she frowned and slapped my chest. The accusations dripping from her eyes managed to make me laugh again, but this time, she didn't remain as calm as before. She grabbed cushions and pillows and threw them my way, hissing while she displayed her warrior self to my utter delight.

"Who were you talking to earlier?" I chuckled and eventually ceased ducking her hardly lethal projectiles and strode back to her. When my arms firmed around her waist, her tiptoes could barely touch the ground.

"My mother," Charlotte cried outraged.

"Your mother?"

"Yes, Marcus. I do have a mother."

Stupidly, the notion seemed so alien, but of course, she had a mother, whose name I didn't even know. I realized I was gritting my teeth when Charlotte cupped my cheeks and pressed a delicate kiss to my lips as if saying she forgave me for seducing her while talking on the phone with her mother.

"I know, it's just that we never spoke about her."

She eyed me sadly, sympathetically, the glint in her eyes saying what her lips refrained from. We never spoke about mine either, and perhaps that was why she had never dared to discuss hers.

"I don't want you to hold back, Charlotte. You can talk to me about anything. Anytime."

"Would you like to meet her?" she asked shyly, offering me a gorgeous smile that I had no defenses against.

"As soon as possible."

She agreed happily, the last agreement we had before we started fighting about her already scheduled return to New York. By the time she finished dressing, her luggage was at the door and so was I. Neither her attempts at rationalizing with me nor her compelling kisses swayed me.

Charlotte fought me although her eyes were pleading for something else. She complained and listed all the obligations that tied her to D.C., but she didn't quite want to fight me, so when she saw me ready to go, all the fight left in her evaporated.

I was not surprised to hear her sighing with relief as she stepped out of her room. The ride to the police station was silent. Charlotte kept kneading her hands in her lap and glancing every so often out the window at the people that went about their business, unaware of the gruesomeness that afflicted their world.

When we arrived at the police station, Vincent Cole met us at the entrance. He said something that indicated he had already been there on business, but I got the feeling he had been purposefully waiting for Charlotte.

"You still look shaken," Cole observed. "Let me represent you, Charlotte. You shouldn't trouble yourself over this ordeal any more than you already have. It would be an honor."

"I can handle it," Charlotte snapped.

I glanced at her, perplexed, and it was at that moment that I noticed the stony set of her features and the glacial look in her eyes. I couldn't quite tell whether it was because I wanted to offer comfort or silently ask for an explanation, but I put my arm around her waist and Charlotte took refuge in my half embrace.

"What's the matter?" I whispered in her ear so only she could hear me.

She shook her head gently, albeit a little rigidly, then confronted Cole's startled eyes.

"I'm a lawyer too, Cole. I can represent myself."

He opened his mouth to protest, but detective Foreman stepped out into the hallway and asked Charlotte to follow. I trailed after them only to be stopped by the woman who pinned me with a critical stare and told me that I was not allowed to accompany

Charlotte when she was supposed to identify the man who attacked her.

My hand tightened around her slim fingers, and my teeth gritted, but the policewoman remained unimpressed by my glares or almost audible growls.

"Follow me," she decreed, motioning to Charlotte.

"I'll only be a moment," Charlotte murmured, prying her little hand from my grasp. "It's procedure."

The sad nature of Charlotte's voice and the resigned look in her eyes did little to convince me to let her go. She nodded to herself, mustering the courage to face her attacker, and made to step away when my arm automatically curled around her waist.

"I'll be waiting for you."

Vincent Cole stepped to the side to allow Charlotte to pass. She followed detective Foreman into a room at the end of the corridor while Cole watched her with a sort of brooding gaze that I couldn't quite make sense of.

He looked spent and absent-minded as he rolled his head from one side to the other then excused himself.

I couldn't even waste a glance on him. My attention was glued to that door at the end of the hallway.

The forced smile Charlotte had offered me before she stepped into that room was a calming companion in the minutes that followed. The moments dragged on, and my mind, suddenly not occupied by Charlotte, was freely whipped by a rage that returned so aggressively that it momentarily choked me.

After a whole night of witnessing Charlotte's tossing and turning, of watching her tense features as dreadful nightmares tormented her mind, after holding her writhing body and feeling utterly powerless, I was furious, and that fury had to be unleashed on somebody. I was especially angry since the damn nightmares were back after a fairly long while of peaceful nights.

Marching up and down the corridor and burning holes in the granite under my feet, I kept staring back at the closed door that separated me from Charlotte. I pressed the phone to my ear, almost slamming my fist through the thin walls when finally, someone answered.

"Hudson," an annoyed voice greeted me as if he didn't know who he was speaking with.

"We need to meet," I snarled, but somehow managed to keep my voice a whisper.

"I'm in New York actually. Should I come by your father's firm? I can be there in twenty."

"No," I said harshly, struggling to ignore the enthusiasm in Hudson's tone. "I'll come to you. Send me the location."

I hung up and covered my face, rubbing at my eyes as though that small, repeated gesture could dissipate the white-hot anger coursing through my system.

When Charlotte emerged minutes later from the interrogation room, looking pale as a ghost and nearly in tears—again—I grew even more furious. I was on the verge of a murderous frenzy.

She flung herself into my arms without a word, muffling her sobs against my chest.

"Don't worry me like this, Charlotte."

"Just take me away from here," she sobbed, teary eyes looking up at me anxiously.

IT WAS PAST NOON WHEN we landed in New York, and it was even later when I parked my car in front of Christina's apartment building. Gripping the steering wheel, I turned in my seat to face Charlotte who had been distant ever since we left the police station in D.C. She eyed me shyly, gifting me with a delicate smile.

"Come upstairs. Christina won't eat you, I promise," she murmured, leaning into my touch when I cupped her cheek and brushed her lips with my thumb.

"I should drop by the office. I think Weston needs me for something."

Charlotte nodded, but her disappointment was clear. I hated lying to her.

I stifled guilt, worry, and frustration with the blissful feeling of her lips trapped between mine. I kissed her softly, massaging her lower lip and nuzzling her chilled nose until she let out a warm moan.

The vulnerability in her gaze tempted me just as harshly as her graceful sensuality. I wanted to wrap her in my arms and hold her tightly, to swallow her in the rooms of my heart where she filled every corner.

The intensity of my feelings scared me. This level of untamed need, this incapability to let her go was bound to scar my heart. I could only hope that Charlotte would be merciful with the fortress she had conquered, that she would treat my heart gently, and that, if need be, she would heal my wounds.

"I love you," I heard myself whispering.

Charlotte sobbed.

It didn't pass my notice that she hadn't said it back. I needed her to tell me she felt the same for me just as I needed to scream to the world my own feelings for her. Yet, I would never pressure her nor trick her into confessing something she wasn't ready for. I smiled sadly when the silence stretched, and her eyes wouldn't travel higher than chin-level.

"Don't say it like it's the last time."

"Never."

I forced her to meet my eyes and kissed her, never breaking eye contact. She seemed troubled, and I suspected that yesterday's events weren't the only cause. Charlotte was tremendously intuitive. She had suspected that something was going on with me since the night I refused Hudson's offer.

"Please call Kai if you need anything and you can't reach me. I don't want you alone on the streets if possible." I grabbed her phone and programmed Kai's phone number, absolutely aware of her puzzled glances.

"Why wouldn't I be able to reach you?"

"Things might happen."

Things like meeting Julian Hudson or actually entertaining the idea of accepting his deal.

Her eyes narrowed. She did not bother to pretend that she had welcomed my explanation since she probably hadn't. After Charlotte slid out of the car and disappeared into the building, I knew I was a fool for imagining I could lie to her for too long.

HUDSON WAS OVERLY WATCHFUL, but I found I liked his prudence. Burton & Associates was definitely not the venue to meet, and neither was the hotel he was staying at since he was undoubtedly monitored by more eyes and ears than he cared to count. When he sent me the address of an abandoned warehouse on the outskirts of the city, I was hardly surprised.

"Were you followed?" Hudson demanded as soon as he dismounted his ride. It was a black and red Harley Davidson, so lush and wild that I could hardly reconcile it with the man who rode it.

Faced with my astonished expression, Hudson smirked and patted the quieted beast. I couldn't tell whether he was trying to get on my good side, or we really had more in common than I thought, but the surprise wasn't going to distract me from the real purpose of this meeting.

"I'm not an idiot, Hudson."

"So what is the meaning of this? Did you reconsider my offer?"

He looked expectant, but my scoff made his spine straighten and his chin rise in some sort of challenge. Then he caught the scent of my inner crisis and prepared to take the final leap before he snatched and added me to his collection of loyal soldiers.

I didn't cope well with being controlled or commanded, but things had changed, and whether I liked it or not, I depended on his help. Although Charlotte wasn't aware of it yet, she was in as much danger as the woman she was looking for. Last night had been a clear proof of that.

"Do you know what happened last night?" I shot at him. "I went back to D.C. to find Charlotte beaten and scared out of her mind. Do you even know how close to a tragedy everything was? Do you know she could have been injected with a lethal dose of cocaine? She could have died. So no, I'm not here to accept your offer. I'm here to ask you—No, I'm here to demand that you do your damn FBI thing and put that scumbag of a mayor and his evil spawn behind bars. And do it now."

"Are you done?" Hudson sighed. His annoyance turned to

compassion, then to something very close to understanding. "I am truly sorry about Ms. Burton's injuries and the danger she is in, but this is exactly why we have to take Mitch Stewart down. I cannot do that without you, Marcus. I know the facts, but I don't have the proof. I need you to collect the proof that will show, beyond a reasonable doubt, that Mitch Stewart is guilty of all the horrible things we know he is."

"Have you listened to anything I told you?" I shouted. "Charlotte is already in a hell of a lot of danger. If I accept your offer, it's like I'm putting a target on our backs."

"If you don't, Charlotte will be in a hell of a lot more danger. Do you think the cocaine is a coincidence? Do you think there's no link between that and the drug trafficking business the mayor runs?"

I did not believe in coincidences. I cursed and really wished I could punch something, hard enough to tear it to pieces.

Anger morphed into fear. My hands started to tremble, and my heart beat madly as if it wanted to come out of my chest. The dread from the previous day returned with an intensity that almost knocked me to my knees. I could have lost Charlotte. Permanently. Like I had lost everything else I cared about in my life.

"Look at it this way," Hudson continued shrewdly. "You help me put the mayor in prison, you help Charlotte stay safe."

"How can that even be possible?" I groaned and remembered my mother's story. She hadn't been kept safe. She had been collateral damage.

"We have resources."

"Then use those damn resources to get her off Jack Stewart's case."

Hudson sighed again and shook his head like he was talking to a child who refused to see reason.

"Ms. Burton is entirely too involved in Stewart's affairs to walk out unharmed. If you want her safe, she needs to be off Mitch Stewart's radar, and that can only happen when he is behind bars. Do you know he has threatened her in the middle of the day? You think staying away will make her safe, but it won't."

"It will be a start," I seethed.

With his hands grasping his lean hips, his back rigid, and his eyes shooting arrows, Hudson studied me and assessed the situation. For some reason, he needed me as much as I needed him. *We are a match made in heaven*, I thought bitterly and almost laughed.

"Very well," he consented. "I'll see what I can do. But, Marcus, the favors are piling up, and you have done nothing to earn them just yet. The next time we see each other, I expect a much different answer."

Chapter 33

Charlotte

"*Did you kill Jennifer Gunnar and Rheya Larsson, then try to do the same with Charlotte Burton to keep her from finding the truth?*" Agent Richard Coulter asked and slammed his fist against the metal tabletop.

Jase Parker jumped in his seat and gave the agent a glassy-eyed look then resumed his hunched posture. It took him a moment before he registered what Agent Coulter had said, then Jase straightened and gaped.

"Rheya is dead?"

"Let's not play games, Parker."

The observation room was dark and still, and the darkness seemed to stretch and swallow Jase too. I heard the rumble of a car and turned around startled, but the room was empty and the door closed. Then the air became cold, and Jase's screams grew louder. When I turned, Jase Parker was staring right through the two-way mirror like there was no barrier between us, like he could see me, like he could reach me.

I gasped and moved backward, but his shouts followed me, and so did the darkness.

"It wasn't me," he screamed and neared the glass wall. "I never went to that hotel. I don't know what happened. It wasn't me."

The two-way mirror disappeared like it had never been there, and Jase

Parker grabbed me by the wrists and yanked me closer, then my knees gave way, and I was falling down a dark, bottomless hole.

I WOKE UP WITH MY HEART in my throat and my damp camisole clinging to my skin. I touched the mattress and fisted my hands around the sheets, but I still felt like I was falling.

The fear from the dream was all the more real when I remembered that despite all evidence, Jase Parker was not my attacker. My attacker was free and roaming around like a vulture.

"Charlotte, what's the matter?" Marcus asked.

He walked into my bedroom, still wearing his pajamas, and cradled me to his chest. It felt safe and inviting to hide there in his embrace, but he wasn't going to tolerate that. Gently, like he didn't want to break me, he pushed the hair out of my face and tilted my chin up so he could stare into my eyes.

I didn't tell him about Vincent Cole. When he thought about that night, Marcus didn't look any better than I felt. If I was correct about Cole, and Marcus found out just how close my attacker had always been, I couldn't guarantee he would not do something stupid.

If I was correct, Vincent Cole should be the last to learn about my suspicions. As long as he didn't know the things I knew about him, I was at an advantage, and that was how I needed things to remain.

Camouflaging the distaste I now felt for Cole with approval or respect was difficult. When he approached me at the police station the previous day, my hair had stood on end. After declining his offer to act as my lawyer, I hoped he would just go away, but he had lurked around like he wanted to assess what I had seen and planned to divulge.

When we exited the police station, he had been leaning against the car Marcus had rented. He had looked concerned, but I wasn't so easily fooled anymore.

"I thought Parker looked suspicious when we talked to him, but I never expected him to act against you," Cole had said. "Maybe the only reason he did talk to us was to have an alibi, when in truth, he had already killed her."

Cole had said it in passing, like a mere comment thrown out there without a second thought, but perhaps his intention had been more calculated then I imagined. Maybe his intention all along had been to plant the seed of doubt, to make Parker look guilty so Cole himself could not be suspected of killing Rheya or attacking me afterward.

If his theory about Jase had a leg to stand on, then he could be a suspect just as well. He could have killed Rheya than come to me to have an alibi and later go on campus to look for Parker so he could lay the blame at his feet.

My head threatened to explode. I groaned but kept all those thoughts quiet. Instead, I told Marcus the other half of the matter.

"I had a nightmare," I admitted, my voice small, my heart still thundering in my chest.

"Brayden?" Marcus all but growled. His jaw set, his eyes turned tempestuous, but his touch remained warm and soothing. Then he continued in a calmer voice. "Look, Charlotte, he's getting help, he's—"

"I know that. It wasn't Brayden," I said and let my fingers play across his stubbled cheeks. "Marcus, I don't think the nightmares were ever about Brayden. I think they were about you saving me."

"It's funny," Marcus chuckled and mirrored my gesture. He caught my face between his hands and pressed his lips to mine. "I'm not the savior in our story."

I shook my head but smiled as I indulged in caressing his face, his hair, his shoulders until finally, I settled on his lap. If he didn't know it in his heart that he had saved me from a world of fears and insecurities and made me bold and daring instead, then no words were going to convince him.

"Then what did you dream about?" he asked and looked away.

Faced with my grateful, loving gestures, I could swear he was blushing. However, as the dream flooded my mind, the desire to tease him waned and finally disappeared altogether.

"Jase Parker. Jennifer Gunnar."

I shuddered. The way Jennifer Gunnar had died seemed ghastlier than ever.

"Charlotte, you are not Jennifer Gunnar. What happened to her will never happen to you."

"I know, but I can't help thinking that the way I was attacked seems so close to how Jennifer was killed. What if—" I trailed off and took my head in my hands. "What if she didn't die by gunshot? What if she had been injected with an overdose just like—my attacker wanted to inject me?"

"The reports never mentioned any substances found in her blood. She was declared dead after being shot," Marcus muttered and frowned, deep in thought. But he was right. The reports had never mentioned any trace of illegal substances found in Jennifer's body.

"I know it's a long shot, but maybe she was shot after she was injected to conceal the actual reason for her death—God, I sound like a madwoman."

Although it wasn't going to solve anything, I had the explicit desire to bang my head against the wall. Marcus sensed my frustration, and cupping my cheek, he gave me a look that urged me to calm down, then he kissed me long and hard and soothing. Neither the kisses nor his touches were going to solve a thing, but they did manage to settle my turbulent nerves.

"Not exactly. Your theory has merit," he continued after some thought. "The mayor is suspected of running a drug trafficking organization. It wouldn't have looked good to have his family tied so closely to a case that involved drugs. The prosecution would have looked into whoever dealt the drugs, and everything would have led back to the mayor's alleged business. So you might be right. They might have tried to cover this up by shooting Jennifer after she had already been killed. But shouldn't the autopsy have shown that?"

"Not if they buried the evidence," I replied in a quiet, staccato voice. Then I frowned and leaned back so I could see Marcus's face. "How did you know all of that?"

He shook his head like it was nothing and unwound his arms from my waist to stand. My phone rang on the nightstand, and Marcus walked to the window, running a hand over his face and looking exactly like he had been saved by the bell. I was baffled and somewhat curious about his sudden change of attitude but decided that I should take the call.

It was my father.

"What in the world have you done to be removed from the Stewart case?"

I didn't know whether it was my father's fury and the harshness of his voice or the shocking news that rendered me speechless, but I found myself unable to reply. Then the part of me that was angry and resented him and was often hurt by his severity took over.

"Is that the only thing that concerns you, Father?" I asked. I was angry with him, but more so with myself. I wanted to be strong and collected just like he always was, but instead, I was crumbling. "You have nearly lost a daughter, and the only thing you care about is why I no longer work for Jack Stewart?"

My question, or perhaps the rage that was laced around it, gave him pause.

"Quit the dramatics, Charlotte," James finally answered. "You have been discharged immediately. I assumed that you were fine, that it was nothing to worry over."

"It wasn't nothing, Father," I sighed and massaged my temples. When had this chasm between us widened so much that I could hardly reach or recognize him? "You know what would have been nice? A call from my father, last night when I was scared and alone."

"Charlotte—"

"You know what?" I snapped. I didn't need his comfort, nor his scolding. "I'm glad that I'm no longer a part of Jack Stewart's case, so deal with it."

I hung up then stared at my phone shocked. I had just hung up on James Burton. Then I started laughing.

Marcus watched me, grinning, his stance relaxed, his eyes proud.

"I thought you weren't so daring as to confront your father," he teased but winked encouragingly.

"Well, a certain someone showed me that I could."

I laced my arms around his waist and stood on my tiptoes to meet him halfway, where our little firestorm started. We chuckled and kissed and almost got lost in our bubble when Marcus pushed me back gently.

"Come on, we have work to do."

HE HAD ME DRESSED AND out the door in less than half an hour. At first, he enjoyed my confusion and curiosity, but little by little, he grew quiet and pensive, almost sullen. Then I remembered his earlier insight into Jennifer's death and the things he knew about Mitch Stewart.

Something was off about Marcus and that feeling only intensified when I laid my hand on his knee, and he didn't even notice.

The car stopped at a traffic light, but the silence didn't. In fact, it expanded until my nervous system threatened to combust at any moment. And all the while, Marcus kept his eyes trained forward, unblinking and unseeing. He was still, except for the occasional cracking of his neck and the overwrought flexing of his hands around the steering wheel.

In his perfect quietness, the brooding quality of his expression, with his narrowed eyes, clenched jaw, and the far-away light in his gaze, would have rendered him mouthwatering if something hadn't been utterly wrong.

I tried again, stroking his knee, then let my fingers travel up his thigh, applying the exact amount of pressure to attract his attention. My wish to comfort him and my endeavor to seduce him were equally ineffective.

I let out a frustrated sigh and glanced out my window, removing my hand from his knee. The car surged forward illegally fast, and firm, unbending fingers coiled around my wrist, forcing my hand back where it had been. Was this his silent demand for comfort?

"Talk to me," I pleaded on a new tension loaded sigh. It might not have been his intention, but emotionally, he was pushing me away, and I hated it.

"I have a surprise for you," Marcus replied quietly as if all of a sudden, he lacked the energy to speak louder, or as if he was working very hard on controlling something dark and raw battling within him.

Eventually, he pulled the car into a nearly empty parking lot, in front of a facility that looked rather like a fortified warehouse. I watched him quizzically, but instead of explaining where we were and why, he climbed out of the Jaguar, rounded the vehicle, and opened my door, waiting tensely for me to join him on the sidewalk.

Troubled eyes assessed me before he leaned close, drinking me in through parted lips. Neither of us spoke. We remained still, close but not quite touching, our eyes locked in a silent, intimate conversation. It was Marcus who finally sighed, ran a hand over his face, then grabbed my elbows and took my mouth as if through that gesture he could remind me that I was bound to him.

"It's for your protection and my peace of mind."

"What is?"

He clasped my hand and led me toward the facility where understanding finally dawned on me.

JH Private Shooting Complex hung written in big bold letters over the entrance. Marcus opened a narrow glass door and nodded for me to walk inside, looking all tense, uncertain, and adorable.

I was not a violent person. I had never considered applying for a firearm license because I had never been in so much danger that I would need a gun to save my life. But times had changed, and Marcus had been so thoughtful and loving that he had taken care of things before I even considered them. I tightened my hold on his hand and forced him to stop in the middle of an almost empty lobby.

His taut expression turned perplexed when he registered the small smile on my face. I wasn't smiling necessarily because I was eager to have a gun in my hands and feel the power it granted. I was smiling because his gesture, a little extreme as it was, proved his feelings more than his words had.

I enjoyed spoken declarations and romantic acts like any other woman, but what I craved was the security of being loved, and that type of protection only came from these gestures that proved more than words ever did.

"Thank you," I whispered, returning his earlier kiss and letting my fingers linger for a few moments on his lips.

Marcus didn't even blink as he pressed his lips against my fingertips, a wispy caress that he couldn't control any more than I could subdue the feelings flaring up in my heart.

"Mr. King? Ms. Burton?" a rough male voice interrupted us, and Marcus turned, snaking a strong arm around my waist. "I am Alexander James. I will be your instructor today. If you please, follow me."

Alexander James looked fierce and rebellious. He had intent downturned eyes and a bald head that glistened under the fluorescent lights. He wore a white polo shirt with olive cargo pants and dark brown boots with the laces left untied. His forearms were covered in monochrome tattoos that matched his daunting physique. His voice was deep and commanding, and his stride was confident as he turned around and led us down a hallway to a vast room that resembled a larger corridor than an actual room.

I wanted to ask Marcus how the instructor knew my name, but I dismissed the problem quickly. The man must have remembered our names from the application forms that Marcus had probably filled out.

We stopped next to five booths each separated by bulletproof glass that overlooked the sizable shooting range ahead. I hardly had any time to get properly acquainted with the new surroundings before James was already pushing safety gear in our hands. Apparently, he was a no-nonsense kind of man.

"I assume neither of you consumed alcohol or any other illicit substances before this session—" James trailed off, waiting for our nods of consent, then went on naturally, ignoring my half-affronted stance. "You should always be wearing eye and ear protection."

He pointed a stiff finger to the safety glasses and black earplugs he had handed us and motioned us to put them on. I was a little intimidated by his commanding nature and instantly decided he had to be some kind of military man. However, my attention was soon distracted, and I had to strain not to gape and moan at the sight.

Marcus laced the earplugs around his neck and put the safety glasses on like he had performed the task a million times before. His eyes gleamed with a tint of danger behind the lenses, and suddenly, my throat went dry, not because of fear, but of unprecedented desire.

"I will always be present while you make use of your weapons," James continued and produced two pistols that suddenly made the whole affair seem dark and serious. We were truly going to learn how to shoot. "The weapons remain unloaded until you are ready to use them."

He turned to an armory and pulled out a box that I quickly realized was full of bullets—lethal, metal bullets. I eyed the ammunition skeptically. I did not enjoy violence, nor did I want to be its performer. Yet, those bullets and the guns Alexander James placed on the counter of a booth only reiterated the danger that had brought me to this shooting range.

"Shall we begin?" the instructor asked sternly, but somehow, he sensed my reluctance.

Marcus stroked my back and kissed the top of my head before he walked to his own stand. He winked encouragingly and nodded for me to take the gun. Eventually, I took a deep breath and reached for the weapon.

It was cold and foreign under my touch. Alexander James grabbed the second gun and pointed it forward, his stance firm and deliberate yet completely natural and relaxed. If earlier I had believed he was a military man, now I had proof. He looked like a man properly trained and disciplined in the military arts.

I mimicked his posture and pointed to the shooting target—a sheet of paper with the black silhouette of a man. My fingers trembled around the gun and my breath hitched. Involuntarily, I glanced to my left and found Marcus smiling appreciatively. He watched me with his arms folded over his chest and a mischievous expression adorning his face.

"*Bad girl,*" he mouthed, making me blush at the same time a sense of tranquility washed over me.

"You always keep the gun pointed forward and your finger off the trigger unless you want to shoot."

"Understood," I replied in a small voice and I could swear my instructor suppressed a smile.

"Good. I will show you how to load your gun, then I will fire a demonstration, so you should put the earplugs on now."

He made quick work of loading his gun. I hardly kept up with his speed, but with a little help from him and reassuring, indulgent stares from Marcus, I eventually loaded my own. Then, Alexander James picked up his handgun, gripped it tightly, and fired without hesitation—two bullets to the heart and one to the head. No mistake, no mercy.

"Your turn, Miss Burton."

This time, Alexander James truly smiled. He took a step behind and put a hand on my waist as if to steady me. There was no mistaking the sudden frown that contorted Marcus's expression, nor the stiffness of his clenched jaw.

"Keep your back straight and firm and your legs slightly apart. It's essential you keep your balance. Now you can grab your gun, but don't forget to keep your finger off the trigger. That's it, good," he praised.

I found it difficult to swallow as I tried to mimic his former posture as accurately as possible. I was a poor copy, though. My arms felt weak and uncertain, and the fingers grabbing the gun were sweaty, cold, and hesitant. What if, instead of using this weapon for self-protection, I ended up hurting people by mistake? What if it misfired? What if—

"You're overthinking, Charlotte," Marcus cut in and curbed my thoughts. "Straighten your arms and take a good hold of your gun."

Somehow, his short, low-voiced instruction carried more weight than everything Alexander James had said. I nodded dutifully and tightened my hold on the pistol, then faced my target. I willed myself to aim and pull the trigger, but I just couldn't.

"May I?" I heard Marcus inquiring, but by the time I shifted my eyes to him, he was already behind me, his front plastered against my back. "Take a deep breath, Charlotte."

Then I understood why it was so difficult to make use of that weapon. Learning how to shoot and actually firing a gun went against every one of my beliefs. I had been taught to defend people against violence. I couldn't be the one inflicting it. I turned pleading eyes to Marcus, and he sighed. He understood, but he wasn't going to budge.

"For your safety. For me, please," he whispered and locked

deep-ocean blues with my own hesitant eyes.

Marcus's hand glided up and down my spine, warming the flesh beneath my clothes. Yet, it was not necessarily warmth he intended to bring but comfort. Under his thoughtful, knowing touches, an inner quietness claimed me. And suddenly, the distance I felt between us earlier, his aloofness and rigidness, it all disappeared.

"Keep your arms straight and lifted like this," Marcus advised and arranged my arms with deft, confident hands before he settled them on my own and molded his fingers around mine. "Use the gun as an extension of your eyes."

"Easier said than done."

"Don't think, just aim."

His lips brushed against my ear and cheek before he straightened. Then I aimed. With his hands guiding my motions and his comforting body blanketing me in safety from behind, I almost forgot about the danger. I squinted, pointed, and fired three times in succession like James had done.

And to our collective surprise, I didn't miss all the shots. The dark silhouette had a big chunk of its chest missing. I had shot my victim right in the heart.

My success didn't bring me any modicum of satisfaction. I hoped I would never have to truly make use of the weapon I was presently holding.

"Beginner's luck," I tried to joke, but couldn't quite bring a smile to my face.

"How did it feel?" James asked.

My forehead crinkled in concentration. "Strange," I admitted. There were a million other words to describe the feeling, but none of them were diplomatic enough to voice out loud.

"Do you have something smaller for her?"

Nodding to Marcus, James turned to the armory and retrieved a black revolver with a polished wooden grip. He showed me its bullets and how it should be loaded. This time, Marcus stepped back beside James and winked at me almost conspiratorially.

The feeling of holding the revolver was completely different. It was smaller and weighed less. My fingers wrapped naturally around it, and its power didn't seem as lethal as that of the first gun I had used. I had more control over it, which offered me confidence, but I didn't fool myself—a gun was a gun, regardless of its size.

I took a deep breath, held it, and fired. This time, I hadn't aimed for the heart, but for spots less fatal that could still cause enough damage to hold back a potential attacker. I missed a shot but hit a shoulder and a spleen. That had to grant me enough time to run or call for help.

"How was that, gentleman?" I put the revolver down and turned to Marcus with a pleased smile on my lips. His concentrated expression morphed instantly into a wide, congratulatory grin. He looked proud and somewhat relieved as he stepped forward and brushed his lips against mine.

"Good," James said. "Although, I'm inclined to teach my students to take a shot for the heart."

"No." My answer was abrupt and curt, and I found myself flinching, but neither man seemed bothered by my reaction. They both nodded before urging me to keep practicing my technique.

Now and again my attention shifted to Marcus, who would wink playfully or nod approvingly, creating a good-natured complicity that had me smiling and relaxing. By the time it was his turn to practice, the muscles in my arms ached, yet I welcomed the discomfort. If sore muscles were what it took to make myself stronger, then I was willing to make the trade.

Marcus leaned to peck my cheek as he returned to his booth and took hold of his gun without blinking. I might not have liked violence, but I was capable of appreciating the sight of a man dressed in black and carrying a firearm. He looked dangerous and absolutely delicious.

Marcus didn't bother with a smaller weapon. I caught myself gasping and blushing when his head snapped back, and his fiery eyes found mine. Then I pinned him with an annoyed frown, but the devilish grin only widened and illuminated his whole face.

I was taken aback to see that the grin soon faded into a scowl, without any apparent reason. Marcus nodded to whatever instructor James had told him and turned to his shooting target with something akin to fury. He didn't even breathe as he shot three times, much as Alexander James had done earlier—two shots to the heart, one shot to the head.

His breath came out raggedly, his hands lowered just a fraction, then the frown deepened, and he lifted the weapon and fired until there were no more bullets to fire. What had once been a regular sheet of paper was now just a frame with a massive hole where the heart of the target had been.

Marcus put the gun away, and the instructor removed it without making any comments or adding other instructions to what he had already said. Marcus's body heaved and trembled, and his head hung low between his shoulders. I hadn't realized how tightly I had been clinging to that sense of playful complicity or to the respite from anxiety it had created until it was completely and utterly gone.

His odd disposition hadn't been a figment of my imagination. He was acting weird, he was distant, and he most definitely was hiding something—like the fact that today was not the first time he was using a gun.

He didn't actually hide that, since you never asked, a voice in my head tried to rationalize with my better judgment. Or were those my hurt feelings?

I stifled the voice before it could go on defending him. Because finding excuses for his actions was the first step down a path of certain destruction.

I had told him that I couldn't do things by halves. Once I was in, I was in—without holding back, without turning back. I needed to be treated as an equal. I needed to receive as much as I offered. I had warned him, so he most definitely didn't have the right to lie to me or play me for a fool.

"Can you give us the papers now?" Although formed as a question, his words had been more of a command to which James merely nodded and gestured to be followed.

I walked out, without giving Marcus time to turn and catch a glimpse of my expression. I experienced a peculiar combination of anger and vulnerability, and I couldn't quite predict how I would react if he denied my conclusions. But I was a fool to imagine that while he could so easily evade me, I was allowed to do the same.

"Charlotte?"

His hand circled my elbow and stopped me in place. He tugged at my hand, gently motioning me to face him, but my gaze remained stubbornly focused on Alexander James's retreating form.

Only when he disappeared around a corner, and Marcus and I were the only ones left standing in the hallway that led to the reception area, did I sigh in defeat and meet his inquiring eyes. Apparently, he could pick up the changes in my mood as instinctually as I picked up his.

"Why are you upset?"

I sent him an incredulous look. Earlier on, I had actually believed that I had exaggerated, but the rage that had poured out of Marcus in waves, and the storm I was witnessing now in his eyes told me I had been right. So the moment he started acting as if he had no idea what was happening, betrayal stabbed at my chest. This very reaction was what worsened the whole situation.

"Sometimes it feels like I barely know you. Like right now."

Marcus stiffened. His eyes were speaking a truth I could not decipher, but his lips were preparing for another lie. I sighed and took a step farther away—into my shell.

"We are still learning. I don't know everything about you either, Charlotte."

"You know I didn't mean what's your favorite food or where you like to go in your free time. How did you book this entire place, for instance? How can you get us permits in less than a day? Why do you know the things you do about Mitch Stewart?"

"A friend helped me."

I scoffed and shook my head. This was just the type of elusive answer that made me suspicious, and eventually, it raised too many questions and an entire chaos in my head. With a heavy sigh that created an ache that ran all the way to my chest, I turned to leave. But he simply wouldn't let me.

"Don't," I snapped, struggling to keep my voice down when his hand closed around my wrist and refused to let me go. "This is what I meant. I only know a man who saves me when I need him to, who impresses me with his charm and silver tongue, and who is a damn good lover. But I don't know this man who is aloof and cold, and who is lying to me. Who are you really, Marcus King?"

"I'm not lying—"

The placating look he had been giving me for the last five minutes changed abruptly into a warning glare. I was the one entitled to be mad, not him, and yet, the fury blended with a potent shade of hurt that I could see clearly in his stare sent my thoughts into a whirl of confusion. Was I the one making a mistake by picking a fight with him?

"Aren't you?"

He did not deny my accusations and that did nothing to improve my mood. Releasing a bitter sigh, Marcus ran a hand over his tense features. When he made an attempt to cup my face, I avoided his hands and those inquisitive eyes that touched me more deeply than his hands could.

"I'm doing my best to be a better man for you, Charlotte, but you need to trust me."

His hands settled on my waist, and his body caged me between its unyielding hardness and the wall. We were perfectly aligned, but he still found space between us to eradicate, so he inched closer. When he spoke next, his lips moved slowly, brushing against mine.

"Ever since you entered in my life, you turned me upside down. You make me want to do things for you that I never wanted to do for any other woman. It's infuriating that you won't let me."

"Let you do what?"

"Let me protect you," he cried in a whisper.

In his pleading eyes, there was despair, the kind of despair that drove sane men to do insane things.

"How?" I demanded with a similarly broken voice. "What have you done, Marcus?"

I had stopped thinking that there was something wrong he was hiding from me. I was starting to believe that he was hiding something actually dangerous. And that caused my heart to constrict with worry and my lungs to burn as I forgot to breathe.

Marcus watched me for so long that I thought he had gone into some sort of stupor. In the end, after gnashing his teeth and glaring at nothing in particular, he rested his forehead against mine with a long, heavy sigh of defeat. When he massaged my lips with his and wrapped his arms around my waist, I found myself unable to deny him.

"You won't stop until you know the truth, will you? Not even if I tell you it's not safe if you know?"

This time it was he who refused to meet my eyes.

"If you are trying to make me stop asking questions, you are failing."

There was no way now he would walk out of that building without telling me what he had done. I only hoped that whatever it was could still be repaired.

"Charlotte—I—I was offered a deal."

That definitely did not sound good. A thousand thoughts ran through my head, and each one was worse than the last.

"What kind of deal?" I eventually asked, nearly not wanting to hear the answer.

"A deal to bring down Mitch Stewart."

"Has Leon Holden propositioned you? Why would he choose you to—"

"No. It was the FBI."

My mouth opened and closed, but my tongue remained lax and unable to form words. This was definitely much worse than what I had been imagining. The FBI, just like any other government agency, was like an octopus that seized you and never let you go.

They didn't make deals. They recruited, then they infiltrated your life until you had no life of your own. And that was the time when you were their perfect agent. I didn't want that for Marcus or for us, not even if he was doing it in good faith.

"Did you accept it?"

"No," Marcus answered curtly, but although he did not accept the deal, it was evident that he was considering it.

"Who exactly made you this deal?"

"Julian Hudson. He runs an operation meant to bring to light all of Stewart's dirty affairs. That's how I know about the mayor's business, and whether his son is guilty or not, he is only a small piece of the whole dark puzzle. There is an organization behind them to back up their actions. If they are not stopped, they will continue killing and destroying lives. If the power is not stripped from Mitch Stewart, if he is not put behind bars, you won't be safe.

The only way to ensure that is to break their organization from the inside."

"That would be your job?"

It seemed I was too numb to properly express how outraged or panicked I was. I realized my hands had been clenched in his jacket only when Marcus took them gently, covered them with his, then cradled them to his chest.

"Yes," he answered like that was the simplest, most obvious thing in the world.

"Why? Why you?"

"Can't you see? I'd be invested in this operation more than anybody else. I couldn't care less about the mayor or his business, but I do care about you, and it seems the only way to ensure your safety."

"Marcus, you don't have to accept the deal. I'll admit I am not safe, and you have no idea what it means to me that you care so much as to want to protect me, but you can do that by being by my side, by supporting me—"

"That is not enough, Charlotte. I'd love to spend every living moment next to you, but it's not realistic, and it's not healthy to think that I would. You will never be safe as long as Mitch Stewart is running free. He and his people know you have been meddling in their affairs. They haven't taken it well."

"But—I can hire a security detail. You don't have to get involved with the FBI. You don't understand—"

My voice grew thinner and shakier. My heart beat rapidly with undiluted anxiety. I was panicking. While Marcus was trying to protect me, it seemed I was completely unable to do anything to protect him.

If he got involved with the FBI, I was terrified that he would become another disposable body they buried under a made-up story. And if that happened, I would be the only one to blame.

"It's just this one time."

I scoffed and looked away, suddenly as weary as if I hadn't been resting for weeks. His intentions were right, but I was afraid that time would prove him wrong. Perhaps what I dreaded as much as him failing was him succeeding. Because then, there was no way the FBI would simply let him go.

Marcus placed his hands once more on the wall, on each side of my head, and nudged my nose with his, urging me to look at him. Through words and gestures, he was trying to appease me, but right now nothing truly could.

"Say something, Charlotte," he pleaded.

"There's no such thing as one time."

"I promise you."

I shook my head hopelessly and pushed against his restraining arms. He didn't offer resistance.

"It is not you I don't trust. It's them."

I walked away before he changed his mind and took me in his arms again. When I was so close to him, and when he had me so tightly wrapped in his arms, I couldn't stop feeling. And at the moment, I dreaded feeling.

I waited by the car, and Marcus followed me outside in less than ten minutes. He carried the permits, a handgun, and the revolver. At the sight of them, I groaned, shook my head, and finally decided on staring out the window.

We drove back to my apartment in silence, and for once, Marcus didn't press me. Then it hit me like a bulldozer right upside the head.

"It was you, wasn't it? You asked this Hudson person to interfere and have me removed from Jack Stewart's case. How did he manage it? Who did he threaten?"

"I don't know, and really, I don't even care. All I care about is keeping you safe, and I will do that even when you don't want me to. Even when you don't like how I do it."

Marcus spoke without even looking at me. We had worked ourselves into a foul state that we didn't know how to come back from. I was not upset about not working on Jack's case anymore. In fact, I was grateful, but what Marcus failed to understand was that I couldn't stop now. I couldn't in good conscious walk away when I knew that another woman's life was threatened.

I didn't miss that on our way up to my apartment, Marcus didn't even try to hold my hand or otherwise touch me. He had grown forlorn, and if his distance was any indication, he was as upset about my reluctance as I was about his decision to accept Julian Hudson's deal.

Marcus held the door and stepped inside my apartment only after I did. An expensive sweet perfume assaulted my nostrils before I swiped a glance around the living room and finally saw *her*.

She was perched on the edge of the loveseat, her hands resting on her knees and her knowing brown eyes studying me with a kind, serene beam. In the light that filtered through the windows, her red hair shone, and her skin glowed a healthy shade of honey.

She stood from her seat, lean, tall, and gracious on her enormous heels and opened her arms wide, just like she used to do when I was little.

"Mom," I whispered and walked over to hug her. She seemed changed, happier, more serene, and yet the same nurturing, sophisticated woman I had always known.

"Oh, Charlotte," she sighed and squeezed me in her arms. For such a frail-looking woman, she was unexpectedly strong.

"I thought you were waiting for me to visit on Christmas," I admonished gently but kissed both her cheeks to temper the reproach.

She rolled her eyes and made an impatient gesture with her hands. "You didn't actually believe that I would stay away while my daughter was in a hospital."

"I'm alright," I assured her and made a pirouette just to appease her. "Besides, you're in a hospital all the time."

"That's different, young lady, and you know it," she said, pointing a finger at me.

Throughout the whole exchange, Marcus's eyes never strayed from us. Mom cupped my cheek, apparently coming to the conclusion that I was indeed safe and sound, then bypassed me to get a long look at him. Although composed and expressionless, I could tell that Marcus was uncomfortable.

"We are quite disrespectful," Mom said and offered Marcus her special smile that seemed to immediately put him at ease. Mom had that way about her that made her agreeable and that ease of interacting that charmed you. "Who is your friend?"

"I'm Marcus King, ma'am."

Marcus stepped forward and kissed her hand, making her wink at me and giggle.

"Call me Lauren," she chirped. "Ma'am is for the queen and old ladies."

Marcus smiled politely and I a little embarrassed. I wished they had met under different circumstances. I wished the cold tension between Marcus and me wasn't there to stain the moment.

"Are you Isaac's son?" Mom asked with half a frown, then she smoothed her forehead immediately. She never really frowned. Frowning caused terrible wrinkles, more so than laughing ever would, she said.

She was quick to make connections and even quicker to make sense of every situation. I wondered how long it would take her to understand that Marcus was not only a friend and read through the tension smothering us.

"Not by choice," he answered.

His tension only intensified at the sound of his father's name, but whether Mom noticed the change in his mood or not, she ignored it and laughed loudly, not surprised that Isaac and his son were on precarious terms. To my astonishment, Marcus laughed too.

"Oh, come on, I made lunch. We have a lot to talk about."

She led the way to the kitchen, but although we followed, neither Marcus nor I had our hearts in her little celebration.

Chapter 34

Charlotte

*A*s expected, it took Lauren Burton about five minutes into our meal to make sense of the whole situation. Her suspicions solidified when Marcus made some poor excuse and left before dessert. It wasn't his hasty departure as much as my collapsing mood afterward that tipped her off about our impasse.

We talked about her new gorgeous home in London and how tiring being a plastic surgeon could get, about ballet, the latest royal drama, and how conservative the British were, but all the while, I knew she was dying to ask me everything about Marcus and me.

Once he left, nothing stopped or deterred her from her newfound mission.

"How long have you been together?" she asked dead on.

After tiptoeing around the topic concerning my father, Mom had finally declared she needed to talk to him immediately. I had a feeling that part of the discussion would involve me, and it wasn't going to be pretty. If I rarely stood up to my father, my mother never had that problem. Hence, the reason their marriage worked better when they were apart.

"Almost two months," I said, sliding behind the wheel of my

car. "It feels much longer than that."

"It always does," she smiled wistfully then ducked her head to gauge my expression. "Is this your first fight?"

"Not exactly, but—I don't know what to do."

I sighed, and while I drove to the firm, I told her everything, from the night I met Marcus to how we ended up quarreling earlier. Mom was partly amused, partly worried.

"Sweetheart, he must care a lot about you to risk so much. Have you considered the issue from his perspective?"

"Mom, I'm not being ungrateful. It flatters me the way he tries to protect me, but if something happened to him because of me, I couldn't live with myself."

"If something happened to you, and he could have prevented it, do you think he would be able to live with himself?"

I sighed sulkily but admitted in my heart that she was right. Mom patted my knee and stared ahead. I had the feeling she was actually siding with Marcus on this.

"Sweetheart," she said eventually, "I think the best way to work through this predicament is to ask yourself what you would do if the roles were reversed. Would you stay on the sidelines or fight against the world by his side?"

I had my father's stubbornness and impetuosity, my mother used to tell me. I was quickly upset and difficult to appease, but when she put it like that, I could neither remain upset with Marcus nor irritated that she was defending him.

The firm was uncommonly quiet when we arrived, and my mother, whether because she was the boss's wife or because she was simply ravishing for a woman in her early fifties, attracted curious glances from everyone around us.

"If you excuse me, I'll have a word with James now," she said then took the private elevator that carried her all the way to the top floor.

I waited for my own ride to my office, deep in thought. Wrecked by worry and remorse, I was about to call Marcus when the doors of the elevator slid open to reveal the stiff figure of Isaac King.

He smiled, a peculiar soundless twist of his features that seemed forced and jeering. I walked inside, straightened my dress, and looked ahead, grateful that he didn't bother with small talk.

"Are you fucking my son, Charlotte?" Isaac turned around and asked.

The phone almost slipped between my fingers as the elevator walls seemed to shrink on me. I felt dizzy, and some invisible weight pushed down on my chest, making it difficult to breathe.

With all that had happened lately, it had seemed ridiculous to worry about who might find about our relationship, but now that Isaac knew, I remembered all the reasons why we shouldn't have let him know in the first place.

"My private life does not concern you," I replied coolly. "And don't forget who you are talking to, Isaac. It's still my family name up on the wall."

Isaac hated to be reminded by a woman half his age that he was just an associate in the firm and most certainly would never occupy the seat he craved. His nostrils flared, and he cracked his neck before his frosty eyes zeroed in on me.

"It's my son's life that concerns me," Isaac spat.

"It's your son's life you want to control," I corrected. "Tell me, Isaac, how does it feel to know you can't do that anymore?"

Isaac smirked without saying a word.

I shuffled a step back and squeezed my eyes shut. My throat felt dry and my muscles rigid. What if Isaac still controlled Marcus? What if the reason he considered accepting the FBI's deal was that Isaac had coerced him after finding out about our relationship? What if he threatened Marcus to send him to prison if he didn't comply?

I was not a violent person, but at that very moment, I wished I could slap the triumph off Isaac's face. He knew I couldn't be Marcus's handler if I were intimately involved with him. If he wanted, he could make it look like Marcus never completed the community service the court ordered. Hell, knowing Isaac, he could make it look much worse than that, and I would be in no position to help Marcus.

"It's because of you that he hadn't accepted the deal," Isaac muttered disdainfully.

Air finally filled my lungs. Maybe Isaac hadn't threatened

Marcus into accepting this deal. Maybe I could still make him understand that there had to be another way to battle against everything that the Stewarts threw at us.

"It's because of me that he won't have to accept any deal at all coming from you."

I walked out of the elevator and didn't look back as I strode to my office. Isaac might not have threatened Marcus yet, but I was going to make sure he would never get the chance to.

"Sophia, get Tanner on the phone now."

She looked startled but nodded and had Reid Tanner on the line in exactly two minutes. He didn't sound happy to have been disturbed from whatever he was doing, and he definitely didn't shy away from expressing his displeasure in a long, colorful speech.

"I need you to run a check on Isaac King," I cut him off impatiently. "Can you do that?"

"Of course, and in the process should I also get your coffee and cook you dinner and maybe warm your bed before you go to sleep because God forbid you get a cold or worse—do these damn things on your own?!"

"Tanner, can you do that?" I snapped.

"Wait a moment. Isaac King, you said? As in your boyfriend's father, Isaac King?"

"You ran a check on me?" I yelled, outraged.

"Sweetie, I run a check on every one of my clients. Periodically."

"Wonderful," I groaned and rolled my eyes.

"I know, for example, that you love to have breakfast at that Italian place when you are irritable, and sometimes you sneak around at night and buy cranberry cider, which, let me tell you, is a total waste of money, and oh, my personal favorite, you love to kick men out of your apartment. Well, it was only the one, what was his name? Oh yes, Carter Pierce."

"Tanner," I groaned again, but this time the sound was tinged with warning.

I slapped my forehead and gritted my teeth. My face and neck felt unbearably hot, and I was grateful that nobody witnessed my shame. Tanner knew things about me that I was definitely not interested in revisiting or sharing.

The only reason I tolerated his behavior, and apparently his stalking tendencies, was because the man did a damn good job every time I needed him to. Today, however, I didn't feel very permissive.

"Jesus, you're no fun," he complained. "I'll have your report within the hour."

One hour later when he called to inform me that he had forwarded his findings to my personal email, he didn't sound as chipper as before.

"Charlotte, I don't think you'll like what's in that report," Tanner warned.

"I need leverage against Isaac. It should be him not liking what I read."

"Don't say I didn't warn you."

Tanner's last words still rang in my head after I finished reading his report twice. I had looked for dirt on Isaac, for some big secret that would put him under my thumb. I hadn't expected the dirt I found on him would be so sickening and utterly devastating to Marcus.

Isaac was most certainly no saint, but of all the questionable deeds that stained his character, one stood out, and it involved his wife.

Jacqueline King had been fatally wounded in a car accident twenty-two years ago. I had no recollection of the funeral ceremony since at the time I was only four, but I had grown up hearing my mother talk with regret about her, about what a beautiful person she had been. I had seen her grave once after paying my respects to my grandparents. I had felt Marcus's boundless pain and longing for the mother who had never been in his life and never gotten the chance to see her son grow up.

But Jacqueline King was alive, and Isaac had always known it.

I slammed my fists against my desk and swiped at the objects on it, sending them smashing to the ground, one by one. The screen of my laptop cracked, and its case broke and skidded onto the floor. My custom pens went clattering, stacks of papers fell with a dull thud, and my favorite mug of coffee shattered to pieces, sending splotches of black everywhere.

Sophia stormed in, her eyes bulging like onions and her mouth hanging so low that it could have fit a coconut. We just stared at each other for what felt like endless minutes, then she walked out and shut the door without intruding or questioning or offering counsel when none was requested.

Nobody disturbed me as I continued crying and trashing my office. I didn't know exactly why I was crying or why I was raging or why I simply couldn't stop.

I was sitting on the carpet in front of the sofa that was now half covered by papers, half drenched in water and coffee, with my phone clasped in my hands when my mother burst in, horror settling on her face the instant her eyes landed on me.

"Charlotte what is the meaning of this?" she cried and raised one hand to her chest and the other to her open mouth. "Are you alright, sweetheart? What happened?"

She sat by my side, not caring that most likely she was going to ruin her clothes. She stroked my cheeks, wiping at the running make-up and studying me like I was a terminally ill patient. I didn't trust my voice to speak, so I pushed the phone into her hands and rested my head in her lap while she read.

If I took after my father where stubbornness was concerned, intuitiveness I had taken after my mother. Perhaps with me more than with other people, she had always been able to tell how I felt and what kind of thoughts tormented me, so after reading Tanner's report, she understood my rage and despondency without explanations.

"How am I going to tell him?" I sobbed.

She cradled me in her arms, rocked me quietly, and after a while, she managed to lift me onto weak, unsure feet. I noticed then that she was pale, and the corners of her mouth were white. She didn't say a thing as she wiped under my eyes at the tears I forgot I was shedding and pressed a kiss to my forehead. There was nothing more to add, and yet, there was a lot more to say.

Marcus stalked in my office and stopped short when he caught sight of my mother and me standing disoriented in the middle of the room.

"Charlotte, what happened?"

His arms were wrapped around me instantly. He gripped my chin, firmly but not unkindly, turning my head this way and that. I imagined how I looked with blotchy eyes and mascara sullying my face, with my hair disheveled and a body that didn't seem to be able to stop trembling.

"Please, talk to me," he whispered in my ear and watched me with pleading eyes.

I nodded and clung to him, but first, I had to gather myself. I asked my mother to give us the room, and she left, saying she was heading home, or more precisely, to my father's house, since their conversation wasn't over yet. As she hurried to the door, she looked like she was running away from what was about to happen.

Then I asked Marcus to drive me to my apartment. I was stalling, but I was also trying to put as much space between him and his father as I could. Once Marcus learned the truth, I wasn't sure what he would do.

We didn't talk during the short drive back home. Marcus glanced at me every now and then like he wanted to check that I hadn't mysteriously combusted. Occasionally, he reached for me but faltered mid-gesture. He wasn't as distant as earlier, but he wasn't himself either. Just because I was a mess, that didn't mean our fight had come to a conclusion.

After he got us to my apartment and I spent a whole hour moving about and not saying anything coherent, it was finally time to tell him about his mother. It was time to break his heart.

"Marcus," I said, sitting next to him on the sofa.

I stroked his forearms while struggling to choose my words, then ignoring the ache in my throat, I found courage where I thought there was none.

"Isaac knows about us," I started.

"And this got you in this state?" he asked with arched brows and half a smile.

"No. Let me say it," I begged. If he interrupted me, I was afraid I wouldn't dare to tell him. "I thought you considered accepting Julian Hudson's deal partly because your father had threatened you in some way. So I asked my private investigator to run a check on Isaac. I thought if we could find some leverage on him, then maybe you wouldn't have to let him make decisions on your behalf. I thought—"

"What have you done, Charlotte?"

"There's no easy way to say it," I murmured more to myself than to him.

At first, I didn't notice it, but right before I spoke those last words, right before I gave him the news that his father should have given him twenty-two years ago, his face lost all emotion like it was petrified, and his eyes turned to ice.

"Marcus, your mother is alive."

As he sprang to his feet, he didn't let my hands go. He shoved at them. He stepped back, planting his feet wide apart and glaring like he had never glared at me before. The veins in his neck strained right beneath the layer of skin, and his fingers curled into stony balls by his sides.

"What right do you have to drag my mother into this?" he snarled.

"You knew?" I gasped.

"Of course, I fucking knew," he roared and threw his arms in the air. "She's my mother."

"But you never said anything. When you talked about her, it was always in the past. I thought Isaac never told you. I thought—"

My head was swimming. My vision blurred. Had I just made a terrible mistake?

"Not even Isaac is that much of a monster. In fact, not saying anything about her was the only noble thing he has ever done. Then you come snooping around, looking for the goddamn truth. You can't stop, can you? You have to know everything, all the time?"

Marcus was angry, but not because he had been kept in the dark for over two decades. He was upset for reasons I could not fathom, and his rage was uncontrollable and completely untamable.

He stared me down with a glower so cold and so wrathful that right then, I could have been mistaken for his worst enemy. He pointed a finger at me and kept shaking his head, but he didn't say another word.

Perhaps if I had known how grossly I would invade Marcus's life, I would have never asked Tanner to run a check on Isaac.

"Marcus, please, I didn't mean to—" I said in a small voice.

He didn't listen. He didn't even hear me.

I felt the wetness on my cheeks, but just as he couldn't rein in his fury, I couldn't control my tears. I pleaded, and I apologized. I tried to reach him, but as soon as my fingers connected with his arm, he shot back like I had burned him. I was not welcomed into his arms tonight.

"So you think I went behind your back, talking with the FBI, and now you are going behind mine, having me and my life investigated? Leave my mother out of it, Charlotte. Whatever mess we make, don't bring her into it."

"Marcus, I never tried to—"

"Just—I've had enough for today."

He ran a hand over his face and cast me a last glance of disappointment, grief, and accusation, then he bolted for the door like breathing the same air I did suffocated him.

"Marcus, please, don't leave like this."

He slammed the door so hard that it shuddered on its hinges. The blast echoed like thunder, then silence settled in heavy, bitter, and taunting.

I remained motionless in the middle of the room for a long time after Marcus left. The world spun, then it finally slowed down. My lungs were working, but I couldn't breathe properly, and the tightness in my chest felt like a giant rock that dragged me down.

When I finally moved, I realized that my phone was ringing, first my mother, then Christina, even my father. I turned it off and curled up on the sofa. With my knees to my chest and my face buried in the cushions, I told myself that everything would be alright. The storm would pass. The disappointment and betrayal in Marcus's eyes would disappear. He would understand. And eventually, the pulsing pain in my chest would subside.

Like a mantra, I kept telling myself all of those things, but the more I said them, the more they felt like a lie.

I MUST HAVE FALLEN ASLEEP at some point because the next thing I knew was the loud banging that came from across the living room. Groggily, I opened and shielded my eyes from the bright sunlight invading the room. This day, radiant, loud, and warm, was a mockery of the murky shadows clouding my heart.

I knew my appearance reflected the desolation in my heart when my mother hugged me so hard that my bones protested. She didn't ask what happened the previous night. She knew if I were ready I would tell her myself, so she simply led me into the kitchen and fed me breakfast, one spoonful at a time.

It was pleasant to be coddled, and a couple of times she actually wrenched a few shy smiles from me, but her pampering couldn't entirely pull the plug on my rampant thoughts or cure the throbbing in my breast.

Where was Marcus? What was he doing? Why had he been so furious?

"The nerve your father has," Mom was saying in an attempt to lift my spirits. "He told me to quit the hysterics, and if I had come all the way to New York, that I should very well attend the festivities tonight."

It sounded just like James Burton to catalog reproaches as hysterics or dramatics and then put the matter out of his thoughts and never ask himself what he had done so wrong as to earn those reproaches.

"What festivities?"

"Some lawyerly fundraising gala. I don't know, sweetie," Mom waved the subject off, fed me another spoonful of rice pudding, then her expression changed completely.

Flashing a huge grin full of mischief, she bumped my shoulder with hers and winked.

"You know what? I think we should go, have a girl's night out, drink some mojitos, and catch up."

"Mom, I'm not in the mood. I think I've just screwed everything up."

The tears came rolling then, just as fiercely as before. I'd had the best of intentions. I'd only wanted to protect Marcus, just like he wanted to protect me, but they didn't say that the road to hell was paved with good intentions for nothing. At the moment, I felt like I was being scalded in my own form of hell.

"Stop it," she ordered, but unlike my father, her manner was warm, and her voice was honey sweet. "I'll have none of that. You deserve the respite, and staying here, crying your eyes out, will not make you or that boy feel better. Let him cool down. He'll be back."

"He knew," I said quietly and looked away before more tears filled my eyes.

She didn't appear pleased that someone who knew his mother was alive would take part in the sham of hiding it, but she wasn't judging either. My mother was the type of person who never judged and never jumped to conclusions. She waited, and only after she knew all the aspects of a problem, did she assess the situation. So, since she hardly knew Marcus or his reasons for keeping his mother's existence a secret, she shrugged and rolled her eyes, then she shooed me to my room with an apron.

"Patience, Charlotte, patience," she chanted behind me, although she knew full well that patience had never been my strong suit.

UNDER DIFFERENT CIRCUMSTANCES, to witness my mother behaving like a girl getting ready for prom would have been truly a delight. She called her hair-stylist, and although she hadn't been in touch with him for over three years, he still spoiled her rotten.

Antoine arrived sometime before noon with his two assistants, who served my mother's every whim, from giving her a gorgeous French manicure to rubbing her feet while Antoine cut and styled my hair. I wasn't really interested or excited, but I managed to be polite and gave him unrestricted freedom to be as creative as he wanted.

He gave me a layered cut with long asymmetrical bangs and styled it in such a manner that it looked rebellious, but still classy. When he suggested in that lovely French accent of his that he should give me some highlights to complement my look, I declined and excused myself.

My mother's watchful eyes followed me as I retired to my

bedroom. I dialed Marcus's number, but he never answered. When I tried for the fifth time, it went straight to voicemail. I gave a sob but forced myself not to cry again.

Let him cool down, I repeated to myself then returned to the living room where Antoine was packing up his things. He air kissed us, then threatened to shave us bald if we let another three years pass before we called him, and eventually, he left with his assistants.

Mom twirled around, showing off her new wavy bob, then produced her make-up kit from her purse and arranged us both. She gave me a Brigitte Bardot look while she ended up looking more like Liz Taylor.

By the time she finished getting us both dressed and ready, I didn't necessarily feel better, but I felt distracted enough to be patient and wait for Marcus to come back to me.

THE SALONS OF THE Baccarat Hotel had been especially redecorated to accommodate this year's Aequitas Awards. If the cinematographic industry had the Golden Globes and the Oscars, the legal community had the Aequitas Awards, a gala that gathered the elite of law from all over the world.

The Baccarat buzzed with people wearing the latest designer's clothes and huge smiles that faked camaraderie when most of them could be found at each other's throats on any other day of the year.

Some people I knew, some I admired, and some I completely wanted to avoid. My eyes stumbled upon my father talking to Cameron Drake like they were best friends then skimmed across the crowd to find Isaac with his assistant at his arm, John Kendrix and Paul Zane, who although they were equal shareholders of Drake Kendrix Zane, had always remained in Drake's shadow.

I saw some of my Harvard professors, who nodded appreciatively, Leon Holden, who smiled and raised a glass in my direction, even my interns slinking among the guests. Yet, all the time I perused the scene, I felt an itch crawling beneath my skin like a thousand ants running up and down my body.

I did a 180-degree turn and finally saw him. He was hiding in plain sight, standing somewhere in the middle of the salon, dressed in an expensive black suit with a purple silk handkerchief in his breast pocket and his eyes trained on me. When our eyes met, Vincent Cole graced me with his peculiar smirk that had my blood cooling and my muscles tightening.

"You look like you've seen a ghost," my mother said and looked around.

"Don't," I said, my voice coming out shrill and alien. "Let's get drinks."

Thankfully, she was easily distracted and led the way to the open bar across the room. I followed stiffly, struggling to control my breathing and the somersaults in my stomach, but out of sheer will, I managed. I wasn't going to show Cole that I feared or suspected him.

"Brandy, please," my mother ordered, her newly acquired English accent embracing her words.

"I thought we were drinking mojitos?"

"Not strong enough. I forgot how much patience these functions require."

I released a laugh and was surprised by how liberating it felt. Mom winked and ordered me the same, then we settled on some barstools in a corner and talked about everything except lawyers, murder mysteries, or family secrets. When the lights dimmed, and I felt a hand on my waist, I flinched.

"You look ravishing," Cameron Drake told me, grinning hugely and giving me a once-over.

He was well-dressed and reasonably attractive himself, but he was not the man I wanted to see.

My father appeared at his side and regaled me with an approving glance. He was oddly happy. Offering my mother his arm in a rare display of affection, he led her away from the bar. His cheerful disposition was certainly due to his wife's presence, which although he was never going to admit it, he often missed.

Five years ago, after things between them had gone from bad to worse, and their marriage had turned into a landmine, Mom decided to accept an offer from a redoubtable plastic surgery institute in London. She never filed for divorce or made a scandal, but she withdrew both physically and emotionally. She only spoke with her husband during holidays when she visited.

My father, on the other hand, in his authoritative, selfish manner still loved her, but he was never going to beg or apologize. At first, he had tried to goad her, welcoming the fights instead of the cruel silence, but when goading her ceased to work, he had grown colder and crabbier than ever.

"Let's find our seats," James said. "The gala is about to begin."

My mother walked at his side, a vision of elegance. If you hadn't known the story behind their smiles, you would have never suspected they had stopped being a couple years ago. They sat at a grand table to the right side of the stage, joining a few of my father's close friends and engaging naturally in the conversation.

"Shall we?" Drake asked, all very thoughtful and gentlemanly.

He escorted me quietly, watching me like I was his treasured possession. He held the chair for me and complimented me again, then right before he took the seat to my left, he swiped the name card and stuffed it in his pocket.

I raised a questioning eyebrow, but he gave me a charming smile and winked. Although he clearly occupied somebody else's seat, nobody came to claim it.

The gala started as usual with the fundraising and dragged late into the night.

"We strongly believe that we must give back to the community and help those whose unfavorable circumstances prevent them from exerting their most basic human rights," the host was saying. She was beautiful and dressed in a silver dress that flowed around her like water. "We do that first by vigilantly upholding the justice system and basing our work on its principles. Tonight, however, in addition to awarding our best members, we have gathered here to help those less fortunate and make sure that every man, woman, and child can employ their right to healthcare."

About halfway through her speech, I tuned her out and turned to my mother. She was deep in discussion with some judge from Norway who happened to have a fixation with his big, flattened nose and was happy to find, in his late fifties, that the monstrosity, as he called it, could be remodeled.

The host invited on stage the CEO of the Aequitas Foundation, their sponsors, and last year's most generous donor to present the cause they advocated for this year.

And so, the donations commenced. I wrote my own check and slipped it into the bowl held by one of the staff girls, who walked from table to table. I was not fooled by appearances, though. Tonight, it was not about some great cause, about people in need, or about generosity. It wasn't even about being awarded for our exceptional performances. It was about bragging.

"Can you see Rolf Krauss's outraged face?" Cameron leaned in to whisper in my ear.

He pointed to a half-bald man sitting three tables from us, pulling at his grizzled mustache and ogling from the check he was holding to the pixie girl collecting the donations. More than outraged, he looked horrified.

"Every year the girl tells him the minimum donation is five thousand bucks, and every year he makes a scene. The stingy idiot."

"Perhaps he can't afford it," I suggested.

"Oh, don't let his avarice fool you. He's filthy rich. He inherited his grandfather's estate, moved from Germany to the States, and multiplied everything since then."

"Perhaps because he doesn't make donations."

Drake laughed and watched me with curiosity and something that looked uncomfortably close to longing.

"And Miss Ingrid du Royer over there," he added after finally regaining his composure. Cameron cupped my shoulders and rotated me slowly to the left. His fingers lingered on my skin longer than was considered sociable. "She donated one hundred thousand dollars last year. When she realized it was not for show, she asked to pay the amount in installments."

"How do you know these things?"

"You'd be surprised the things a good assistant knows."

I smiled but refrained from expressing my opinion. His notion of a good assistant defined a nosy one in my book.

"You know, I never got the chance to tell you that we miss you in D.C.," he said and stroked my hand with a finger.

I pulled my hand into my lap and took a sip from the champagne the waiter had just brought. Drake's change of attitude was not only odd but worrying. He acted friendlier, more attentive, even courteous.

"I'm certain you can manage very well in my absence."

"There is a good part about your leave, though. I've been meaning to invest in a few fields in New York, and I hoped you'd help me. Actually, I'm staying here at the Baccarat until next Sunday."

Drake flashed his white teeth and bent until he invaded my space. His cologne was sweet and cloying, and his warmth unwelcome next to my side.

"Join me tomorrow for dinner," he whispered. His nose grazed my cheek, and I inhaled sharply. Drake smiled. "I'd like to have a talk with you in private. You are a magnificent conversational partner. You know, not many people dare to argue with me the way you did."

His low voice, the smoldering riveted look in his eyes, even the way he licked his lips alluded to another kind of partnership.

"Let's discuss this later," I proposed and moved uncomfortably in my seat. *Or never.*

I straightened in a fruitless attempt to put some distance between Drake and me when my eyes accidentally met my father's. He was studying me keenly, and when our eyes locked, he nodded, displaying the earlier approval, a gesture so rare and bizarre that I could not even decode it.

I was thankful when the host announced that the donations would continue throughout the night and proceeded to present the nominees for Best Corporate Lawyer of the year.

The widescreen above the stage showed the pictures of every lawyer and every team nominated for the various categories of the Aequitas Awards before the winner took the stage for a short acceptance speech then left with a Lady Justice statue made of crystal and gold.

"Charlotte, we'd love to have you in D.C. more often," John Kendrix said at some point, startling me with his raucous voice.

His black hair was cut short which made him look like a chunky bear that lost its fur. He always sounded stern when he spoke, but his eyes were kind and playful. John pulled at the knot of his tie and eventually discarded it altogether.

"Actually, we would love to steal you completely," he went on.

"I don't think James would allow us to poach his daughter," Drake said, sharing a private smile with my father. Then he turned to me and murmured in a tone that was meant to be seductive, "You'd be a wonderful addition to our team, though, and a sight for sore eyes."

"I'm exactly where I should be," I said both to Kendrix and Drake, but softened the firmness of my words with a good-mannered smile.

I had never considered practicing law someplace other than at Burton & Associates, but if I had, it would have never been under Cameron Drake's tutelage. Despite his charming and gallant attitude, I could not forget the questionable manner with which he liked to handle his cases.

At the end of the night, when Drake won Best Litigation Lawyer, and Burton & Associates won Best Finance Team I was not surprised. I was surprised, however, when out of nowhere, the host called my name.

"The award for Pro Bono Initiative of the year goes to Charlotte Burton of Burton & Associates from New York City, United States."

My mother wiggled and clapped excitedly in her seat like she had done every time I had ever won a diploma, medal, or award, and somewhere from the crowd, Philip Foster whistled and punched at the air with his fists like he had just won the award himself. As I stood and walked to the stage, I finally understood my father's unexpected disposition.

I delivered a succinct speech that regarded the importance of pro bono work and fighting for the right cause even when financial remuneration was out of the question. I received my Lady Justice statue and was astonished by the gratifying feeling that took over me once I had it in my hands. More than any other award, this meant the most to me, and while I walked off the stage and back to my table, I wished Marcus had been there with me.

"Sweetheart, this is wonderful," Mom cheered, her eyes big and bright. She kissed my cheek and clapped again under the table, too happy to help herself.

It was Drake who surprised me again. He placed his hand on my knee and massaged it softly over the satin folds of my dress.

I had never known how to decline the advances of a man. I did it brusquely, and given tonight's setting and company, it was not suitable, or I didn't do it at all and I waited until he got the hint that I was not interested and just stopped trying.

"I'm proud of you Charlotte," he said and grinned so widely that crinkles appeared at the corner of his eyes.

I was so stunned that I had almost missed the host introducing on stage the man behind a variety of causes that ranged from supporting patients with rare conditions to funding medical innovations, a man as noble as he was just—Mayor Mitch Stewart.

I nearly dropped the champagne flute in my lap. The way Mitch Stewart was acclaimed and the way he humbly spoke about the causes the foundation supported, nobody would have suspected that he had a son accused of murder or that he had probably destroyed more lives than Jack ever would.

"I need to use the restroom," I excused myself, queasy and not really interested in the mayor's speech.

Mom made to join me, but the judge with his monstrous nose started a new barrage of questions, and she dropped back in her seat, taking another gulp of brandy. What had begun as an interesting conversation was getting on her nerves now, but she was too much of a lady to let it show.

Thankfully, the restroom was empty save for the attendant who made sure the area was clean and in perfect order. I dipped a napkin in cold water and dabbed at the nape of my neck.

Perhaps because I hadn't eaten much all day, or the emotional stress was getting to me, but all of a sudden, I didn't feel quite well. I pulled out my phone to call Marcus, to beg if that was what it took to call a truce tonight and adjourn the anger and the hurt for another day.

"You called," I breathed in the quietness of the room and leaned my hip against the sink. While my legs wobbled under my weight, my heart pounded crazily in anticipation.

The cleaning woman glanced at me, undoubtedly wondering if

lawyers sometimes went mad, then returned to folding towels and arranging them under each sink.

Without sparing another second, I bolted from the restroom in search of a quiet spot with better mobile signal.

Mitch Stewart and Vincent Cole were arguing less than five feet away from the ladies' room. My feet dug into the carpet and my breath hitched.

Unlike the serene act he had put on up on stage, the mayor looked tense and slightly displeased. He was talking to Cole, while the latter listened, but the words didn't drift to the small alcove where I was hiding. Cole nodded and peeked around before holding out his hand. The mayor told him something more then pulled out a banker envelope from the inner pocket of his suit jacket and handed it to Cole.

The mayor studied his surroundings like he wanted to make sure nobody had witnessed the exchange, forcing me to pull back into my nook. When I glimpsed again around the corner, both Cole and the mayor were gone.

Too drained to figure out what the whole incident had been about, I walked outside onto the terrace as fast as my feet would carry me.

The terrace had a magnificent view, embellished with painted floors and bordered by a sculptured marble railing that dipped down to guard a spiral flight of stairs that led to the back gardens where daisies and anemones bloomed.

I called Marcus as soon as the signal strength allowed it, but it went to voicemail again. Sometime between calling me and now, he must have switched his phone off. I felt like screaming in frustration, but when a waiter surfaced out of nowhere, I was glad I had refrained.

"Miss, are you Charlotte Burton?" the waiter asked.

"Yes."

"This is for you then."

He handed me a white banker envelope and left. There was no inscription on the envelope, and from the feel of it, it only carried a slip of paper.

"Wait, who asked you to give it to me?"

The waiter opened a glass door and disappeared inside where he mingled with the attendants of the gala and the staff. I examined the envelope and felt a cold grip get a hold of me. It was exactly like the envelope Mitch Stewart had given Cole.

I pulled out the card and stared at it, strangely detached and unfeeling. The text was made of letters cut out from magazines and glued to a hard paper sheet.

Curiosity killed the cat, it said.

"Charlotte, is everything alright?" Cameron called from behind and approached me with quick, decisive steps. "Your mother was worried."

"I'm fine," I said, hearing my voice as if it came from somebody else.

"What's this?"

Drake stopped in front of me, bowing to study the card I was holding. The worry morphed to a look of shock, then anger. He looked around, circling me a few times in his attempts to peruse the terrace and the darkened garden.

"Have you been threatened before?"

I shook my head, not mentioning the time the mayor had threatened me in the middle of the day or that most probably he had just done it again.

"I'm going to call the police," Drake said and pulled out his phone.

"No," I protested in a high-pitched voice.

I gripped his wrist, not quite sure why I was stopping him, but before I figured out the meaning of this threat, I didn't want anybody else knowing about it. I put the card back in its envelope and placed it in my clutch.

"Charlotte, this is very serious."

"I know, but I don't want to ruin tonight."

That was actually my last concern since the night had been more or less ruined from the start, but he bought the lie.

"God, you're shivering," Cameron muttered, the frown between his brows deepening again.

He took his coat off and pulled it around my shoulders, keeping it closed with his fisted hands. He squatted just a bit so he could see my eyes. When he found whatever he had been looking for, he smiled and wrapped an arm around my waist.

"Don't be afraid. Jase Parker is in prison. You will not be attacked again. I'll make sure of that."

He wrapped his other arm around me, then his mouth covered mine, and his tongue probed at my lips. I was so shocked and so repulsed by the slow and sloppy glide of his mouth that I remained immobile in his embrace. Then I heard a sound that blasted so familiarly and so dreadfully in my ears.

I shoved Cameron aside just in time to see the shadow of a slate gray Jaguar speeding from the driveway like hellhounds were on its tail.

"Marcus—" I breathed and covered my mouth with my hands. He had seen us.

"What is the matter?" Drake demanded, coming close again.

I finally exploded, and the civility I had struggled to keep up the whole night vanished.

"The matter is that you should have never kissed me," I hissed. "And you will never do it again."

"But, Charlotte, I thought you and I had something going on."

He reached for my hand, but I pushed at him, exasperated. It felt wonderful to finally be able to tell him that I didn't appreciate his advances. It felt wonderful to hiss and see the gallantry slip from his face.

"You thought wrong. Don't touch me."

Drake scoffed and cast me a look of disdain that felt more real than every word and every glance he had given me the entire night. He was not familiar with rejection.

"I don't even know why I let your father get in my head. It's evident you do not live up to my standards."

"My father put you up to this?" I shrieked as I realized that James's show of approval had had nothing to do with my award but with the man he had somehow convinced to conquer me. Sometime between yesterday and tonight, Isaac must have shared his concerns with my father about my relationship with Marcus, and together, they had decided it would be better to split us up.

I let Drake's coat slip off my shoulders and ran down the stairs to the garden then out the back entrance and to the parking lot. My legs trembled, but they had purpose. I wasn't going to let Marcus think for another moment that there was something between Drake and me.

I dialed a phone number I never thought I would ever use. Kai answered after the second ring, his voice loud but not loud enough to drown out the background noise or the soft giggles of a woman.

"Hello?"

"Kai, it's Charlotte. I want you to tell me if there is a race tonight."

He gasped, hesitated, and mumbled something incoherently, then a little louder he added, "Why are you asking?"

"Because I'm afraid Marcus is about to make a big mistake."

Chapter 35

Charlotte

"*There's fun in the races too,*" Marcus had told me, but he wasn't racing for the fun or the adrenaline. He raced to purge the anger, the frustration, or the grief. He raced to quiet his thoughts and let his heart beat without hurting. He raced to forget, and tonight he wanted to forget me.

I could imagine the misplaced betrayal that fueled his anger and the rabid wish to drive it out. I suspected to some extent this outburst of his was meant to punish me, to make me feel the anguish he had felt when he saw Drake hold and kiss me like I was his.

I understood all that because I was jealous and possessive by nature, but most of all, I understood it because I had already experienced it when I found that redheaded woman in his apartment. The worst thoughts had come to my mind then, so I knew without a shadow of a doubt that Marcus was not in the right frame of mind to race tonight. His judgment was not soaked with alcohol, but it was equally inebriated.

I knew I had come to the right place when I heard the noise. It was loud and terrible. Music boomed from unseen speakers, and a cacophony of hoarse voices and liquor-fueled laughter mingled with the screeching of tires against the pavement.

I parked somewhere on the side of the road then hurried on foot, right into the middle of the unleashed crowd. My body wasn't completely recovered from the last time I was attacked, and my mind hadn't forgotten the dread or the despair, but the fear of knowing that Marcus could be in danger eclipsed whatever fear I had left for my own safety.

Men cast me vile and lewd glances while some drunken ones stumbled into me and slurred obscenities that had my stomach rolling. My skin crawled, and my heart pounded like it wanted to dig a hole through my chest. They hooted, and they laughed as I cringed, but I pushed forward until I finally saw him.

Marcus mounted a motorcycle that I noted wasn't his. He arched his back and grabbed the handlebars with a sort of fury that couldn't easily be curbed. I could only see the side of his face, but it was enough to confirm all my fears. He was mad and out of control. He wasn't even wearing protection.

"Marcus," I screamed. "Marcus, stop, please don't do it."

He didn't hear me, or if he had, he didn't even spare me a glance. It was Kai, who finally noticed me and came my way.

"Charlotte, what's going on?" he shouted.

"Kai, please stop him. He'll get hurt."

He stared confused at Marcus's crouched back, then shaking his head, he returned his attention to me.

"He's a damn good rider. Well, he'll still lose, but he'll be safe," Kai laughed. "Why don't you bet on him, and after I beat him, and you lose, you'll let me paint you?"

"You don't understand. He saw me kiss somebody else. He's not thinking clearly."

I felt the tears in my eyes and heard the trembling in my voice, but I couldn't bring myself to care. Kai paled, then he glanced again at his cousin. He looked terrified like it wasn't the first time he witnessed Marcus riding in this condition, like he was fully capable of predicting the outcome.

"Damn it," he cursed and spun around.

People all around gave him a wide berth as he jogged to the

booth where a man with a microphone was working the crowd. Kai wrestled the microphone from the man's grasp, but it was too late to stop the race now. Marcus had already set off.

"King is cheating," the announcer said with a gasp after regaining control of his mike. "That's highly unethical, Mr. King, but two seconds advance won't win you the race. Haralson and The Fox are hot on his tail, and oh, look at that, The Fox just outstripped him.

Kai ran back to where I was, his eyes fixed someplace over my shoulder. He shot a warning glare at somebody, but I lacked the strength to turn and check what was happening behind me. My full attention was focused on Marcus's disappearing form.

"He will be fine," Kai said, wrapping an arm around my shoulders.

I didn't realize I had needed the support until I leaned into him and noticed that my legs were shaking so badly that my knees bumped against each other. It was suddenly very cold and very difficult to breathe.

"I cannot see Reed, however," the announcer yelled into his microphone. "Oh, look, he's in the crowd with a stunning lady. Hmm, now we understand why he is not racing tonight, but what will The Fox say about this? We have some interesting stuff to look forward to, people."

Kai glowered where the scrawny man was gesturing madly and moving gracelessly to the music. He made a sharp gesture with his hand that effectively shut him up.

"Marcus will be fine," Kai repeated, more to himself than to me, but he didn't sound so sure of it.

I bounced on my feet, staring ahead but not quite seeing. If anything happened to him, if Marcus got hurt, I could never forgive myself.

"Looks like Haralson has a pretty good advantage now, while King is furiously catching up," I heard the announcer saying like I was underwater, and he was talking from somewhere far off. "King has overtaken Haralson, who I think doesn't like it very much. Hey, he should be disqualified. Haralson almost hit the back of King's motorcycle."

Time stood still, and so did my heart.

They were getting back now, and Marcus's usual controlled way of mastering his motorcycle was lost. The bike wobbled as it moved at a blinding speed, and somebody sped past him, grazing his side and pushing him off the road.

A roar split the night, and it drifted to me like a punch to the gut. I bent at the waist and covered my face with my hands, sobbing quietly, uncontrollably.

"Definitely not the night for King. His motorcycle has a blowout. Why isn't he stopping? That's insane, he's going faster. This can go very bad, very fast. People, move aside, he's losing control of the bike."

"What are you doing, you moron?" Kai muttered then cursed again and stepped forward, dragging me with him.

The bike rolled down the pavement like a bullet uncertain of its target, then it came tumbling to the ground in a cloud of smoke and gravel. A scream tore from my chest right before Kai let go of me and darted to his cousin.

I begged my feet to move, but they were firmly rooted to the ground. Marcus was trapped under that motorcycle, and he was not moving.

His limbs were lying askew, and his neck was bent at an odd angle. His head was resting on the cement, in a pool of his own blood. His eyes were closed, and his face was covered in more blood. His beautiful, cocky face was twisted in an ugly grimace that left his mouth half open but not speaking. He was quiet. Everything was painfully quiet.

"Charlotte, he's fine," Kai was saying.

It was when he shook me a little that I realized all those lurid images had been glimpses from a dreadful, nonexistent nightmare, but one that could have been real.

"The motorcycle is a mess, but Marcus is fine," he reiterated and glanced back where a few cars created a closed area that looked quiet and empty. "His left foot is a little banged up, so we pulled him to the side to—"

I stormed off, and Kai neither stopped me nor followed.

Marcus was leaning against a red Mustang with his left foot

stiffly stretched forward and a scantily dressed blonde wrapped around him like a bandage.

Or scabies.

His arm was loosely curled around her waist, and with closed eyes, he was leaning against her invasive touch.

"Oh, you hurt yourself, babe," she told him, stroking his hair. She kissed his cheek but was aiming for his mouth.

Worry switched to hurt and anger of my own, and I let it all out, lashing at the woman.

"Take your hands off him," I rasped.

The blonde jerked and glanced at me, at first shocked, then annoyed that I was disrupting her fun. Marcus's arm dropped from her waist, and in its absence, she lost the confidence that drove her to his chest, to the place she did not belong.

Scoffing and rolling her eyes, she finally got lost, leaving Marcus and me alone.

"You don't like what you see?" he challenged, lifting his chin and regarding me with impenetrable, unfamiliar eyes.

"You are behaving like a little boy throwing a tantrum because somebody else took his toy."

"Are you calling this a tantrum?" he barked, shooting to his feet. "I saw you in another man's arms. I saw him touching you, kissing you."

Limping, Marcus walked to me, his fists clenched, his teeth bared. He didn't resemble the deadly image that had flashed in my head right after the crash, but as Kai had pointed out, he was a little banged up, with a few scratches on his jaw, above his left eyebrow, and around his wrists and certainly some bruises under his clothes.

"You're trying to hurt me on purpose while I didn't mean to hurt you at all. If you had stuck around just for another second, you'd have seen that I pushed Drake away and declined his attention. You'd have seen that I immediately ran after you. *To you.*"

We glared at each other, standing close but not close enough, our chests heaving, our mouths open but not talking, our hands half outstretched but not really reaching. When I couldn't bear the distance anymore, I spun around and hugged myself. We were both hurting now, and I was at a loss as what to do or what to say.

"You're shivering," Marcus said, and I could feel him stepping closer.

He wrapped his leather jacket around my shoulders and turned me gently to him. He looked nonplussed and ashamed and just as miserable as I felt. He opened his mouth, then closed it, then repeated the same process twice before he settled on hugging me. He kept me there, tightly pressed to his chest, a hand clenching my hair and the other arm circling my waist.

I let him hold me and kiss my temples, and I let myself feel with every bone and every cell of my blood that he was safe and whole. Then I disentangled myself from his arms and walked away.

At first, I thought Marcus would stay behind, but eventually, waddling on his feet and grunting every few steps, he did follow me back to my car and slid into the passenger seat without a word.

I drove to his apartment in silence, and when I pulled up behind his building, I squeezed the steering wheel and looked hesitantly out the windshield. It was easier to run back to the comfort of my shell and follow the patterns that were already familiar. It was easier to withdraw, but we had come too far, and our hearts were too deeply involved now to take the easy way out.

So I stayed. I stayed to fight and ache and finally mend.

I helped Marcus out of the car and all the way to his apartment. Kinga barked and scratched at the door the instant we stepped out of the elevator.

"Easy, girl," Marcus muttered to her after we let ourselves in, patted her head, and gave her a handful of treats.

She sleepily returned to her snuggle sack, and it was quiet again save for her chewing and our ragged breaths.

I walked to the bathroom, and Marcus once again followed, not really knowing what to make of my mood. I turned on the water and looked for some ointment and hydrogen peroxide to clean his scratches. When I could think of nothing else to occupy my hands or my thoughts with, I turned around.

Marcus was leaning against the doorframe, watching me cautiously, a little astonished and a lot chastened.

"Why would you do this to me?" I finally said. "Why would you make me fear that I could lose you?"

Lately, I had feared for myself on more than one occasion, but I had never experienced such a paralyzing fear as I did when I saw Marcus collapsing to the ground, unable to stand on his own.

"Charlotte, the only other option was to come up there and beat that Drake character to a pulp."

He straightened, as much as he was able to on his wobbly foot, and walked to me. His warmth seeped through my dress.

"I can't live worrying that every time you feel remotely jealous, you're going to do something to punish me."

"I wasn't punishing you."

"Weren't you?"

Marcus fell silent, and his silence confirmed what I had already suspected. He was a Scorpio, after all, and just like a scorpion he had lifted his tail and struck, inflicting the venom of his anger deep into the one he suspected of betrayal. Into me.

I shook my head, disoriented, and wiped at the errant tears on my cheeks. The bathroom was large enough, but I suddenly felt claustrophobic. I tried to dodge him, but Marcus stalked closer, ignoring the pain in his leg and advancing until I had no other option but to confront him.

"I had come there to apologize for how I acted yesterday. When I saw him all over you, I didn't think clearly. I have bad habits, sugar, and they die hard. I didn't go racing to punish you. It was the only thing I knew that could wrench that image from my mind."

"But you did punish me, whether you realize it or not."

Marcus cupped my cheeks and lifted my face until his mouth brushed softly against mine. He kissed both my cheeks and sipped the tears that tumbled down from bloodshot eyes, then nuzzled his nose against mine and sighed.

"I'm sorry," he whispered. "I'm sorry I scared you tonight, but most of all, I'm sorry you had to go there alone. If I hadn't acted like a complete idiot, we wouldn't have fought in the first place. I would have been there with you, and that man would have never dared to touch you."

I planted my hands on his chest, but Marcus never stopped chasing me, step by little step, until he had me corned in the shower.

The water was raining down on us. We were fully clothed and thoroughly drenched, but as we touched and drowned in each other's eyes, none of that really mattered.

"If you ever race again, no matter the reason, I am done. I am done, Marcus."

"I promise, I won't."

He pulled the straps of my dress off my shoulders and bent to kiss each one gently, licking and nipping at the skin. If my mind hesitated, my body never did. I leaned into his touch and pressed against him as much as he pressed against me. It was soothing after all the turmoil to surrender to his caresses and the flames they ignited in my flesh.

"You're just saying it to take my mind off it," I cried softly but let my head fall back and rest against the tiled wall as Marcus continued trailing kisses up and down my neck. "You don't mean it."

He stopped mid-kiss and cupped my face again, his jaw set, his eyes blazing.

"I swear."

Not the vehemence in his voice convinced me, but the look in his eyes, the look that had told me that I could trust him from the very beginning.

I thrust my hands into his hair the instant he yanked me closer. Our mouths smashed together, lips warring and tongues wrestling while our hearts pounded against our ribcages.

Marcus fumbled for the zipper of my dress, and I struggled to free my arms from the confines of the wet straps. Neither one of us was successful. He groaned and spun me around, placing a hand on my hip to steady me, then the sound of fabric being torn to shreds muffled the furious drizzle of the shower.

"Marcus," I gasped, and he mumbled something unintelligible before he bowed his head and nibbled on the flesh between my neck and shoulder, at first softly as to incite me, then harsh enough to mark me.

As the bite of pain subsided, I realized I had just marked him too. My fingernails had dug crescent patterns in his forearms, but he was not complaining. If anything, he was growing wild and feverish.

He ripped the clothes off himself with a haste that made him desperate and let them pool at our feet.

"Tell me you forgive me," he rasped and sucked my earlobe in his mouth.

My eyes rolled back, and my whole body trembled with desire. That delicious fire started burning once again in my loins, and with every touch, every kiss, and every whisper, Marcus aroused it.

"Tell me, Charlotte," Marcus pressed and pushed me flush against the wall. I was captive between the steamy wall and his raging, muscled body, and I couldn't think of a better place to be.

"I forgive you," I said and let him take my mouth, my body, and my soul.

With an arm clenched around my waist and the other propped against the wall, Marcus thrust inside me and used each stroking motion to drive me insane. I kept my cheek flattened against the tile and my eyes closed, succumbing to sensation.

It was quick and fierce and yet so gentle that it appeased all the chaos in our hearts. I felt the tension building deep in my stomach, and when Marcus tensed behind me, I knew we were about to fall off the brink together.

We remained under the stream for a long time, panting and holding each other. After we managed to wash ourselves, and I cleaned Marcus's small wounds, we returned to his bedroom. I made him sit on the edge of the bed while I applied salve to his scratches, and Kinga watched us from the hallway.

Later, I was looking out the window and brushing my hair when I felt Marcus coming from behind. He plastered his chest to my back and rested his chin on my shoulder. His leg was aching especially after the stunt we had pulled in the shower, but he was doing a good job hiding the pain.

"What are you thinking?" he asked, tapping his finger against the tip of my nose.

"My mind remained stuck on something your father said."

"What is that?"

"He said it's because of me that you didn't accept the deal. He sounded shocked and resentful at the same time, and I didn't understand why he'd think that since it's because of me that you want to accept it in the first place."

Marcus sighed and stroked my arms. He led me to his bed and settled me on his chest. I thought he had fallen asleep when he finally started speaking.

"It's because of my mother," he said softly.

To finally hear him mentioning his mother startled me. I looked up at him to find him staring at the ceiling, his jaw rolling, and his eyes narrowed with grief.

"You asked why Julian Hudson would be interested in me. It's because Isaac stoked that interest. He's a damn agent. He's been one his entire life, and it's because one of his missions failed that Mom—that Mom—I lost her because of him, and I'm terrified that history could repeat itself, that I could make a poor decision and do to you what Isaac did to my mother."

"Marcus, look at me," I ordered and crawled up his chest until we were eye level. "No matter what happens, I will never blame you."

He shook his head and tried to escape my piercing eyes, but I held him in place as I continued, "You are not your father. You could never make a decision that would actually harm me."

"Isn't tonight proof enough?"

"Tantrum," I murmured and kissed his lips chastely until he smiled and kissed me back.

Then I remembered I should be apologizing as well. I licked my lips and watched him from under my lashes. It gave me a heady rush to know that I was the only woman who had the privilege of seeing him after he had shed the armor. His head lolled from one side to another, his hair shot in all directions, and his sleepy eyes glimmered sensually.

"I get it now," I sighed. "What you said, that you will protect me even when I don't like how you do it. Marcus, I've tried to do the same. I never intended to go behind your back or expose you. I only—"

"Charlotte, I know," he stopped me and stroked my bottom lip with his thumb. "I really do. It's not you who should apologize. It's me, so please forgive me."

He took my hand and kissed each knuckle before kissing my mouth and begging me with his eyes to understand. I had always felt that his mother was a touchy subject, but I had never anticipated the rampant rage and the ease he unleashed it with when Jacqueline was mentioned.

It still hurt a little to remember how he had ambushed me with all that rage, but I did understand. When you loved somebody unconditionally, you defended that person against the whole world. Sometimes, the line between friends and enemies blurred.

"Where my mother is concerned, I cannot think clearly. She's—" Marcus trailed off, sighing heavily and throwing his head back on the pillow. "With the enemies my father has and the ones we are making, it's better if the world doesn't know that she is alive. I wasn't mad because you found out. Sooner or later, I was going to tell you everything myself. I was mad because I realized that if you knew, somebody else must have known too. If the wrong people find out about her and they do something to her—"

"We won't let them," I promised and knew I would do anything in my power to help him keep his mother out of harm's way.

Millions of questions about Jacqueline came to mind, but I stifled each one of them and waited. Sooner or later, he was going to tell me everything himself. I trusted he would, and I respected him enough to let him do it when he was ready.

I WAS REVELING IN A pleasant dream for once, lying on the beach, the warm waves lapping at my thighs and Marcus resting his head on my stomach, playing absentmindedly with my fingers. It was peaceful and quiet, except for the distant shriek of a seagull and the balanced tune of the ocean as its waves rolled and broke against the shore.

Then the peacefulness, the sun kissing my skin, and the salty breeze wafting across my face dissipated with Kinga's loud barking. Yet, it wasn't precisely her barking that startled me awake. It was the unexpected voice coming from the living room. It took me a moment to realize that it was Kai's.

Marcus groaned then threw a leg over my hips and started

kissing my neck while I couldn't cover my almost bare body fast enough.

"How did he get in?" I hissed and dashed to the bathroom where Marcus kept his bathrobe.

"Kai has a key for when I come home late so he can walk and feed Kinga."

"Perfect," I mumbled and tied the sash around my waist.

I returned to the bedroom just as Kai was shamelessly bursting in with Kinga joyously hopping around him. Marcus yawned and rolled out of bed, completely untroubled that he was only wearing a pair of boxers.

"Oh my God, the lewdness and sin you live in," Kai gasped and covered his eyes. "I'm permanently scarred. You should pay me moral damages."

"That coming from someone who paints naked women for a living," I scoffed and rolled my eyes. Kai boomed with laughter then kept grinning, looking very proud of his occupation.

"Get out of my bedroom," Marcus grumbled and started guiding Kai toward the door, but he didn't budge. Kai cast him a slashing glance then directed a more cordial look at me.

"I would if I could," Kai said. "But there's a guy in my workshop, and he's already demolished an easel and broke a few things, so please, can you come and just make him disappear as quickly as possible? Pretty please?"

"Can you get out of my bedroom now?" Marcus insisted and grabbed Kai by his arm.

He wasn't exactly bothered by his cousin's unannounced visit, but he still sounded like he wanted to tell him something that wasn't entirely pleasant.

"Philip?" I asked.

Kai nodded, putting in that motion all the exasperation he was capable of, and let Marcus sway him out into the hallway.

"Oh, and for your information, I cuffed him," Kai yelled, just before Marcus shoved him out of the room and closed the door.

My heart pounded in anticipation, and my hair stood on end. If Philip wanted to talk outside of the firm, it only meant one thing. He had found something more on Elana Beckham.

I showered and put on some leggings and a gray sweatshirt which were the only clothes I had in Marcus's wardrobe, except for the completely ruined dress from the previous night.

From the living room, upset voices drifted to me. In the end, it sounded like Kai was the one telling Marcus something not entirely pleasant. Although Marcus was the older and usually the responsible and mature one, it was Kai scolding him now.

When we arrived at Kai's workshop, I was shocked to find that he hadn't lied when he told me that he had cuffed Philip. He was sitting on an upturned paint box with his left arm hanging above his head from a pipe.

"He cuffed me," Philip complained as if it wasn't already evident and tugged forcefully at the handcuffs.

"He destroyed my easel," Kai snapped. "What? I wasn't going to let him wreck everything while I wasn't here."

"Uncuff him," I ordered with a warning glare but couldn't completely hide the grin that tugged at my lips. Although Kai looked so dismayed because his easel had been destroyed, I suspected he was secretly amused too.

After Philip was uncuffed and Kai left with Marcus to get coffee from the shop across the street, we sat at a small table in the middle of the room, which although littered with drawings and all sorts of crayons and brushes, was fairly clean.

"Do you have something for me?"

Philip nodded and pulled some papers from his briefcase.

"We didn't find Elana, but Tanner found something. What if this is the secret Jennifer shared with Rheya and Elana?"

I read each file, completely rigid, with a hand covering my mouth and the sound of my blood rushing to my ears. I blinked every so often, but the words on the papers didn't change. Jennifer Gunnar had been pregnant.

"How did you get these files?" I eventually gasped.

They were Jennifer's complete gynecological history, including medical results, exams she was supposed to take, ultrasounds, even the appointment schedule throughout her pregnancy.

"You know how," Philip said quietly, shaking his head.

"If they were not legally obtained, then they are not admissible in court."

"But if the doctor were to be subpoenaed, then he would have to come forward and admit to these," Philip countered with a proud grin.

"And if he admitted to this," I added. "It might be sufficient to request an exhumation and a new autopsy, which will prove whether Jennifer had been injected with an overdose before she was shot."

"This is it," Philip chimed excitedly and almost started clapping.

His enthusiasm was contagious, and I shared a smile. Coming down from the clouds, I frowned at the papers I was still holding. I shook my head, and Philip's proud excitement slowly dissolved.

"This is still only speculation," I sighed. "We haven't found who killed Rheya and probably Jennifer too. Elana is still in danger."

"But this is a lead," he whined and started drumming his fingers on the table.

"It is," I agreed, although we both knew it wasn't enough. "And if Jennifer was pregnant then this changes everything. If she was pregnant, I don't think Jack would have killed her."

"Probably—"

"Unless the child wasn't his."

Marcus and Kai returned before Philip could cover his gaping mouth or regain his composure. I thanked him and ushered him out the door before he got a chance to reveal everything. I had to test my theory, and to do that, I had to do something that Marcus wasn't going to like and wasn't going to let me do if he knew.

So I deflected the best way I could and tried to join their conversation about Brayden and the rehab facility where he was receiving treatment, then I told them I would drive home while they went to visit their friend.

THREE HOURS LATER I WAS BACK in D.C., about to pay Jack a visit.

My legs were unsteady as I climbed out of the cab that drove me from the airport to his apartment building, but they eventually carried me to his door. I knocked and waited, shuffling my feet and glancing over my shoulder at every little noise. If somebody wanted to attack me again, nobody would have witnessed it.

"It will be fine," I whispered to myself once, twice, then as many times as needed until I was convinced of it.

When Jack finally opened the door, I jumped and clenched my fingers until the nails dug into my palms. I hadn't planned an elaborate questioning. I only needed to tell him about Jennifer's pregnancy. I didn't even need him to comment on it. I only needed to see his face, and I would know the truth.

Whether by Drake or by Cole, the official papers, including the autopsy results, had clearly been manufactured.

If Jack knew about Jennifer's pregnancy, he was going to be furious that I found out and their charade wasn't as well orchestrated as they thought, which would indicate her pregnancy played a role in her death and he was involved.

If he didn't know, he was going to be just as shocked as I had been when I found out, which would mean the child could be somebody else's, and this was motive to kill for the person in question. Either way, Jack was going to lead me to the truth whether he intended to or not.

"What are you doing here?" he snapped and curled his lip over his teeth. "You are not working for me anymore."

"I just heard something, and I thought I should congratulate you in person," I spoke more brazenly than I felt. "You were going to be a father."

I realized I was a little cruel since both the mother and the child were dead, and perhaps macabre, but I chose my words specifically for the utmost impact.

"What are you talking about?"

Jack's eyes turned big and incredulous, and his whole expression became stony. He drew in a breath but forgot to let it out, and in that second, he looked more like a marionette than a killer.

"Forgive me, I should have said that you could have been a father. Jennifer was pregnant."

"You don't know what you're saying. I always used protection."

Jack had never suspected that his fiancée carried a child, and as he tied the loose ends, he turned white as a ghost. The father was somebody else.

"Who are you trying to protect, Jack?"

He swallowed the lump in his throat and continued glaring my way.

"Don't ever come back here," he said, but his mind had drifted someplace else. "You are not my lawyer anymore."

He slammed the door after finally having said something truthful. I was not his lawyer anymore. And because of that, I had no remorse for anonymously forwarding Leon Holden the papers Philip had brought me plus a personal note that informed him that Jack was not the father.

Most certainly, Holden was going to recognize my writing. In court, though, he could claim the papers had landed on his doorstep, and that he had no knowledge of who sent them, so the judge couldn't reject them on the grounds that the prosecution obtained the evidence unlawfully or colluded with the defendant's former lawyer.

I smiled to myself and returned home, where I was sure I had some explaining to do.

Chapter 36

Marcus

I knew Charlotte was planning something the moment she left Kai's shop, but I never suspected that something would be a journey into the wolf's lair. Again.

I spun the phone between my fingers then tracked her location for the twentieth time in less than half an hour, and for the twentieth time, I growled under my breath and clenched my jaw.

After Kai and I left Brayden, who had finally shown glimpses of his old self, I drove straight to Charlotte's apartment to find it completely empty as was the parking lot. Trying not to overreact, I had driven to the firm then to her sister, but nobody had seen Charlotte since the night of the gala. So I finally gave in to paranoid instincts and just tracked her phone to find that she was carelessly roaming the streets of the capital.

I had nearly boarded the next flight to D.C., but twenty minutes after the initial tracking of her location, she went dark. I assumed she was on a plane back home, so I forced myself to breathe, calm down, and wait. One hour later, I was leaning against my car, with my eyes narrowed and my arms crossed over my chest, watching Charlotte walking absentmindedly to her car.

"Marcus," she breathed when she spotted me.

Surprise flickered on her face, then it was immediately replaced by such a sweet look of bashfulness that I almost forgave her for making me worry. Almost.

I didn't ask where she had been, and to her credit, she didn't even try to lie or fake innocence. She walked to me with big, repentant eyes and pressed a kiss to my closed mouth.

"Don't be upset with me. Philip showed me evidence that Jennifer was pregnant prior to her death. I only wanted to confirm if Jack knew or not. Nothing happened to me. Plus, I had the revolver with me."

Charlotte gifted me with a shy grin that still managed to be mischievous, then she locked her hands behind my neck and bent for another quick kiss.

"Get in," I said, stepping to the side and holding the passenger door open.

She cast a hesitant glance at her car, parked precisely next to mine, but I shook my head and pointed to the Jaguar, urging her to get in.

"Give me your keys," I ordered once she climbed in and fastened her seatbelt.

Charlotte frowned but didn't protest. After I hid the key above the rear passenger wheel, I returned to my car, turned on the ignition, and put the car in motion while completely ignoring her.

"Kai will drive your car home," I said eventually then resumed driving, faster than Charlotte favored but much slower than I needed to.

"Are we going to talk about this?" she murmured. In the charged silence, her voice sounded uncommonly loud and trembling.

"No need."

"Marcus, please, you have to understand. There's not just my safety at stake here."

My head snapped in her direction, and my cutting stare efficiently quieted her. Her safety might not have been the only one at stake, but it was the only one that mattered to me.

I drove to the forest house in relative silence after that. I parked in the clearing behind the house, then moving somewhat unsteadily, I walked over to Charlotte's side to help her out. She said nothing as we strolled to the back porch, but her small hand slipped into mine and clasped it tightly.

It was pleasant outside, and the pond looked especially inviting today, but I went straight inside, and Charlotte followed. When I stopped in the middle of the room and let out the breath I had been holding, she circled my waist from behind with her supple arms and kissed my back.

"You are off the case now," I burst and whirled around. "I thought this was what you wanted from the beginning."

She had the grace to flush and look just the tiniest bit contrite, then her features hardened, and she regarded me with a harsh look that was equally determined and stubborn.

"Yes, but it's too late to choose the easy way out," Charlotte cried and shoved a hand through her brown locks. "I know too much to simply be able to walk away. I cannot let a murderer walk free, and I cannot allow an innocent woman to spend the rest of her life fearing for her safety. If you don't know this about me by now, maybe you don't know me at all."

Lifting her chin and clasping her hips, Charlotte took a step back and watched me head-on. It astonished me how she had quietly permitted her father to control her life when she had no problem confronting me and driving me insane in the process.

"All I want is for you to stay safe," I said through clenched teeth. "I am trying to protect you, and if you don't know the lengths I am willing to go to, maybe you don't know me at all, sugar."

Charlotte flinched, and her mouth parted enough to allow the tip of her tongue to glide over her rosy bottom lip. I followed the motion with narrowed, hungry eyes, and Charlotte bit her teeth into the plump flesh, making me groan. Her exceptional appeal, however, was not going to deter me.

I strode forward, caught her by the hips, and before she realized what was happening, I slung her over my shoulder and carried her upstairs to the bedroom.

"Next time you are off playing Sherlock on your own, remember that naughty girls get caught and punished, Charlotte."

The air wheezed from her sweet, enticing lips as I tossed her on the bed, and my own breath came out spasmodically.

She had scared me enough. And the result wasn't going to be pleasant.

There were no concessions I was willing to make and no lines so unimaginable as to not cross to ensure her wellbeing. Charlotte inhaled harshly and fidgeted under my stare then attempted to stand.

I blanketed her with my body and pushed her down against the mattress, pillaging her mouth without delicacy. The notion of losing her made me reckless and in desperate need of her. I tore at her blouse, sending the first three buttons scattering on the ground, then dived in to taste the creamy flesh I had just exposed.

Charlotte threw her head back, offering her body instinctively and clutching my shoulders as if I were her anchor. Licking between her breasts, I lingered close to one puckering areola then detoured back to her hot, delicious mouth. She whimpered and squirmed under my body, pressing her breasts against my chest, frenzied to appease the ache throbbing in their peaks.

"I want you to understand me," she pleaded, hooking her fingers around my collar and moaning when I unbuckled my belt and pulled it out.

"I do," I muttered and returned to her arms. Understanding, however, didn't equal agreeing with her methods.

"I'm not being stubborn," she went on between moans of pleasure. "I'm following the right lead. My gut knows it, I know it, and I think you know it too. I am part of this case now whether I want it or not, and I need to see it through. I'm not doing it to defy you. Please just listen—"

Desire grew so fierce that it muddled Charlotte's thoughts. I felt no remorse for taking advantage of the confusion it created and laced my belt around her wrists. When she realized I had her hands tied to the bedpost, her eyes glinted sexily, then realization finally dawned on her.

"Marcus, what—what are you doing?" Charlotte demanded once I climbed off the bed. She looked properly horrified and outraged.

"You are making me lose my mind," I told her calmly. "But I knew you could do that from the start, so I can't quite blame you."

I bent to kiss her again with a possessiveness that bordered on aggression, but the pliable Charlotte, wrecked by passion, was completely gone now. She glared and seethed and basically looked gorgeously safe.

"Marcus, don't turn this into something sexual," she demanded, struggling against the bindings. The leather belt was soft but firm, and while the little snare wasn't going to loosen, it wouldn't damage her sensitive skin either.

"You weren't complaining a second ago," I teased and turned to the mirrored wall to put order in my completely rumpled appearance. "But no, I am not turning it into something sexual. I'm making sure you stay put while I go to work."

"Work?" she shrieked and kept on fighting against the restraints. "It's Sunday."

"Sugar, you know better than anyone that work doesn't stop just because it's Sunday. Plus, I have to catch up on the things I should have done while chasing a certain someone."

Once satisfied that I looked decent enough to walk out the door, I winked at her and headed for the stairs, enjoying the annoyed sounds she was making.

"You are not going to leave me here, are you?"

"You left me no choice," I said glumly then grinned shamelessly at the sight of her bound and furious little body. "Use the time to take a nap. You look—restless."

"Argh, Marcus?" Charlotte growled, a sound so primal and yet so sexy that it elicited torturous awareness in my whole body. "What if I need to use the bathroom?"

"Make sure you don't stain the sheets, darling."

"MARCUS," she yelled and spit threats and promises of retaliation probably long after I left the house.

THE DELICIOUS SMELL OF FRESHLY baked brownies wafted all the way to the back porch, and so did Kai's enthusiastic ramblings and Charlotte's reserved but genuine chuckles.

Half an hour after I left Charlotte fuming and shrieking, I called Kai to retrieve her car from the airport and drive it to the forest house. That he stuck around to save the damsel in distress or babysit her in my absence was no surprise to me. It was a little surprising though that, after the way they met, Charlotte had let her guard down enough to honestly enjoy Kai's company.

"I'm just in time for dessert," I muttered as I stopped in the entryway. "Wonderful."

Kai seldom cooked, or baked for that matter, but a few years back, when he had an affair with a baker from Toulouse, between extended and steamy sessions of coupling, she had taught him the secrets of baking. Truth be told, he hadn't been a sensational pupil, but he had managed to memorize a few recipes he still used to charm women when it suited him.

"Look who deigns to make an appearance," Kai said with a smirk.

Charlotte stiffened then hissed under her breath, and eventually, looking up from the strawberries she was cutting into tiny pieces, she smashed the knife against the marble counter and lifted her chocolate stare to pin me with the most fabulous of glares.

"This should be fun," I muttered and walked over to her.

Following my movements with her brows still narrowed and her delightful lips pressed tautly, Charlotte resumed cutting the fruits and chucking them with unrequired force into a bowl.

"It definitely will," Kai laughed and leaned back against the cupboards to enjoy the show.

I wrapped my arms around Charlotte's waist and intentionally pressed my body into hers, garnering a quiet but exquisite moan that made my skin tingle and my hands itch to explore her body. Then, kissing her neck, her jaw, and finally her cheek, I bent forward, grabbing a strawberry and popping it in my mouth, letting its juice trickle from the corner of my lips.

Charlotte was far from ignoring me. She stealthily eyed the juice trailing all the way to my chin, and her hands stopped working as she drew in a sharp breath. Clenching her jaw stubbornly, she licked her lips then bit down hard enough to remind herself that she should stay mad at me.

"I can think of a much better way to use those enticing lips of yours," I whispered and freed her bottom lip from the brutish assault of her teeth.

Inching my chin closer, I waited for her to lick clean the mess I had made. She tipped her head back and regarded me standoffishly before her features lightened up into an unconsciously seductive smile. I responded in kind, feeling something deep inside me quiver in anticipation, but as soon as the back of my finger stroked her cheek, the smile faded into a scowl.

Arching a challenging brow, Charlotte shoved a paper towel into my hands then moved to the sink where Kai intercepted her and washed the few dishes that had gathered.

"Messy little boy," she threw over her shoulder, inflicting insult to the words but only managing to make me laugh.

"I might be messy," I said, pulling her back in my arms and pressing my mouth to her ear. "But we both know there's nothing boyish about me, sugar."

Kai pressed a fist to his mouth to cover his grin then turned to the oven and pulled out a tray of hot, decadent brownies. The air was rich with the aroma of chocolate and rum, but it was Charlotte's fragrance that filled my nostrils and made me crave a sample.

"Tantrum," I mouthed her words back at her and gave her a smug look.

"This should be about perfect," Kai declared, bowing close to the pan and sniffing greedily.

His phone rang, and by the way his eyes softened when he checked the display, I knew it was The Fox. Wiping his hands on a towel, he hurried out onto the porch and answered with a smile that turned from dumb to dumber.

"And about gone by the time you get back," I called after him and shoved a piece in my mouth. It seared my tongue, and I hardly tasted it before I swallowed, but I still knew that it was phenomenal.

Charlotte sneaked closer, leaning her hip against the counter, and watched me with a calculated look that assessed and schemed and promised all kinds of incredible torment.

"I am so nice that I am going to forgive you," she said, sounding so proud of her generosity.

This time, *I* arched a challenging brow.

"Strangely, on this occasion, I'm not looking for forgiveness," I replied.

She groaned low in her throat, and the little smile slipped from her face before she recovered and ignored my total lack of remorse.

"But there will come a time," she continued like I had never stopped her. "When you least expect it, and you'll find yourself tied to a post with the greatest erection of your life and an even greater disappointment that nobody will take care of it."

"Does this mean that I aroused you? Because I can get rid of Kai, and we can definitely continue from where we left off earlier."

She shook her head slowly, regaling me with a sassy grin that was likely to earn her a new sort of punishment if she kept teasing without delivering.

"It means that I intend to even the score, little boy."

Standing on her tiptoes, Charlotte smacked my lips and patted my cheek cockily then left me in the middle of the room dreaming about the day she would have her revenge.

"Naughty. I like that."

CHARLOTTE DIDN'T HOLD GRUDGES, and that was another reason why she had crept into my heart so quickly and so easily. When I woke up, she was already in the shower. I slipped in behind her and lavished the smooth expanse of her back. My chest slid across her back, creating a slow friction that made my blood simmer with need.

Turning her around to devour her mouth, I breathed her in. She smelled fresh and without a doubt mine, with my shower gel coating her silhouette in tiny white bubbles and my fragrance not quite eradicated from her skin.

She and I were two pieces of a puzzle that against all odds, fit to perfection. It didn't matter if we fought or if Fate tried to separate us. Ultimately, we ended up on the same side.

"Good morning, little boy," she chuckled, but I knew she wasn't upset with me anymore.

"I thought we settled the little boy matter last night," I muttered against her lips.

"We did," she moaned and let her head roll back against my chest.

The peaceful, lazy smile that danced on her face brought to mind the ravished look I had put in her eyes the previous night and her soft, lithe body thrashing in my arms, giving as much as it received.

I brushed quick, gentle kisses from her forehead to her chin, until she eventually opened her eyes and granted me that smile of hers that was sweet, intimate, and reserved especially for me.

"I know it might not be the proper time, but—" I trailed off, struggling to find the perfect words, but in the end, I just let out the question in one relieved breath. "Would you like to meet my mom?"

Charlotte became very still, and if I hadn't been so close that I could hear her breathing, I would have thought her lungs had ceased working altogether. She splashed her hands on my chest before a smile bright as the sun broke on her face, and she rose on tiptoes to softly kiss my lips.

"I'd love to," she whispered with earnest joy and enthusiasm.

Between good-humored teasing and furtive kisses, we finished showering and dressing. We skipped breakfast and left early. Charlotte joined me in the car with a delicate smile. I kissed the knuckles of her left hand, winked, then turned on the ignition and drove to The Hamptons.

I didn't race, for a change, and Charlotte gradually relaxed in her seat, except for when she thought I wasn't paying her attention, and she wrung her hands in her lap and worried her lower lip between her teeth.

"I never got the chance to compliment your new haircut," I said, breaking the silence.

"Thank you," she replied a little awkwardly and blushed a wonderful shade of pink.

"It suits you," I went on, unashamedly exploiting her uneasiness. Eventually, she was going to learn to accept compliments without feeling embarrassed or undeserving. "Especially when my hands are in it to muss it up, and you are under my body moaning in pleasure."

"Marcus," she shrieked and smacked my shoulder.

"Yes, darling?" I said innocently.

"I'm about to meet your mother. Can you, please, behave?"

I threw my head back and laughed while she wrinkled her nose at my lack of chivalry and pulled her denim jacket tighter around herself. I suspected she was only doing that to conceal the hardening nipples that poked at her blouse.

The drive was short and uneventful. Charlotte rolled down her window, and the salty breeze wafted in like the flapping of wings, soft and soothing. The streets were less frenzied with people, and the usual clamor faded into a pleasant background buzzing.

I veered east and drove down the street that led to the estate that Isaac had bought twenty-two years ago. Wrought iron gates opened to grant us access, and the keeper on duty saluted me with two fingers placed to his temple. He motioned us forward as the gates closed behind us.

The road was flanked by old maple trees that created a breathtaking tunnel of flaming leaves and twisted, gnarly branches.

The maples thinned until the winding labyrinth gave way to a greensward. The turf girdled the two-story manor and ended somewhere far to the west where a thin stretch of white sand separated the estate from the ocean.

I parked the car in the ample cobblestoned driveway, but my fingers never loosened and never let go of the steering wheel. Sucking in a harsh breath and flinching slightly, I glanced down at Charlotte's hand stroking my knee and closed my eyes.

After decades of keeping Mother's story under lock and key, it was excruciating to start digging up all the horrible memories. My chest ached, and my throat constricted as wounds that never properly healed opened once again.

"We can come back when you're ready," Charlotte whispered with immense patience and kindness. I hadn't realized a lone tear had trailed down my cheek until Charlotte reached to wipe it then kissed the skin that had chilled in its wake.

Shaking my head, I kissed her hand and took comfort in the warmth of her palm tightly pressed to my cheek. Charlotte was a sanctuary, the balm to my despair and the hope that cast light in the dark and sinful recesses of my life.

"Mom was a ballerina. She traveled all around the world. She even stayed in Russia for a few years and was a part of the Bolshoi Ballet, then she came back home and met Isaac. She thought she had met her future, but he was her doom."

I gasped. Invisible knives stabbed and sliced me from the inside out. I hated Isaac for what he had done to such a beautiful creature, so pure and elegant and full of life that she was otherworldly, but I hated more the idea that I could be the same kind of demon for Charlotte.

"She gave up everything for him, her dreams, her job, eventually her life. She stopped dancing and started teaching so she could spend more time with him. Then, they had me, sooner than expected and definitely long before I was wanted. Mom has always loved me, I'm sure of it, but Isaac, well, I doubt he ever has. My arrival was the event that tipped his perfectly balanced world into chaos."

I flexed my fingers around the steering wheel and averted my gaze. I didn't want Charlotte to witness the abounding hatred and rage festering there. I couldn't handle it if she were disgusted by what she saw, or worse, if she feared me.

"I only have pieces that I gathered from the people who knew them. The puzzle is far from being complete," I grunted, struggling to keep my voice calm and quiet. "My aunt says that pregnancy changed Mom. She required more stability, more comfort, more care. And while she gave up everything to be with him, Isaac never could do the same. He was a damn agent. He had missions, and they were always more important than his wife and son."

Charlotte's hand never left my knee, and her touch gave me comfort as well as strength to carry on. My hair stood on end, my skin crawled, and dark spots swam around in my vision, but in the end, I managed to paraphrase the story Isaac had told me.

I told her about how betrayed Mom must have felt, how she went searching for her husband, how he so recklessly made her part of his operation, and how he took the risk of losing her instead of risking the mission he had been working on.

Eventually, through a jaw that hardly moved and eyes that had visualized the same horror for an entire lifetime, I told her about the accident, about how the doctors thought she would not survive, about how I had been a boy of seven, missing a mother that had never really returned to me.

"In the accident, her spine was sectioned in the lumbar area, and she has never walked again. My beautiful, exuberant mother trapped in a wheelchair—"

I still remembered the first time I saw her after that cursed accident. I was nine, and after almost two years of living with the conviction that Mom had abandoned me because I had been a very bad boy for having put a frog in one of her little pupil's backpack, we met again.

The meeting was not the fairy tale I had so joyously hoped for. It had been a complete nightmare. Mom had been unable to say whether or not she had forgiven me.

In fact, she had been so troubled that she had some sort of seizure. She had nearly dropped from the peculiar chair she had been sitting in when I entered her room. The unripe mind of the boy I had been soaked up the dreadful image and let it scar its way into my brain forever.

"Her brain was also injured. She speaks very little, and most of the time she has difficulty understanding what we want to tell her, but she is not crazy, Charlotte. My Mom is still in there."

My head fell against the headrest, and a harsh breath left my lungs in a rush. My insides twisted, and the ache was searing and vicious, much like a razor that slipped under my skin and cleaved my veins open.

Charlotte unfastened her safety belt and crawled into my lap, wrapping her hands around my head and nestling me tightly to her chest. She didn't speak as harrowing sobs wracked my body, but in the warmth of her embrace, I found all the comfort I needed.

I grieved and panted for breath, and through it all, I almost wished I could have cried. Yet, no more tears left my eyes. I had flooded universes with my tears. I had no more to spill.

"She needs around the clock care," I explained. "The fact that she cannot speak properly or call for help if she needs it makes it very difficult to leave her unsupervised. And I think, struggling every day to make herself understood would have been a painful fight, and she has already been hurt enough.

"So I can't blame Isaac that he took her to this place. He bought the manor and had it staffed and fully equipped for my mother's every need. At first, she was alone in there, and the doctors advised Isaac that she shouldn't be cut from the world so drastically, that interaction with people with similar conditions could be helpful. It was eight years after her accident that Isaac finally allowed for the east wing to host other patients as well. Like I said, providing for her and keeping the truth about her a secret has been the only good thing he has ever done."

The white door of the Victorian house opened, and a nurse dressed in pink floral scrubs stepped onto the porch, gazing a little surprised at how Charlotte was cocooned in my arms. Taking a deep breath, I straightened and steeled myself.

"It's the lack of trust that broke them and Isaac's arrogance that destroyed my mother," I said, staring deeply into Charlotte's eyes. "You have to trust me, Charlotte. I don't need you to always agree with me, but I need you to trust me even when we are at odds."

"I trust you," Charlotte promised, stroking the hair out of my face, then sucking my lips between hers in a long, fiery kiss.

She didn't understand the desperate, bottomless need I had for her complete, unrestrained trust. She didn't understand, not yet, but she was going to.

Charlotte rotated in my lap and hopped out of the car first, then taking her hand and lacing my fingers with hers, I joined her in the driveway. The nurse smiled encouragingly as we climbed the short flight of stairs that led to the porch and eyed Charlotte with an examining look that wasn't actually prying.

"Hello, Khloe. How are you today?"

"Very well, thank you," she replied brightly. "I see you have brought a friend."

Khloe was a petite woman who sheltered in her small, slender frame herculean strength and an unwavering will. With sandy blonde hair, a sharp and slightly long nose, and eyes so dark they were almost black, the nurse did not embody a staggering beauty, but that sincere ever-present smile of hers breathed a sort of radiant charm into her features that few people had.

She never complained and never let sadness creep past her resplendent grin. She was the sunshine in a facility where reasons for grief and despondency abounded, and because of that, she was Mom's favorite nurse and therefore, mine.

"It was about time," I said, glancing fondly at Charlotte.

She blushed, shaking Khloe's hand more hesitantly than she usually did, and greeted her in a small voice that made her seem younger than she really was. I wrapped my arm around her waist and kissed her temple just as Khloe winked and opened the manor's door to let us in.

"How is she today?" I asked, bracing myself for an answer that was not always favorable.

Khloe led us to the west wing where my mother lived with the sure step of someone who crossed the same distance on a daily basis. Her stride never faltered, and her smile never left her face as she answered.

"A little better than yesterday, but she is still rather agitated."

It wasn't uncommon for my mother to be agitated, but I still found myself asking, "Why?"

Khloe kept walking, but her features tightened, and the corners of her mouth dipped downward in a disapproving contortion that I had yet to see on her. My hold on Charlotte's hand tightened until I heard her gasping. My heart started pounding a dangerous warning in my chest.

"Khloe, do you need to tell me something?" I demanded roughly, all but growling.

"Your father visited her yesterday morning," she answered cautiously, her eyes shifting away before she could witness the rage that took hold of me. "Her disposition has been hectic ever since."

My whole body turned to stone. Isaac and I had an unspoken arrangement. He stayed away from my mother, and I didn't completely forget he was my father and make him regret the day he was born. He strayed from that arrangement now and then, and every time he did, things did not end up well.

Charlotte massaged my back, kneading knots out of stiff muscles. Gradually, my nerves settled, and my breath regained its normal, controlled rhythm.

"Would it be alright if we saw her?" I asked Khloe, and only when her soothing smile fluttered across her face, did I realize how nervous I had been.

Khloe placed long, bony fingers on my arm and ushered Charlotte and me toward my mother's door.

"She loves whenever you come. It would do her good."

"Thank you," I sighed then looked down at Charlotte for confirmation that she was ready.

She smiled, a nervous tension etched on her features, but it was affection and enthusiasm that prevailed in her gaze. She tightened her fingers around mine and nodded bravely then turned to face the slightly open door.

"I'll leave you to it," Khloe said and hurried down the hallway that connected the west wing to the rest of the building.

Chopin's *Joie de Vivre* flowed from wireless speakers placed all around the ample room. Mom's chair faced the glass wall that looked over an English landscape garden, and her fingers moved slowly over the leather armrest, with the same grace I supposed she would have embraced if she had played the piano herself.

Where a door was opened, the curtains coiled and shivered as fresh, salty air filtered inside. Mom absorbed it greedily, with eyes closed and chin held high. If she heard our approaching footsteps, she made no gesture of acknowledgment. Sinking to my knee, I waited for the song to end then bowed and kissed her hand.

"How are you today, my princess?"

"Ma-argh-kus," Mom croaked and smiled, and just like that, all the hurt and the anger disappeared.

Everything was peaceful and uncomplicated when we were together. I didn't have to be strong or defiant or rebellious. I didn't have to pretend when I was with her. I only had to be her boy. I only had to love her, and that was the only thing that came naturally. Or it had been the only one until my heart learned to love somebody new.

"Mom, I'd like you to meet someone." I murmured and stroked her soft, ageless cheek. "She is very important to me, just like you are."

I held my hand for Charlotte, who walked closer, one small step at a time. Her bottom lip was between her teeth, and her eyes crinkled at the corners with a cautious smile as I sat her on the cream leather footstool facing Mom.

The two women analyzed each other, chocolate eyes meeting hazel in a tangle of sifting glances. Eventually, their faces broke into genuine smiles. While they silently became acquainted with each other, I sat at their feet, marveling at their beauty and my good fortune of holding the affection of such angelic, softhearted women.

"I'm Charlotte, ma'am," Charlotte said simply and covered my mom's hands instead of a handshake.

"No," Mom gurgled and gave a soft shake of her head.

Charlotte retracted her hands like something had burned her, and those soft brown eyes turned hurt and uncertain.

"No," Mom repeated, glancing at Charlotte's hands then at the quiver of her lips, which she disguised in a taut line that curved slightly downward at the corners.

When Charlotte looked at me for guidance, she looked so adorably clueless, that I almost bent to kiss the worry away.

"She doesn't like to be called *ma'am*," I explained with a grin. "And she doesn't like that you let go of her hands."

"Oh," Charlotte breathed appeased and cupped my mom's hands again. Mom smiled and blinked approvingly, and so did Charlotte.

"Jackie," Mom instructed, with a wise look about her.

"Jackie it is then," Charlotte agreed and stroked her hands like they had known each other for a lifetime.

Undoubtedly, Mom felt better. I could tell by the discreet widening of her eyes and her smiling mouth that remained mostly quiet, but in its silence, it still participated in the conversation. Those were little gestures, but they were indicative of her understanding what Charlotte and I so enthusiastically told her.

We gave her the edited account of how we met and what

happened in our lives in the short time since then, excluding the part Kai had played that first Friday night or the treacherous waters we waded in because of Jack Stewart's case.

"You look happy," I told Mom after Charlotte and I finished our recount. Mom nodded slowly and pointed to me, which meant that she knew how happy Charlotte made me and in return she was happy.

Khloe came in just as the music stopped again. She went about her business as if nothing out of the ordinary was taking place, but as she administered Mom's late morning pills and helped her sip from her mug of tea, I could see the furtive smiling glances she was trying to hide.

"All done," Khloe said, fondly pinching Mother's cheek. "Now, let's brush this gorgeous hair of yours, Jackie."

Mom stiffened and started shaking her head. Charlotte stood to her feet and intercepted Khloe.

"May I?" she asked, holding out her hand for the brush Khloe had just picked up from a nightstand.

"Of—course—" Khloe said, slightly hesitant, but definitely pleased with the outcome.

Mom and Charlotte smiled at each other, and I found myself turning away in an attempt to hide the raw emotion in my eyes. There was a tightness that clawed at my throat and a heaviness that seemed to expand within my ribcage, but the sensation was not unpleasant. It was an aching kind of pleasure, an unbearable load of relief that came so unexpectedly that it proved to be overwhelming.

I fixed the audio system and replayed *Joie de Vivre*, Mom's favorite, then leaning against a windowsill, I watched them.

"You are so very beautiful," Charlotte was telling Mom.

Mom smiled wistfully. She directed her gaze out the window, out of the confines of her body, and back to a time when she was happy and glorious and extolled.

Charlotte brushed her long hair, touching reverently the white threads mingling with her thick, hazelnut curls. When she finished getting all the tangles out, she weaved Mom's mane into an elaborate French braid that she tied with a lilac bow made of satin ribbon. Gently, she placed the braid over Mom's shoulder and pressed a quick kiss on top of her head.

"Thank you," Charlotte mouthed when I caught her eye.

"I love you," I mouthed back, and she blushed then looked away.

Mom became sleepy soon after, and although she wasn't quite pleased to see us leave, she grudgingly complied with her favorite nurse's command. Khloe returned and shooed us as sternly but just as kindly as she had received us.

I was holding the door for Charlotte when her hand slipped from mine, and she took a step backward, closer to my mom.

"Can I?" she asked softly, a little uncertain.

I nodded although I wasn't exactly sure what she wanted to do. Charlotte returned to my mother and knelt, cupping her cheek with a gentleness so immensely affectionate as if Jacqueline King was her own mother. She gestured and whispered animatedly but quietly enough so I didn't hear a word. After a few moments, Mom broke into the most brilliant smile I had ever seen.

Standing and blowing Mom a kiss, Charlotte returned to me. A weight I hadn't been aware existed lifted from her shoulders, and she seemed carefree as she walked by my side. Even the tense frown that used to knit her brows was gone, and her countenance resembled the sated look that danced on her face after we made love.

"What was that all about?"

"Something that I needed her to know," Charlotte smiled and kissed my lips softly, as softly as she had handled my mom.

After we left, Charlotte withdrew and became utterly quiet. I imagined there were a lot of things she had to understand and adjust to, so I made an effort to give her the time and space to process everything. When all of a sudden she seemed to be suffocating and started grabbing at her chest, I looked over in horror.

"Stop the car, Marcus," she panted. "Just stop the car."

I hit the brake so hard as I halted the car on the shoulder of the road that gravel spit everywhere. Charlotte lounged forward, hanging with stiff fingers onto her seatbelt. I shoved the door open and circled the car to get to her side in a single, delirious heartbeat.

"What's going on?" I demanded, unfastening her seatbelt and pulling her out of the car and to my chest.

Her body was trembling, and her hands were ice cold as she kept panting for breath. The way she was panicking for no apparent reason and the lost look she gave me brought a heavy lump to my throat.

"Charlotte, please, talk to me," I begged, clutching her shoulders. Something was wrong, and my heart knew it as it kept pounding an insane rhythm in my chest.

"I love you," she burst, fisting unsteady fingers in my collar. "I love you so much that I can hardly bear it."

My sigh of relief was so loud that it drowned out her sobbing as well as the buzzing in my ears. My joy was so tremendous and so terribly soothing that I almost missed the total desperation in Charlotte's eyes.

Then she started crying in earnest, her hands still fisted around my jacket and her breathing still coming out in jagged bursts. She was on the brink of a precipice, and more than anything in my life, I wished she would just fall.

"But?" I asked, fearing the answer.

"There are no buts," Charlotte gasped and grabbed my head between her quivering hands. "I was afraid to say the words, but I can't hold them inside anymore. I love you, Marcus."

Her eyes were wild and passionate as they studied me. At that moment, I grasped that it hadn't been a weight that had lifted from her shoulders but a truth she had emboldened herself to accept. The undeniable truth of her heart.

I cupped her face and kissed her forehead, gentling the storm whirling in her blood. She sobbed and clung tighter to my collar, as scared of losing me as I was of losing her.

"Then why are you crying?"

"You don't understand," she cried and thrust a hand through her hair, ravaging the beauty of her braid. "You have invaded every fiber of my body, every little thought in my head, every corner in my heart. I don't know how to put a stop to how I feel. I don't know how to control my emotions. They are rampant, and they have taken over me altogether. My worst day gets better only because I know at the end of it, I will be back in your arms. You make me feel strong and safe. You make me feel confident and beautiful. And you make me utterly unable to picture my world without you in it. I don't know how to let go, Marcus. I'm falling so deeply for you that I know without a doubt that I won't be able to function without you. You have the power to break me, and I'm terrified."

"Oh, my sweet, sweet Charlotte."

I pulled her to my chest, hugging her tightly, perhaps tighter than I should have, but Charlotte welcomed the discomfort with arms wide open that clamped around my waist just as fiercely.

After a long time of just standing there on the side of the road, with the car parked askew and countless other vehicles speeding past us, I pushed her back enough so I could lean down and smash my mouth against her quivering lips. They welcomed my invasion with a lust so strong and contagious that the more I kissed them, the more addicted I became.

"I'm going nowhere," I promised, stroking her cheeks with my thumbs. "All those words you've said, I feel them too. You are etched in my heart. You are in my blood. You are permanent, Charlotte."

"I love you," she repeated. This time her voice was steady, and her words, although full of affection, didn't sound as desperate as before but precise and unwavering.

I let myself smile then, with relief and gratitude. I smiled until my cheeks hurt and my eyes watered. I smiled until she smiled back and kissed me so thoroughly that by the time the kiss was over both of us were flushed and breathless.

"I love you too, woman," I told her in a low growl. "But never scare me like that again."

She chuckled. The little minx chuckled and batted her eyelashes at me like the most innocent of creatures. Looking very proud of herself, she slid back in the car and nodded for me to follow.

WE WERE BACK AT THE forest house when I realized she

was once again too quiet and shooting out all kinds of nervous vibes that made me instantly frown and pull her into my lap.

"Is there anything else on your mind?" I asked, tipping my head back so I could fully see her face.

She smoothed the crinkles between my brows and resumed playing with her fingers. Picking at her nails, she considered whether or not she should tell me whatever was bothering her.

"Charlotte," I urged, raising both eyebrows and pulling at her lower lip in an attempt to make her speak.

"I was thinking that since we are not hiding anymore..." she said softly, trailing off and gazing at me from under her thick, dark lashes.

"That was never really my intention," I interrupted.

Charlotte immediately cast me a reproachful look then shook her head gently, making the curls framing her face bounce with the motion.

"Because you are reckless and arrogant and fail to consider the consequences," she said sternly and with a touch of bossiness.

"Because you are too important to me and deserve much more than a man who does not dare to take any risks needed to have you."

"Not a little boy after all," she murmured with a coy smile and flushed as I arranged her weight in my lap and made her aware of the evidence a little boy could not provide.

"Agreed," I grinned while she missed a breath and struggled to find a better sitting position, one that wouldn't make her body temperature skyrocket.

"So since we are not hiding anymore, are you willing to be my plus-one?" she asked, her brown eyes wide and expectant.

"Always." My answer was vehement, and so was my possession of her body as she kept struggling in my arms. "No other man will escort you anywhere else as long as I breathe."

She gasped loudly and shut her eyes so tightly that her lashes caressed the rosy tops of her cheeks. I brushed my lips against the heated skin of her face, breathing in her fire and letting it consume me from the inside out.

"You do realize that the more you struggle, the more you arouse both of us, don't you?"

Charlotte pulled sluggish eyelids open then watched me lustfully, with a focused gaze baring me of clothes and secrets until I was left raw under her voracious mouth. I caught her between my chest and the smooth cushions of the sofa, groaning as she arched to alleviate the aching in her breasts.

"It's a black-tie event," she muttered on a sharp intake of breath.

"Any special occasion?" I breathed as I drew an earlobe in my mouth and nipped on it gently.

It could have been a carnival for all I cared. My unrelenting attention belonged wholly to Charlotte and her exposed body waiting avidly to be brought over the edge.

"You can say that, but since you are so keen on taking risks, let's make it a surprise."

She gave me a grin full of mischief, and after an incredulous look of my own and a menacing growl, I grinned as well. If she wanted to provoke me, then I might as well let her feel the full extent of the outcome.

Chapter 37

Charlotte

S pending five interrupted days at Marcus's forest house was like stepping into our own nirvana. Nothing touched us but the firestorm we provoked, and we did provoke it until we collapsed lax and breathless and nearly incoherent with pleasure.

I still felt deliciously sore and much too aware of Marcus's pull as I placed a small, dark box in his lap. I watched him fervently, a little too fervently, absorbing the shimmering blue of his eyes and the sharp contour of his lips, those lips that worked miracles and drove me insane, kiss after tormenting kiss.

Marcus winked, reading my thoughts and my hunger with a sort of ease that both scared and aroused me further.

He was breathtaking, dressed in a black tuxedo with shawl lapels and matching pants that hugged him tightly, showcasing the virile power under the silk garment. His white shirt had dark pearl buttons that I had fastened myself after indulging in the exquisite feel of his perfectly hard abdomen.

Putting on his rectangular diamond cufflinks, Marcus observed the box in his lap. "A gift?"

He stared suspiciously at the box then placed it on the bed and stood up to knot his bowtie in a diamond point shape.

"Not exactly. It's part of your attire."

I licked my lips, and when the sight of him proved too much, I turned to the mirror to put on my teardrop diamond and amethyst earrings. The jewelry contrasted splendidly with the soft lavender of the mermaid gown I was wearing. I smoothed the lace with my palms and applied a fresh coat of lipstick before turning around and smashing right against Marcus's chest.

"So it's not far from a carnival," he muttered under his breath and hovered his mouth above mine, a brash tease that almost made me whimper. He straightened with a crooked smile that became a full laugh when he caught sight of my glare and heard my groan.

Taking the filigreed silver mask from its silk wrappings and discarding the box on the dresser, he tried it on with economical grace. I sucked in a breath and massaged slowly at my unbridled heart.

"It's a masquerade ball. You'll love it," I said, winking and taking tremendous pride in being able to tease him back.

No matter how much he had insisted during the past days and how artfully he had played with my senses, he hadn't gained the leverage to force me to tell him who was throwing the party we were supposed to attend or what the event was about.

When we finally arrived at the *Exterus*, a rooftop restaurant that had been fully rented and decorated for the occasion, and the whole mystery was dispelled, Marcus looked downright incredulous.

I nudged him to don his mask again, and I tied mine as well, which was the feminine counterpart of his own. While the only adornment to his mask was the elegant filigree, mine was a more complex work of art.

It had almond-shaped holes to reveal my eyes and tiny diamonds embossed on the upper lids. Threads of white gold curled on one side, all the way to my forehead like a feather blown by the wind and frozen in place.

"You remember Rachel and Ethan," I told Marcus, waving to the two of them. "They decided to renew their vows instead of divorcing."

"And since we've done it so many times before, we thought we should have a theme on this occasion," Ethan muttered as he walked arm in arm with his former, present, and future wife. He cast a dubious look at his own jet-black mask, which proved to whoever had entertained any doubts that the whole idea had been Rachel's all along. "Maybe it will bring us luck."

Rachel elbowed him in the ribs and dashed into Marcus's arms with an enthusiasm that made me chuckle and question her sobriety. She wore a fabulous A-line dress made of cream tulle and lace, with a square neckline that was embroidered with tiny pearls which weaved around her shoulders in delicate, shiny straps. The laurel leaf tiara she wore atop her head shone against coppery strands that had been curled and were hanging loosely around her face.

"Oh, Marcus," she gushed and hugged him tightly. Noble features had been enhanced by the tiniest bit of makeup, offering her an even lovelier appearance. Marcus caught her awkwardly with a huff and a scowl, but Rachel couldn't care less. "You worked on all those divorce papers in vain."

"Does she suffer from multiple personalities?" Marcus mouthed over Rach's head, looking adorably helpless in her tight embrace.

I imagined Rachel hadn't been so cheerful or friendly the first time they met. At the time, she had been dead set on divorcing Ethan although she had been secretly entertaining an idyll with him in the interim. She was volatile like the wind, but the love she had for her husband was the only constant in her life. No matter how viciously they quarreled, they didn't manage to stay away from each other for too long.

Ethan threw his head back and laughed. "She might."

"Don't get on my nerves," she growled.

Marcus caught my eye then rolled his own. He nodded toward Rachel like he wanted to say he was more familiar with the angry, unbalanced side of her than with the joyous woman who had just hugged him.

She and Ethan were superbly entertaining, but definitely an acquired taste, and while Marcus got used to them, he was an enjoyable sight of incredulity. To my complete amusement, he shuddered slightly. Then banding an arm around my waist, he pulled me flush against his side.

"I've got a feeling I'll like your partner, Lottie," Ethan said and clapped Marcus's shoulder. "Come, have a drink. Join the party. We have games and a prize after midnight."

The thought of nuptial parties and mysterious games caused goose bumps to pop on my skin, but after gritting my teeth and stiffening my spine, I forced myself to put Jack Stewart and everything involved with him out of my mind.

Rachel and Ethan led the way to an open bar, tastefully adorned with pastel colored roses and big, white candles that flickered gracefully in the otherwise darkening evening.

Ethan whispered something in her ear, and Rachel laughed, tipping her head back to kiss her husband's lips. The chaste kiss, however, was coupled with an agile hand that slid from Ethan's waist to his butt. Naughty fingers pinched his derriere, which earned her a growl of protest. Rachel glanced back and winked at me from beneath a cream, lace mask, looking very pleased with herself.

"Lottie?" Marcus inquired, distracting me from Rachel's antics.

My grin died down, replaced by what I supposed were annoyingly deep red stains on my cheeks. "That's the disadvantage of keeping friends from childhood."

"Why the blush?" He touched my cheek with the back of his index finger and ended the sweet caress with a lingering thumb against my lips.

"It just sounds girly."

"Oh, Charlotte. You are all woman to me."

His eyes smoldered, and so did my insides. There were a thousand things he wanted to do to me and a thousand more I would have gladly let him, but in the end, he settled for a searing, knee-buckling kiss.

Someone from very close by cleared his throat, and Marcus reluctantly let go of me, but not before he whispered against my lips, "I'm not nearly done, sugar."

"Get a room," Logan, Christina, and my mother cried in unison.

That the first two were making an overt remark concerning the electrifying passion between Marcus and me was no surprise, but that Mom joined them left me gaping and staring dumbfounded.

"Mom," I groaned while Marcus grinned and shook Logan's hand.

"Oh, don't get shy now. You weren't shy at all earlier."

"I need something to drink," I said and waved to the barman, who was bare-chested except for a waistcoat, certainly another one of Rachel's great ideas.

"Mojitos?" Mom asked excitedly.

"Are you sure? No brandy tonight?" I teased.

She made such a funny face, entirely inappropriate for her age and social status that I burst out laughing and was quickly followed by Christina, who was so fond of Lauren that she rarely sided with me against her.

The bartender took our orders, and he prepared our drinks while complimenting my mom's pink gown and throwing covert glances at Christina, which proved to be more forthright than he intended. A menacing sound rumbled in Logan's chest just as Ethan took the stage at the center of the restaurant and caught our collective attention.

He thanked the guests for attending, again, then professed his love for Rachel, again, then he warned he might screw things up, again, and eventually he announced the start of the games he had told us about earlier.

It turned out they had hidden clues all around the restaurant, and whoever pieced the puzzle together first was going to win the grand prize after midnight. Knowing them, I would bet the prize was some sexual toy or embarrassing moment that I could really do without.

"Do we want to play?" Marcus asked cautiously, looking at the excited crowd that had actually started searching for clues.

"No," everyone in our corner shouted, then we resumed a pleasant conversation that flowed smoothly and was full of laughter and harmless teasing.

"Take it easy," Marcus murmured against my temple when the bartender placed a second glass of mojito on my napkin. "We're going to have a very long night."

The heat that coursed through my veins like molten lava had nothing to do with the rum in my drink. I bit my lip and inhaled deeply. His dazzlingly masculine scent hinted at the primal beast beneath the luxurious clothes, and something inside me started throbbing with desire.

"Let's dance," he drawled, his voice low and raspy and dripping with red-hot promise.

Mom was stolen by the bride's parents at their table, and Christina and Logan mingled, probably playing Rachel and Ethan's game, contrary to their earlier refusal.

I watched Marcus with bated breath as I slid my hand into his and let him draw me to his savagely powerful chest. His arms went around my waist, and my hands locked around his neck as we swayed on the gentle rhythms of Lara Fabian's *Adagio*.

He was normally stunning, but with the added mystery of the silver mask that hid half of his face, he was downright devastating. His lips seemed redder and his eyes a deeper blue, like the ocean on a sunny day. Flawless skin, except for the few scratches he had gotten himself at the last race, pulled tightly against a sharp, freshly shaven jaw that rolled with hardly restrained force.

"You should have let me cover this," I muttered, stroking the fading red signs on his jaw.

Marcus looked down at me and growled, just like he had done when I had determinedly walked up to him earlier at the forest house with concealer in one hand and a blender in the other.

"Men don't wear makeup," he grunted.

"You'd be surprised," I laughed.

He shivered and wrinkled his nose, acting adorably willful. Unable to contain myself, I rose on my tiptoes and pressed a kiss to a small, pinkish scar under his jaw, right where his pulse thrummed the most hypnotic songs of all. I surrendered to him completely, and like everything else Marcus did, he twirled me around, then caught me between strong arms with graceful ease and innate firmness.

I had been so enthralled by Marcus and so deeply attuned to him, with my head resting against his heart and my hands randomly caressing his jaw and the nape of his neck that I had to do a double take before I recognized the red-haired silhouette that slinked at the skirts of the crowd. I knew she had realized that I had seen her when emerald irises stood out against the glistening white of her eyes.

"Elana," I breathed, the word drowned out as the song reached its peak and Lara Fabian's voice boomed through the speakers.

"What was that?" Marcus asked.

The faraway smile in his gaze shattered as I disentangled my arms from his neck and hurriedly stepped away.

"Charlotte, where are you going? The ceremony is about to begin."

"I'll be right back," I told him, placating his advance with a gesture of my hand. "Wait here."

He tried to follow, but the movement was too fast and too brusque, and although he had never complained, his leg was still hurting after the debacle at the races. He winced, and his hand darted to clasp his thigh as he pinned me with knitted brows and questioning eyes.

I hated to leave him like that in the middle of the crowd, taking advantage of his injury, but if he learned of my intentions, he would have never let me follow the woman who was making a fast escape down the emergency stairs.

I discarded my stilettos right before taking the emergency exit then ran after her as fast as my bare feet could carry me. The blood in my body seemed to have gathered in my skull where it created a tempest that beat against the confines of bone and flesh and made it impossible to hear anything except its maddening, relentless pounding.

"Elana, wait," I shouted.

She halted in the middle of the corridor, and only after she hesitantly turned around, I slowed down my pace and allowed myself a full unsteady breath. I had anticipated this meeting for weeks now and had considered so many questions that I was sure she had the answer to, but now, face to face with Elana Beckham, I could only stare and wonder why she had followed me here.

My heart twitched uncomfortably in my chest, but I convinced myself the only cause for that was Marcus's absence. I had grown to depend on his protection, and for some reason, the thought didn't seem as bothersome as it used to. When you loved, you had to offer protection as well as know when to seek and accept it from your significant other.

"Elana, please, talk to me," I pressed and inched a step closer.

She looked around uncertainly, but thankfully, she didn't flee. I nodded encouragingly, taking yet another step closer, and gauged her appearance. She wore the *Exterus* staff uniform, which looked a size or two bigger than her slender frame.

She had dark strawberry blonde hair and green eyes that were loaded with trepidation. She seemed a little too pale and a little too raw-boned to be traditionally beautiful, but she had a reserved appeal about her that made her agreeable.

Her hair cascaded down her shoulders, all the way to the middle of her back, and the tangled, almost greasy strands were the only indication that she might not have enjoyed a proper bath in as many days as I had been looking for her.

"You are on the run," I noted. "But you don't have to run anymore. I know you have contacted me before. You can trust me, Elana. You can tell me what you know about Jennifer's death. That's why you are here, isn't it?"

Elana shook her head, hugging herself and scanning the empty corridor through frantic eyes. I was afraid if I raised my voice, she would set off running again.

"Coming here was a mistake," she muttered.

"No," I said sternly, walking determinedly to her and gently clasping her shoulders. I needed the connection to make sure she wasn't going to suddenly disappear. "Coming here was the bravest thing you could possibly do. Tell me what you know about that night, Elana."

"That it didn't go down like Jennifer had planned it." Her voice was flat and her tone disapproving.

"What's that supposed to mean?"

"That night was supposed to be her golden ticket to paradise," Elana explained and brushed my hands off her shoulders to pace up and down the narrow width of the hallway. "Instead she was injected with cocaine and silenced, just like Rheya. I'm not going to be the next one."

"Do you have proof of this?"

The shivering, the furious beating of my heart, even the blood rushing to my ears, all settled down into an oddly detached numbness as my grimmest theory was confirmed.

"Dumb me. Why didn't I think about taking some snapshots while Jennifer was murdered?" Elana shouted and made a face that hinted at her fickle disposition. "And before you ask, no, she had never done drugs, and she wasn't doing drugs then because she couldn't afford to put the baby in danger. She was pregnant."

"She loved the baby, that's understandable, but I already knew she was pregnant."

Elana stopped the pacing that had quickly become disturbing and fixed me with an unexpectedly sickened look. She rolled her eyes as if she was having a conversation with a stupid little child and had already grown tired of it.

"She loved the fortune the baby was going to provide."

My eyebrows lifted so high that I could feel the crinkles forming across my forehead. "I don't understand," I mumbled.

"Jack was not the father of the baby. Mitch Stewart was."

Her words, partly revolted, partly resentful, literally sent me staggering. I leaned against the wall for support, looking at Elana in shock and horror. She scoffed then resumed her pacing, every now and then glancing at the exit door that led back to the restaurant.

"The night of the party, Jen told him and asked him for a lot of money to keep quiet. It seems like the mayor didn't take well to blackmail. I told her, but she wouldn't listen."

Mitch Stewart was in full campaign to become Senator, so if Jennifer had made good on her threats, the ensuing scandal would have ruined the mayor's family as well as his chances to win the elections. Although such a drastic way of having her removed from his life was repulsive, I had to admit that it made sense.

"Elana, that is a serious allegation to make," I finally managed to say on a shaky breath.

"I have proof," she snapped and whirled around. Scared eyes

turned stonily vehement.

"Then if you come forward—"

"Oh, you got me all wrong," she chuckled bitterly. When she vigorously shook her head, her hair fell over her shoulders to reveal a peculiarly bruised neck. I frowned but didn't have the chance to comment on it as she fervently continued, "I am not interested in making Jennifer's killer pay. I'm interested in staying alive. So let the mayor know that I have copies of Jennifer's medical records including the baby's DNA. If something were to happen to me, those records would become public."

"Elana, I'm not the enemy here," I pleaded. "I want to help you. I want justice as much as you do. If you don't come forward, you'll be running and looking over your shoulder your entire life."

"I'd rather run than lay in a coffin five-feet underground."

"I can protect you."

"How can you protect me if you can't even protect yourself?" she shrieked out.

At first, I noticed the shrill quality of her voice, which I suspected was caused by fear rather than being her natural timbre. After a long moment of just staring thunderstruck at her, I realized what she alluded to and why she was in possession of such information.

"It was you that night in the parking lot at the Willard Intercontinental?" I gasped. "Did you attack Vincent Cole to save me, Elana?"

Elana let out a breath, then she slid down the wall until she plopped on the granite floor. Sitting cross-legged, with her head propped in one hand and her eyelids almost drifting closed, she looked young, exhausted, and afraid, but what made me crouch next to her was the lonely, desolate character of her gaze.

"Look, I'm not blaming you," I whispered, touching her hand tentatively. Her skin was chapped and cold. "If anything, I'm grateful. Thank you, Elana."

"It was not Vincent Cole," she muttered without meeting my inquisitive stare.

I let out an exasperated sigh and rolled my eyes. "Elana, please, I know it was not Jase Parker."

"It wasn't Jase Parker, either."

"Pardon?"

She took a deep breath, and when she let it out, she looked like it pained her. "It was—"

I didn't hear whether or not she finished her sentence. A massive, earsplitting noise whipped my eardrums so violently that I could swear something had popped in my head, then the floor and the walls and the ceiling quaked and crackled. I fell on my side with my hands pressed against my ears, and my eyes shut as my head hit the ground.

Before I got back on my feet, the air turned very hot. Then I noticed the smell. I could taste it on the roof of my mouth, a sickening stench of burning plastic with overtones of cement powder and chemicals.

It hadn't been an earthquake.

It had been an explosion.

"Oh my God, it's them," Elana cried and fisted her hands in her dirty hair. "They're trying to kill us."

For the first time, I looked at her and considered that she might have gone crazy, that she had been crazy all along, and that I had made a grave mistake by seeking her out. Then I followed her petrified gaze, and *I* felt crazy. Crazy with dread.

The emergency door that led to the restaurant was blocked with a thick metal bar where it hadn't been there before, and dark smoke was filtering through the cracks between the door and its frame.

"We are not alone," I breathed and looked around, but apart from the thickening smoke, the corridor was still empty.

"Of course, we're not," Elana spat, gesturing to the metal bar that hadn't been there before. "They were watching. They are always watching. They know. We have to leave. Now."

From upstairs, a second smaller explosion reverberated across the walls, followed by the smashing of glass and the cracking of wood. And then I heard the screams.

They were terrible and frightened, and the helplessness made me choke and blubber. Everyone I loved was in there, and with them were the flames.

"Oh no, no, no, no," I chanted and sprang to my feet, horror and despair in my eyes.

I knew the fire gained strength by the smothering smoke that grew thick and dark and invaded the entire hallway. It was pure adrenaline rush that kept me standing and functioning. My eyes smarted and watered, but I plunged right through the thick veil of smoke.

"Please, don't let them be hurt," I cried and pleaded and walked faster.

Marcus. Mom. Marcus. Christina. Logan. Marcus. Marcus. Rachel. Ethan. Marcus. Marcus. Marcus.

Their names were a litany that kept throbbing in my head, but I couldn't voice them. If I entertained the idea that something might have happened to any of them, I was going to lose the remaining drop of sanity I had left.

If something happened to them, I wouldn't be able to bear it, but most frighteningly of all, if something happened to *him*, I didn't think I could survive it.

I gripped the metal bar blocking the door, but as soon as I laid hands on it, I pulled away, hissing in pain. The metal was burning hot, and so was the air coming from the restaurant.

Stiff fingers wrapped around my elbow and yanked me backward. "What are you doing? Are you insane? We have to leave."

"I can't leave. Everyone is in there. We have to help them."

I ripped my dress and pulled it taut around my hands like bandages, then I grabbed the metal bar again and channeled all my strength into dislodging the damn barrier. Someone was banging and scratching at the door, but the bar didn't budge, and the screams turned louder.

I became desperate, my motions wild as uncontrollable sobbing tore my chest apart. Then I became hopeless, and my knees almost buckled under my weight.

Desperation was empowering—it drove me mad, but it spurred me into action. Hopelessness, on the other hand, was paralyzing. It put an end to a tragedy that hadn't been written yet, that I had to avoid, that—

"Charlotte? Are you there?"

"Marcus?" I shouted back, so relieved to hear his voice that fresh tears burst from my eyes. They were hot as the fire burning on the other side of that door.

"Sugar, tell me you are alright."

"It's—it's a bar blocking the door. I can't get it off. It's not working."

"Okay, look around. Can you see something you can use to knock it loose? A chair or hammer or a crowbar?"

I spun around and halted mid-sob as I stumbled into Elana. Disbelieving emerald eyes examined my unhinged expression for an infinite heartbeat, then she looked around as if pondering her options. Exhaling exasperatedly and rolling her eyes, she dragged me forward.

"Damn it," she growled. "Come on, I know a way."

Elana tugged me through the unbreathable air and into a room to the right side of the emergency door. It looked like a storage room. There was a vent hole in the ceiling that must have led upstairs to the kitchen of the Exterus. Narrow windows were placed high, close to the ceiling, and a stepladder was propped up against the wall.

"Good, this is good," I muttered, looking around for something, anything I could use to smack that bar off the door. Anything that could help me get everyone out of that burning restaurant. "Elana, help me look for—"

"I'm so sorry," she whined, sounding strange and unstable.

"What are you talking about?" I rasped. "Look for something to knock that bar down."

"I'm sorry," Elana repeated quietly. "It was the only way I had to protect myself."

I felt that nagging ache in my chest return, which only intensified when I glanced at the woman and found her huddling in a corner. Her arms were wrapped around herself, and she was shaking her head violently. Her splendid emerald eyes appeared bloodshot and goggled, and bitter tears were coursing down her cheeks.

"What have you done?" I demanded on a cough.

She stilled, and her eyes shifted behind me. The plagued

contortion of her face turned deadpan, and whatever light she had had in her eyes was suddenly snuffed out. Then, the door of the storage room was slammed shut with destructive intent. I jumped, swallowing heavily and spun around.

The color drained from my face. Cameron Drake stood rigidly with his feet planted wide apart and his eyes roaming the storage room. He was holding a gun in one hand and a black square device with a red button in his other. He looked poised and detached despite the circumstances.

My thoughts reeled at the sight of him, but the primal part of me was suddenly very alert and immediately recognized the danger.

"Huh," he grunted when his frighteningly centered gaze stopped on a ramshackle cabinet. "We won't be needing this."

Drake launched to the sideboard, and with a firm shove, he knocked it right in front of the closed door. The raucous screech made me cringe. A cloud of dust merged with the dense, stifling vapors coming from the vent that led to the restaurant above, briefly cloaking the man from view.

I fooled myself that there was no danger, that if I turned around, I would find a way to get out.

"What are you doing? How are we getting out? You promised, you promised if I did this, you'd let me go."

Elana clung to Drake as if he was her lifeline, and her wild eyes danced desperately between him and the collapsed cabinet blocking the entrance.

Drake's sneer was cunning and merciless. He had hurled the cabinet down in front of the door not only to block our way to safety but also to prevent any potential rescue from the outside. As my gaze raked over him, his feat as well as his unruffled demeanor became painfully clear.

We were trapped in a small room, with fire raging above us and toxic fumes cramming the space, making it very difficult to breathe, and the only way out was blocked now. But Drake had never intended to use that door to escape.

He wore a black jumpsuit with leather reinforcements for his knees and back. Elastic fabric wrapped around his wrists and ankles and curled up around his throat, finishing with a hood that could have hidden his face if necessary. He carried on his shoulder what looked like a backpack, but was, in fact, his parachute.

His head snapped to Elana, and the motion caused the steel buckles on his full-body harness to clink. His lip curled over his teeth, and his eyes narrowed disdainfully at the trembling hands of the woman who was still tugging at him hysterically.

"It was so sweet of you to believe me," he mocked and shoved at Elana's grabbing hands so viciously that she went teetering to the ground.

My lungs squeezed out a tension loaded breath as Elana's body toppled against a frail working table, sending tools and glass clattering everywhere. Under the weight of her body, the wood gave way, and it collapsed in a pile of splinters and rusty metal. Elana groaned, a low, breathless sound that spoke of pain and fear.

Her fingers constricted around her torso, just under her left breast where a screwdriver had lodged deep between her ribs. Blood coated her hands, and pain tightened her features as she struggled for breath and started crying in earnest. I wanted to move, to run to her, and offer the little help I could, but my legs didn't seem to cooperate as my body stood frozen in the middle of the room.

Watching her curling into a tight ball on the floor and Drake towering maliciously over both of us, I realized what Elana had been about to say before the explosion. It had been neither Vincent Cole nor Jase Parker who attacked me. It had been Cameron Drake.

She had known that, and she had been foolish enough to believe his promises of clemency. She had made a deal with the devil to protect herself, and in return, it was going to cost us both our lives.

Drake's arm thrashed in the air like a whip, whacking the particles of dust out of his way as he stepped closer. His eyes were cold and punishing when they finally found me, and when he smiled, he appeared cruel and menacing.

I wasn't sure if my lungs still functioned or if my heart still pumped blood. There was a disconcerting heaviness dragging me down as if molten lead was sluggishly rolling through me.

I brought my hand to my nape and gripped the flesh hard until my nails punctured the skin. I felt slickness under my fingertips and ice pervading my flesh.

"It's so nice to see you again, Charlotte," Drake drawled in what he certainly believed was his most seductive voice. The light flickered, creating a sinister image of Drake, who shuffled forward and gesticulated with his gun. "After how we parted the last time, I was not so sure that you'd be happy to see me."

Drake ducked to see my face and stomped like a child when all he found was contempt. I narrowed my eyes to keep the dizziness at bay and looked around for a way out, which made him chuckle and throw his hands in the air.

"Now, don't be sullen," he said. "I made all this effort to bring you here, and you already want to leave? Shame on you, Charlotte."

"You're deranged," I coughed.

"Mouth, please. It doesn't suit a lady to speak so rudely."

His manner was so polite and collected, much like it had been the night of the Aequitas Awards, and I wondered, with a suffocating load of frustration, how I could have missed the signs. How could I have missed the crazed glint in his eyes or the danger he emanated like a poisonous, invisible twin?

Drake followed my gaze to Elana, who was whimpering and clutching tighter at her wound. "Oh yes, fascinating conversation you two had. Not quite what is expected from defending counsel, or better said, former defending counsel. But then again, you were never interested in defending Jack, were you?"

"I was interested in the truth, and I think you are right. Jack needs to be defended—from you and his father."

My voice sounded stronger than I felt, a possible effect of the adrenaline rush still propelling me.

Drake shook his head and pursed his lips. "See, it's this exact attitude that brought you here. Elana, on the other hand, was smarter, but well, not smart enough."

At the sound of her name she whined and hugged her knees tighter with the little force left in her. She sensed Drake walking to her before she saw him and made a sound so terrifyingly pained that I shuddered in sympathy.

"I did say I would spare you," Drake told her, poking her legs with the tip of his shoe. "And I would have kept my promise if you had been wise enough to leave and skip the chit-chat."

I looked with eyebrows squished together and clouded vision from Drake to Elana's rocking body, wondering why she had gone to all the trouble of filling the gaps in the story if she had already planned to sell me to Drake. The taste of betrayal rankled like a savage insult in my brain, but the sight of her, terrified and hurt, didn't let me despise her.

"You seem confused," Drake muttered, spinning back to me so fast that my world spun with him. "Why did she tell you everything if she had already stabbed you in the back? Because she had already decided to trade your life for hers. That's what smart people do."

I shook my head vigorously, not sure whether to show my disagreement or disgust.

"Oh, don't give me that judgmental look," Drake complained. "Being a coward and staying alive is more productive than being brave and dead. What good does it do you to know the truth?"

Regrettably, Drake was right. Searching and finding the truth behind Jennifer Gunnar's death had brought me no benefits, yet I couldn't convince myself that bowing my head and mindlessly complying would have been the better option.

"But now that you possess this truth you have been avidly looking for, let's put the cards on the table. I didn't kill Jennifer Gunnar because she threatened the mayor's family and career with her unborn spawn, but because she was a gold-digger and a whore who deserved to die."

My nostrils stung, and my throat ached as I sucked in a breath. I moved a step back for every step forward that Drake took. With his eyes wholly concentrated on me and his nostrils flaring, he looked just like the sociopath he was.

"Come on, ask the question you are dying to ask. Ask me if I enjoyed it."

"You are a monster," I breathed and covered my mouth with both my hands.

"What did I say about that mouth of yours?" he barked and flung himself into me with such force that he knocked the air right out of my lungs.

I hated the shriek of fear that escaped the taut line of my lips and the maddened satisfaction that gleamed in his gaze. I hated how I cowered when his hand fisted in my hair, and he shoved his gun between my eyes. And I hated even more that my body failed me. My legs quivered, and my hands limply gripped the arm he used to restrain me.

"You should think twice before taunting me," Drake spat out each word, enforcing the threat and hatred behind them with a merciless shove of his gun against my forehead. "Now, ask me the damn question."

I flinched and shut my eyes as his snarl reverberated around the room. "Did—did you enjoy killing Jennifer?"

"Oh, damn, yes," he sighed heavily and looked as euphoric as a normal man would have after having an orgasm. "She was lucky number 33."

My eyes bulged, and my feet, although bare, wobbled and almost bent at the ankles. Jennifer hadn't been the only one. She had been the 33rd victim on a horrendously long list of fatalities.

"When she came into that room to find me sitting on the edge of the bed with a syringe between my fingers and a gun lying on the mattress, she was as surprised as you are right now. She begged, you know? She used her despicable child to try to save herself. I didn't like that, not one bit. And I didn't like either that I couldn't make her hurt for every little stupid thing she had done. The bruises would have messed everything up. The police had to believe that it had been a crime of passion, that Jase Parker killed Jennifer because he couldn't stand the idea that she would marry another man."

With the gun still pressed to my head and his hand pulling at my hair, Drake looked into the distance, almost nostalgically. He recollected the whole ordeal through the eyes of a serial killer, enjoying his crime but still considering ways of perfecting it, ways that might come in handy for his next crime.

"Then you came snooping around, asking the wrong questions and ruining my hard work," he snarled. "But you see, Charlotte, there will be no problem if you die with a few bruises and some broken bones because by the time they find you, they'll need to run your dental records to identify you."

I sniveled and braced myself for the impact of his strike, yet when he used the full force of his fisted hand coupled with the butt of his gun and hit me, I lost my balance and dropped like a lifeless puppet to the floor.

"You'll be number 35," Drake crooned and kicked me in the stomach.

I curled into a ball, exactly like Elana in the other corner of the room, and tried uselessly to get away from him. I crawled, ignoring the pain in my side and legs as shards and splinters and the cemented ground itself scraped at my skin. Drake kicked me again with all the anger he must have gathered ever since this nightmare began.

"Rheya was number 34," I moaned as he planted his foot in my stomach again.

"Smart girl," he laughed and clapped his hands mockingly.

The all-consuming pain of his onslaught, combined with the choking smoke drifting inside the building, made me gasp and convulse, unable to draw in oxygen. Then I saw the hammer seated a mere three feet from where I was tossing and turning like a wounded animal.

If only I could reach the handle, if only my fingers could wrap around it and hold tight just for a second. I only needed a second to swing the hammer at Drake's crotch, a blow that was certainly going to make him double over. I just needed a second of distraction, then this nightmare would be over.

But first I needed to reach it.

I slithered across the floor, my arm extended and my nails digging into the cement as my fingers groped for the hammer. My ribs ached with the movement, and my skin burned as fragments of dirt scratched it raw, but I forced myself to keep going.

"That would have been too easy, wouldn't it?" Drake ridiculed and placed his foot over my fumbling hand.

I lifted my eyes to a diabolical face screwed up with severe loathing and wondered how I could have ever considered him beautiful. Drake winked right before his foot pressed down on my hand, and the bones in my fingers crunched noisily in protest.

I screamed so loud that my anguished howl boomed long after

my jaw clenched, and my bones shattered. My small and ring finger hurt the worst like thick needles were inserted beneath my nails, right through my bones.

Drake chuckled.

The fluorescent lamps flickered again, then they were out with a sizzling cracking sound, leaving the room in shadows and lit only by a small poorly-functioning candle bulb that hung above a series of empty shelves.

"Charlotte," I heard Marcus's wild scream, and for the first time since I left his side on the dance-floor, I felt a glimmer of hope.

Once Drake had shut and blocked the door of the storage room, fear had been a constant clamor in my head, so loud and crippling that it had drowned out the screams and pleas for help and the crackling of fire from upstairs.

Now that Marcus's voice permeated the fear and agony, every sound, thought, and smell bombarded me with keen accuracy.

I propped my weight on my elbow and pushed myself against the ground, closer to the door. I was almost smiling as I opened my mouth to shout back, to tell him that I was locked inside with a murderer, to tell him to get everyone out, to save himself. But Drake sucked the hope and happiness out of everything. He hit my calf and tsked while shaking his head in disapproval.

"You don't want to do that," he cautioned. He sounded unflappable and sympathetic, but his counsel was the clever disguise of a menace. Drake dangled the small black device he was holding in his left hand and smirked. "One tiny twitch of my finger on this little, red button and he goes poof."

"You're not getting away with this. If you kill me, everything I know will be on Leon Holden's table by the morning."

Drake read right through my bluff and laughed. He circled me slowly, venom dripping from his gaze.

"Pathetic," he spat. "The most important piece of information you hold is right here." He gestured to himself and took an unflinching hold of his gun, training it at my head. "And we both know you are not getting out of this room to share it with the prosecutor or anyone else for that matter. So there's nothing you can threaten me with and nothing you can do to save yourself. I'm really sorry, Charlotte. If only you weren't so nosy and so stupid…We'd have made an exquisite couple."

I heard the furious roaring of the fire, and although dreadful, it was also comforting. I remembered the incandescent logs in the chimney of a Swiss chalet and the fire smoldering on a cold late night. I remembered the smell of freshly baked apple strudel and boiled cinnamon wine. I remembered peace, and I was dearly tempted to just close my eyes and let Fate have its way.

The flames kept crackling loudly, and the smoke threw the already dimly lit storage room into shadows. I glanced up at the ceiling just in time to see the vent grid blazing red, then a small explosion sent the grid to the ground like a projectile launched with the sole purpose of damaging everything in its path.

Elana, who I thought had already lost consciousness, hissed loudly just before I managed to roll over and out of the flaming grid's radius. The grate only grazed Drake's shoulder, but the collision had been so unexpected and so brutal that he fell to his side, cursing and snarling in pain. He cradled his shoulder, holding the gun awkwardly while completely forgetting about the black device he had used as a bargaining chip earlier.

I swiped the ground with my eyes and saw the small gadget flash a red light somewhere halfway between me and the blocked door. I lurched toward it, managing to prop my battered body on shaky, bruised hands and knees. If Drake couldn't detonate another bomb and no harm would come to Marcus and whoever was still in the building, I could scream for help, I could—

Slick fingers gripped my ankle and pulled hard enough for it to dislodge. My arms gave up, and my body crashed to the floor with a dull thud. I cried as my chin connected to the ground, and my teeth chattered.

"Where do you think you're going?" he demanded furiously as his fingers dug painfully into my ankle.

The vent hole spat flame after vicious flame, and the room started catching fire like a torch. Part of the ceiling crumbled down, pieces of concrete falling in a curtain of dust and ashes. The flames grew thick and merciless and scorched everything in their wake.

I looked in horror at the blazing inferno and struggled to pull myself to my feet. The firestorm had taken an ugly, painful form. And from its untamed flames stepped the perverted killer I had been hunting for. It was he who hunted me now, and he was ruthless.

Staggering and hunching in pain, Drake was no less lethal than he had been all this time, yet in his arrogance and physical agony, he'd granted me the only second of distraction I had needed.

I fished the revolver from the leather holster that was clasped around my thigh and forced my broken fingers to wrap around its handle. With every movement of my hand, it was like Drake was stepping on it all over again. But I had to learn to make the pain my dearest strength.

"Oh, that's unpredictable," Drake laughed as he watched my trembling hand aiming for him. "You want to shoot me with a toy and a broken hand?"

I nodded, not because he had expected an answer, but because I needed to believe that I could. While my right hand was severely hurt and my aim wavering, I knew it would have a more significant chance at succeeding than if I used my left one, which wouldn't be able to hit a target even if it were glued to it.

"Very nice, but useless, nonetheless."

With eyes full of hatred, Drake pointed his own gun at my head.

The thought that crossed my mind then was so ridiculous that it made me laugh. It was Friday. The story Marcus and I had written started on a Friday night, and sadly, it was about to end the same.

Two months was all we'd had, but I didn't regret one second of it. What I regretted was that the last face I saw was the one of a murderer instead of the face of the man I loved.

Drake kept his gun pointed at me and walked to the step ladder that led up to the windows. "Goodbye, Charlotte."

I didn't know who pulled the trigger first.

The revolver shook and fell from my hand, then the most excruciating pain warmed my chest. I gasped, one last toxic breath before I hit the ground and rolled listlessly to my back.

Someone screamed for help and glass rained down from above, but my attention was solely focused on the fire. It was wild and incessant and beautiful. And it was burning as mercilessly as the pain in my chest.

"Charlotte," I heard again and smiled.

In the dark, among the falling ceiling and through the chaos that had been unleashed, I fumbled for Marcus's touch. But he was out of reach, and I was running out of time.

My vision clouded, and I reached one last time for him. There were no warm, soothing hands waiting for mine, no tender lips to brush across my forehead and urge me to be brave, nor strong arms to protect me.

There was only pain and fire. I coughed blood, feeling oddly cold except for the flames pounding a lulling rhythm in my breast.

Then fear finally wore off, and everything went slowly, peacefully dark.

About the Author

Michelle crafts love stories that go beyond the flesh and touch the heart. She loves the perfect imperfections of her characters and favors alpha males with a soft side, who live by a code of honor, and witty ladies who are willing to risk everything for their men.

When she is not writing, she likes to read, travel, and watch her favorite TV shows. Among other things she is in love with chocolate, sunrises, and the sea.

Her debut novel is called *Darkside Love Affair*. She is currently working on her second novel, *Love in Disguise*, which is the sequel to *Darkside Love Affair*.

Michelle would love to connect with her readers. You can reach her at:

www.michellerosigliani.com
www.facebook.com/MichelleRosigliani
www.twitter.com/michelle_rsgli
www.instagram.com/michelle.rosigliani

Don't forget to subscribe to her newsletter at www.michellerosigliani.com/Newsletter. You will be notified about new book releases, promotions, and other exciting news.

If you enjoyed this book, consider leaving an honest review. This would help the author immensely to improve and bring to you, the reader, a better sequel

The story continues in:

Love
in
DISGUISE

Preface

The heart is an exquisite machine—a little fist pumping life into your body, from the day you are born until you fall in love.

And then, it stops working properly.

The clockwork mechanism becomes faulty and unreliable. The cadenced heartbeats turn erratic until the pounding threatens to tear a hole through your chest. Then they falter and turn slower, soundless, until you fear your heart has stopped working altogether.

Love is an irrational, painful feeling.

And yet, as I bolted into the cavernous room, I couldn't bring myself to regret one ounce of the love I bore for Charlotte. Shuddering at the desolation that stretched mercilessly all around me, I pushed forward until the faintest glimmer of light penetrated the darkness.

Then I saw her. Floating like an angel, the light creating a halo around her head.

I pulled out my gun, aimed for my target, and took one precise shot. Charlotte collapsed right into my arms, her hair stuck to her face, her lashes powdered with frost, caressing the soft peaks of her cheeks, her lips blue and parted as if she wanted to confess a secret.

I was battling against time, and I was losing again.

Chapter 1

Marcus

"Charlotte," I called for the hundredth time, but her eyes remained closed, and blood oozed from lips void of color.

Under the dirt and the bruises, she was shockingly pale and frighteningly still. Her head was rolling listlessly from one side to the other as the nurses and the paramedics whisked her stretcher down an endless corridor to an elevator that seemed miles away.

Grime and blood clogged her nostrils. Tears that had already dried left winding trails on cheeks that looked hollow and chalky-white. A mouth I had feasted on a mere couple of hours ago was tipped into a grimace that spoke of a load of pain that she did not deserve.

I jogged numbly by her moving bed, holding onto her hand more determinedly than if I were holding on for dear life. Doctors emerged from unseen hallways and shot directives every which way.

"Don't leave me," I muttered while my vision clouded, and my racing heart slowly joined Charlotte in her stillness.

She had crept into my heart, and like a thief, she had possessed it. She had become my world, and now, she was lying there, bruised and in pieces. She was the fire in my veins, and she was dwindling.

Her cold fingers slipped from my grasp, and I felt the earth shifting under my feet.

"Sir, you must step aside," a nurse dressed in teal scrubs told me while blocking my way. She was grave and unyielding. "We're taking her to the OR. A doctor will update you on the progress of—"

"You're not taking her away from me!"

The commotion and the shrill voices came to a grinding halt. Shocked and disapproving eyes settled on me, but it was the nurse's wholly horrified expression and the way she cowered a full step back that snapped me out of my trance.

The convoy stopped, and the elevator doors finally slid open. A rather short doctor, with thick fingers and a serious lack of neck length, stepped in front of the startled nurse.

"Sir, the patient has lost a lot of blood, and there is no exit wound, so the bullet is still lodged in her body. We need to operate immediately. Please, step aside."

The doctor placed a gentle hand on my fist, which had closed tightly around the side rail of Charlotte's stretcher. Rationally, I realized he was right and that time was of the essence. But how could I convince my heart to let go, to allow my sweet, sweet Charlotte to dive into the unknown by herself?

"Marcus, you need to let the doctors do their job," Lauren Burton called from the middle of an adjacent hallway. She sprinted to her daughter with yet another doctor flanking her side.

She appeared devastated, but somehow, she managed to stay together despite the desperation and the terror of what might happen. When warmth enveloped my frozen fist, I looked down to see Lauren's hands deftly peeling finger after finger from the cold bar of the stretcher.

The lump in my throat expanded. It filled my lungs and pressed over my chest. It was impossible to breathe and difficult to see through eyes that misted once again, but by dint of great effort and with a voice that broke after every word, I managed, "I'm sorry."

Lauren nodded mechanically and cradled my hand in hers like she needed the contact to stop from grabbing at her daughter in my stead. Drawing in a sharp breath, she lifted her chin, clicked her heels together, then focused her undivided attention on the shrewd-eyed doctor who had left her side to check on Charlotte.

He looked no more than a few years younger than Lauren, but they must have been colleagues at some point. He had a somber, authoritative countenance that portrayed him as competent. The precise way he checked Charlotte's vitals *and ordered his team around only confirmed that assumption.*

"She is my daughter, Roman," Lauren said, stopping the doctor in his tracks for half a second. "You must save her."

"I will. I promise."

He spared only the other half of that same second to squeeze Lauren's shoulders, then they both nodded to each other, and the cavalcade of doctors and nurses disappeared inside the elevator with Charlotte lying quietly in her bed, so achingly, despairingly quiet.

The lights flickered as a sharp breath wracked my chest. I shut my eyes to curb the ache, but behind my closed eyelids, Charlotte's sweet, tormented face was imprinted like a tattoo—too still, too ashy, too bereft of life.

MY EYES FLEW OPEN, AND I almost jumped from the chair that had been my home lately. I heard the cadenced beeping of the machines and the whirring noise of the ventilator before I regained control of my sight and focused on Charlotte's motionless form.

My heart lurched in my chest and squeezed uncomfortably. The constant ache that had tormented me since Friday night regained new strength and threatened to shatter me from the inside out.

I stroked a trembling finger down Charlotte's cheek and wished it were me in that bed, inanimate and speechless, instead of her.

Her once flushed skin was turning paler by the second. A horrible tube was coming out of her mouth, pumping air into lungs that were too weak to breathe on their own. She also had a concussion. Although the neurologist had seemed hopeful, she couldn't tell the extent of the injury until Charlotte woke up. Seeing her unchanged, swollen, and bruised face didn't help me feel as optimistic.

Her right hand, tightly contained in a cast, with her small and ring finger immobilized as well, was carefully placed beside her body. The exposed purplish skin of her other fingers contrasted harshly with the pure white bedspread.

Her midsection was covered and protected, and a drain tube was implanted in her incision. The bullet had done more damage than just the cut on her formerly perfect abdomen, but I couldn't think about that now.

Her lower body hadn't escaped unscathed either. The thin hospital sheet was pulled to the side to reveal her left leg, slightly elevated and severely marred by cuts that had been cleaned and stitched.

I couldn't bear to watch her so defenseless, so fragile, but the thought of leaving her side, even for a single moment, was torturous enough to make me lose my mind.

"My beautiful, stubborn angel, wake up," I pleaded, bowing over her good hand and kissing her knuckles, her fingers, even her palm.

I cradled her limp hand in mine and nestled my cheek against her inert fingers, a sob escaping my throat. Charlotte's touch was alarmingly cold, but I could feel the feeble pulse at her wrist, and that brought me a shadow of comfort.

It had been days since the surgery, and she had yet to wake up. I assumed my mind was still too muddled to understand the medical ramblings about Charlotte's diagnosis, but Lauren had seemed sufficiently appeased when Dr. Bryce informed us that keeping her under deep sedation was the best option. She had suffered severe injuries, on top of losing too much blood, and her body needed time to recover, to rest.

"Her condition is stable now. We have taken her off the sedatives, and she should be waking up any moment now," Doctor Roman Bryce had told us that morning as the nurses rolled Charlotte's bed from the ICU to a private room. *"Have patience, have faith,"* he had said.

I'd had both, for over four thousand excruciating minutes. I couldn't be patient anymore. The only thing that I truly understood was that Charlotte hadn't come back to me.

The soft squeak of the door filtered through my thoughts. I gave an involuntary jerk, but otherwise, I didn't acknowledge the intruder. I couldn't remove my eyes from Charlotte to check who had come to prod at her now.

"You look worse than she does, you know?"

Warm fingers clamped my shoulder, then the softest pat on my head, like the flapping of wings, finally convinced me to straighten from my contorted position.

"You have to rest, Marcus," Lauren whispered.

Her calm had settled me at first, then it infuriated me. How could she remain so calm when her daughter hardly had any life left in her? But now, her collected demeanor was the only anchor I had in my never-ending turmoil.

"What will Charlotte say when she wakes up to find you in worse a shape than she is? She will be very disappointed that I didn't take better care of you."

Lauren's baby talk was soothing, or perhaps it was her melodious voice, so much like her daughter's, that acted as a balm to my frayed nerves. I almost smiled, almost let her sway me.

"I can't leave," I sighed and pressed my cheek again to Charlotte's immobile hand.

"Marcus, she'll still be here when you return," Lauren tried to rationalize. "She is out of the woods now. She's healing."

"Is she?"

Lauren's brave façade slipped, and I could catch a glimpse of her own fear. She was a doctor. She understood Charlotte's condition better than I ever could, but although her mind firmly believed in her daughter's recovery, uncertainty still tormented her heart. Just like it tormented mine.

"She'll be fine. I promise."

Her voice was decisive once again, but I suspected she was trying to assure herself of Charlotte's wellbeing more than she was trying to convince me.

"I can't—I can't let her out of my sight. She's in this damn bed because I allowed it once."

"You are only a man, Marcus. You couldn't have done more than you did."

But I had done nothing—nothing at all to protect her like I should have. And that was precisely the matter.

"That filth is only a man too," I spat. My jaw clenched, and the vein in my forehead throbbed madly until it spread sheer venom in my bloodstream. "And he was able to do so much more damage than I was able to prevent."

"She is safe now. We all are. If we let the fear he caused rule us, then we let him win."

I was afraid—afraid of permanently losing Charlotte—but I wasn't afraid of Cameron Drake. If it were possible, I would kill him again and again and again…and again.

"Go home, Marcus. If anything changes, anything at all, you'll be the first to know."

When she realized that I wasn't going to leave if I wasn't forcibly removed from Charlotte's side, Lauren stepped outside for a moment. She was quiet as she stepped back inside. Watching over Charlotte, each of us suffered and fought our own demons until a muted knock at the door disrupted the perfect quietness.

I lifted my head to see Kai sneaking inside, his eyes swiping over Charlotte then settling on me. Behind him, through the half-opened door, Bryson stood with his hands locked in front of him and his head bowed, not quite sure what to do with himself, or maybe not quite sure how to handle me.

He had seen me devastated, but not quite to this extent. I would have laughed if I'd had any power left—their strategy was so evident that it was amusing.

Lauren must have called Kai, realizing over the past days that he was my voice of reason, the one, in Charlotte's absence, who had a modicum of influence over me. Then Kai had called Bryson, who was supposed to act as the muscle if Kai's silver tongue failed to persuade me.

"I am not leaving," I told all three of them and nobody in particular.

Kai took three uncertain steps inside the room and fixed me with kind eyes. "Look, it's not about you, Marcus. It's about Charlotte. She'll need you when she wakes up more than she needs you now. How will you be able to support her if you break down by then?"

He knew just the right words to say and which buttons to push. He wasn't a bandmaster because he knew how to orchestrate his life like a masterpiece, but because he was quite talented at manipulating everything and everyone around him.

"Bryson will take you home, and I will stay here. Nobody goes through these doors, and nothing will happen in this room without you knowing."

I shook my head, but when Kai wrapped his hands around my shoulders and pulled me up, I found I lacked the strength to oppose him. I was drained and more of a mess than I wished to admit, but the thought of leaving slashed at me viciously. It brought me to the fine edge of despair.

"You call," I managed in a whisper. "Even if the slightest gust of wind blows over her, you call me. You call me immediately, Kai."

"I swear. You know I will."

Lauren smiled encouragingly as I wobbled to the door with Kai's help. When I stopped in the doorway, she glanced at me like she had expected the hesitancy.

"Lauren, I'm sorry I didn't take proper care of her."

She gulped down almost noisily, and the corners of her eyes reddened. She still remembered that heinous night just as well as I did. Although she had never uttered an unkind word, I knew part of her blamed me for what had happened.

I wasn't sure how I managed to walk to Bryson's car or when the ride from the hospital to my apartment came so rapidly to an end. Bryson parked in front of the building, then he accompanied me upstairs just as quietly as he had been driving.

"I'll be here if you need anything," he said, patting Kinga and slumping into a loveseat.

Bryson knew me well. He never hovered, and unlike Kai, he rarely forced me to spill out my feelings. But without fail, he was always there when I needed him, quiet and blending into the background, but there nonetheless.

I nodded absently and ambled to my bedroom. The quiet was maddening. Whereas at the hospital I had been focusing on Charlotte, in the soundless emptiness of my room, where her scent still lingered, I could only focus on the memories.

"CHARLOTTE!"

I knocked the emergency door open with her name wrenched from my throat. My heart felt strangled in my chest as I pushed through the smoke and struggled to spot her. She had been right next to the emergency door, but she hadn't been alone. And now, she was nowhere to be seen.

"I'll get everyone out," Logan shouted over the screams and the wild crackling of fire burning everything in its path. "You look for Charlotte."

I inspected the corridor that seemed an endless road to nowhere, then I darted back inside the burning restaurant. Without help, I was never going to find Charlotte.

"Marcus, what are you doing?" Lauren yelled.

Thankfully, she didn't follow. It was already unbearable to worry for Charlotte, to think that I might be already too late. I couldn't fear for her loved ones too.

"Get them out," I barked to Logan then strode purposefully to a half-naked bartender collapsed by a high table near the edge of the dance floor.

"Help me," he croaked as I knelt next to him and clasped his chin, pulling his head back to face me. His eyes widened with pain and terror.

"The emergency door," I said. "Where does it lead? Where is the nearest room?"

"I don't—my leg hurts. I think it's broken—there's blood…and the fire—please, help me."

"Help is on the way. Now focus. What is below us? Where is the nearest room?"

"The storage room," he gasped. "Below Exterus."

I jumped back to my feet and sprinted away. If there was a storage room under the restaurant, there had to be a door on the left side of the corridor. I ran like a madman, pushing people aside, ignoring pleas for help, cries of agony, and protests as I made for the storage room.

And there it was. A white door, firmly shut, with part of its frame collapsed as if the door had been slammed.

"Charlotte," I screamed again and struggled to listen.

No answer came. The fire and the terrorized people were loud enough to drown out anything else.

Then something much louder and deadlier than anything I had hoped to hear boomed like thunder. Not one, but two gunshots in a row.

I could hardly tell how I managed to blast through the door and stumble over a nearly dilapidated cabinet, but I found myself kneeling beside Charlotte's still form, frenziedly absorbing the sight of her.

She was covered in smut and bruises, and her limbs were misaligned, almost like they didn't constitute a part of her body anymore. Her small revolver was covered in blood and swung from her fingers. Beneath her wilted body, there was a pool of crimson, and the bloodstain expanded terrifyingly fast.

Despite the horror of the situation, a small smile curved her lips like she was finally at peace, like she couldn't feel the pain anymore, like she had embraced it.

"Oh, no, no, no," I screamed and looked for her wound.

Her lilac dress was punctured right in the middle of her stomach, and the blood seeped freely. I applied pressure to the wound, glancing frantically around us. The fire was wild, an incensed fiend that swallowed everything all around. I had to take her out of that room immediately, but I couldn't do it while still keeping pressure on her wound. I hadn't been able to protect her, and now, I couldn't save her.

"Damn it," I growled.

It was then that I heard the whimper, and it was not coming from Charlotte. My eyes searched crazily through the smoke and the flames. In a corner, next to a shabby table, a woman curled into a ball, rocking slightly, like an infant trying to fall asleep. Her eyes were narrowed to slits, and I realized then that she must have been hurt as well.

"He's gone," she sniffled and glanced unseeingly upward at the window that was now broken.

But whoever he was and whatever his condition, he was not my concern. What I feared was that I might have just lost her—my own beating heart.

"Charlotte," I called as I cradled her to my chest and lifted her body off the ground. "Sugar, please wake up. Goddammit, you can't do this to me. You have to wake up."

FINDING REST IN A BED where Charlotte didn't warm my body and the sheets underneath us as she lounged in a graceful, quiet sleep of her own was a stupid notion. I crawled out of bed and dragged my feet to the window. The curtains had been pulled to the sides by Charlotte herself to allow the light to spill freely inside the bedroom. She had played with the tassels of the curtain belts while luring me in with her deliciously timid smiles. Now she wasn't smiling, and the light had dissolved into darkness.

I showered and pulled on a fresh set of clothes because of necessity, not because I required the change. I couldn't be sure how long it had been since I left the hospital, but it felt unbearably long. My heart couldn't tolerate the distance anymore.

When I emerged from my bedroom, Bryson was just unlocking the front door, walking in with Kinga, who was happily padding after him. He watched me, slightly startled, then his brows dipped into the smallest frown.

"I took her for a walk," he explained, nodding at the dog. Kinga gave a bark, but when she realized her request for attention was ignored, she hopped to her bowl and wolfed down the dry kernels.

"I'm surprised she hasn't run off to you or Kai by now. You're taking better care of her than I do."

Bryson shrugged like the notion of taking care of someone else's dog didn't bother him, then he gestured to the door. "Do you want to go back to the hospital?"

"Yes, but I'm going to drive."

"Marcus, I don't think you should. Plus, I promised Kai that I would—"

"I need the time to think," I stopped him and snatched my keys from the mahogany entry table.

He didn't seem convinced but nodded although his thoughts were evident in his eyes. I'd had three days' worth of time solely dedicated to thinking.

Our eyes locked, and a small part of me noted the difference in him. Lines crossed his forehead, and dark rings circled his eyes, but that was not why he looked older. He must have finally realized that life was too short to waste it recklessly, and with his newfound maturity, came wisdom.

"Thank you," I said. "For everything."

"She'll be fine," he replied, a robot-like comfort.

Once behind the wheel of my car, I lacked the enjoyment I experienced each time I drove. However, it hadn't been the adrenaline rush I had sought out, but privacy. I pulled the phone out of my pocket and called a number that was already on speed dial.

"Hudson," came the grating voice I recognized now all too well.

"Any updates?"

"Look, Marcus, I can't talk right now. I'll be in touch very soon."

"You can't—What do you mean you can't talk? You dare to—"

"Have a pleasant evening."

Then he hung up.

I could almost see the fumes seeping from my nostrils. I held Julian Hudson responsible for what had happened to Charlotte as much as I did myself. I had failed her, but if Hudson hadn't failed at his job in the first place, nothing of this nightmare would have happened.

I slammed my fist against the steering wheel and shoved my foot on the gas pedal. I was volatile and violently furious. It was in this frame of mind that I stepped inside the hospital.

It didn't take long to spot the Armani-suited man pacing back and forth down the corridor that led to Charlotte's room. He was talking to Dr. Bryce, and Lauren was standing with her back to them, her spine rigid, her disposition unreadable.

"James, stop this nonsense," Lauren cracked and finally turned around. "Charlotte is perfectly taken care of—"

She trailed off when she found me, standing still in the middle of the hallway, a hardly contained animal about to distance himself from judgment and go berserk.

"You self-centered bastard," I lashed out.

Breaking free of invisible chains, I slammed into him. A puff of air left his lips as I smashed his body against the wall. My hands were fisted around the lapels of his luxurious jacket, but what I really wanted to do was wrap my hands around his throat and squeeze. I felt murderous—I had felt so since Friday night, and James Burton was definitely the wrong man to cross my path.

"What are you doing here?" I snarled and smashed his body repeatedly against the wall. "*You* did this to her. *You* brought those monsters into her life. *You* put your own daughter in the hospital."

Lauren gasped and wrapped her fingers around her throat, just like Charlotte did when she was nervous. "For Heaven's sake, Marcus, stop."

"But it wasn't enough that you forced her into a world she had no business exploring, was it? You had to push her into the arms of a killer."

James Burton's face caught a peculiar shade of red. His eyes were bloodshot and unfocused. His lips were twisted in a deplorable grimace. As I bit each poisonous word out, he remained a pitiful puppet in my grasp. More than his arrogance of coming here, showing affection and concern well past the point when it mattered, his lack of reaction infuriated me.

"Don't have anything to say? Has your ludicrous lawyerly talk left you? No more commands to bark?"

"Now, gentlemen, let's get control of ourselves," Dr. Bryce intervened, taking my elbow in an unexpectedly hard grip. When I shoved his hand off me, he didn't even flinch.

"Marcus, please, we are in a hospital," Lauren begged and tried ineffectively to push me off her husband.

"I can't understand how a despicable man like you could have fathered a creature so pure and brilliant as Charlotte. You don't deserve her. You have no business being here."

I released him so brutally that he stumbled and collapsed right onto his knees. His tie hung loosely around his neck, his lapel was half torn, and his Rolex shattered as he broke his fall. His head sagged, and something akin to a sob infected the shocked silence. The great James Burton toppling from his clouds in the misery he had unleashed was a disgraceful sight. He disgusted me more than my own father ever had.

Kai stepped out of Charlotte's room, his mouth agape. "What in the world?"

He must have heard the exchange, but it was evident from his stunned expression that he hadn't expected the recipient of my rage to be Charlotte's father. He strode to me and pushed me a safe distance away. I wasn't done, and Kai could sense that the storm hadn't passed yet.

"Settle down," he hissed. "Pointing fingers won't help anybody. Come on, let's take a walk."

He elbowed me another step away, then the terrible commotion started. The machines beeped furiously from Charlotte's room, and three nurses came running from their station. Dr. Bryce scowled, and Lauren paled, then they both jogged after the nurses. Someone slammed the door shut, muffling the noises coming from inside.

My world stood still.

"God," I breathed, bumping my head against the wall. When was this turmoil going to end? When was she going to wake up?

While we waited, Kai hovered close, standing between Charlotte's father and me. James Burton had crawled back up to his feet, and his face had frozen into an inscrutable, constipated expression.

"You're right, you know," he spoke eventually. He planted himself in the middle of the hallway, staring at the closed door of his daughter's room. His hands were shoved in the pockets of his trousers, and his head was still somewhat bowed. "But she is still my daughter. I've never meant for this to end this way. I never imagined this would ever happen to her when I gave her the case."

An eternity later, Lauren walked out with Roman Bryce following her. They acted relieved, and unlike me, hopeful and composed.

"There was only a small issue with the machines," the doctor announced, glancing at me with an apologetic glint in his eye. "Charlotte's condition is still stable."

Nobody could have stopped me from being by Charlotte's side then, and they were all wise enough not to try.

She didn't appear changed. Her expression was serene as if she were dreaming. I bent to press my lips against her stiff mouth and realized that I was crying only when my tears pooled between her closed lips.

"I know I have failed you, but you have to stop punishing me. I can't take it anymore. It's killing me."

I staggered into the leather chair by her bed and rested my head against her uninjured hand. Her touch, unresponsive as it was, had been the single solace I'd had during the past days.

At some point, I must have dozed off for when I opened my eyes again, something had changed.

The window was open, causing the cream curtains to sway restlessly. My hand drifted back, searching for the gun I'd learned to keep religiously tucked beneath the band of my jeans. I heard a noise, a soft, almost imperceptible sound coming from the adjacent bathroom, and my fingers tightened around the grip of my gun.

I pulled it out slowly, then just as a man was coming out of the small bathroom, I lifted my arms and aimed.

"Put that away, will you?" Julian Hudson muttered as neutrally as if he were telling me to clear the breakfast table.

Gritting my teeth, I thrust the gun back where it belonged. "First, you cannot talk to me, and now, you are sneaking around like a thief?"

"There are well-founded reasons why I do things a precise way. I don't appreciate you questioning my methods."

I cracked my neck as my nostrils flared. Hudson cast me a knowing glance, sighed, then took a wiser approach. It was definitely not the best time to scold me as if I were a stupid child he could dictate over.

"It's better if we keep our association under wraps," he explained, peering over at Charlotte. His expression was genuinely concerned. "How is she?"

"I wish everyone would stop asking me that," I sighed and leaned against the window frame.

"I assume nothing has changed. No change is good news."

"If you tell me to be patient, I swear you won't like my reaction."

Hudson almost chuckled. Although he was a calculated man, he seemed to understand my affectionate relationship with impatience.

"I need to do something, anything to stop feeling this useless."

My eyes were fierce as I watched him, but Hudson remained as cool as ever. He studied me in silence, perhaps checking if I was still capable of aiding him in his plans. In the end, his attention drifted out the window. He mirrored my stance, leaning against the frame.

"You know what you can do. Charlotte will only be safe when Mitch Stewart's affairs are exposed and he is behind bars."

"It was not Mitch Stewart who pulled the trigger, though," I reminded him. The gnashing sound of my teeth drowned out the beeping of the machines.

"Cameron Drake will have nothing if the mayor goes to prison."

I snorted and glanced back at Charlotte's still body. Cameron

Drake already had much more than he deserved—he had a life.

Hudson followed my gaze, but unlike me, he remained detached and logical. His blood wasn't boiling, and his heart wasn't shattering each time he perused the comatose face of the woman he loved.

"The only reason he's still able to hide," he continued, "is because he has protection. If the leader falls, the others will follow. He'll have no support to rely on, no money, nothing."

"So the only way to lure him out of his lair is to hunt his master down."

"Exactly. Look, Marcus, I can imagine that every instinct in your body is telling you to hunt Drake instead, but that would be a waste of time and resources. We don't even know if he is still alive, and if he is, he must be extremely well hidden. Any effort in locating him would be futile, and in the interim, he will get his strength and power back. He'll be once more a step ahead of us. We have to force them to play by our rules."

"Your rules, you mean." Hudson eyed me stiffly but did not bother to contradict me. "I'm going to ask you one question. If this operation goes south, what will your priority be?"

He seemed an honorable man, honorable enough to care if the lives of innocent people were at risk, yet he was willing to sacrifice the welfare of the few for the benefit of the many.

The only sacrifice I was ready to make was for Charlotte. I was willing to sacrifice the world itself if it meant that no harm would come to my sweet Charlotte ever again.

"If something goes wrong, we'll salvage whatever is left of the operation, and you'll be extracted immediately. You might be alone in the field, but we'll have eyes on you."

"Wrong," I snapped. "See, our priorities do not align. If something goes wrong, my first priority will always be Charlotte. So keep that in mind. She'll always come first. Always."

"Let's hope the moment you realize that endangering the mission equals endangering your lover never comes."

"One more thing," I said before he could put an end to our discussion. "I have a condition, and it is not negotiable."

"You have just made it clear that you will never accept my offer.

Why should I be interested in any more of your conditions?"

"Because if you don't honor it, you might as well be an enemy," I said, tearing my scrutiny from Charlotte to pin it on the FBI agent.

"What is your demand?" he asked, sighing and meeting my stare with a raised chin and locked jaw.

He didn't seem entirely surprised. As I replied, I even got the feeling that he had been expecting my words.

"When I find that lowlife, he's mine."

Hudson nodded grimly. Straightening, he let his head fall back, and his gaze roamed the bleach white ceiling.

"Have you ever killed before, Marcus?" Hudson asked eventually.

In my nightmares, a thousand times in a thousand different ways, I thought bitterly. The low growl that rumbled from my chest must have tipped Hudson off about my grim train of thought. He shook his head as if saying that the imaginary would never weigh as heavily as the real kill.

"Although you might not believe me, I understand much of what you're going through, so I won't stand in your way if it comes to that. But hasn't Drake taken enough from you? Hasn't he already ruined too much between Charlotte and you? Will you give him the satisfaction of ruining more even in death?"

"She will be safe."

Hudson shook his head, looking disappointed. "You leave me with no other option but to take measures I hoped you wouldn't force me to take."

"What is that supposed to mean?"

"You're blinded by grief, and your idea of going after Drake on your own might ruin everything my team has managed to put together up to this point."

I blinked at the fog that fell like a curtain over my eyes, but I couldn't clear my blurry vision fast enough. It frequently happened these days, and although exhaustion was the rational explanation, I believed rage was the actual reason for those strange spells.

Cracking my neck and rolling my shoulders, I let Hudson get acquainted with some of that rage. "I warn you, Hudson, don't stand in my way."

He didn't appear impressed, let alone intimidated, and somehow, that made me want to fight him all the more.

"I'd warn you to think carefully before threatening a federal agent, but I know you won't listen. We're done negotiating. Expect a package from me, and when you receive it, don't think you have the option to refuse me anymore."

Presenting me a stiff back, he walked to the door, making it clear that he was done talking. I was done talking too. I wanted to act. But what Hudson didn't understand was that I wasn't about to serve as his spy.

"I thought you only wanted to work with willing people," I muttered, an afterthought right before the agent vanished from the room.

Halting in the doorway, he looked over his shoulder. "I'm running out of options, and I cannot afford to have you running around, seeking revenge."

"You don't want to make an enemy of me, Hudson," I warned, feeling the blood rolling hotly in my veins and the fury craving to be unleashed.

"Neither do you. So think long and hard before you act."

17208247R00323

Printed in Great Britain
by Amazon